I0576397

Anna Glover

Glover Memorials and Genealogies

Anna Glover

Glover Memorials and Genealogies

ISBN/EAN: 9783742887771

Manufactured in Europe, USA, Canada, Australia, Japa

Cover: Foto ©Andreas Hilbeck / pixelio.de

Manufactured and distributed by brebook publishing software
(www.brebook.com)

Anna Glover

Glover Memorials and Genealogies

AN ACCOUNT

OF

JOHN GLOVER OF DORCHESTER

AND HIS DESCENDANTS.

WITH

A BRIEF SKETCH OF SOME OF THE GLOVERS

WHO FIRST SETTLED IN

NEW JERSEY, VIRGINIA, AND OTHER PLACES.

BY ANNA GLOVER.

BOSTON:

DAVID CLAPP & SON, PRINTERS.

1867.

TO THE MEMORY OF

HORATIO NELSON GLOVER, Esq.

DECEASED, OF QUINCY,

THESE

MEMORIALS

ARE MOST GRATEFULLY AND RESPECTFULLY INSCRIBED

BY

THE AUTHOR.

He beareth Sable, a Chevron Ermine, between three Crescents, Argent.

This patent was granted by William Camden,
April 3, 1604, and descends to the
name and family of Glover.

The above Coat of Arms, with the accompanying inscription, corresponds with those referred to on pages 14, 15 and 44. It was taken from one obtained of a London Herald by Capt. Russell Glover, and is now in the possession of John J. Glover, Esq., of Quincy.

PREFACE.

In offering these Memorials of the preceding generations of the name and family of GLOVER, the writer gratefully acknowledges the kind words of encouragement received from many individuals in each branch of the families contained in the work, as also the ready response to her call for ancient original documents and private records. In addition to such sources of information, an extensive correspondence has been the means of gathering in much valuable and reliable information. Letters have been addressed to every person bearing the name of Glover, not only in New England but the United States, whose records and history could not be otherwise obtained. More than one thousand letters have been sent to such persons, and to others from whom there appeared to be any chance of gleaning information. To those who have responded promptly, the most grateful acknowledgments are here tendered. In some few instances inquiries have remained unanswered; and in others, where another name was borne although of Glover descent, an indifference has been made apparent by the doubtful character of the reply. The best has been made of it, however, and if such should chance to see an error in the arrangement of their names or a discrepancy of dates, they must impute it to the deficiency of their own communications, for no expense or labor has been spared in the endeavor to obtain the correct dates and facts in every case. It is earnestly hoped that those who may discover errors or omissions, will be kind enough to make them known to the author.   .

There have been found to be six original progenitors or American ancestors of the name of Glover—four only of whom are here Memorialized. Of Charles Glover, of Salem and Gloucester in 1632, and subsequently of Southold, Long Island, N. Y., and of Henry Glover, who settled early in New Haven, Ct., there has been a large amount of information gathered and their descendants traced as far as practicable ; but they could not be noticed in this volume, without too much increasing its size.

A. G.

STOUGHTON, JUNE, 1867.

CONTENTS.

PART I.

	Page
GLOVERS OF ENGLAND	1

First Generation in New England.

Mr. JOHN GLOVER, of Rainhill Parish, Lancashire, England, and of Dorchester and Boston in New England, and his five sons . .	39

Second Generation.

I. Mr. THOMAS GLOVER, of Dorchester, N. E., and London, Eng., and his Descendants	81
II. Mr. HABACKUK GLOVER, of Boston, and his Descendants . . .	99
III. Mr. JOHN GLOVER, of Dorchester and Boston	149
IV. Mr. NATHANIEL GLOVER, of Dorchester, and his Descendants . .	162
V. Mr. PELATIAH GLOVER, of Dorchester and Springfield, and Descendants	453

DESCENDANTS OF THE FIRST SON, MR. THOMAS GLOVER.

Third Generation	82
Fourth Generation	82

DESCENDANTS OF THE SECOND SON, MR. HABACKUK GLOVER.

Third Generation	104
Fourth Generation	112
Fifth Generation	129
Sixth Generation	135
Seventh Generation	138
Eighth Generation	143
Ninth Generation	147

DESCENDANTS OF THE FOURTH SON, MR. NATHANIEL GLOVER.

Third Generation	176
Fourth Generation	218
Fifth Generation	257
Sixth Generation	299
Seventh Generation	344
Eighth Generation	400
Ninth Generation	442

B

DESCENDANTS OF THE FIFTH SON, REV. PELATIAH GLOVER.

Third Generation 468
Fourth Generation 481
Fifth Generation 491
Sixth Generation 492
Seventh Generation 497
Eighth Generation 501

PART II.

HENRY GLOVER, of Rainhill, England, and Dedham and Medfield in New
  England, and his Descendants 505
Second Generation 507
Third Generation 510
Fourth Generation 513
Fifth Generation 518
Sixth Generation 526
Seventh Generation 538
Eighth Generation 545

Supposed Branch from Henry Glover 516

THE NEW JERSEY GLOVERS 550

Mr. RALPH GLOVER, of England, and Dorchester and Watertown in New
  England 554

Rev. JOSEPH GLOVER, of Sutton, England, and his Descendants in Cambridge,
  New England 560

RICHARD GLOVER, of England and Virginia 573

NORTH AND SOUTH CAROLINA GLOVERS 577

ADDITIONS AND CORRECTIONS 581

COLLEGE GRADUATES 587

SOLDIERS OF THE NAME OF GLOVER 589

INDEX TO CHRISTIAN NAMES OF GLOVER 591

INDEX TO SURNAMES 594

INDEX TO WILLS AND OTHER DOCUMENTS 600

EXPLANATION.

In order to render the work as plain as possible and avoid elaborate numbering, as a means of designating the places of each individual member of so large a family, the plan kindly suggested by a distinguished genealogist has been adopted, and the sign of addition (+) placed before each name designed to be noticed in the succeeding generation. This rule has been followed as far as practicable. In a few instances, however, the sign will be found placed before a name which does not appear in the next generation, on account of a deficiency in the additional facts obtained, as in the following numbers :— Nos. 67 and 68, on page 252 ; 171 and 177, on p. 273 ; 227, on p. 285 ; 413, on p. 306 ; 601, on p. 323 ; 731, on p. 336 ; 846, on p. 346 ; and 113, on p. 522. The numbers before which the sign was omitted, and which were intended to be again noticed and have been carried forward to their proper places in the next generation, are as follows :— No. 97, on page 255, is carried forward to p. 298 ; 200 and 201, p. 280, to pp. 332 and 333 ; 204, p. 281, to p. 333 ; 358, p. 300, to p. 346 ; 451, 452 and 453, p. 310, to p. 362 ; 587, p. 382, to p. 370 ; 600 and 602, p. 323, to pp. 370 and 371 ; 1040, p. 363, to p. 420 ; 1060, p. 364, to p. 423 ; 1061 and 1063, p. 365, to p. 423 ; 1234, p. 383, to p. 433 ; 1284, p. 383, to p. 433 ; 1294, p. 387, to p. 434 ; 1305 and 1306, p. 388, to p. 435 ; 1361 and 1364, p. 396, to p. 437. An error on page 301, No. (123), and carried forward to page 347, may be found corrected on page 582, under the head of Additions and Corrections. No. 1393, on page 398, was received too late to be carried forward to its proper place in the next generation, and is inserted among the Additions and Corrections. On page 402, No. 835, the account of the children was received too late to be inserted in the proper place, and is placed among the Additions and Corrections. On page 408, is an erroneous communication in relation to the children of No. 888, which is corrected among the Additions and Corrections. Also No. 83, of Part II., may be found noticed there.

Very few abbreviations have been used :—the letter b. for born, m. for married, d. for died, unm. for unmarried, comprising nearly all.

PART I.

GLOVERS OF ENGLAND.
HON. JOHN GLOVER AND HIS DESCENDANTS.

THE GLOVERS OF ENGLAND.

GLOVER is an ancient name in England, and from what has been gathered of its origin, is indisputably Saxon. In some of the oldest counties, as Warwickshire and Kent, it was, at a very ancient date, written Golofre — then Glove, and in the middle of the fourteenth century it was written as it now is, Glover. It has undergone no change since, excepting that some of the earliest settlers of New England occasionally wrote it with a u, instead of a v, as may be sometimes seen in the oldest documents, viz., Glouer; although there is no record of the name being spelled in that way in England at any time. It was a corruption, which soon went into disuse, and the name written Glover again, according to the English orthography, and has continued to be so written to the present day.

Families of Glover, of the Christian names of William and John, were recorded in Buckinghamshire, Berkshire and Warwickshire, about the middle of the fourteenth century. To distinguish one family from another, it became necessary to have some rule established by which to preserve to their children the remembrance of their origin and race, and the titles to their estates. The Norman nobles first used surnames in England, to avoid confusion and the extinction of family origin — and surnames were taken by some from the places from which they came, from their office or their trades — and various other circumstances induced them to adopt some sur-

2

name. The Saxon race who were living at that time under the rule
of the Norman kings, soon found it not only convenient, but honorable, to adopt the same rule, and surnames became universal throughout the kingdom. To perpetuate the remembrance of their estates,
William of Normandy, called the Conqueror, who invaded England
in 1066, caused a survey to be made of his English kingdom, and
a record kept of all the estates as they then were possessed and
occupied, with the titles to them, and ordered that this record should
be made in a book, called the Dooms-Day Book, and preserved in
the Tower of London, to enable all persons who had a desire to
know to whom these estates had once belonged, and other particulars in relation to them, by examining that record book, to obtain
the desired information.

Another rule or plan adopted by the Norman Conqueror, was to
appoint competent persons, to whom he gave the name of Heralds
or Norroys, and send them throughout his English kingdom to collect
and preserve the origin and pedigrees of all English, Saxon or Norman families. These visitations were made not long before his
death, in A.D. 1087, and the records of all such families as then
existed, with their rank and pedigrees, were ordered to be preserved
in the Tower of London, and may be seen at the present time.

These visitations were called "Heralds' Visitations," and continued to take place once in about thirty years, through all succeeding reigns, for a long period.

The office is referred to in the times of Edward I., II. and III.
The Norroys, or Kings of Arms, as Burke writes, were always attended throughout their circuit by a register, a draughtsman and
proper attendants.

Fuller, in his Worthies of England, written in the 15th century,
gives an account of one of these Heralds' Visitations among the
gentry and worthies of England, which occurred in the twelfth year
of King Henry VI., as returned by the commissioners in A.D. 1433.

Titles came into use about this time, which were very convenient
in designating persons and classes, as a kind of dignity granted to
the most worthy and enterprising. Master was one of the earliest
in use for expressing Lordship, according to the definition given by
writers on the science of language. In those times it was a title
of honor and regard, but in the lapse of time has become so pro-
miscuously applied to all classes and grades of people, that it has

long ceased to be a distinguishing title expressing Lordship, and other names have been and are at present used to express the same rank. It was at first Master, then modified to Mister, which was a title expressing worth, honor and probity. In the 16th and 17th centuries, the appellation or affix of Mr. to a surname expressed dignity and rank, distinguishing those to whose name it was applied, from the common classes. It was in those times very carefully used, and but few names, and those only of the distinguished class, were honored with the title. It has been stated by writers of the time of the early emigration to New England, that in a list of one hundred freemen, not more than four or five persons bore the appellation of Mr.

Knighthood was a very ancient title. Certain qualities of mind and manner, certain courses of action which distinguished persons for bravery and honorable conduct, and brought them into favorable notice with their sovereigns, were rewarded with the appellation of Knight, and such individuals became a favored class.

According to a survey made in the following counties, the name of Glover is recorded thus:

Among the worthies of the County of Berkshire — Johannis Glover, Sheriff in the 12th year of King Henry VI., A.D. 1433.

Buckinghamshire — John Glover, of Kimball.

Bedfordshire — Gentry, Johannis Glover, and John Glover, Junior.

Warwickshire — Robert Glover, of Monceter, Gentleman, martyred at Coventry Sept. 20, 1555.

Middlesex — William Glover, Sheriff in the time of Queen Elizabeth, London, Middlesex, about 1588.

Kent — Robert Glover, Somerset Herald, son of Thomas and Mildred, was born at Ashford, in this County. By the epitaph on his monument, he died not 46 years old, Anno 1588, and was buried without Cripplegate, London, St. Giles, on the south wall of the choir.

The names of John, William, Robert, Thomas, Richard and Henry, are among the earliest Christian names of Glover that have been noticed by writers. These names have been perpetuated, and have descended down like their estates, through many generations, both in Old and New England.

1423. There was a William Glover, who lived in A.D. 1423

and is noticed thus: " Feoffment of a Burgage in the town of Stratford upon Avon, in the second year of King Henry VI. (1423), being a conveyance of Land to William Glover and others."

1469. William Glover, in Wiltshire, collected fifty shillings for the Charities of that Church during the week on which falls the nativity of St. John the Baptist.

Of the John Glovers we have dates from English records as follows:

1446. Mr. John Glover, incumbent at the Rectory of Sutton, in Surrey County, as early as 1454, resigned in 1466. Records from 1416 lost, also from 1616 to 1628.

1571. John Glover, Vicar of Docking, in Wiltshire, in 1571. After the death of John Glover, Stephen Richman succeeded to the vicarage. He was Master of Arts; sometime one of the fellows of Magdalen College, and became vicar immediately after the death of John Glover, who died in 1571.

1593. John Glover, page 236, Charities from County of Kent: "Mr. John Glover, of this Parish, gave by Will, five Shillings per Annum forever for the Poor, to be paid out of his Lands to the Surveyors for the time being, towards mending the highways of this Parish, which Lands are now in possession of Matthew Parker."

1685. John Glover, at St. John's Church, Margate, County of Kent. This Church was one of three Chapels belonging to the Church of Minster, in the Island of Thanet, and very probably was begun to be built as early as the year. A.D. 1050. It is situated on the open sea, at Margate, in Kent.

A Memorial to John Glover, Gentleman, who died at London in 1685, aged 56 years, born in 1629. He had a wife Susanna, whom he left a widow, according to the following inscription underneath his obit:

" Mrs. Susanna Glover, his wife, Obiciit in 1713, aged 75 years " (born, therefore, in 1638).

In the second volume of Stowe's Survey of London, not in Index, the following is found:

" John Glover, Church Warden in 1701 — buried in St. James, Checkinwell, and Anne Glover his wife, buried also in 1689."

1551–2. John Glover, a Patron, resigned Feb. 3, 1551–2, the Vicarage which is in the Deanery of Stoke. " County of Surrey," vol. i.

ROBERT GLOVER, THE MARTYR.

Robert Glover, who suffered martyrdom in September, 1555, noticed by Fuller in his Worthies, had brothers John, William and Thomas, and possessed estates in Monceter, Baxterly, and other places in the County of Warwickshire.

John and Robert were married, William died unmarried. The name of John's wife was Agnes; the name of Robert's, Mary. Thomas left Warwickshire, and settled in Ashford, County of Kent, according to the testimony of some — and undoubtedly it is correct. His Coat of Arms refers him back to Warwickshire. Robert, the Somerset Herald, was probably nephew to the Martyr. Robert the Martyr had several children, the names of but two of whom have been given: Hugh, whom he named, it is said, from Hugh Latimer, who was often a guest at the house of his brother John Glover; and Edward, who succeeded, in the reign of Elizabeth, to the Baxterly estate.

We find the following in "Fox's Acts and Monuments," at pages 814, 817 and 819:

"The persecution of Mr. Robert Glover* and his two brothers John and William Glover, in September, 1555.

"To this month pertains the memorable Martyrdom of Glover, Gentleman, in the Diocese of Litchfield and Coventry, in Warwickshire County, England.

"I must intermix with his history some mention of his brother John Glover, for whom this commission was chiefly sent down; and not for Robert, although it pleased Almighty God that John escaped, and Robert was apprehended instead. I thought therefore in one history to comprehend them both together in describing some part of their virtuous lives.

"And, first, to begin with John Glover, the Eldest brother, being a Gentleman and heir to his father in the Town of Monceter, he was endowed with fair possessions of Worldly Goods. But yet was much more enriched with God's Heavenly Grace and inward Vir-

---

* A detailed account of the sufferings of the Martyrs Glover and Lewis has been written by Rev. Benjamin Richings, Vicar, incumbent of Monceter, to which the inquirer who desires more copious details, is referred.

2*

tues. Which Grace of God so working in him he with his other
brothers William and Robert not only received and embraced the
happy light of Gods Holy Gospel, but also zealously professed and no
less diligently in their living and conversation followed the same.
Who though he suffered sharp temptations, yet the Lord Graciously
preserved him all the While, and not only at last did rid him out of
all discomfort, but also framed thereby to such mortification of Life
in that his conversation was in Heaven, and being dead to this
World, he in Word and meditation led a life altogether Heavenly;
Abhorring in his mind all profane doings. Neither was his talk
different from his life; never using any vile or vain language. The
most part of his lands he distributed among his brethren, and committed the rest to the arrangements of his servants and officers, by
which he might the more quietly give himself to his Godly study, as
to a continual Sabbath rest.

"This was about the latter part of King Henry Eighth's Reign,
and continued a great part of the time of King Edward Sixth.*

"After this, in the persecuting days of Queen Mary, As soon as
the Bishop of Coventry heard of the fame of this Mr. John Glover,
he wrote his letters to the Mayor and Officers to apprehend him.
But it chanced otherwise by Gods Holy Providence, disposing all
things after His Holy and own secret pleasure, Who seeing His old
and trustworthy Servant, so many years broken with many torments;
would in no wise heap too many sorrows upon one poor sheep;
neither would commit him to the flames of fire, who had been already scorched with the sharp fires of inward Affliction and had sustained so many burning darts and conflicts of Satan.

"God therefore of his Divine Providence Graciously provided
his brother Robert Glover, being both stronger of Body and also
better furnished with the helps of Learning to answer the Adversaries (this Robert being a Master of Arts in Cambridge), should sus-
tain that conflict.

---

* "Edward VI. was taken to his rest, and his sister Mary—alias, Bloody Mary—ascended
the Throne as Queen of England in Anno Domini 1553. The system of persecution which
she put in force was the most awful exhibition of cruelty and of cold and deliberate blood-
guiltiness that the records of our race presents to us. There may have been at other times
and in other lands persecution as terrible and bloody; but this continued through the whole
five years of her Reign. The Loftiest in the Land were its Martyrs, and a Woman was its
perpetrator."

Fox's Acts and Monuments, Editor's Preface, p. 3.

"As soon as the Mayor of Coventry had received the Bishop's Letter for the apprehending of John Glover, he sent forthwith private word to John to convey himself away, who with his brother William was not so soon departed out of his house; but yet in the sight of the Sheriff, the Searchers came and rushed in to take him according to the Bishop's Command. But when John could not be found, one of the officers, going into an Upper chamber, found Robert* there lying ill on his bed and sick of a severe disease, who was immediately brought before the Sheriff. The Sheriff would fain have dismissed him, and did what he could, saying he was not the Man for whom they were sent; yet nevertheless the Officers contending with him to have him stayed until the Bishop's coming, he was constrained to carry him away against his Will."

We shall now give some account of the history of Robert Glover. From a narration which was sent to his wife, in his own hand writing, we give extracts as follows:

"*To my Entirely beloved Wife, Mary Glover.*

"The peace of Conscience which passeth all understanding, the sweet consolation, comfort, strength and boldness of the Holy Ghost, be continually increased in our heart, through a fervent, earnest and steadfast faith in our most dear and only Saviour Jesus Christ. I thank you most heartily, my most loving Wife, for your letters sent to me in my imprisonment. I read them with tears more than once or twice: With tears, I say, for Joy and gladness that God had wrought in you so merciful a Work. First, an unfeigned repentance; secondly, an humble and hearty reconciliation; thirdly, a Willing submission and Obedience to the Will of God in all things, which, when I read your letters and judged them to proceed from the bottom of your heart, I could not but be thankful to God, rejoicing with tears for you; and these his great mercies poured upon you. These your letters and the hearing of your most Godly proceedings and constant doings from time to time much relieved and comforted me at all times, and shall be a goodly Testimony with you at the Great Day against many worldly and dainty Dames who set more by their own pleasure and pelf in this world than by God's Glory, little regarding the everlasting health of their own souls or

* A younger brother.

of others.   My prayer shall be while in this world that God, who
of his great mercy hath begun this good work in you, will finish it
to the Glory of His name, and by the Mighty power and inspiration
of His Holy Spirit so strengthen, establish and confirm you in all
his ways, to the end that we may together show forth his praises in
the World to Come to our unspeakable consolation everlastingly.
Amen.   So long as God shall lend you a continuance in this miserable World, above all things, give yourself Continually to prayer,
lifting up, as St. Paul says, clean and pure hearts and hands, without
anger, wrath, or doubting, forgiving, as he saith also, if you have
any thing against any Man, as Christ forgiveth us.

"If I would have given place to Worldly reasons, these might
have moved me.   First, the foregoing of you; and the consideration
of the state of my children, being yet of tender age; apt and in-
clinable to Virtue and Learning, and so haveing the more need of my
assistance — being not altogether destitute of gifts to help them —
possessions also above the common sort of Men.   Because I was
never called to be a Minister or Preacher, and because my sickness,
fear of death in imprisonment before I should come to my answers
to the Bishop; and so my death to be unprofitable.   But these
things and such like, I thank my Heavenly Father, which of his Infinite mercy inspired me with his Holy Spirit for his Son's sake, My
only Saviour and Redeemer, prevailed not in me."

The letter closes; and then follows, viz.:—"In the same fire with
Robert Glover was burned Cornelius Bungy of Coventry, and William Wolsey and Robert Pigot of the Isle of Ely, about the 20th
of September, 1555."

JOHN AND WILLIAM GLOVER.

An account of John and William Glover is given in the same
work as follows:

"After the Martyrdom of Robert Glover, John Glover, the eldest
brother, seeing his brother apprehended for him, had little joy of
his life, and would gladly have put himself in his brother's stead if
friends had not otherwise persuaded him.   About the latter end of
Queen Mary's Reign there was a new search made for him.   The
Sheriffs with their under Officers being sent to seek John Glover,

came into the house where he and his wife were. It chanced as he was in the Chamber by himself the Officers bursting into the house and searching other rooms came to the chamber door where he, holding the latch, softly with his hand, perceived and heard the Officers bustling about the door, amongst whom one of the Officers, having the string in his hand, was ready to draw and pluck at the door. In the mean time another coming whose voice he heard and knew, bade them come away, saying that they had been there before, upon which they went to search other corners of the house, where they found Agnes Glover his wife, who being taken to Litchfield and there examined before the Bishop, at length after much ado was constrained to give place to their tyranny. John Glover in the mean time, partly for care of his wife and partly from cold taken in the woods where he lay hid, had an ague, and not long after gave up his life which the cruel Papists had so long sought for. Thus by the protection of Almighty God, John Glover was delivered and defended from the hand of his persecuting enemies during all the time of his life. Now what befel him after his death, both to him and to William his brother, is not unworthy to be remembered. After he was dead and buried in the Church-yard without Priest or Clerk, Doctor Dracot, then the Chancellor, Six weeks after sent for the Parson of the Town and demanded how it chanced that he was there buried; The Parson answered that he was then sick and knew not of it. Then the Chancellor commanded the Parson to go home and to cause the body of John Glover to be taken up and to be cast over the Wall into the Highway. The Parson answered that he had been six weeks in the Earth, and so smelled that none was able to abide the stench of him. Well, said Dr. Dracot, then take this bill and pronounce him in the pulpit a damned soul, and a twelve month after (for then the flesh will be consumed) take up his bones and cast them over the Wall, that the horses and carts may tread upon them, and then I will come again and hallow that place in the Church Yard. Similar usage was practised upon the body of William, the Third brother, whom after it had pleased Almighty God about the same season to call him out of this vale of misery, the good disposed people of the Town of Wem in Shropshire where he died, brought the body into the Parish Church, intending there to have it buried, but one Bernard being the Curate of the Church, to stop the burial rode to the Bishop, to have his advise. The body in the mean time lay there two whole days and one night; when Bernard the Curate comes with the Bishop's Letter, of which we here have a copy word for word:—

" 'Understanding that one Glover a heretic is dead in the Parish of Wem, which Glover hath for all the time of my being in this Country been known for a rebel against our Holy Faith and Religion, a contemner of the Holy Sacrament and Ceremonies used in the Holy Church;—and hath separated himself from the Holy Communion of all good Christian men and never requested to be reconciled to Our Mother Holy Church, nor in his last days did call for his Ghostly Father, but died without all those Rites belonging to a Christian Man, I thought it good not only to command the Curate of Wem that he should not be buried with a Christian burial, but also will and command all the Parish of Wem that no man procure, help, nor speak to have him buried in Holy Ground. But do charge and command the Church Warden of Wem in special and all the Parish of the same, that they assist the said Church Curate in defending and rendering and procuring, that he be not buried either in the Church or within the limits of the Church Yard. I charge those that brought the body to this place to carry it away again, and that at their Charge as they will answer at their peril.

" 'At Ecclish, this 6 day of September, 1555.

" By your Ordinary Rudulph, Coventry and Litchfield.'

" It fell out that those who brought the corps thither were at their own charges to carry it back again. But as the body was corrupted and smelt so strongly that no man could come near it, they were forced to draw it with horses into a broomfield and there he was buried."

Something more about John Glover is gathered from the History of Warwickshire, Vol. 3, page 1054.

" Baxterly in Warwickshire.

" Within this Moiety is a fair Mansion call Baxterly Hall, built in King Edward 6th's time by John Glover, then a retainer to Lord Ferrers, as may appear by the Arms and Badges carved upon the timber work (but formerly attached to the Abbots of Heresdale, as by tradition I have heard), unto Whose house did that famous asserter of the Protestant Faith, Hugh Latimer, Sometime Bishop of

Worcester, resort. Whose Ghostly instructions so well grounded Robert Glover, brother to the said John, that rather than that he would recede from them he chose to lay down his life, being burnt at Coventry in the 5th or 6th of Philip and Mary, as Mr. Fox in his Catalogue of Martyrs has deduced. Which Robert had issue Hugh Glover, who inherited these Lands as Cousin and heir to his Uncle John Glover, in whose line they continued until John Glover, descendant of said Hugh Glover, by deed dated 22 July, 1704, sold the same to Thomas Strong, Esq., who by Sarah his wife, one of the daughters of Lovisagod Gregory of —— Hall in this County, Esq., hath Issue one son now living (1788), and one daughter named Lucy."

Page 1063. " Hurley Manor, Edward Glover, of Baxterly. Maria, wife of Edward Glover of Baxterly in Warwickshire, was daughter of Thomas Willington and Alicia, who were married in 1599."

John Glover, of Barcester, in Warwickshire. A notice of John Glover occurs on page 1076 of " History of the County of Warwickshire," which reaches further back than the time of Robert the Martyr. He may have been the father of Robert.

" William Harper, Nicholas Rowley and Thomas Arblaster, of Langdon, County of Staffordshire, Esquires, were in the 10th Year of Henry Sixth of England (1432), joyntly possessed of the manor of Monceter. Thomas Harper, the last of that name, sold his share to John Glover of Baxterly, in whose line it still continues now at this writing (1788), the manor house being a part of it."

" Robert Glover, martyred in September 20, 1555, wife Mary and several children; one named Hugh, another Edward. John Glover, his brother, of Monceter, wife Agnes, children. John was the elder brother; was arrested, escaped, and died of disease in 1555.

" William, another brother, met with similar usage; he escaped to Wem in Shropshire, and died there."

Thomas, of Coventry in Warwickshire and of Ashford in Kent, may have been a brother of the above martyrs; he was father of Robert the Antiquary. The conjecture is not improbable, as after the death of Queen Mary, who was succeeded by Elizabeth, times were changed in relation to those families whom she persecuted on account of their absolving themselves from the Catholic religion. Elizabeth's reign commenced in 1558, and those families which had been so persecuted by her predecessor, were treated by her with marks of especial favor. Where estates had been confiscated by Mary, they were restored to them or their children by Elizabeth, as in the case of the Glovers of Warwickshire.

Frequent instances are on record at the present time, by which it appears that many of the name have continued to enjoy the power and patronage of their Sovereigns — both Kings and Queens — one of which may find a place here.

Among the members of the Camden Society in London, for the year 1838–9, and previous years, are mentioned Ambrose Glover, Esq., F. S. A.; John Hurlburt Glover, Esq., F. S. A., Librarian to Her Majesty Queen Victoria.*

" Lancashire Visitations. Robert Glover, Somerset Herald. In the time of Queen Elizabeth, 1567, William Flowers, Norroy. The celebrated Robert Glover, Somerset Herald, accompanied his Father-in-law Flower in his Lancashire Visitations in 1567. The Rare Manuscripts were in the hand writing of the celebrated Glover, very neatly written, and marked L. 2086."

" List of Heralds appointed in the happy days of Queen Elizabeth, as set down in Burke's General Armory : — John Cooke of Lancaster, Robert Cooke of Chester, William Flower of Chester, William Colbarne of York, Ralph Langman of York, Richard Turpyn of Camden, and Robert Glover, who died in 1588. In the time of his being Herald he was employed to carry the Garter to the Emperor Maximilian, and afterwards was joined an Ambassador to the Earl of Shrewsbury to carry the Garter to Henry 4th, King of France."

Fuller, in giving an account of the distinguished writers of that time, 1588, speaks thus of him:

" Robert Glover, son to Thomas and Mildred, was born at Ashford, in Kent. He addicted himself to the study of Heraldry, and in the reward of his pains was made first a Pursuivant Port-Cullis and then Somerset Herald. When the Earl of Derby was sent into France to carry the Garter to King Henry Third of France, Mr.

---

* There are living at the present time in Coventry, in the County of Warwickshire, several families of the name of Glover, as shown in the Post Office Directory of 1859. The boundaries given of the County of Warwickshire may assist in directing the reader to the part of England whence many of the name originated. Warwickshire is bounded on the Northwest by Staffordshire, on the Northeast by Leicestershire, on the Southeast by Oxfordshire, on the East by Northamptonshire, on the Southwest by Gloucestershire, and on the West by Worcestershire. The London and Birmingham Railway passes through it. Its chief city is Coventry.

Glover attended the Embassage, and was, as he deserved, well rewarded for his pains. He by himself began in Latin a book called the Catalogue of Honour of our English Nobility, with their Arms and Mottoes. It being the first book of the kind, he therein travelled untrodden paths, and therefore no wonder who since succeeded him found a nearer way and exceeded him in acuteness therein. Being old rather in experience than years, he died not Forty six years old, Anno 1588, and lieth buried under a comely Monument in Saint Giles, without Cripplegate, London, on the south wall of the Church Choir. Let Mr. Camden's commendation pass for his Epitaph."

Stowe, in his "Survey of London," speaks thus of him (not in index):—

"The Skilful Robert Glover, Somerset Herald, a man of as good wit and great reading, so of infinite industry. He began the book called the Catalogue of Honour, in Latin (but finished by Thomas Milles, his kinsman), wherein he undertook to clear the descent of Royal Pedigrees of our Kings and Queens. He had an abundance of Rolls and Pedigrees and Ancient Writings of Heraldry, which he had gathered for his use, besides vast collections made by his own hands and travel, touching the Arms and Visitations of Twenty-four Shires, and Miscellaneous matters, all written by himself."

"Camden mentions him oft with honor, and acknowledges he had made much use of him in making out Genealogies.

"Glover also communicated to Dr. David Powell a copy of the History of Cambria, Translated by H. Lloyd.

"He was thus useful in prosecuting the knowledge of the Ancient Britons, and would have been much more had he not been taken away so early, being at his death but Forty five years old. In the Parish Church of Cripplegate, where he lies buried, is a fair monument got up to his memory, with an inscription in Latin."

The following notice from Chalmers appears to refer to this Robert Glover:—

"Thomas Glover, a Herald and Heraldic Writer, was the son of Thomas Glover of Ashford, in Kent, the place of his Nativity. He was first made Portcullis pursuivant, and afterwards, in 1571, Somerset Herald.

"Queen Elizabeth permitted him to travel abroad for improvement, and in 1582 he attended Lord Willoughby, with the order of

3

the Garter, to Frederic II. of Denmark. He waited as Clarencieux to the Earl of Derby, with that Order to the King of France.

"No one was a greater ornament to the College than this Gentleman. The Suavity of his manners was equal to his integrity and skill. He was a most excellent and very learned man, with a knowledge in his profession which has never been surpassed or exceeded, perhaps has never been paralleled. To this the best writers of his own and recent times bear testimony. He left two treatises — de Nobilitate Politica vel Civili, and a Catalogue of Honour, both of which were published after his death by his nephew Thomas Milles, the former in 1608, the latter in 1610 — both folio — to revive the name and memory of his deceased uncle and friend, whose private studies for the public good deserved a remembrance beyond the forgetfulness of time. His Answer to the Bishop of Rose's book, in which Mary Queen of Scots' claim to the Crown was asserted, was never published. He made great collections of what had been written by preceding Heralds, and left his own labors relative to Arms and Visitations of Twenty-four Counties, and miscellaneous matters belonging to this science, all written by himself. He assisted Camden in his Pedigrees for his Britannia — communicated to Dr. David Powell a copy of the History of Cambria, translated by H. Lloyd — made a collection of inscriptions upon the funeral monuments in Kent — drew up a most curious survey of Herewood Castle in Yorkshire, in 1584 — and his Catalogue of Northern Gentry, whose surnames ended in *son*. He died in London, says Stowe, April 14, others say 10, Anno Dom. 1588, aged only 45 years, and was buried in St. Giles Churchyard, Cripplegate. His loss was severely felt by all our lovers of English Antiquity. His Ordinary of Arms was augmented by Edmonson, who published it in his first volume of his Body of Heraldry."

Extract from Edmonson: "Glover, London, 1604, of Coventry, in Warwickshire, of Ashford, in Kent.

"Sa, a Chevron Ermine between three Crescents arg. Crest a Crossbow az. between two wings or.

"Another Crest on a round Chapeau, sa turned up, or two wings expanded of the first, granted in 1577."

From Burke's General Armory: "Glover, Norfolk, 1611, Romney, Kent, London. Also borne by Robert Glover, Somerset Herald, time of Elizabeth.

"Sa, Chevron Ermine between three Crescents argent. Crest an Eagle az. charged, or, with three spots of Erminites. Another Crest a dragon."

" Glover, London, 1604, Ashford, Co. of Kent and Coventry, in Warwickshire, granted 4 March, 1577. Sa, Chev. Erm. bet. three Cres. ar. Crest a Crossbow az. bet. two wings expanded of the first."

From Berry's Cyclopedia of Heraldry: " Glover, London. Sa, a Chev. Erm. between 3 Crescents argent. Granted to Thomas Glover, of London, in 1604."

Another writer gives an account of the Somerset Herald, and gives him the Christian name of Thomas. In some places, where the name is Robert in the index, on looking at the page, as in the Gentleman's Magazine, the article in relation to him is under the name of Thomas. There is a mystery in this synonyme of names as applied to the Somerset Herald by different writers, that has not yet been elucidated; but the accounts are correctly transcribed by the different authorities.

Hugh James Rose, D.D., Principal of Kings College, London, in his latest Heraldic Dictionary, writes thus: — Glover, Thomas. A Herald and heraldic writer, born in A.D. 1543, at Ashford in Kent. He was first made Portcullis, and afterwards, in 1571, Somerset Herald. In 1582 he attended Lord Willoughby with the Order of the Garter to Frederick of Denmark. In 1584 he waited as Clarencieux to the Earl of Derby, with that Order to the King of France. He wrote *de Nobilitate rel Civili*, and a Catalogue of Honour, published by his nephew, Mr. Thomas Milles; the former in 1608, the latter in 1610, fol. His answer to the Bishop of Rose's book, in which Mary Queen of Scots' claim to the Crown of England was asserted, was never published. He assisted Lord Camden in making out his Pedigrees for his Britannia, and communicated to Dr. David Powell a copy of the History of Cambria, translated by H. Lloyd. He made a collection of the Inscriptions upon the Funeral Monuments in Kent; and in A.D. 1584 he drew up a History of Herewood, with a Survey of Herewood Castle in Yorkshire. He died in 1588. His Ordinary of Arms was augmented and improved by Edmonson, who published it in his first Body of Heraldry."

The following references to Robert Glover are extracted from a work called the " Collectanea Topographica Genealogica." They relate principally to the different families of whom Robert Glover assisted to make out pedigrees and genealogies.

In Vol. vii., pages 256 and 320. Robert Glover: an account of assistance in tracing out the family of Willoughby, and the place where his collections were preserved. "N. B. Glover's Collections marked A contain Genealogical matter relative exclusively to the ancestors of Lord Willoughby, with a prefatory note in his hand-writing, deposited in the College of Arms."

"In a Pedigree for Sir George Shirley, drawn out in 1583, by Robert Glover, the most learned, Skilful Herald that ever lived." Other authorities are introduced, but are said " to weigh nothing against the authority of Glover."

Page 258, Vol. vii., Glover is referred to as getting a Pedigree of Robert De Spencer.

On page 320, Robert Glover, Somerset Herald, is noticed as being the author of several manuscripts, which Chartres asserts are in his own hand-writing, contained in a volume in the College of Arms, and marked Philpot E. I., and were derived immediately from the Monument Room in Cobham Hall, with notices of the family of Brooke.

In Vol. viii., page 299, the name of Glover may be found in a catalogue of "Whatsoever persons owning estates manorial or des-mesne, messuage, or mansions, within the County of Warwickshire, in the 20 year of Queen Elizabeth's Reign, being in the year A.D. 1577."

CRIPPLEGATE WARD.

Tolerandum, Seperandum.

Roberto Glovero, Alias Somerset, Teciali celeberrimo; Heraldi-cæ Scientiæ & veritatis antiquæ, vindici acerrimo; Summam lau-dem et benevolentiam ob præclarum ingenium, peracre Judicium ex multa veterum scriptorum (labore Indefesso) perscrutatione; ob mo-rum facilitatem, vitæque innocuæ sanctimoniam apud omnes consecu-to; Avunculo chariff (or ss). Thomas Milles Nepos, amoris hoc Monumentum mœrens posuit.

Robertus iste, natus Ashfordiæ Cantii emporio, parentibus inge-nius, liberaliter educatus, in multis apprimè, versatus Heraldicæ unice peritissimus evasit. Fratrem unicum Gulielmum ex Thomas & Mil-dredæ, pp. Sorores autem 5 habuit, ex Elizabetha Flower Conjuge, 5 tantum, superstices reliquit liberas, filios scilicet 3, filiasque 2.

Tandem cum jam Patriæ orbiq. post varia exantlata studia acuminis, peritiæ & diligentiæ stupendæ gustum insignem præbero, atque Principi Sereniss. Suis meritis gratissimus esse ceperit, 10th April, 1588, ætat Suæ 45 vitam erumnosam cum morte piè & placidè in uno Christo commutavit. Idque omnium cum Doctissimorum, tum optimorum undiquæ pro tanto literar pietatis & virtutis — alumno dolore ac gemium; utpote, Quem fata tantum terris ostendisse videantur, nec-amplius esse sinant.

R. G. Moriens ut vixerat, vixit ut moriturus.

TRANSLATION, BY W. S. LEACH.

" Enduring, Hoping.

" To Robert Glover, alias the Somerset Herald, celebrated as a powerful defender of the art of Heraldry and Antiquarian Truth. From a thorough examination of his old writings, a man of great honor and benignity, of a noble nature and indefatigable labor; of easy manners, living honestly and uprightly before his successors.

" This sad monument was erected by a loving Nephew, Thomas Milles, to his most beloved maternal uncle.

" This Robert was born in Ashford, in Kent, a market town, of free parents, was liberally educated and became eminently learned in many things, but was particularly well versed and skilful in Heraldry. He had only one brother, William, from Thomas and Mildred, and also five sisters. He left five surviving children by his wife Elizabeth Flowers, viz., three sons and two daughters. Robert Glover dying as he had lived, lived as if he was about to die. His life closed with death, and he departed piously and calmly united in Christ."

The following is another translation, procured from the Rev. T. Wilson :

" Abiding, Hoping.

"To Robert Glover, alias, sometimes called Somerset Herald; a most strenuous maintainer of Heraldic Knowledge and Antiquarian Lore; a man of the highest worth and benignity, on account of his excellent ability and subtle judgment, derived from a thorough reading and searching with unwearied toil of many old writings; in view of the courteousness of his manners, and in consequence of the probity

3*

of his blameless life before all; Thomas Milles, a Nephew sorrowful erects this monument of Love to his most beloved Maternal Uncle.

"This Robert was born in Ashford, a market town in Kent, of respectable parents. He was liberally educated, and died eminently skilled in many things, but remarkably well versed in Heraldry. His only brother, William, was born of Thomas and Mildred, but he had five sisters. He left only five surviving children, viz., three sons and two daughters by his wife Elizabeth Flower. Most thankful for his worth, he may have reached the 10th of April, Anno 1588, in the 45th year of his age. He has exchanged a life suddenly broken off, for a devout and tranquil death in Christ. So when he was of all the most learned, he became one of the most happy."

The translator was obliged to pass over some sentences, which were obscure, and could not be made into good English.

Thus it appears that the parents of this Robert Glover were Thomas Glover, of Ashford in the County of Kent, England, and Mildred his wife. Thus:

Robert, b. 1543, m. Elizabeth Flower, died April 10, 1588.
William, b. 1545, m. Anne ——, d. Dec. 17, 1603, London, æ. 58.
Joanna, m. Richard Mylles, of Ashford in Kent.
Elizabeth, m. Thomas Deedes, of Wythe.
—— —— m. John Philpot.

T. Moule published a work on Genealogies in 1660, in which he notices Robert Glover thus:—

"Robert Glover wrote de Nobilitate Politica vel Civili, of 190 pages." (An extract therefrom in Latin, accompanied by the following remarks of the author, T. Moule.) He says, referring to the Latin extract, " It is only a portion of the original of the next article, which was compiled by Robert Glover, Somerset Herald, in the reign of Queen Elizabeth. A man fully qualified by industry to fulfil the laborious duties of his office. He died on the 10th of April, 1588, and was buried at Cripplegate Church, where, on the south side, is a monument to his memory. His authority in Genealogy and Heraldry is much relied on by the officers of Arms at the present day.

" Thomas Milles revised this work in 1608, and in 1610 got it printed. The title-page is engraved by Renald Elstrache. At the top are the Royal Arms and supports. The lower part is occupied as a group of three figures, Honor, Nobilitas, Pax. It is inscribed,

Catalogue of Honour, London, printed by William Jaggard. The Epistle is dedicated to Robert Cecil, Earl of Salisbury, and Henry Howard, Earl of Northamptonshire. It explains that his intention in publishing this work is to revive the name and memory of Robert Glover, his uncle, who had taken such uncommon pains to clear the descents and Pedigrees of our Kings and Nobility. At the death of Mr. Glover, his nephew, with the assistance of several friends, undertook to translate and reduce it to method, acknowledging, at the same time, the aid he received from the good antiquaries of that day, viz., Lord William Howard, nephew to the Earl of Northampton, Sir Robert. Cotton, Robert Brooke, Clerk to the Council, William Camden, Clarencieux, and Nicholas Charles, Lancaster Herald, Michael Hennage, keeper of the Records in the Tower, Thomas Talbot and Matthew Patterson."

The Epistle contains six pages, according to J. Leslie, who speaks thus of another of Mr. Glover's manuscripts, written in Latin, but never published.

"The Title and interest of the most excellent Mary Queen of Scots. The defence to that Title, and of the right of Queen Elizabeth to the English Crown against the plea set up by Bishop Ross, and in answer to the claim of the House, was considered by Sir William Dugdale as one of Glover's best performances."

Thomas Milles, Esq., of Davington Hall, near Feversham in Kent, the translator and publisher of this work, was the son of Richard Milles, of Ashford, by Joann, the sister of Robert Glover, Somerset Herald. He appears to be a man of some consideration as well as learning, and discharged a trust reposed in him by Queen Elizabeth, on a mission in which he was sent to King Henry the Fourth of France with credit and distinction. He afterwards held the following offices as custoder of the Port of London, Keeper of the Roche Castle and Esquire to the Body of King James the First of England.

Upon the death of his uncle, Mr. Glover, it appears he first applied to George Earl of Shrewsbury, respecting the manuscripts of that industrious Herald. There is a letter extant, the copy of which is in the Gentleman's Magazine, Vol. 90, part 1st, p. 595, from Thomas Milles to that nobleman in behalf of the widow of Somerset, left with five children, offering the manuscripts to his Lordship in consideration of an annuity of one hundred pounds sterling per annum. They were afterwards published by Lord Burleigh.

A William Glover was married to Anne Gaveiard, in Rainehill, November 6, 1578, and may have been the one whose history follows. He could not have been the father of Thomas Glover of Rainehill, as Thomas himself was married only fourteen years after, in 1594, but there is evidence that he was collaterally related.

He had a Coat of Arms granted him in A.D. 1602. It is said to be the same arms which Fuller finds recorded in the Worthies of Middlesex, granted to William Glover, Sheriff, at an earlier date.

The arms granted to William Glover of London, "Arg. a Chev. Ermine betwixt three Cross Crosslets," were granted to him by Queen Elizabeth one year before his death.

William Glover was buried in London, Colman Street Ward.

A fair monument in chancel is erected to his memory.

"Here lyeth in peace the body of Sir William Glover, Knight, late Citizen and Alderman of London, who for his many good gifts both in sincere religion, Wisdom and Gravity wherewith he was very plentifully endowed and graced, was elected Sheriff of London, and served the same in 1611. He had lived in good name and fame Fifty Eight years, and very blessedly departed this life the 17 of December, 1603· Leaving two sons, Thomas and William, and five daughters, viz., Anne, married to Barne Roberts of Willesden, in the County of Middlesex, Esq.; Susan, Elizabeth, Mary and Alice, behind him to mourn the loss of so loving a Father. To whose deceased memory the Lady Anne Glover, the most Sorrowful Widow of the deceased said Sir William, lamenting his death and unrecoverable loss, at her own charge erected this monument in testification of her love and duty."

In 1612, Dame Anne Glover, the widow of Sir William Glover, late of London, gave a stock of £10 to the poor of the Parish.

In 1660, William Glover, son to Sir William Glover, gave to the Hospital in London, Two Hundred Pounds.

Thomas Glover, son of Sir William Glover and the Lady Anne his wife, was born in London, was created Knight, married Jane Roberts, daughter of Francis Roberts, Esq., of Willesden in Middlesex. He died in London, and his widow, the Lady Jane Glover, married George Purefoy, Esq., died 8 June, 1664, æ. 77 years.

William, the second son, married Elizabeth Harlakenden, daughter of Henry Harlakenden, Esq.

Anne, the eldest daughter, married Barne Roberts, son to Francis Roberts, Esq., her cousin.

Susan, the second daughter, married Thomas Philpot, Esq., Norroy Somerset Herald.

ASHTON, GLOUCESTERSHIRE, GLOVER.

Sir Thomas Glover, having purchased Franklin's estate, in Ashton Underhill, he, with Mr. Wakeman, took a fresh grant of the manor from the Crown in the reign of King James I., of England, and afterwards by deed, reserving to himself and his heirs certain manorial rights over his own lands, conveyed all other manorial rights over the residue of the manor to Mr. Wakeman; and Henry Wakeman, of Beckford, Esq., is the descendant of that Wakeman from whose son is this account derived. See Beckford.

Ashton Underhill. One part of this Parish lies in the Hundred of Tibblestone, the other in the upper divisions of Tewksbury, seven miles distant, from which it comes six miles North-East from Tewksbury and sixteen North-East from Gloucester. It was anciently a member of the Manor of Beckford (and by corruption, Aston). King Henry VIII. granted this Manor to Sir Richard Lee, who had two daughters co-heiresses, who made a division of their estates, and the Manor of Beckford, of which Aston was a part, was sold to Richard Franklyn and Edward Wakeman. Therefore, from Sir Richard Franklyn to Sir Thomas Glover, and from Edward Wakeman to Henry Wakeman, his son and heir.

Lady Jane Glover was the wife of Sir Thomas Glover, Knight, of Hayes Park, in the County of Middlesex. After the death of Sir Thomas Glover, she married the second time to George Purefoy, Esq., the eldest of Wadley in the County of Berkshire.

In the Church of Feecham, on a black grave-stone before the communion rails, is the following inscription, viz.:

"Here sleepeth the Body of Dame Jane Purefoy, who was the dau. of Francis Roberts of Willesden in the County of Middlesex, Esq., wife of Sir Thomas Glover of Hayes Park in the said County of Middlesex, Knight, and relict of George Purefoy, the eldest of Wadley, in the County of Berkshire, Esq., who exchanged this life for a better the 8 of January, 1664, aged 77 years."

ROBERT GLOVER, HELLIDON, NORTHAMPTONSHIRE.

Hellidon, in ancient records Elidon, may possibly be derived from the Saxon Holb, sleep, and sundown is at least descriptive of the situation of the village.

The Lordship contained about one thousand five hundred and ten acres. Part is old enclosure, and the open fields were enclosed by act of Parliament, in 14 George III., 1774.

Sir Thomas Wenham, of Carswell, County of Oxon, sold Hellidon in 1556, and died 22 July, 19 of Elizabeth, 1577. Sir Thomas Wenham and Ursula his wife sold this manor, in 1556, to Robert Glover of Hellidon, Yeoman, who died the year following, 1557, seized of a capital messauge and seventeen vergates and a quarter of land in Hellidon, leaving William Glover his son and heir to the inheritance, aged 20 years.

This estate has been alienated in parcels, but a considerable portion is now vested in the devisees of the late Joseph Ashley, of Ashley Ledges.

William Glover, son of William Glover, Esq., and Anne ——, was married to Elizabeth Harlakenden, the daughter and co-heir of Henry Harlakenden, Esq., had one daughter Susan Glover, who married to John Philpot, Esq., Norroy, Somerset Herald, and had one daughter, Susan Philpot.

The monumental inscription reads thus:

"Here lies the Bodye of Susan Philpot, late wife and Widow of John Philpot, Esq. Norroy, Somerset Herald, in the Chancel of this Church.

"She was the daughter and sole heir of William Glover, Esq., and Elizabeth his wife, the daughter and co-heir of Henry Harlakenden, Esq. Her daughter Susan lies buried near her."

SIR WILLIAM GLOVER, MANORIAL ESTATE, ANSLEY MANOR.

Ansley belonged to the family of Culpepper. The manor passed in mortgage unto Wm. Glover, citizen and dyer in London, in the thirty fourth (1592) reign of Elizabeth, by George Wightman, who in the forty-third of Elizabeth (1601), obtained a release from Thomas Wightman, son and heir to the said George, of all his right and title therein. To which William Glover, afterwards a Knight and alderman of London, succeeded Sir Thomas Glover of Williston, Commonwealth of Middlesex, his son and heir, who with the Lady Anne, his mother, sold it in the sixth year of James (1609), unto James Wightman, of Beachman.

"Here lyeth the body of Barne Roberts, eldest son of Francis Roberts, of Williston, Esq., in the County of Middlesex, who took to wife Anne, the eldest daughter of Sir William Glover, Knight and Alderman of London, by whom he had three sons and five daughters. The said Barne Roberts dyed January 30, 1610, aged 34 years. Thereon his said Wife Anne, of her very kind and loving affection, at her own proper expense and charges, hath caused this monument to be erected, A.D. 1611."

J. Bernard Burke, in his Heraldic Dictionary of the Landed Gentry of Great Britain and Ireland, published in London in 1853, comprising, as he affirms, "a faithful and worthy record of that class of Gentlemen who, though indistinguishable by hereditary titles, possess an undeniable right, from antiquity of race, extent of property, and brilliancy of achievements, to hold foremost rank among the lesser nobility of Europe," under article Glover, gives the following names, with the figures attached to them, which refer to the description of their estates, the manner of their receiving and holding them, &c., viz.: —

Glover, of Mount Glover, Co. of Cork, 3368; Anne and Robert, 596; Edmund, 31–8; Elizabeth, 501; Elizabeth and Robert, 320; Hannah, Elizabeth and William, 168; James, 447; John Jackson, 73–8; Jonathan, 1531; Mary, 1473, 1958; Mary and Philip, 1048; Mary and Samuel, 151; Miss Glover, 464; Miss and James, 261–8; Rachel, 99; Richard and Daniel, 234–8; Sibella and Samuel Codrington, 1040; Thomas Glover, 827.

Of the above names of Glover, Burke gives the lineage of James of Mount Glover, Co. of Cork, Ireland. "James Glover, Esq., of Mount Glover, eldest surviving son of the late James Glover, Esq., by Mildred his wife, daughter of Robert Freeman, Esq., of Ballingait Castle, is the representative of John Glover, Esq., who settled in Ireland in the middle of the 17th Century. Arms, Sa, a Chev.-Erm. between three Cres. arg. Crest, an Eagle, displayed, arg. charged on the breast with three spots of Erminites.   Motto, Nec Timeo nec sperno."

Copy of lineage, as given by Burke:

"John Glover, the first of the family who settled in Ireland early in the 17th Century, was a near relation of Robert Glover, Esq., the famous Genealogist of the 16th century, and Somerset Herald at Arms. He was a captain in command of a large body of troops under one of the Percivals, and greatly distinguished himself by his obstinate and gallant defence of the Bath at Arms; which he suc- ceeded in holding against the attacks of an immense body of Irish, who continued to check his small and gallant band for three days; when they were compelled to retire with much slaughter. For his remarkable bravery and success on this, as well as for other services in the local wars of the times, he obtained possession of extensive and valuable estates in the Counties of Cork and Limerick, in Ire- land. He married a Miss Mills, sister of Thomas Mills, Esq., and had issue, one son and three daughters, viz.:

"1. Edward, b. 1668; d. 24th April, 1753; married, in 1695, to Eleanor, daughter of James Barry, Esq., of Ballinvauve, and had issue four sons — 1. Edward, b. 1696; d. April, 1747, a. 45 years; m. a Miss Quinn, and had issue only one daughter, who m. her first cousin, Philip Barry, of Ballinvauve. 2. James, of Fourmile Water, b. 1705; d. April, 1753, æ. 48 years; m. a Miss Maunsell, and died leaving no issue. His estate devolved on his next brother. 3. Thomas Glover, of whom presently. 4. John Glover, m. a Miss Pole, of Kinsale, and d. without issue."

Thomas Glover, the third son of Edward and Eleanor (Barry) Glover, b. in 1712, d. 22 April, 1772, æ. 60 years, succeeded to the Mount Glover estate. He m. April 1, 1751, Mary, only daughter and heiress of William Martin, Esq., of Corroden, by his wife Anne Purdon, of Bally Clough Castle. Thomas Glover married, 2d, Mary, only daughter of Edward Brailing, Esq., of Dublin, widow of Chas. Maccarty, Esq., of Bathduff. By the first wife only he had issue — three sons and three daughters. The 2d, and eventually only sur- viving son, was James Glover, Esq., who succeeded to the estate of Mount Glover; m. Mildred, eldest daughter of Robert Freeman, Esq., of Ballindale Castle, by his wife Mildred, daughter of William Seeley, Esq., by his wife Mildred, daughter of Col. Frederick Mul- lens, direct ancestor of Lord Vantry. By this lady Mr. James Glover had fourteen children, as follows:

1. Thomas Glover, who died in 1812, unmarried.
2. Edward, M.D., died unmarried.
3. James Glover, of Mount Glover.
4. William, Lieutenant in the army, died unmarried.
5. Stirling Freeman, Lieut.-Colonel in the army; married Georgianna, 2d daughter of Lord Charles Henry Somerset, fifth Duke of Beaufort.
6. George Freeman, who married a Miss White of Cork, and died leaving two sons, George and Robert Glover.
7. Mildred, who married Maurice Newman, Esq.
8. Ellen, who married William Hudson, Esq., M.D.
9. ——, died unmarried.
10. Margaret, died unmarried.
11. Bridget, married Edward Power, Esq., of Kildare.
12. ——, died unmarried.
13. James Glover, of Mount Glover, succeeded to the Mount Glover estate; married in 1813, Ellen, only daughter of John Power, Esq., by Abigail Ballen his wife, and had issue as follows: Edward Auchmuty, J. P., barrister at law. James, M.D., died unmarried. Marlboro' Parsons Stirling Freeman, died unmarried. Piercy Power, died young. Ellen Alicia, married —— Crafts. Mildred Lavinia Freeman, married Townsend McDermot. Anna Maria Stirling. Mary Georgiana Somerset, married J. Abollaram, Esq.

Thus we have the succession to the Mount Glover estate in a direct line — from John Glover to his only son Edward; from Edward devolving on Thomas, third son of Edward; from this last to James; then James again, the present occupant, who married in 1813 — five generations.

OF THE RICHARD GLOVERS.

"Here lyeth buryed the Bodye of Richard Glover, Citizen and Pewterer of London; who was twice master of his Company and one of the Common Council of this City, having two wives, Elizabeth and Mary — had issue by his first, three sons, and by his second wife five sons and four daughters — he deceased the 16 day of August, A.D. 1615, being aged 59 years."

This appears to be the earliest date of the Richard Glovers that has been gathered. He was born in 1556, and was twice married, 1st to Elizabeth, 2d to Mary.

Richard Glover, born in 1649, is the next date: of Waldingham, Surrey, Chelsham; married, had children; son Richard born in 1676.

The next, taken from the monumental inscriptions in the Church or Chapel at Chelsham. Richard Glover, born in 1676.

" Underneath this Stone lye buried the Bodye of Mr. Richard Glover, heretofore of Waldingham, but late of Slines in this Parish, afterwards of Sanderstead, Eldest Son to Mr. Richard Glover, heretofore of Waldingham, who also lies buried in this Parish, and which the said Richard his son departed this life 13 August, 1753, in the 77 year of his age.

Also

" The bodye of Mrs. Susanna Glover, widow of the said Richard Glover the younger, and eldest daughter of Mr. Richard Harswell, heretofore of Westerham, in the County of Kent, who departed this life the 24 of March, 1761, in the 87 year of her age.

Also

" The Bodye of Mr. John Glover, one of the sons of the said Richard and Susanna Glover, who died a Bachelor in the 54 year of his age, and was buried on the 8th of March, 1760."

Richard Glover, son of Richard of Waldingham and Chelsham, was married to Susanna Hayward, daughter of Mr. Richard Hayward of Westerham in the County of Kent, born there about 1674. She died in Chelsham the 24 of March, 1761, and was entombed at Chelsham, Surrey. Her inscription, on a monument in the Church-yard or Chapel, together with that of the elder Richard Glover, and Richard Glover his son, is given above.

Richard and Susanna Glover had children: a son John Glover, born in 1706; a son Richard, born in 1704, who settled at Waldingham. A monumental inscription at Waldingham on the floor of the Church—" Here lyeth the Bodie of Richard Glover, yeoman of this Parish, who died 19 March, 1772, aged 68 years."

On another tomb-stone, much obliterated, is a memorial of a Richard Glover, of Croydon in Surrey, who was born in A.D. 1698. The inscription reads thus:

" Here lyeth the Bodye of Mr. Richard Glover, late of Croydon in Surrey; an eminent Attorney at Law. He died 22d of January, A.D. 1766. Aged 68 years."

Richard Glover, an eminent Poet, Merchant, and Member of Parliament, was born in St. Martin's Lane, Cannon St. London, in 1712, and died there in 1785, æ. 73 years. He was the son of Mr. Richard Glover, an eminent merchant of London, who was a brother of Phillips Glover, Esq., of the family of Robert Glover, the Somerset Herald, and bore the same arms.

This Richard Glover acquired a distinguished reputation as a poet. He composed an epic poem called Leonidas, and published it in 1737. In 1739 he published a poem entitled the "Progress of Commerce." In 1742 he was elected by the merchants of London to conduct an application complaining of the neglect of trade. He made a speech at the Bar of the House of Commons, on the subject, which was highly applauded. It was afterwards printed.

In 1751 he was an unsuccessful candidate for the office of Chamberlain of London. He wrote the Tragedy of Boadicea, which was performed at the Drury-Lane Theatre in London, in 1753, with good success. In 1761 he wrote another tragedy. His Medea, which was imitated from Euripides and Seneca, appeared in 1761. His rare wit and humor is thus referred to on the occasion of the Degree of LL.D. being conferred at Cambridge on Sir W. Calvert, Lord Mayor of London, who, in his address before that honorable assembly, says: "I remember a mournful example in the fate of an ingenious Author and Merchant. The Poet ruined the Merchant. Had this distinguished Genius studied the Mercantile more, and the Epic less, he might have been an Alderman, although that Right Worshipful (Bodye) Corps would perhaps have apprehended dangerous consequences from admitting so great a Wit among them."

May 21, 1737, he married Hannah Nunn, daughter of Jonathan Nunn, Esq., a lady said to possess a handsome fortune. The Manor of Passamere descended to her, being sole heir to her father. Several other estates were possessed by her as her inheritance.

The Manor of Passamere took its name from the Passamere family, who settled here in the third year of King Henry III. (1219). It was sold to Mr. Pink, and by him to Jonathan Nunn, Esq., who died in 1630, and his widow enjoyed it after him. It then descended to their daughter and sole heir, Hannah Nunn, who married Richard Glover, Esq., of London, author of Leonidas.

Richard Glover, of London, Esq., the Poet, was in possession of Downe Court Manor, in 1785. From him it descended to his son Richard, who was in possession of it in 1788 and afterwards.

Appleton's Cyclopedia of Biography, Art. GLOVER:—"Richard Glover, a distinguished Greek scholar and poet. Popularly known as the author of Leonidas, Hosier's Ghost, &c., 1712–1785—London."

The portrait of Mr. Richard Glover, merchant-poet, was engraved by Fitler, and is preserved in the Cheatham Library.

"The Parish of Waldingham was in the possession of a Mr. Richard Glover in 1809 — two farm houses and two cottages. The mansion house is now a farm house known by the name of Fickleshole, and near it is a considerable pond, which from the scarcity of water on the high grounds of Chelsham and the country thereabouts, appears to have been resorted to by the neighbors so long ago as the 16th year of King Edward II. (1323). A deed of that date in Mr. Glover's hand describes land as abutting on a highway which led to a place called Fickles-hole-water. The demesne lands called Fickleshole consist of seven hundred and two acres, as it appears by a plan and the deed above mentioned, and were of consequence enough to deserve particular attention, which Mr. Glover has caused to be done according to the papers in his hands." Co. of Surrey, Vol. ii. p. 423. Mr. Glover has in his possession a quantity of brass and Roman coins from the lower empire, which were found in this Parish about fifty years ago (1809), preserved in an earthen vessel, which had been broken by the wheel of a carriage on the highway leading from the village of Nutfield towards Ham. He is also in possession of some original papers addressed to Audsley (1809).

Richard Glover, born in 1700, wife Mary, died Dec. 20th, 1768, æ. 68 years. Mary, wife of Richard Glover, died July 14, 1775, æ. 71 years; born A.D. 1704.

Henry Glover, of Worcestershire. His name appears among a list of benefactors. "Henry Glover of this Parish (old Swinston), gave four hundred pounds, which have been laid out in Lands and vested in the Governors of the Free Grammar School in Stourbridge, in trust, that out of the Rents, they do cause six boys to be instructed in English Writing and Arithmetic at the Free School for six years each; and provide them all necessary books, pens, ink and paper, and place one of the said boys out at apprentice annually with five pounds to be given as a premium." Hist. Co. Worcester, Vol. i. p. 213.

It is presumed the above Henry lived about the last of the 16th century; but there is no date to the old book from which the record was extracted. He is probably the Henry who was in Lancashire in 1572, and married there about that time.

GLOVERS OF RAINHILL PARISH, PRESCOT, LANCASHIRE, ENGLAND.

Lancashire is one of the Northern counties of England, and the town of Prescot, in that County, is one of its most extensive towns. It is bounded on the south by the River Mersey; on the west, by Walton Parish; on the north-north-west by Ormskirk Parish; and on the east, by the Parish of Warrington. Its extreme length is twelve miles, from Dalton on the south to Mumford on the north; its breadth is eight miles. It is situated in the western part of the county, about ten miles from Liverpool in the same county, and two hundred and twenty-five miles from London, by railway. It is at the present time divided into Parishes, one of which is Rainhill, the birth-place of John Glover, who in 1630 emigrated, with others under Gov. Winthrop, to New England, and became the American ancestor of numerous descendants. In 18th Edward III. William Daniell held the towns of Dutton, Rainhill and Eccleston. His possession of them was temporary, and in 12 Henry IV. they were held by Alan de Norrys, under the Baron of Holton. The Ecclestons for a long time were Lords of the Manor of Barton head, in Dutton. The family of Norrys acquired Rainhill in the time of Edward II., and held the Manors, of Dutton, Rainhill and Eccleston, under Thomas, Earl of Lancaster, who held the Duchy in the time of Henry VIII., and sold portions of it in the time of Elizabeth to Thomas Glover, Esq., father of the American emigrant. Thomas Glover conveyed these lands to his eldest son, Mr. John Glover, of Rainhill, afterwards of Dorchester and Boston—who, in 1652, by deed of gift, conveyed them to his eldest son and heir apparent, Mr. Thomas Glover, of London, merchant.

The Glovers were not early in Lancashire. The County history does not give any account of them until nearly the close of the sixteenth century.

There is a record among some old manuscripts in the Tower of

4*

Londen, of a William Glover who owned lands at Derby, and a Thomas Glover who owned lands at Rainhill, in Prescot, Lancashire, in the sixteenth century, but the particulars in relation to them, which were undoubtedly given there in detail, were not communicated.

These three marriages are recorded on the Parish Records, which, if faithfully communicated, appear to be the first notice of them there—viz.:

"Henry Glover was married to —— ——, 22 Dec., 1574.

"William Glover and Anne Goverard were married the 6 Nov., 1578.

"Thomas Glover and Margery Deane were married the 10 Feb., 1594."

From what county these individuals had their origin, or what line they connect with, has not been ascertained. It is confidently believed, however, that they were led to the northern counties by the religious persecution which occurred about the middle of the sixteenth century, and by which some of the families of Glover and others suffered severely.

Henry, the first above recorded, appears to have remained and settled there, some of whose descendants are still living in the same place.

Of William, the records give nothing further, and evidence seems to indicate that he settled in London, and was the William Glover, dyer and Alderman, afterwards Sir William Glover—wife Anne, who after his elevation became the Lady Anne, and distinguished herself by her benevolence.

Thomas Glover, whose marriage is given above, remained and lived in Rainhill. He purchased lands there of Thomas Lancaster, Esq., son of the Earl of that Duchy, and of Edward Eccleston, Esq., in Eccleston; also of Thomas Gerard, Esq., of William Woodfall, in Appleton, and of Lyman Garnet, Esq., and became the possessor of several estates there, all of which he conveyed, before his decease, to his eldest son John Glover. There is a link wanting in the genealogical chain, which would give a certainty to the family he connects with, as the names of the parents of Thomas Glover, of Rainhill, have never been obtained. Tradition says they originated in some of the oldest counties of England, as Kent or Warwickshire. Heralds confirm this by the armorial bearings they grant to the families of this line, and from all that has been gathered the strongest presumption, aided by tradition, evinces and determines his relationship and connection with the family of Robert, alias Thomas Glover, Somerset Herald, whose parents were from Coventry in Warwickshire, and from Ashford in Kent—either by direct descent or by collateral ties of consanguinity; and the same evidence obtains in the belief that there was a relationship or kinship existing between Robert the martyr, of 1555, and the Somerset Herald, who died in London in 1588.

There is a tradition which has come down among some branches of his descendants, from father to son through long generations, which fixes their original county to be that of Warwick, and the city of Coventry, in that County, one of their original places of abode. This tradition has been attested and confirmed by Heralds. Charles L. Cole, Esq., who was an Heraldic transcriber and writer, attested this assertion in the year 1804, to some of the descendants of Mr. John Glover, of Dorchester and Boston, whose history was well known in London, from his connection with the London Company and other institutions and societies there. This descendant, who had at that time a personal interview with Mr. Cole, and a conversation on Glover origin and Glover genealogies, was informed that a pedigree of Glover had been written out, reaching back many centuries, by a distinguished genealogist of his name and kin, in England; and that a transcript of it could be obtained by applying to the Herald's College, at London. The application has never been made.

MR. THOMAS GLOVER, FATHER OF THE EARLIEST EMIGRANT TO NEW ENGLAND.

The place of his birth cannot be given with certainty. He lived in Rainhill from the time of his marriage, and died there Dec. 13, 1619. He was married to Margery Deane, daughter of Thomas Deane, of Rainhill, Feb. 10, A.D. 1594. The following list of the children of Thomas and Margery (Margaret) Deane Glover, born in Rainhill Parish, has been copied from the records there, and arranged as in the original. Ten in number.

1. Ellen, bap. Feb. 2, 1595; m. William Barnes.
2. John, a Twin, bap. July 27, 1599, died the same day.
3. Elisabeth, a Twin to the above, bap. July 27, 1599, died the same day.
+4. John, bap. 12 Aug., 1600; m. Anna ——, went to New England.

+5. Henry, bap. 15 Feb., 1603 ; m. Abigail ——, went to New
      England.
  6. Anne, bap. Oct. 19, 1605, died Oct., 1605, 1 month.
  7. Thomas, b. 1607 ; m. Deborah Rigby, of Cranston.
+8. William, b. 1609 ; m. Mary Bolton, of Rainhill, 24 Nov., 1664.
+9. George, b. 1611 ; m. Margaret ——.
  10. Jane, bap. 13 Sept., 1612 ; m. —— Watts.
+11. Peter, bap. 22 March, 1615 ; married.

Will of Thomas Glover, of Rainhill.

The following is a copy of the remains of the Will of Mr. Thomas Glover, of Rainhill, deposited in the Registry office at Chester in the County of Chester, in England. It bears date 1519, is written on parchment, but portions of it have become so obliterated by damp and mould, that they cannot be read.

In the name of God Amen.

This 10 day of December, A. D. 1619, I Thomas Glover, of Rainhill, in the County of Lancashire, (Tanner) being sicke in body yet whole in mynde ; nevertheless being in good and perfect memory (Praise be to God) Doe make and ordayne this my last Will and Testament, in manner and form following.

First and principal I commit and bequeathe my soul to Almyghty God my Maker and Redeemer, and my Bodye to be buried in the Parish Church, or Church Yard of Prescot by the direction of my Executors hereinafter named. * * * * * * * *

Item, Concerning my Worldly Goods. It is my mynde that *
* * * * * * * * * * * *
out of my whole Goods after the * * * * *
* * * * * * * * * * * *
* * * * * * * * * * * *
hundredth pounds in full satisfaction * * * * *
* * * * * * * * * * * *
* * * * * * * * * * Goods
* * * * * * * * * * Also
I do give unto my * * * * * * * *
* * * * * * * * * * *

Also, * * * give unto William Barnes my Son-in-law
* * * * * * * * * * *
Also I do give unto my men Servants each and every of them *
* * * * * * * * * * * *
* * * * * * * * * unto my women
Servants each and every of them * * * * * *
* * * * * * * * * * * *
* * * * * * * * * give and bequeathe
all the rest and residue of my said Goods unto my six youngest children—viz. : Thomas, Henry, William, George, Peter and Jane Glover, equally to be divided among them. * * * * * *
* * * * * * * *
Item further it is my mynd * * * * * * *

* * * * * * * * * * * * *

so given unto my said youngest children as aforesaid shall come short of One hundred and fifty pounds a piece, then my land shall be charged to make up their said portions every one of them one hundred and fifty pounds as aforesaid. * * * * *

* * * * * * Item, further, it is my mynde that (it if please God) my said wife shall be with child at the time of my death—then my mynde is that such child so to be borne as aforesaid, shall have out of every of my youngest childrens portions so bequeathed to them as aforesaid Twenty pounds towards its preferment *

Item, I doe ordayne and make my said wife * * * * *

* * * * * * * * * * *

and John Glover my sonne my true and lawful Executors. * *

* * * * * * * * * * *

well as my trust is in them so to doe * * * * *

* * * * * * * * * * *

* * * * * * * * * * *

John Alden, Vicar of Prescot * * * * * Thomas Woods, of Whiston, and Edward Deane, my Brother-in-law to be Overseers of this my last Will and Testament, as I hope they will, to see the same performed accordingly * * * * * *

Witnesses at the publishing hereof
  Edward Deane,
  Thomas Woods,
  Thomas Deane,
  Edward Stockley.

The name of Thomas Glover as a signer to this will is obliterated or destroyed by mould, so that it cannot be read without difficulty.

The portion to his son John, who was his eldest, cannot be read, but it appears from other evidence that he gave him his estates in Rainhill, Eccleston, Knawlesby, and elsewhere in Lancashire County, who afterwards conveyed them, in 1652, to his son Thomas Glover.

(4) John emigrated to N. England and settled in Dorchester in 1630.

(5) Henry also, his second son, came over about 1640, and settled in Medfield—had grants of land in Dedham as early as 1640, and died in Medfield in 1655.

(8) William Glover, son of Thomas and Margaret (Deane) Glover.

There is a notice of him in 1652, in which he is styled a mercer, or dealer in silk, and in another place a merchant, and lived in Whiston, Lancashire Co., England; but no record appears of his having remained in Rainhill after his arrival at the age of manhood.

A tradition of him has reached the present generation, or some branches of it, and which is confirmed by references, that he also came to New England, and was in Dorchester at one time towards the close of the 17th century.

The precise date has not been given by those who assert the fact, but it is certain that his name appears on a document called Glover's Agreement, dated at Dorchester in 1680. It relates to a division of Newbury Farm, which belonged to the heirs of Mr. John Glover, who was his eldest brother, and it appears that William was an acting attorney on the share of one of his nephews. Information from other sources renders it certain that he was in New England at one time, and at Dorchester with his eldest brother. Tradition says that "he was the owner of lands there, and intended to settle in Boston, and that he returned to England to make arrangements for that purpose. He was requested by his brothers to gather up and get all the copies of manuscripts which related to the Glover pedigree, and in relation to their ancestral line, which it was said had been written out and were preserved by one of their own progenitors, and could be easily obtained." It was feared that those who had come to New England would lose, in their succeeding generations, a knowledge of their ancestry, which the brothers had a great desire to perpetuate. This William Glover was instructed to obtain not only the Glover pedigree as far back as it could be traced, or had been traced, that it might be perpetuated among the generations in New England, but all copies of records and documents which related in any way to the grants of lands originally laid out to Glover proprietors who had settled in Dorchester and Boston. The tradition continues that "having accomplished this mission fully and gathered up all his treasures, he embarked again for New England, but never arrived. The vessel in which he was coming, destined for Boston, was wrecked on a rock near the coast of Maine, in Portland harbor, and the passengers were all lost." How many of the crew of the ship escaped to tell the sad story, or if any, has not been ascertained, but the fate of the ship was in some way communicated to the family of Glovers who lived in Dorchester, and were looking anxiously for his arrival. The tradition closes with this remark: "The rock on which they were wrecked was named, from that time, 'Glover's Rock,' and has borne that name to this day"—meaning the time of the last narrator.

[NOTE.—The foregoing tradition has been transmitted down through the descending generations in the line of Mr. Nathaniel Glover, of Dorchester, commonly distinguished as "Nathaniel Senior," and is probably known in other branches—but has reached the sixth generation from Nathaniel to his son Thomas, and from Thomas to his sons.]

There is a Glover's Rock situated midway between Cape Small Point and Cape Elizabeth, about three leagues at sea, near the coast of Maine, midway of the entrance of Portland harbor. The date or year when it took that name has not been ascertained. It is laid down on all the charts of that part of the coast, and is represented by ship masters as being a very dangerous place and much to be avoided. Sea captains are familiar with the name of this rock. But only one historian has noticed it. Williamson, in his History of Maine, Vol. i. p. 33, gives the following account, which proves its identity, but does not give any history or dates respecting it.

" Glover's Rock. Cape Small Point, lying about two leagues south-eastwardly of New Meadows River, at its mouth, has a high ground and rocky shore. Above this Point on the north-west and below the west extreme of the Point is Lovell's (' Glover's ') Rock, which is one mile west by north of Seguin Light House."

He further writes that " one mile west by north-west from Glover's Rock is Small Point Ledge." Thus it appears that the Rock on the coast of Maine, which has been above described by Williamson, was anciently called Lovell's, and subsequently changed to " Glover's " Rock, and this inference is identified with the incidents before related.

Efforts have been unceasingly made, and many letters written, to procure more information respecting the name of the ship in which Mr. William Glover sailed, the time of the wreck, and other circumstances connected with the disaster, but they have proved unavailing as to any further knowledge. It is said that the disappointment to those who were looking for the arrival of this ship was very great, and irreparable in some respects to his relatives and friends. The last notice of him in England is in 1664, at the time of his marriage at Rainhill.

(9) George Glover, another son of Thomas and Margaret (Deane) Glover, was first a schoolmaster at Liverpool. He built a house there, married Margaret ———, and had two children, Jane and Ellen. He was afterwards a tenant on Moore's Rental. Moore writes of him thus : " Mr. George Glover is a very honest man, and has a good woman for a wife. Use him and his family well whenever it may please God they shall have occasion to use you, that when they can see virtue rewarded it may encourage their honesty. His rental is worth out of lease Seven Pounds per annum, and if it be fined three times, it is worth fifty Pounds per annum, and to

receive an old rent upon it One Pound. In doing this you will use his children very well. The lives at present are Jane, Ellen, and his wife Margaret. The second Rent liens at Christmas, and for other Covenants occurring to the Rents of the new Tenants I built the Gable ends of the house—cost Ten Pounds. Rent at present— five Shillings.   EDWARD MOORE, *Moore's Rental.*"

The Free school at Liverpool no longer exists. The building was destroyed in 1673. It was a great piece of antiquity—once a Chapel, then a Free school, at the west end whereon, next the River, stood the Statue of St. Nicholas. Moore alludes to the former schoolmaster, Mr. George Glover, and Bishop Cartwright states that after Mr. George Glover vacated, he licensed Mr. Thomas Bryant to be the schoolmaster of the Free school in Liverpool. It will be recollected that George Glover, by his father's will, was to receive but one hundred and fifty pounds.

There is a notice of him on the records of Harvard College, in Cambridge, N. E. Among the donors of cash gifts which were applied to the erection of College buildings, credit is given to Mr. George Glover, of Liverpool, Eng., of Two Pounds. Another notice, from another source, informs us that the gift was collected by Rev. Joseph Glover, of Sutton, in Surrey, who was shortly to embark for Cambridge in New England, with funds for the College lately established there. It was entrusted to his care—and although he never reached the place of his destination, having died on his passage in 1639, the property collected for Harvard College was faithfully transmitted and recorded.

1766. Power of Attorney was granted to George Glover of Poole, in the County of Dorset, England, by Mary Dawes, widow, and Mary Dawes, Jr., of Worgate in the same County, bearing date March 7, 1766, witnessed and certified by Robert Harris, Mayor of Wareham, and John Glover, Jr., of the borough of Wareham, in Dorset, England. Both the Power of Attorney and the Certificate are recorded in Boston on the Registry of Deeds for Suffolk County, Vol. 108, p. 263.

There may have been a relationship existing between the above-named Glovers and those who settled in New England, but no direct evidence has yet appeared to substantiate the belief.

The following is a copy of the Power of Attorney and Certificate alluded to.

Power of Attorney.

Know all men by these presents, That we, Mary Dawes, late of Boston in the County of Suffolk, and in the Province of Massachusetts Bay in New England, but now of Worgate in the County of Dorset, Widow, and Mary Dawes the Younger, of Worgate aforesaid, Spinster, only daughter and heir apparent of the said Mary Dawes, Widow; have and each of us hath made and ordained, and by these Presents; and each of us doth make and ordain, and in our place and stead put George Glover, of the town of Poole, in the County of ———— , Merchant, to be our true and lawful Attorney, as the said George Glover shall see fit.

[*Obliterated.*]

MARY DAWES, Sen.,
MARY DAWES, Jun.

Signed and sealed in presence of Robert Harris,
Mayor of Wareham, and John Glover, Jr., Borough
of Wareham, in Dorset, England.

A Certificate.

I, Robert Harris, Mayor of the Borough of Wareham aforesaid, do hereby Certify whom it may concern, that Mary Dawes of Worgate, in the said County of Dorset, Widow, and Mary Dawes the Younger, of the same place, Spinster, the only daughter and heir apparent, did on the day of the date hereof, Sign, Seale, and as their Act and Deed, and deliver this writing or Letter of Attorney bearing even date herewith, and that they the said Mary Dawes and Mary Dawes the Younger did execute the same in my Presence and in the Presence of John Glover, Junior, the other Witness attesting the same.

In Testimony of the truth hereof, I, the said Robert Harris, have hereunto set my hand and the Seale of the said Borough and Corporation, this Seventh day of March, A.D. 1766.

March 7, 1766.   Entered and Examined, Accepted and Recorded,
By EZEKIEL GOLDTHWAIT,
Register of Deeds for Suffolk Co.

(11) Peter Glover, of Rainhill, youngest son of Thomas and Margaret (Deane) Glover, was born 22 March, 1615; died there 26 April, 1700, in his 86th year. He married and settled in Rainhill, and had children. Several of his descendants are at the present time

5

living there, and are the owners of estates. Peter Glover, of the seventh generation, his wife Agnes, and children, are residents there. He is a descendant in a direct line from Peter the elder.

Some of the descendants of the above emigrated to the United States about the year 1812, and settled in New Jersey, of whom an account will be given in another place, under the head of the New Jersey Glovers.

MRS. MARGARET GLOVER.

She was left a widow at the decease of her husband, Mr. Thomas Glover, of Rainhill. She was co-executor with her son John Glover to the Will of Thomas Glover, and nothing further of her appears on the Parish Records to indicate the time or place of her death. Her death is not recorded on the records at Rainhill, if they have been faithfully transcribed. But records of Kent County furnish some evidence that she married a second time to Mr. William Glover, of Mildred, in the County of Kent, and died there in 1654, aged 79 years, and that she was buried in the Church-yard of St. Mildred. The Church of St. Mildred is situated at the south-west extremity of the city, near the old Castle and River Stour. In this Church-yard is a memorial, partly obliterated, of

" Mr. William Glover, Gentleman, deceased in 16—.
" Mrs. Margaret Glover, his wife, died ——, 1654, aged 79 years."

Born, therefore, in or about 1574 or 5, and would have been 19 years old at the time of her first marriage with Mr. Thomas Glover.

The will of Mr. Thomas Glover, of Rainhill, provides for another child, whom it appears he anticipated as an event not at all doubtful.

It has been suggested by some who were making searches for Glovers in England, that the Mr. Glover of Dorchester and Boston had a brother Nathaniel. If this conjecture is true, he must either have been posthumous, or, which is more probable, only a half brother, and child of his mother by her second marriage with William Glover, of Mildred, County of Kent. The name of Nathaniel has been found but once, in all previous and after searchings. The following memorial is recorded:

" Here lyes the Bodye of Mrs. Lydia Glover, widow of Mr. Nathaniel Glover, heretofore of this Parish, but late of Wood Church in the County of Kent, Gentleman, deceased. Which said Lydia died on the 21 day of January, 1764, in the 69th year of her age.

Also the bodye of Lydia Glover, Spinster, only child of the above-named Mr. Nathaniel and Lydia Glover his wife, who died on the 5 of February, 1766, in the 35 year of her age "— (born, therefore, in 1732).

This line of Nathaniel became extinct in 1766, at the decease of his only child Lydia. The time of his death has not been ascertained.

JOHN GLOVER, OF PRESCOT, ENGLAND, AND OF DOR-CHESTER AND BOSTON IN NEW ENGLAND.

(4) John Glover, the eldest son of Thomas and Margery (Deane) Glover, was born at Rainhill Parish, Prescot, Lancaster County, England, August 12, 1600, and died in Boston, in New England, "11, 12, 1653," in his fifty-fourth year.

By his father's will he came into possession of large estates in England, situated in Rainhill, Eccleston, Knowlesby, and other places. Being the eldest son he inherited a double portion by right of primogeniture, and was named as an executor, with his mother, to carry out the provisions of that will — although at that time (1619) he was not of full age.

He appears to have attained the age of manhood at Rainhill, living on his estates there, and was married to Anna ——, about 1625. He had three children born and baptized in that Parish, the last in 1629. Previous to that, in 1628, his name appears on the Records of the " London Company," organized at London in 1628. He was a member of the Ancient and Honorable Artillery Company of London, established there at a very early date, and was a Captain of that company. He was also a member of a Lodge of Freemasons, and in fellowship with them before his emigration. He was sometimes called " the Worshipful Mr. Glover."

So much has been said and written of the London Company, formed in England in 1628, its origin, its objects, present and prospective—of the early planting of New England and the worthy gentlemen who joined themselves to that Company; its whole history has been so many times brought before the historic reader in the various accounts of New England, that it may be deemed superfluous to attempt further notice of this matter, in these memorials. But as the

following pages are designed to notice and give an account of one of
the members of that Company who came to New England, and for
the benefit of whose descendants this work has been chiefly prepared, it is hoped that a few dates and facts selected from some of
the most faithful and reliable writers on that subject, and which will
help to explain the condition, motives, and social position of their
honored ancestor (Mr. John Glover), will be generously allowed by
them.

In 1628, three years after his marriage, the name of John Glover
appears on the records of the London Company, which was being
organized at London for the purpose of emigrating to New England.

"May, 1628, London, England.

"Allotments of land to the adventurers for New England who
intend to become planters there. The following is a list of the
names of the Joint-stock Company, and their subscription to that
stock."

Sir Richard Saltonstall, Knight,	£100
Isaac Johnson, Esq.,	100
Mr. Samuel Aldersey,	50
John Venn,	50
Hugh Peters,	50
John Humfrey,	50
Thomas Stevens,	50
George Harwood,	50
John Glover,	50
Matthew Craddock,	50
Simon Whetcomb,	50
Francis Webb,	50

May 13, 1629, London. "At a meeting of the Company forming
for New England, First Election Day.

"Present this day—the Governor, Deputy Governor, Mr. Treasurer,
Mr. Glover, Sir Richard Saltonstall, Mr. Adams, Mr. Offield, Mr.
Whetcomb, Mr. Foxcroft, Mr. Vassall, Mr. Perry, Mr. Nowell, Mr.
Pynchon and ten others."

To understand more fully the persons and particulars of the London Company, who subsequently emigrated to New England and laid
the foundation of the Massachusetts colony, we have the following
contract, and two specific contracts with Messrs. Bright, Higginson
and Skelton.

The Contract.

"London, May 1, 1628. In the name of God Amen. Sundrie men owe unto the general stock of the Adventurers for a plantation intended at Massachusetts Bay in New England, in America, the sum of Two thousand One hundred and fifty pounds (£2150)—and is for so much undertaken by the particular persons mentioned hereafter, by their several and general stock for the aforesaid plantation. Subscriptions to be by them adventured in this joint stock Company. Whereunto the Almighty grant prosperous and happy success—that the same may redounde to His Glory, for the propagation of the Gospel of Jesus Christ, and the particular good of the several adventurers that now are or hereafter shall be interested therein. The persons now to be made debtors to the general stock being as followeth.

Sir Richard Saltonstall, Knight, oweth 100 pounds.
Mr. Isaac Johnson, Esq.,   "   50   "
Mr. Samuel Aldersey,   "   50   "
Mr. John Venn,   "   50   "
Mr. John Humfrey,   "   50   "
Mr. Thomas Stevens,   "   50   "
Mr. George Harwood,   "   50   "
Mr. John Glover,   "   50   "
Mr. Matthew Craddock,   "   50   "
Simon Whetcomb,   "   50   "
Francis Webb,   "   50   "
Increase Nowell,   "   50   "
Mr. A. C.   "   50   "
Richard Tuffneale,   "   50   "
Richard Perry,   "   50   "
Joseph Offield,   "   50   "
John White,   "   50   "
Joseph Caron,   "   50   "

Twenty-one others were also subscribers to this contract, viz.: Thomas Adams, Richard Davis, Abraham Palmer, William Darbie, John Endicott, Daniel Hudson, Edward Foorde, Daniel Bullard, Thomas Hewson, Andrew Arnold, Richard Bushrod, Richard Younge. "George Harwood, Treasurer for the Plantation of the Massachusetts Bay, oweth unto sundrie accounts for moneys received by him of Sundrie Adventurers," viz.:

To Sir Richard Saltonstall, Knight,   £50
Isaac Johnson, Esq.,   25
Mr. John Glover,   25
Mr. Increase Nowell,   25
Mr. Matthew Craddock,   25
Richard Perry, Esq.,   25
Hugh Peters,   25
Joseph Offield,   25

Captain John Venn,	25
Abraham Palmer,	25
Samuel Aldersey,	25
Simon Whitcomb,	50
Richard Younge,	
Joseph Caron,	
Edward Foorde,	
Thomas Hewson,	
Daniel Ballard,	
Thomas Stevens,	
Job Bradshaw,	
Joseph Bradshaw,	
Andrew Arnot,	
Nathaniel Manstreye,	

A. C. ——, George Harwood, Abric ——, and John Smythe, each 50 pounds.

The gentlemen who composed this Company, which had been formed in London, and who afterwards emigrated to New England and became the first planters of the Colony there, it is recorded were strictly and devoutedly religious Non-conformists. They were styled Puritans, from their strict adherence to the doctrines of religion, and from their having set themselves apart to promote a holy work — that of planting a colony for religious growth and freedom. They were all members of some church in England previous to their embarkation, and those of their company who came out under Gov. Winthrop, met together at Plymouth, a seaport town in England, and formed themselves into a church body gathered from other churches. They elected their ministers, and assembled themselves together at the New Hospital in Plymouth, the Sabbath previous to their departure for New England, and bound themselves together in Christian unity and love. A sermon was preached to them by the Rev. John White, and instructions given in relation to the future course to be pursued. The ship which was to take them to New England was at this time waiting in the Downs, to receive them and bear them to their destination.

It is recorded that the Dorchester Company came in the *Mary and John*, which set sail from England the 20th of March, 1629–30, commanded by Capt. Squeb, and who is said to have arrived on the coast of North America the 31st day of May, 1630. The manner in which he treated his passengers, and deceived them by putting them on shore at Nantasket, when he had promised to land them at Charlestown, is too well known to require any detail here. Some of them took boats and found their way to Charlestown; and others, who remained at Nantasket, found out a way to Dorchester Neck, adjoining a place called by the Indians Mattapan, to which they gave the name of New Dorchester, and commenced a settlement about the first of June. The place was afterwards called Dorchester Plantation. The same writer says our people were settled here a month before Gov. Winthrop, and the ships that came with him, arrived.

Mr. Glover came to New England in the *Mary and John*. It has been questioned by some as to the ship in which he came over, probably on account of a note of Mr. Frothingham, in his History of Charlestown, by which it might appear that he arrived earlier. Frothingham, in a list of those who stayed and became inhabitants of Charlestown in the year 1629, gives the names of Increase Nowell, Esq., Mr. William Aspinwall, Mr. Richard Palsgrave, Edward Converse, William Penn, William Hudson, William Blackenbury, and Mr. John Glover. He also says that Mr. Glover removed to Dorchester, where he became a prominent man, being a Selectman and a Representative from 1637 to 1652. He also writes that Mr. Glover died in 1654, which does not agree with Dorchester Town Records. The above from Frothingham has led many to doubt of his coming over in the *Mary and John* with the Dorchester Company; but he was always associated with them, his interests were identified with theirs, and he served them in a public capacity until his death, although he had removed to Boston. His name stands among a list of inhabitants at the incorporation of the town of Dorchester in 1631, according to Blake's Annals. When the Church was re-organized there (in 1636, Richard Mather, Pastor), he and his wife Anna were among the first signers to the covenant. He may have remained in Charlestown until that time, but there is no evidence of it.

He brought over with him a great number of cattle, and all the provisions and implements, with men servants, to set up and carry on the tanning trade, according to the laws and regulations of the London Company requiring each member to establish some trade on his estate. He selected the business of tanning, and was the first one of the Company who carried on that trade in the Colony. He established it first at Dorchester, very probably as early as the incorporation of the town. The pits still remain to be seen on the land of one of his descendants. He afterwards established the business in Boston, and left it in his will to his second son. A very reliable writer on the early history of New England asserts the following in relation to Dorchester: "The first inhabitants of Dorchester were a godly and religious people, and many of them persons of note and figure, being distinguished by the title of Master or Mr., which but few in those days were. Their ministers were the Rev. John Maverick and the Rev. John Warham. Others of note, who came passengers in the *Mary and John*, were as follows:—Mr. Newbury, Mr. Rossiter, Mr. Ludlow, Mr. Glover, Mr. Johnson, Mr. Terry, Mr. Smith, Mr. Gallop, Mr. Duncan, Mr. Hull, Mr. Stoughton, Mr. Cogan, Mr. Hill, Mr. Pinney, Mr. Richards, Mr. Way, Mr. Williams, Mr. Tilley and others; Capt. Southcote, Capt. Lovell, and among them came Capt. Roger Clap," whom he describes as being a very worthy and religious gentleman.

This account may seem to conflict with Mr. Frothingham's, but the conclusion is that the above is the correct one, as all circumstances confirm it, and it is probable that Mr. Glover was one of those who took boats and went to Charlestown settlements, where were a few English families, and possibly he remained there a short time. It could have been but a short time, as he never removed his family there, or his servants or cattle, nor the goods which he brought over to establish his trade.

He was made Freeman in England before his emigration, and took the oath of allegiance, which exempted him from that ceremony after his arrival here.

The prefix of Mr. he brought with him, and he has been more generally designated by that than any other title. It was then one of honor and dignity, but has depreciated in its original significance, from its general usage. His armorial bearings were those granted to Thomas Glover, Esq., of the Body of King James I., who was son of Thomas Glover of Coventry in Warwickshire, Knighted 17th of August, 1606. "This Coat, with a star for a difference, was confirmed by William Camden, April 3d, 1604, and is a fac-simile of the arms granted to the Somerset Herald, Robert Glover, after being enlarged and improved by Edmondson, with the exception of the star."

Mr. Glover was called a godly and upright man. His religion was that of a strict Non-conformist, or Puritan, which appears to have been the ruling motive of his life, and led him to leave his English home and forego all the comforts and conveniences of an English life, to settle on the cold, uncomfortable, cheerless shore of New England.

Johnson in his History writes thus of him: — "Mr. Glover was a man strong for the truth, a plain, sincere and godly man, and of good abilities." The following lines appear in his work entitled *The Wonder-working Providence*, in which he notices Mr. Glover, with some others of that company who were his associates: —

"And Godly Glover his rich gifts thou gavest,
Thus thou by means thy flock from spoiling savest."

His age thirty years, well settled in life with a wife and three children (the youngest but a year old), inheriting large landed estates from his father, and living in the enjoyment of a competent estate at the time this enterprise was undertaken, the inquiry naturally arises, what motive could have induced him to choose such a life of hardship and endurance?

His life, after his arrival and settlement at Dorchester, was evidently one of unceasing action and service to the Colony. During a period of nearly eighteen years his name appears not only as a public officer in Dorchester, but in other towns, among those who sat in judgment. In Salem, Charlestown, Cambridge, and at Barnstable and other places in the Plymouth Colony, he was frequently called in council in cases which required judicial decisions.

The following references to Mr. Glover are from various documents.

1631. "A Shallop of Mr. Glover's was cast away on the rocks about Nahant. Crew all saved."

1636. Mr. Glover was chosen one of the Selectmen for the town of Dorchester, and continued to fill that office until his removal to Boston about 1650. He was a Representative to the General Court at Boston from 1636 to 1652, when he was chosen an Assistant.

1649. John Glover's house is said to have been situated at the head of the Dock in Boston, but his name appears to continue on the Town Records of Dorchester until after that time.

1651. Mr. John Glover, Deputy from Dorchester. Assessments made and certified 7 May, 1651. Capt. Leverett, Mr. Clark, and Mr. John Glover.

27, 3d, 1652, at a Court of Elections, was chosen John Endicott, Governor. Thomas Dudley, Esq., Deputy Governor. Assistants, Richard Bellingham, Esq.; Increase Nowell, Gentleman; Lyman Bradstreet, Gentleman; Samuel Symonds, Gentleman; William Hibbins, Gentleman; John Glover, Gentleman; Capt. Daniel Gooken,

Gentleman. Edward Rawson, Secretary; Richard Russell, Treasurer, and twenty-eight deputies.

May 18, 1653, the same gentlemen were chosen for Governor and Deputy-Governor and Assistants. Mr. John Glover therefore continued in the office of Assistant at the General Court up to the time of his decease, which, according to the Dorchester Town Records, occurred in December, 1653.

He was also appointed to other offices of trust and honor, as appears from the Massachusetts Colonial Records, Vol. 3d, under the following dates:

1637. He was surety for Mr. Aspinwall. "Mr. John Glover and Mr. Aspinwall are each of them bound in the sum of one hundred pounds apiece for Mr. Aspinwall's departure by the time limited." *Book* 3, p. 206, *Col. Rec.*

1638. A Deputy, and power to execute judgment against the men if they neglect to defray the charges at Castle Island.

" Mr. Glover to allow and direct Bray Wilkins to set a house and keep a ferry over the Neponsett River."

1640. Mr. Glover, with others, to dispose of lands to Hingham inhabitants.

1641. Mr. Glover propounded for a magistrate. June 2, 1641, Mr. Glover appointed, with Humphrey Atherton, to lay out the highway in difference in the town of Braintree. Mr. Glover, with another, appointed to settle offences between Hingham Plantation and Nantasket. Appointed Clerk of the Writs at Dorchester.

1642. Mr. Glover one of a committee to settle a highway at Braintree,

1642. Mr. John Glover's grant of an iron mine, in Worcester County, is as follows:

Upon a petition of Mr. John Glover and another of Dorchester for the improvement of a supposed mine in Neipnett, about forty or fifty miles hence. It is ordered that they shall have the privilege granted by a former order so as they go effectually on with it within one year, and if they think fit to plant a convenient number of families there which may make a village, they shall have such quantity of land and meadow fit for their occasion as the place will afford, provided they be ready and go effectually to work about it within three years next after such mine shall be opened; provided also, that such grant of a village shall not hinder the Power of this Court in ordering and disposing of any mines otherwise than hath been already or hereafter shall be granted. June 14, 1642.

Neipnett lies in Worcester County, Massachusetts, now Grafton. It had its name of Neipnett from the Indians. Gov. Winthrop and others visited it as early as 1632. The present town of Oxford also lies in the Neipnett country.

June 10, 1652. "It is ordered that Capt. Hawkins, Mr. Glover, Ensign Tomlins and Mr. Stevens are chosen a committee for the drawing up of an order about ship carpenters, and respecting their engagements to those that employ them."

From the Records of the General Court, at Boston:

"8 (7) 1642. Mr. Glover present at this meeting — a Deputy from Dorchester."

Sept. 27, 1642. Appointed a committee, with Mr. Duncan and two others, to seek out a convenient place for the highway and ferry at Dorchester, and certify at the next Court.

May 10, 1643. Mr. Glover, Mr. Prichard, Mr. Atherton and others, appointed a committee about the receiving of Mr. Ahdros's gift.

June 22, 1643. In a transaction with the Indians, John Winthrop, Governor, Thomas Dudley, Deputy Governor, Richard Bellingham, John Glover, Joseph Weld, Hugh Prichard, Humphrey Atherton, William Aspinwall, appointed to settle their claims.

Sept. 7, 1643. Mr. Glover and others appointed a committee to take the names of all the teachers, and what they have paid, and certify to the next Court.

Sept. 7, 1643. Mr. Glover, Mr. Russell, Ensign Weld, and Mr. Edward Tyng, are appointed a committee "about the Children, to dispose of them, call for their beds, and see that satisfaction is provided and paid in."

"It is ordered that the charges of the soldiers to go with Capt. Cooke to Providence, should be paid by Mr. Glover and the rest of the Committee about the Children, and to be repaid to them again when it cometh in."

Mr. Glover and others appointed a committee "to view the place Dover, and certify at the next Court."

May 27, 1643. "Advice respecting the Estates and Cattle belonging to the Country, referred to Mr. Glover and Mr. Prichard, or either one of them."

At a Court of Elections, held at Boston,

"4, 5, 1644. The several names of the Towns with their Deputies that were returned with their warrants to serve at the Court."
"Dorchester, Mr. John Glover."

May 20, 1644. "It is ordered that Mr. Downing of Salem, Mr. Glover of Dorchester, and Mr. Rawson, are chosen a Committee to consider one half of the petitions presented to this Court, and to make a return of their thoughts and conclusions of them endorsed upon said petitions."

May 31, 1644. "It is ordered that Mr. Speaker, Capt. Cooke, Mr. Glover, Mr. Sparhawke and Mr. Rawson, are chose a Committee to Examine the French business — to state the case and to draw the bills — to lay the charges — to procure the Testimony, and to present it to the House."

May 17, 1645. Mr. Glover, Lieut. Atherton, Edward Goffe and Edward Oakes are appointed a committee "to lay out the way through Roxbury Lots to Boston Farms, and to Judge what is meet satisfaction for the Proprietors for the way, and that they have power to impose an equal part on all, and upon all such of Boston or other Towns as shall have the benefit of such way."

Oct. 1, 1645. Mr. Glover with others appointed a Commissioner "for Laws, to meet at Boston for Suffolk, at Cambridge for Middlesex; and at Ipswich for Essex Counties."

Oct. 1646. "The Court understanding that there are several suits of the children belonging to the Country and in the hands of Mr. Glover, think it meet to join Mr. Treasurer with Mr. Glover to appraise them, and then deliver them to Capt. Davenport in part of what the Country stands indebted to him for the Castle."

Nov. 4, 1646. "Mr. Glover, Capt. Atherton and Mr. John Wiswall, appointed to end small causes in Dorchester."

May 26, 1647. "Mr. Glover, present at this Court as a Deputy from Dorchester, is appointed, with Mr. Duncan, to regulate the affairs at Hull, and see the orders of the Court carried out." Appointed also, with Mr. John Wiswall and Capt. Atherton, "to end small causes."

Nov. 11, 1647. Mr. Glover and others, a committee of Deputies appointed "to Judge upon the petition of John Daniel, and to settle the rates of Wharfage."

Nov. 11, 1645. Mr. John Glover appointed a Surveyor General with Edmund Rice and Mr. Hibbins, "to view and appoint a place for a Bridge at Watertown."

March, 1647-8. Mr. John Glover one of a committee to view Mystic Bridge.

March, 1647–8. Present at the General Court, Mr. John Glover.

May 11, 1648. " Neponsett Ferry. Upon a certain information to the General Court, that there is no ferry kept over Neponsett River between Dorchester and Braintree, whereby all that are to pass that way are forced to head the River, to the great prejudice of Towns that are in those parts, and that there appears no man that will keep it unless he may be accommodated with house, Land and a Boat, at the charge of the Country. It is therefore ordered by the authority of this Court, that Mr. John Glover shall, and hereby hath full power given him; either to grant it to any person or persons for the term of seven years, so it be not in any way chargeable to the Country, or else take it himself and to his heirs as his own inheritance forever. Provided that it be kept in such a place and at such a price as may be most convenient for the Country and pleasing to the General Court."

May 28, 1647. Mr. Glover, William Parks and Mr. Duncan are appointed a committee " to see the order of Court for the advancing of Fisheries duly observed."

May, 1650. Mr. Glover and others are appointed to examine the case of Marmaduke Matthews, of Charlestown.

Boston, June 1, 1650. " At a special commission instituted to examine Mr. Matthews of Charlestown (of the first Church), on doctrinal points. The Commission consisted of the following Gentlemen, viz., Mr. Simon Bradstreet, Mr. Simonds, Mr. John Glover, Capt. William Hawthorne, Mr. Eleazer Lusher, Mr. Richards, Capt. Daniel Gookin, Capt. Humphrey Atherton." They were instructed to call on the Rev. Elders in case of difficulty.

It is further stated that Mr. Matthews was formally examined by these gentlemen from Boston, and not being able to give satisfaction, he was adjudged to be fined ten pounds, providing he did not make an acknowledgment within a month for consenting to be ordained over the Church in Charlestown.

Mr. Matthews was asked to appear the 11th of June, 1650.

Report of the Commissioners on the case of Marmaduke Matthews to the General Court of Massachusetts, June 17, 1651: —

" Upon serious consideration of the charges brought against Mr. Matthews, together with the answer to them by himself given; as also upon conference with himself concerning the same ; We the commissioners yet remain much unsatisfied, finding him in several

6

particulars weak, unsafe, and unsound, and not being retracted by him, some whereof are contained in this paper, with his last deliberate answer thereto.

Simon Bradstreet,	John Glover,
William Hathorne,	Eleazer Lusher,
Richard Browne,	Humphrey Atherton."
Edward Johnson,	

April 15, 1652.   John Glover was one of a committee appointed with John Endicott, Thomas Dudley, Richard Bellingham, Increase Nowell, Simon Bradstreet, William Hibbins, Samuel Symonds and Robert Bridges, to examine a work written by Mr. Pynchon, said to contain pernicious sentiments.   They speak thus of him: That although they loved and respected the Author, they thought a book he had written too pernicious to be published. "Signed by your unworthy Servants."   [*Com. Names.*]

Mr. Glover's death is thus noticed in the Town Records of Dorchester, page 53 : —

"Dorchester, 15 (12) 1653. — Whereas Mr. John Glover was Chosen with William Sumner and William Clarke to lay out Mrs. Stoughton's farm in Dorchester, and now the said Mr. Glover being deceased this 11th day of the 12th month, 1653; at a Town meeting the town hath chosen John Wiswall in the room of Mr. Glover, to be joined with the said William Sumner and William Clarke, for doing that work."

The evidence is conclusive that Mr. John Glover continued to be appointed to and hold offices in Dorchester after his removal to Boston, and until his death, which, according to the above, took place on Feb. 11th, 1653.

Children of Mr. John Glover and Anna his wife, born in Rainhill Parish, Prescot, Lancashire, England, and in Dorchester, New England.

+1. Thomas, b. Jan. 8, 1627 ; m. Rebecca ——, 1652.
+2. Habackuk, b. May 13, 1628 ; m. Hannah Elliot, of Roxbury.
+3. John, b. Oct. 11, 1629 ; m. Elizabeth Franklin, of Ipswich, 1683.
+4. Nathaniel, b. 1631 ; m. Mary Smith, of Dorchester, 1652.
+5. Pelatiah, b. Nov., 1637 ; m. Hannah Cullick, of Boston.

In 1652 Mr. Glover conveyed to his eldest son, Thomas Glover, the title and possession of all his estates in Lancashire, England, by the following indenture:

John Glover to Thomas Glover.

THIS INDENTURE, made the first day of February in the year of our Lord God, One thousand six hundred and fifty two, between John Glover of Dorchester, in New England, Gent^{lmn}, upon the one part, and Thomas Glover, sonne and heir apparent of the said John Glover, upon the other part, WITNESSETH—that the said John Glover for and in consideration of the natural love and affection which he beareth unto the said Thomas Glover, his sonne, and for the better maintenance and preferment of the said Thomas Glover, and the heires of his body, lawfully begotten, and likewise of intent to enable him the said Thomas Glover to make a complete jointure to Rebeckha now his wife, with whom he is to have and receive a considerable portion, and for other good and valuable considerations, him the said John Glover hereunto moving, hath given, granted, enfeoffed and confirmed, and by these presents doth fully and absolutely give, grant, enfeoffe, and confirm, unto the said Thomas Glover his heires and assignes, all that messuage and tenement, with the appurtenances in Rainhill in the County of Lancaster within the Commonwealth of England, heretofore in the tenure, holding or occupation of Thomas Glover, deceased, late father of the said John Glover, and late in the holding or occupation of the said John Glover, or his assignes, and by him purchased and obtained from Thomas Lancaster, late of Rainhill aforesaid, Esq., deceased; together with one Court or entry newly enclosed leading from the said messuage into the high land before the said messuage; and all that one parcel of land, meadow and pasture with the appurtenances parcel of a Close of the demesne land of Thomas Lancaster, late of Rainhill, Esq., deceased, and called the High field, which parcel of land containeth by estimation One Acre and three quarters of an Acre, or thereabouts; with free liberty to and for the said Thomas Glover his heires and assignes at all times hereafter to have, take, digge and carry away at their will and pleasure, stones, malle, clay, sodds, gravel, sands, furrs, gorse and other necessaries in, of and from the land, common and waste grounds of Rainhill aforesaid: and of, in and from all or any of them. And also all that Close, enclosure or parcel of land with the appurtenances in Rainhill aforesaid heretofore used as demesne lands by the said Thomas Lancaster, and late in the occupation of the said John Glover or his assignes, commonly called or known by the name of the great High field, and all that messuage and cottage, with their and either of their appurtenances, lying and being in Rainhill, aforesaid, heretofore in the houlding and several occupations of Richard Johnson otherwise called Thompson deceased, and John Harrison deceased, their assign or assignes, and heretofore purchased and obtained by the said Thomas Glover deceased, in his lifetime, from Edward Ecleston Esq., deceased, and all that one enclosure or parcel of land lying and being in Rainhill aforesaid, and heretofore in the occupation of the said Thomas Glover, deceased, commonly called and known by the name or names of the Long marled hey or the marled earth, and was sometime parcel of the tenement of Thomas Gerrard late of Rainhill aforesaid Gent^{lmn} deceased, containing by estimation four acres of land, or thereabouts, of the large measure:

and also all that messuage and tenement lying and being in Eccleston
near Knowlsby in the said County of Lancaster, heretofore purchased
and obtained by the said Thomas Glover deceased in his lifetime from
William Woodfall, late of Apleton, deceased; and all those two
Closes and parcels of land with the appurtenances, in Rainhill aforesaid, commonly called and known by the name of the Dobbfields, or
by whatever name or names soever they now are or heretofore have
been called or known by, heretofore purchased and obtained by the
said Thomas Glover deceased in his lifetime from Lyman Garnett late
of Rainhill (aforesaid) deceased : and also all and singular, houses,
edifices, buildings, yards, orchards, gardens, meadows, pastures,
woods, underwoods, waters, fishings, mines, quarries, delfs, enclosures
from the waste and commons and common of pasture and turberry,
wayes, entryes, passages, liberties, easements, profits, commodityes
and heredittaments whatsoever, to the said several messuages, lands
and tenements severally and respectively lying, belonging or in
any wise appertaining to or therewith usually occupied or enjoyed as
part and parcel or member thereof, and the reversion, and reversions,
remainder and remainders, of all and singular their premises, with
their and every of their appurtenances, and all rents, suites, service,
reserved, due or payable upon or out of the premises, or any part or
parcel thereof: and all other the messauges, lands, tenements, rents,
reversions, services and heredittaments whatsoever of him the said
John Glover, lying and being in Rainhill and Eccleston aforesaid, or
elsewhere within the said County of Lancaster: And the said John
Glover does further give, grant and confirm unto the said Thomas
Glover, his sonne and heir apparent, his heirs and assignes, all deeds,
evidences, writings, counterp[ts] of Leases, escripts and miniments
whatsoever touching or concerning the premises only : or only any
parte or parcel thereof. To have and to hold the said severall messuages, lands, tenements, heredittaments, and all other the premises
before mentioned with the appurtenances, unto the said Thomas Glover, sonne and heir apparent of the said John Glover, his heirs and
assignes forever, to the sole and only proper use and behoofe of the
said Thomas Glover, his heires and assignes forever. Without any
revocation at all, in any wise, to be holden of the Lord or Lords of the
ffee or ffees of the premises, by the rents and services therefor due
and of right accustomed.
     And the said John Glover for himself and his heires, executors, ad-
ministrators and assigns, and every of them doth covenant, promise,
grant and agree to and with the said Thomas Glover, his sonne and
heir apparent, his heires and assignes by these presents, that he, the
said Thomas Glover his heires and assignes, shall and may forever
hereafter quietly and peaceably, have, hold, occupy and enjoy the
said several messuages, lands, tenements, heredittaments, and premises, with the appurtenances, without the lett, hindrance, contradiction or impediment of him the said John Glover or of any person or
persons, lawfully claiming the premises or any part thereof, by, from
or under him the said John Glover or his estate in any wise. And
lastly the said John Glover hath constituted, made, ordained, and
by these presents doth constitute, make, ordaine, and in his place
and stead put, his well beloved friend, John Latham of Whis-

ton, Gent^{lmn}, and William Glover of Posset aforesaid, Mercer, his true and lawful Attorneyes, joyntly, or, either of them severally to enter for him and in his name and stead, into the said Messuages, lands, and premises, or some part thereof in name of the whole, and possession and seizure thereof to take and have, and after such possession and seizure, so thereof taken and had, to deliver over the same unto the said Thomas Glover, to have and to hold unto the said Thomas Glover his heires and assignes forever, according to the purport, true intent and meaning of these presents. *In Witness* whereof, the parties abovesaid to these present indentures, interchangably their hands and seales have put, the day and year first above written. 1653.   JOHN GLOVER   (*and a Seale*).

Sealed and delivered in the presence of us, Increase Nowell, Jno^a Leverett, William Robbins, George Halsall, Nathaniel Souther, Notary Public^{ns}.

Acknowledged to be sealed and delivered by the within named John Glover, the day and year aforesaid, before me,

RICHARD BELLINGHAM, Dep^t Govr.

Entered and Recorded, 5 Nov. 1653.   EDWARD RAWSON,
                                                            Recorder.

A true copy from the Records of Deeds, for the County of Suffolk. Lib. 1, fol. 333.

Dorchester Estate.

Mr. Glover's Dorchester homestead estate was passed by him to his fourth son, Nathaniel Glover, of Dorchester, about the year 1651 or 2, and continued in his possession about five years. He died May 21, 1657, leaving a widow and three children as co-heirs to his estate of inheritance. His widow, marrying again (March 15, 1659) to Gov. Thomas Hinckley, of Barnstable, relinquished her right of dower in the estate to the children of Nathaniel Glover, and removed to Barnstable. The estate was held in trust, and rented for the benefit of the three minor children until the year 1674. At this time the eldest son of Mr. Nathaniel Glover had arrived to the age of 21 years, was married, and the estate was ordered by the General Court at Boston to be divided. It was then, in 1674, and for a short time after, owned conjointly by Nathaniel Glover, John Glover of Dorchester, and Mrs. Anna (Glover) Rawson, wife of William Rawson, of Boston, as their inheritance. Nathaniel Glover, the eldest son, being in possession of the house and a portion of the land, occupied it and lived there. He continued to carry on the tanning business, which had been set up there by his grandfather, Mr. John Glover, the original owner of the estate. He purchased the shares of his brother, John Glover, cooper, who lived in Boston, and of Mrs. Raw-

6*

son, his sister, as soon as they were of age to dispose of them, and in the year 1676 became the sole owner and occupant of the Dorchester homestead. He had seven children born there, by his wife Hannah Hinckley. He continued to occupy it until 1700 — twenty-four years — when his eldest son, Nathaniel Glover, Jr., was of an age to receive it. In that year the whole estate was, by deed of gift, confirmed and passed to Nathaniel Glover, Jr. The date of this deed and transfer is January, 1700.

Nathaniel Glover, Sen., at this time removed with his family to Newbury Farm, beyond the Neponset River in Dorchester, and left his Dorchester estate in the possession and occupancy of his son Nathaniel, who continued there until March, 1726, a period of twenty-six years. He continued the business of tanning on the estate, and had seven children born to him there, by his wife Rachel Marsh. In March, 1726, he went out to London as an agent for the original Proprietors of Dorchester Common and Undivided Lands, of which he had become an extensive shareholder, both by purchase and inheritance. He left his wife in possession and occupancy of the estate — his children being all minors. He died in June, 1726, in London, of smallpox, soon after his arrival there. His widow continued to occupy and possess the estate until her death, in 1752.

When her second son, Mr. Alexander Glover, arrived to the age of twenty-one years, the estate was passed to him as joint occupant, but it was not divided. Alexander continued there until his death, March 15, 1770. He had ten children born there by his wife Sarah White. He engaged in the lumber business, and discontinued the tanning, which has never been resumed by any of his successors. The pits are still to be seen on a portion of land belonging to one of his grandchildren. In 1752, on the death of his mother, the widow of Nathaniel Glover, Jr., the estate passed into the possession of her children, six in number, viz.: Mr. Nathaniel Glover, of Boston, eldest son; Mrs. Rachel Salter, of Boston; Mrs. Hannah Bass, Dorchester; Mr. Alexander Glover, Dorchester; Miss Mary Glover, Dorchester; and Mr. Pelatiah Glover, of Boston. It was owned conjointly by the above heirs but a short time. Alexander became the purchaser of the shares of the other children from time to time, but the final settlement of the estate was not until 1785. Alexander died in 1770, having been in possession of a portion of the estate from 1732 to that time, and occupying it first as co-heir, and conjointly, then sole heir for a period of thirty-eight years. He left a widow, who continued there by right of dower, and the estate was then owned conjointly by Alexander Glover, Jr., the second son, and his mother, Mrs. Sarah Glover, widow.

Alexander Glover was the sixth occupant there in a direct line from the original proprietor. By inheritance and by purchase he came in possession of a considerable portion of the estate, and remained on it until his death in 1813, a period of forty-three years. He had six children born to him there, by his wife Hannah Pope. After his death his widow continued by right of dower, and died there in September, 1825. The estate was then owned conjointly by the heirs of Alexander Glover, Jr., his eldest son Alexander, Jr., and the third of the name, being a retainer of the house and homestead, and a portion of the land as his inheritance. He continued to occupy and possess the original mansion for a time. The old house was taken down and a new one built near the spot. A house has been built since for one of his sons over the old cellar, and portions of the land remain in possession of the other sons. A considerable portion of what was the original homestead has been sold. Alexander, Jr., the last occupant and successor to the estate, was a retainer until his death in 1842, a period of forty-eight years. He had ten children born to him there, by his wife Jemima Tolman.

The last successor was the longest occupant. The estate has been divided into various divisions and subdivisions, to accommodate the heirs. Oliver Glover, Esq., of Dorchester, and James Glover, Esq., of Boston (brothers to Alexander the last successor), are now in possession of portions of it as their inheritance. Other portions of it have been sold. The above are of the seventh generation. Another portion has passed on to the sons of Alexander, third, who are still in possession and occupancy. The original bounds of the estate may be seen as given in the Deed of Gift from Mr. Nathaniel Glover, Sen., to his son Nathaniel Glover, Jr., which is inserted among the acts of Nathaniel, Sen.

It will be seen that this estate, which was first possessed by the Hon. John Glover, of Dorchester, who lived upon and occupied it about twenty-two years, and had two children born to him there, has descended down in a direct line, from father to son, to the seventh and eighth generations, and that sixty children have been born there who bore the name.

The mansion house belonging to this estate was built by Mr. Glover. It was fashioned after the English style, but with thatched roof and large open chimney. It was situated on the shore road, now Commercial Street, fronting the water.

Winthrop, in his Journal, Vol. 1, page 42, relates an incident connected with it, under date of 1636. "Mr. Glover of Dorchester, having about sixty pounds of powder in bags to dry in the end of his chimney, it took fire and some of it went up chimney; other of it filled a room and blew up the gable end. A maid which was in the room having her arms and neck naked was scorched and died soon after. A little child in the arms of another was scorched upon the face, but not killed. Two men were scorched, but not much injured: various pieces of furniture which lay in the room were scorched. The room was dark with smoke, so that those in the room could not find door or window; and when neighbors went in, none could see each other a good time for smoke. The house was thatched, but took not fire, yet many things were burned and many were found injured. Another great Providence was, that three little children being at the fire a little time before; they went out to play, although it was a very cold day, and so were preserved."

Estate and House in Boston.

It appears from the following that John Glover owned and occupied a house in Boston as early as 1644.

"Dec. 6, 1664, John Glover, of Dorchester, sold to Jonathan Oliver, of Boston, " a little plot of ground in Boston, as it is set out by Mr. Jonathan Oliver, being now within my garden fence, between my new Dwelling house and George Burden's and William Hudson's * * * * so as William Tyng * * * * The said John Glover to make and maintain in his garden a little higher towards my house a close, well, and channel there within the ground for the convenience of Water."

Mr. William Tyng's house, " Close, Garden, great yard and little yard before the Hall window." Description of bounds — " John Glover, William Hudson, Jr., George Burden, Hugh Gunnison and the street East."—*Boston Book of Possessions ; History of Boston, page* 786.

" John Glover's house and yard bounded by the street South East,

. George Burden South West, William James North West and North East."

In the description of bounds of George Burden's land, it is said to be bounded on the eastward by John Glover.

Gov. Winthrop says, in his Journal, under date of 1649, that Mr. Glover's house was situated at the head of the cove in Boston.

By his will, his Boston estate passed to his second son, Habackuk Glover, who owned and occupied it until his death in 1692. It then passed to Mrs. Rebekah Smith, who was his sole heir. She was Rebekah Glover, and his only daughter, and at the time of her father's death was the widow of Capt. Thomas Smith, of Boston, who died in 1688. She owned and occupied it until her second marriage with Capt. Thomas Clarke, in 1691, when it came in possession of her eldest son, Capt. Thomas Smith, and was confirmed to him by her will made in his favor after her second marriage. Capt. Thomas Smith died at Saco in 1742. The estate then passed to his heirs, who occupied and possessed it until about 1798, a period of fifty-six years or more, when it was sold by them to Dr. Eliakim Morse and Samuel Torrey, Esq., of Boston, who owned it conjointly for a time. In 1812 it passed to the heirs of Samuel Torrey, Esq., and in 1828 the whole estate became the property of Samuel Torrey, Jr., Esq. who is the present owner, and describes it as follows: "This estate measured fifty-six feet in front on Dock Square, and extended through to Elm Street. The mansion house was a large double house, built of brick, with a wide front door at the entrance, which opened into a hall from which two winding staircases led to the second floor. The house remained standing till about 1830, when it was destroyed by fire. Three stores have since been erected on the site, and are now occupied by Brooks, Darling, and Walker."

It appears that the estate has passed down in the possession of succeeding generations, under the conditions expressed in Mr. Glover's will, which will hereafter be noticed.

John Glover owned a house and land in Weymouth, and sold it to Nicholas Byram in 1647, by his power of attorney, as follows:

"5: 8: 1647. John Glover, Power of Attorney. John Brabrook, of Watertown, Granted to Nicholas Byram, by virtue of a Power of Attorney from John Glover, of Dorchester, all that piece of land which was formerly John Glover's, lying in Weymouth, viz., Sixty acres of Upland adjoining to Nicholas Byram on the East and on the West part.

" Also Two Acres of Meadow by the Waterside, and Four acres of marsh.   Also four acres of Frog's Meadow in the Woods, and a Great Lott of Twenty-five Acres adjoining, by absolute Deed of Sale made the 5 day of the 8ᵗʰ Month in 1647."

The above was purchased by Mr. Glover in 1644, of John Goffe.

" At a County Court held at Cambridge, County of Middlesex, in 1643, on the account of John Glover, son of Rev. Joseph Glover, Deceased, and Step-son of Rev. Henry Dunster, against Henry Dunster, immediately following the death of his wife Mrs. Elizabeth Dunster, who was the Widow of said Rev. Joseph Glover, and the mother of the said Complainant " —

Present, Mr. John Glover, Dorchester and Boston.

> Mr. Nowell,   "
> Mr. Gookin,   "

1653.   Extract from first book of Court Records for Middlesex County. " In an Action of 'Foster against Stowe,' purporting to be a suit or action for the recovery of some Rents for Houses and Lands in Maidstone, County of Kent, in England, wherein Mr. John Glover, Senior, Deputy, with Hopestill Foster, bound themselves in the sum of One hundred Pounds to the Court to prosecute the appeal against Thomas Stowe."

The Last Will of Mr. John Glover, of Boston, made as followeth.

It being written that the Earth is the Lords ; and the fulness thereof: the habitable world and they that dwell therein.   Again I have prayed to the Jehovah, I have said, Thou art my trust, my portion in the land of the living.   And again none of us liveth to himself, neither doth any die to himself, and I accordingly believing, do therefore also speak and unto God say, I am thine and Thou art mine, and pray, Oh that I and mine, the souls that Thou hast given me, if we live we may live to Thee: if we die we may die to Thee : both if we live and also if we die, we may be thine.   And as for what also Thou hast given me to possess, Thou hast trusted me to dispose, that Thou wilt be pleased to be with me in disposing of it, and bless it so, in their hands to whom I give it.   Amen.

And first I will all former Wills be revoked, and whereas I have by deed given to my son Thomas Glover all my lands in England, with the promise that they shall be freed of my Widows dower, and that besides I have promised to give him four hundred pounds : and have also promised to my son Nathaniel, to give him so much in good payment, as would make the lands, the which I delivered him, worth four Hundred pounds : And have also given to my son Habakuck, that one half of the new house in Boston nearest Mr. Webb's house, with half of all the other housing, half of the Yard and pits in it, and other accommodations for tanning, and promised to make it up to him four hundred pounds.

All these with all other my debts, I will to be duly paid in the first place out of my goods, debts due to me, and out of the profits of all my lands in Dorchester and Boston, saving my Widow's dower, not already expressed to be given.

And next unto these my Will is, that my two sons John and Pelatiah shall have either of them, One Hundred pounds paid unto them, out of my goods and out of the profits of my two farms on the further side of the River in Dorchester, and out of the one half of my house, yard and other housing, and tan pits not herein expressed to be given to my son Habakuck, as soon as my widows necessary maintenance out of the aforesaid estate will permit.

And further after these performed, my will is, my beloved wife relinquishing her right of dower in England, shall have all the rest of my goods, and all the profits of my two farms in Dorchester, and of my aforesaid half house, yard, housing, and tan pits in Boston, undisposed of, for and during her natural life. And further that my son Habakuck shall have the said half of my house next Goodman Hudsons, with the half of the yard and other housing and tan pits : my son Habakuck paying within one year to my son Thomas Glover ten pounds, and to my son Nathaniel Glover forty pounds : and to Harvard College at Cambridge, for and towards the maintenance of a fellow there, five pounds a year forever. And if my beloved wife can spare to give the said five pounds a year in her life-time I doubt not that she will give it. And of this my last Will I make and ordain my well beloved wife my sole Executrix, desiring my respected loving friends Mr. Richard Mather and Mr. Henry Withington, as overseers, to advise and further the performance of this my Will. Now, O ; God ! as for me, let me see thy face in righteousness. I shall have sufficient in the awakening of thine image.

As for my children with them which I leave behind me, Oh that thy grace and peace may be with them. And as for thy Majesty, to Thee be glory and might, both now and for the day of Eternity. Amen.

If my said sons John and Pelatiah shall have occasion to sell Mr. Newbreys farm, my desire is, that it be sold to my son Nathaniel if he desires to buy it. Written with my own hand this Eleventh day of April, 1653.   JOHN GLOVER.

Upon further consideration of what my sons John and Peletiah have already received in their education, my Will and mind is, that after the decease of my beloved wife, they the said John and Pelatiah shall have and receive out of my two farms in Dorchester, either of them, the sum of two Hundred pounds, which sum of four Hundred pounds being first paid unto them the said John and Pelatiah, I do hereby give the reversion and inheritance of the said two farms unto my sons Habakuck, John, Nathaniel and Pelatiah, and to their heirs forever : to be equally divided amongst them in four severally. And that this is my Will I have caused this Codicil to be annexed and affixed to my Will and testament, as part thereof, and have thereunto put my hand, this twenty sixth day of the Eleventh Month, 1653. Witness hereof,   JOHN GLOVER.

The Will itself, with these words interlined, "saving my Widow's dower," with the Codicil, to both which he hath subscribed his name, was acknowledged by the said Mr. John Glover to be his last Will and testament the Twenty Sixth day of the Eleventh month, 1653, before me WILLIAM HIBBINS, the 9th Feb., 1653.

Mr. Habakuck Glover appeared before the Magistrates and presented the above and within written, to be the last Will and testament of his father, Mr. John Glover deceased. Mr. William Hibbins being a witness thereunto, having deposed, saying that he saw the said Mr. John Glover sign the above mentioned premises, and that when he signed it he heard him publish it as his last will and testament, and that then he was of a sound disposing mind, when he signed it; which the Magistrates approved of, present the Deputy Gov'.

A true Copy, Attest   Mr. HIBBINS, *Recorder*.
H. M. WILLIS, Reg'.

An Inventory of the Goods and Chattels of Mr. John Glover, of Boston, prized and drafted 6 : 12 : 1653, At his Newbury Farm in Dorchester, Beyond Neponset River, and now in the Occupation of John Gill and Roger Billings, by Vs whose names are Underwritten.

Imp'. The Farm House, Barn, Housing and Lands broken and Pasture, with Meadow thereunto belonging	£700 00 00
Wheat, 130 bushels at 5 shil and 8 pence pr bush .	82 10 00
Indian Corn, 3-8 " " .	45 00 00
Oats, 40 bushels, 2-6 " " .	5 00 00
Mares	80 00 00
Stone Horse	56 00 00
Young Mare two years old	56 00 00
2 young Colts	7 00 00
4 Oxen at 16 pounds the yoke	32 00 00
2 Oxen more	14 00 00
9 Cows, 6 having Calves, 3 being at hand to Calve .	47 05 00
10 Cows more	50 00 00
3 Bulls, One 3 years Old and 2 at two and a half yrs .	08 00 00
2 Heifers	09 00 00
6 young beasts	15 00 00
One Old Cow	3 05 00
5 Heifers, 8 shill per "	10 00 00
4 young Bullocks one with another	15 00 00
2 young Heifers	6 00 00
1 Cow more	
12 Calves, 3-8d	05 05 00
Swine	10 00 00
12 Pigs	1 00 00
4 Ox Chains	1 06 08
1 Old Plow	1 06 08
1 Indian Plow	0 08 00
1 Whip Saw	0 08 00
33 Harrow pins	0 16 00
Wheels	01 06 08
2 yokes and other irons	00 12 00

Harrow of 50 Pins	2	00	00
1 Cops Axletree, Pin and Pot Racks	2	05	06
2 Scythes (old)	0	13	00
1 Mattock	0	6	08
Hammer	0	1	04
Sickles	0	2	06
2 Muskets, 2 Swords, and 2 Bandeliers	2	07	04
6 Coverlits	2	02	00
3 Ruggs	1	04	00
Old Twill	0	02	00
Old Ruggs	0	05	00
3 Beds and 1 half Bed	0	18	00
Pillows and Old Bolster	0	03	00
3 Bedsteads	0	05	00
2 Bedsteads	0	05	00
1 Flock-bed	00	06	08
Frame Table and Mould and Trough		13	00
½ bush measure, Cases		05	00
Boat and Grappling	3	10	00
Cannon 2 pounds	2	00	00
1 more Cops and Pin	0	02	00
Sundry other articles about the House and Farm	6	16	8
	£1226	02	08

An Inventory of Goods and Chattels of Mr. John Glover of Boston, prized and drafted 6 : 12 : 1653, at his Farm in Dorchester, beyond the Neponset River and now in the occupation of Nicholas Wood, by vs whose names are underwritten.

Imp'. The Farm House, Barn, Out-housing, Uplands, broken and unbroken, and all Meadow-lands thereunto belonging	£350	00	00
3 Yoke of Oxen,	45	00	00
1½ Yoke	12	00	00
Old Mare,	16	00	00
Young Mare 3 years old and yearling	13	10	00
4 acres of Rye growing in the field, estimated 4ˢ 8ᵈ	20	00	00
70 bushels of Wheat a 5ˢ 8ᵈ per bush	17	10	00
30 bushels of Rye	06	00	00
3 Cows	12	00	00
Wheels and Pins	2	00	00
Plow Irons	1	04	00
2 Harrows	1	06	00
5 Chains, 6ˢ 8ᵈ	1	13	04
4 Ox Yokes, 3ˢ 8ᵈ	0	14	00
Rent for 9 acres of land	3	12	00
Pot Racks	0	02	00
	£502	11	04

7

An Inventory of the Goods and Chattels belonging to Mr. John Glover, of Boston, prized and drafted 7 : 12 : 1653, at his Dwelling House in Boston, by Vs whose names are under Written.

Imp'. The Dwelling House wherein Mrs. John Glover now dwelleth with the proportionable part of the Land thereunto belonging, prized at	£300 00 00
Wearing Apparel	17 00 00
3 yds Kersey	01 07 00
1 piece colored Fustian	1 12 00
5 yds White Kersey at 3ˢ 8ᵈ per yard	0 17 00
5½ yards Demi Stone 4ˢ 8ᵈ	1 02 00
3 yards Red Broadcloth 16ˢ 8ᵈ per yard	2 08 00
3 yds Gladen 3ˢ 8ᵈ	0 10 00
Nagorie and Linen	10 14 06
1 Bed and bolster and Clothes-bedding	7 00 00
Some old things in the Little Chamber	1 00 00
1 Bedstead, Bolster, Pillows and Coverlit	8 00 00
1 Bedstead and Clothes	3 00 00
1 Bedstead	1 17 00
1 Bed	2 10 00
Muskets, Swords and other Arms	4 15 00
2 Chairs and 4 Stools	2 00 00
1 Table	1 08 00
1 Bedstead, Feather Bed, Bolster and Pillows, Coverings and Curtains	10 00 00
6 Chairs and Stools	1 03 04
Covering to Bed	1 00 00
7 Cushions	1 16 00
Small	6 06 00
Silver Plate	6 06 00
Pewter	4 03 00
Brass Pots and other brass	5 04 00
Wooden Vessels	1 06 00
1 Seat, Chairs, Stools, Kitchen table	0 08 00
3 Chairs	0 05 00
Handirons, Grate, Bellows, and other Iron things	2 06 00
————	30 00 00
Books English and Latin	4 00 00
110 Bushels of Barley	27 10 00
16 Bush. Wheat	8 08 00
1 Clock and Warming pan	8 08 00
Dry Leather	102 00 00
415 Hydes in the Bark	600 00 00
45 Hydes in the Lyme	33 00 00
313 West India Hydes	187 00 00
500 Weight of	4 10 00
Bark	10 00 00
Boards, Plank, Shingles, and Sawed Timber	6 00 00
———— ————	19 00 00
	£1436 19 10

Debts owing the Estate.

William Phillips of the Ship ——, lying at Boston	£97	00	00
Goodman Coleman of Boston, Shoemaker	04	00	00
by William Robinson, sold him by John Gillfora for Mr. Glover's Use	4	00	00
Mr. Thomas late of Boston, Principal and forbearance, not paying in Old England	60	00	00
James Ashwood	20	00	00
Mr. Valentile Hill, Principal and forbearance and not paying in Old England	25	00	00
Capt. John Sturtevant	03	00	00
William Shattuck	14	13	04
Joseph Jewett of Rowley	214	19	01
Sampson Mason of Dorchester	007	10	00
Capt. Gookin to pay in Old England	010	00	00
More by Capt. Gookin	3	13	00
Mr. Holman of Dorchester	30	07	00
Thomas Broughton of Boston	100	00	00
John Gurnell	04	00	00
Mr. Rawson	02	00	00
	£600	**02**	**05**

4 Barrels of Pork	£18	00	00
1 Hhd Beef	07	00	00
3 hhd Mackerel	4	00	00
1 Press for Clothes	00	10	00
Plank and Boards	15	00	00
5 Servants at 8 Pounds each	40	00	00
	£84	**10**	**00**

Whole amount of estate contained in the above
Inventories, £3850 06 03

Mrs. Anna Glover appeared before the Magistrates and Recorder the 4th day of January, 1654, and deposed that this is a true Inventory of the Estate of her late husband Mr. John Glover, of Boston deceased, and promised that when she knew more she would discover it to the Recorder. pr EDWARD RAWSON,
Recorder.

Humphrey Atherton, ⎫
John Wiswall, ⎬
John Smith. ⎭

On the records of Harvard College, under date of 1642, Mr. Glover and two others are credited with a "Gift of Utensils," for the use of that institution, amounting to twenty pounds.

He was one of those who allowed themselves to be assessed for the expenses and benefit of that College, and was called upon from time to time to furnish provisions and all such articles as were needed there, according to his ability.

At his decease he left them a token of his remembrance in a legacy of " five pounds a year forever, as a perpetual annuity for the aid of indigent students." It was directed to be paid out of that portion of his Boston estate which was given to his second son Habackuk Glover, after the decease of his mother.

That event occurred in 1670. At this present writing, 1866, it is two hundred and twelve years since the above annuity became due and payable to the treasurer of the College. The amount of five pounds, or in Federal money sixteen dollars and sixty-seven cents, has been paid annually by those who inherited the estate, and their successors — which sum, though it may seem small at the beginning, has amounted, in the aggregate, to three thousand five hundred and sixty-seven dollars and thirty-two cents.

Samuel Torrey, Esq., of Boston, is the last successor and present owner of Mr. Glover's Boston estate, and paid the last annuity in April, 1866.

Mr. Glover owned another estate in Dorchester. He mentions in his will his " two farms in Dorchester, out of which his widow, relinquishing her right of dower in England, was to draw the income until her death." One of these was his " Newbery farm," and the other a tract of land of one hundred and eighty acres, situated directly south of Milton Hill, and extending westward (according to the bounds described in the deed) on the flat fronting on the northwest by the brook which now bears the name of " Aunt Sarah's Brook," and south-east by the central line of the town of Milton. He laid out a farm here, and built a house and barn and other out-houses convenient for farming. It is said the house stood near where the brook reaches the road, by the house now occupied by Mr. Davis. The furniture of the house, stock and farming utensils were all owned by Mr. Glover. This farm was leased to Nicholas Wood, who came over to New England as Mr. Glover's agent, and was a tenant there at the time of Mr. G.'s death, and continued to occupy it until it was sold in 1654 by the heirs of Mr. Glover, to Robert Vose. It has descended down in the Vose line to the present time, although portions of the land have been sold, from time to time, so that the original farm is now much diminished. This estate now lies in the town of Milton. The following deed is copied from the original document:

John Glover's Heirs to Robert Vose.

To All Xpean People to whom these Presents shall come. Mrs. Anna Glover, Widow, Executrix of the last Will and Testament of the Worshipful Mr. John Glover, One of Our Honored Magistrates Deceased, Mr. Habackuk Glover, Mr. John Glover, Mr. Nathaniel Glover, and Mr. Peletiah Glover, sons of the said Mr. John Glover, deceased; now abiding inhabitants of Boston in the County of Suffolk and in the Colony of Massachusetts Bay in New England; Send Greeting in Our Lord God Everlasting. Know Ye,

That the said Mrs. Anna Glover, Mr. Habackuk Glover, Mr. John Glover, Mr. Nathaniel Glover and Mr. Peletiah Glover, for and in consideration of the sum of Three Hundred and Forty-Seven Pounds to be paid by Robert Voss, of Dorchester in said County, Gentleman, Have Given, Granted, bargained, sold, enfeoffed and confirmed, and by these Presents do hereby give, grant bargaine, Sell, enfeoffee and confirm unto the said Robert Voss his Heirs and Assigns Forever,

All that Dwelling House and Farm where now Nicholas Wood dwells; with the Barn, Cow House, Out House and Yards, Orchards, and Gardens; with what Fences and Privileges to the said House is thereunto belonging, with all appurtenances belonging or appertaining, with Ten Acres of Upland and Meadow more or less within the close, lying about the said House and upon which the said House standeth.

Also a Parcel of Land about Tenne Acres, more or Less, lying betweene the Calf Pasture and Robert Redman's.

Also One Hundred Acres of Upland more or less in a Plain called the Great Plaine, about a Mile from the said House, most of it fenced in.

Also Twenty Acres of Meadow joyning the said Hundred Acres, near Little River on the South side thereof.

Also One half of the Division which the said John Glover purchased in the time of his life of John Phillips, the said half containing Sixty-Four Acres or thereabouts. It to be of that part of the Division that butts upon or is nearest adjoyning the said Farm.

Also One half of the Five Divisions of Commons that were the said Mr. John Glover's, owned undivided before his death, lying on the West side of the said before named, that were the Divisions of said John Phillips, containing about Forty Acres More or Less; to be laid out at that end of said Divisions that is nearest the said Farm. Also half the Divisions that were the Divisions of the said Mr. John Glover in the time of his life properly belonging to himself elsewhere, that lye in common on the South side of the Naponsett River so far as the Blew Hills.

Also One half of Five Divisions which the said Mr. John Glover purchased in the time of his life of several other Persons on the south side of said River.

Also Forty Acres of Meadow lying on the South side of the said River Neponsett near to Mr. Glover's sons Farm.

Also Forty acres of Upland near or about the Blew Hills.

Also a Certain Tract of Land lying by the Out side of the fence towards the Playne as it is now bounded with a straight line between

7*

the lands of several other men, with all Timber, Woods, Underwoods upon any part of the said premises, fallen or unfallen.

Also Three quarters of Land for a Landing place adjoyning to the River Neponsett, below Mr. Stoughton's Mill.

Also Six Acres of Salt Marsh which the said Mr. John Glover Deceased, in his Life time purchased of the Town of Dorchester, that formerly did belong unto the House that the said Town purchased of one Mrs. Hill, and lying upon the South side of the said River where the said Marsh Lot was, and now in the tenure and occupation of Stephen Kinsley.

Excepting and reserving unto ourselves the said Mrs. Anna Glover, Mr. Habackuk Glover, Mr. John Glover, Mr. Nathaniel Glover, and Mr. Peletiah Glover, Our Heirs and Assigns forever, the liberty of the said landing place for her or their necessary Use. As also liberty of passage to and from said landing to the Highway; and of all such passages belonging to said farm or the before reserved and demised premises, for her or their, or any of their necessary use.

To Have and to Hold the before mentioned and bargained Premises, butted and bounded as aforesaid, of all and singular the Appurtenances thereunto belonging.

Except what was before Excepted to the said Robert Voss, his Heirs and Assigns Forever. And that the said Mrs. Anna Glover, Mr. Habakuck Glover, Mr. John Glover, Mr. Nathaniel Glover, and Mr. Peletiah Glover, their Heirs, Executors, Administrators and Assigns, now is the first conveyance   *   *   to the said Robert Voss, his Heirs and Assigns forever, by these Presents that now is the first Estate and conveyance and assurance of the above mentioned Premises, and every part thereof with their appurtenances unto him the said Robert Voss, his Heirs and Assigns forever, According to the true intent and meaning of these Presents, and shall stand seized of them in the Premises or every of them with their appurtenances, in their or every of their Own Right to give, convey of their own   *   *   * The said Anna for the term of her natural Life, and the said Mr. Habackuk, John, Nathaniel and Peletiah as an Estate of Inheritance as true and lawful heirs of the said John Glover, Esq., and of the said Anna their Mother according to the gifts and bequests the said Mr. John Glover Deceased gave to her.

And are the true, proper and Lawful owners of all and every of the before mentioned Premises and of every part and parcel thereof with their appurtenances in nature as before expressed.

And have good right and Lawful authority to give, grant, bargain, sell and convey the same Premises with all their appurtenances unto the said Robert Voss, his Heirs and Assigns, in full manner and form as before in these Presents is mentioned and declared.

And the said Anna Glover, Habackuk Glover, John Glover, Nathaniel Glover and Peletiah Glover, for themselves, their Heirs and Assigns, Executors, or Administrators, further Covenant and grant to and with the said Robert Voss, his Heirs and Assigns, Executors and Administrators by these Presents, that the said Premises and every part and parcel of them with their appurtenances now and at all times hereafter shall remain and abide unto the said Robert Voss his Heirs and Assigns Forever, freely acquitted, Exonerated and discharged as aforesaid, from time to time and at all times hereafter fully secured and defended from all manner of former bargains, gifts, grants, mortgages, Leases, Joyntures, Executions and incumbrances whatsoever from the said Anna Glover, Hubackuk Glover, John Glover, Nathaniel Glover and Peletiah Glover, or any of them or their Heirs, or any person claiming under them the said Anna Glover, Habakuck Glover, John Glover, Nathaniel Glover and Peletiah Glover in the before mentioned and bargained Premises unto the said Robert Voss his Heirs and Assigns forever.

And the said Anna Glover, Habackuk Glover, John Glover, Nathaniel Glover and Pelatiah Glover, and their Heirs and Assigns, Executors and Administrators shall cause to be delivered unto the said Robert Voss, His Heirs and Assigns, All Writings, Deeds, Evidences and whatsoever, answering to the Premises, of true Copies and Plans, wherein the said Premises or any part thereof is intermixed with other Lands in the Possession of the said Anna Glover, Habakuck Glover, John Glover, Nathaniel Glover and Peletiah Glover, if he the said Voss shall have just ground and reason to require them.

Provided, however, that in case the aforesaid sum of Three Hundred and Four score Pounds Sterling be not paid according to the several obligations given by the said Robert Voss, Then he the said Robert Voss stands bound to the said Mrs. Anna Glover, * * * bearing date the 11th day of the fifth month, called July, in the year of our Lord 1654, according to the several times and Payments as all provisions of Payments in the said obligations expressed in part or in the whole at the time and at all times hereafter * * * And it shall be lawful for the said Anna, Habakuck, John, Nathaniel and Peletiah, her or their Heirs and Assigns, Executors and administrators, to enter in and upon the Premises and to hold possession as in their former Rights.

In Witness whereof, the said Anna Glover, Habakuck Glover, John Glover, Nathaniel Glover and Peletiah Glover have hereunto set our hands and seals this Thirteenth day of the fifth Month (July) in the Year of our Lord 1654.

ANNA GLOVER,
HABAKUCK GLOVER,
Signed, sealed and delivered in presence of   JOHN GLOVER,
   Humphrey Atherton,   NATHANIEL GLOVER,
   Richard Mayor,   PELETIAH GLOVER.
   John Wallys,
   Robert Howard.

Entered and Recorded Oct. 4, 1654.   EDWARD RAWSON,
   Recorder.

[Suff. Records, Vol. 2, fol. 60.]

On the margin:

Know all Men by these Presents, that Mrs. Anna Glover, Habackuk Glover and John Glover do Authorize Nathaniel Glover, one of the said Venders, to give Possession unto Robert Voss of Dorchester of the Houses and Lands contained in the within written order or convey-

ance after the order lately enacted in a session of the General Court, in the Year 1652. In witness whereof we have thereunto set our Hands and Seals.   ANNA GLOVER,
HABAKUCK GLOVER,
JOHN GLOVER.

Seizing of possession accordingly given of the said Houses and of the said Lands in the name of the Whole,

In the presence of   (Signed) JOHN GLOVER.
John Spig,
Nicholas Wood.

Mrs. Anna Glover lived about sixteen years after the death of her husband, and died at her mansion house in Boston, in the 11th month of 1670–71.

16 : 11 : 1670–71. Administration was granted on the Estate of Mrs. Anna Glover to John Glover, her younger son (by consent of Habackuk Glover, his elder brother), he bringing an Inventory of said Estate and giving security to administer thereon according to law.

An Inventory of the Goods and Estate of Mrs. Anna Glover of Boston deceased, taken and prized by the subscribers the day abovesaid.

Imp'. One Feather bed, boulster and pillows . .	£3	00 00
Another Boulster and pillows	1	00 00
Her Wearing Apparel	7	00 00
Small Rugg	7	05 00
2 Old Rugs	0	14 00
Curtain Stuff	0	10 00
Linen	1	10 00
4 Chairs	0	12 00
2 pots, one Iron, the other brass	0	10 00
2 pot hooks or Racks	0	10 08
pr Tongs and Candlestick	0	04 00
Silver Spoon	9	07 00
One and One Chamber	0	05 00
Debt in the hands of Robert Vose	40	00 00
Debt in the hands of Jonathan Lewis	2	00 00
Debt in the hands of Thomas Broughton . . .	120	00 00
	£194	07 08

John Glover made oath this 16 : 11 : 1670–71, before the Governor Richard Bellingham, Esq. and Edward Tyng, Esq., that this is a true Inventory of the Estate of his late Mother, Mrs. Anna Glover, and that when he knows more he will disclose the same.

Attest :   FREEGRACE BENDALL.

A donation of £10 is credited to Mrs. Glover on the records of Harvard College, under date of 1642, as a gift towards furnishing

books for the College Library. Other instances appear of her enlarged benevolence and of her hospitality. The name of her family
has not been ascertained, although diligently sought for; nor has
even a clue to her origin or English life been discovered by the examination of any records found here. But through her New England
life and acts, aided by tradition, she has become known to us as a
woman of superior endowments, and of remarkable grace and dignity of manners, well fitting her high station. She was a church
member beforeher emigration. Her name appears on the records of
the Dorchester Church, 23 : 6 : 1636. She remained in that connection about twenty-five years, and on the 4 : 9 : 1660, was dismissed to
join the old Church at Boston. She was received there 1 : 3 : 1661,
and continued a member until her death. She stands at the head
of the descending generations as their first American ancestress, and
her Christian name has been perpetuated among them successively to
the present time.

Mr. Glover's Newbury Farm.

Mr. Thomas Newbury, who came from England in the same ship
with Mr. John Glover, was first in possession of this farm, by grants
of land from the Proprietors of Dorchester, and by purchase from
Mr. Pynchon, who removed to Springfield and became one of its
first founders.

The following extracts are from the Proprietors' Records:

1634. "It is ordered that Mr. Newbury shall have Thirty Acres
for the purchase that he bought of Mr. Pynchon; the house that
Mr. Pynchon built; and Forty Acres of Upland ground to the
house; and Forty Acres of Marsh and Twenty acres of Neck in
Brantry Neck." Mr. Newbury's one hundred acres to be laid out
to him next Israel Stoughton's, six miles above his mill at Neponset
River.

"Likewise it is ordered and agreed upon, that Whereas Mr. Newbury hath relinquished a former Grant of Forty-one Acres of Marsh
and Twenty Acres of Upland in Squantum Neck, he is now to have
all the land from his house to Mr. Wilson's Farm, in consideration
thereof."

There appears to have been no deed given to Mr. Glover, but the
title was confirmed to him by the heirs of Mr. Newbury, and is recorded on the records of the General Court at Boston, as follows:

1645. "Upon petition of the heirs of Mr. Thomas Newbury, viz., Henry Wolcott, Daniel Clark, Joseph Newbury, Mr. John Warham and William Gaylord, in the behalf of the three youngest daughters, that the farm bought of Mr. Pyncheon with its appurtenances, the Sixteen Acre lott, with the Barn upon it, and Forty Rods in the Little Neck, should be ratified and confirmed to Mr. John Glover."

Oct. 2, 1645. "In Answer to the Petition of the Children an. Executrix and Overseers of the Last Will and Testament of Mr. Thomas Newbury, late of Dorchester, Deceased, for the confirmation of the said Farm of said Thomas Newbury to Mr. John Glover, of Dorchester, of Whom they acknowledge to have received full satisfaction, and in consideration thereof, their Petition is hereby Granted, and the farm confirmed to the said John Glover and to his heirs and Assigns forever."

This farm, containing four hundred acres, was situated in Dorchester, on the south side of the Neponset River, and was bounded on the north by the River, on the south by Mr. Wilson's farm in Braintree, on the east by the sea at low water mark, and on the west extended to near the bounds of what is now Milton, a precinct of Dorchester until 1662. In 1640 the whole farm passed into the possession of Mr. Glover, Mr. Newbury relinquishing, with the intention of removing to Connecticut River. Mr. Glover leased the farm to John Gill and Roger Billings. There were two houses upon it — one built by Mr. Newbury, and occupied as his homestead, the other built by Mr. Pynchon. The lessees occupied these houses, and carried on the farm, paying an annual rent. Mr. Glover owned the stock and farming utensils; also the furniture of the houses. He gave it the name of "Newbury Farm." In 1649 he renewed the lease to John Gill and Roger Billings for another term of ten years. They were the occupants there at the time of Mr. Glover's death, in 1653, and continued there for some time after, the lease being renewed by his heirs.

By his last will Mr. Glover reserved the income of his Newbury Farm as the dower of his widow, who dying in 1670, the estate reverted to his four sons, and was for the next ten years owned conjointly by Mr. Habackuk Glover of Boston, Mr. John Glover of Boston, the heirs of Mr. Nathaniel Glover of Dorchester, and the Rev. Pelatiah Glover of Springfield. They continued the lease to Roger Billings, Sen., until the year 1680, at which time they had a survey made of the farm, and a plan drawn indicating the divisions and sub-divisions, according to the purport of the will and each one's right of inheritance. They entered into the following agreement at this time, bearing date with the plan.

Glover's Agreement (a Quadripartition).

Articles of Agreement Quadripartite, Indented, made and concluded upon the Twelfth day of November, Anno Domini One Thousand Six Hundred and Eighty, between

1. Thomas Hinckley of Barnstable, in the Colony of New Plymouth in New England, Esqr. on the behalf of himself, and

Nathaniel Glover, son of Mr. Nathaniel Glover, late of Dorchester, in the Colony of Massachusetts in New England, Deceased, on the One part; And

2. Habakuck Glover of Boston, in New England aforesaid, on the Second part; and

3. John Glover of Boston aforesaid, merchant, on the Third part; and

4. Pelatiah Glover of Springfield, in the Colony of Massachusetts in New England, Clergyman, on the Fourth part, are as followeth:

Imp. That the said Thomas Hinckley, in behalf of himself and the said Nathaniel Glover, and the said Habakuck Glover, do hereby Covenant and Promise, agree and grant to, and with the said John Glover and Pelatiah Glover so far as their, or either of their interests doth extend, that they the said John and Pelatiah Glover shall have and enjoy to their own proper Use and Uses, All the Rents, Profits, Benefits and improvements which are arising or growing from, or issuing out of, a Certain Farm, scituate and lying within the Township of Dorchester in the Colony of Massachusetts, Commonly called and known by the name of the Newberry Farm, said Farm formerly belonging unto Mr. John Glover, Esq., Deceased, and now in the tenure and occupation of Roger Billings for the full term of Three years from the Twenty fifth day of March last past (1680) before the date of these presents: from thence next ensuing and fully to be completed and ended.

In consideration whereof, the said John Glover for himself, his heirs, Executors, Administrators and Assigns; and also for, and in the name and behalf of his Uncle William Glover of Prescott, in the County of Lancaster in the Kingdom of Great Britain;

the which he the said John Glover is Attorney to the said William Glover;

and Pelatiah Glover for himself and his heirs and Executors and Administrators and Assigns; and also for and in the name and behalf of his brother Thomas Glover, of the City of London in the said Kingdom of Great Britain, Merchant,

Have remised, released, and forever quitclaimed, and do by these presents, for their several and perspective heirs, Executors and Administrators and assigns, do remise, release and forever quitclaim unto the said Thomas Hinckley, Nathaniel Glover and Habakuck Glover, and each and every of them, and each and every of their heirs, Executors and Administrators and Assigns.

And all manner of suites, actions, causes, or causes of actions, con-
troversies, bills, bonds, accounts, reconings, sum or sums of Money,
rents, moveables, Houses, Lands, tenements, Judgments, Executions,
and demands whatsoever which they the said Thomas Glover, William
Glover, John Glover and Pelatiah Glover, or either or any of them
ever had, or either or any of their heirs, Executors, Administrators,
or assigns, or either or any of them can or may have in, for or against
the said Thomas Hinckley, Nathaniel Glover and Habakuck Glover,
their heirs, Executors, Administrators or Assigns, for or by reason of
their father the said John Glover's Estate, or any thing relating to
the said Farm in the Last Will and Testament of the said John Glover, Esq., Deceased, Excepting only that the said Pelatiah Glover
doth hereby except his own personal interest in the farm that is now
in possession of Robert Vose, of Milton, in New England aforesaid,
and his assigns. And it is mutually agreed between the said parties
to these Presents, in manner and form following (that is to say) that
at the expiration of the above said Term of three years, the aforesaid
Farm Commonly called and known by the name of the " Newberry
Farm," shall be divided into four equal parts, according to the tenor,
purpose and true meaning of the last Will and Testament of (Mr.)
John Glover, Esq', deceased. And also, as well Thomas Glover and
William Glover, as the several parties above mentioned, shall have,
retain, and keep, possess and enjoy all such part and parts of that
Estate as did formerly belong to John Glover, Esq', deceased, and the
Rents and proceeds of the said Estate or any part thereof, which is
now in their several or respective hands, custody and possession,
without any manner of trouble, molestation or disturbance whatso-
ever of either or any of the said parties, their heirs, Executors, and
Administrators and Assigns.

And for the true and real observation and performance of all and
singular, the covenants, promises and agreements, and of all other
things above rehearsed, the said parties have bound, and hereby do
bind themselves, their heirs, Executors and Administrators and
Assigns, unto the other heirs, Executors, Administrators and Assigns,
in the penal sum of One thousand Pounds lawful money of New
England well and truly to be paid by virtue of these presents.

In Witness Whereof, the parties first above mentioned and named
to these present articles, interchangeably their hands and scales have
set the day and year first above Written.

	THOMAS HINCKLEY,
Signed, sealed and delivered in	HABAKUCK GLOVER,
presence of us,	JOHN GLOVER,
Elisha Cooke,	PELATIAH GLOVER.
John Hayward.	

This Instrument was acknowledged by the abovenamed Thomas
Hinckley, Habakuck Glover, John Glover and Pelatiah Glover, as
their free will act and deed, this Twelfth day of November, One thousand six hundred and Eighty (Nov. 12th, 1680), before
                                          WILLIAM STOUGHTON.

Joseph Dudley,
John Richards.

Entered and Recorded on Suffolk Records of Deeds,
        Nov. 19, 1680.

Oct. 8, 1681, Mr. Habackuk Glover, of Boston, sold and confirmed his one fourth part of Newbury farm to Roger Billings, as marked on the plan. Consideration one hundred and seventy pounds. Signed by Habackuk Glover and Hannah Glover.

In 1686, Mr. John Glover, of Boston, conveyed and confirmed to his "beloved Nephew, Nathaniel Glover, eldest son to his brother Nathaniel Glover, of Dorchester, who died in 1657," "one twelfth part of this farm, which fell to the share of Anna Glover, now wife unto William Rawson and one of the heirs of his said brother Nathaniel, and conveyed by her to her Uncle John Glover." Signed John Glover and Elizabeth Glover. From 1686 to 1692, the farm was owned conjointly by Mr. John Glover, of Boston, in his own right one fourth; Roger Billings, in right of Habackuk, one fourth; Nathaniel Glover, Sen., eldest son of Mr. Nathaniel Glover, of Dorchester, deceased, in his own right of inheritance, one twelfth, and by purchase of his brother John Glover (cooper), one twelfth, and by Deed of Gift, from his uncle John Glover, of the remaining one twelfth part which accrued to his sister Mrs. Anna Rawson, as her right of inheritance, being the only daughter of Mr. Nathaniel Glover of Dorchester deceased — which last named three twelfths comprised one fourth; and the Rev. Pelatiah Glover, of Springfield, one fourth.

Rev. Pelatiah Glover dying in 1692, his share, or one fourth part, devolved on his son Pelatiah Glover, Jr., of Springfield, who sold it in 1699 to Nathaniel Glover, Sen., and William Rawson. The farm was then owned conjointly by the heirs of Roger Billings, one fourth; Nathaniel Glover, Sen., in his own right, one fourth; Mr. John Glover, of Boston, one fourth; Nathaniel Glover, Sen., and William Rawson, one fourth, in the right of Pelatiah Glover, Jr.

In 1700, they made a new division among themselves, and with Roger and Ebenezer Billings, sons to Roger Billings, Sen.

Nathaniel Glover, Sen., was a retainer of both houses, and all the out buildings, with his share of the land; he removed there and became an occupant in 1700. He remained in possession until his death, which occurred in 1723–4, about twenty-four years. At his death he left his house and homestead by Deed of Gift to his youngest son, Mr. Thomas Glover, Esq., reserving the right of dower for his widow.

Mr. Thomas Glover, of the fourth generation, owned and occupied

8

it until his death in 1758, a period of thirty-four years, and had twelve children born to him there, by his wife Elizabeth Clough. 'He left it by will to his two youngest sons, William and Ebenezer. They owned it conjointly for a time, when they divided, and Ebenezer retained the homestead, comprising the houses and land which lay convenient to it. In 1798, Ebenezer Glover, successor to Thomas, took away the old house and built a new one just in the rear of the old cellar. It is still standing, having been remodelled and repaired several times. Ebenezer Glover occupied and was in possession nearly fifty years. He had three children born to him there, by his wives Sarah Wadsworth and Mary Davenport, and left it by will, in 1807, to his only son, Benjamin Wadsworth Glover, who succeeded him and occupied there until his death in 1814 — a period of seven years. By his wife Mehetable Willard Baxter, he had two sons born to him there. In 1823, the homestead estate of Newbury Farm was settled on his eldest son, Horatio N. Glover, Esq., who succeeded to the occupancy, and had ten children born to him there, by his wife Martha Turpin Hovey. At his death, in 1863, he had been in possession forty years, and had made great improvements on the buildings and land. The estate is now, in 1866, held in trust by his widow and his sons Horatio N. and William B. Glover, Esqs.

Thus it appears that Mr. Glover's Newbury Farm, which was possessed by him in 1640, has passed down in a direct line of succession, through his descendants, until it has reached the eighth generation, covering a period of two hundred and twenty-six years.

Undivided Lands apportioned to Mr. Glover in the Three Divisions, Dorchester Neck, and in Dorchester New Grant.

The members of the London Joint Stock Company were entitled to a share of two hundred acres of land for every fifty pounds adventured, and additional acres under other conditions, or according to the men they employed in their business, and the number of their servants. As soon as practicable after their settlement at Dorchester, apportionments were made by the Proprietors, to each man, according to the laws of the Company.

The following apportionments were made to Mr. Glover, and recorded on the Proprietors' Records.

"March, 1636. It is ordered that Mr. Glover shall have Thirty Acres of land and Meadow beyond Neponset River, about one mile from the Mill, in Lieu of a Twenty Acre Lott which he leaves to the Plantation, in the Great lotts beyond the Fresh Marsh." "The proportion which Mr. Glover is to have in the lands on the Neck is Twenty Acres, and the same in the Cow pasture."

"26 (3) 1644. It is ordered that Mr. Glover shall have that Upland he so much desireth, being and lying to the Brook from the Upper part of the Great Plain, beyond his farm; the said John Glover giving Upland and Meadow for the same, to the Town, out of his own Propriety of the 'Three Divisions,' or out of the next land divisible or elsewhere to the full value according to the Judgment of Nathaniel Duncan, Thomas Jones, William Sumner, Hopestill Foster and William Blake."

Mr. Glover had lands apportioned to him on Dorchester Neck (now South Boston), some of which he sold (29: 6: 1644), to Nicholas Ball, as follows:

"Land in the great Neck in the further end of his lott; together with half of the Way granted and quality considered: said land lying next to the Moat of the Neck on the further end of his lott. To have and to hold to the aforesaid Nicholas Ball, and to his heirs forever. Whereby the aforesaid John Glover doth acknowledge to have had full satisfaction for the aforesaid Tract."

Dorchester New Grant, in which were comprised the Proprietors' Undivided Lands, extended from the Blue Hills southward to the Colony line which separated it from the Plymouth Colony. The lines were run parallel from North to South. The swamps were set off as the "Twenty-five Divisions;" the Upland was, when divided, called the "Twelve Divisions" of land. The Proprietors were an organized body, and received their proportions according to the stock invested and accredited to them on the Company's Records.

"In the years 1636, 1637, and 1638, the lands in 'Dorchester New Grant' were ordered to be divided, in such proportions that Mr. Glover, of Dorchester, one of the Original Proprietors, should have Thirty-Six Acres, two quarters and Twenty-five Rods out of every Division of land."

"7 (4) 1642. It was agreed that Mr. John Glover, being one of the Original Proprietors of the Town of Dorchester, should with Mr. Baker and Mr. Breck, run the line at the head of Braintry Bounds; and then run the line unto the Country for the laying out of the New Grant."

The line was accordingly run about that time, but the divisions were not made until 1667.

"At a General Town Meeting (1: 1: 1667), in the Town of Dorchester, It was voted that there should be Twelve Divisions laid out altogether, in the good land beyond the Blue Hills. The first lott to be nearest the Town; and so each man to have his lott successively in the Good land Lotts lying so near as may be, not above Eight Score or Two hundred Rods long. And, if it so turn out that a Plott of bad land falls in a lott, then allowance may be made by the Surveyor and those men that the Town shall appoint to go with him."

Another survey was made, commencing in the year 1714, and ending in the year 1716. Most of the original proprietors had passed away before this last was undertaken, and the allotments were made to their grandchildren or their legal representatives.

In the "Twenty-five Divisions," there was allotted and laid out to Mr. Glover, in the year 1716,

9th Division — Burnt Swamp and Iron Mine Meadow, 12 acres.
48th Division — Dead Swamp,   10 acres.
45th Division — Purgatory Swamp,   45 acres.

At the western extremity of the New Grant, where the towns of Foxboro' and Wrentham now meet, there was laid out to him one thousand acres in five hundred acre lots.

In the Twelve Divisions of Upland, there were apportioned and laid out to him two hundred acres in the 48th lot.

In the 67th lot, Twelve Divisions, three hundred acres (sold by his heirs to Nathaniel Stearns).

These two last lots of two and three hundred acres were in the South precinct of Dorchester, which was subsequently set off from Dorchester and took the name of Stoughton.

Final Settlement of the Estate of the Hon. John Glover, Esq., of Boston.

March 19, 1724.   Suffolk ss.   Vol. 67, pp. 213, 214, 215.

Whereas John Glover, Esq., of Boston, in the County of Suffolk, and in his Majesty's Province of Massachusetts Bay, in New England, by his last Will and Testament did therein give and bequeathe unto his five sons, viz., Thomas Glover, Nathaniel Glover, Habackuk Glover, John Glover and Pelatiah Glover, Several Tracts of Land, Housing, Moneys, and other Estate, as expressed in and by his last Will and Testament, dated the Eleventh day of April, 1653, as upon record may appear: All of which said lands, Housing and other Estate, as expressed in said Will, was prized to each son, viz.:   To

Thomas Glover, of London, in the Kingdom of Great Britain ;
Nathaniel Glover, of Dorchester, in New England ;
Habackuk Glover, of Boston, in New England ;
John Glover, of Boston, in New England aforesaid ;   And
Pelatiah Glover, of Springfield, in New England ;
and delivered and paid ; and the said Will being fully performed and
finished and completed, We who have hereto subscribed do own and
acknowledge.

And Whereas, there was also belonging unto the said John Glover,
Esq., considerable former and after divisions, in the Common and
Undivided Lands in the Township of Dorchester and elsewhere, none
of which was laid out to him in his life time, nor by the said John
Glover devised, either before or at his death, to any person or persons Whatsoever, and as to which he died intestate ; All which Common and Undivided Lands still do remain to be divided among the
heirs and Legal Representatives of the aforesaid five sons, viz.,
Thomas Glover of London, Nathaniel Glover of Dorchester, Habackuk Glover of Boston, John Glover of Boston, and Pelatiah Glover
of Springfield, heirs of the above-named John Glover, who are justly entitled to and do own one full share or part each, of the abovesaid common and Undivided Lands.

And We whose names are hereto subscribed, do also hereby bind
and oblige Ourselves, Our heirs, Executors, Administrators and Assigns in the full sum of Five Hundred Pounds, Currant Money of
New England aforesaid, never in any Wise, to, or by any means, dispute or disallow or contest the same, but always and forever hereafter to allow the same thereof.

In Testimony Whereof, We have hereunto set our hands and seals,
This Twenty fourth day of December, One Thousand Seven Hundred
and Twenty four, and in the Eleventh Year of his Majesty's Reign,
Our Sovereign Lord George the Second, King of Great Britain.

Nathaniel Glover, and a seale.	Wm. Rawson & Anne Rawson.
Nathaniel Rawson.	Mary Glover.
Pelatiah Rawson.	Hannah Glover.
Thomas Smith.	Elizabeth Glover.
John Smith.	John Glover.
John Jeffries and Anne Jeffries.	Thomas Glover. [and a seale.
Rebecca Gore.	John Glover, cordwainer,

Signed, Sealed and delivered by Nathaniel Glover, Nathaniel Rawson and Pelatiah Rawson, Thomas Smith and John Smith, in presence
of Us, Jonathan Waldo and David Butler.

Also Signed, Sealed and delivered by John Jeffries, Anne Jeffries,
and Rebecca Gore, in Presence of Jonathan Waldo and David Butler.

Signed, Sealed and delivered by William Rawson and Anne Rawson, in Presence of Us, Mercy+Wells and Thomas Wells, Nathaniel
Glover.   Her mark.

Signed, Sealed and delivered by Mary Glover, Hannah Glover, and
Elizabeth Glover, in Presence of Us, Roger Billings and Elizabeth
Glover.

Signed, Sealed and delivered by John Glover, in Presence of Us,
John Quincy and Hannah Glover.
            8*

Signed, Sealed and delivered by Thomas Glover, in presence of Us, Cornelius Thayer, Isaac Casno. .

The Instrument on the other side, Signed, Sealed and delivered by John Glover, in Presence of Us, Cornelius Thayer and Isaac Casno. Suffolk ss. Dec. 24, 1724.

Nathaniel Glover, Nathaniel Rawson, Pelatiah Rawson, Thomas Smith and John Smith, subscribed to the within written Instrument, and personally appearing freely acknowledged this Instrument to be their free Will, Act and deed, January 14, 1724–5, before me,

JOHN CHANDLER.

William Rawson and Anne Rawson, Mary Glover, Hannah Glover, Elizabeth Glover and John Glover, personally appeared and severally acknowledged the above written Instrument to be their free Will, act and deed, before me, JOHN QUINCY, January 28, 1724–5. ·

Mr. Thomas Glover appeared personally and acknowledged the above written Instrument, on the other side, to be his free Will, Act and deed, before me,   SAMUEL CHECKLEY, Esq.

Boston, March 19, 1724.

John Glover, Cordwainer, appeared personally and acknowledged the above written Instrument, on the other side, to be his free Will, act and deed, before me,   SAMUEL CHECKLEY, Justice of the Peace.

Entered, Examined and Recorded in the Registry of Deeds for the County of Suffolk, February 22, 1743.   EZEKIEL GOLDTHWAIT,

Registrar of Deeds for Suffolk County.

Shubael Seaver's Deposition.

Roxbury, May 11, 1725.   Liber 67, folio 214.

Shubael Seaver, aged about Eighty-Seven years, Testifieth and saith that formerly he well knew John Glover, Esq., of Boston, who was one of the Original Proprietors of Dorchester and Boston. And that he also knew his Five sons, viz. : Thomas Glover, that went for England ; Nathaniel Glover, of Dorchester ; Habackuk Glover, of Boston, married to Mrs. Hannah Eliot, daughter of the Revᵈ John Eliot, formerly of Roxbury. And that he well knew Mrs. Rebecca Glover, daughter to the aforenamed Habackuk Glover and Hannah Eliot, and that the said Rebecca Glover married with Captⁿ Thomas Smith of Boston, now deceased, and that Mr. Thomas Smith and John Smith, now of Boston, and their Sisters, are the reputed children of the aforenamed Captⁿ Thomas Smith and Rebecca Glover his wife.

SHUBAEL SEAVER.

Boston, May 23, 1726. Shubael Seaver personally appeared and made Oath to the truth of the above written Statement by him subscribed in Perpetual Memoriam, before Us,   SAMUEL CHECKLEY,

HABIJAH SAVAGE.

Entered, Examined and Recorded at the Registry of Deeds for Suffolk County, Boston, February 2, 1743.   EZEKIEL GOLDTHWAIT,

Registrar.

Joshua Seaver's Deposition.

May 11, 1725.   Liber 67, folio 215.

Joshua Seaver, aged Eighty-four Years, Testifyeth and Saith, that when he was young he well knew Mr. John Glover, of Dorchester (otherwise called John Glover, Esq.), he being then one of the Original Proprietors of Dorchester and Boston ; and also he knew him afterwards when he was one of the Magistrates of this Province, and dwelt at Boston in the house now possessed by Capt⁰ Thomas Smith, and that he also knew Four of the sons of the said John Glover, Esq., viz. : Nathaniel Glover of Dorchester, Habackuk Glover of Boston, and his son John Glover of Boston, and Pelatiah Glover of Springfield ; and that this deponent entered into the family of the Rev⁴ Mr. John Eliot, of Roxbury, deceased, to dwell with him, on the same day that the aforenamed Habackuk Glover was married unto Mrs. Hannah Eliot, only daughter of the aforesaid John Eliot.

And that this deponent was one of the family and in service of the said John Eliot when Rebecca Glover, daughter of the said Habackuk Glover and Hannah Eliot, was born there (in Roxbury). And that he continued to dwell in the aforesaid family until the said Rebecca Glover was married to Capt. Thomas Smith of Boston, deceased. And that Capt⁰ Thomas Smith and Mr. John Smith now of Boston, with their sisters, are the reputed children of the aforesaid Capt⁰ Thomas Smith and Rebecca Glover his Wife.

Suffolk ss.   Roxbury, May 11, 1725.

Mr. Joshua Seaver personally appearing, made Oath in perpetual Memoriam to the above-written statements subscribed before us,

SAMUEL CHECKLEY and
SAMUEL SEWALL, Esqrs.

Entered, Examined and Recorded on the Register of Deeds for Suffolk County at Boston, February 22, 1743.   EZEKIEL GOLDTHWAIT,
Registrar of Deeds for County of Suffolk.

Deposition of Nathaniel Glover, Jr., of Dorchester, Great Grandson to Mr. John Glover of Dorchester and Boston.

The Deposition of Nathaniel Glover of Dorchester, aged about 49 years, Testifieth and saith that he very well knew Mr. Habackuk Glover, formerly of Boston, when he dwelt in the House now possessed and occupied by Mr. Thomas Smith in Boston, and that he also knew Mr. John Glover when he dwelt in Seven Stars lane, or Summer Street, in Boston ; and that the said Habackuk Glover, John Glover and Pelatiah Glover, late of Springfield, Deceased, and Thomas Glover, Esq., of London, Eng., deceased, and Nathaniel Glover, deceased, Grandfather of this deponent, were all reputed brothers, and also the Five reputed sons of Mr. John Glover, alias John Glover Esq., formerly of Dorchester and Boston.   And this deponent further saith, that Mr. Thomas Smith, Mr. John Smith, Anne Kay, Elizabeth Brenton, Rebecca Gore, and Anne Jeffries, are all of them the reputed grandchildren of the aforesaid Habackuk Glover.

(Signed)   NATHANIEL GLOVER, Boston, March 25, 1725.

Nathaniel Glover, Jr., personally appeared and made Oath to the truth of the above written Statement, Instrument and Deposition subscribed by him in perpetual memoriam, before me,

SAMUEL CHECKLEY.

Vol. 67, p. 259, *Suffolk Reg. of Deeds.*

It is thus seen that seventy years after Mr. Glover's death, his lands in the Dorchester New Grant came in possession of his descendants of the third and fourth generations as their inheritance, and were set off as far as possible by a just and equal division among themselves. At that time, a large portion of these lands had been settled on by those who had no title, and could not be dispossessed without resorting to a course of law. A very small portion of it remains in the possession of one of his descendants at the present time. That tract of two hundred acres which was situated in Stoughton, and which fell to the share of a great grandson, Thomas Glover, Esq., of Newbury Farm, Dorchester, was passed by will to his eldest sons, Thomas and James, in 1752. They divided it, each taking one hundred acres. Thomas had built a house there previous to that time, or about 1750, and occupied it until his death in 1811, a period of forty-one years. He had eleven children born to him there, by his wife Rebeckah Pope, and left the homestead to his youngest son, Mr. Elijah Glover, who owned and occupied it until his decease in 1855, forty-four years, having had ten children born to him there by his wives Martha Pope and Sarah Howe. His third son, Mr. John Clough Glover, has built a house near the original one (which is still standing), and inherits a portion of the land. He resides there at the present time. Other portions are in possession of his brothers. Thus after a period of two hundred and thirty years from the first order for apportionment, the estate has reached the seventh generation in regular and direct succession.

And here closes what has been gathered of Mr. JOHN GLOVER — his ancestors, his birth, life in England, life in New England, his manorial estates, and his disposition of them. He has justly been styled by writers as one of the founders of New England, and ranks as the earliest American ancestor of more than one thousand descendants, whose lives are noticed in the pages which follow.

[Second Generation.]

THOMAS GLOVER, OF LONDON, ENGLAND, AND HIS DESCENDANTS TO THE FOURTH GENERATION.

I. Thomas Glover, the eldest son of Mr. John Glover, of Rainhill, Lancashire, England, and Anna his wife, was born in Rainhill Parish, Prescot, in Lancashire, England, the 8th day of January, 1627; and died in the Parish of St. John, Hackney, London, England, the 3d day of October, 1707, æt. 80 years and 9 months. His will bears date April 18th, 1707; proved November 7th, 1707. He left a widow and three children, five grandchildren and four great-grandchildren.

In 1630, when at the age of three years, he was brought by his parents to Dorchester, in New England, and lived there until the age of manhood, 1648. Very little information can be gathered of him from New England records. He never took the freeman's oath, and never joined any church while a resident here. In 1644, with five others from Dorchester, he joined the Ancient and Honorable Artillery Company, which had been formed early in New England, and was a branch of the parent association in London. He was at that time but seventeen years of age. He returned to England, and was married there before February, 1652, to Rebeckah ———. The first day of February, 1652, he received from his father, Mr. John Glover, by Deed of Gift (see page 51), all the lands, houses, and edifices which belonged to the latter, lying in Rainhill, Eccleston and Knowlesby, and other places named in the deed, in the County of Lancashire. It appears he was on a visit to New England at that date, and returned to England immediately after, probably in the same ship with Rev. George Moxon, the first minister of Springfield, and Mr. Pynchon. He was at that time twenty-five years of age. His estates of inheritance in Lancashire had been left in trust, and were ordered to be delivered to him by Mr. John Latham, of Whiston, and Mr. William Glover, of Prescot, brother and attorney to Mr. John Glover, of Dorchester. He was to receive them immediately after his arrival at Rainhill. There is no evidence of his ever having settled on his estates at that place, or lived there after his marriage. He resided in London, was a merchant there, and probably had been established in business there ever since first going from Dorchester, in 1648 or '49. He never engaged in any business while here, being destined by his father, as his eldest son and heir apparent, to an English life.

Children of Thomas and Rebeckah (——) Glover, born in London, England:

6. Rebeckah, m. 1st, Joseph Moxon ; 2d, —— Bard.
7. Elizabeth, m. 1st, Richard Chiswell ; 2d, Thomas Trench.
8. Mary, m. Joseph Thomson.

Rebeckah had by her first husband, one son, Joseph Moxon. Her second husband, —— Bard, died before her father's will was made in 1707.

Elizabeth had by her first husband, one son, Richard Chiswell; and by her second, two daughters, Elizabeth and Rebeckah French.

Mary, wife of Joseph Thomson, had five children — two sons and three daughters.

[*Third Generation.*]

Grandchildren of Thomas and Rebeckah Glover, of London:

+ 9. Joseph Moxon, son of Joseph and Rebeckah Moxon.   Wife Rebeckah ——.
+10. Richard Chiswell. ⎫ Wife ——.
11. Elizabeth Trench, ⎬ Children of Elizabeth Glover.
12. Rebeckah Trench, ⎭
13. William Thomson.   Wife Judith.
14. Joseph Thomson.
15. Francis Thomson.
16. Mary Thomson.
17. Elizabeth Thomson.

[*Fourth Generation.*]

Great-grandchildren of Thomas and Rebeckah Glover, of London:

18. Joseph Moxon.
19. Rebeckah Moxon.
20. Richard Chiswell.
21. A daughter, Thomson.

By the last Will and Testament of Mr. John Glover, bearing date April 11th, 1653 (p. 58), the estates in England which were granted to his son Thomas in February, 1652, were confirmed to him, and he was also to receive the sum of four hundred pounds in money, to be paid by his executors at his decease. And the additional sum of ten pounds was ordered to be paid to him at the decease of his mother, by his brother Habackuk, who at that time came into full possession of his father's Boston estate. He was not to share in the division of the estate called Newbury Farm, which was retained as the widow's dower, and immediately after her decease was, with all its incomes, to be divided into four equal parts and given to his four brothers.

In 1680, when Mr. Glover's Newbury Farm was surveyed and divided, Thomas Glover, Esq., of the city of London, merchant, was noticed and legally represented in Glover's Agreement. (See p. 71.)

In 1724, at the final settlement of the estate of Hon. John Glover, the name of Thomas Glover occurs again, in a compact or agreement drawn up and signed by the surviving heirs in relation to the Common and Undivided Lands lying in Dorchester New Grant, in the town of Stoughton. (See p. 76.) This transaction took place seventeen years after the decease of Thomas Glover, of London. All the other sons were also dead, and were represented by their children and grandchildren. It is not known at the present time by whom Thomas was represented. He had three daughters at the time of his death in 1707, and probably at this time, who may have appointed some person to represent them, but it is not expressed in the agreement. There are signers to that compact, however, whose names could not have been attached to it in their own right, as those of Nathaniel Rawson and Pelatiah Rawson, and who may have been appointed to act for Thomas's heirs.

In 1654, he was appointed an attorney by Judith Holland, of Dorchester, in New England, and by Henry Ashurst, creditor to her estate, to settle her affairs there. (See next page.)

He was visited in 1661 by gentlemen from Boston, who were witnesses to a writing drawn up by his hand, appointing his brother Habackuk Glover to be his attorney in relation to lands and property in Boston and the adjacent towns; and they brought back with them to Boston this Power of Attorney, delivered it to Mr. Habackuk Glover, and testified to it, personally appearing on the 26th of May, 1664.

28 (6) 1669, Mr. Habackuk Glover appears to have recovered a debt of Nathaniel and Peter Duncan, and transmitted it to London for his brother Thomas Glover.

There has been preserved an original letter written by him to his brother-in-law, Gov. Thomas Hinckley, of Barnstable, in Plymouth Colony, in New England, bearing date August 2, 1684, which, with documents above named, are given in succeeding pages.

In 1689, Judge Sewall, of Boston, on going to London, made him another visit, and records it in his diary. Mr. Glover probably wrote to his friends by Judge Sewall, who immediately after his return to New England, made a visit to Gov. Hinckley; and he writes in his diary of the entertainment which he received as his guest, and the attention shown him by Madam Hinckley, whom he said read letters to him from her children — and also that the conversation turned on friends and relations whom Judge Sewall had seen and visited when lately in England.

Judith Holland to Thomas Glover.

Vol. 2d, folio 291.   Out of Boston.   Suffolk Registry of Deeds.

Be it Known unto all Men by these Presents, That I, Judith Holland, of Dorchester, in New England, in the County of Suffolk, Spinster, being Executor and Administrator of the last Will of my late husband, John Holland, Deceased, being by my own knowledge in the lifetime of my husband satisfied that my said husband stood indebted unto Mr. Henry Ashurst, of London, in Old England, Woolen Draper, in the sum of Four Hundred and Ninety Pounds, or thereabouts, and now the sum having been demanded of me by Mr. Thomas Glover, of London, Attorney for Mr. Henry Ashurst aforesaid; and being further so granted to be the just debt of the aforesaid Mr. Henry Ashurst, and for the securing and satisfying of him the aforesaid Mr. Henry Ashurst for the debt aforesaid of Four Hundred and Ninety Pounds, or thereabouts, have given, granted, mortgaged and made over, and by these presents do give, grant, mortgage and make over the Dwelling House of my late Husband, situate in Dorchester, wherein I now dwell, and all the Lands and accommodations thereunto belonging, Together with all Out Housing, Gardens and Orchards, with all appurtenances thereunto belonging, as valued and prized in the Inventory at Two Hundred and Eighteen Pounds, Ten Shillings, £218 10s. As also all the brass and Pewter, Andirons, Pots, Tubs, all Linen, Beds and Bedding, Chests, Trunks, Tables, Stools, Carpets, Cushions, Silver Plate, Saddle and Pillion, Barrels and Tubs, prized at Ninety Six Pounds, Ten Shillings and Sixpence, £96 10s. 6d. Also One Eighth part of the Good Ship called the Goodfellow, near whereof for the present voyage is Mr. George Dell, of Boston, in New England. Prized at Two Hundred Pounds, £200 00 00. Together with all the produce of the present voyage. As also a Parcel of Land, called by the name of Munnings Moon, prized at Twenty Eight Pounds, £28 00 00, with all which Lands and Goods, Moveables and immoveables, with the One Eighth part of the Ship and Produce thereof, according to the prizers and according to the Inventory thereof delivered unto Mr. Thomas Glover, Attorney to Mr. Henry Ashurst of London aforesaid, I acknowledge now to be and shall forever remain to be unto the aforesaid Mr. Thomas Glover to and for the use of Mr. Henry Ashurst so long and until the sum of Four Hundred and Ninety Pounds, or thereabouts, be fully satisfied and paid without any fraud or ——.

And I do hereby acknowledge the Right and equity of the said premises to be in and unto Mr. Thomas Glover for the uses aforesaid, and hereby engage myself to be ready from time to time, and at all times, to ratify and confirm, warrant and defend, by all acts and doing according to law for the making valid and firm the said premises against myself or any person or persons claiming whatsoever.

Witness my hand and seal this first day of the Seventh month—1: 7: 1654.   JUDITH HOLLAND.

Signed, sealed and delivered in presence of
    Thomas Holland,
    John Wiswall.
                    Brought by J. Woodmansey.

This Deed was Acknowledged by Judith Holland to be her free Act and Deed the 12th day of September, 1654, before me,
                                                HUMPHREY ATHERTON.

Entered and Recorded the 20 Sept., 1656.   EDWARD RAWSON,
                                                        Recorder.

Know all Men by these Presents, That I, Judith Holland, of Dorchester, in New England, as Executor to my Late husband John Holland, Dec^d, have acknowledged myself to be indebted to Mr. Henry Ashurst, of London, Woolen Draper, in the Sum of Four Hundred and Ninety Pounds or thereabouts, as by my Deed, bearing date the 1ˢᵗ day of September, 1654, more at Large appeareth.

In Consideration of the same, I do make over, relinquish and confirm unto the said Henry Ashurst in part payment of the said debt, All my Right, Title and Interest in One Hundred and Ninety four Pounds Sterling, or thereabouts, with the Produce of One Eighth part of the Ship belonging to my late husband, and sold by Mr. George Dell; Together with all due damages and Interest for the said money since the sale of the said Ship, hereby empowering the said Ashurst and his Lawful Attorney to Ask, Demand, and require and receive of the Executor or Administrator of the said George Dell whatsoever is justly due to me in the Premises.

Witness my hand and Scale, this 29 day of Sept., 1656.
                                                JUDITH HOLLAND.

Signed, sealed and delivered in presence of
    John Gill,
    John Woodmansey.

John Woodmansey deposed the 29 of Sept., 1656, that this was the free act and Deed of Judith Holland, whom he saw sign and Deliver it. Taken on Oath before me,   ANTONY STODDARD.

Entered and Recorded with the Suffolk Records of Deeds, Sept. 29, 1656.   EDWARD RAWSON, *Recorder.*

The following is copied from a letter of Power of Attorney,
by Thomas Glover, of London, to his brother Habackuk Glover, in
Boston.

[Vol. 8, page 265, Suff. Reg. of Deeds.]

To all people before whom this present writing shall come, Thomas
Glover, of the City of London, in the Kingdom of Great Britain,
Merchant, sendeth greeting. Know ye, that I the said Thomas Glover have, and by these presents do constitute, put, authorize, ordain
and appoint and make and in my stead put and ask my brother Habackuk Glover, of Boston, in New England, and in the Province of
Massachusetts Bay, Merchant, or his Assigns, to be my true and
lawful Attorney, To act for me and in my name and to and for my
own proper use and behoof, to ask, demand, Levy and receive of and
from all and every person or persons in New England and the parts
adjacent, of all debts, sums and sums of money, Lands, Goods, Chattels whatsoever and wheresoever as are or shall be due or owing,
payable or belonging unto me, my Executors or Administrators, by
any manner of ways or means whatsoever or howsoever. And I do
hereby give and grant unto my said attorney and his assigns, my full
and whole strength and power and Lawful Authority in my name and
for my use, the debtor or withholder or destroyer of the premises, or
of any part thereof, or any of their Executors or administrators,
Lands, Goods or Chattels to cause to be arrested, attached, seized,
&c. &c. to call all my debtors and delayers and withholders to an
account, and with them to confer, compound and agree as occasion
shall require.

And to make, sell and deliver, with one attorney or more under him,
to substitute and make, and at his pleasure to revoke and in my
name and for my use to enter into and upon all and singular of my
lands, messuages and tenements in New England and the parts
adjacent.

And also to demand, receive and discharge all the rents, Issues and
profits thereof for non-payment of the same or any part thereof, and
to recover and get the same by suit, distress or otherwise that shall
be, to retain and keep until you and they shall be fully satisfied.

And to Let, sell or assign all and every of my lands, messuages,
Tenements, Heredittaments aforesaid and generally, as well as to
manage all my affairs and business in New England aforesaid, as also
to do, execute, transact, effect, perform, finish, and cause to be done,
executed, transacted, performed and finished, in, about or surrounding
the premises, or to any part thereof, as to my said attorney or his
assigns shall seem meet and convenient, and that as fully, firmly and
effectually in all respects and to all purposes and subjects whatsoever
as I myself might or would do were I from time to time personally
present, holding firm and stable all and whatsoever my Attorney shall
do or cause to be done, And shall and will justify and assent to all
and whatsoever my said Attorney or his assigns shall do or cause to
be done in or about or under the premises, or any part thereof, by
virtue of these Presents.

In Witness whereof, I the said Thomas Glover have hereunto set my
hand and seale, bearing date the 14th day of May, 1661, and within

the 13 year of the Reign of Our Sovereign Lord, King Charles the Second, by the grace of God King of England, &c.

THOMAS GLOVER, and a Seale.

Signed, sealed and delivered in the presence of
  Benjamin Gillam,
  Thomas Savage,
  Thomas Payne,
  Thomas Gilbert,
  William Browne.

Boston, May 26th, 1664.

 William Browne and Thomas Savage, two of the Witnesses, did come before me personally and declare that they saw Thomas Glover Sign, Seale and deliver the above Power of Attorney herein specified, this 26 day of May, 1664. THOMAS SAVAGE, *Commissioner.*

 Aug. 17, 1669. The next notice of Thomas Glover on any record appears to be in relation to an Execution, as follows:

 Habackuk Glover of Boston, in New England, and in the Province of Massachusetts Bay, Merchant, Attorney to Thomas Glover, of the City of London, in the Kingdom of Great Britain, Merchant, obtained of the General Court, then sitting at Boston, an Execution against Nathaniel and Peter Duncan, for the recovery of Seventy-Nine Pounds ten Shillings and ten pence Sterling, due to his brother Thomas Glover.

Execution and Warrant.

[Page 635, Suff. Reg. of Deeds.]

To the Marshal of the County of Suffolk or his Deputy:

 You are hereby, in virtue of these Presents, required to levy on the Goods and Chattels of Mr. Nathaniel Duncan and Mr. Peter Duncan, to the value of Seventy Nine pounds ten Shill. and ten pence Sterling, and deliver the same to Mr. Habackuk Glover, of Boston, Attorney to Mr. Thomas Glover, of London, Merchant, together with two Shillings for two Executions granted by the County Court then sitting at Boston the 26 day of July, 1669, that is in satisfaction of a Judgment of that Court, and if you find not Goods you are to seize the persons.

 Hereof you are not to fail. Dated the 17 of August, 1669.

EDWARD RAWSON, *Recorder.*

 Aug. 17, 1669. "Mr. Habackuk Glover, of Boston in New England, Acknowledges the receipt of Twenty Pounds Sterling from the hands of Nathaniel and Peter Duncan, of Boston, as Attorney for his brother Thomas Glover, of London, England."

Aug. 27, 1669. " Mr. Habackuk Glover acknowledges the receipt of Twenty Pounds Sterling, of the said Nathaniel and Peter Duncan, on account between them and himself as Attorney for his brother Thomas Glover.   Witness my hand,   HABACKUK GLOVER."

28 : 6 : 1669. " Mr. Habackuk Glover did acknowledge the receipt of Twenty Pounds Sterling, in full of this Execution betwixt Messrs. Nathaniel and Peter Duncan and himself.
                    Witness my hand,   HABACKUK GLOVER."

The following is a copy of a letter from Mr. Thomas Glover, of London, England, to his brother-in-law, the Hon. Thomas Hinckley, of Barnstable, New England, dated August 2d, 1684. The top of the letter, which probably contained the address, was missing.

SIR,
          I received your kind letter wherein you express yours and my Sister's respects to me. I am glad to hear from you, and rejoice to hear of the welfare of any of my relations.
          We live in bad times, wherein our privileges, especially our Spiritual enjoyments, are obstructed and our lives made uncomfortable thereby.
          I doubt not the same evil will at last in a great measure reach you. Were it not for fear of the loss of those enjoyments which are enjoyed in New England, very many of us should certainly retire to New England.
          All comfort in our outward enjoyments are much abated by want of Spiritual Liberty. It is made a very great crime with us to hear a good minister preach Christ or Pray to God.
          If it please God that I live, I may another time order something for some of my relations. Pray present mine and my wife's respects to my Sister, your Wife, whom I commit to God, and so rest your loving brother,   THOMAS GLOVER.
          2d Aug. 1684.

          Thomas Glover had three brothers living in New England at that time, but they all died before he did — the last in 1696. There were also the three children, heirs of his brother Nathaniel Glover, of Dorchester, who were his nephews and niece.

          Judge Sewall corresponded with him, as shown by the following letter from his Letter Book:
                                        Boston, N. E., July 15, 1686.
Mr. THOMAS GLOVER.
          SIR, I received yours pr Mr. Clarke, with the cottons and penistons and 2 doz. books, which with the bill of Exchange of 80£,

amounts to 119 : 9 : 0, or one hundred and nineteen pounds and nine shillings. Have delivered Mr. Rawson his kerseys and crape. I thank you for your ready acceptance of my bill, of which I was informed, and of the payment by my correspondent before yours came to hand. Am grieved at the afflictions of France (that is, the afflictions by France of the Protestants), but am glad to understand it seeing it is so. Our letters that come by vessels do now pass through the hands of Councillor Randolph. We are here exercised with a very sore drought. Yesterday was observed as a public fast for that occasion. Except God make haste to help us, we shall be greatly straitened for want of grass and corn. The only son of Mrs. Holland, Widow, is to be buried this afternoon. The smallpox is in town. Only one hath died of it yet that I hear of.

Sir, your friend and Servant,   SAMUEL SEWALL.

1689, April 22. Judge Sewall visited Thomas Glover, and writes in his diary, under the above date, thus: "I went on foot to Hackney, through brick lane, about ¼ a mile long, and dined with Mr. Thomas Glover, his sons Bard and Thomson, their wives, Mrs. Trench and several Grandchildren. Eat part of two lobsters that cost 3–9^d apiece, 7–6 both."

This visit of Judge Sewall appears to be the last notice of him before his decease. Two notices occur after his death, in relation to the distribution of property accruing to him or his heirs, both in 1724, at the final settlement of the estate (or reversion of it) left by his brother John Glover, of Boston, merchant, and in the final settlement of the estate of his father. His estates at Rainhill may have been sold, or they may have been held in trust for some future distribution under other conditions, and so not devised — as in case his line might at some time become extinct.

Thomas Glover was in good health on the 8th day of April, 1707, as is stated in his will, had wife Rebeckah and three daughters, several grandchildren and great-grandchildren. He appointed his eldest daughter Rebeckah Bard, widow, sole Executrix. His death occurred October 3d, 1707, and his will was proved November 7th, 1707.

His wife Rebeckah survived him, and died at Hackney, in the Parish of St. John, the 13th day of May, 1711. She was buried in Trench's vault.

This latter information is gathered from a letter received in 1862, from the present incumbent of the Church of St. John, Hackney, in London.

Thomas Glover in his will makes no allusion to the Rainhill es-
9*

tates, which were given him by his father, in 1652, but devises the following as owned by him, viz.:

Estates, messuages and lands lying in the Cock and Pye Fields, near the Seven Dials in the Parish of St. Giles in the Fields, in the County of Middlesex, England; a freehold estate in Bartholomew Square, in or near Old Street, in the County of Middlesex, purchased of Antony Ball and John Brown in fee simple; a copy-hold estate situate in the Parish of St. John, Hackney, by the name of Brookes Field; a messuage and house new built, in St. John, Hackney; an estate in Westham, County of Essex, consisting of houses, lands and tenements, held by lease from the Mayor of the City of London, lying in that Parish of Westham.

His donations from his personal estate amount to about three thousand pounds sterling, as expressed in his will. His legatees were his wife Rebeckah, three daughters, five grandchildren and four great-grandchildren; with gifts to his minister, Mr. Billis; Mr. Bates, his daughter Trench's chaplain; his vicar, Mr. Newcome; his nephew, Daniel Poyntell; cousins Charles Watts and Priscilla Lucas; cousin Margaret Lightman; Lydia Davis, his servant; nurse Watrous; Mrs. Ratcliffe and Mary Talbot; and to Christian Owen, his daughter Bard's maid servant, and his poor neighbors at his wife's discretion.

Thomas Glover's Will.

[Extracted from the Registry of the Prerogative Court of Canterbury.]

In the name of God, Amen. The Eighteenth day of April, One thousand seven hundred and seven, Thomas Glover, of the Parish of St. John, Hackney, in the County of Middlesex, being in good health of body and disposeing minde and memory, for which I bless God, but not knowing when it may please God to call me out of this present World by death, I doe make this my last Will and Testament in manner and forme following:

In the first place, revokeing all former and other Wills by me yet aforemade and declareing the same void, I doe committ and commend my Soul into the Hands of God, my Saviour and my Redeemer, the Lord Jesus Christ, and my bodye to be decently buryed according to the discretion of my executrix hereafter named. As for what Worldly estate God hath blessed me with, I doe hereby give and devise the same as followeth:

Imprimis. I devise and bequeath and give unto my loveing and beloved Wife Rebeccah, all my messuages, lands and estate whatsoever situate, lying and being in Cock and Pye Field near the Seven Dials, in the Parish of St. Giles in the Fields, in the County of Middlesex, which I hold by three distinct leases, granted to me by Squire

Neale, James Ward and others, for a term or terms of years unexpired and undetermined, together with all the rents, issues and profitts thereof, To hold to her my said loveing Wife and her assigns for and dureing soe long only of the said terms as she shall happen to live.

Item. I doe devise, bequeath and give unto my said loveing Wife all my freehold or fee simple estates situate in Bartholomew Square, in or near Old Street, in the said County of Middlesex, and by me formerly purchased of Mr. Anthony Ball and John Browne. To have and to hold unto my said loveing Wife and to her assignes for and during her natural life only, and from and after my said Wife's decease Then I doe devise all and singular my said lands and tenements aforesaid to my loveing daughter, Rebeccah Bard, Widow, her heirs, executors and administrators absolutely for ever. But in trust, however, and to the intent and purpose that the same may be sold with all convenient speed after the decease of my said loveing Wife, to the best purchaser, and the money arising from such sale to be equally divided, one third part thereof to be retained by or paid to my loveing daughter Rebeccah Bard, And one third part thereof to be paid to my loveing daughter Elizabeth Trench, And the other third part to be paid to my loveing daughter Mary Thomson.

Item. I doe devise and bequeath unto my said loveing daughter Rebeccah Bard, her heires and assignes for ever, All that my Copyhold estate situate and being in the Parish of St. John's in Hackney, and afore purchased by me of John and William Brookes, and knowne by the name of Brookes his ground, garden and field, and by whatsoever other name called or distinguished, the better to enable her to raise money to pay my legacies hereinafter given or devised (except out of this present devise one part of my said Copyhold estate, one house, or messuage, or tenement lately new built, and now in the tenure, occupation or possession of William Clarke.)

Item. As for my estate consisting in Limekilns, Wharfes, houses, land and tenements, which I hold by Lease from the Mayor and City, of London, scituate in the Parish of West Ham in the County of Essex, in the occupation and tenure of William Penkett and John Watkins Miller or his assigns, I doe hereby devise the same to my loveing Wife, for soe many years of the term I have as she shall happen to live, And from and after her decease Then I devise the same and all my estate, interest, and right of renewal therein and thereto to my said daughter Rebeccah Bard, her executors, administrators and assigns absolutely for ever. And whereas by a certaine Indenture, bearing date the Twentieth day of December, one thousand six hundred eighty one, and made between Joseph Thomson my Son-in-law, and me the said Thomas Glover, wherein is recited or notice taken of certaine articles made upon or before the intermarriage of the said Joseph Thomson with my aforesaid daughter Mary Thomson, to the effect, That if at any time thereafter I should give anything to either of my said other two daughters, I should give the like at the same time to my said daughter Mary Thomson, it is conditional that in regard that what estate I had given or settled upon my two daughters Rebeccah and Elizabeth was of less value than what I had given to the said Joseph Thomson with his said wife Mary Thomson, That it should be lawful for me to give Six hundred pounds apiece to each of my said two daughters, reference thereto may more fully appear, Now I doe hereby devise and bequeath and give unto my said loveing daughter Rebecca Bard Five hundred and fifty pounds to be paid to her, or retained by her as my Executrix.

Item. I give and devise and bequeath to my loveing daughter Mary Thomson, the sum of three hundred and fifty pounds, to be paid her by my Executrix within two months after my death.

Item. I give, devise and bequeath unto my loveing and beloved wife Rebeccah the sume of Three hundred and fifty pounds, to be paid her by my Executrix within Two moneths after my death.

Item. I doe further give and bequeath unto my said loveing Wife all my household goods, silver plate, leaden cesterns, pipes, pumpes, coppers, grates, and alsoe all other moveable goods whatsoever.

Item. I give to my said loveing Wife Twenty pounds to buy her mourning.

Item. I give to my loveing daughter Rebecca Bard Twenty pounds to buy her mourning.

Item. I give to my grandson Joseph Moxson and Rebecca his Wife, each of them Twenty pounds to buy them mourning, and to Joseph and Rebecca Moxson their two children each Six pounds to buy them mourning.

Item. I give and bequeath to my loveing daughter Elizabeth Trench, Twenty pounds to buy her mourning.

Item. I give to my grandson William Thomson and to his Wife Judith Thomson, each of them Twenty pounds to buy them mourning, and to their little child my great-granddaughter Six pound to buy mourning.

Item. I give unto my grandson Richard Chiswell and his Wife each of them Twenty pounds to buy them mourning, and to their little daughter Six pounds.

Item. I give my granddaughter Elizabeth Trench Twenty pound to buy her mourning.

Item. I give unto granddaughter Rebeccah Trench Twenty pounds to buy her mourning.

Item. I give to my son in law Joseph Thomson Twenty pound to buy him mourning.

Item. I give to my loveing daughter Mary Thomson, his Wife, Twenty pounds to buy her mourning.

Item. I give to my granddaughter Frances Thomson Twenty pound to buy her mourning.

Item. I give to my grandson Joseph Thomson Twenty pound to buy him mourning.

Item. I give to my granddaughter Mary Thomson Eight pounds to buy her mourning.

Item. I give to my granddaughter Elizabeth Thomson Six pound to buy her mourning.

Item. I give to Mr. Billis, our Minister, Ten pounds.

Item. I give to Mr. Bates, my daughter Trenches Chaplin, Ten pounds.

Item. I give to my nephew Daniel Poyntell Ten pounds.

Item. I give to my cosin Charles Watts Six pounds.

Item.   I give to my cousin Priscilla Lucas, Sister to Charles Watts, Ten pounds.

Item.   I give to my cosin Margaret Lightman Eight pounds.

Item.   I give to Mr. Newcome, our Vicar, Six pound.

Item.   I give to Lidia Davis, my Servant, Four pounds.

Item.   I give to Nurse Waterers Five pound.

Item.   I give to Mrs. Ratcliffe four pound.

Item.   I give to Mary Talbut Five pound.

Item.   I give to Christian Owen, my daughter Bard's Maid Servant, four pound.

Item.   I give four pounds to be distributed to such poor neighbours as my loveing Wife shall name ; all which legacies I doe appoint and order to be paid by my Executrix hereafter named.

Item.   For the disposal of the said house part of my Copyhold estate, before herein excepted and not devised and mentioned to be in the tenure or possession of William Clarke, and is likewise mortgaged by the said William Clarke to my daughter Elizabeth Trench, her heirs and assigns in trust, I doe hereby devise the same to my said loveing daughter Elizabeth Trench and to her heirs and assigns, with what interest is due upon it, and doe declare the sume for and in lieu and in discharge of one hundred pounds, part of the sume of Five hundred and fifty pounds before herein devised to her.   And whereas by a Deed Poll or writing under my hand and seale Dated the one and thirtieth day of May, one thousand six hundred eighty six, I am under covenants to and with Anthony Ball and John Browne for augmenting at their request and charges of giving an additional term of Ten years after the expiration of the term of Forty years, of a pecce or parcel of ground situate in Bartholomew Square aforementioned, Now I doe hereby order, will and direct that if any suite doe hereafter arise and be prosecuted for, because or for the performance of said covenant or other reason, that my said respective other daughters, Rebecca, Elizabeth and Mary, shall be at equal costs and charges thereof, though I believe the said Anthony Ball and John Browne, nor any other never will nor have ground for such Suite, for that many of the persons they let leases to never finished nor performed the covenants of their leases, soe that Mr. Anthony Ball and John Browne never performed on their parts, or complyed with true consideration of the said Deed Poll on their parts to be performed and done, or to be done on the part of their Representatives or assigns.   And as for and concerning the rest and residue of my estate whatsoever not herein devised, as all debts due to me by Bonds, bills, notes, book debts, or any other waies as money or cash in my possession, I doe devise the same to my said loving daughter Rebecca Bard, she paying all legacies herein devised and discharging funeral charges, and performing all the trust herein in her reposed by this my last Will and Testament.

And lastly I doe hereby nominate, constitute and appoint my said daughter Rebecca Bard to be my sole and only Executrix of this my last Will and Testament.

In Witness whereof, I the said Tho: Glover have to this my last Will and Testament set my hand and seal the day and year first above written.   Tho: Glover.

Signed, sealed, published and declared by the Testator
as his last Will and Testament, in the presence of us, who
do subscribe our names hereto in the presents of the Testator.   John Applebie,
                                    Roger Lidyard,
                                    Joseph Armroide.

Whereas, by my last Will and Testament above written, I have devised my Lime Kilns, Wharfes, Houses, lands and Tenements mentioned to lye or to be scituate in the Parish of West Ham, in the County
of Essex, to my loveing Wife for soe many years of the term I have
therein as she shall happen to live, and after her decease to my
daughter Rebecca Bard, or to that effect ; Now I doe by these presents, which I declare to be a Codicil to my said Will and to be accepted as part of my said Will, Revoke the said devise thereof to my
said Wife, and doe hereby devise the said Kilnes and other the premises in the said County of Essex, and all my estate and interest therein and right of renewal thereof or thereto, unto my said daughter
Rebecca, her executors, administrators and assigns absolutely, and
to and for her sole use and benefit.

In Witness whereof, I have hereunto these presents set my hand
and seale this Twenty Sixthe day of August, one thousand seven
hundred and seven.   THO: GLOVER.

Signed, sealed, published and declared by the Testator, Thomas Glover, as a Codicil to his Will above written, and to be accepted as part of his said Will, in the
presence of us who have subscribed our names thereunto in
the presence of the said Testator.   Thomas Wellman,
                                     Thomas Combe,
                                     Joseph Armroid.

Witnesses: John Appleby, at the Signe Oxford Arms,
in Warwick Lane ; Roger Lidyard, Tinman, at Fleet
Bridge ; Joseph Armroid, my Servant.

I add this as a Codicill to my Will, That I give unto my Wife one
hundred pounds over and above what I have already given her in my
Will, and that my Executrix pay that arrear of Ground rent in Cock
and Pye Field which shall be due at my decease.

Witness my hand and seale this Ninth day of September, in the
year of our Lord one thousand seven hundred and seven.
                                                THO: GLOVER.

Signed, sealed and delivered in presence of us,
      Thomas Wellman,
      Tho: Combe,
      Joseph Armroide.

PROBATUM fuit hujusmodi Testamentum cum duobus Codicillis eidem
annexis, apud London, Septimo Die mensis Novembris, Anno Domini
millessimo Septingentesimo Septimo, Coram Venerabili Viro Henrico
Raines, Legum Doctore Surrogato ; Venerabilis et egregij Viri domini

Richardi Raines, Miletis Legum etiam Doctoris Curiæ prerogativæ Cantuariens, Magistre Custodis sive commissarij legitime constituti juramento Rebeccæ Bard, Filiæ dicti defuncti et Executricis in dicto Testamento nominat, cui commissa fuit administraco omnium et singularum Conorum jurium et creditorum dicti defuncti de bene et fideliter administrando eadem ad Sancta Dei Evangelia Jurat.

CHA. DYNELEY,   ⎫   *Deputy*
JOHN IGGULDEN,   ⎬   *Registers.*
W. F. GOSTLING,   ⎭

His armorial bearings were those granted and confirmed in 1604 to Thomas Glover, Esq., of the body of King James I., son of Thomas Glover, of Coventry, knighted the 17th of August, 1606.

"He beareth Sable a Chevron Ermine between three Crescents Argent, By the name of Glover, and is borne by Mr. Thomas Glover, of the City of London, Merchant, and descends to the name and family of Glover. This Patent was granted by William Camden, April 3d, 1604. A true copy from Heraldry, attested by Charles L. Cole," Feb. 2, 1804. Mr. Cole also bore testimony that the above was the same Arms which was originally granted in 1577, and subsequently enlarged and improved by Edmonson, to Robert Glover, Somerset Herald, a description of which is given on page 15 of this work; and that Mr. Glover of Dorchester and his descendants were entitled to bear the same by hereditary descent. Heralds in London and from there invariably confirm this statement whenever consulted. By the writings of Edmonson and Burke, we learn that there are seventeen of the name and family of Glover who are entitled to and have been granted Coats of Arms; and by an examination of all, it appears that the one granted to Somerset Herald is the only one which corresponds with those which have been granted at different periods to this branch of New England Glovers. We have also the testimony of William Camden, a distinguished herald who was cotemporary with Robert Glover and survived him, who has confirmed the right of this branch to the same arms, by his description, and that the family was first of Coventry in Warwickshire and Ashford in Kent.

RICHARD CHISWELL.

Richard Chiswell, who was a son by her first husband of one of the daughters of Thomas Glover — or there may have been another daughter who died previously to the date of the will in 1707 — was a grandson, and had a wife and one child, at the time the will was made.

Of the Chiswells in London, the following has been gathered:

Mr. Richard Chiswell, a noted bookseller of London, lies buried in St. Peter's Church-yard. He was one of the proprietors, says Stowe, " of this book " — meaning his Survey of London.

" He lies here in the North Isle of this Church, and also his father and mother, John and Margaret Chiswell, and his first wife Sarah, daughter of John King — and also five children who died young, whom he had by Mary, daughter of Richard Royston, bookseller, by whom he had three sons more, viz., John Chiswell, who died in India, Richard, and Royston. Richard Chiswell, Sen., was born in this Parish, January 4, 1639, and died here May 3d, 1711 (aged 72 years), and was a man Worthy of Great Praise, whereof his son Richard Chiswell of London, Merchant, caused a Monument to be erected, which is against the Wall of the South Isle of this Church."

Notices of Richard Chiswell are as follows:

St. Butolph, Aldergate Ward. Among a list of benefactors, " Mr. Richard Chiswell, late of this city, bookseller, besides his charity to this School in his lifetime, did at his death give Twenty-five Pounds."

Another, of the date of 1708:

" Mr. Richard Chiswell, abovesaid, besides his charity to this School in his lifetime, did at his death give Twenty-five pounds, and to the Workhouse at Bishop's Gate Street he gave Two hundred Pounds; and in January, 1708, he gave Fifty Pounds."

The above notices probably relate to the father of Richard Chiswell, merchant, who married a daughter of Thomas Glover. He must have died young, and of him little has been gathered, or of his wife. He may have been one of the five children by the first wife Sarah King, as the son Richard by the second wife survived him and erected the monument to his memory.

1717. The following notices seem to relate particularly to the Richard Chiswell, grandson of Thomas Glover, and named in his will as a legatee; also the Joseph Thomson named must be another grandson associated with him under the head of " Governors of the Royal College of St. Thomas Hospital, in Southwark, A.D. 1717:— Mr. Richard Chiswell, Esq., Mr. Joseph Thomson, Esq."

The following from Essex County History, published by the Camden Society in 1838 or 9, appears to indicate the place of his death and the name of his wife, which show he could not have been the son of Elizabeth Glover, who married Thomas Trench.

"Against the east wall of the south Isle of the church is a very handsome marble monument, on which is this inscription: 'Hereunder lieth the remains of Mr. Richard Chiswell, Esq., of London, Merchant, who purchased and improved and settled his whole estate at Depden upon his posterity, and died in 1751, aged 78; and also of Mary his wife, the daughter and sole heiress of Mr. Thomas Trench of London, merchant, whereby was brought into this family the estate of Finchenfield, which they now enjoy. She died in 1726, aged forty-three years, and had by her said husband five children, whereof her two sons, William and Trench Chiswell, died at Constantinople, aged about eighteen years, and lie buried there. Also Richard Chiswell, his second son, who survived him; also his second daughter, who married Mr. Dudley Foley and Peter Muilman, merchants of London; in commemoration of which particular this monument was erected by the direction of the said Richard Chiswell, Deceased.'

"Upon the north wall there is another, having the following inscription:

" 'In the adjacent corner of this Church lie Interred the remains of Mr. Dudley Foley, Ob. 1747, and likewise his Wife, Ob. 1742, who are both further mentioned in the monument of Richard Chiswell, Esq. The only two children they had lie buried at Cheaum in Surrey, one a son aged fourteen, the other a daughter aged sixteen years.'

"Upon the ground, on a black marble stone, is engraved in two graves arched with brick:

" 'Mr. Richard Chiswell, Esq., Obit. A.D. 1751.
Mary, his only Wife, Obit. 1726.
Mr. Dudley Foley, Obit. 1747.
Elizabeth, his only Wife, Obit. 1742.' "

Of Joseph Moxon, another grandson of Thomas Glover, the presumption is that he was the son of Rev. George Moxon, who was the first minister of Springfield, and returned to England with Mr. Pynchon in 1652. Joseph, if he had such a son, married, in all probability, one of the daughters of Thomas Glover.

10

JOSEPH THOMSON.

Joseph Thomson was the husband of Mary Glover, second daughter of Thomas and Rebeckah Glover of London.

Judge Sewall writes, April 18, 1689: "Go to Hampden Court, in company with Mr. Hutchinson, John Appleton and Mr. Mather. Sir Samuel Thomson, Mr. Whiting and Mr. Joseph Thomson, rode in another coach. Cost 21 Shill. and 8 pence apiece, beside money for the driver."

Children of JOSEPH and MARY (GLOVER) THOMSON, born in London:

William, married Judith ———.
Joseph.   Mary.
James.   Elizabeth.

Hackney, the Last Residence of Thomas Glover, Esq.

The following description is from "Stowe's Survey of London":

"The circuit walks on the northwest parts bordering upon London, viz., Hackney, Stoke Newington, Islington, Paddington, Highgate and Mary-le-bone.

"St. Augustine, alias St. John, on turning westward on the other side of the river Lea, is situated in the pleasant and healthful town of Hackney, where divers nobles in former times had their country seats, as one of the Earls of Northumberland, the Countess of Warwick, Lord Brooke and others.

"This Church at Hackney has been of late called by the name of St. John's at Hackney, as though it belonged to the Knight Templars of St. John at Jerusalem; certainly they had a mill there once, and some tenures in the Parish. But in an ancient record in the Tower, it is found to have been written St. Augustine de Hackney, and in the Cotton Library there is a volume about the Knight Templars, wherein mention is made of St. Augustine's at Hackney, and of the lands and rents they had there, viz., about twelve acres, quit rents, and a small mill commonly called Templars' Mill. There are, besides, many antiquities concerning this Parish of Hackney, in the time of Edward I., in the 19th of whose reign (1290) free warren was granted to Richard of Graves and Bishop of London.

"Hackney Church had, five hundred years ago, a distinct Priory and Vicarage, as appears by a record in the Tower of London, of the value of that ecclesiastical preferment."

It appears that Thomas Glover removed from London, where he was at the time of Judge Sewall's first visit, in 1686, to St. John: Hackney, and there passed the remainder of his life. One of his daughters was settled there, viz., Mrs. Elizabeth Trench, and perhaps others, probably at the time he retired from business. At the time of Judge Sewall's last visit, in 1689, he had arrived at the age of seventy-two years, and had undoubtedly sought this place as a quiet resort in which to close his life.

[*Second Generation.*]

HABACKUK GLOVER.

II.   Habackuk Glover, the second son of Mr. John Glover and Anna his wife, was born at Rainhill Parish, Prescot, Lancashire, England, May 12, 1628, and died in Boston, in New England, in the early part of the year 1693, in his 65th year. His remains were deposited in the Granary Burying Ground.

At the age of two years he was brought by his parents to New England, and lived in Dorchester until he attained the age of manhood. At the age of twenty-two years (1650), he was admitted to join the first Church in Dorchester, Richard Mather being pastor and was admitted freeman the same year. He continued to be a member of the Church in Dorchester ten years, and on the 4 (9) 1660, was dismissed to join the first Church in Boston, Rev. John Wilson, pastor.

While an inhabitant of Dorchester, he resided at the homestead and carried on the business of tanning, which had been established there by his father. He was a man of extensive business, and became a large landholder, both by inheritance and purchase, not only in Boston, but in the adjacent towns, as Charlestown, Dorchester, Milton, and other places.

3 (4) 1653 — he was married to Hannah Eliot, and resided for a short time at the house of her father, the Rev. John Eliot. In 1654, he removed to Boston, and succeeded to the inheritance of his father's "Boston Estate," which, according to the will of Mr. Glover, was to be "one half of the new house in Boston nearest Mr. Webb's house, one half of all the other housing, half the yard and tan-pits in it, and all the other accommodations for tanning, with the sum of four

hundred pounds in money." After the decease of his mother he was
to come in possession of the whole or other half of the new house,
with all the other half of the housing, yard and tan-pits, goods, chattels, and all the residue and remainder of the estate which was reserved as the widow's dower, under the following conditions: by
paying to his brother Thomas Glover in London, England, ten
pounds; to his brother Nathaniel Glover of Dorchester, forty pounds;
and to Harvard College, at Cambridge, five pounds a year forever.
The conditions were punctually fulfilled, as gathered by evidence on
record.   The annuity to Harvard College was paid regularly by him
during his life, and since his decease in 1693 by his successors to
that estate.

Children of Mr. HABACKUK and HANNAH (ELIOT) GLOVER, born
in Roxbury, at the house of Rev. John Eliot:

1. Hannah, b. 3 : 5 : 1654;   bap. 3 : 7 : 1654; died in infancy.
+2. Rebeckah, b. 24 : 5 : 1655; bap. 29 : 5 : 1655;
                             m. { 1st, Thomas Smith, of Boston.
                                 { 2d, Capt. Thomas Clarke, of Boston.

Among the public references to Habackuk Glover during his lifetime, we find the following.

He appeared before the magistrates, January 4, 1654, with Mrs.
Anna Glover, his mother, and presented his father's will for probate.

Again in 1654, July 6th, his name appears in a lease of the farm
in Milton, which had been assigned as a part of the widow's dower.
(See Lease, p. 65.)

May 18, 1660.   Robert Mousall, merchant, of Boston, sold to
Habackuk Glover, of Boston, his house and land at the sea side, near
Mr. Harrison's house, the "Ropemaker." Signed by Robert Mou-
sall; witnessed by Anna Glover and John Glover.

In 1661, Habackuk was appointed attorney to his brother Thomas
Glover, with full power to settle all his affairs in New England.
(See p. 86.)

10 mo. 11 day, 1661.   An Indenture between Habackuk Glover
and Hannah his wife, and William Hudson, for a house twenty feet
square from outside to outside; the house situated at the head of the
Dock in Boston.

20 (1) 1662.   Thomas Mousall to Habackuk Glover: A mortgage of his house and land in Charlestown, County of Middlesex;
consideration, eighty pounds. Signed by Thomas Mousall, Mary

Mousall, and Alexander Mousall. Witnessed by Benjamin Lothrop and Edward Burt.

July 13, 1663, Habackuk Glover makes a conditional sale of the house and land in Charlestown, conveyed to him by Thomas Mousall. Signed by Thomas and Mary Mousall. Witnessed by Jonathan Howe, Jr., James Russell and Andrew Belcher.

Aug. 8, 1663. William Hudson, of Boston, sold to Habackuk Glover "his Brew house and the land on which it stands;" bounded by land of Habackuk Glover; consideration, twenty-five pounds.

March 22, 1665, he bought a house and land of William Hudson near the Dock in Boston. Witnessed by his brother John Glover, and John Loring.

June 11, 1666. Habackuk Glover bought land in Boston of Francis and Elizabeth Smith. Witnessed by his brother John Glover, and Richard Goulding.

Nov. 28, 1666, he discharged a mortgage to John and Mary Mousall.

March 28, 1668. Habackuk Glover purchased a house and land of James Penniman, bounded easterly and northerly on land of Nathaniel Woodward.

January 3, 1666, John Woodmansey mortgaged a piece of land in Boston, which was discharged by Habackuk Glover, June 2, 1675.

Nov. 28, 1666, he sold a piece of land in Boston to Capt. Thomas Smith, mariner.

In 1669, a transaction is recorded of him with Nathaniel and Peter Duncan, for the recovery of a debt due to his brother Thomas Glover of London. (See p. 87.)

In 1671, Habackuk Glover and John Glover sold to Robert Babcock, of Milton, two acres of land laid out to their father, John Glover, Esq., of Boston, by the Proprietors of Dorchester, on the south side of Neponset River.

March 2, 1673. A conveyance of house and land from Habackuk Glover to his beloved daughter, Rebeckah Smith, wife of Capt. Thomas Smith.

Nov. 20, 1674, he makes another conveyance of land to his son-in-law, Capt. Thomas Smith, of Boston.

March 18, he visited Newport, R. I., and while there wrote a letter, addressed to the Rev. Increase Mather, on doctrines of religion which seemed to be a subject of discussion at that time. The

10*

letter was concise and very neatly written. The original has been preserved.

Nov. 12, 1680, his name appears again in Glover's Agreement (before referred to) in behalf of himself and his brother Thomas Glover of London.

The next year after the division of Newbury Farm, Oct. 8, 1681, Habackuk Glover sold one fourth part of that farm, which was his share in its division in 1680, to Roger Billings; consideration, one hundred and seventy pounds. Signed Habackuk Glover and Hannah Glover. (See p. 73.)

Will of Mr. Habackuk Glover.

I Habackuk Glover of Boston, in New England, being under bodily weakness, but of sound, disposing mind and memory, and knowing the uncertainty of life, do make my last Will and Testament, in manner and form following—hereby revoking and making void all former Wills by me formerly made. And first, I commit my soul unto God who gave it, and my body to the Earth to be decently buried at the discretion of my Executrix hereafter named.

For my Worldly Goods and Estate, I will that these be employed and bestowed as by this my last Will expressed. *Imp.* I will that all my just debts and funeral expenses be well and truly paid, or ordained to be paid by my Executrix, with what convenient speed may be after my interment.

Item. I give and bequeathe unto Hannah, my Well-beloved wife, the use, profits and incomes of all my moveables and personal Estate whatsoever, and of all my housing and lands situate at the Dock Head, adjoining to the housing and lands of my son-in-law Thomas Clarke, for the comfortable subsistence of my Wife during the term of her natural life.

Item. At the decease of my said Wife, I give and bequeathe all my remaining moveables and personal estate whatsoever, and the rents, issues and profits of all my aforesaid Housing and Lands, unto my beloved daughter Rebeckah Clark, to her Use and benefit, for and during the full time and term of her natural life.

The reversion of all the Housing and Lands at the decease of my said daughter Rebeckah Clark, I give, devise and bequeathe unto the heirs of her body, and to their heirs and assigns forever.

And of this my last Will and Testament I do make, constitute, appoint and ordain my before named Wife and Daughter to be full and whole Executors of all my Estate.

In Witness whereof, I the said Habackuk Glover have hereunto set my hand and seale, this Seventeenth day of September, One thousand Six hundred and Ninety two, in the Twenty fourth Year of the Reign of William and Mary, King and Queen of England.

Published by the Within named Habackuk Glover, in presence of Us,

Benjamin Walker, Daniel Allen, Jonathan Jackson.

JONATHAN ADDINGTON, *Registrar.*

There appears to be no account of his death, either by any record or by tradition.

His will was made the 17th day of September, 1692, being then, as he says, under bodily weakness, but of sound mind. He lived six months after that event. Letters of administration on his estate were granted to Mrs. Hannah Glover, widow and relict of Mr. Habackuk Glover, April 4, 1693, and to Mrs. Rebeckah Clarke, his only daughter. No inventory of his estate was ever rendered to the Court of Probate.

There appears to be a mortgage deed from Jonathan Pratt to Mrs. Hannah Glover, widow of Mr. Habackuk Glover, which was discharged and exonerated by Mrs. Rebeckah Clarke, only child and heir of Mr. Habackuk Glover and Hannah his wife, she personally appearing after the decease of her mother and acknowledging that she had received full satisfaction. (Boston, Feb. 25, 1708–9.)

HANNAH ELIOT, the wife of Mr. Habackuk Glover, was born in Roxbury, the 17th day of the seventh month, 1633, and died in Boston the 8th day of February, 1708-9, æt. 75 years. She was the daughter of the Rev. John and Hannah (Mountfort) Eliot, of Roxbury. She is noticed by those who have gathered up memorials of the life of her father, the well-known Apostle to the Indians, as being eminently devoted to religious duties in early life; as "a dutiful daughter — the only one who survived her parents — and who administered to their comfort in their declining years." She was married to Mr. Glover, 3 : 4 : 1653, and removed to Boston in 1654, it is said, although both their children were born at the house of her father in Roxbury, and baptized by him. (See depositions of Shubael and Joshua Seaver, pp. 78, 79.)

16 2 mo. 1654, she was admitted to join the first Church in Boston.

Judge Sewall writes in his diary, under date of July 18, 1705, "I visited this day Mrs. Hannah Glover, widow, who is blind. Father and Mother Eliot were there."

Feb. 9, 1708. "The widow Hannah Glover dies, in the 76th year of her age; widow of Mr. Habackuk Glover, and daughter of Mr. John Eliot, who married here, and this daughter of his was born at Roxbury, so that this gentlewoman, tho' born in New England, passed not only sixty but seventy years, and became a Great Grand Mother in our Israel."

"Feb. 11, 1708–9.   Mrs. Hannah Glover is buried in a tomb in the new burying place (the Granary).   Bearers — Winthrop, Sewall, Addington, Sargeant, Fayerweather and Checkley.   Very cold day."   •

[Third Generation.]

(2) REBECKAH GLOVER, only surviving daughter of Mr. Habackuk and Hannah (Eliot) Glover, was born in Roxbury the 25th day of the 5th month, 1655, and baptized there by her maternal grandfather, the Rev. John Eliot, 29 : 5 : 1655.   She died in Boston, Nov. 10th, 1711, in her 57th year, and was buried in the Stone Chapel yard.

She was twice married; first, in 1672, at the age of about eighteen years, to Capt. Thomas Smith, of Boston, mariner, by whom she had eight children.

"May 16, 1680, Capt. Thomas Smith, with his wife Rebeckah, was admitted to join the first Church in Boston in full communion." (Rec. 1st Church.)

Three of their children had been baptized previously under the half covenant, as it was called, which was at that time admissible in the New England churches.   Capt. Thomas Smith died Nov. 8th, 1688; and April 30th, 1691, she married a second time to Capt. Thomas Clarke, a wealthy merchant of Boston.   By him she had one daughter, who married but left no issue.

Capt. THOMAS SMITH, the first husband of Rebeckah Glover, was born in England (the place not ascertained), and died in Boston, Nov. 8, 1688.   He was the son of Capt. Thomas Smith, Esq., who was undoubtedly one of the Smythes of Essex County in England. "In the parish of Blackmore, at the end of the Chancel, is the burial place of the Ancient family of Smythes of this Parish, and in which is a very old and decayed tomb erected to the memory of Thomas Smythe, Esq., who died in the year 1594; and also of Margaret his wife, and relict of Stephen Parvel.   Their effigies at full length are fixed in this monument.   Upon the floor are several other inscriptions upon the gravestones of different branches of the family."   Capt. Thomas Smith, the husband of Rebeckah Glover, was a mariner and shipmaster, in command of his own ship, making foreign voyages.   He was also a landholder to some extent in Boston and vicinity.   At the time of his death he owned lands in Wenham, Bradford, and other places in Essex County in New England. By his wife he succeeded to the possession of the estate of Mr. Habackuk Glover on Dock Square, and occupied the mansion house. He was the owner, also, of several pieces of land which were conveyed to him by his father-in-law, both before and after his marriage.

Children of Capt. THOMAS and REBECKAH (GLOVER) SMITH, born and baptized in Boston:

+ 3. Anne, bap. Dec. 2, 1677; m. Nathaniel Kay, Esq., of Newport, R. I.
   4. Rebeckah, bap. same day; died in infancy.
+ 5. Thomas, bap. May 19, 1678; m. { 1st, Mary Corwin, of Salem. { 2d, Sarah Oliver.
   6. Habackuk, a twin, bap. July 7, 1680; d. same day.
   7. Samuel, a twin, bap. July 7, 1680; d. same day.
+ 8. John, bap. July 11, 1681; m. Martha Brenton, of Bristol, R. I.
+ 9. Elizabeth, bap. Feb. 14, 1685;
      m. { 1st, Nathaniel Lyndall, of Salem. { 2d, Ebenezer Brenton, Esq., of Bristol, R. I.
+10. Rebeckah, bap. Dec. 25, 1687;
      m. { 1st, John Gore, A.M., of Cambridge. { 2d, Nathaniel Hubbard, Esq., of Dorchester.

And by Capt. THOMAS CLARKE:

+11. Anne, born Sept. 2, 1694; m. John Jeffries, Esq., of Boston.

The following notices of Capt. Thomas Smith are taken from the diary of Judge Sewall, by the kindness of the Rev. Samuel Sewall, of Burlington, Mass. The Judge says:

"Oct 28, 1688. I visited Capt. Thomas Smith, who lies very ill."

"Nov. 8th. Capt. Thomas Smith dies at 5 o'clock in the morning."

"Nov. 10th. Capt. Thomas Smith was buried this day. I attended the funeral. Where the Corpse was set, was the room where my father Hull first led me to see the manner of the merchants and Lords of the trade, I suppose now about twelve years ago.

"The Bearers were Capt⁰ˢ Prout and Fayerweather, William Clarke, Foye, Savage, Legg. Mr. Peter Sargent and Benjamin Brown, Esqrs., led the Widow. He was buried in the Old Burial Place" (or Stone Chapel yard).

Will of Capt. Thomas Smith.

Liber 10, folio 435–6.

In the name of God, Amen.   The 30 day of October, Anno Domini
1688, &c.   I Thomas Smith of Boston, within the Territory and common of New England, being sick of body, but, through the mercy of
God, of sound disposing mind and memory, do make and ordain this
my last Will and Testament, in manner and form following; hereby
revoking and making null and void all former Wills by me made.

First and principally, I recommend my spirit into the hands of
God who gave it, and my body I remit unto the dust, to be devoutly
interred at the discretion of my Executrix hereinafter named.   And
for such Worldly Goods and Estate as it has pleased God to bestow
upon me, the same shall be disposed of in the following manner as
hereafter expressed.

Imprimis.   My Will is that all my just debts and funeral expenses
be well and truly paid, or ordered to be paid, by my Executrix, with
what speed may be after my decease.

Item.   I give, devise and bequeath unto Rebecca, my Well beloved
Wife, for her heirs and assigns forever, one full third part of all my
housing, lands, farms, goods, chattels and Plate, whatsoever and
wheresoever it may be found, as well Real as Personal.

Item.   I give, devise and bequeath the other two thirds part of all
my housing, lands, farms, goods, chattels and Plate, whatsoever and
wheresoever it may be found, unto my five children, vizt.:

Anne Smith, Thomas Smith, John Smith, Elizabeth Smith, and Rebeckah Smith, and to such other child as my wife may now be preg-
nant, to be equally divided and distributed to them and among them,
part and part alike, within the space of two years after either of my
children shall attain the age of Twenty One Years, or on the day of
Marriage, which may first happen and come.   And if any of my children happen to die before the age aforesaid, then the part or share of
such child or children who die young or before they marry, is to be
equally divided amongst all my remaining children, part and part
alike, and also my wife is to share with them in such division.

Item.   I do nominate and constitute my said dear Wife Rebecca
Smith sole Executrix of this my said Will during the time of her widowhood; but upon her intermarriage or decease, I do hereby nominate and appoint my father-in-law Mr. Habackuk Glover, and my
good friends Mr. Peter Sargeant and Mr. Benjamin Brown, and my
brother-in-law Obadiah Gill, or so many of them as will be then living,
to be my Executors in trust in behalf of my children, to see this my
will duly performed.   And to each of my said Executors I give the
sum of four pounds apiece in money, in testimony of my respect and
love.

And I do give full power and authority unto my aforenamed Executrix succeeding her, to make sale of my house and land situate in Boston, and my farm and land lying in Wenham, and my farm and land
lying in Bradford, or any of them, or any other land to me of right
belonging, if opportunity offer, and to seal and execute loyal Deeds
of Conveyance of the same in due form, and to employ and improve
the produce thereof according to their good discretion, for the most

benefit and advantage of my said wife and my said children, according to their respective shares thereof.

Lastly, I do solemnly charge and command all my children that they acquiesce and rest satisfied in this my last Will and disposal to them. And that they carry it well towards their mother and consult and take her advice in the disposal of themselves in márriage or otherwise.

In Witness whereof, I have hereunto set my hand and seal the day and year first above written.

THOMAS SMITH, and Seal.

Witnessed by

Daniel Allen,   John Talbot,

Jeremiah Fitch,   *(Signum)* E Elizabeth Bussey.

June 7, 1688. The above-written Daniel Allen, Jeremiah Fitch and Elizabeth Bussey, three of the Witnesses to this Will, appeared personally and made Oath that they saw Thomas Smith subscribe and sign and seal, and heard him publish and declare this Writing to be his last Will and Testament, and that he was of sound mind and memory, according to the best of their proving.

Sworn the 7th day of June, 1688, before me,   PAUL DUDLEY.

Thomas Smith's Estate.

Sept. 18, 1702.   Prob. Rec., Vol. 15, fol. 68.

Letters granted cum Testament unto Peter Sargeant, Esq., and Benjamin Brown, Esq., Executors in trust of the Will of Thomas Smith, of Boston, mariner, Dec^d, and of his Estate.

ELISHA COOKE, Esq., Judge of Probate of Wills for the County of Suffolk in New England, *Greeting:*

Whereas Thomas Smith, late of Boston in the County aforesaid, Mariner, Dec^d, did in his last Will and Testament duly proved and approved (a copy of which is hereunto annexed), make and order his wife Rebecca sole Executrix of his Will during her widowhood, but upon her intermarriage or decease did recommend and appoint his father-in-law Habackuk Glover, and his friends Mr. Peter Sargeant and Mr. Benjamin Brown, and his brother-in-law Obadiah Gill, or so many of them as should be then living, his Executors in trust in behalf of his Children, and to see his Will duly performed;

And whereas Rebecca Smith, late wife of the said Thomas Smith, and Executrix as aforesaid, hath intermarried since his decease, whereof her Executorship is determined; And it hath been made to appear unto me that Habackuk Glover and Obadiah Gill, before-named Executors, have since deceased; Therefore, Know Ye, that all and singular of the Housing, Lands, farms, goods, chattels, Plate, &c., of the said Thomas Smith, is hereby committed to Peter Sargeant and Benjamin Brown, Esqrs., and they are also to render a plain and true inventory of the remaining value of said estate, and to give an account of their Executorship upon Oath within one year from the date hereof.   ELISHA COOKE, *Judge of Probate.*

Boston, September 18, 1702.

Mrs. Rebeccah Clarke lived twenty years after her second marriage. She made her will, which bears date Nov. 8, 1711, and is as follows:

Will of Mrs. Rebeckah (Glover) Clarke.

Suffolk ss.   Vol. 17, p. 344.

In the name of God, Amen.

I Rebeckah Clarke, Wife of Thomas Clarke of Boston, in the County of Suffolk in New England (Pewterer), and formerly the Wife of Thomas Smith, Mariner, deceased, being weak in body, but of sound disposing mind and memory, praised be God for the same, do make and ordain these Presents to be and contain my Last Will and Testament. That is to say, first and principally, I commend my soul into the hands of Almighty God, and my body to a decent interment in hopes of a Joyful resurrection to Eternal life through the alone merits of Jesus Christ my only Saviour and Redeemer.

And as touching such Worldly and separate Estate which in and by a Certain Deed under the hand and seale of my said husband, bearing date the Twentieth day of February, 1695, is prescribed wholly to me and to be at my disposal, and wherein and whereby my said husband doth Covenant, promise and agree to and with Peter Sargeant of Boston, Benjamin Brown of Salem, Esquires, and Obadiah Gill of said Boston, Housewright, Trustees for and on the behalf of me the said Rebeckah Clarke, to and with the survivor of them, their Executors and Administrators, that it shall and may be lawful for Me the said Rebeckah Clarke, notwithstanding the overture from time to time to employ, bestow, alienate and dispose of all and singular the Estate and Estates therein mentioned by my former husband or of my late father so far as my Right and interest therein can reach or extend, according to my own free will and pleasure, either by my last Will and Testament or by any other Testament, and that he my said husband, in case of his surviving, shall and will freely consent and allow of the Probate of any such Last Will and Testament, by Me signed in the Presence of Two or more Credible Witnesses as in and by the said recited Deed or Instrument, reference thereto being had among other things, may more fully appear. I therefore say, by virtue of the Power and Authority to me therein given, I do give, devise and bequeathe as followeth.

Imp. I do give and bequeathe Anne Smith, Elizabeth Lindall and Rebeckah Smith, One Hundred and Forty Pounds apiece in Money and Province Bills.

Item. To my daughter Anne Clarke, my Gold Chain, wearing apparel and Twenty Pounds in Money or Province Bills.

Item. To my daughter-in-law, Jane Coleman, Ten Pounds in Province Bills.

Item. To my Grandson Thomas Smith, a piece of Land at the Eastward, bought by my son John Smith of James Russell, of Charlestown, Esq., or in lieu thereof my Will is that my said son John Smith shall pay to his brother Thomas Smith, for the use of my said Grandson, Fifty Pounds in money of New England.

Item. I do hereby remit and forgive unto my son John Smith half of the Interest he owes me for money due by bonds, due March 1st,

1712. (The note and bond was given by the Executors to perform the Will and desire of their mother Mrs. Rebeckah Smith, and pay the debts of the estate, and is on file.)*

Item. All the rest and residue of my Estate, Whatsoever and Wheresoever the same is or may be found, which does in any way belong to me, I do give and bequeathe the same as followeth, To Wit —Two thirds part thereof to my son Thomas Smith, and the other Third part unto my son John Smith. And I do hereby nominate and appoint my said Two sons, Thomas Smith and John Smith, to be the only Executors of this my Last Will and Testament. And I do hereby revoke and make void all former Wills and Testaments at any time heretofore made by Me, in word or Writing, and declare these Presents to be and contain my only last Will and Testament.

In Witness Whereof, I have hereunto set my hand and Seale this Eighth day of November, One Thousand Seven Hundred and Eleven.

REBECKAH CLARKE, and a Seale.

Signed, Sealed, Published and delivered by the said Rebeckah Clarke, to be her last Will and Testament, in presence of us,
> Samuel Tyley,
> Jonas Clark,
> George Basin.

Boston, November 17, 1711. I do hereby consent and allow of the Probate of this Will of my late Wife Rebeckah Clarke, and confirm the same.
THOMAS CLARKE.

Jonas Clark, } *Witnesses.*
Richard Kilby, }

PAUL DUDLEY, *Register.*

Capt. THOMAS CLARKE, the second husband of Rebeckah (Glover) Smith, was born in Charlestown, Middlesex County, and baptized there at the Old North Church (of which the First Church in Boston was a branch), when four days old. "22 (6) 1657, Thomas, the son of brother Thomas Clarke, was baptized by Rev. John Wilson." He afterwards became an honorable and useful member of that Church, and in his will gave to it a suitable portion of his substance as a memorial of his love and interest. He was one of the most eminent merchants of the early times of Boston, where he resided. The house where he lived is said to have been situated at the North End of Boston. A street and a square have since been named for him, near the location. He died there December 16, 1732, in his 76th year.† He was twice married; the name of his first wife

---

* The above in parenthesis is on the margin.

† The father of Capt. Thomas Clarke was also an eminent Boston merchant, and engaged largely in other enterprises of profit and trade.

There is a record on the books of Mr. John Pynchon, of Springfield, that Mr. William Payne and Capt. Thomas Clarke, merchants of Boston, in 1657, 1658, and 1659, employed

was Jane ——, by whom he had one daughter Jane, born March 16,
1679–80; married Rev. Benjamin Colman, D.D., and died October 26, 1731. He married, second, April 2, 1691, Rebeckah (Glover)
Smith, widow of Capt. Thomas Smith, by whom he had one daughter,
Anne Clarke, who married John Jeffries, Esq. It is said also that
he married a third time, August 13, 1713, Abigail Ketch or Keach,
who died January 28, 1729. His grandchildren were two daughters
of Rev. Benjamin and Jane (Clarke) Colman, born in Boston, and
named in his Will, viz.:

Jane, b. Feb. 25, 1708; m. Rev. Ebenezer Turell, of Medford, Aug.
  17, 1726.
Abigail, b. 1710;   m. Albert Dennie, of Boston.

Will of Capt. Thomas Clark.

Liber 31, folio 112, Suffolk Prob. Rec.

In the name of God, Amen.

This 8th Day of December, 1730, I Thomas Clarke of Boston, in
the County of Suffolk and in the Province of Massachusetts Bay in
New England, Merchant, being aged and infirm of body, although of
sound disposing mind and memory, do make and publish this my last
Will and Testament, as follows, viz.:

Imp. I recommend my soul into the hands of Almighty God, and
my body to a decent burial, in the hope of a Joyful Resurrection to
Eternal Life through the merits of Jesus Christ my only Saviour and
Redeemer.

2dly, As touching my temporal Estate which God hath bountifully
given me, after my just debts and funeral charges are paid by my Executors, I hereby give, devise and bequeathe thereof as follows:

That is to say, I give to my Sons-in-law, Mr. Benjamin Coleman and
Mr. John Jeffries over and above what I have already given them,
the Sum of Five Hundred Pounds each in token of my love to them.

Item. I give to the Poor Communicants of the Church of Christ
usually assembling at Mr. Coleman's Meeting-House, the Sum of One
Hundred Pounds, to be let out for their use by the Committee who
shall from time to time be appointed by the Church: and the Interest
thereof to be by the said Committee yearly and every year forever,
distributed among such poor communicants as the said Committee in
their discretion shall think fit.

Item. I give unto the children of my son-in-law Mr. Benjamin
Coleman by Jane his Wife, my loving daughter lately deceased, and

---

men to work at a Black Lead Mine, which was situated in what is now Sturbridge. Mr.
John Pynchon was agent for them till 1659, when his agency ceased. In 1651, Mr. John
Pynchon purchased twenty-six barrels suitable to contain black lead, and Clarke and Payne
paid for them. In October, 1651, Capt. Thomas Clarke sent to Springfield a large number
of cattle, horses and swine, to be sold or wintered. Gov. John Winthrop afterwards came in
possession of the mine referred to.

to their heirs forever, to be equally divided among them, My House and Land lying in Brattle street (so called), Boston, aforesaid, with all the Privileges and Appurtenances as now enjoyed by Benjamin Dyer.

Item. I give unto my loving daughter Anne Jeffries, the sum of One Thousand Pounds to be at her own disposal forever (notwithstanding the coverture).

Item. I give One Third part of all my Silver Plate unto my said daughter Anne Jeffries forever, and I give the other Two thirds parts unto my two Grand-daughters, Jane Turell and Abigail Coleman, to be equally divided between them.

Item. I give, devise and bequeathe unto my two said Grand-daughters Jane Turell and Abigail Coleman all that my certain Farm and Tract of Land lying in Charlestown in the County of Middlesex in Massachusetts aforesaid, with all the privileges and Appurtenances thereto belonging, which Joseph Frost hired of me. To Have and To Hold the said Land and Premises unto them the said Jane Turell and Abigail Coleman, the one half unto the said Jane Turell and the heirs of her body lawfully begotten or to be begotten and their heirs forever, and the other half or part thereof unto the said Abigail Coleman and the heirs of her body begotten of her in lawful Wedlock and their heirs forever.

Item. I give and devise unto the said John Jeffries and Anne his Wife, my loving daughter, and to their heirs forever, All that my Mansion House, Brick Ware House, Shops, Coach House, and Lands thereto belonging, with the privileges and appurtenances to the same appraised, with the rest of my real Estate in Boston not otherwise herein disposed of.

Item. I give my Negro Man Bristol his freedom within Seven years after my decease.

Item. I devise my worthy friends, viz., Addington Davenport, Thomas Fitch, Thomas Palmer and Stephen Minot, to be Overseers of this my last Will and Testament, and I do hereby bequeathe unto each of them Five Pounds in token of my respect for them.

Lastly, I give and bequeathe All my land at the Eastward which I bought of Mr. Edwards, and all the residue and remainder of my Estate, both Real and Personal, in Goods, Chattels, Rights or Credits, unto my two sons-in-law, viz., Benjamin Coleman and John Jeffries, to be equally divided between them, and to their heirs, Executors, Administrators and Assigns forever.

And I do hereby Constitute and appoint the said Benjamin Coleman and John Jeffries sole and only Executors of this my last Will and Testament: hereby revoking all former Wills by me made.

In Testimony whereof, I the said Thomas Clarke have hereunto set my hand and seale the day and year therein before written.

THOMAS CLARKE, and Seale.

Signed, sealed, published and declared by the said Thomas Clarke to be his last Will and Testament, in Presence of Us,
John Simpson,
Nathaniel Galpin,
Samuel Tyley.

The foregoing Will being presented for Probate by the Executors within named, Jonathan Simpson, Nathaniel Galpin and Samuel Tyley made Oath that they saw Thomas Clarke sign the above written Instrument, and heard him declare it to be his last will and Testament.

JOSIAH WILLARD, *Judge of Probate.*

Boston, December 26, 1732.   JOHN BOYDELL, *Register.*

[*Fourth Generation.*]

(3) ANNE SMITH, eldest daughter of Capt. Thomas and Rebeckah (Glover) Smith, was born in Boston, baptized at the first Church, Dec. 2, 1677, and died at Newport, R. I., about 1740, aged 63 years.

Oct. 14, 1715, she was married by the Rev. Samuel Myles to Nathaniel Kay, Esq., of Newport, R. I., and went there to reside. The date of her death has not been obtained, but it is known that she survived her husband about six years. They had no children.

A bust portrait of NATHANIEL KAY, Esq., " Collector of the King's Customs," has been preserved at Newport, and was in the family of the Brentons a few years since. An interesting account of him may be found in Updike's History of the Narragansett Church. He was born in England about 1675, and died in Newport, R. I., April 14, 1734, aged 59 years. The following inscription is engraved on a stone which covers his grave in Trinity Church yard, where his remains were deposited. It is on the left of the entrance at the gate.

" This covers the dust of Nathaniel Kay, Esq., Collector of the King's Customs at Newport, whose spirit returned to God on the 14th day of April, Anno Domini 1734, after it had tabernacled in the flesh here 59 years. He, after an example in life of Faith and Charity, did, by his last Will at his death, found and largely endow two Charity Schools in Newport and Bristol within his Collection."

He was one of the early friends of the Church, for we find his name as one of the Vestry as soon as the year 1720. He was in Newport as early as 1713. The records of Trinity Church notice him thus: " Mr. Nathaniel Kay, Esq., Collector of the Queen's Revenue in Rhode Island, who afterwards liberally endowed a school connected with this Church, was among the signers to a petition to the Queen for the establishment of Bishops in America."

His house stood on the site now occupied by George Engs, Esq., on the hill near the head of Towne Street. It was, when built, one of the most spacious and elegant of private dwellings in the town. In his will, made a short time before his death, he bequeathed his dwelling-house, coach-house, and other valuable property to his wife Anne during her natural life; after which he gives both his lots of land to Trinity Church, at Newport, and four hundred pounds in money of the currency of New England, to build a school-house for the minister of the Church of England in Newport, Mr. Honeyman — the lots of land lying in Rhode Island. In 1740, six years after his death, the estate of Mr. Kay is said to have come into the possession of the Church; probably his wife died in that year. This estate has since been sold, and it is said that at the present time none of it remains in the hands of the Church. An account of the rents of the lands and houses left by Mr. Kay for the use of a grammar master at Newport, commencing April 1, 1765, shows the income to have amounted to 64 pounds and 5 shillings sterling.

(5) THOMAS SMITH, eldest son of Capt. Thomas and Rebeckah (Glover) Smith, was born in Boston, May 16, 1678, and died in Saco, District of Maine, Feb. 19, 1742, in his 64th year.

At the age of twenty-one years he succeeded to the estate on Dock Square, which formerly belonged to his great-grandfather, John Glover, Esq., and passed by him to his grandfather, Mr. Habackuk Glover, who left it to his only surviving child and heir, Rebeckah, the widow of Capt. Thomas Smith, Sen., who on her second marriage with Capt. Thomas Clarke, left it in trust to Peter Sargeant and Benjamin Brown, Esqrs., until her eldest son Thomas arrived at the age of manhood. His share in the estate being only one fifth, the other four-fifths were subsequently obtained from his brother John and his sisters by deeds bearing date March 13, 1707, wherein "John Smith, Merchant, of Boston, conveys to his brother Thomas Smith one fifth part of a house and land situated at the head of the Great Dock in Boston, with all its privileges and appurtenances;" and Anne Smith and Rebeckah Smith in their rights, and Nathaniel Lyndall and Elizabeth his wife in her right, also each convey to him one fifth part of the same estate. The trustees, Peter Sargeant and Benjamin Brown, Esqs., having performed their duty in carrying out the purport and intention of the will of Capt. Thomas Smith, Sen., were discharged from their bonds, and Thomas Smith the successor assumed the payment of the perpetual annuity to Harvard College, which before had

11*

been paid by the trustees. He became a prominent man in Boston and resided there till about 1730, at which time he left and settled in Saco, Maine. He was largely engaged in the speculation of lands at the eastward, and kept a block house or store-house for the supply of the Indian tribes located in that region, and was some time known as Truck Master for the Indians at Saco and the adjacent villages. He left a large estate to his widow and surviving children.

Thomas Smith was twice married, and had, in all, thirteen children. First, May 9, 1701, he was married to Mary Corwin, of Salem, by whom he had eight children. She was the daughter of Judge Corwin by his wife Elizabeth Sheafe, and was born in Salem about 1680, at the "Old Corwin House," which is said to be still standing on the corner of Essex and North Streets. She died in Boston, July 27, 1716, aged thirty-six years, and Capt. Thomas Smith was married a second time to Sarah Oliver, of Boston, daughter of Nathaniel and Elizabeth (Brattle) Oliver, Oct. 9, 1717. By her he had five children, who all died in infancy, or at a very young age. Sarah, his second wife, survived him and held her right of dower in the estate at Dock Square, and assumed the payment of the perpetual annuity to Harvard College from the income during her life. The date of her death has not been ascertained.

Children of Capt. THOMAS and MARY (CORWIN) SMITH, born in Boston and baptized there:

+12. Thomas, b. March 10, 1701–2; m. Sarah Tyng, of Woburn.
+13. John, b. Feb. 2, 1703; m. Mercy Bridgham, of Boston.
  14. Samuel, b. Nov. 29, 1705; d. Aug. 23, 1712, aged 6 years.
  15. Mary, b. May 30, 1708; m. Owen Harris, of Boston (perhaps).
  16. Rebeckah, b. Jan. 24, 1710; d. in Boston, Aug. 6, 1740, aged 30 years.
  17. Margaret, b. Dec. 11, 1711; d. Jan. 12, 1742, aged 32 years.
  18. Hannah, b. Oct. 26, 1713; d. Sept. 14, 1714, aged 11 mos.
  19. Elizabeth, b. March 2, 1715; d. April 24, 1724, aged 9 years.

By wife SARAH OLIVER:

  20. Sarah, b. Sept. 16, 1718; d. Oct. 28, 1721, aged 3 years.
  21. Anne, a twin, b. Nov. 3, 1719; d. Dec. 2, 1719, aged 1 mo.
  22. Bethiah, a twin, b. Nov. 3, 1719; d. Jan. 2, 1720, aged 20 ms.
  23. Anne, 2d, b. April 22, 1721; d. Oct. 1, 1725, aged 15 months.
  24. Sarah, b. May 15, 1724; d. May 27, 1724, aged 12 days.

Capt. Thomas Smith died intestate.

March 3, 1742, Letters of Administration were granted to Sarah Smith, his widow, and to John Smith, of Boston, merchant.

Inventory of the Estate.

Boston, June 22, 1742. We the subscribers, being appointed to make an appraisement of the estate of Thomas Smith, Esq., late of Boston, Dec^d, intestate, have valued the foregoing articles as exhibited by the Administrators on the estate, the amount whereof is five thousand seven hundred and forty three pounds, ten shillings and three pence, in bills of old tenor.   WILLIAM TYLER,
                                                JEFFE BEDGOOD,
                                                DANIEL HENCHMAN.

Suffolk ss. Sarah Smith and John Smith, Administrators, presented the aforegoing under oath, that it is a true and perfect inventory of the estate of Thomas Smith, Esq., Dec^d, so far as hath come to their knowledge, and that if more appear hereafter they will cause the same to be added. The subscribers and Appraisers were all at the same time sworn as the law directs. JOSIAH WILLARD, *Judge of Probate.*
                              ANDREW BELCHER, *Register.*

Boston, June 22, 1742.

By the HON. JOSIAH WILLARD, *Judge of Probate.*

Suffolk ss. To Caleb Lyman, Jonas Clarke, Thomas Hubbard, Esq., Capt. William Downes and Deacon John Phillips: You or any three of you are hereby empowered to make a just and equal division and partition of the Real estate of Thomas Smith, Esq., late of Boston aforesaid, Dec^d, intestate, of which he died seized, by setting off to his relict Widow, Sarah Smith, her Dower or Thirds therein according to your best Skill and judgment, as the law directs; the which you have been shown. And you are to make return of your doings hereof unto the register's office as soon as may be. Given under my hand and seal of the said Court of Probate at Boston, this 2^d day of August, 1742.   J. WILLARD, *Judge of Probate.*

Pursuant to the Within appointment to set off to the Relict Widow, Sarah Smith, her Dower or Third part of her late husband's estate Thomas Smith, Esq., Dec^d, Real estate shown to us, We have accordingly attended to that service, and unanimously agreed that her Right of Dower or Third part of said Dec^d estate on Dock Square, Boston, viz., measuring in the front twenty-nine feet and five inches on a South West line, bounded by the house and land of Joshua Blanchards and there measuring Fifty ft. thereon, a return on the back part of said Blanchard's yard, and there measuring fifteen feet and one inch; then running on a Northerly line, and bounded by the land of Mr. John Holyoke and there measuring twenty-six feet; then running on the back part of said Holyoke's land three feet, may then run on a rear line bounded by a Warehouse now in possession of Mr. Joseph Sherburn and measuring Seven and a half feet; and on a return by the said Warehouse on a South East line measuring eighteen feet and five inches, and on a North East line measuring sixteen feet and two inches; and from thence measuring through the Entry of the Mansion house home to the Front on Dock Square on a South East line Fifty-nine feet. Together with the Dwelling house and buildings on said Land and now in the possession of Mr. Joseph Lewis, Tobac-

conist; with the privileges of the Entry into the Street, excepting a Shop included within said lines, and in the possession of Mr. Thomas Eastwick, Jeweller, running in the Front on Dock Square seven feet and nine inches, and on the rear seven feet and four inches ; and on the East side Thirteen feet and six inches ; which house and land as above described we agree to be her Dower. Provided she pay annually to the Treasurer of Harvard College the sum of Five pounds passable money of New England; being an encumbrance on the estate of said Deceased.   CALEB LYMAN,
                                                              JONAS CLARK,
                                                              THOMAS HUBBARD,
                                                              WILLIAM DOWNES,
                                                              JOHN PHILIPS.

    Boston, 6th August, 1742. The foregoing being presented by the subscribers as the Widow's Thirds on the Estate of Thomas Smith, Esq., Dec⁴, I do hereby allow and approve.

                              JOSEPH WILLARD, *Judge of Probate.*

    The following items are extracted from the inventory. Among the household articles prized was one family picture, 30s.; two small ones, 60s.; one family picture in a gilt frame, 15s.; a family Arms in a gilt frame, 4s.; 145 oz. plate, £210–5 shill.; Negro Man named Henry and Clothes, £90; Negro Man named Robert and Clothes, £180; Negro Woman named Tamar, £150; houses and Lands in the occupation of Mr. Sherburn, Mr. Randall and Mr. Lewis, £4000. Whole amount, £5743 10 3.

    (8) JOHN SMITH, second son of Capt. Thomas and Rebeckah (Glover) Smith, was born in Boston, July 1, 1681, and it is supposed died there about 1737. He was a merchant in Boston, and was at one time largely engaged in land speculations at the eastward. It is stated in the Journal of his nephew, Rev. Thomas Smith of Portland, that he was at one time Proprietors' Clerk in North Yarmouth, before that town was incorporated, and largely interested in the ancient town of Falmouth, now Portland.
    In 1706 he purchased Long Island* of James Russell, of Charlestown, Mass. A reference is made to this transaction in the will of his mother, Mrs. Rebeckah Clarke, of Boston.
    Under date of July 13, 1717, his name is enrolled among a list

---

* Long Island was one of the Islands in Casco Bay, near Portland, and was said to contain six hundred and fifty acres of land belonging to the town of Falmouth, in the Province of Maine, but under the jurisdiction of Massachusetts.

of petitioners to the General Court of Massachusetts for protection to the Proprietors' lands, and aid in building up the waste places made desolate by ravages of the Indians.

He was co-Executor to his mother's will, in 1711–12. In 1724 his name appears on the agreement of the heirs of John Glover, Esq. of Dorchester and Boston, as a sharer in the Common and Undivided Lands in Dorchester New Grant.

Feb. 5, 1707, he was married, by Rev. Benjamin Colman, to Martha Brenton, of Bristol, R. I., eldest daughter of Major Ebenezer Brenton, and grand-daughter of Gov. Brenton, of Rhode Island. By her he had eight children:

25. Martha,   b. Dec. 7, 1708 ;   d. Nov. 6, 1709.   (Boston Rec.)
26. Rebekah, b. July 31, 1710 ; d. Sept. 8, 1716, aged 6 years.
27. Martha,   b. April 27, 1712 ; d. Jan. 29, 1714, in her 2d year.
28. Anne,   b. July 14, 1715 ; d. Oct. 14, 1716, aged 15 months.
29. Jahleel, b. Nov. 20, 1717 ; d. same year.
30. Sarah,   b. April 9, 1719.
31. John,   b. Nov. 4, 1720.
32. Martha,   b. April 21, 1723.

As no deaths are found recorded of the last three children, it is supposed they lived to attain the age of maturity, and perhaps have descendants; but none of them have been identified or become known to us.

(9) ELIZABETH SMITH, third daughter of Capt. Thomas and Rebeckah (Glover) Smith, was born in Boston, Feb. 10, 1685; baptized at the first Church there, Feb. 14, 1685, and died in Bristol, R. I. She was twice married: first, to Nathaniel Lyndall, Esq., of Salem, May 21, 1706, by whom she had two children. He was son of the Hon. Timothy and Mary (Veren) Lyndall, and was born in Salem, Nov. 4, 1679. He became a merchant, and established himself in Boston, where he resided at the time of his marriage, and died there Sept. 2, 1711, in his thirty-second year, leaving a widow and one child.

Children of NATHANIEL and ELIZABETH (SMITH) LYNDALL, born in Boston:

33. Nathaniel, b. Feb. 16, 1707–8, H. C. 1728; settled probably at
        Newport, and died there in 1776.
34. Elizabeth, b. April 17, 1711 ; died in infancy.

And by Major Ebenezer Brenton, her second husband:

35. Anne, m. { 1st, —— Concklin.
              { 2d, Martin Howard, Esq.

Will of Nathaniel Lyndall.

Sept. 1, 1711. Nathaniel Lyndall, of Boston, Shopkeeper, being sick and weak in Body, but of sound mind and memory—After providing for just debts and funeral expenses, gives his beloved wife Elizabeth Lyndall, in view of her thirds, Five hundred Pounds in Money, with all his household stuff and furniture, she paying to "my brother Thomas Smith a debt due to him of Sixty pounds and interest."

Gives to his Honored Mother, Mary Lyndall, a decent suit of Mourning Cloaths; his seal and Ring to his two brothers, James Lyndall and Timothy Lyndall; his wearing apparel, linen and woolen, to be equally divided between them, and to his aforenamed brother Timothy his watch.

All the rest and residue of his Estate, both Real and Personal, he gives to his son Nathaniel Lyndall and to his heirs forever, to be possessed and enjoy edas soon as he shall attain to the full age of twenty-one years; And if he should die before he attain that age, he gives all that accrues to his son of his Estate to his aforenamed James Lyndall and Timothy Lyndall, to be equally divided between them and their heirs; and the residue of his personal Estate to be equally divided between his brothers and sisters. Constitutes and appoints his beloved wife Elizabeth to be sole Executrix.

                            (Signed) Nathaniel Lyndall.

Witnessed by
          Isaiah Fay,
          Jonathan Barnard,
          Edward Weaver.   Will proved Sept. 17, 1711.

Elizabeth (Smith) Lyndall was married a second time to Ebenezer Brenton, of Newport, R. I., March 6, 1712–13, and went there to reside. She had one child by Ebenezer Brenton, and perhaps others, a daughter Anne, who married first a Concklin, who died; and on the 29th of December, 1749, she was married to Martin Howard, Esq., at the house of her father, Major Ebenezer Brenton, by the Rev. James McSparrow, D.D., Incumbent of St. Paul's Church in Narragansett. They resided, it is said, at Newport. There was issue from this marriage—two daughters, one of whom married James Center of Newport, R. I., and died soon after, and he married the other daughter. There was issue from this marriage — Mary Center, a granddaughter of Judge Howard, who married Capt. Harris, of the revenue service, and resided in the mansion house of her grandfather, situated on North Main Street. Mrs. Harris has since died.

Thus it appears that there were descendants in this line from Ebenezer and Elizabeth (Smith) Brenton, which reached three generations, in the names of Howard, Center and Harris, who were lineally descended from Habackuk Glover. Probably there were others who have not been noticed.

Will of Major Ebenezer Brenton.

Made the 8 day of June, 1706.   Suff. Prob. Rec., Vol. 16, p. 541.

In the name of God, Amen. I Ebenezer Brenton of Bristol, within the County of Bristol, in the Province of Massachusetts Bay in New England, Merchant, being in Good health and perfect memory, do make and ordain this my last Will and Testament. That is to say, first of all, I recommend my soul, &c. 2dly, his lawful debts and funeral charges are provided for. 3dly, Gives to his son Ebenezer Brenton and to his heirs and assigns forever, One half of his Whole Estate, when he shall arrive at the age of Twenty One years. To his two daughters, Martha Brenton and Sarah Brenton, the other half of his Estate equally divided for their support and maintenance in the time of their minority, and the residue to be delivered unto them when they shall come of lawful age. Constitutes and ordains his honorable and beloved brother, Jahleel Brenton, of Newport, R. I., and Col. Nathaniel Byfield, of Bristol, aforesaid, his Executors.

(Signed)   EBENEZER BRENTON, and Seal.

Witnessed by
Joseph Torry,
Martha Church,
John Cary.   Will proved April 14, 1709.

Brenton's Children's Bond to Nathaniel Byfield.

Vol. 18, p. 174, Suff. Rec.

Know all Men by these Presents, That We, Ebenezer Brenton of Bristol, in the County of Bristol and in the Province of Massachusetts Bay in New England, Merchant, and John Smith of Boston, within the County of Suffolk and in the Province aforesaid, Merchant, are held and firmly bound and obliged unto Nathaniel Byfield, Esq., of the aforesaid Bristol, Executor of the last will and Testament of Major Ebenezer Brenton late of the same place, Deceased, in the full and just sum of Five Hundred Pounds Current money of New England, to be paid unto him the said Nathaniel Byfield, his heirs, Executors, Administrators and Assigns, to the true payment whereof we bind ourselves and each of us by himself, our and each of our heirs, Executors, Administrators and Assigns Joyntly and Severally for the whole and in the whole firmly by these Presents.

Sealed with our seals and dated the fifth day of February, Anno Domini 1713, in the 12th year of Her Majesty's Reign.

The Condition of this present Obligation is such, that Whereas the above bounden Ebenezer Brenton and John Smith in the Right of Martha his wife, son and daughter of the abovenamed Major Ebenezer Brenton, have had and Received of and from the abovenamed Nathaniel Byfield, Executor as aforesaid, their several and respective parts and shares and portions of and in the surplusage of the clear Estate of their said father Major Ebenezer Brenton, Deceased, according to his last will and Testament, all debts, legacies and incidental charges being first proved and discharged according to the said Executor's account of his Administration exhibited upon oath to the Court of Probate (relation thereto being had), have likewise had and received of the said Nathaniel Byfield the part and share and portion of and in the Estate of the said Major Ebenezer Brenton accruing to their sister Sarah Brenton lately deceased, who died a Minor within age, and to whom the said Ebenezer Brenton and John Smith, their Executors and Administrators and each of them respectively, in case it happen that other debts do hereafter appear to be due from the Estate of their said late father Major Ebenezer Brenton (not now known), do refund and pay back to the said Nathaniel Byfield in his capacity of Executor as aforesaid, their several rates, parts and shares of such debt or debts, or Executor's charges, without cover, fault or delay, then the within written Obligation to be void and of none effect, or else to remain in full force and virtue.

EBENEZER BRENTON, and a Seal.
JOHN SMITH, and a Seal.

Signed, sealed and delivered in Presence of us—
        John Spurrier and
        Edward Little (Bristol, R. I.)

Edward Little, one of the witnesses of this Instrument, personally appeared before me the subscriber, one of his Majestic's Justices of the Peace for the County aforesaid, and made oath that he was present and did see Ebenezer Brenton and John Smith sign, seal and deliver this Instrument as their Act and Deed, and that he, with John Spurrier, did set their names thereunto as Witnesses.

Bristol, Sept. 11, 1714.

Thomas Palmer and
Samuel Tyley, for
PAUL DUDLEY, *Register.*

Received, Examined and Recorded, Sept. 11, 1714.

(10) REBECKAH SMITH, third daughter of Capt. Thomas and Rebeckah (Glover) Smith, was born in Boston, Dec. 22, 1687, was baptized on the 25th of the same month, and died after 1748. The place of her death is not known. She was twice married: first, May 12, 1713, to John Gore, A.M., by the Rev. Benjamin Colman. He died November 12, 1720, and left no children. She married, second, Nathaniel Hubbard, Esq., of Dorchester, December 5, 1725.

JOHN GORE, the first husband of Rebeckah Smith, was the son of John and Elizabeth Gore of Roxbury, born there in 1682, and died of smallpox at sea, on his return voyage from England, Nov. 7, 1720, aged 38 years. He graduated at Harvard College in the class of 1702, was Librarian there from 1706 to 1707, and was admitted to the first Church in Cambridge, January 6, 1707.

A sermon occasioned by his death, with an appendix containing something of Mr. Gore's character, was prepared by Rev. William Cooper, of Brattle Street Church; the appendix by Rev. Benjamin Colman, pastor of the same Church. The former was entitled "A Sermon on the lamented death of that ingenious Gentleman, Mr. John Gore, A.M., of Harvard College, in Cambridge, N. E., who died of Small Pox on his return voyage from England, Nov. 7, 1720." In the Appendix it is said :

" The death of Mr. John Gore, which occasioned it, was as lamented a death as has of late been among us. There were several of his near relations and mournful friends in the assembly to whom it was preached."

In the preface it is written: " Mr. Gore was truly an ornament to his country, to the College and to our Church. He was very much the Honor of his order among us, a glory to his Profession, the beauty of the Sea, of Sobriety, Modesty, Literature, and (in a Judgment of Charity) of sincere unaffected piety, makes up his Just character. He was fit to teach either in the school or the pulpit. He was the same abroad as at home, in his ship as well as in his house. To conclude, the last act of his life shewed his generous regard to the safety of his country; for knowing well the terror the Town is in, of the Small Pox, and having had seven of his company ill of that contagious distemper on his voyage from London, he being the only person remaining on board who had not had the distemper, when he cast anchor, and having reason hourly to expect he might be taken down with it, as indeed he was the next day, yet he would not come on shore to his own house, but chose to keep on board his ship, in so cold a season of the year and at such a distance from needed help, rather than to endanger the Town by bringing sickness into it."

The Doctor adds also an observation by Mr. Prince of the News Letter: He says, " Mr. Gore seemed to be set as a rare example for all ship commanders and sea-faring men to observe; that he excelled in Mathematics and Philosophy. A young gentleman who

12

came over passenger with Capt. Gore, writes of him to his brother from Spectacle Island, Nov. 15, 1720, speaking in the highest terms of his dearly beloved Captain."

Will of John Gore.

In the name of God, Amen.

I John Gore of Boston, in the county of Suffolk, in his Majesty's Province of Massachusetts Bay in New England, Mariner, Being bound on a voyage to Sea, and considering the uncertainty of human affairs, especially those attended with such a variety of accidents, and knowing it to be appointed for all men once to die, do make and ordain this to be my last Will and Testament, vizt. Principally and first of all I give and recommend my soul into the hands of God who gave it, and my body to the Earth or Sea to be buried in a decent Christian manner, nothing doubting that at the Resurrection I shall receive it back again by the Almighty Power of God.

And as to my Worldly Estate it hath pleased Almighty God to bless me with in this life, I give, devise and dispose in the following manner. *Imprimis.* I give and bequeathe to my Honored Mother Eliza-beth Tucker, for her support and maintenance during her natural life, Six Pounds of Lawful money of that Province, to be paid yearly, and at her death Six Pounds to defray her funeral charges.

Item. If it shall please God to take away my life abroad and prosper my interest that goeth with me, or if the vessel I proceed in shall miscarry and the insurance I have ordered to be made shall be paid and arrive safe, I give and bequeathe to my brothers Samuel Gore and Obadiah Gore, and my sister Margaret Healy, each of them the sum of Ten Pounds, to be paid to them after the death of my Mother.

Item. I give and bequeath to my dearly beloved wife Rebecca, All and singular my Real and Personal Estate (except the above mentioned), if she shall have no issue by me, but if she shall have issue, be it son or daughter, I give and bequeath to such issue the sum of Two Hundred Pounds, and utterly disannul the paragraph to my brothers and sister.

I likewise constitute, make and ordain my wife Rebecca above-mentioned my sole Executrix of this my last Will and Testament, if she shall have no issue by me. But if God shall give her a son or daughter by me, I desire my very good friend and brother Mr. John Jeffries will act as an Executor with my wife.

And I do hereby utterly disallow, revoke and disannul all and every former Will, Testament, Legacy and bequest executed by me in any ways before named, willed, bequeathed, Ratified and confirmed, and this and no other to be my last Will and Testament. In witness whereof, I have hereunto set my hand and seal, this 8th day of November, 1717.   JOHN GORE, and a seal.

N. B. If my house be destroyed by fire, or any part of my Estate be destroyed by fire, or any Extraordinary Providence of God, I revoke all and every of the above Legacies. JOHN GORE, and a seal.

Signed, Sealed, Published and Declared by the said
John Gore as his last Will and Testament, in presence
of us,   Richard Love,
                               Thomas Laneklin,
                               Henry Gibbs.

The above will was made three years before his death, and was
presented for probate by his widow Rebeckah Gore, in December,
1720.

NATHANIEL HUBBARD, Esq., the second husband of Mrs. Rebecca
(Smith) Gore, was born in Boston, Oct. 13, 1680; graduated at
Harvard College in the class of 1698, and died at Rehoboth, Bristol
County, R. I., in 1748. He was the son of John and Anne (Leverett)
Hubbard, and grandson of Rev. William Hubbard, the historian of
New England. His father was an eminent merchant of Boston, and
for some years a resident in Braintree, where he was the owner of
extensive Iron Works, and carried on the iron business largely until
the time of his death. He died in Boston, January 8th, 1709–10.
His mother was Anne, daughter of Gov. John Leverett, of Mass.,
who died in Boston, March 16th, 1678–9. She died in 1717.

Nov. 29, 1693, Mr. Nathaniel Hubbard was chosen by the Church
at Braintree to go to Dedham as delegate to assist in the ordination
of Rev. Joseph Belcher. Mr. Torrey, Mr. Hubbard and Mr. Danforth laid their hands upon the head of Mr. B., and Mr. Fiske gave
the Right Hand of Fellowship.

In 1708, he is said to have been a petitioner, with others of
Dorchester, for liberty to dig iron ore in the Undivided Lands in
Dorchester New Grant.

He was of Braintree in 1713–14, and is said to have purchased
twenty-one acres of land there, situated near the Iron Works, and
bounded on the highway. There was a dwelling house, also a barn
and shop on this land, which, Oct. 12, 1720, he sold again to Thomas Vinton, the former owner and grantor. He was soon after in
Dorchester, and makes another conveyance to Thomas Vinton, bloomer, of Braintree, of one acre and a half of land in Braintree, adjoining Monotaquod River, upon a part of which the Braintree Iron
Works now stand. He removed to Dorchester about this time, took
an active part in the affairs of town, and was chosen Moderator at
the town meetings. He owned land in the south part of the town,
now Milton. His name stands among a list of those who were
liable to pay province tax in the years 1720 to 1734.

He was twice married: first, at Braintree, Aug. 25, 1707, to Mrs. Elizabeth Nelson, by Francis Malauny, Esq. They had four children, born and recorded in Braintree, as follows: Elizabeth, born Dec. 9, 1708, m. —— Munday; John, born March 28, 1709-10; Nathaniel, born Feb. 28, 1711-12, m. Hannah Wiswall, of Dorchester, in 1763; Anna, born Nov. 12, 1713. Another son was born in Dorchester and recorded on Milton town records as follows: "Leverett, the son of Nathaniel Hubbard, Esq., was born in Dorchester, Dec. 23d, 1723." He had also a daughter Margaret, of whom no record of birth has been found. His wife dying in 1724, he was married the next year to Mrs. Rebeckah Gore, widow of John Gore, A.M., who survived him. It has not been ascertained at what time he left Dorchester. He paid taxes there in 1739, but he was at Rehoboth some time before that, and it is believed he removed there soon after his second marriage. It is said he was a man highly distinguished for his ability, learning and sound judgment. He became a prominent man in Rehoboth, owned large estates there and in Bristol, was elected Judge of Probate for the County of Bristol, and continued to serve in that honorable position until his decease in 1748. He was also elected to other important offices, which he filled with honor and distinction.

Will of Nathaniel Hubbard, Esq.

In the name of God, Amen.

I Nathaniel Hubbard of Rehoboth, in New England, do make and ordain and declare this to be my last Will and Testament, revoking all former Wills by me heretofore made.

And first of all, before I settle my Worldly affairs, I do most seriously and humbly recommend my Soul and bodye into the hands of God in our Lord Jesus Christ, hoping for pardon and Salvation through his alone merits and Righteousness. Let my bodye be buried according to the custom of God's people amongst whom I now live, without pomp or vanity, at the disposition of my Executors, save only that they be restrained as to the funeral charges, so far that my wife only have liberty to take and make for herself such a suit of mourning apparel as she shall choose, and no money shall be allowed the other Executors, or any of their children, but each one find themselves out of what I have given them by Will.

And for settling that portion of my Worldly Goods which it hath pleased God to bestow upon me, I do order and bestow the same as followeth.

Imp. Let all my just debts and dues, with expenses of my funeral, be discharged as soon as conveniently may be after my decease.

Item. I give and devise to my Kinsman Nathaniel Ruggles, son of my Sister Mary Ruggles, deceased. One Tenth part of my Lands at the Place called Amos Congers, in the Eastern part of and near to George's River (so called), to be to him and his heirs forever; Provided he deliver up to my Executors, cancelled, my Bond given to Mary his Mother conditionally for my giving her a Deed of said tenth part. Yet if I shall give him a Deed thereof or otherwise discharge said Bond in my lifetime, then is this Gift or lease to become entirely void.

Item. I give and bequeath unto my Kinsman William Hart, and to my Kinswoman Rebecca Ruggles, the children of my Sister Rebeckah Hart, One tenth part, that is to say, two parts of said one tenth to William Hart, and one third part thereof to Rebeckah Ruggles, to be to them and their heirs forever; This Gift on condition that they deliver up to my Executors, cancelled, my Bond conditional for my giving them a Deed of One tenth part.

Item. I give and devise to my three sons, Nathaniel, Leverett and John Hubbard, All the remaining part of my Lands and Estates at Amos Congers or anywhere to be found at the Eastward of Kennebeck River. Also the aforesaid two tenths if I should discharge the before mentioned Bonds in my Life time, otherwise than by giving Deeds of the Lands. To have and to hold the same in manner and proportion as follows. That is to say, One moiety or half part of all the Main Lands, also the whole of my Right in the Islands, unto my eldest son John and his heirs forever. Also One fourth part of all on the Main Land to my Son Nathaniel and to his heirs forever. And One fourth part of all the Main Lands to my son Leverett Hubbard.

Item. I give to my son John, my Silver hilted sword, and my Watch and Seal, and my yellow stocked gun.

Item. I give to my son Nathaniel my other gun and sword, a clock I have already given into his hand, one half of my books, save the Bibles hereafter named and those books brought by my Wife, my Spanish Secretary, and all that is due to me either by Bond or by Books from him.

Item. I give to my son Leverett my clock, one of my desks, and one half of all my Books save the Bibles named, and those brought by my Wife, Four pictures, two of them —— pictures, and two of them Lings; and two more that used to hang up in my green room at Bristol; and two servants, Jacob and his Wife, saving the use of the servants to my Wife during her lifetime. Also I give him all my utensils of husbandry, my Chair and Caravan, saving the use of my Caravan to my Wife during her life. And I also give him my Bible, with the Genealogy of the Tribes and Line of the Blessed Saviour.

Item. I give to my daughter Munday All that she is indebted to me by Bond or Books or Note, with what I have given her at marriage, makes her about equal with her sisters.

Item. I give to my daughter Anne Hubbard, my Silver Tankard, my largest walnut frame Looking-Glass, my finest Damask Tablecloth, with Six Napkins the same; One Feather bed, bolster and pillows, and two or three blankets, my Wife shall choose; my Diamond Ring, with a Pearl Necklace which I have given unto her already. I give her also one of the Bibles and half of the Books that came by my Wife.

12*

Item. I give to my daughter Margaret Hubbard my best feather bed and bolster and pillows I had with her mother, my best diaper Table Cloth, with eleven napkins of the same ; Also a silver Porringer, with six spoons marked N.* E. ; 10 Leather Chairs, 1 Couch, a Walnut frame Looking Glass, with square Chamber Table ; my Negro named Kate, with time remaining in Phillis by Indenture ; Also my Bible with silver Clasps, and One half the books brought by my Wife. And Let my daughters Anne and Margaret have my Scarlet Cloak between them.

Item. I give to my Wife and Margaret my Wearing Linen in equal parts, and all the rest of my Wearing Apparell I give to my three sons to be equally divided between them.

Item. I give to my sister Anne Ten pounds of Province bills of Old tenor, to be paid by my Executors within six months after my decease ; and it is my will that my Wife pay to my Sister Anne yearly Six pounds Old tenor in discharge of my Bonds as an Annuity for that sum. And my children out of what I have given them shall each of them, after my Wife's decease, pay to her yearly the sum of 4 pounds Old Tenor during her mortal life, in Lieu of said Annuity.

Item. All the rest of my household goods I give to my two daughters Anne and Margaret, to be equally divided between them. Saving the use thereof to be to my Wife during her natural life.

Let my Executors sell all my Stock of Cattle, Sheep and Horse and Swine, except what I shall hereafter dispose of, to enable them to pay my debts.

And whereas I have laid out Ten Lotts of Land on the East side of my farm at Bristol, in the Colony of Rhode Island, fronting on Bristol Harbor on the East, and lying between an enclosed Meadow on the North, called the Meadow before the House, and an enclosed Meadow on the South, called the East Meadow (bounds described), I give to my eldest Son John the 1st and 10th Lots, to Nathaniel the 2d and 9th Lots, to daughter Anne the 4th and 7th Lotts, to daughter Margaret the 5th and 6th Lotts ; to hold to them and their heirs forever. The 3d and 8th Lotts I give the use and improvement to my daughter Elizabeth Munday during her natural life.

To my Son John the South Westerly part of my farm at said Bristol, being Forty five acres (bounds described).

[Disposes of all his lands and farm to his six children, they paying to his wife fifty-six pounds five shillings and sixpence annually during her natural life.]

Item. I give to my faithful and beloved Wife Rebeckah, in Lieu of her Dower, the sum of 150 pounds in bills of Credit ; One half my Dwelling House, with Yard, Garden and other Lands.

[Appoints his wife Rebeckah and sons Nathaniel and Leverett his Executors.]   Signed, &c.   NATHANIEL HUBBARD, and a Seal.

Witnessed by
Daniel Carpenter,
Eleazer Tiffany,
Benjamin Sheldon.

Inventory taken Feb. 25, 1747–8.   Value of Estate, £4678 0 6.

Nathaniel Hubbard, the eldest son of Nathaniel Hubbard, Esq., married in Dorchester. He and Hannah Wiswall were published Dec. 24th, 1763. They probably went to Bristol, and settled on his estate of inheritance there.

Leverett Hubbard, the youngest son of Judge Hubbard, married Anne Jaffrey (widow of Nathaniel Pierce), Dec. 6, 1769, and died Jan. 2, 1793. She was the daughter of George, Jr. and Sarah (Jeffries) Jaffrey, of Piscataqua, and was born there or at Portsmouth, N. H., Oct. 26, 1723. She married 1st, Nathaniel Pierce, Dec. 20, 1744, who died Aug. 27, 1762; and 2d, Leverett Hubbard, Esq., of Bristol. She died Dec. 17, 1790.

(11) ANNE CLARKE, daughter of Rebeckah (Glover) Smith and Capt. Thomas Clarke, was born in Boston, Sept. 2, 1694, and died there, or, perhaps, in Dorchester. She was married to John Jeffries, Esq., of Boston, Sept. 24, 1713. She was living in 1724, as her name appears, with her seal affixed, to a bond which was signed by the grandchildren and great-grandchildren of the Hon. John Glover, Esq., of Boston, at the time of the surveying of his undivided lands in the town of Stoughton. (See p. 77.)

The only child of JOHN and ANNE (CLARKE) JEFFRIES was

36. Anne, b. June 25, 1719 or 20; d. Aug. 23, 1730, aged 10 yrs.

JOHN JEFFRIES, Esq., the husband of Anne Clarke, was born in Boston, Feb. 5, 1688, and died there Dec. 15, 1777, aged 89 years. He was buried in Lidgett's Tomb, No. 83, in the South Burying place. In December, 1710, he visited London and remained there three years, returning in April, 1713, and was married to Anne Clarke the September following. He was a merchant, and lived in Boston, on Tremont Street, opposite the King's Chapel. His parents were David, Sen., and Elizabeth (Usher) Jeffries, who were married in Boston, Sept. 15, 1698. His father was born at Rhoades, in England, Nov. 18, 1658, and came to Boston in New England, arriving there May 9, 1677, and became a respectable and wealthy merchant. His mother was the only child of John and Elizabeth (Lidgett) Usher, born June 18, 1669, and died June 27, 1698, leaving eight children.

Abstract of the Will of John Jeffries.

Prob. Rec. Suff.   Lib. 69, fol. 76.

After the payment of his just debts he orders his estate to be distributed as follows, viz. :   To his

Nephew David Jeffries, Esq., houses and lands situated in Brattle Street, Boston, in Crooked Lane and Exchange Lane, which I bought of my Honored father, David Jeffries, Dec^d, to be to him my said nephew forever, and to his heirs after him.

To Dr. John Jeffries, son of my brother David Jeffries before named, my Mansion house which is in Tremont Street (so called), and which I bought of George Craddock, Esq., Dec^d (in 1727), to be to him the said Doct. John Jeffries and to the heirs of his body forever.   Also to him the said Doct. John Jeffries, all my interest and claim to Tracts of Land at the Eastward.   Also two large Silver Candlesticks.

To John Jeffries, the third son of the aforesaid Doct. John Jeffries and Sarah his Wife, all my land lying in Rutland in the County of Worcester.

To Anne Jeffries, daughter of Dr. John Jeffries, all my Land lying in Dorchester in the County of Suffolk, now under the improvement of Mr. Edward Bird.   Also to Anne Jeffries aforesaid, my Gold Necklace, Diamond Rings and Gold Buckles which of late belonged to my Wife* Anne (Clarke) Jeffries as they stand in her cabinet.

To George Jeffries, Esq., Anne Hubbard, Wife of Leverett Hubbard, Esq., and Samuel Wentworth, all of Portsmouth, New Hampshire, children of my deceased Sisters Sarah Jeffries and Rebecca Wentworth, Thirty pounds in money each.

To Sarah Usher, Kinswoman of my Dec^d Wife, Ten pounds in Lawful money.

To Hannah Goffe, who now lives with me, a bed and bedding and Twenty pounds in money.

To David Jeffries, Esq., and Doct. John Jeffries, my nephews, all my household Goods, Furniture, Pictures and Plate, to be equally divided between them.

(The residue of the estate he gives to David Jeffries, Esq., before named, and appoints him his sole Executor.)

(Signed)   JOHN JEFFRIES.

Feb. 17, 1777.

> Robert Pierpont,
> William Breed,   } *Witnesses.*
> Thomas Edwards,

Oct. 28, 1733, George Craddock, Esq., and Mary his wife, sold to John Jeffries, Esq., a messuage, land and tenement, the same being the mansion house of Samuel Myles Clark, in Boston, bounded by Col. Townsend.   Consideration, £3000.

---

* Anne Clarke, daughter of Capt. Thomas and Rebeckah Glover (Smith) Clarke, who died childless.

[*Fifth Generation.*]

(12) THOMAS SMITH, eldest son of Capt. Thomas and Mary
(Corwin) Smith, was born in Boston, March 10, 1702, and died in
Portland, Monday, May 25, and was buried on Friday, May 29, 1795.
He graduated at Harvard College in the class of 1720, gave himself
'to the study of Divinity, and became a clergyman. After preaching
as a candidate in several towns in New England, he was finally settled in the ancient town of Falmouth (now Portland), in Maine. A
biographical memoir has been written of him by his colleague and
successor in the ministry, which is accessible to the public. It contains an account of his life and acts, aided by his Journal, which he
commenced in 1719, and continued until within a few years of his
death, to 1788. This Journal covered a period of nearly seventy
years, and is exceedingly interesting, showing that both in public and
private life he was a man of uncommon excellence and ability, and
fulfilled all the duties which devolved on him with distinction and
honor.

Rev. Thomas Smith was thrice married: first, to Sarah Tyng, Sept.
12, 1728. She was a daughter of William Tyng, Esq., of Woburn,
was born there, and died in Portland, Oct. 1, 1742. They had eight
children.

March 1, 1744, he married, second, Mrs. Olive (Plaisted) Jordan,
the widow of Samuel Jordan, of Saco, Maine. She was a native of
Berwick in that State, and died suddenly in Portland, Jan. 3, 1763,
in her 65th year.

He married, third, Aug. 12, 1766, the widow Elizabeth Wendell,
who survived him and died March 16, 1799, at the age of 83 years.

Children of Rev. THOMAS and SARAH (TYNG) SMITH, born in
Falmouth, now Portland:

37. Thomas, b. Sept. 19, 1729 ; d. the next February, aged 5 mos.
+38. Peter Thacher, b. June 14, 1731 ; m. Elizabeth Wendell, of
    Boston.
+39. Lucy, b. Feb. 22, 1734 ; m. Hon. Thomas Saunders, of Glou-
    cester.
+40. Thomas, b. Sept. 12, 1735 ; m. Lucy Jones, of Portland.
+41. William, b. Dec. 18, 1736 ; d. Oct. 16, 1754, aged 18 years.
+42. John,   b. Oct. 14, 1738 ; d. unm. Dec. 26, 1773, aged 35 yrs.
+43. Sarah,   b. Nov. 14, 1740 ; m. Dea. Richard Codman, of Port-
    land, Maine.

The following memorandum is prefixed to Mr. Smith's Journal in the year 1750:

I was born on the 10th of March, 1701–2.
I was admitted to College July, 1716.
Took my first degree in 1720.
I began to preach April 19, 1722.
I came to Falmouth June 22, 1725.
I was ordained March 8, 1727.
I was married Sept. 12, 1728.
My Father died Feb. 19, 1741–2.
My Wife died Oct. 1, 1742.
I was married the 2d time, March 1st, 1743.
Thomas went to Boston, April 12, and was bound to Mr. Scollay for 6 years and nine months, July 3, 1750.
William went to Mr. Grant, Nov. 24, 1750.

1742. Jan. 2. I got home from a journey to Piscataqua, where I have been to observe and affect myself with Gods Grace.
Jan. 29. I rode with my wife and preached a Lecture at Mr. Frost's, where the work broke out.
Jan. 31. The blessedest Sabbath Falmouth ever knew.
Feb. 19. My Father died Last night.
March 12. I set out with my brother on a Journey to Boston.
April 3. I returned from Boston.
June 14. I set out with my brother on a journey to Boston.
June 17. Got to Boston. July 10, got home.
Oct. 1. My dear Wife died Last night between 2 and 3 o'clock in the afternoon.
June 22, 1743. I rode with my Sister* to a Ministers' meeting in Scarborough; had a Lecture; we went to declare our sense of the late religious appearances.
Nov. 1757. My Son Peter keeps school and preaches at Weymouth.
May 17, 1765. Wiswall returns from London.
Aug. 10, 1766. I was married to the Widow Wendell.
Jan. 10, 1773. (An account of his son John, who died with apoplexy.)
Jan. 10, 1774. My Son Saunders died.
Feb. 10, 1776. A fatal day. Hear of the death of my son Thomas. He has left a widow, but no children. Died intestate, 41 years of age.

He was a landholder, and gives the following estimate of his estates after the death of his father.

Oct. 3d, 1742. *An Account of what Estate belongs to Mr. Thomas Smith, on pages 16, 17 and 18 of his Journal.*

Imprimis. His Mansion House, barn, &c., upon a three acre lot of land, given him by the town of Falmouth.

* Mary Smith was the only unmarried sister living at this time.

Joining hereto under the same enclosure, is a three acre lot bought of the widow of Mr. Walton.

Another 3 acre lot bought of Mr. Dunnevan.

Another, bought of Mr. Bowman. These lie to the westward of the house.

Then to the eastward a three acre lot bought of Mr. Cob, and about an acre and a half bought of Mr. Wheeler.

Item. Joining to these, but not in the same enclosure, is a three acre lot bought of Mr. East, which extends from said Smith's fence to the burial place, and is bounded by the fence or line that shuts in Munjoy's neck.

Item. A three acre lot joining the ministry lot, which was given to Mr. Smith by the Town, as his three acre lot, and which lies between Mr. Wheeler's on the East and Mr. Bramhall's on the West.

Item. About Sixty Acres and a part of an acre on Munjoy's Neck, as may be seen by the particular deeds on record.

Item. A third part of Peak's Island, and a third part of House Island.

Item. A sixth part of Ammoncongan farm, bought of John Munjoy, together with a third part of salt marsh belonging to it, which lies at Capisick, before Dea" Cobb's land and others.

Item. A sixth part of a large tract of land being formerly the half of the same Estate, but sold by Mr. Munjoy to Mr. Ingersoll, whose son-in-law, Mr. Chapman, I bought it of.

Item. My third part of the land the General Court gave to the Tyngs of Major Tyng, in a new Town called Gorham Town, and lying on Presumpscot river, as may be seen by plan on Secretary's Books.

Memorandum. Mr. John Tyng gave my son Peter half of his share in it, which he has often promised, and will give a deed of it if desired.

Item. A sixth part of Col. Gedney's Estate on Royal's River in North Yarmouth, as may be seen by several conveyances on County Records.

Memorandum. I gave bond to Capt. Wear and Mr. Fellows to pay their part of the charge that should arise in trying the title of the whole, and I have done it. I expect they have given me receipt therefor on bond.

Item. Estate my Grandmother Clarke* left me by will, as may be seen by looking at the Will.

Item. My share in the remaining part of my father's estate.

Item. My Library, watch, firelock, wearing apparel and my wife's, and the furniture of the house.

Item. Several bonds, viz., Mr. Bayley's, Capt. Larabee's, Mr. Clough's, &c.

Item. Several debts, more especially some hundreds of pounds, the parish and town owes, which was, as I could recon on September 1, 1742, about £800, besides other years not cleared, and I know nothing about. But I would not have the parish ever sued for the same,

* His grandmother Clarke was Rebeckah, daughter of Habackuk and Hannah (Eliot) Glover.

nor for the old arrears five years back, only would have the account settled that they may know that I give them something considerable, and that I never had it in view to get their money, but to do them good and save their souls.

Item.   My stock of Creatures, my Chaise, Saddles and bridles.

Item.   My share in several tracts of land belonging to Munjoy's estate, which are something in the dark, and therefore never purposely sought after by me.

Item.   My share in my Aunt Corwin's Estate and my aunt Thacher's in Mr. Walley's hands.

There is a remark on page 16 of the Journal to the import that "Parson Smith" was probably drawn to the eastern country, and acquired a taste for speculation in real estate from his kinsman John Smith, a merchant of Boston, who was largely interested in lands in North Yarmouth, before that town was incorporated, and was Clerk of the Proprietors of Lands in that place and in Falmouth. He purchased into the Munjoy estate titles and other claims of the old proprietors, which required his presence there. Mr. Smith made other purchases and speculations, which proved successful, as is stated by his biographer.

Among his cotemporaries in the ministry were Thacher, Sewall, Checkley, Prince, Webb and Chauncey, with all of whom he frequently exchanged. In the year 1725 he preached seventeen sabbaths at ancient Falmouth (Portland) before accepting a call there. He preached at Malden, Sandwich and Bellingham, and received a call to settle at the latter place, but declined. He was invited to preach in several other towns in Massachusetts and also in Maine. He lived in an easy and hospitable style, suited to his wealth, entertaining not only the clergymen of that day, but all the most distinguished gentlemen of the age who visited that city were at times his guests, and were freely and generously entertained by him. Among these, he writes in his Journal, were the Governor and Lieut. Governor and other State officers, Winthrop, Hancock, and Bowdoin. Masters of vessels who arrived there from Boston and other cities, were welcomed to his house, and partook of his bounties. He enjoyed festivals and entertainments, public and private, liked to attend dinner parties when given, and gave them often himself, and always wrote and expressed himself highly gratified.

His funeral was attended by the Rev. Mr. Kellogg. A sermon was preached on the sabbath after his funeral, by Rev. Samuel Deane, his colleague and successor, a few extracts from which, it is hoped, will not be deemed superfluous.

The Church in ancient Falmouth was organized on the same day Mr. Smith was ordained its pastor. It was the first Church that was formed to the eastward of Wells. " His pastoral relation was a very happy one, and continued to the day of his decease, which was sixty-eight years and two months and a half, and brought him into the ninety-fourth year of his age. He preached in his turn until the close of the year 1784, and has assisted in the work of the sanctuary until within a year and a half of his decease, by his public prayers. His faculties continued unimpaired, and he performed the service with ability and edification. Not more than one instance is recollected of a ministry in this country so long protracted. For a long course of years he has been considered the most distinguished preacher in this part of the country.

"Though his voice was feeble, the excellency of his elocution, accompanied with a venerable and becoming gravity, rendered his performances very acceptable. Possessing in a high degree the gift and spirit of prayer, devotion could not but be excited in the breasts of the serious part of the audience.

"In sermons his composition was elegant, and his language chaste and correct. Nor was he wanting in animation and pathos in delivery. He was endowed with exquisite sensibility, a lively imagination, and with an extraordinary strength of memory, which he retained with but little abatement to the last. His house was noted for the resort of foreigners and distinguished strangers from all parts of the country, and of his clerical brethren, where they were ever generously entertained."

(13) JOHN SMITH, second son of Capt. Thomas and Mary (Corwin) Smith, was born in Boston, Feb. 2d, 1703, and died there April 6, 1768, aged 65 years. He graduated at Harvard College in the class of 1722. He never studied any profession, but established himself as a merchant in Boston, and was largely engaged in the importation of goods from France and England, and became one of the most distinguished among the early merchants of Boston.

He is thus noticed in the Journal of his brother, the Rev. Thomas Smith, of Portland, old edition, p. 37: —

13

Oct. 31, 1744.   Brother John returned from England to York with Mr. Whitefield.

Nov. 1, 1757.   Brother John returned from England with a vast deal of Goods.

July 31, 1761.   My brother came here in the Capt. Target with the Man of War that went from hence to Boston to take and carry to France the Merchants' money, viz. 22,000 Pounds Sterling.   The Fleet consists of the Man of War, Mr. Target, Three Mast Ships, Darling, Haggart, and Mallard, and two Brigs, making Seven in all.

July, 1765.   Brother John sailed for England ; had a new Coat and Wig.

April 6, 1768.   Brother John dies.

John Smith was married Nov. 24, 1728, to Mercy Bridgham, daughter of Joseph Bridgham and wife Mercy Wensley, or Winslow,* of Boston.   She was born in Boston in 1706, and died there Nov. 26, 1772, aged 66 years.   Her father, Joseph Bridgham, Esq., was an early settler of Boston, and a prominent man; was Representative from 1690 to 1697; lived a short time in Northampton; returned to Boston, and was chosen Deacon and Ruling Elder of the First Church there.   He continued in that office until his death, June 5, 1709.   Her mother was daughter of John and Elizabeth Winslow, of Boston.

Children of JOHN and MERCY (BRIDGHAM) SMITH, born in Boston:

44. Mary,   b. Dec. 29, 1729.
45. John,   b. May 29, 1731 ; d. in infancy.
46. Joseph,   b. May 29, 1733 ; d. before 1761.
47. Margaret,   b. 1735 ; m. Rev. Ebenezer Pemberton, of Boston.
48. Hannah,   b. 1737 ; d. May 2d, 1762, unmarried.

Will of John Smith.

Prob. Rec.   Vol. 67, p. 77.

John Smith of Boston, in the County of Suffolk in New England, being indisposed of body but of sound disposing mind and memory, &c., after his just debts and funeral charges are defrayed, Bequeaths to his loving wife Mercy Smith, one third of all his Estate, Real and personal, The remaining two thirds to his three daughters, viz., Mary, Margaret and Hannah Smith, and to their heirs forever.   Constitutes his wife Mercy sole Executrix, assisted by his Good friends Isaac Royal of Medford and Richard Cary of Charlestown, Merhants, both in the County of Middlesex, as co-Executors.

(Signed)   JOHN SMITH, and Seal.

* Mercy Winslow was twice married: 1st, to Joseph Bridgham, Esq.; 2d, to Hon. Jonathan Cushing.   She died in 1746, and left a will.

Witnessed by
   Samuel Edwards,
   Abraham Chamberlain,
   William Winter.   Probate, May, 1768.

Inventory taken Nov. 11, 1768, by Samuel Grant, Ebenezer Storer and John Timmins. Presented by Mercy Smith, Widow. Amount, £2832 12 9 4.

House and Land in Boston, value, £300. Negro man James.

[*Sixth Generation.*]

(38) PETER THACHER SMITH, second son of Rev. Thomas and Sarah (Tyng) Smith, was born in Portland, June 14, 1731, and died in Windham, Maine, Oct. 26, 1826, in his 96th year. He graduated at Harvard College, and took his first degree in 1753, at the age of twenty-two years. After leaving college he followed the occupation of school-teaching for some years — part of the time at Weymouth, Mass. He also studied divinity. In 1759 he was called to be a minister at Windham, and was ordained there in 1762. In 1790 he was dismissed from the ministry. He continued to reside in Windham, and passed the remainder of his days at that place: was appointed a magistrate, and filled several public offices in the town. His biographer writes of him thus: " He was a man of rare wit and humor, which he was never anxious to restrain; and of free and agreeable address. He was tall and portly in his person, resembling more his mother's than his father's kindred. His venerable appearance in the costume of the bygone age — his breeches, three-cornered hat and ample coat — attracted general observation as he occasionally visited the town of his birth (Portland), over the ruins of which, after it was burned by the British troops in 1775, he bitterly grieved, and which drew from him a sermon preached in the old and shattered meeting-house soon after the sad event, from the memorable words — ' He beheld the city and wept over it.' "

Peter Thacher Smith was twice married. First, to Elizabeth Wendell, daughter of Jacob and Elizabeth (Hunt) Wendell, in Boston, Oct. 8, 1765, by Rev. Dr. Lowell. By her he had all his children. She died Oct. 16, 1799, aged 57. He married, second, Mrs. Jane Loring, third daughter of Shrimpton Hunt and widow of Dr. Loring, of Boston, Nov. 1, 1801.

Children of Rev. PETER THACHER and ELIZABETH (WENDELL) SMITH, born in Windham, Maine:

49. Elizabeth Hunt, b. Aug. 16, 1766 ; m. John Farwell, of Tyngs-
    borough, and died Nov. 28, 1807, aged 41 years.
+50. Sarah, b. April 9, 1767 ; m. Hezekiah Smith.
+51. Lucy, b. Aug. 24, 1769 ; m. Abraham Anderson.
+52. Thomas, b. Oct. 2, 1770 ; m. Polly Barker ; d. Feb. 27, 1802,
    aged 32.
+53. John Tyng, b. March 6, 1772 ; m. Mary Duguid.
 54. Mary, b. July 6, 1774 ; m. Jonathan Winslow, of Albion, Me.
 55. Peter Thacher, b. Nov. 6, 1775 ; d. Nov. 9, 1775, 3 days old.
 56. Anne Wendell, b. March 31, 1777 ; m. Charles Barker.
 57. Rebeckah, b. June 15, 1778 : d. April 19, 1782, aged 4 years.
 58. Susannah Wendell, b. March 31, 1781 ; m. George C. Thomas,
    of Tyngsborough. No issue.
 59. Rebeckah, b. Sept. 25, 1783 ; d. Oct. 31, 1808, unmarried.
+60. Lucretia, b. Nov. 12, 1786 ; m. William Codman, Esq., of
    Portland.

(39) LUCY SMITH, eldest daughter of Rev. Thomas and Sarah
(Tyng) Smith, was born in Portland, Me., Feb. 22, 1734, and died
in Gloucester, Mass., June 5, 1780, in her 47th year.

She was twice married : first, Oct. 2d, 1751, to the Hon. Thomas
Sanders, of Gloucester, born there Aug. 22d, 1739, and died in
Gloucester, Jan. 10, 1774, aged 35 years. They had eleven children. He was a lineal descendant of Thomas Sanders, one of the
first settlers of Cape Ann, who was for many years in the service of
the Provincial Navy. His parents were Thomas and Judith (Robinson) Sanders, who were married in Gloucester in 1728. Thomas
Sanders was their eldest son. He was prepared for College under
the instruction of the Rev. Moses Parsons, entered Harvard College,
and graduated there in the class of 1748. After leaving College, he
engaged in commercial pursuits, became a distinguished citizen in
the town of Gloucester, and was elected to many public offices, in
which he served faithfully. He was Representative from 1761 to
1771, and a Councillor until 1773. He resigned that office at the
close of the year for a more quiet life. He lived seven years after
his retirement from office.

She married, second, the Rev. Eli Forbes. They had no children.

Children of Hon. THOMAS and LUCY (SMITH) SANDERS, born in
Gloucester, Mass. :

+61. Lucy, b. Nov. 24, 1752 ; m. Paul Dudley Sargent, Esq., of
    Boston.
 62. Thomas, b. Dec. 8, 1753 ; d. July 26, 1754, aged 7 m. 18 d.
+63. Judith, b. June 1, 1755 ; m. Thomas Saunders, of Gloucester.
+64. Harriet, b. April 2, 1757 ; m. Major Peter Doliver, of Boston.

+65. Thomas,   b. Mar. 25, 1759 ; m. Elizabeth Elkins, of Salem.
+66. Sarah,   b. Mar. 1, 1761 ; m. Thomas Augustus Vernon.
 67. Charlotte, b. —— 1762 ; d. in 1847, aged 85.   Unmarried.
 68. William, b. —— 1764 ; d. young.
 69. Charles, b. —— 1766 ; d. young.
+70. Joseph,   b. —— 1768 ; Lieut. in U. S. Navy in 1800.
+71. Mary,   b. —— 1770 ; m. Erasmus Babbitt, of Sturbridge.

(40) THOMAS SMITH, third son of Rev. Thomas and Sarah
(Tyng) Smith, was born in Portland, Sept. 12, 1735, and died in
Gloucester, Mass., Feb. 10, 1776, at the house of his sister, Mrs.
Lucy Sanders, aged 41 years, "having earned the epitaph inscribed
on his tombstone, ' That man of honor and integrity.' " He was
married Oct. 20, 1758, to Lucy Jones, daughter of Phineas Jones,
Esq., of Portland. They had no children. He was a merchant. His
store was on the corner of Middle and Franklin Streets, where he
was engaged in an extensive business, at one time with his brother
John Smith, and subsequently with John Fox. It was said of him
that "he was a man of fine personal appearance, dressed in good
taste, in the style of his day, full bottomed wig and all, and was gentlemanly in his manners."

(41) WILLIAM SMITH, the fourth son of Rev. Thomas and
Sarah (Tyng) Smith, was born in Portland, Dec. 18, 1736, and died
at ——, Oct. 16, 1754, aged 18 years. He was preparing for commercial life, away from his home, as stated in the Journal of his
father.

(42) JOHN SMITH, fifth son of Rev. Thomas and Sarah (Tyng)
Smith, was born in Portland, Oct. 14, 1738, and died there Dec. 26,
1773, aged 35 years. He was designed for the profession of medicine, and commenced his preparatory studies under the instruction
of Dr. Benjamin Dearborn, of Portsmouth, N. H. Dr. Dearborn
died soon, and he was transferred to Dr. Nathaniel Sargent, of the
same place, with whom he boarded and completed his studies. He
commenced practice in Portland, and opened an apothecary shop in
the same store in which his brother Thomas kept. He was never
married.

(43) SARAH SMITH, the second daughter of Rev. Thomas and
Sarah (Tyng) Smith, was born in Portland, Nov. 14, 1740, and died
13*

there Sept. 10, 1827, aged 87 years.   In 1763 she was married to
Deacon Richard Codman, of that city, and was his second wife. They
had four children.   He was the son of Mr. John and Mrs. Parnell
Codman, of Charlestown, Mass., and was born there in 1730.   In
1775, having been bred a merchant, he left his native place and settled in Portland, where he became an eminent merchant, a deacon of
the Church of which Rev. Thomas Smith was pastor, and died there
of dropsy, Sept. 12, 1793, aged 63 years.   He was twice married:
first, to Anne, daughter of Phinehas Jones, Esq., by whom he had
two children, Richard and Anne.   His wife Anne died the 31st
of March, 1761, and he married a second time to Sarah, daughter of
Rev. Thomas Smith.   His father, John Codman, was a man of eminence and of wealth.   He was a merchant, and was extensively
engaged in foreign traffic.   He came to his death in 1775 by means
of three of his negro servants, who inhumanly poisoned him.   They
were arrested, and two of them were executed; the other transported.

   Children of Dea. RICHARD and SARAH (SMITH) CODMAN, born in
Portland, Me.:

   72. James, b. —— 1764; m.
   73. Sarah, b. —— 1765; m. Timothy Osgood, Esq., of Portland.
   74. Catharine, b. —— 1767; m. Ebenezer Mayo, Esq., of Portland,
        in 1811.
+75. William, b.   —— 1769; m. Lucretia Smith (60), of Windham.
   76. Mary,   b. —— 1772; m. William Swan, Esq., of Portland.

                    [Seventh Generation.]

   (50) SARAH SMITH, daughter of Rev. Peter Thacher and
Elizabeth (Wendell) Smith, was born in Windham, Me., April 9,
1767, and died there January 3, 1854, aged 87 years.   January 22,
1797, she was married to Hezekiah Smith, of Windham.   They lived
in Windham, and had six children, as follows:

   77. William,   b. Nov. 5, 1801.
   78. Thomas,   b. July 18, 1803.
   79. Anne Wendell, b. July 4, 1805; d. March, 1830, aged 25 yrs.
   80. Sarah C.,   b. Sept. 9, 1807; d. May 12, 1813.
   81. Rebecca,   b. April 9, 1859.
   82. Mary J.,   b. Jan. 14, 1811.

   (51) LUCY SMITH, third daughter of Rev. Peter Thacher
and Elizabeth (Wendell) Smith, was born in Windham, Me., August

24, 1769, and died there April 17, 1844, aged 75. She was married about 1790 to Abraham Anderson, of Windham, Me. They had a son —

+83. John, b. 1792; m. Anne Jameson, of Freeport, Me.

(52) THOMAS SMITH, eldest son of Peter Thacher and Elizabeth (Wendell) Smith, was born ih Windham, Me., Oct. 2, 1770, and died there Feb. 27, 1802, in his 32d year. In 1792 he was married to Polly Barker, daughter of Thomas and Eunice Barker, born in Salem, Mass., Aug. 30, 1770, and died in Windham, Jan. 12, 1846, in her 76th year.

Children of THOMAS and POLLY (BARKER) SMITH, born in Windham, Me.:

84. Tyng, b. Feb. 24, 1793.
85. Eliza Wendell, b. May 24, 1795.
86. Thomas, b. Nov. 3, 1797.
87. Mary Anne, b. Nov. 30, 1800.

(53) JOHN TYNG SMITH, second son of Rev. Peter Thacher and Elizabeth (Wendell) Smith, was born in Windham, Me., March 6, 1772, and died in Gorham, Me., about 1863, in his 92d year. He was a magistrate, a Justice of the Peace, and served in several offices of trust and honor, both in his native town and in Gorham. He was married April 15, 1798, to Mary Duguid, a Scotch lady, connected with the family of Alexander Ross. She was born in Boston, April 22, 1772, and died at Gorham, Feb. 19, 1855, in the 83d year of her age.

Children of Col. JOHN TYNG and MARY (DUGUID) SMITH, born in Gorham, Me., as reported by him in 1855:

88. ———, b. Aug. 6, 1799. Stillborn.
89. William Tyng, b. Sept. 21, 1800; d. July 15, 1801, aged 10 m.
90. William Tyng, b. June 19, 1802; m. Margaret Duncan, of Portland. He died in Portland, Friday, March 10, 1854, aged 52 years. He was a military man, and was at the time he died a Major of a battalion of Artillery.
91. Peter Wendell, b. June 6, 1805; m. Mary Shaw, of Portland. He is a military man, and is Major-General of the Fifth Division of the militia of Maine.
92. Edward Tyng, b. Dec. 17, 1807; m. Margaret Foster, of Gorham, Me. Is Brigadier-General of the Fifth Division, Second Brigade.

93. **Arthur McLellan**, b. Dec. 18, 1810; d. at Mobile, Aug. 4, 1847.
   He was, at the time of his death, master of the ship Emblem,
   of Portland, of 700 tons burthen, then loading at Mobile for
   a voyage to Europe. He died of yellow fever, and was
   greatly lamented by his relatives and many friends and acquaintances, for his sincere and warm affections, his great
   worth and true manly qualities. It has been said of him that
   " he was a true man and an honest one — ' the noblest work
   of God.' "
94. **John Duguid**, b. Sept. 2, 1813; d. May 29, 1836, in the 23d
   year of his age, at Livingston, Sumpter Co., Alabama, to
   which place he had gone in the hope of benefiting his health.
   He had been suffering under a severe affection of the lungs
   for some considerable time previous. He was preparing for
   the ministry, and was distinguished for his early piety and
   learning.
95. **Thomas Sutherland**, b. Oct. 16, 1816. Living at the homestead
   in Windham, in 1855. Is a military man—Major-General
   of the Fifth Division of Militia, Second Brigade.

(61) LUCY SAUNDERS, eldest daughter of the Hon. Thomas
and Lucy (Smith) Saunders, was born in Gloucester, Mass., Nov. 24,
1752, and died in Sullivan, Me. The date of her death has not been
communicated. In 1794 she was married to Paul Dudley Sargent,
of Boston, who was born there in 1745, and died at his farm in Sullivan, in 1827, leaving a widow and several children. He was the
son of Col. Epes and Catharine (Winthrop) Sargent, of Salem, who
by further tracing is lineally descended from Gov. Thomas Dudley,
of Roxbury, by his son Gov. Joseph Dudley, whose daughter Anne
Dudley, born Aug. 27, 1784, married John Winthrop, H. C. 1700,
F.R.S., who was a son of Hon. Waitstill Winthrop, of New London,
Ct. Paul Dudley Sargent was a distinguished patriot in Revolutionary times, and shared its military honors. He served his country as a Colonel in the army. None of his children or descendants
have been traced, except one daughter, born in Gloucester, Mass.:

+96. Lucy, b. 1774; m. Rev. John Turner, of Randolph.

(63) JUDITH SAUNDERS, second daughter of Hon. Thomas
and Lucy (Smith) Saunders, was born in Gloucester, Mass., June 1,
1755. She was married about 1775, to Thomas Saunders, her first
cousin, who graduated at Harvard College in the class of 1772, and
of whom it is stated that he expended a large fortune, and died in
1795, leaving a widow and two daughters. This account does not
seem to accord with another which has been given of him, and which
is as follows:

"Thomas Saunders was the son of Joseph and Elizabeth Saunders, and was born at George's River, in Maine, June 15, 1753. His father was drowned when Thomas was four years old. He was adopted into the family of a relative, Mrs. Gibbs, by whom his expenses were paid. He graduated at Harvard College in 1772, and except occasional employment during the war of the Revolution, is believed to have spent his whole after life in teaching school. He was a teacher of the town school in Gloucester for several years; and subsequently was employed by individuals to take charge of a select school. He had been in their employment but a short time, when, in consequence of a severe and unmerited censure of his course as a teacher, he gave way to a depression of spirits, which induced such a state of mind as caused him to put an end to his existence, April 23, 1795."*

(64) HARRIET SAUNDERS, the third daughter of the Hon. Thomas and Lucy (Smith) Saunders, was born in Gloucester, Mass., April 2, 1757, and died in Boston. She was married about 1780, to Maj. Peter Doliver, of Boston, and went there to reside. They had one son and three daughters, as follows:

97.	Peter,	b. in 1782.
98.	Harriet,	b. in 1784.
99.	Charlotte,	b. in 1786.
100.	Sarah Elizabeth,	b. in 1788.

(65) THOMAS SAUNDERS, eldest son of Hon. Thomas and Lucy (Smith) Saunders, was born in Gloucester, Mass., March 25, 1759, and died in Salem, June 5, 1844, aged 84 years. He is said to have resided in Portland, Me., before the Revolutionary War, was

* It is confidently believed from evidence gathered, that the above were the parents of Mrs. Judith (Foster) Saunders, who was for many years an accomplished and successful teacher of young ladies. In the early part of the year 1803 she came to Dorchester and opened a boarding and day school for young ladies, and continued in that occupation until her death, which took place in 1842. She was buried in the ancient Cemetery in Dorchester, and has a gravestone on which her age is given as 67 years, which would make the year of her birth 1775. Her school was kept in the large house situated on the slope of Meeting-House Hill, and was the most celebrated one of the kind ever kept in Dorchester. She received and educated not only young ladies in the town, but others from all parts of the United States and the British Provinces. She was at first assisted by Miss Clementina Beach, who subsequently became her co-worker and partner, and continued with her till her death in 1842, when she closed the school, it having been in continuance about forty years. Miss Sarah Elizabeth Doliver (No. 100), a near relative, was also an assistant at one time in the school.

clerk in a store with his uncle Thomas Smith, and was present at the bombardment of the town in 1775. He afterwards removed to Salem, and became a wealthy and respectable merchant. In 1782 he was married to Elizabeth Elkins, of Salem. She was descended lineally from the distinguished Peregrine White, of Plymouth notoriety — born in Cape Cod harbor, in November, 1620, and died in Marshfield, July, 1704, aged 83 years. She attained to a great age, being 87 years old in 1849, and died not long after.

Children of THOMAS and ELIZABETH (ELKINS) SAUNDERS, born in Salem, Mass.:

+101. Charles, b. in 1783 ; m. Charlotte Nichols, of Portland.
  102. Catharine, b. in 1785 ; m. Dudley L. Pickman, Esq., of Salem.
+103. Mary Elizabeth, b. in 1787 ; m. Leverett Saltonstall, Esq., of Salem.
+104. Caroline, b. in 1789 ; m. Nathaniel Saltonstall, Esq.
+105. George Thomas, b. Oct. 30, 1804 ; m.

(66) SARAH SAUNDERS, fourth daughter of Hon. Thomas and Lucy (Smith) Saunders, was born in Gloucester, Mass., March 1, 1761, and died in St. Petersburg, in Russia, about 1800.

She was married about 1782 to Thomas Augustus Vernon, an English merchant, and went with him to St. Petersburg to reside, where they both died, leaving four children — two sons and two daughters — names not reported.

(70) JOSEPH SAUNDERS, fifth son of Thomas and Lucy (Smith) Saunders, was born in Gloucester, in 1768, and died at Edgartown, Mass., July 13, 1804, aged 36 years. He was a lieutenant in the United States Navy. He was married — no children reported.

(71) MARY SAUNDERS, sixth daughter and eleventh child of Hon. Thomas and Lucy (Smith) Saunders, was born in Gloucester, Mass., about 1770, and died in Sturbridge in 1816, aged 46 years, leaving two daughters.

She was married in or about 1793, to Erasmus Babbitt, Esq., who graduated at Harvard College in 1790, and was by profession a lawyer. He settled in Sturbridge, where he practised law, and became eminent in his profession. They had two children, as follows:

+106. Mary Eliza, b. in 1794; m. Elkanah Cushman, of Boston.
107. A daughter, b. in 1796; not further reported.

(75) WILLIAM CODMAN, Esq., second son of Dea. Richard and Sarah (Smith) Codman, was born in Portland in 1769, and died there. He was married to Lucretia Smith (60), of Windham, Me., about 1810. They resided in Portland. He was by profession a lawyer. She was the daughter of Rev. Peter Thacher and Elizabeth (Wendell) Smith.

Children of WILLIAM and LUCRETIA (SMITH) CODMAN, born in Portland:

108. William Henry, b. in 1812. Counsellor at law, and lives at Camden, Me. Was for several years a clerk in the Treasury Department at Washington, D. C. He was married to Mary Eager, and has four children.
109. George C.; m. Harriet Louisa Bradstreet, in Nov., 1846; lives in Portland. They have no children. Mr. Codman has in his possession many relics and antiquities of Parson Smith. The baptismal suit of linen cambric, and the blanket of white satin, which were used at his christening, at two days old, in 1701, have come down in this family.

[*Eighth Generation.*]

(83) JOHN ANDERSON, son of Abraham, Esq., and Lucy (Smith) Anderson, was born in Windham, Me., about 1792, and died there an honored and distinguished citizen.

He was married about 1817, to Anne Jameson, of Freeport. Me., a daughter of Capt. —— and Anne (Hichborn) Jameson. They had three sons:

110. John, b. ——; m. —— Winter. He inherited his father's estate at Windham, and resides there; has a wife and children.
111. Samuel, b. ——; m. Jane Drew, lives in Portland; is a counsellor at law. The portrait of Rev. Thomas Smith, taken in 1706, when at the age of five years, has descended to him, and hangs in his library. He also possesses many other relics of silver plate and valued antiquities, which have come down to him in the descending generations, and have been carefully preserved.
112. Edward, b. ——; m. Fanny Purley, of Bridgeton.

(96) LUCY SARGENT, daughter of Paul Dudley and Lucy (Saunders) Sargent, was born in Gloucester, Mass., in 1774, and died at Sullivan, Me., Feb. 13, 1853, aged 79 years. She was married about 1794 to Rev. John Turner, of Randolph. He was the son of Col. Seth Turner, of Randolph, and was born there Nov. 4, 1768, graduated at Brown University in 1790, and after preparing for the ministry, became a preacher and was settled at Alfred, in Maine. He resided there until 1808, when he was dismissed, and again settled over the second religious society at Biddeford. He remained at Biddeford about nine years, and was dismissed again in 1817. He died in Dorchester, Mass., Sept. 29, 1839, aged 71 years.

Children of Rev. JOHN and LUCY (SARGENT) TURNER, born in Alfred and Biddeford, Maine, and in Stoughton, Mass.

113. Lucy Sargent, b. June 29, 1795 ; m. David Hall, of New York.
114. Maria Sophia, b. Aug. 30, 1797 ; m. Rev. Joseph Searle.
115. Charlotte Saunders, b. 1799 ; d. in 1813, aged 14 years.
116. Rebecca,   b. June 26, 1803 ; d in infancy.
117. Martha Walker, b. Feb. 13, 1809 ; m. Edward Dunning, of Mobile.
118. John Newton,   b. Jan. 6, 1811 ; m. Harriet Dana.
119. Samuel Hubbard,   b. Feb. 9, 1814.
120. Catharine Winthrop, b. June 22, 1819 ; d. Jan. 25, 1839, aged 20 years.
121. Rebecca Vinton,   b. in 1820.

(101) CHARLES SAUNDERS, eldest son of Thomas, Esq., and Elizabeth (Elkins) Saunders, was born in Salem in 1783, and died there. He graduated at Harvard College in 1802, and was Steward there from 1827 to 1830. Previous to that he was engaged as a merchant in Salem, where he had established himself in a flourishing and successful trade. He was married to Charlotte Nichols, daughter of Rev. Dr. Nichols, of Portland, and the successor of Rev. Thomas Smith. Since his retirement from business, he has resided in Boxford, North Parish, and is there esteemed as a valued and useful citizen.

(103) MARY ELIZABETH SAUNDERS, second daughter of Hon. Thomas and Elizabeth (Elkins) Saunders, was born in Salem, in 1787, and died there January 11, 1858, aged 70 years. March 7, 1811, she was married to Leverett Saltonstall, Esq., who graduated at Harvard College in 1802. He was the eldest son of Dr. Nathaniel

and Anna (White) Saltonstall, and was born in Haverhill, June 13, 1783. He read law with the Hon. William Prescott, Esq., of Salem, and after completing his studies, opened an office in Haverhill. He practised law there but a short time, and in May, 1806, he removed to Salem, where he devoted himself to his profession and acquired great eminence as a lawyer and advocate. He held various offices, and served the public with distinction and honor. He was the first Mayor of Salem. He was elected Representative to the State Legislature, and was chosen Speaker of the House of Representatives; and subsequently, when a Senator, became President of the State Senate. He was afterwards elected Representative to the Congress of the United States. He was President of the Bible Society, of the Essex Agricultural Society, and of the Essex Bar, A. A. and S. H. S. In 1838 he received from Harvard College the honorary degree of LL.D. He was elected a member of its Board of Overseers, and continued to fill that office until his decease. He died in Salem, May 8, 1845, in the 62d year of his age.

Children of Hon. LEVERETT and MARY ELIZABETH (SAUNDERS) SALTONSTALL, born in Salem :

122. Anne Elizabeth, died unmarried.
123. Caroline, died unmarried.
124. Richard Gurdon, b. June 29, 1820 ; died Feb. 22, 1821.
+125. Lucy Saunders, b. Feb. 10, 1822 ; m. John Francis Tuckerman.
126. Leverett, born March 16, 1825, H. C. 1844, LL.B. 1847 ; a lawyer in Boston. He was married Oct. 19, 1854, to Rose Lee, daughter of John Cabot and Harriet (Rose) Lee, of Salem, born there in 1835. No children reported.

(104) CAROLINE SAUNDERS, third daughter of Hon. Thomas and Elizabeth (Elkins) Saunders, was born in Salem, 1789, and died there. She was married Nov. 30, 1820, to Nathaniel Saltonstall, a merchant in Salem, born there Oct. 1, 1784, went to Baltimore, Md., was a merchant there, and acquired a handsome estate. He returned to Salem, and died there Oct. 19, 1838, aged 54 years. He was a brother of Leverett Saltonstall, and both of them lineal descendants of the honorable and worthy Richard Saltonstall, who was among the earliest settlers of the Massachusetts Colony, and was an honorable and active member of the Joint Stock Company of London, England. They married sisters.

14

Children of NATHANIEL and CAROLINE (SAUNDERS) SALTONSTALL, born in Salem:

127. Gurdon, b. Aug. 14, 1821 ; d. Aug. 30, 1821.
128. Catharine Pickman, b. May 18, 1823; m. Edward Brooks Peirson, of Salem.
129. Elizabeth Saunders, b. May 26, 1825 ; m. George B. Silsbee.
130. Henry, b. March 2, 1828 (H. C. 1848), a merchant in Boston.
131. William Gurdon, b. Dec. 22, 1831, a merchant in Boston.
132. Richard, b. 1834, through whom the ancient name of the first Saltonstall progenitor has been preserved.

(105) GEORGE THOMAS SAUNDERS, the youngest child and only son of Thomas, Esq., and Elizabeth (Elkins) Saunders, was born in Salem, Oct. 30, 1804. He graduated at Harvard College in 1824. He was married to Marianne Browne, daughter of Samuel Browne, Esq., of Salem, and has a family of sons and daughters. Children have not been reported.

(106) MARY ELIZA BABBITT, eldest daughter of Erasmus, Esq., and Mary (Saunders) Babbitt, was born in Sturbridge, Mass., in 1794, and died in Brixen, England, May 7, 1865, aged about 70 years.

She was married in 1815 to Elkanah Cushman, Esq., of Boston, and went there to reside. She was his second wife, and survived him. He was the son of the Hon. Isaac Cushman, of Plymouth, and was born there about 1790; became a lawyer in Boston, where he maintained a fair and honorable practice, and died there in 1841, leaving a widow and two daughters and one son. They had, in all, six children. The three youngest died in infancy, or at a very young age.

Children of ELKANAH, Esq., and MARY ELIZA (BABBITT) CUSHMAN, born in Boston:

+133. Charlotte Saunders, b. in Richmond Street, Boston, July 23, 1816 ; resides in London, England.
134. Charles Augustus, b. Nov. 14, 1818. Lives in London, England, and is a Topographical Engineer.
+135. Mary, b. in 1820 ; m. James Sheridan Muspratt, and lives in Liverpool, England.
136. ——, b. in 1822 ; d. in infancy.
137. ——, b. in 1824 ; d. young.
138. ——, b. in 1827 ; d. young.

[*Ninth Generation.*]

Children of DAVID and (113) LUCY SARGENT (TURNER) HALL, born in New York:

142. Lucy Turner.
143. Laura.
144. Charlotte.
145. Martha Eliza.

Children of Rev. JOSEPH and (114) MARIA SOPHIA (TURNER) SEARLE:

146. Joseph Hall.
147. Turner.

Children of EDWARD and (117) MARTHA WALKER (TURNER) DUNNING, born in Mobile, Alabama:

148. William Hall.

And by a second husband, ARTHUR WILKINSON:

149. Martha Elizabeth.
150. Arthur.

Children of (118) JOHN NEWTON and HARRIET (DANA) TURNER:

151. Nathaniel Dana, b. June 28, 1840.
152. Catharine Winthrop, b. Feb. 10, 1842.

(125) LUCY SAUNDERS, daughter of Hon. Leverett and Mary (Elkins Saunders) Saltonstall, was born Feb. 10, 1822; and June 10, 1847, was married to John Francis Tuckerman. He was a graduate of H. C. 1837, M.D. 1841, Surgeon in the U. S. Navy in 1847, M.M.S.S. in 1854. Now lives in Salem.

Children of JOHN FRANCIS and LUCY SAUNDERS (SALTONSTALL) TUCKERMAN, born in Salem:

139. Leverett Saltonstall, b. April 19, 1848.
140. Francis,   b. June 11, 1849.
141. Charles Saunders,   b. Jan. 31, 1852.

(133 and 135) CHARLOTTE SAUNDERS CUSHMAN and MARY CUSH-MAN, daughters of Elkanah and Mary Eliza (Babbitt) Cushman, were born in Boston in 1816 and 1820. The property left by their father at his decease being insufficient for the support and education of his family, the eldest daughter, who was then twenty-five years

of age, and her sister four years younger, prepared themselves, under competent teachers, and went on the stage, as it has been stated, "to obtain the means of support for themselves and their mother." They were both highly educated, and richly endowed with rare natural gifts, which were developed by the choice they made, and they soon attained excellence in the histrionic and dramatic art. Their first appearance in public was at the old Tremont Theatre, on Tremont Street, in Boston. They were eminently successful: and after continuing there for a season, visited other cities, and have performed in most of the large cities in the United States and in Europe. They have acquired a competent fortune, and have contributed largely to benevolent objects. They have always maintained an irreproachable character. A few years ago, Miss Charlotte retired from the stage, and has devoted herself to public readings whenever she appears before the public. She resides at the present time with her brother, in London. In 1862 she visited Boston, and was present at the opening of the Grand Organ, on which occasion she recited or read to an admiring audience.

There are descendants in the line of Habackuk Glover in the ninth and tenth generations, but few of them have been ascertained. His line has been perpetuated mostly through his great-grandson, the Rev. Thomas Smith. There may be some of the descendants of his grandson, John Smith; and of Howard, from Elizabeth Brenton. There may also be some of the descendants of John Smith, the brother of Parson Smith, by the name of Pemberton, but they have not been reported or reached. There are descendants of Rev. Peter Thacher Smith, of the names of Farwell and Winslow, living in Tyngsboro,' Mass., and in Albion, Maine; also of the name of Anderson in Windham, and Saunders in Salem, who have not been reported. The whole number collected is one hundred and fifty-two, including the few which have been gathered of the tenth generation.

[*Second Generation.*]

JOHN GLOVER, A.M.

III. John Glover, the third son of John Glover and Anna his wife, was born at Rainhill Parish, in the town of Prescot, Lancashire, England, Oct. 11, 1629, and died in Boston, Sept. 23, 1696, in his 67th year. He was buried Sept. 25, in the Granary Burial Ground. Judge Sewall attended his funeral, and enters the following notice of it in his diary.

"1696. Sept. 23. Mr. John Glover dies." " Sept. 25. Mr. John Glover is buried; Col. Pyncheon, Col. Cook, Mr. Peter Sargeant and Mr. Oakes were there."

In 1630 he was brought to New England by his parents, and lived with them at Dorchester until he attained the age of manhood. In 1647 he entered Harvard College, and graduated there in the class of 1651. Soon after leaving College he engaged in commercial pursuits, and became a merchant of some eminence, importing goods largely from London and other cities.

He was married late in life, or at the age of about fifty years, and it is not known that he ever had any children. He was an extensive landholder, both by purchase and inheritance. By his father's will he was to receive two hundred pounds in money in addition to what had been paid for his education, and at the decease of his mother his share in Newbury Farm and other lands was one fourth part, which was disposed of by Deeds of Gift and Sale a short time before his death. He resided with his mother at the mansion house in Boston, and in 1670 was appointed to continue the administration of the Hon. John Glover's estate, in the place and by the consent of Habackuk, his elder brother, after the decease of Mrs. Anna Glover their mother. In 1671 he joined with his brother Habackuk in the sale of a tract of land which belonged to the estate of their father John Glover, Esq. of Dorchester and Boston, to Robert Babcock of Milton, of two acres in the division of land which was laid out to Mr. Glover on the south side of Neponset River. Habackuk and John Glover certified to their father's hand writing.

In 1672 he purchased an estate of Joseph Lowell, of Boston (cooper), situated as follows, viz.:

14*

"House and land situated near the Exchange in Boston, bounded Westerly by and with a Lane that runs from the head of the Great Dock to Samuel Shrimpton's house; extending from the front to the rear sixty feet or thereabouts; and on the West side thirteen feet and eighteen inches; Southerly and Easterly by land of Samuel Plummer; Northerly by land of the said Joseph Lowell to the said Plummer's house, from the front to the rear sixty feet or thereabouts; extending from the North East Corner of said Joseph Lowell's house to said Plummer's house.   Jan. 6, 1672.   (Signed) JOSEPH LOWELL.
                                                    ABIGAIL LOWELL.

Witnessed by
Habackuk Glover,
John Hayward.

This estate was sold six months after, July 11, 1672, by John Glover to Thomas Skinner, in presence of Thomas Pecke, Samuel Plummer and John Williams.   Acknowledged by John Glover, Aug. 20, 1672, before Edward Tyng, Assistant.

March 2, 1673, his name appears as a witness to a deed from his brother Habackuk Glover to Rebeckah Smith.

July 10, 1673, John Glover sold his house and land to Samuel Skinner, of Boston.

Nov. 20, 1674, he witnessed a deed for his brother Habackuk Glover.

He was of Boston in 1675, and sold land to William Griggs, known by the name of Hudson's land, deed bearing date April 6, 1675.

In 1677 he sold to Roger and Ebenezer Billings, of Dorchester, a piece of salt marsh and meadow which formerly belonged to John Glover, Esq., "lying in Dorchester, and containing about six acres, more or less — being a part of Mr. Glover's Newbury Farm and his inheritance, with all the Creeks and Ponds thereunto belonging; Bounded partly on a Creek called Newbury Creek, and partly by the Salt Marsh Meadow of his Brother Nathaniel Glover, late of Dorchester, Dec^d; Southerly by Sagamore Creek; Northerly by a Salt Water Creek, and partly by a meadow of William Rawson."

Dec. 4, 1679, John Glover of Boston, merchant, accepts and receives, for the consideration of fifty pounds, one sixteenth part of Newbury Farm, which belonged to his nephew John Glover (cooper), the son of his brother Nathaniel Glover, who deceased in 1657, as may more fully appear by a deed recorded among the transactions of the said John Glover, his nephew.   Signed by John Glover the younger, and acknowledged Dec. 4, 1679.

May 20, 1680, the above deed of sale was made void and conveyed back to John Glover (cooper), his nephew, with all the rights and privileges and power of sale.

In 1680 he purchased a piece of salt marsh lying in Dorchester, of Katharine Smith, "relict, Widow and Executrix of the late John Smith, Quarter Master."

In 1680 his name appears in Glover's agreement as an acting attorney to and for his uncle William Glover of Prescot, in Lancashire, England, and also in his own right.

In 1684 he purchased a tract of land in Swansea, of Samuel Miles and Anne Miles.* The following is a copy of the conveyance, as recorded at the Probate Office in Plymouth, Lib. 5, fol. 294.

Samuel Miles and Anne Miles to John Glover, of Swanzey, Merchant.

To all persons to whom this present Deed of sale shall come. Anne Miles of Swanzey, Executrix, and Samuel Miles Executor to the Last Will and Testament of Mr. John Miles of Swanzey, Merchant aforesaid; The receipt whereof, &c., send Greeting: Know ye, That for and in consideration of the full Sum, &c., of Current Money of New England, to us in hand well and truly paid, by John Glover of Swanzey, Merchant aforesaid; The receipt whereof we do by these Presents acknowledge, and fully acquit the said John Glover, his heirs, Executors, Aministrators and Assigns Forever;

We the said Anne Miles and Samuel Miles of Swanzey in the County of Plymouth have given, granted, conveyed and confirmed, and do by these Presents hereby give, grant, convey and confirm unto him the said John Glover of Swanzey, one half of a Seventeenth Right of all the Lands lying in the New Meddow in Swanzey in New Plymouth, Undivided, Together with all woods, brush, underwood, &c., thereon;

And all manner of Rights, immunities, Profits, Privileges and Appurtenances to the same belonging, or in any wise appertaining thereunto.

To Have and to Hold the aforesaid Seventeenth Right of Land which now lieth in common and Undivided, unto him the said John Glover, his Heirs and Assigns Forever. And that We, the said Anne and Samuel Miles, have full Power and good right to sell, &c., and that it is clear and free from all incumbrances. And it shall and may be lawful for the said John Glover, his Heirs and Assigns, to use, occupy, possess, &c., And that we will Warrant and defend, &c., unto him the said John Glover.

---

* John Glover was the owner of lands in Swansea at the time of his death, and there is no record to be found of any disposition having been made of them by any of his administrators. Elizabeth did not dispose of them, and they are not included in the account of Thomas Smith.

In Witness whereof, &c., this 5th day of November, 1683.
                    (Signed)   ANNE MYLES,
     Witnessed by   SAMUEL MYLES.
Nicholas Boone, John Brown.
Received, Entered and Recorded June 10, 1684.
                              DANIEL SMITH, *Assistant.*

John Glover was married in or about 1680, to Elizabeth Franklin, of Ipswich, who survived him and was appointed Executrix of his estates in his last will. He was, at the time of his marriage, residing in Swansea, in the County of Bristol, and was a merchant there. In 1684 he bought a mansion house and several tracts of land of Joseph and Abigail Curtis, of Sudbury, in the County of Middlesex, and soon after removed there from Swansea, and was there in 1686. Dr. Stevens includes among his list of the early inhabitants of Sudbury, from 1684 to 1686, the names of "John Glover, Gent", and Elizabeth his wife." He resided in Sudbury but a short time, and appears not to have attended to any business, except the occasional buying and selling of lands. In 1690 he removed again to Boston, and lived in Summer Street until the close of his life. He was admitted to join the first Congregational Church in Boston in 1693, three years previous to his death.

In 1682 he sold a piece of salt marsh lying in Dorchester, to Isaac Jones. Deed signed by John Glover and Elizabeth Glover.

He owned estates at Boston, Dorchester, Swansea, Milton, Sudbury, and other places in the vicinity of Boston.

In 1684, John Glover, merchant, of Swansea, purchased of Joseph Curtis and Abigail his wife, an estate, house and land in Sudbury, in the County of Middlesex. Extract from deed:

Joseph Curtis of Sudbury, and Abigail his wife, for and in consideration of divers good causes me thereunto moving, and also one hundred pounds in money paid by John Glover of Swansea, merchant, in the County of Bristol, conveys the following, viz. : A house lot containing two acres, situated in Sudbury ; Two divisions of land containing twelve acres, Eight acres more of Upland, with ten acres more of Upland on Pine Plain ; a half acre of Upland, a Town Right, Three quarters of an acre of Meadow, Two acres and a half of land ; Also one acre more and three and a half acres more ; Also five acres of bog Meadow ; Also one half of five and a half acres of Meadow ; Also all their Dwelling house that stands upon the house lot formerly granted to John Ruddock, with appendages, Commonage, &c. Signed, April 3, 1684, by   JOSEPH CURTIS,
     In presence of   ABIGAIL CURTIS.
John Green, Hugh Duane, —— King.

In 1687, three years from the purchase of the above of Joseph and Abigail Curtis, John Glover sold the same to Thomas Knapp, of Boston. Consideration one hundred and twenty pounds. Signed and acknowledged by John Glover and Elizabeth Glover, Dec. 6, 1687, in presence of James Bernard, Thomas Halsey and Thomas Browne.

In 1689, John Glover, gentleman, purchased the house and land which he sold to William Rawson in or about the year 1677; the latter, with Anne his wife, for two hundred pounds in money, conveying to Mr. Glover and to his heirs forever,

" All their Dwelling house, Messuage or tenement, situate in Boston, at the Southerly end of said Town, near Capt. Samuel Sewall's land, containing three lower rooms, two chambers, one cellar, woodhouse and Brewhouse, with all the Land on which they stand. Likewise all the Garden on the Southeasterly side of the said house, and all the land on the Southwesterly end of said house ; the whole land being bounded at the Southeasterly end from the Street to the Widow Morse's Land, on Land of Capt. Samuel Sewall ; Southwesterly by Land of the Widow Morse ; Northwesterly by Land of said William Rawson, and Northeasterly by the Street or lane leading to the water side ; and measures at said Southeasterly end Sixty Seven feet and three inches or thereabouts. From that corner near the Lane or Street aforesaid to the Widow Morse's land is Eighty one feet ; Thence to the Street in a straight line is Sixty four feet and three inches, or thereabouts. Then along the street, beginning three feet Westward of the Woodhouse and Brewhouse aforesaid, Eighty-four feet or thereabouts to the South End. Together with all the appurtenances thereunto belonging. To Have and to hold, &c., unto him the said John Glover, &c. (Signed) WILLIAM RAWSON, ANNE RAWSON.

In presence of
James Groom,
Joseph Webb.   Oct. 14, 1689.   Acknowledged June 13, 1692.

Attest : JOSEPH WEBB, *Clerk*. SIMON BRADSTREET, *Gov.*

In 1689, John Glover sold to William Rawson his one fourth part of Newbury Farm, "lying in Dorchester on the south side of Neponset River, which said one fourth part was devised to me by my Honoured father, John Glover, of Boston, Dec^d, Together with one fourth part of all the houses, barns, stables, woods, trees, fences, &c., and all appertaining thereto." Signed the fourteenth day of October, 1689, by John Glover and Elizabeth Glover, in presence of Habackuk Glover and Ralph Perkins.

Deed of Gift.

John Glover of Boston in New England, to his beloved Nephew
Nathaniel Glover, of Dorchester, Sen'.

To all Christian people unto whom these Presents shall come. John
Glover of Sudbury, in the County of Middlesex, within His Majesty's
Territory of New England, Gentleman, sendeth Greeting: Know ye,
That Whereas Roger Billings, late of Dorchester in the County of
Suffolk within the Territory aforesaid, did for me and in my behalf,
treat and bargain, and with my money did purchase of William Rawson of Boston, Shopkeeper, who married with Anne the daughter of
my brother Mr. Nathaniel Glover of Dorchester Dec^d, A Third part
of a Quarter or One Twelfth part of all that farm commonly called and
known by the name of Newbury Farm, situate and lying within the
Township of Dorchester, aforesaid, formerly in the possession of my
father the Worshipful John Glover Esq. Dec^d, for the which part of
said Farm the said Roger Billings and his heirs, who were then and
still continue in the tenure and occupation thereof, have from the time
of the said purchase (being in Anno Dom. 1677, or thereabouts) ever
since paid me yearly rent.

Now I the said John Glover, for and in consideration of the love and
affection which I have and do bear unto my beloved Nephew Nathaniel Glover of the same Dorchester, Tanner, Eldest son of my aforesaid
brother, Nathaniel Glover of Dorchester, Dec^d; and for divers other
good causes and considerations, me hereunto moving, have given,
granted, surrendered, released, enfeoffed and confirmed, and by these
Presents do hereby give, grant, release, enfeoffe and confirm unto my
said Nephew Nathaniel Glover his Heirs and Assigns Forever,

All that One Third part of a Quarter, or One Twelfth part of said
Newbury Farm, heretofore purchased of William and Anne Rawson
(it being her right in her father's estate), situate and lying in Milton
or on Squantum Rock. To Have and to Hold unto him the said Nathaniel Glover, his Heirs, Executors, Administrators and Assigns,
with all the rents, privileges and appurtenances from and after my
decease, with all the lands belonging thereunto as well arable as pasture. The whole farm containing Four Hundred Acres; and all the
profits to be had or raised unto him the aforesaid Nathaniel Glover
to his only proper use and behoof forever.

Without any power of reclaim or challenge whatsoever or contradiction of my Heirs, Executors, Administrators or Assigns, without
any account or reconing or answer thereof to be given, made, or rendered, or power of Thirds to be had or claimed therein by Elizabeth
my wife.

And I do hereby Covenant and oblige my Heirs, Executors, Administrators and Assigns from time to time and at all times forever from
and after the decease of Me the said John Glover, to Warrant, maintain and defend the above granted and released premises unto him the
said Nathaniel Glover, his Heirs, Executors, Administrators and
Assigns Forever, against the Lawful claims and demands of all
persons.

In Witness whereof, I the said John Glover, with Elizabeth my
Wife, have hereunto set our Hands and Seals this 20th day of September, Anno Domini 1686. (Signed)   JOHN GLOVER, and a Seale.
                                   ELIZABETH GLOVER, and a Seale.

Signed, sealed and delivered in presence of us,
    Habackuk Glover,
    Ralph Perkins.

    Boston, December 7, 1686.

Mr. John Glover personally appeared before me, underwriter of His Majesty's Council of His Territory in New England, and acknowledged the above written Instrument to be his free will, act and deed.

WAIT WINTHROP.

John Glover died Oct. 8, 1696, ten years after the signing of the above instrument; and on the 10th of August, 1697, Ebenezer Billings confirmed to Nathaniel Glover, by the following indenture, the one twelfth part of Newbury Farm, above described and conveyed.

Indenture of Billings to Glover.

    Aug. 10, 1697.   Liber 14, folio 434.

To all Christian People before whom these Presents shall come.
Know ye,

    That in the ·Ninth Year of the Reign of Our Sovereign Lord King William of England, and on the 10th day of August, 1697, Ebenezer Billings and Roger Billings of Dorchester, in the County of Suffolk, and within His Majesty's Province of Massachusetts Bay in New England, Yeoman, on the one part ; and Nathaniel Glover of the same Dorchester, County and Province aforesaid, Tanner, Nephew of the said John Glover heretofore of Sudbury in the County of Middlesex and Province aforesaid, Gentleman Deceased (but late of Boston), on the other part, Witnesseth :

    Whereas the father of Said Roger and Ebenezer Billings purchased in his lifetime for and in behalf of the said John Glover, of William Rawson, sometime of Boston but now of Dorchester, Shop-keeper, who married with Anne the daughter of Mr. Nathaniel Glover of Dorchester, Deceased, One Third part of a quarter or One Twelfth part of all that farm called Newbury's Farm, situate and lying in Dorchester Township aforesaid, formerly in possession of the late Worshipful John Glover, Esq. Dec^d, for which part of the said farm (which was purchased by the said Roger Billings in his lifetime in 1677 or thereabouts), and for which he the said Roger and his sons Roger and Ebenezer aforesaid have ever since paid the said John Glover Yearly Rent.

    And Whereas the said Roger Billings by a Writing bearing date December 7, 1680, acknowledged that the said One Twelfth part of the said Newbury Farm belonging to the said William Rawson in Right of his Wife Anne, with all the other lands belonging to them whether in Milton or on Squantum Rock was by his purchase henceforth the true and proper Estate of the said John Glover from whom and for which the said William Rawson had received full pay.

And whereas the said John Glover by virtue of a Deed of Gift bearing date December 7th, Anno Dom. 1686, did give, grant, surrender, enfeoffe and confirm unto his said Nephew the first above-named Nathaniel Glover, and to his Heirs and Assigns forever, All that One Third part of a Quarter or One Twelfth part of Newbury Farm purchased of the said William Rawson and Anne his Wife, and of all the lands arable, pasture and Wood land Marshes belonging thereto, The whole farm containing four Hundred Acres, and One Twelfth part of all Houses, Barns, Edifices, &c., Woods, Trees thereon growing or standing, and One Twelfth of all the other Lands situate in Milton or on Squantum Rock belonging to the said Farm or parcel, with all his Estate, Right, Title or Interest whatsoever in said One Twelfth part of said Newbury Farm.

To Have and to Hold unto him the said Nathaniel Glover, the above named nephew of the said John Glover, his Heirs and Assigns Forever, from and immediately after the decease of him the said John Glover, as by the Deed of Gift, Reference may be had to the Records of Deeds for the County of Suffolk.

And whereas the said John Glover hath been dead for the space of One Year or more, since which time and to this day the above said Nephew Nathaniel Glover hath been and now is by virtue of said Deed in peaceable and quiet possession of all the aforementioned and granted Premises.   *   *   *   *   *   *

Confirmed by the said Roger Billings and Ebenezer Billings, sons of the said Roger Billings late of Dorchester, Deceased, this Tenth day of August, 1697.   ROGER BILLINGS,
                                              EBENEZER BILLINGS.

Acknowledged before Timothy Dwight of Dedham.

Received, Entered and Recorded with the Records of Deeds for the County of Suffolk, October 3, 1697.

The Last Will and Testament of John Glover, of Boston.

Suffolk Prob. Vol. 11, fol. 218.

I John Glover, of Boston, being in health of body, and of sound and disposing mind and memory, do thus make and ordain this my last Will and Testament.

My soul I resign into the hands of Jesus Christ my Saviour and Merciful Redeemer, and my body I commit unto the Earth whence it was taken, to be decently buried by the discretion of my Executrix.

And as for the Worldly Goods which the Lord hath lent me, I do give and bequeathe All unto my beloved Wife, my Houses and Lands in Boston and at Swansey, or wherever else ; in case I depart this life and leave her surviving, to sell and dispose of it as she shall like best, and to give it to whom she pleaseth (my debts being first paid). As also all my moveable estate and debts whatsoever of my personal Estate. And of this my last Will I do appoint my Well beloved Wife Elizabeth Glover my sole Executrix.

In Witness whereof, I have hereby set my hand and seale this Eighth day of April, In the year of Our Lord One thousand six Hundred and Ninety two (1692).   JOHN GLOVER, and a Seale.

This Will is to stand in force until another shall appear. Signed, sealed and published by John Glover as his last Will and Testament, in Presence of us,   Jonathan Marion, Jun.
                              Joseph Tolman,
                              Benj^a Tolman.

Examined by JONATHAN ADDINGTON, *Register.*

ELIZABETH FRANKLIN, the wife of John Glover, was born in Boston the 3d day of the 8th month, 1638, and died there June 21, 1705 aged 67 years. She was the daughter of William and Alice (Andrews) Franklin, of Boston. Her mother was the daughter of Robert Andrews, Esq., of Ipswich, who died in Boston in 1641, and Elizabeth her only child was removed to Ipswich and cared for by her relations. Robert Andrews, after the death of his daughter Alice, entered into an agreement (of which the following is an extract) with William Franklin, the father of Elizabeth: —

" As concerning the forty pounds portion of Alice, the late wife of William Franklin and daughter of said Robert Andrews, it is to be reserved for Elizabeth the daughter of said William Franklin and Alice his late wife." Dated April 2, 1641, and signed by Robert Andrews and William Franklin.

William Franklin's estate was said to be situated at or near Bendall's Dock. He died in 1644. Elizabeth was educated by her maternal uncle Thomas Andrews, who was for many years a celebrated teacher in Ipswich. He died in 1683, intestate, and Elizabeth, who was at that time Elizabeth Glover, inherited one eighth part of his estate, in common with the other nephews and niece.

"Inventory of the estate of Thomas Andrews, Teacher, who died July 10, 1683, taken by John Appleton and Nathaniel Rust, Sept. 16, 1683, and returned in Court, Sept. 25, 1683. Amount, Five hundred and fifty one pounds sixteen shillings and ten pence. Amount of debts, twenty six pounds seven Shillings and ten pence."

Certificates of heirship were presented to the Court of Probate in Salem, Essex County, by John Andrews and Sarah Cannon, children of John Andrews, brother of Thomas ; by Mrs. Elizabeth Glover, daughter of his sister Alice ; and by Daniel Hovey, John Hovey, Nathaniel Hovey, Joseph Hovey, Thomas Hovey, children of his sister Abigail.

15

Copy of Certificates, as presented.

A Certificate that John Andrews, the son of the brother of Mr. Thomas Andrews of Ipswich, Schoolmaster, Dec[d], and Daniel Hovey the son of his sister, are the nearest relations of the said Thomas Andrews ; and their desire is to have administration granted to them on his Estate.

July 13, 1683.   JOHN ANDREWS,
                                                          DANIEL HOVEY.

John Choate, about 58 y. ; Joseph Goodhue, 43 y. ; James Gregory, 42 years, testifieth that the above John Andrews of Salem is the reputed son of Corporal John Andrews, Dec[d], formerly of Ipswich, who was a brother of Thomas Andrews, Schoolmaster.

Sept. 25, 1683.

Sept. 27, 1683. Certificate to the Court from Daniel Hovey, Sen., wherein he mentions that Mr. Thomas Andrews was his truly and loving and well beloved brother, and says, More than 40 years ago I did match with his loving and well beloved Sister Abigail Andrews, by whom the Lord blest me with six sons and a dafter (daughter), five of which sons are yet living ; so that by these it may appear that we are nearly related to this Deceased Gentleman ; but in brief he hath six nephews and two nieces as follows, viz. :

There is the son and daughter of his brother John Andrews, Dec[d], who are John Andrews and Sarah Cannon his Sister, which are considerably debtors to his estate, as also,

Mrs. Elizabeth Glover, who is married to Mr. John Glover, formerly living at Boston, now at Swansey, who is debtor to this Estate.

There is myself (Daniel Hovey, Sen.), also debtor to the Estate Thirty-five Shillings upon the paying of some things he sent me for my present use, and gave me order to take and keep them 'til he called for them.

There is Daniel Hovey and John Hovey, two of his nephews, debtor to the Estate for schooling their children, about four pounds.

There is also Thomas Hovey, Joseph Hovey and Nathaniel Hovey, three of his nephews who never had the value of one Shilling of the Estate of their uncle, that I know of.

                    (Signed)   DANIEL HOVEY, Sen.

Elizabeth, after the decease of Mr. John Glover in 1696, married a second time in a very few months (Nov. 5, 1696), to Dr. John Cleverly, of Braintree and Boston. He died in Boston, May 5, 1703. She was married a third time, July 27, 1703, to James Mosman, of Roxbury, who survived her and died in 1722. She commenced an administration on the estate of John Glover, but never finished ; and the estate, after a series of years, was settled by an order from the Probate Court.

Feb. 24, 1697, John Cleverly of Boston, with Elizabeth his wife, " who is Executrix of the last Will and Testament of Mr. John Glover, late of Boston, Shopkeeper, Dec⁴," sold a piece of land "lying and situate near the Meeting-house in Dorchester, containing one acre and one quarter and a half rod," to Nathaniel Glover, Sen., of Dorchester — "said land some time appertaining to the estate of John Smith, Esq., late of Dorchester, Dec⁴, bounded Northerly and Easterly by land of Widow Susannah Breck; Westerly by the Highway leading from the Meeting House to Dorchester Mill, commonly called Neponset Mill; Southerly by land and orchard of Katharine Smith, Executrix of the Estate of John Smith, Esq., Dec⁴, recovered by the said Elizabeth Cleverly against the estate of the said John Smith by a Judgment of Court in October, 1696." Signed by John Cleverly and Elizabeth Cleverly, in presence of Thomas Harper and Eleazer Moody.

James Mosman lived after the death of Elizabeth his wife about seventeen years, and used the income of John Glover's estates devised to his wife, until the Court appointed an administrator, Feb. 9, 1721. The remainder of the estate was then committed for settlement to Thomas Smith, Esq., of Boston, an heir at law, who finished up the administration in 1724, and the residue was distributed among the surviving heirs.

Administrator appointed on the Estate of Mr. John Glover, of Boston.

Suff. Prob. Rec., Liber 22, folio 191.

Samuel Sewall sends greeting to Thomas Smith, and grants to him letters of Administration, &c.

Whereas John Glover, heretofore of Boston, Gentleman, deceased, made and published his last Will and Testament, bearing date the Eighth day of April, One thousand Six Hundred and Ninety two, and therein appointed his beloved Wife Elizabeth Glover sole Executrix, who is since deceased, intestate, and without having fully administered on the Estate of the said John Glover, whereby the power of committing further administration of his remaining Goods, Chattels, Rights and Credits doth appertain unto me. Trusting therefore in your care and fidelity, I do by these Presents commit unto you full Power to administer all and singular on the remaining Goods, Chattels, Rights and Credits of the said deceased left unadministered upon by his Executrix Elizabeth Glover aforesaid at the time of her decease, and well and faithfully to dispose of the same according to Law.

Also to ask, gather, levy, recover and receive all and whatsoever Credits of the said deceased John Glover which to him while he lived was due, and at the time of the decease of the said Executrix did appertain, and to pay all debts which the said deceased stood bound and yet remaining unpaid, and to make a true and perfect Inventory of the remaining Goods, Chattels, Rights and Credits, according to the value thereof, so far as his Goods, Chattels, Rights and Credits can extend ; and to exhibit the same into the Registry of the Court of Probate for the County of Suffolk aforesaid, before the Ninth day of May next ensuing ; and to render a plain and true account of your Administration, upon Oath, at or before the 9th day of February, 1722.

And I do hereby ordain and constitute and appoint you Administrator of the remaining Goods, &c., aforesaid, with the Will Annexed.

In Testimony whereof I have hereunto set my hand and seal of the said Court of Probate, holden at Boston the 9th day of Feb., 1721.

SAMUEL SEWALL.

Commissioners appointed to settle Creditors' Claims to the Estate of John Glover.

SAMUEL SEWALL to John Noyes, William Downes and Cornet Thayer, Greeting :

Whereas The Estate of John Glover, Gent[n], heretofore of Boston, is represented to be Insolvent and not sufficient to pay the debts, I nominate and appoint the abovesaid Gentlemen with full power to examine into the Claims.   Dated at Boston, December 27, 1722.

SAMUEL SEWALL, Judge of Probate.

Prob. Rec. Suff. County, Liber 23, fol. 147.

Boston, June 29, 1724.

The Account of Thomas Smith, Administrator *de bonis non* on the Estate of John Glover, of Boston, Gentleman, deceased. The said Accountant charges himself with a House and Land belonging to the said deceased, exhibited into the Registry of the Court of Probate for the County of Suffolk aforesaid, amounting to £145 00 00 0

What said House and Land sold for more than appraised at, ...   105 00 00 0

Item received for Rent before the sale of the House,   9 00 00 0

259 00 00 0

Thomas Smith abovenamed, petitions for Allowance, as follows, viz. :

To the several charges and expenses by him disbursed, for Writing from the Registry Office, Searching of Records, and the expenses of the Commissioners for examining claims and for receiving claims, as an account of particulars herewith exhibited,   .   .   10 12 09 0

Item, for a certain debt of Fifty Eight pounds seventeen shillings and Eight pence, which the Commissioners appointed by the Hon[b] Judge of Probate for receiving claims, &c., as by their returns made into this Court under their hand is found due to the heirs of Mrs. Anna Glover (Widow) heretofore of Boston, deceased, deducting therefrom Three pounds, Five shillings, Five pence and two farthings, being William £45 15 10 2

leaving

Rawson's Third part or share in the Right of his wife
Anna (Glover), who was one of the Grand-children
of the said Mrs. Anna Glover; He, William Rawson,
having heretofore received the same: And deducting
also Nine Pounds, Sixteen Shillings, three pence and
one farthing, being what was the Administrator's
own part or share of his uncle John Glover's Estate,
so that the remainder is to your Administrator for
Time, extraordinary trouble, ... 10 00 00 0
For Allowing and Recording the Account, . . . 10 00 00 0
For distributing and Recording, &c. 5 00 00 0
Remaining in the hands of your Administrator, . . 67 04 08 2

THOMAS SMITH.

Remaining in the hands of the Administrator, of Des-
perate debts, viz., amounting to 15 19 10 0
A note from under the hand of Mary Mosman,* widow, 3 08 00 0
A note under the hand of Sarah Phillips and Bridget
Morefield, ... 2 11 10 0
To the above sum is also added an Old Mortgage from
Joseph Parker, of 10 00 00 0
    Boston, June 29, 1724.
                                            31 19 8 0

Thomas Smith presented himself before me, and made Oath that the
above contained a just and true Account of his Administration on the
Estate of John Glover, deceased.   SAMUEL SEWALL.

Suffolk Prob. Rec., Liber 23, folio 146.

By the Hon^b SAMUEL SEWALL, Esq., *Judge of Probate.*

Whereas it appears to me by an inventory and account presented
by Thomas Smith, Administrator *de bonis non* on the Estate of John
Glover, heretofore of Boston, Gent^m, deceased, of his administration
thereon: that his clear estate at present remaining in the hands of
the said Administrator amounts to the sum of One Hundred and Ninety one pounds fifteen shillings and three pence half penny, after the
charges of administration and other payments by him made are deducted, which is and remains to be divided among the four brethren
of the deceased, their heirs or legal representatives, viz., Thomas
Glover, Habackuk Glover, Nathaniel Glover and Pelatiah Glover, in
equal parts and proportions.
And I do hereby order the said Administrator to pay the aforesaid

---

* Mary Mosman was the widow of James Mosman, whom he married after the decease
of Elizabeth Glover. She was his third wife, and survived him. James Mosman made his
will the 20th day of July, 1722, and died the same year. He left all his money and moveables to his wife Mary Mosman, with all the income of his dwelling house in Roxbury. Left
to his son George, daughter Elizabeth, and his five grand-children, the children of his son
Timothy, the residue after his wife's decease.

sum accordingly to each party or to those that legally represent them.
They bearing their respective proportions of all such debts as shall
hereafter appear to be due and owing from the Estate of the said deceased John Glover.

Dated in Boston, the 29th day of June, One thousand Seven Hundred and twenty-four.

Examined, Entered and Recorded.   JOHN BOYDELL, *Register.*

[*Second Generation.*]

NATHANIEL GLOVER.

IV. Nathaniel Glover, the fourth son of John Glover, Esq., and
Anna his wife, was born in 1630–31, died in Dorchester, May 21,
1657, and was buried in the ancient burial ground of that town.
The grave-stone has gone to decay. There are but few acts of his
short life to be found on record. He attained the age of manhood
in Dorchester, and succeeded to the homestead at the time of his
father's removal to Boston in 1652. In that year he was married to
Mary Smith, of Dorchester. On the 22d of the 3d month he was
admitted to the Church there, in full communion. May 3, 1654,
he took the freeman's oath, and was recorded among the New England Freemen. In 1655 he was chosen one of the Selectmen of Dorchester, and again in 1656 and 1657. In 1655 he was appointed,
with others, to settle the bounds between Dorchester and Dedham.
He was also chosen to fill other offices in the town. By his father's
will, in addition to the Dorchester homestead estate already given
him, he was to receive four hundred pounds in money, and forty
pounds more to be paid to him by his brother Habackuk after the
death of his mother, Mrs. Anna Glover; also one fourth part of Mr.
Glover's Newbury Farm, and one fourth part of the other lands reserved as the widow's dower. He left a will, which is on file, proved
June 5, 1657. Inventory of his estate taken and sworn to by the
underwriters, Roger Clap and William Clark, the 5th day of the 4th
month, 1657:

Imp. His wearing apparell, ... £10 00 00
Household furniture, ... 13 06 00
In a debt of his father's Will, ... 200 00 00
In a debt of Mr. Habackuk Glover, after the decease of
    his mother, ... 40 00 00

House and Land, ...	200 00 0
Meadow, ...	30 00 0
	493 06 0

Reversion of one fourth part of Newbury Farm after the decease of his mother. Said farm situate in Dorchester, beyond Neponset River.

Children of NATHANIEL and MARY (SMITH) GLOVER, born in Dorchester:

+1. Nathaniel, b. 30: 1: 1653; bap. 8: 2: 1653, by Rev. Richard Mather; m. Hannah Hinckley, of Barnstable.
+2. John, b. 15: 12: 1654; bap. 18: 12: 1654;
     m. { 1st Mary ——.
          { 2d, Miriam Smith, of Boston.
+3. Anne, b. 1656; m. William Rawson, of Boston.

MARY SMITH, the wife of Nathaniel Glover, was born at Toxteth Park, near Liverpool, Lancashire, England, the 20th day of July, 1630, and died in Barnstable the 29th day of July, 1703, aged 73 years. She was the daughter of Quartermaster John Smith and his first wife Mary Ryder of Toxteth Park. She was twice married; first, in 1652, to Mr. Nathaniel Glover, of Dorchester, who died there in May, 1657, aged 27 years. She was married, second, to the Hon. Thomas Hinckley, of Barnstable (afterwards Governor of the Plymouth Colony for many years), March 2, 1659–60." Her parents are thus noticed in a manuscript Journal of the Rev. Mr. Prince:

"She was the only child of Mr. Quartermaster Smith, by his first wife, formerly of Lancashire in England, and afterward of Dorchester in New England. Her father had been a Quartermaster in the army of the Netherlands, her mother a gentlewoman of a creditable family and of eminent natural powers, piety and acquired accomplishments. Of them she was born in Lancashire in England, in 1630. Her parents living under the ministry of the Rev. Richard Mather at Toxteth in that shire; they came up and brought her with them to Bristol, in order for New England, in April, 1635; young Nathaniel, the son of the said Mr. Mather, being carried on one side in a pannier, and this young Mrs. Mary on the other, as I have often heard her say. May 23, 1635, she, with her father and mother, the said Rev'd Richard Mather and Wife, their sons Samuel and Nathaniel, Mr. Jonathan Mitchell, then about 11 years of age, &c., set sail from Bristol. In the night, between Aug. 14 and 15, coming on the

New England Coast, there arose an extreme hurricane, wherein they were in the utmost danger and wondrously delivered (see the account in the Life of Revd Richard Mather in the Magnalia), and on Aug. 17th arrived at Boston. Her father and others settling at Dorchester, and a new Church being gathered there, Aug. 23d, 1686, the said Mr. Richard Mather became their teacher, under whose ministry she lived, unless when sent to school at Boston, where she enjoyed Mr. Wilson's and Mr. Cotton's ministry."

Rev. Mr. Prince adds: " In ——, she married to Mr. Nathaniel Glover, a son of the Hon. John Glover, Esq., of said Dorchester, by whom she had Nathaniel and Ann. And then this husband dying, she remained a widow until when she married the Honble Thomas Hinckley, Esq., of Barnstable, whither she removed, and had by him Mercy, Experience, John, Abigail, Thankful, Ebenezer and Reliance, who all grew up and married; and all but Ebenezer, before she died.

" At Barnstable, to the day of her death, she appeared and shone in the eyes of all as the loveliest and brightest woman for beauty, knowledge, wisdom, majesty, accomplishments and graces throughout the Colony. And there her first son Nathaniel married to Hannah, a daughter of the said Mr. Hinckley by his former wife. Her said daughter Anne married to Mr. William Rawson, a son of Mr. Secretary Rawson, Secretary of the Massachusetts Colony; her daughter Mercy to Mr. Samuel Prince, of Sandwich; Experience, to Mr. James Whipple, of Barnstable; her son John, to Mrs. Trott, of Dorchester; her daughter Abigail, to the Rev. Mr. Joseph Lord, of Dorchester, South Carolina, afterwards of Chatham, on Cape Cod; Thankful, to the Rev^d Mr. Experience Mayhew, of Martha's Vineyard; Reliance, to the Rev^d Mr. Nathaniel Stone, of Harwich; and after her death, her son Ebenezer to Mrs. Stone, of Sudbury. Mrs. Hinckley died July 29, 1703, in the 73d year of her age."

The writer visited her grave in the ancient cemetery at Barnstable, in the summer of 1856, and copied the following from her gravestone :

" Here lyeth Y^e Body of Y^e truly Virtuous and Praiseworthy Mrs. Mary Hinckley, wife unto Mr. Thomas Hinckley, who departed this life July 29th, 1703, in Y^e 73^d year of her age."

Mary Smith joined the Church at Dorchester previous to her mar-

riage, and was subsequently dismissed from it to join the Church at
Barnstable. The following is taken from the records of the Church
at Dorchester: " The 22⁴ day of the 2ᵈ month, 1660, Mrs. Mary
Glover, whose maiden name was Mary Smith, and who lately married with Gov. Thomas Hinckley, about Sandwich, desired letters
of dismission to the Church there; but they were not at that time
granted, It being so suddenly after her removal thither, and they
not being in a capacity for the enjoyment of the ordinances, having
no officers to dispense the same."

" 23 (4) 1664, Was Mrs. Hinckley, who formerly was the wife of
Mr. Nathaniel Glover, dismissed to join the Church at Barnstable."

Mary Smith was promised a marriage portion by her father* on
her marriage with Mr. Nathaniel Glover, but, from a clause in her
father's will, it appears she did not receive it until some time after.
Quartermaster Smith's will, made December 30, 1676, was proved
July 25, 1678. The following are extracts from it: " Wife Katharine and sons John and other children." " Whereas it is said my
daughter Mary Smith hath received part of her portion, it is to be
understood of my daughter Mary Pelton, who hath received about
twenty pounds or more, as by my books will appear, p. 166." " Lastly, as far as my daughter Mrs. Mary Hinckley is concerned, she is paid
what I promised her upon her marriage with Mr. Nathaniel Glover,
as will appear by a writing under her hand and seal, bearing date
1 : 9 : 1660. Therefore I do not give her anything in this my Will."

Mrs. Mary Glover's marriage with the Hon. Thomas Hinckley
was, for a time, resolutely opposed by the relatives and friends of her
former husband. She being young, or at the age of twenty-nine
years, at the time the grave subject was first presented for her consideration, with three children of the tender ages of three, five and
six years, and possessing a competent estate and ability to rear and
educate them, it seemed absurd to those who were nearly connected
with her children, for her to enter into new relations with a man,
however exalted his worth or elevated his position, who had a

---

* John Smith, Quartermaster, was thrice married: first, in England, at Toxteth Park,
Lancashire, to Mary Ryder, who was the mother of Mrs. Glover. She died soon after her
emigration, and he married a second time to Mary ———, of Dorchester. She died, and he
married a third time to Katherine Pelton, widow, who survived him, and died in Boston,
July 17, 1710, aged 90 years. He had by his second wife Mary, several sons and daughters, one of whom was John, who married Miriam (probably Deane), and died in Boston
in 1676. His widow was the ancient schoolmistress of Dorchester, and is buried in the cemetery there. She has a gravestone.

family of eight children, and was much her senior. To remove the children to a new home in a distant Province or Colony, could not at once be acquiesced in; and to leave them at their tender age, seemed equally inconsistent and unmotherly. Accordingly the Governor's suit was rejected, although, it seems, not entirely abandoned by the parties. The marriage was delayed for several months; but after a time the relatives became reconciled and gave their assent to it. The following arrangements were accordingly entered into and agreed upon.

An inventory of the estate of Mrs. Mary Glover was taken at her request before her marriage with Gov. Thomas Hinckley, and presented to the Court by the "Honorable Thomas Hinckley and Mrs. Mary Glover, he resigning all right and interest which his marriage with her may give him in her Estate."

Mrs. Mary Glover's Inventory, taken and Drafted the 18 : 12 : 1659, by Us, whose names are Underwritten, and by the request of Mrs. Mary Glover.

Imp. Her Husband's Wearing Apparel, . . .	£5 13 00 0
Chairs and Stool, ...	1 00 00 0
Cradle, ...	0 02 00 0
Warming pan, ...	0 04 00 0
In Brass, 10s. ; Brass Pot and Iron Pot, 5, . .	0 15 00 0
Pewter, £1 10s. ; Earth. Ware, 10 2 ; Wooden Vessels, 8,	2 08 02 0
Cooking Utensils, 16s. ; One Still, 12s. ; Cradle Rugg, 1,	1 09 00 0
Shaving Kuife, 2s. ; Books, 8 ; ——, 2, . . .	0 12 00 0
Trundle Bed, ...	2 10 00 0
Standing Bed, ...	6 00 00 0
Tubbs and Barrels, 6d. ; Frying pan and Spit, 4d. ; } Pot Racks, 4d.	00 01 02 0
Table and Carpet, ...	10 05 00 0
Two Silver Spoons and Cups, &c.	17 00 00 0
Wine Cups and other Cups, ...	12 00 00 0
4	12 00 00 0
One Bed and Furniture, ...	08 10 00 0
One Court, ...	02 15 00 0
Two Chests and Boxes, ...	00 16 00 0
Napkins, £1 08 ; Table Cloths, £1 08, . .	02 16 00 0
Pillow Cases, £2 02 ; sheets, £11, . . .	13 02 00 0
One Musket, One Rapier, One Case Pistols, . .	03 02 08 0
One Table, 10s. ; Pillion, 8 ; two —— Iron, 3s. .	01 01 08 0
One Cart and Things Appertaining to it, . .	4 00 00 0
One Horse, £12 ; Stone Horse, £7, . . .	19 00 00 0
Four Cows, £17 ; Two Oxen, £12 ; Thirteen Sheep, £15,	44 00 00 0
Plow and Irons, 10s.	00 10 00 0
Meadow, ...	34 00 00 0
House and Land Tw—, ...	220 00 00 0

Debts due the Estate.

Imp.	Quartermaster Smith,	.	.	.	.	. 113 00 08 0
	Thomas Davenport,	.	.	.	.	. 8 10 08 0
	Samuel Chandler,	.	.	.	.	. 1 00 00 0

548 04 00 0

Roger Clap, } *Appraisers.*
John Gurnell, }

This Inventory was presented to the County Court by Thomas Hinckley, Esq., of Barnstable in the Plymouth Colony.

Mary Glover, the Widow of Nathaniel Glover (the elder), to her Children.

Suffolk Rec., Liber 1.

Know all men by these presents, The Relict and Administratrix of Mr. Nathaniel Glover of Dorchester, Deceased, Sends Greeting :

Being about to Change my Condition, yet sensible of the duty incumbent on me in my Relations to my Deceased Husband in thereby securing the Portions and Inheritance of my Three Children, viz., Nathaniel Glover, John Glover, and Anne Glover my daughter, I have therefore Granted, Assigned and Confirmed, and do by these Presents Grant, Assign and Confirm unto Edward Rawson, Recorder for the County of Suffolk in Massachusetts Jurisdiction in New England, All my Now Dwelling House, Barn, Corn Barn and other Buildings, Orchard, Yard, Garden, Plow Ground, Farming Land, Woodland and Meadow, with all the Liberties and Appurtenances thereunto belonging, Late in the Possession of the said Nathaniel Glover, Deceased.

To Have and to Hold to the said Edward Rawson, &c., giving him full power to act for my Children from time to time until they become of Age to have their full and Just Proportions, or that they shall arrive at the Age of Twenty One Years, Being satisfied and paid as they shall grow and become due and Payable.

The said Nathaniel, John and Anne.

This 15 day of March, 1659–60.
MARY GLOVER, and a Seale.
THOMAS HINCKLEY.

Witnesses.
Samuel Rigbee,
Humphrey Atherton.

Entered and Recorded, 16 : 1 : 1659–60, pr EDWARD RAWSON,
Recorder.

Suffolk ss.

At a County Court Holden at Boston, the 31st day of August, One Thousand Six Hundred and Sixty. Recorded as by the Records may appear. And Whereas The Inventory of the Estate of Mr. Nathaniel Glover, late of Dorchester Deceased, being Recorded in the County Court and entered and Recorded on the Court Books of Records, as it may appear, amounting in value to Five Hundred and Fifty Pounds, One Shilling and Eight-pence. And on the Marriage of Mary, the Relict Widow of the aforesaid Nathaniel Glover, with Mr. Thomas Hinckley, an Inventory of the said Estate being brought and presented to the Court of what remained, which appears to be in value Four Hundred and Seventy Eight Pounds, One Shilling and Sixpence. The Court on Request of said Mr. Hinckley (in Right of Mary the said Relict) Judged meet to make Division of said Estate which hath been under the Management of the said Mary, Relict (Widow) aforesaid and Administratrix to the said Estate, as follows, viz. :

That the said Thomas Hinckley, in Right of Mary the said Relict and Widow of Mr. Nathaniel Glover, now his Wife, shall have One full Third part of the aforesaid Four Hundred and Seventy Eight Pounds, One Shilling and Sixpence : To the amount of One Hundred and Fifty Nine Pounds, seven Shillings, and Two-pence, to be deducted out of the Goods and Chattels.

The other Two Thirds of Lands and Goods to remain as the Portions and dues of the Children of the said Mr. Nathaniel Glover. The Court Drawing the Reversion* left by the Will of Mr. John Glover and the Forty Pounds (left by the said Will) and due from Mr. Habackuk Glover, to be divided amongst the said Children of Mr. Nathaniel Glover and their Mother as they shall grow and become due according to the above said Will.

And it is further ordered that the Administratrix shall deliver up into the hands of Mr. Habackuk Glover and John Gurnell, who at this Court are hereby appointed Guardians to said Children of the said Nathaniel Glover Deceased, the remainder of the Goods, amounting to Sixty Five Pounds, with the Lands thereto belonging, in behalf of the children ; And that the abovenamed Habackuk Glover and John Gurnell be required to give security to the Recorder for the sum of Sixty Five Pounds in behalf thereof, With the increase of the Lands to run for the Benefit of the said children.

Mrs. Anna Glover and Mr. Habackuk Glover engaging on their own Charge and account, without looking to the Children's Estates for satisfaction, to bring them up to School and find them meat, drink and clothing until they be fit to be disposed of in good hands.

EDWARD RAWSON, *Recorder.*

May 28, 1659, Mrs. Mary Glover was permitted by the General Court at Boston, to convey a piece of land by a legal deed to Thomas Davenport of Dorchester.

Vol. 4 Mass. Col. Rec., p. 319. " This Court being satisfied of the reality of the sale of a piece of land numbered in a draught of a bill of sale presented to this Court and is on file, do judge meet to empower Mrs. Mary Glover, Administratrix and relict of Mr. Nathaniel Glover, to make and sign a legal deed of conveyance of the said land unto Thomas Davenport, his heirs and assigns," &c.

---

* Newbury Farm.

After the necessary preliminaries were settled, Mrs. Mary Glover was married and removed to Barnstable. Her children by Mr. Nathaniel Glover were placed among their relatives and sent to school in Boston.

Order of Court for a Division of Nathaniel Glover's Estate.

At a County Court held at Boston, April 28, 1674, Two of the children of the late Mr. Nathaniel Glover deceased, who are now of age, and Mr. Antony Checkley as guardian to the third child, being under age, appearing in Court and moving the Court to order a settlement of the estate late the said Glover's, the eldest son with the allowance of the Court made choice of ensign Richard Hall; the other with the Guardian made choice of Joseph Holmes; the Court appointed Capt. Hopestill Foster as a third man; being all three of Dorchester, to be a Committee, who are hereby impowered to Divide the said Glover's late estate into two equal parts, and to make a division of one of the said parts into two equal parts again, and to make their Return to the next Court of this County of what they do herein. This Committee are thus impowered as above said, in case the said Children with the Guardian do not agree upon a Division of the said Estate amongst themselves, to their mutual satisfaction, by the last day of May next following.

Endorsed upon the Order as follows :

Dorchester, 1st May, 1674.

The partys concerned in the Order of this Honorable Court on the other side, repaired to Dorchester, and prevailing with the Committee appointed therein, to accompany them to the Dwelling-house and land of the late Mr. Nathaniel Glover, where, on a view of the land and after several proffers and considerations made between Nathaniel Glover the eldest son and the other Children concerned, with the full consent and approbation of the said Committee, It was amicably and fully agreed, consented to, and concluded, that Nathaniel Glover the Eldest son should have and enjoy to him and his heirs the Dwelling house and land adjoining thereto, the full breadth to the Sea, and dead low water mark, all the land fenced in running from thence to the Highway, or Road leading to Dorchester Mill, being fourteen Acres more or less, with the second Division or Wood Lott lying for Thirty six acres, be it more or less, into the Woods. And that the Thirty six acres of land, Right against the said Nathaniel's Division on the other side of the Highway, be the same more or less, with the first Division of Wood lott lying in Dorchester Common next unto the said pasturing bordering on that Highway leading from Ensign Hall's Fence to the Mill, and also the Third Division of the Wood lott, being Thirty six Acres, with all the Wood and trees thereupon, lying about two miles from the Thirty six acres of Pasture land fenced in, All lying for One Hundred and Eighty Acres more or less, to be and belong to William Rawson in Right of Anne his Wife, and to John Glover the youngest son of the late Mr. Nathaniel Glover and their heirs, to be in their own time equally divided between them; and

16

that the several parcels of Salt Marsh over against or between the Mr. Glover's Newbury Farm and Squantum Neck to be equally divided between them. The said Nathaniel Glover to have One half of the meadow here or there, and the other half to be and belong to William Rawson and John Glover and their heirs. And so the rest of the Goods, Rents and Whatsoever else belonging to the said Mr. Nathaniel Glover Deceased, and left under the care of Mr. Habackuk Glover, to be and belong and to be divided between them in like proportions as above. As Witness Ye* hands the day and year above Written, in presence of and with the Approbation of the said Committee.   NATHANIEL GLOVER.
                                         ANTONY CHECKLEY, Guardian
In presence and with the Approba-   to John Glover.
    tion of   WILLIAM RAWSON.
    Hopestill Foster,
    Richard Hall,
    Joseph Holmes.   The Court approves of this Division,
                              and orders it to be recorded.
And is witnessed by   May 2, 1674.
    · Thomas Hinckley, Sen.   As attest,   IsᴬADDINGTON, *Clerk.*
    Edward Rawson,
    John Richards.

A true copy as of Record.
                    Examined by EZEKIEL GOLDTHWAIT, *Clerk.*

THOMAS HINCKLEY, the second husband of Mary Smith, was the son of Samuel and Sarah (———) Hinckley, who came to New England in the ship Hercules, of Sandwich, England, which sailed about March, 1634. They brought with them four children, of whom Thomas was the second son. The family originally was from the County of Kent, in England. At a small Parish called Egerton (Tenderton), Thomas Hinckley was born in 1618, and baptized there by the Rev. John Lathrop, a few days after his birth. His parents, on their arrival in this country in 1634, settled first at Scituate, and in 1639 removed to Barnstable, where he attained the age of manhood, and soon took an active and prominent part in the affairs of the Colony. He was chosen Deputy as early as 1645; a Magistrate and Assistant for the Colony of Plymouth from 1658 to 1680; elected Governor in 1681, and continued in that office — except during the interruption caused by the appointment of Sir Edmund Andros — until the union of the Colony of New Plymouth with the Massachusetts Colony in 1692. From 1678 to 1692, a period of fourteen years, Gov. Hinckley was chosen a Commissioner in the General Board held by the two Colonies before their union. He died suddenly at Barnstable, in April, 1706, aged 86. He was

twice married: first, Dec. 7, 1641, to Mary Richards, daughter of
Thomas and Welthean (Loring) Richards, of Weymouth. She died
June 24, 1659, and he was married a second time, March 16, 1660,
to Mrs. Mary Glover, widow of Mr. Nathaniel Glover, of Dorchester.
By his first wife, Mary Richards, he had eight children, born in Barn-
stable, as follows:

Mary, b. Aug. 3, 1644; m. Peter Wybourne.
Sarah, b. Nov. 4, 1646; m. Nathaniel Bacon, of Barnstable,
    Mar. 27, 1673.
Melatiah, b. Nov. 24, 1648; m. Josiah Crocker, of Barnstable.
Hannah, b. April 15, 1650; m. Nathaniel Glover, of Dorchester.
Samuel, b. Feb. 14, 1652; m. Sarah Pope, of Sandwich.
Thomas, b. Dec. 5, 1654; d. unmarried, 1688; will proved same
    year.
Bathshua, b. May 15, 1657; m. Samuel Hall, of Dorchester.
Mehetable, b. Mar. 24, 1659; m. { 1st, Samuel Worden, of Boston.
                                  { 2d, William Avery, of Dedham.

Children of THOMAS HINCKLEY and MARY (SMITH) (GLOVER)
HINCKLEY, born in Barnstable:

Admire, b. July 28, 1660-1; d. two weeks after.
Ebenezer, b. Feb. 22, 1661-2; d. two weeks after.
Mercy, b. Jan. 1, 1662-3; m. Samuel Prince, of Sandwich.
Experience, b. Feb. 2, 1664; m. James Whipple, Esq.
John, b. June 9, 1667; m. Thankful Trott, of Dorchester.
Abigail, b. April 1, 1669; m. Rev. Joseph Lord, of Dorchester,
    South Carolina.
Thankful, b. August 20, 1670; m. Rev. Experience Mayhew.
Ebenezer, b. Sept. 23, 1673; m. Mary Stone, of Sudbury.
Reliance, b. Dec. 15, 1675; m. Rev. Nathaniel Stone, of Mar-
    tha's Vineyard.

Gov. Hinckley was a man of large estate — an extensive landholder. He made a will dated Oct. 16, 1700, when he was 82 years old.
Appoints his beloved wife Mary to be sole executrix, and in the
event of her previous decease, sons John and Ebenezer to be her
successors; bequeaths one half of all his estates to his wife Mary,
the other half to sons John and Ebenezer, who are to succeed to
the whole at her decease — including two hundred acres of land at
Little Compton, R. I., granted him by the General Court for his services in the War of King Philip.

His will was signed Dec. 31, 1700, and witnessed by Jonathan
Russell, James Whippo, John Jenkins and Martha Russell.

" BARNABAS LOTHROP, Commissioned by the Governor and Council for the County of Barnstable.

To all persons before whom these Presents shall or may come or concern—Greeting :

Know Ye—That on the 27th day of April, 1705, before me at Barnstable, the Will Within Written was proved, approved, and allowed so far as it concerns and relates to the Real Estate of said Thomas Hinckley, Dec^d, who having while he lived and at the time of his death Goods, Chattels and Credits in the aforesaid County—but by reason that Mary Hinckley, Wife of the Deceased, died before the Testator, Therefore the said Will is not allowed to be of any force for the disposing of the personal estate of the said Deceased, but Administration of all and singular of the Goods, Chattels and Rights and Credits of the said Deceased was committed to Samuel Prince of Sandwich, Son-in-Law to the Testator, as witness my hand and seale of office set this 27th day of April, 1705.   BARNABAS LOTHROP."

There appears to be an uncertainty as to the date of his death. It is said by those who have written of him, that he died in 1706. The following is the inscription on his gravestone or tomb-tablet, which was erected to his memory in 1829, by one of his descendants*— the old gravestone having been demolished by time.

" Beneath this stone, erected A.D. 1829, are deposited the mortal remains of Thomas Hinckley, Esq., Gov. of Plymouth Colony. He died A.D. 1706, aged 86 years. History bears witness to his piety, usefulness and agency in the public transactions. The important offices he was called to fill evidence the esteem in which he was held by the people. He was successively elected an Assistant and Governor of Plymouth Colony, from 1658 to 1680, and continued to discharge that office, excepting during the interruption of Sir Edmund Andros — resumed the office of Governor in 1681, and continued until the junction of the Plymouth and Massachusetts Colonies in 1692."

His death is thus noticed in Freeman's History of Cape Cod.

" In 1706, April 25, died suddenly in Barnstable, Gov. Thomas Hinckley, at the advanced age of 86 years. A gentleman of distinquished reputation and of great energy of character, who, as we have

* Capt. Matthias Hinckley, of Barnstable, is the descendant who caused the Tablet in memory of Gov. Hinckley to be erected in 1829. He has in his possession the shattered fragments of the gravestone of Mrs. Mary (Glover) Hinckley. A letter has just been received from him stating that he is making arrangements for a monument to be erected over her grave with a suitable inscription, and to have the lot which contains the Governor's family inclosed with an iron fence.

Capt. Hinckley is a descendant of the Hon. Thomas and Mary (Glover) Hinckley, by the line of their son John Hinckley, who married Thankful Trott.

seen, filled a large space in the history of the County of Barnstable, and especially in the affairs of the Plymouth Colony. In truth it may be said it was his to fill a large space in the world's history. He had stood by the cradle of the Colony in its infancy, and had been, from first to last, the associate of its great and good men, in weal or woe, and had lived, himself the chief among the surviving, to see the last chapter written in its immortal annals."

Gov. Hinckley's verses on the death of his second consort, Mrs. Mary (Glover) Hinckley, in which he enumerates her remarkable virtues and traits of character, have been preserved and are here given:

" Pity me, Oh my friends, and for me pray
   To him that can supply what's taken away.
My Crown has fallen from my head, and Wo,
Wo is unto me that has sinned so,
As to provoke the Lord to shew such ire,
Which I deserve against me should burn like fire.
God righteous is in all that he hath done ;
Yea, Good in lending her to me so long.
A blessing rich Forty three years and more
Had I been wise to have improved such store
Of Gifts and Grace wherewith she was endu'd,
I might in Grace have also much improv'd.
How prompt in heavenly discourse was she,
That to her own, and others good might be !
Out of her store came things both new and old,
Which she had read, or thought, or had been told.
How great my Bond to God for thankfulness
For such a Gift, for all my worthlessness.
The *only Child* her gracious Mother bore,
Ordained of God as a return of Prayer,
For which she with her friends employed a day
In private, and soon found it good to pray
Unto the God of Nature and of Grace,
Who thus approved their seeking of His Face
In forming this fair child to shew his Praise.
Endowed with virtues in her early days,
Which grew and shined in young and riper age,
And to her Maker's Praise did much engage
All those who knew her, both of late and old,
And proved as divers Godly Wise foretold.
She by her wisdom built the house, and by
Her prudent care kept all in such a way
And in such order, so as nought might be
A let or (hindrance) to worship in the family,
Or cause distraction on God's Holy day.
Yes, both at *morn* and *even* as it was need,

She did in *Household Worship* always lead
Her family while in her widowed state ;
And in my absence, since she was my mate.
Whose good example may rebuke all those
Who slight this duty and themselves expose
Unto the Wrath of God which hangs o'er all
Those families who on him do not call.
To rise up *very early* was her way ;
Enter her closet strait to read and pray,
And then to call and raise her family,
And lived to see a blessing great upon
Her prayers and prudent education
Of children, such a number for the Lord
Under his Gracious Covenant and Word,
That now may say, I am through Grace divine
Thy servant, daughter, son or handmaid thine.

She highly prized a Gospel ministry,
For its support was an example high ;
And while a Widow chose the Town should say
What was her part; lest self from right should stray,
And always gave more than her Rate away.
Yea, ever first would pay that pious due,
Then other debts, and on the residue
Would wisely live, and help the poor she knew.
Nor ever any want she found thereby,
And counselled her friends the like to try.
But if they would till last let that alone,
They would find nought to pay it, all would be gone.
Which some have tried and found what she said true,
And so God was not robbed of his due.
As by God's grace she lived piously,
So by the same she lived righteously,
Chusing that she and hers might wrongs receive
Than even the least to others give ;
Always a pattern of Sobriety,
Meek, lowly, peaceful, prone to Charity
And freely given to Hospitality ;
Behaved wisely in a perfect way
Both in the brightest and the darkest day.
She come in nothing short with count of many
Of highest praise of tongue or pen of any.
Great cause we have of pious thankfulness,
For that tho' sharpest pains did her distress,
For *six weeks* almost constantly that she
Could take no rest, nor in the night nor day,
Yet God preserved her mind and senses clear
With exercise of Grace, that we could hear
Not the least murmuring nor impatient word,
But meek submission to her Sovereign Lord
Full of heart melting prayer and savory words

Which joy and wonderment to all affords,
Whose hearts were moved to leave your homes and see
And help her in her great extremity.
Her last words were, " Come, dear Lord Jesus, come,
And take me quickly to thy bosom dear,"
And in a few minutes had her soul's desire,
With Him whom she did love with heart entire.
Death was no terror to her nor fear,
No Ghastliness did in her face appear.
But sweet composure in her life and death, }
When her dear soul she in her final breath }
Resigned to him whom she beheld in faith ; }
Whose own she was and with him longed to be
Where she is free from sin and misery :
She entered into perfect endless rest,
And with the blest above is ever blest.

So that we have no reason to repine,   }
But thankfully and humbly to resign ;   }
To his most Wise and Righteous hand therein. }
Nor mourn for her, in plenitude of joy,
But for ourselves whom evils still annoy.

As a great loss to all the wisest deem,
Then sure to me and mine a loss extreme.
Now she has left, the gap is made a way
For evils to bear on us every day,
Where our iniquities deserved have
Unless the Lord please, as I humbly crave,
To give repentance and remission free
Of all our sins, of mine especially.
My great defect in point of Gratitude
In prizing and improving such a good
Which as a *second* miracle of Grace,
After the first, who no less pious was,
And love *consort*, both free gifts most rare
And both in answer unto humble prayer.
As soon as I my will resigned so
To God, as to be free that he should do
As most for his own Glory He should see,
Then did their several relatives agree
To say that they had opposed our match so long
They neither dared, nor would it more prolong.
Which was so far above all expectation
As made us to admire the Dispensation.
Yet that I such wondrous works could ere forget,
Does my offences greatly aggravate :
Which has so much dishonored his name
As justly may me fill with grief and shame.
And Oh that by his grace enabling me,   }
I may with hate, yea, self abhorrency   }
Turn from all sin, and unto Jesus flee ; }

176 MEMORIALS AND GENEALOGIES.

Whose meritorious and precious blood
Can cleanse from sin and reconcile to God.
Oh, may he be most highly prized by me,
And as most precious may embraced be ;
May I to Him eternally be joined,
And in Him rest and satisfaction find.
By His good Spirit's mighty energy   }
My heart be purged from all impurity, }
And filled with all grace and sanctity. }
Awakened out of all my drowsy frames,
Raised up to lively heavenly views and aims,
Ever composed, humble, watchful be,
Especially upon God's Holy Day.
And when I read, hear, meditate and pray,
In holy duties never slightly be,
As if to approach the Glorious Majesty
Of God a light and trifling thing it were,
But ever look and speak to him with fear.
May bring forth much good fruit in my last days,
Living and doing more unto His praise,
Gaining much profit by Our Father's Rod,
Who can make all work out eternal good.
For all such merits great I beg the prayers
Of all who see these drops of aged tears,
That I and mine may by his mighty hand
Be kept through faith unto salvation.
And that we may neither slack or slothful be,
But follow him and that blest company,
Who through their faith and patience now possess
The full completion of the promises,
And we may fitted be at death to say,
Lord Jesus, come, and take us quick away,
To be with thee unto Eternal day.

Afflicted and distressed, but through undeserved Mercy not wholly forsaken.

T. HINCKLEY,

aged 85 years.

[*Third Generation.*]

(1) NATHANIEL GLOVER, the eldest son of Mr. Nathaniel and Mary (Smith) Glover, was born in Dorchester, 30 : 1 : 1653, and baptized 3 : 2 : 1653, by Rev. Richard Mather. He died at Newbury farm in that town, January 6, 1723–4, aged 71 years, and was buried in the westerly part of the ancient burial yard, where his gravestone still remains, but the inscription is so much worn by time as scarcely to be deciphered. At the age of seven years, in 1660, he was placed under the guardianship of his uncle, Mr. Habackuk

Glover, of Boston, who succeeded his mother in that appointment at the time of her marriage with Gov. Hinckley and removal to Barnstable. He was placed at school in Boston, and resided in the family of his grandmother, Mrs. Anna Glover, and after her decease, in 1670, with his uncle and guardian until about the time of his own marriage. In 1672–3, at the age of twenty years, he was married to Hannah Hinckley, of Barnstable, and occupied the homestead at Dorchester a part of which was his inheritance, although, on account of his minority, the estate remained as yet undivided.

In 1674, when he had attained the age of twenty-one years, the homestead estate at Dorchester was ordered to be divided amongst the children of Mr. Nathaniel Glover, deceased. (See page 169.) Whether by the will of his father, or as the eldest son by right of primogeniture, it is not stated, but the Court ordered one half of the estate, with the house and buildings, to be settled on him as his portion, and the other half part to be shared equally between his only brother and sister, when they were of full age. He succeeded to his inheritance, and continued the business of tanning, which had been followed on the estate since the first occupation by his grandfather in 1631, and was carried on by his father until his decease in 1657, and by the lessees until the period of his succession in 1674, forty-three years from its commencement. In 1700 he resigned the business to his eldest son Nathaniel Glover, Jr., and the next year removed with his family to the Newbury farm estate, a portion of which was his by inheritance. By a deed of gift from his uncle John Glover, and by purchase from the other heirs, he soon came in possession of a considerable portion of that estate, with the houses and buildings, which he retained until his death in 1723–4.

In 1677, the second day of the eighth month, he was admitted to the Church at Dorchester;* also "Mrs. Hannah, the wife of Mr. Nathaniel Glover." In 1683 he was elected constable, and was afterwards chosen to serve as selectman, and continued in that office a few years, the last in 1715.

---

* "A list of those who were adults, and have personally and in public submitted themselves to the government of the Church, and have assented to the doctrines and given satisfaction to the Elders concerning their knowledge, and afterwards being proposed to the Church for their satisfaction as to their conversation and regular walking sometime before their calling forth to own the Covenant, viz., 29 (5) 1677, these persons under named were called upon in the public and owned the Covenant: Mr. Timothy Mather, Thomas Andrews, Mr. Nathaniel Glover, John Smith, and others."

Division of the Dorchester Estate by Nathaniel Glover and William Rawson.

April 28, 1674. The Honorable County Court now sitting at Boston, by their Order for the settlement of the House and lands lately belonging to the late Mr. Nathaniel Glover Dec⁴, son of Mr. John Glover of Boston Dec⁴, amongst the children of the above named Nathaniel Glover, viz., Nathaniel Glover, John Glover, and Anne Glover now wife unto William Rawson of Boston, did settle and divide all the said houses and lands, and apportion the one half to the said Nathaniel Glover for himself and his heirs forever, and the other half to the said William Rawson in Right of his Wife Anne, and to John Glover the second son as aforesaid, to be held by them in equal halves and by their heirs forever. Leaving only sixteen acres of Salt Marsh for themselves to divide.

And Whereas the said William Rawson hath purchased this Right of the said John Glover in said Marsh, and hath received the sum of ten shillings of the said Nathaniel Glover the eldest son, that he might take his choice of the said eight acres of said Salt Marsh lying in two nearly equal parts on a Creek running between them, and lying between the farms of the late Mr. Hawkins and Mr. Glover's Newbury Farm. The said Nathaniel Glover having chosen that eight Acres that lyeth on the Northerly side of said Creek to enjoy to him and his heirs forever. And it is agreed between them, the said Nathaniel Glover and William Rawson, that the said William Rawson shall have and hold and keep the other eight Acres of Salt Marsh to himself and to his heirs forever, lying next to the Newbury Farm. With which division as forever to enjoy to them and to their heirs and assigns forever, and they hereby declare themselves to be fully satisfied.

(Signed)   NATHANIEL. GLOVER,
28 April, 1674.   WILLIAM RAWSON.

Acknowledged in person by the above parties, June 29, 1681.

HANNAH HINCKLEY, the wife of Nathaniel Glover, was born in Barnstable, April 15, 1650, and died in Dorchester at Newbury farm, April 30, 1730, in her 81st year. She was buried in the ancient burial ground on the westerly side, and has a grave-stone. She was the fourth daughter of Gov. Thomas Hinckley by his first wife Mary Richards, granddaughter of Thomas and Welthean (Loring) Richards, of the early settlers of Weymouth. By the will of her maternal grandmother, made in 1679, she received five pounds as her equal and just proportion as a grandchild; and by the will of her maternal uncle, the Hon. John Richards, of Boston, she received the sum of two hundred pounds in money, and silver plate to the amount of ten pounds. From her father she received a competent portion upon her marriage with Mr. Nathaniel Glover. After her marriage and removal to Dorchester, she was admitted to join the Church there, 2 (8) 1677.

Children of NATHANIEL and HANNAH (HINCKLEY) GLOVER, born in Dorchester:

4. Nathaniel, b. Feb. 24, 1674; bap. (in private) when 3 days old; d. soon.
5. Nathaniel, b. Aug..7, 1675; bap. (in private) two days old; d. same year.
+6. Nathaniel, b. Nov. 10, 1676; m. Rachel Marsh, of Braintree.
+7. Mary,   b. April 12, 1679; died after 1743.
+8. Hannah,   b. July 26, 1681; m. Thomas Laws, Esq., of Marblehead.
+9. Elizabeth, b. July 26, 1683; d. April 11, 1725, aged 41 years; unmarried.
+10. John, b. Sept. 18, 1687; m. { 1st, Susannah Ellison, Boston.
                                  { 2d, Mary Horton, Milton.
+11. Thomas, b. Dec. 26, 1690; m. Elizabeth Clough, of Boston.

The last six children were baptized at the Dorchester Church within a few days of their birth, but not all by the same pastor. The two youngest sons, John and Thomas, were baptized by Rev. Jonathan Bowman.

In 1687, Nathaniel Glover, Sen., made a division of land with Ebenezer Billings, who had purchased some of the rights in Newbury farm.

Nathaniel Glover to Ebenezer Billings — A Division.

To all Christian People to whom these Presents shall come — Nathaniel Glover of Dorchester, in His Majesty's Territory of New England, Sendeth Greeting: Know Ye, That Whereas John Glover, Esq., late of Dorchester Deceased, did by his last Will and Testament devise and bequeath unto his four sons, viz., To Habackuk Glover, John Glover, Nathaniel Glover and Pelatiah Glover, a Certain Messuage or Farm in said Dorchester, commonly called and known by the name Newbury Farm, to be equally divided to them and their Heirs: And Whereas Ebenezer Billings having purchased the Right of Habackuk Glover, and John Glover, and Nathaniel Glover in right of the Heirs of his father Mr. Nathaniel Glover of Dorchester Dec^d, and Pelatiah Glover, have by mutual consent made a Division of said Farm in Four equal parts as by a Deed of Division under their hands and Seales may appear: And Whereas Ebenezer Billings aforesaid hath purchased a fourth part of that Share belonging to the Heirs of Nathaniel Glover Dec^d, of John the son of said Nathaniel Glover Dec^d, Now Know Ye, That I the said Nathaniel Glover have by my full and free consent set and laid out unto Ebenezer Billings aforesaid, as his Fourth part of the said Division, in right of my brother John

Glover aforesaid, That is to say, Six Acres of Land in the Bay Field, and by consent of my Uncle John Glover laid out his Fourth part of the field adjoining to Ebenezer Billings from the Highway to the Sea. Also a Fourth part of the Second Division of Land that fell by Lot to me in right of the Heirs of my father Nathaniel Glover of Dorchester Deceased, lying next adjoining to said Billings his Second Division. Item, the First division of Squantum Marsh, being the first lot that was staked out and bounded ; as also Two Acres of Marsh, more or less, near Nine Acre Marsh ; and is bounded on the South by a line from a Pine Tree to a small Hammock, or in a small Creek where is set a stake, which line runneth through a small Pond ; And from said Stake bounded by a small Creek till it comes to a Great Pond of Thatch ; and from thence to another Pond, there being a Stake at the head of each Pond ; and from said Pond by a Small Creek that runneth out of a Creek that divideth between Nine Acre Marsh and Smith's Marsh : Also a just Fourth part that fell to me in the Orchard in Right as aforesaid, adjoining to said Billings in said Orchard ; As also a full Sixteenth part of the Old Houses, Barns, Common Land and Springs laid in common to the whole concerned.   Which several parcels of Land and Meadow aforesaid, I the said Nathaniel Glover have set out and delivered to the said Ebenezer Billings in full of his Right bought of my brother John Glover, his Right in said Newbury Farm as aforesaid.   Excepting what Right said Billings may have in any divisions of Land in Milton, formerly improved with or appertaining to the said Newbury Farm or the Proprietors thereof.

To Have and to Hold the said Parcels and divisions of Land to the said Ebenezer Billings, his Heirs and Assigns Forever.   Without the Least Lett or Hindrance, Suit, Denial, Challenge, Claim or Demand of me the said Nathaniel Glover, my Heirs and Assigns, &c.

In Witness Whereof, I have hereunto set my hand and seale this Fifteenth day of April, 1687.   NATHANIEL GLOVER, and a Seale.

Signed, sealed and delivered in Presence of us,
        Richard Hall,
        John Breck.

Certificate.

These may Certify All Whom it may concern, that I Ebenezer Billings do freely accept the above parcels of Land as they are described and bounded in the above-written Instrument under the hand and seale of Nathaniel Glover, in full of what I bought of John Glover his brother, Excepting what is there excepted.

In Witness Whereof, I have hereunto set my hand and Seal this Fifteenth day of April, 1687, The day of the date above-written.

        In presence of   EBENEZER BILLINGS.
        Joseph Hall,
        John Breck.

In 1688, Nathaniel Glover, Sen., conjointly with his uncle John Glover, Sen., of Boston, acted as attorney in the leasing of Rev. Pelatiah Glover's one fourth part of Newbury farm to Ebenezer Billings for a term of years.

To all Christian People to whom these Presents may come: John Glover Senior, and Nathaniel Glover in his own Right, being fully empowered by his Uncle Pelatiah Glover to act and do in all things concerning and about the division of the Newbury farm as if himself were present; and Ebenezer Billings in his own Right, all in his Majestic's Territory and Dominion of New England. Now know ye, that we John Glover Senior, and Nathaniel Glover for ourselves and Pelatiah Glover aforesaid, and Ebenezer Billings aforesaid in his Right and for himself (which was the Right of Habackuk Glover and purchased by him in 1681), have upon second thoughts and mature considerations, notwithstanding our former determination at our former division of said farm (which was to let all the old houses, barns and yard lye in common to all the said Proprietors), mutually and with one free and full consent joyntly agreed and fully determined to make a division of all the houses and lands not formerly divided at the Newbury farm aforesaid, and have by ourselves this Ninth day of April, in the fourth year of our Sovereign Lord King James the Second and in the Year of Our Lord 1688, made a full and final division of said Newbury farm to our mutual content and satisfaction, and by these presents have and do ratify and confirm against ourselves, our several heirs and successors of each other in the free and full, quiet and peaceable possession of our respective shares and just rights as now laid out, viz., to Ebenezer Billings in the full right of Habackuk Glover and John Glover Junior's share and right in said farm : We John Glover Senior, and Nathaniel Glover for himself and for his Uncle Pelatiah aforesaid, do by this deed of division, give and grant, alien and confirm unto him the said Billings and to his heirs and assigns forever, the great barn standing next said Billings's new house, with all the land square off with the North end of said barn as it is now staked out, with convenient way through the yard before the old housing (houses) down to the Spring for man and beast, with free use of said Water, with egress and regress thereunto. The land is to extend from the North end of the said barn to the said Billings's own lot where his house stands ; together with all the privileges and appurtenances thereunto belonging, to have and to hold, use, occupy and enjoy forever.

In consideration whereof, the said Ebenezer Billings doth give, grant, alien and confirm unto them the said John Glover Senior, and Nathaniel Glover, and to their heirs and Assigns, all his just Right, Title and Interest in and to all the other old Dwelling Houses, Barns, Yards, Back-yards, Trees, Fruit trees or others, with the land square to and with the North end of the Great Barn aforesaid, with liberty of a convenient way through the Yard at the East end of the orchard into the field or pasture. Together with all and singular the privileges and profits and appurtenances thereunto belonging.

To have and to hold the above granted premises as above expressed, with all the appurtenances, forever. And in witness whereof, the aforesaid premises and of our Joynt Consent therein and thereunto, we have joyntly set our hands and peaceably and with full consent possessed each other in his rightful and lawful possession, according to the true intent of this Instrument, on the 9th day of April, Anno Domini 1688.   (Signed)   JOHN GLOVER, Sen.
In presence of us, Joshua Stone, Moses   NATHANIEL GLOVER,
     Belcher, Abigail Thompson.   EBENEZER BILLINGS.

17

August 17, 1692, Nathaniel Glover, Sen., with Daniel Preston, were appointed by his Excellency William Stoughton, to divide the estate of Timothy Tileston. The division was completed, and accepted August 20, 1698.

July 21, 1696, his name occurs as a witness, with those of Ralph Stoughton and Samuel Topliff, to the last will and testament of Ellis Wood, who married Miriam, the widow of his uncle John Smith, deceased.

In 1697–8, Nathaniel Glover, Senior, of Dorchester, purchased a piece of land containing one acre and one quarter, situated near Dorchester Meeting-House, on the road leading to Dorchester mill, of Elizabeth Cleverly, widow, and Executrix of his uncle John Glover, deceased. (See p. 159.)

In 1699 Nathaniel Glover, Senior, with William Rawson, purchased the one fourth part of Newbury farm which belonged to their uncle, the Rev. Pelatiah Glover, of Springfield. April, 11, 1700, they agreed to divide it in equal halves. The agreement was as follows:

WILLIAM RAWSON and NATHANIEL GLOVER agree to divide the One Fourth part of Newbury Farm which they bought of Pelatiah Glover their Cousin, as follows:

Whereas Pelatiah Glover, son and Executor of the last Will and Testament of Pelatiah Glover late of Springfield in the County of Hampshire and in the Province of Massachusetts Bay in New England, Clergyman, deceased, who was one of the sons of John Glover Esq. of Boston in the Province aforesaid, Esq., Dec^d, by him duly executed, bearing date the Fourteenth day of February last past, before the date of these presents, did bargain, sell and convey unto William Rawson of Brantry in the Province aforesaid, Yeoman, and Nathaniel Glover of Dorchester in the said Province, Tanner, their heirs and assigns forever in equal halves, One quarter or Fourth part of a Certain farm situate and lying in Dorchester aforesaid, being that quarter or fourth part thereof that was set forth upon division thereof to the said Deceased Pelatiah Glover; the whole of said farm being formerly the before named John Glover's, and by him given to his four sons, whereof the deceased Pelatiah was one.

Now these Presents Witness that the said William Rawson and Nathaniel Glover have and hereby do Covenant, grant and agree to and with each other that the said one fourth part of said farm shall be divided between them: and that each of them shall have and enjoy to him, his Heirs and Assigns forever in severalty, the several parcels of said farm hereafter mentioned as his share or dividend of the said fourth part thereof sold to them as aforesaid. (That is to say)

That the said William Rawson for his divided or half part of the said fourth part of said farm aforesaid shall have, hold and enjoy to him, his Heirs and Assigns, forever in severalty, One Acre of land in the

Bay-field, so called, next to his the said Rawson's meadow. Also Thirty acres of land lying in the Rye-field, so called. Also One half the Meadow lying in the quarter part of the aforesaid farm, both for quantity and quality; Also one half the Woodland belonging to said quarter part of said farm, lying in the Town of Milton; Also one half the Orchard called Pelatiah's Orchard, and so much more of said Orchard as shall suit to the like quantity with one half of the Three Cornered piece of Land, so called, lying before the House.

And that the said Nathaniel Glover, for his half part of the said fourth part of said farm aforesaid, shall have, hold and enjoy to him, his Heirs and Assigns forever in severalty, All the remainder of land in the Bay field, other than the One Acre allotted thereout to the said William Rawson as aforesaid; All the Upland on the Neck of Land called Pine Neck; Also all the Common land about and behind the House standing on the fourth part of the farm aforesaid, Together with all the said Rawson's Right and Interest in and to the said House. Also One half the Meadow in said fourth part of the farm abovesaid, both for quantity and quality; Also Half the Woodland belonging to said quarter part of said farm lying in the town of Milton; Also the Three Cornered piece of land so called, lying before the House; And such part and so much of the Orchard aforesaid as shall remain when the part thereof allotted to the said William Rawson shall be measured out to him.

And further, the said William Rawson and Nathaniel Glover do hereby respectively Covenant, Grant and agree to and with each other, that within the space of Three months from the date hereof, they will reciprocally make, seal, duly execute and deliver articles of partition for said premises so divided as aforesaid, in due form, wherein the butts and bounds and certain quantities of the respective parcels of Land to them severally set forth as aforesaid shall be particularly mentioned and expressed.

In Witness Whereof, the said William Rawson and Nathaniel Glover to these Presents have interchangeably set their hands and seals this Eleventh Day of April, 1700. WILLIAM RAWSON.

Signed, sealed and delivered in presence of
James Addington and
Edward Turfrey, Esqs.
Roger Billings.

A duplicate signed at the same time by NATHANIEL GLOVER.

An indenture was afterwards drawn on the fourth day of July, 1702, and the bounds more fully expressed. It was signed by both parties, in presence of Edward Turfrey and Roger Billings.

In 1700, the 27th day of December —

An Indenture to divide three several lots of Woodland, in the Township of Milton, between Nathaniel Glover, Senior of Dorchester, Tanner, and William Rawson and Roger Billings, Yeomen. Bounded as follows, viz.: The first lot, containing Eighty acres more or less, is Abutting on the South East on the boundary line of the Township of

Brantrey: South Westerly on the land of John Daniel and Samuel
Miller; North Westerly on the land of Capt. Thomas Vose; and
North Easterly on land of Daniel Henshaw. The lot containing twen-
ty acres also abutting on the boundary line of the Township of Bran-
trey South Easterly; South Westerly on the land of John Wadsworth;
North Westerly on land of Thomas Swift; and South Westerly on
the land of Joseph Belcher. The third lot, containing Twenty Eight
Acres more or less, also abutting on the boundary line of the Town
of Brantrey South Easterly; and on the land of Ezra Clapp South-
Westerly; on the land of Henry Glover Jun. (lately Capt. Thomas
Vose's), North Westerly; and on land of Henry Glover, Senior,
South Easterly.

The said party's by and with the assistance of their Surveyor,
Samuel Thaxter, mutually chosen for the said purpose, have divided
the above three lots of Woodland into four equal parts, and have
mutually guaranteed each unto the other their respective Rights as
Shareholders, the said Nathaniel Glover by his inheritance, the said
William Rawson in Right of his wife Anne Glover, and the said Roger
Billings by purchase of another Right.   NATHANIEL GLOVER,
                                                 WILLIAM RAWSON,
Signed, sealed and delivered in presence of   ROGER BILLINGS.
          Samuel Gooking,
          Edward Turfrey.

          [The above appears never to have been recorded.]

In 1706, Nathaniel Glover, Senior, purchased of William Rawson,
his brother-in-law, a portion of Newbury farm called the Bay-field.
Date of deed, July 20, 1706. Signed by William Rawson and Anne
Rawson, in presence of Samuel Shepard and William Rawson, Jr.

May 20, 1714, he sold to Edward Glover, of Milton, yeoman, a
tract of wood-land in Milton, containing fourteen acres; bounded
South on the parallel line of Braintree; West by Roger Billings.
Consideration, fifty pounds. Signed by Nathaniel Glover and Hannah Glover, in presence of Roger Billings and Edward Turfrey.

In 1715, Nathaniel Glover made a gift to the trustees of the New
South Church in Summer Street, Boston, towards the building of that
house. The following is from the Church Records:

" A Gift for the building of a Meeting House.

" *Voted*, That the money received from Mr. Nathaniel Glover, except the charges arising thereon, viz., the balance, be given towards
the erecting a Meeting House at the South end of Boston, where the
major part of the Proprietors shall be concerned."

In 1719, Nathaniel Glover, Sen., conveyed to his son Nathaniel
several tracts of land in the Common and Undivided Lands in Dorchester New Grant.

Deed of Gift from Nathaniel Glover, Sen., to Nathaniel Glover, Jr.,
his eldest son.

To **All** People unto whom this present Deed of Gift shall come, I Nathaniel Glover of Dorchester, in the County of Suffolk, within the Province of the Massachusetts Bay in New England, Tanner, send Greeting.

Know Ye : that I the said Nathaniel Glover, for and in consideration of the natural Love, good will and affection which I have and doe beare unto my Loving Son Nathaniel Glover of Dorchester aforesaid, Tanner : As also for Divers other good Causes and considerations Me hereunto at this present time Especially moving, I the said Nathaniel Glover Have given, granted, alienated, enfeoffed, assigned, conveyed and confirmed, and by these Presents for myself and my heirs, Doe fully, freely, clearly and absolutely, give, grant, alien, enfeoffe, assigne, convey and confirme unto my son the said Nathaniel Glover and to his heirs and assigns forever—

All that my House Lott of Land scittuate, lying and being in Dorchester aforesaid, containing by estimation Fifteen Acres, be the same more or less : being butted and bounded on the Easterly end upon the Sea or Salt Water ; on the Northerly side by land of Widow Pelton and Joseph Hall ; on the Westerly end upon the Highway leading to Tilestone's Mill, standing upon Neponsett River ; and on the Southerly side by land of Mrs. Brick [Breck]. Also one other parcel of land, containing by Estimation One Acre and one half of an Acre nigh unto the former parcel ; bounded Northerly and Easterly upon Mrs. Brick's Land ; Southerly upon the Land of the late Quarter Master Smith deceased ; and Westerly upon the aforesaid Highway. Also One Acre of Meadow lying adjoyning to the above-mentioned House lott, and bounded Easterly upon the Sea, Westerly upon a Highway leading along by the East end of the House, upon the aforesaid House Lott.

Also Six Acres of Salt Marsh, called and known by the name of Smith's Marsh, lying without the ditch of, and by the Farm called Glover's Farm ; bounded North-West upon Neponsett River ; South-east upon the Land of Roger Billings, and upon land of Me the said Nathaniel Glover, Senior, Southerly.

And also a Certain piece or parcel of Woodland, lying and scittuate in Dorchester aforesaid, containing by Estimation Thirty Six Acres and one half, bounded Easterly by Land of Goodwife Henshaw, and Northerly by Land of Widdow Smith, Southerly by land of Samuel Capen, and Westerly by Land of Samuel Capen, or however otherwise bounded ; Together with all and singular the Housing Edifices, buildings, Barns, Shedds and Fences standing thereon, Yards, Tan-Yards, Gardens, Orchards, Wayes, easements, timber-trees, woods and underwoods, profits, privileges, rights, commodityes, hereditaments, emoluments and appurtenances whatsoever, to the said given and granted Premises, and to every part and parcel thereof, belonging or in any wise appertaining, or therewith now or heretofore used, occupied or enjoyed, accepted, reputed, taken or known as part, parcel or member thereof. And the reversion and reversions, remainder and remainders, thereof. And also all the Estate, right, title and Interest and Inheritance, Use, possession, property, claim and demand

17*

whatsoever, of Me the said Nathaniel Glover, Sen', and my heirs of, in, and to, the same and every part and parcel thereof.

To Have and to Hold all the above before mentioned, given, granted and confirmed premises, with their and every of their Appurtenances, unto my son the said Nathaniel Glover, Jun', his heirs and assigns forever, To his and their own solo and proper use, benefit and behoofe from henceforth and forevermore, freely, peaceably and quietly, without any manner of reclaime, challenge or contradiction of Me the said Nathaniel Glover Sen', My heirs, Executors, Administrators or Assignes, or of any other person or persons whatsoever, by mine or any of our meanes, Title or procurement in any manner or wise, and without any accompt and reckoning or answer thereof to me or in my name to be given, rendered or done in time to come. Soe that Neither I the said Nathaniel Glover Sen', My heirs, Executors, Administrators or Assignes, nor any other person or persons whatsoever by me, for me, or in any of Our Names, or in the name, right and stead of any of Us, at any time or times hereafter, shall or may aske or claime, challenge or demand in or to the Premises, or any part or parcel thereof, any Estate, Title, Interest or possession.   But from All Action of Right, Title, Claime, Interest, Use, possession and demand thereof, I Myself and every of Us, to be utterly excluded and forever debarred by these presents.

And furthermore, I the said Nathaniel Glover Sen', and my heirs, Executors and Administrators, the above given and granted Premises with the appurtenances, and every part and parcel thereof, unto the said Nathaniel Glover, Jun. my son, his heirs and Assignes, against the Lawful Claimes and demands of all persons and every person whomsoever, shall and will Warrant, Uphold and forever defend by these Presents.

And furthermore that I the said Nathaniel Glover Sen', upon the consideration aforesaid, Have and hereby doe fully and absolutely give, grant and confirm unto my said Son Nathaniel Glover Jun. and to his heirs, Executors, Administrators and Assignes, to his and their own and sole and proper use, benefitt and behoofe forever, All my stock of Leather of every sort and kind, lying and being or belonging to my pitts of the aforesaid Tanyard, with all my Barks and Utensils and Tools belonging to the Tanners' Trade, in and about the said Yard.

In Witness whereof, I the said Nathaniel Glover Sen', and Hannah my wife In token of her free consent to these Presents and full relinquishment of all Right of Dower and Thirds to be by her Claimed or had of, in, to, and out of, the above given and granted Premises, have hereunto sett our hands and seales this Twenty fifth day of December, Anno Dom. One Thousand Seven Hundred.

NATHANIELL GLOVER, and Seale.
HANNAH GLOVER.

Signed, sealed and delivered by the said Nathaniel
 Glover, Sen', in Presence of Us,
  Richard Hubbard,
  Eliezer Moody, *Scr.*

Suffolk ss. Boston, 26 December, 1700. The above named Nathaniel Glover personally appearing before me the Subscriber, one of his Majesty's Justices of the Peace in the said County, acknowledged this Instrument to be his voluntary Act and deed.

JEREMIAH DUMMER.

Hannah Glover Signed, Sealed and Delivered
this Instrument as her act and deed, the 18th of
January, 1700–1, in the presence of us,
      Edward Webb,
      Jonathan Dixwell.

Suffolk ss. Hannah Glover acknowledged the above Instrument to be her act and deed Voluntarily, the 18 day of January, 1700–1, in the presence of me,   JEREMIAH DUMMER, *Just. of the Peace.*

Boston, May 5, 1702. Entered and Recorded with the Records of Deeds for the County of Suffolk, Liber 21, folio 8–9.

By ADDINGTON DAVENPORT, *Registrar.*

In 1718 Nathaniel Glover, Sen., purchased of John and Moses Billings a piece of land containing eight acres and one quarter. The deed was signed the 2d of May, and was witnessed by John Mills and Gregory Belcher.

The above appears to be his last purchase of land. He disposed of all his estates by deeds of gift to his children, and died intestate.

November 20, 1723, he made or executed a deed of gift to his three daughters, viz., Hannah, Mary and Elizabeth Glover, and confirmed unto them several pieces of land in equal proportions, viz., twenty-six acres of upland, salt marsh on the south side of Pine Neck, and four acres bounded by Horse Hammocks. This deed was witnessed by Thomas Glover and David Rawson.

Deed of Gift

From Nathaniel Glover, Sen., to Thomas Glover and Hannah Glover of Dorchester, of the portion which was to come to him in the final settlement and distribution of the estate of his uncle John Glover.

To all People before whom these Presents may come. Know Ye, That I Nathaniel Glover Senior of Dorchester, in the County of Suffolk and in the Province of Massachusetts Bay in New England, Yeoman, send Greeting:

That I the said Nathaniel Glover, for and in consideration of the Love and Affection that I have and do bear towards my well beloved son Thomas Glover, Gentleman, And my daughter Hannah Glover, Spinster, both of Dorchester aforesaid, Have given, granted, conveyed and confirmed, and do by these Presents fully, freely, clearly and absolutely give, grant; convey, and confirm unto them the said Thomas Glover and Hannah Glover in equal proportions, All my

Share, Right, Title and Interest in and to a Certain House and Land in Boston belonging to my Uncle John Glover Deceased. And all the Estate, Right, Title, Interest and Inheritance, Property, Possession, Reversion, Claim or Demand whatsoever, to the said John Glover's Estate which shall or may come to my Share.

To Have and to Hold the above mentioned Premises, with all the Privileges and Appurtenances belonging to them, to the said Thomas Glover and Hannah Glover their Heirs and Assigns Forever, as their own proper Estate in fee simple, and to their own proper uses and behoofe forever.

And I the said Nathaniel Glover do hereby Covenant, Promise, bind and oblige myself, my Heirs, Executors and Administrators, from henceforth and forever to Warrant and defend all the above-mentioned Premises, with the privileges and appurtenances thereof, unto the said Thomas Glover and Hannah Glover, their Heirs and Assigns, against the lawful Claims and Demands of all persons Whomsoever claiming any Right, Title or Interest in or to the Premises or any part thereof, by, from, or under Me.

, And in witness whereof, I the said Nathaniel Glover have hereunto set my Hand and Seale this 7th day of November, 1723; And in the Tenth year of his Majesty's Reign King George the Second.

NATHANIEL GLOVER, and a Seale.

Signed, sealed and delivered in presence of us,
>Mary Glover,
>Elizabeth Glover:

Suffolk ss. Boston, July 17, 1724. At a Court of General Sessions of the Peace sitting in Boston within and for the County of Suffolk Aforesaid, on the 17th day of July, 1724, the above named Mary Glover and Elizabeth Glover personally appeared before the Court and made oath that they saw the above-named Nathaniel Glover Sign, Seal and Deliver the Above Written Instrument as his free Act and Deed, And that they subscribed their names as Witnesses to the Execution thereof at the same time.

Attest: JOHN BALLANTINE, *Register.*

Boston, July 17, 1724. Received, Entered and Recorded with the Records of Deeds for Suffolk County, Lib. 37, fol. 265.

Brought by Capt. Thomas Smith.

Deed of Gift from Nathaniel Glover, Senior, to his Well-beloved Son John Glover.

Suff. ss.   Liber 62, fol. 181.

To All People unto whom this present Deed of Gift shall come. I Nathaniel Glover of Dorchester, in the County of Suffolk and in the Province of Massachusetts Bay in New England, Yeoman, send Greeting: Know Ye, that I the said Nathaniel Glover, for and in consideration of the Parental Love and affection which I have and do bear unto my Well beloved son John Glover of Dorchester aforesaid, Husbandman, and for sundry other good causes and Considerations me hereunto moving, I the said Nathaniel Glover Sen' have given, granted, aliened, enfeoffed and assigned, conveyed and confirmed, and by these Presents for myself and my heirs, Doe fully, freely, clearly and absolutely give, grant, alien, enfeoffe, assign, convey and confirm unto my beloved son the said John Glover, and to his heirs and Assigns forever, Certain Part and Parcels of Land situate and lying partly in Dorchester and partly in Braintree, as follows, viz. :

One Piece containing Seven or Eight Acres, with Rye-field, with a Dwelling House and Barn thereon. One parcel of Land containing Thirty-Three Acres, which I bought of Edward Rawson. Also a piece or parcel of Land called Pine Neck, being about Twenty Acres, with a piece of Meadow called Damm Meadow, containing Sixteen Acres; and One Acre of Salt Marsh Lying below the said Damm Meadow, which distinct parcels that joyn together, the Whole being bounded as follows, viz. :

Easterly on land of David Rawson : Westerly partly on a Marsh and partly on a Creek ; Northerly on Horse Hammocks, so called, on a way leading to Pine Neck and on a Swamp called Ryefield Swamp ; and Southerly partly on Land belonging to Ebenezer Hinckley's Heirs, and partly on a Marsh called Sagamore Marsh.

To Have and to Hold unto him the said John Glover my Well beloved and loving son, with all the privileges and appurtenances, the above granted premises, and to his Heirs and Assigns Forever.

In Witness whereof, I the said Nathaniel Glover, with Hannah my Wife in token of her full consent and in full relinquishment of all her Right of Dower and Power of Thirds, have hereunto set our hands and Seales this Twenty-fifth day of November, 1723.

NATHANIEL GLOVER,
HANNAH GLOVER.

Signed, sealed and delivered in presence of us,
> Thomas Glover,
> Hannah Glover.

Received, Entered and Recorded with the Records of Deeds, 1741.

Deed of Gift from Nathaniel Glover, Senior, to his Well-beloved Son Thomas Glover.

To All People before whom this Present Deed of Gift shall come — Nathaniel Glover Sen', of Dorchester in the County of Suffolk within the Province of Massachusetts Bay in New England, Yeoman, sendeth Greeting : Know Yee, That I the said Nathaniel Glover Sen', for and in consideration of the Parental Love and affection which I have and do bear towards my Well beloved son Thomas Glover of the same Dorchester, Husbandman, as also for divers other good and Valuable Considerations me hereunto moving, Do by these Presents convey and confirm freely, clearly and absolutely—give, grant, aliene, enfeoffe, assigne, convey and confirme the same unto my loving son, the aforesaid Thomas Glover, and to his heirs and Assigns forever; And with Hannah my Wife, she thereunto consenting,

All my now Dwelling House, Barn, Corn-Barn and other buildings, with the land on which they stand and adjoining thereto, situate in

Dorchester aforesaid near the House of Captⁿ John Billings, containing about Two Acres. Bounded Eastwardly and Northerly on Captⁿ John Billings his Salt Marsh, South on his upland, and West on the Way leading to the Spring. Also My Orchard and Garden; Bounded East and West on Captⁿ Billings's Orchard, and North and South on his other Lands. Also One Piece of Land called the Bay Field, containing Fifty Two Acres ; Bounded East on the Sea or Salt-Water, West on the Highway, North on Land of Captⁿ Billings aforesaid, and South on the Lands of David Rawson. Also one Piece of Salt Marsh called Squantum Marsh, containing Six Acres ; Bounded East by John Hersey's Marsh, West on Marsh belonging to John Tolman, North on Salt Marsh belonging to Ralph Pope and on a Creek, South on the aforesaid John Hersey and Stephen French their Salt Marsh. Also Four Acres of Salt Marsh lying on the North side of Horse Hammocks, Bounded East and South on the said Hammocks, and West on Neponset River, and North on Land of Nathaniel Glover Junʳ partly, and partly by a Creek and Ditch, all lying in Dorchester aforesaid ; or howsoever otherwise Bounded or reputed to be bounded as the aforesaid parcels may be ; Together with a Way to the said Four Acres, where I usually go to it, through Damm Meadow, with all such other Rights, Liberties, Immunities, Profits, Privileges, Commodities, emoluments and Appurtenances, as to each and every of the said Parcels of Land as above described and bounded in any way or kind appertaining. And all the Estate, Right, Title, Interest and Inheritance, Claim or Demand Whatsoever of Me the said Nathaniel Glover, of, in and to, each and every of the above-mentioned Premises and their Appurtenances thereof. To Have and to Hold unto him the said Thomas Glover my Well-beloved and Loving son, with all the privileges and appurtenances, the above granted Premises, and to his Heirs and Assigns Forever.

In Witness whereof, I the said Nathaniel Glover Senior, with Hannah my Wife, in token of her full consent and in full relinquishment of all her Right of Dower and Power of Thirds, have hereunto set our hands and Seales this 20ᵗʰ day of November, 1723, and in the Tenth Year of His Majesty's Reign King George the Second.

NATHANIEL GLOVER,
HANNAH GLOVER.

Signed, sealed and delivered in presence of us,
　　　David Rawson,
　　　Hannah Glover (jr.)

Suffolk ss. November 24, 1723. The above-named Nathaniel Glover personally appearing, acknowledged this Instrument to be his free Act and Deed, before Me,　　ELIJAH DANFORTH, *Just. of the Peace.*

Received, Entered and Recorded with the Records of Deeds for Suffolk County, Feb. 25, 1723–4.　Lib. 37, fol. 171.

Depositions

Of Henry Leadbetter and Elizabeth Weeks, taken at Dorchester, January 13ᵗʰ, 1718, in relation to the heirship of Nathaniel Glover Senior.

We Henry Leadbetter of Dorchester in New England, aged Eighty Six Years, and Elizabeth Weeks of said Dorchester, aged Eighty Five Years, do testify and say that in the year 1648 we both of us lived with Mr. John Glover of Dorchester aforesaid, who was afterwards a Magistrate, and continued with him during his life.

And we do further testify that the said Mr. John Glover, who upon the Records of the said Town of Dorchester is called " Mr. Glover," was one of the first or Original Proprietors of said Town.

And we do further testify and say, that the said Mr. John Glover left his son Nathaniel Glover in the possession of his House and Homestead in said town of Dorchester, The which House and Homestead was afterwards possessed by Nathaniel Glover Sen', now living, who was the reputed son and heir to Mr. Nathaniel Glover aforesaid deceased, and Grandson to Mr. John Glover the Original Proprietor in said Town of Dorchester.

HENRY [L] LEADBETTER.
his mark.
ELIZABETH [O] WEEKS.
her mark.

The above-named Henry Leadbetter and Elizabeth Weeks personally appeared before Us the subscribers, and made oath to the truth of the above-written deposition in perpetual Memoriam.

PENN TOWNSEND, } Justices of the
TIMOTHY CLARKE, } Peace.

(Endorsed January 13, 1718)

Recorded with the Records of Deeds
for the County of Suffolk, Lib. 38,
fol. 186.

The above depositions were taken when it became necessary to determine who were the heirs of Mr. John Glover, in order to make a division of his Common and Undivided lands.

Towards the close of his life, Nathaniel Glover, Senior, was brought into an unpleasant controversy with the proprietors of Dorchester New Grant about the Common and Undivided Lands, which embarrassed and annoyed him. He was a shareholder of these lands in the right of his grandfather, and in his own right he was entitled to one half of the quantity of land as set out to Mr. Glover in every single division of the proprietor's lands, as stated in the first apportionment. It appears that in 1713 these lands were surveyed, new proprietors admitted, and a new apportionment made, which was so disproportionate to the grants made by the original proprietors, that it caused much dissatisfaction among the shareholders, and they continued to keep possession in some places according to the original apportionment. The controversy commenced in the year 1718–19, by a petition for a partition of land in the possession

of Glovers, to which the petitioners claimed a right in common with
them in a tract containing eight hundred and eight acres, lying in the
township of Dorchester New Grant. It was brought by Ralph Pope
of Dorchester, Sherebiah Butt of Boston, Samuel Butt of Canterbury, Ct., Benjamin Billings of Dorchester, and Thomas Maudsley,
administrator on the estate of Samuel Rigbee, against Nathaniel
Glover, Sen., and Nathaniel Glover, Jr., as a suit for partition.
Judgment was rendered in the Inferior Court in favor of the petitioners, and the Glovers appealed to the Superior Court, selecting
for their counsel the most able men of the time — Robert Auchmuty
and R. Buckminster, Esqrs. — whose ability, superior judgment and
knowledge of the English law were unsurpassed. The appellees also
employed eminent counsel. The Glovers appeared and entered a
Plea of Rights in their own names, and the case was committed to
a jury who returned for their verdict a reversion of the former
judgment of the Inferior Court, and decided that the Glovers should
receive, out of the twenty-five divisions, five hundred acres instead of
the two hundred which were granted at the Inferior Court, or three
hundred pounds in money and costs of court. The Glovers were
still dissatisfied, as were also their counsel.

The following documents, from original papers, give some account
of the controversy and the issue, commencing in 1719 and terminat-
ing in 1725. Nathaniel Glover, Sen., had passed to his rest, and the
case was continued by Nathaniel Glover, Jr., who was also himself a
proprietor in his own right and in the right of his father. Other
proprietors also, in other names, were dissatisfied with their apportionments by the new proprietors, and on being sued for partition,
defended their claims, and consequently the controversy was prolonged to the period above stated.

Depositions were taken from the following persons: Henry Leadbetter and Elizabeth Weeks, January 13, 1718; and from John Blackman and John Blackman, Jr., on March 18th, 1719, after the trial
and decision of the Inferior Court.

Suit for Partition.

Suffolk ss.   GEORGE, by the Grace of God, of Great Britain, France
and Ireland, King, Defender of the Faith, &c.

To Nathaniel Glover Sen', Yeoman, and Nathaniel Glover, Tanner,
both of Dorchester in Our said County of Suffolk, as they are Proprietors of Dorchester aforesaid, Greeting :

We command you, that you Appear at Our next Inferior Court of Common Pleas to be Holden at Boston within and for Our County of Suffolk aforesaid, on the First Tuesday of April next ensuing. Then and there to Answer to Ralph Pope of Dorchester aforesaid; Sherebiah Butt of Boston aforesaid; Goodman Samuel Butt of the Town of Canterbury in the County of New London in the Colony of Connecticut, Husbandman; Benjamin Billings of Dorchester aforesaid, Husbandman; and Thomas Maudsley of Dorchester aforesaid, yeoman, as he is Administrator to the Estate of Samuel Rigbee aforesaid of Dorchester, Cordwainer, Dec⁴. In a Plea of Partition, for that the Plaintiffs and you the Defendants, together and undivided hold and enjoy in Common, A Certain Tract or Parcel of Land Containing Eight Hundred and Seventy Eight Acres Lying in the Township of Dorchester aforesaid, being called Dorchester New Grant in the County Aforesaid.

For that Whereas, by a Meeting of the Proprietors of Dorchester aforesaid, the said Tract was heretofore divided in several Lotts and Ranges: and the Twenty First and Twenty Second Lotts containing part of the Sixth and all of the Seventh and part of the Eighth Range falling to the place of the Plaintiffs, as by a certain plan may appear, according to their several shares and numbers therein mentioned. And the Plaintiffs say that you ought to come to a Division with them of the said Lotts, so that they may lay out their shares and Division thereof in severalty, and may be at Liberty to Improve the same.

Yet you the defendants, though often requested to make Partition of the same according to the forme of the Statute in such Cases made and Provided, Do deny and refuse to permit or suffer the same to be done, contrary to the forme of the Statutes Aforesaid.

Whereupon the Plaintiffs say they are made Worse, and have sustained Damage, as they say, Three Hundred Pounds.

Which Plea the said Ralph Pope, Sherebiah Butt, Samuel Butt, Benjamin Billings, and Thomas Maudsley, Adm⁰, &c., have commenced against you, to be heard and Tryed at the said Court; And your Goods or Estate are attached to the Value of Three Hundred Pounds, being for Security to satisfy Judgment, which the said Ralph Pope, Sherebiah Butt, Samuel Butt, Benjamin Billings, and Thomas Maudsley (Admin'), may recover on the Aforesaid Tryal. Fail not of your Appearance at your Peril.

Witness, Penn Townsend, Esq., at Boston, the Twenty First day of March, in the Sixth year of our Reign, Annoque Dom⁰ 1719.

JOHN BALLANTINE, *Clerk.*

Suffolk ss.   October 20, 1718.

Glovers against Allen — Reasons for Appeal.

Nathaniel Glover, Senior, and   } Of Dorchester in New England,
Nathaniel Glover, Junior,   }   *Appealants.*

To the Honorable His Majesty's Judge of the Supreme Court of Judicature, to be holden at Boston within and for the County of Suffolk, on the first Tuesday in November, Anno Dom⁰ 1718.

The Appealants Reasons of Appeal from the Judgment of an Inferior Court of Common Pleas, holden at Boston on the First Tuesday in October, 1718.

The Action was a Plea of Partition brought by the Appellees then Plaintiffs against the Appealants for not dividing a certain Tract or Parcel of Land containing Seven Hundred Acres, as described in the Writ, to which for Issue the said Appealants pleaded " Not Guilty." Nothing held in Common with them.

Thereupon the Cause was committed to the Jury, who find for the Plaintiffs the Partition sued for, and costs of suit and Judgment Accordingly. Which Judgment is wrong, erroneous, and ought to be reversed : for the Reasons following.

That Judgment ought to have been for the Defendants (now Appealants). The Costs of Court.

For that the Defendants upon tryal disclaimed holding any part of the said Premises in Common with the Appellees. Therefore upon such disclaiming it is held to be absurd that they should be compelled to make Partition or Division before the Appellees, by Trespass of Ejectment, hath Established a Right in Common with the Now Appealants. The Title whereby the Appellees pretend to hold in Common with the Appealants is by a Vote of the Proprietors of Dorchester, dated September, 1713. At which time the said Proprietors took upon themselves to make Divisions of the Common and Undivided Lands of the Town, and stated proportions contrary to Justice, as by the Original Records of the Town upon Trial will appear.

Therefore the said Votes and Divisions should be made void and of none effect, and the Appellees' Title consequently illegal.

But admitting the Appellees have a controverted Title to a Division in the Premises ; surely that matter must be first tryed before they can be admitted to a Partition, because in Partition the Law presumes the Title is not disputed, but admitted by the Defendants, which Title the Appealants in this Case doth not admit.

Therefore the Appellees must by Judgment of Court establish their Title before they can bring Partition. 4thly, The said Proprietors took upon themselves to divide and distribute Lands that were by former Votes of the Town of Dorchester appropriated ; and the Appealants having a particular stated interest therein, the same cannot be restrained and Lessened but by a Jury of Twelve Men. For no man's Property can by law be taken from him but by a Judicial Trial, and cannot be Voted away by a Convention of Men.

Whereupon, for all which Reasons offered upon Tryal, the Appealants doubt not but your Honors, the Gentlemen of the Jury, will see sufficient Cause to reverse the former Judgment and give your Appealants Costs of Court.   R. AUCHMUTY, *for Appealants.*

Nathaniel Glover, Senior, Nathaniel Glover, Junior, *Appealants.*	} *v.* Allen and others. *Appellees.*

Filed in the Office of the Supreme Judicial Court, Oct. 20. 1718.
                    Attest :   JOHN BALLANTINE *Clerk.*
A True Copy, Examined.

Statement of Judge Auchmuty in the Case of Glovers vs. Dorchester Proprietors.

Nathaniel Glover Sen', of Dorchester, within the County of Suffolk and in the Province of Massachusetts Bay in New England, Yeoman; and Nathaniel Glover Junior, of the same Town and County aforesaid, Tanner. Being one of the Proprietors of the Undivided Lands in the Township of Dorchester aforesaid, Appealed from the Judgment of the Inferior Court begun and holden at Boston the first Tuesday of March, 1718–19, wherein the Appealant was Plaintiff and the Appellees Defendants in a Plea of a Case, viz. : Whereas, the said Proprietors in the Year of Our Lord 1636, 1637 and 1638, stated the Propriety and did order that the Lands within the Township of Dorchester aforesaid, should be divided in such proportions as follows, viz. :

That Mr. Glover of Dorchester aforesaid, Deceased, One of the Original Proprietors of the aforesaid Dorchester Lands, under whom the Plaintiffs claim as true and Lawful Heirs, Should have Thirty-Six Acres, Two Quarters and Twenty-Five Rods of Land out of every single division aforesaid.

Now the Plaintiffs in fact saith that Whereas the said Proprietors have laid out Twenty-Five Divisions of Land so called, beyond the Blew Hills in Dorchester New Grant (so called), as in Court shall fully appear, in which said Divisions the Plaintiff saith there should be laid out to him Nathaniel Glover Senior, son of Mr. Nathaniel Glover of Dorchester Deceased (in 1657), and Grandson to the Honorable John Glover, alias " Mr. Glover of Dorchester," Deceased 11 (12) 1653, the number of Thirty-Six Acres, Two Quarters and Twenty-Five Rods of Land in each Division of the aforesaid Twenty-Five Divisions of Land, which will amount to Nine Hundred and Sixteen Acres in the Right aforesaid.

Yet Notwithstanding the Proprietors aforesaid have allowed or laid out but Eight Acres in every single Division, which amounts to but Two Hundred Acres in the Twenty-Five Divisions aforesaid, and which is Seven Hundred and Sixteen Acres and One Quarter less than his due Proportion. To the damage of the said Nathaniel Glover Sen', of (£1000) One Thousand Pounds.

At which Inferior Court Judgment was rendered for Nathaniel Glover Senior, and the Plaintiffs to recover against the Now Appellees the sum of Seventy One Pounds, Twelve Shillings in money, damage and Costs of Court.

Both Parties appeared, the which Judgment, Reasons of Appeal, and all things touching the same, being fully heard; the Case was committed to the Jury, who returned their Verdict upon Oath—1st, That they find for the Plaintiffs a Reversion of the former Judgment of the [Inferior Court.]

Also Five Hundred Acres of Land in the Twenty-Five Divisions of Land, over and above the Two Hundred Acres which he now possesses; or, as an equivalent (£300) Three Hundred Pounds in Money and Costs of Court ; and that it therefore be considered that the Judgment of the Inferior Court be reversed at his Majesty's Superior Court, begun and Holden at Boston in the County of Suffolk on the first Tuesday, 1719. Robert Auchmuty,

R. Buckminster, for Plaintiffs,

vs. Dorchester Proprietors.

Plea of Nathaniel Glover, Senior, and Nathaniel Glover, Junior, for a just Division of the Common and Undivided Lands.

We the Proprietors of the Common and Undivided Lands in Dorchester New Grant, send Greeting: Know ye, That a rule of proportion was made to Four Hundred and Eighty Proprietors on the 9th of May, One Thousand Six Hundred and Thirty Seven, and every Inhabitant then Incumbent in that Town had each man his proportion made according to the Rule, a list whereof has been preserved to this day. And an Order made the 16th of January, 1637, that all the land within Dorchester (Common and Undivided Lands) shall be divided according to said Rule, &c. The records of which in Court will appear.

And the Law relating to said Lands stated each man's proportion in each Division. And the law also gives the Proprietors a power to order, improve and divide said lands; But does not give a power to state a new proportion thereby to cut off the former, being orderly and regularly made as aforesaid. Yet notwithstanding some persons privately, in the year 1713, took it upon themselves to make out a List of Proprietors as they are called, with a new proportion, and thereby cut off the former stated Proprietors. And they, being so great and so numerous when come together, that they carried all before them like a flood. And they got them a Book and entered therein the names of their new Proprietors. And for the support thereof a Warrant was obtained from Chief Justice Lynde for a Proprietors' Meeting. And a Meeting was accordingly called. Edmund Quinsy was chosen Moderator, and Samuel Paul (as he calls himself) Proprietor's Clerk. And now they suppose themselves to be strong and unmovable, and empowered to act for the former Proprietors. But they had no particulars inserted in their Warrant to appoint any other way for the calling of Meetings. And the Law says nothing shall be acted at a Proprietor's Meeting but what is inserted in the Warrant of the Chief Justice. And these Proprietors met by the said Warrant and adjourned their Meeting, and no Moderator appearing, nor a new one being chosen, the Warrant was dissolved, and the whole pretended Proprietors dropped with it, having nothing else to support it; and there being now no Warrant subsisting, and therefore no other Lawful Proprietors, it was thought needful and Lawful by Six of the Proprietors to go to a Justice for a Warrant for a Proprietors' meeting, for the purpose of reviving and bringing to life the Original Proprietors who had been cut off, wronged and excluded by the aforesaid new Usurpers.

But the New Proprietors being now somewhat afraid of such a movement, they had proposed that so many of the Justices should decide the case, and that there was a Warrant subsisting, which was false. We were obliged to travel near Seventy miles to procure from Mr. Justice Chandler a Warrant according to law for a Proprietors' Meeting, in order to recover and maintain the Ancient Rights of the Original Proprietors of the Town of Dorchester as aforesaid in 1713. And a Proprietors' meeting of the Original and lawful Proprietors was in December, 1719, called by virtue of a Warrant from Justice Chandler, and as many as met accordingly chose Mr. Brewer Moderator,

and Preserved Capen was chosen Clerk, and another way appointed to call Proprietors' Meetings for the future, agreeably to the law as we consider it.*   (Signed)   NATHANIEL GLOVER, Senior.
                                    NATHANIEL GLOVER, Junior.

Deposition

Of John Blackman and John Blackman, Junior, in the case between Dorchester Proprietors and Nathaniel Glover, Senior.

Dorchester, March 18, 1719. John Blackman Senior, and John Blackman Junior, in the house of John Blackman, testifieth and saith that on the fifth day of February last past, We the deponents did hear Increase Robinson, of Taunton, in the County of Bristol say, that in the Case between Dorchester Proprietors and Nathaniel Glover, he did not fear that the Glovers would get the case if they could have justice done them, but Col. Townsend had taken a false oath and was not fit for a Jury.

Sworn April 5, 1720, and signed   JOHN BLACKMAN,
                                         JOHN BLACKMAN, Jun.

   Attest:
   John Ballantine.

   The name of Nathaniel Glover, Sen., does not appear in these transactions after this date, and the further progress and issue of the

---

* The notification for the calling of the meeting, as copied from Vol. 1, page 13, of Dorchester Records, is as follows : " A Notification to the Original Proprietors of the Common and Undivided Lands within the Township of Dorchester in the County of Suffolk, to meet on the 21 December, 1719, to consider and transact affairs hereafter mentioned.

" 1st, To choose a Moderator.

" 2d, To choose a Clerk.

" 3d, To choose a Committee to sue any person or persons illegally possessed of any lands in said Dorchester, beyond the Blew Hills, called the New Grant.

" 4th, To appoint some other way for calling a meeting for the future, by virtue of a Warrant.   [*December* 4, 1719.] "

   Dorchester, December 21, 1719. " At a meeting of the Original Proprietors or their legal representatives, of Dorchester, at the Meeting-House, on the aforesaid day, Legally Warned by virtue of a Warrant from Mr. John Chandler, &c. The same day Preserved Capen was chosen Clerk for the Proprietors ; and Nathaniel Brewer, Timothy Tilestone, Joseph Hall, Nathaniel Glover, Junior, and Preserved Capen, were chosen to be a Committee to call meetings for the future."

   The above Committee proceeded to act, and to carry out the laws and rules laid down by the Original Proprietors, as had been given and recorded at stated times since the first action and recognition of their claims by the Joint Stock Company, viz.: In 1636, 1637, 1638, meetings were held and agreements were made as to rights of propriety and modes of division. In 1651, the 1 (10), another meeting was held and apportionments made in the Three Divisions, which did not extend to Dorchester New Grant. The 1 (14) 1663-4, William Stoughton, Esq., at a meeting of the Proprietors, brought in a return list of the rights of the Proprietors under his own hand, as copied from his father's book, attested by Edward Rawson. In 1667, 1681, 1697, and 1698, the Proprietors had met, and their proceedings were on record. The Committee of 1719, above chosen, based their course of action on the transactions and agreements of their predecessors, and continued to call their meetings by virtue of a Warrant.

controversy, which was prolonged until about six years after, will appear in the history of his eldest son, Nathaniel Glover, Jr.

(2) JOHN GLOVER, second son of Nathaniel and Mary (Smith) Glover, was born in Dorchester, 15 (12) 1654, and baptized 18 (12) 1654, by Rev. Richard Mather, when three days old. He died August 26th, 1690, in his 36th year, and was buried in the ancient burial yard, on the westerly side. He has a grave-stone.

In 1660, at the age of six years, his mother was married to Gov. Thomas Hinckley and removed to Barnstable, and he was placed under the guardianship of his uncle Mr. Habackuk Glover, and went to reside with his grandmother, Mrs. Anna Glover, of Boston, where he attended school until of a suitable age to acquire a trade. In 1668, or about that time, when at the age of fourteen years, Antony Checkley, Esq., of Boston, was appointed to be his guardian in the place of his uncle Habackuk Glover. He learned the cooper's trade; but to whom he was apprenticed is not known. In all land transactions or transfers he is designated by his trade, as "John Glover, cooper," to distinguish him from his uncle John, who was "John Glover, Gentleman," or "merchant." He was twice married: first, at the age of about eighteen years, in 1672, to Mary ——,* who died in Dorchester, April 30, 1687, and is buried there. It is supposed there were more children by this marriage than the one given below, but they have not been identified or become known in this branch of the family. The unfortunate circumstances which seem to be connected with the life of John Glover (cooper), from the time of his early marriage to the close of his short life; his disposal of his birthright and estate of inheritance; his protracted illness, &c., conspire to cast an obscurity around his history, which if elucidated and explained would be very interesting now to know. The tracing and following out of those children which are inserted here, have been attended with almost insurmountable difficulties, especially the one by his first marriage, and the work is still incomplete. That connected with the son by his last marriage has been almost as difficult;

---

* From such evidence as could be collected, it appears that Mary, the first wife of 'John Glover (cooper), was in some way connected with the family of Proctor. She may have been a daughter of Samuel Proctor, who made a conveyance to John Glover in 1672. When the estate was sold to Joseph Lowell, in 1675, Mary joins in the sale as an estate of inheritance. The evidence is, however, too slight and indefinite to allow of any certainty in the conclusion.

but in some lines the eighth generation has been reached. In 1688 he was married a second time, to Miriam Smith, of Boston (a daughter of John Smith), who survived him, and died in Dorchester August 23d, 1720. They had one son.

Child of JOHN and MARY (——) GLOVER, born in Boston:

+12. Robert, b. 1673; married ——.

And by his second wife, MIRIAM SMITH, born in Dorchester:

+13. John, b. May 6, 1689; bap. May 12, 1689;
m. { 1st, Hannah Capen, of Dorchester.
{ 2d, Lydia Norcott, of Roxbury.

In 1672, at the age of eighteen years, he purchased a house and land in Boston, of Samuel Proctor (cooper). The conveyance is from Samuel Proctor and Mary his wife to John Glover (cooper), of Boston. The consideration, £150. They alienate to him as follows: " All that my now dwelling-house and the land on which it standeth. Butted and Bounded as followeth — Northerly, on that part of the house I formerly sold to Thomas Sheepcote, and now in his possession; Southerly, on land of Richard Wood; Westerly, on land of Mrs. Oliver (widow). And also all my piece of land lying between the said housing and the land of Jonathan Balston, containing six feet in breadth, always excepting and reserving unto the said Sheepcote and his heirs and assigns for ingress and egress and regress through the said six feet as aforesaid, so far as the Southernmost part of said house extends and no farther; which is to the middle of the Chimney. To have and to hold the said Dwelling-house and land unto him the said John Glover, his heirs and assigns forever. He and they paying to the use of the free schools in Boston the sum of Eight Shillings yearly and every year forever."

The above conveyance, although bargained for in 1672, was not signed, as it appears, until three years after.

The instrument by which the above transfer was made, was acknowledged in person, January 15, 1675, by Samuel Proctor and Mary Proctor.

In 1674, two years after his first marriage, the Dorchester homestead estate was settled by an order from Court (see page 169), and one fourth part was assigned to him as his share or portion. He was still a minor, and Antony Checkley, Esq., of Boston, who had been appointed his guardian, acted for him in the division with his elder brother Nathaniel Glover, and in the subsequent subdivision which was to be made between him and William Rawson, the husband of his sister Anne.

He disposed of this inheritance soon after to his brother Nathaniel; and also to William Rawson, 5 (11) 1675, of four acres of salt marsh.

March 13, 1675, John Glover (cooper) and Mary his wife sold his house and land, purchased of Samuel Proctor, of Boston (cooper), to Joseph Lowell — his wife Mary joining in the sale of the premises, as an estate of inheritance.

John and Mary Glover to Joseph Lowell.

Vol. 9, page 316, Suffolk Reg. Deeds.

To all People before whom this present Deed of Sale shall come. John Glover of Boston (in the Colony of Massachusetts in New England), Cooper, and Mary his Wife, send Greeting : Know ye—That the said John Glover and Mary his Wife, for and in Consideration of the Sum of Fifty Pounds Lawful Money of New England, to them in hand paid before the Ensealing and Delivery of these Presents, by Joseph Lowle [Lowell] of Boston aforesaid, Cooper, well and truly paid, the receipt whereof they do hereby acknowledge themselves fully satisfied and contented, and hereof and of every part thereof, do acquit, exonerate and discharge the said Joseph Lowle, his Heirs, Executors, Administrators and Assigns. And by these Presents have Given, Granted, Bargained, Sold, Aliened, Enfeoffed and confirmed unto the said Joseph Lowell, his Heirs, Executors, Administrators and Assigns, All that Messuage or Tenement, situated and being in Boston aforesaid, with all the Land on which the same doth stand. Being butted and bounded Northerly by the house and Land of Thomas Sheepcote ; Southerly by the Land of Richard Wood ; Westerly by the Land of Sarah Oliver, Widow ;

Also all that Parcel of Land that lieth on the Easterly side of Thomas Sheepcote's house, and between the house hereby Granted and Sold, and Jonathan Balston, measuring in breadth six feet, and running from the Street Southerly to the land of Richard Wood, Together with all the buildings, Lights, Easements, Waters, and Water-courses, fences and Profits, Privileges, Commodities and Appurtenances to the said Messuage and Tenement and Land belonging or in any wise appertaining. Excepting only and hereby referring out the parcel of Land above granted unto the above-named Thomas Sheepcote, his Heirs, Executors, Administrators and Assigns, forever free liberty of ingress and egress and regress through the said parcel of Land that lieth before the House of the said Thomas Sheepcote and the land of the said Jonathan Balston ; that is to say, from the Street to the Southernmost part of the Chimneys that belongeth to the said Sheepcote's House and no further. The said Joseph Lowle, his Heirs, Executors, Administrators, &c., yielding and paying for the use of the Free

Schools in Boston the Sum of Eight Shillings yearly and every year forever. To Have and to Hold the said Messuage and Tenement and Land, with all the other above-granted and bargained Premises (excepting only before excepted) unto the said Joseph Lowle, his Heirs, Executors, Administrators and Assigns, to his and their only, sole and proper use and benefit and behoof forever. He the said Joseph Lowle, his Heirs, Executors, &c., paying the said sum of Eight Shillings in money for the use of said Free Schools yearly and every year forever.

And the said John Glover and Mary his Wife, for themselves, their Heirs, Executors, &c., do hereby covenant, promise and agree to and with the said Joseph Lowle, his heirs, Executors, &c., that at the time of the ensealing hereof they are the true, sole and Lawful owners of all the afore bargained Premises, and are lawfully seized of and in the same and every part thereof, in their own proper Right of Inheritance and Lawful Authority to sell and dispose of the same as aforesaid.

And that the said Joseph Lowle, his Heirs, Executors, Administrators, &c., shall and may by virtue of these Presents from time to time and at all times forever hereafter, Lawfully, Peacefully and Quietly Have, Hold, Use, Occupy and enjoy the above-granted Premises.

And also that the said John Glover and Mary his Wife, their Heirs, Executors, Administrators, &c., shall and will from time to time and at all times forever hereafter warrant and defend the above-granted House or Messuage and Tenement and Land against the Lawful claims and demands of all and every person claiming under them, their Heirs, Executors, &c.

In Witness whereof, the said John Glover and Mary his Wife have hereunto set their Hands and Seals, this 13 day of March, 1675.

(Signed)   JOHN GLOVER, and a Seale.
MARY GLOVER, and a Seale.

Signed, sealed and delivered in presence of us,
John Baker,
John Hayward.

This Writing was acknowledged by John Glover to be his Act and Deed, Mary his Wife consenting hereunto, this 14th day of March, 1675.

Recorded and Com. April 6, 1676.

FREEGRACE BENDALL, *Recorder.*

His next act is a contract with his brother-in-law, William Rawson, for a deed which was sometime to be confirmed and delivered. He was then at the age of 20 years.

Glover to Rawson.

Vol. 9, fol. 277, Suff. Reg. Deeds.

Know all Men by these Presents, That I John Glover of Boston in New England, Cooper, have received the day of the date hereof, of

William Rawson of Boston, Shopkeeper, the full sum of Twenty Pounds (£20) in money, and Twenty Pounds in Cooper's Staves at money price, in part payment of the Sum of One Hundred and Fifty Pounds which I am to receive of the said William Rawson for several parcels of Land, viz.: Pasture Land and Meadow, with all other my Rights and Privileges within the Township of Dorchester in New England aforesaid, which I do acknowledge to have sold to said Rawson, excepting only my Right and Interest in that Farm that is now in the tenure and occupation of Roger Billings or his Assigns. And further, I do hereby covenant, and my heirs and assigns shall and will give unto the said William Rawson, his heirs and Assigns, Executors or Administrators, full, absolute and Legal conveyances of the said parcels of Land, with all my Rights and Privileges above-mentioned, to be granted and sold on demand, as witness my hand this 9 day of October, 1674–5.   JOHN GLOVER.

John Hayward, ⎱ *Witnesses.*
James Couch, ⎰

John Hayward testified upon oath that he drew this Writing by the Order of John Glover, and that he saw him the said Glover sign and deliver it in the presence of the said John Hayward and James Couch, whose hands or subscribees as witnesses taken, 5 : 11 : 1675.
                SIMON BRADFORD,
                THOMAS CLARK, *Ass't.*

Recorded and Com. Jan. 6, 1674–5.   FREEGRACE BENDALL, *Rec.*

The deed above referred to as being contracted for, follows on page 279 of the Records.

The following deed from John Glover, cooper, to William Rawson, is confirmed February 21, 1675, immediately on his coming of age.

Glover to Rawson.

To All Xpean People to whom this present Deed of Sale shall come. John Glover of Boston in the County of Suffolk in New England (Cooper), Sendeth Greeting.. Whereas the said John Glover several months since sold unto William Rawson of Boston aforesaid, Shopkeeper, all his Right, Title and Interest in and to all his Pasture Grounds within the Township of Dorchester in New England, containing Eighteen Acres and a half, with his Eighteen Acres and a half in a Woodlot not far from Mr. Withington's Land ; and Eighteen Acres and a half in another Woodlot about two Miles in the Woods ; with his Four Acres of Salt Marsh, All adjoining to the said William Rawson's Land and Marsh that he had in Right of his Wife Anne, as the portion he had with her yet undivided between them.

And all his Rights and Privileges within the said Township of Dorchester (excepting only in the Farm that is now in the tenure and occupation of Roger Billings).

In consideration of the Sum of £150 to be paid in Money and Goods within the space of Three years. And whereas the said William Rawson hath, notwithstanding the said bargain and sale, at the earnest request of the said John Glover, condescended and agreed that the said John Glover should have liberty to sell unto Mr. William Stoughton his part of the said Pasture containing 18½ Acres, Be the same more or Less. Now know all Men by these Presents, that the said John Glover and Mary his Wife, for and in Consideration of Eighty-three Pounds of Lawful Money of New England to them in hand paid at and before the Ensealing and Delivery of these Presents, by the said William Rawson, the receipt whereof they do hereby acknowledge themselves fully satisfied and contented, and thereof and of every part thereof do acquit and discharge the said William Rawson his Heirs and Assigns Forever. And by these Presents have hereby Given, Granted, Bargained, Sold, Aliened, Enfeoffed, Conveyed and confirmed, and by these Presents do Give, Grant, Bargain, Sell, Alien, Enfeoffe, Convey and confirm unto him the said William Rawson his heirs and Assigns Forever, All that their Right, Title and Interest in the said Two Woodlots and pieces of Salt Marsh-Meadow, with all other those Rights and Privileges in the said Township of Dorchester (Excepting only in that Farm that is now in the tenure and occupation of Roger Billings). Together with all Rents, Arrearages of Rents and Profits, Privileges and Appurtenances to the said part of said Woodlots and Salt-Marsh belonging or in any wise appertaining, with the Rights and Privileges aforementioned, to him the said William Rawson, his Heirs and Assigns, Executors and Administrators, to his and their own and proper use forever. And the said John Glover and Mary his Wife, for themselves, their Heirs, Executors and Administrators, do hereby Covenant, Grant and agree to and with the said William Rawson, his Heirs, Executors, Administrators and Assigns, that at the time of the ensealing hereof they are the true, sole and Lawful owners of all the said bargained Premises, and that the said William Rawson, his heirs, Executors, &c., shall and may, and by virtue of these Presents from time to time and at all times hereafter forever Lawfully, Peaceably and quietly, Have, Hold, Use, Occupy and enjoy the above-granted Premises, with all their Privileges and Appurtenances freely and clearly acquitted and discharged from all manner of former and other Gifts, Grants, Bargains, Sales, Leases, Mortgages, Jointures, Dowers, Titles of Dowers, Judgments, Executions, Contracts, Entails, Forfeitures, and of and from all other Titles, Troubles, and Incumbrances whatsoever.

And further that they the said John Glover and Mary his Wife, their Heirs, Executors, Administrators or Assigns, shall and will at all times Warrant and Defend all the above-granted Premises, with all their Profits, Privileges and Appurtenances, unto him the said William Rawson, his Heirs, &c., against the lawful claiming of all and every person claiming or demanding the same or any part thereof from them the said John Glover and Mary his Wife, or either of them, their Heirs or Assigns, by their or either of their means, Act, Consent, Title, Privilege or Procurement.

And Lastly, that they the said John Glover and Mary his wife shall and will give unto the said William Rawson, his Heirs, Executors, &c., such further and ample assurances of the aforegranted Premises as in Law or Equity can be desired or required.

In witness whereof, the said John Glover and Mary his Wife have hereunto set their hands and Seals this 15th day of January, 1675.

(Signed)   JOHN GLOVER, and a Seale.*
MARY GLOVER, and a Seale.

Signed, sealed and delivered in presence of
> William Pitman,
> John Hayward.

January 15, 1675.

This Instrument was acknowledged by John Glover and Mary his wife personally appearing.

Recorded and Com. January 17, 1675.   FREEGRACE BENDALL,
Recorder.

February 21, 1675. The above-named John Glover acknowledged this Instrument as his free act and deed, he being now of age.
EDWARD TYNG, *Assistant.*

Dec. 4, 1679, John Glover (cooper) made out a Deed of Sale, which is conditional, to his uncle Mr. John Glover, of Boston, merchant, of all his right of inheritance in Newbury farm. Extract from the deed:

To all Christian people unto whom this present Deed of Sale shall or may come. Know ye, That I John Glover, Cooper, of Boston, son of Mr. Nathaniel Glover of Dorchester, deceased, sendeth Greeting: Whereas I the said John Glover in consideration of the sum of Eighty Pounds Current Money of New England, to me in hand paid before the delivery of these Presents, by my uncle John Glover of Boston in New England, Merchant, the whereof to my full content and satisfaction I do hereby acknowledge, do acquit and discharge, &c. unto the said John Glover my Uncle, all this my estate, Right, Title and Inheritance, Interest and Proportion in a certain Farm lying in said Dorchester, commonly called and known by the name of Newberry Farm, sometime the Estate of my Grandfather the late Hon. John Glover, Esq., Deceased, and in the present tenure of Roger Billings. Being One Sixteenth part of said farm, &c. And of all land, whatsoever, both Meadow and Upland, thereunto belonging or in any way appertaining, &c.

Also all my Share, Right, Title or Inheritance in all lands whatsoever, and of all Rights, &c. in houses, Edifices, Buildings, Fences, Woods, Underwoods, Fruit-Trees, &c. Being One Sixteenth part in all the Right, Title, &c., in all such lands as do belong unto my aforesaid Grandfather, the said John Glover, Esq., Deceased, which accrued to me in Right of my father the above-named Nathaniel Glover, Deceased, Lying on the South side of Neponsett River. To Have and

---

* Written on the margin of this deed is the following :—

" John Glover, the son of Mr. Nathaniel Glover, was baptized in the Church at Dorchester, the 18th day of February, A.D. 1654 — as attest,   JOHN CAPEN, *Deacon.*"

to hold unto him my said Uncle John Glover, his heirs and assigns, &c. And I do hereby covenant and agree with my said Uncle John Glover, his heirs and assigns, &c.

In witness whereof, I the first named John Glover do set my hand and seale this 4th day of Dec. 1679.   (Signed)   JOHN GLOVER.

Acknowledged by John Glover, jr., before   EDWARD TYNG, *Assistant.*

[Suff. Rec. Deeds, Vol. 11, p. 257.]

May 20, 1680, John Glover of Boston, merchant, conveys back to his "Nephew John Glover of Boston, cooper, the one sixteenth part of Newbury Farm, together with all the other rights and titles to land which he received from his said Nephew by a deed of sale bearing date Dec. 4, 1679." Consideration, fifty pounds, paid to him by his nephew, and also "in consideration of several Deeds of Sale, Writings, Mortgages, &c., by which he received the above named real estate, he releases to his said Nephew, and makes void the Deed of Sale, and guarantees and confirms unto him all the above-named Rights so conveyed to him."

Four days after the above was confirmed, May 24, 1680, John Glover of Boston, cooper, sold his right of inheritance in Newbury farm, being one sixteenth part of said farm, to Ebenezer Billings of Dorchester. Bounds described in deed, which was signed by John Glover and Mary Glover, and acknowledged in person before Edward Everett.

Soon after the confirmation of his inheritance in Newbury farm to Ebenezer Billings, John Glover removed to Barnstable — or perhaps before, as the following notice appears on the Plymouth Colony Records, 1679, Vol. 6, p. 130: "Yᵉ names of such as stand propounded or approved to take their Freedom, were Samuel Sargent, John Glover, William Bradford, Jun." July 7, 1680, the name of John Glover appears in a list of witnesses in a protest made the 13th of November, 1679, in regard to the shipwreck of the sloop Anne and Elizabeth, of New York, commanded by Alexander Watts. "It is stated that he the appearer (Watts) being bound on a voyage from New York to Boston, in the government and jurisdiction of Massachusetts, and being on his course from Martha's Vineyard towards Boston, and being over night, gotten over or past the pitch of Cape Cod, intending to fetch Cape Anne for a harbor, &c., was shipwrecked and cast away on Cape Cod." Affirmed and witnessed by Alex-

19

ander Watts, Henry More, John Glover, Robert Pelton, Isaac Norton.

John Glover was for several years an inhabitant of Barnstable. He owned a house and land there, and a cooper's shop. It is recorded on the Town Book of Records, in 1680, that in laying out a new road, it is to "pass the shop of John Glover." January 9, 1684, at a meeting of the inhabitants of the town of Barnstable, John Glover was admitted townsman. He took the oath of freeman in Barnstable, June 5, 1684. " The names of Freemen who stand propounded and approved to take their Freedom, and who took the oath of fidelity at this Court, were Samuel Sargent, John Glover, and William Bradford, Junior." Thomas Hinckley was then Governor of the Plymouth Colony. In 1688 he was again in Dorchester, and married to his second wife. In 1689 he had a son born to him there, and in 1690 he died.

Copy from the inscription on his grave-stone:

" Here lies buried y* body of John Glover, a son of Mr. Nathaniel Glover, of Dorchester. Deceased Aug. 25, 1690, aged 35 years."

Letters of administration were granted on the 21st day of August, 1693, to Timothy Thornton, on the Estate of John Glover (cooper), deceased, intestate.

The following is a copy of the order for administration:

To Timothy Thornton, of Boston, in the said County of Suffolk, Merchant, Creditor to the estate of John Glover, late of Dorchester, cooper, Deceased, Intestate, Greeting. Trusting in your care and fidelity, I do by these Presents commit unto you full Power to administer all and singular, on the Goods, Chattels, Rights and Credits of the said John Glover, and well and faithfully to dispose of the same according to Law. And also to ask, gather, levy, Recover and receive all whatsoever of the said Deceased, which to him while he lived and at his death did appertain. And also to pay all debts in which the deceased stood bound, so far as his Goods, Chattels, Rights and Credits can extend. And to make a true and perfect inventory of all and singular of Goods, Chattels, Rights and Credits of the said Deceased; and to exhibit the same into the Register's office in the above said County before the 21st day of November next ensuing, and to render a plain, true account of your Administration upon Oath, at or before the 20th day of August, A.D. 1694. And I do by these Presents ordain and constitute and appoint you Administrator of all and Singular of the Goods, Chattels, Rights, Credits, &c.

In testimony whereof I have hereunto set my hand and seal at the said office, dated at Boston, this 21st day of August, 1693.
(Signed) WILLIAM STOUGHTON.
Attest: JONATHAN ADDINGTON.

It has not been ascertained whether Timothy Thornton ever acted on the above administration. No inventory appears on the Probate Records of Suffolk County at the time required, or subsequently to that time. It appears from the foregoing that all Mr. Glover's estate in Boston had been disposed of, and all his rights of inheritance in Dorchester and Milton, with his share of one sixteenth part of Newbury farm. Of his property in Barnstable, also, there appears to be no mention after he returned to Dorchester, which could have been only about three years before his decease.

The following inventory and account was rendered to the Probate Court in 1730, which, although forty years had elapsed, appears unmistakably to relate to the above John Glover, cooper.

An Inventory of the estate of John Glover, late of Boston, Dec^d. taken and apprized by the Subscribers, March 2, 1730, viz. :—

Books, ...	£5 14 00 0
Linen, ...	39 02 00 0
Bed and Bedding, ...	16 00 00 0
Wearing Apparel, ...	7 00 00 0
Sundry small things, such as brushes, scales & weights,	5 6 00 0
5 oz. Plate, ...	4 08 00 0
5 Gold rings and a Tweezer Case, ...	1 00 00 0
[Save error.]	83 10 00 0

By the Hon. JOSIAH WILLARD, Judge of Probate.

Richard Hall and Asa [William ?] Rand presented the foregoing, and made oath that it contains a true and perfect inventory of the estate of John Glover, aforesaid, Deceased. The Appraisers were at the same time sworn as the law directs, by the Subscriber,

JOSIAH WILLARD, *Judge of Probate.*

Samuel Gerrish,
Bartholomew Gedney, } *Appraisers.*
David Mason, Boston, March 8, 1730.

[Suff. Prob. Rec., Vol. 39, fol. 8.]

Richard Hall and William Rand, Administrators on the estate of John Glover, late of Boston, Deceased, intestate.

The Accountants charge themselves with all and singular of the Goods, Chattels, Rights and Credits of the said deceased, specified in an Inventory thereof by them exhibited into the Registry of the Court of Probate for the County of Suffolk, of the said amount of Eighty three pounds, ten Shillings

and six pence, viz.	£83 10 6
By money found in his trunk, ...	10 6 7
By money received from Daniel Coffee, . . .	22 00 4
	£115 17 5

And the said Accountants pray allowance as follows, viz.:

Paid for Letters of Administration and Bond, . .	£00 10 06 0
Exhibiting the inventory and Oaths, ...	16 00 0
For his board, Nursing, Medicine and attendance at your Accountant William Rand's house, being Seventy eight Weeks at twenty Shillings pr Week, in his last sickness, ...	78 00 00 0
For Coffin and Wine at the funeral, . . .	5 10 00 0
For Gloves at the funeral and Grave-stones, . .	10 00 00 0
For Ringing Bells and Porter, &c. . . .	3 08 00 0
For Drawing, Recording and allowing this Account, and for a Copy thereof, . - . . .	10 15 00 0
	98 19 06 0
To a Cloak allowed the Accountant, Richard Hall, .	2 17 00 0
Paid William Payne, Esq. and Order from the Judge,	12 13 09 0
Paid to John Dolbear of the same, . . .	1 05 00 0
	115 17 3 0

Richard Hall and William Rand, Administrators on the Estate of John Glover, late of Boston, Deceased, intestate, appeared personally and made oath that it contained a just and true account of the aforesaid John Glover's estate, so far as they have proceeded therein, and produced receipts and vouchers for the several payments therein, which I allow and approve.   JOSIAH WILLARD,
Boston, April 15, 1730.   *Judge of Probate.*

MIRIAM SMITH, the second wife of John Glover of Boston and Barnstable, was born in Boston, and died in Dorchester, August 23, 1720. She was the fourth daughter of John and Miriam Smith, of Boston. Her father was the eldest son of Quarter-master John Smith, by his second wife Mary, and was born in Dorchester. He died in Boston, September 17, 1676, and left a widow and six children. January 30, 1676–7, power of administration and letters were granted on the estate of John Smith, Jr., late of Dorchester, to Miriam his widow and relict — she bringing in an inventory of said estate upon oath, and giving bonds according to law. Inventory entered and recorded 18 (12) 1676, vol. 12, folio 153, Suffolk Probate Records. Taken by Richard Hall and Enoch Wiswall.

Miriam, the widow of John Smith, married a second time, about 1680, to Ellis Wood, of Dedham and Dorchester, who died in 1696. He left a will, dated July 21, 1694, wherein he appoints his beloved wife Miriam sole executrix, and his worthy friends Elder James Blake and Samuel Clapp, overseers. Witnessed by Ralph Houghton, Nathaniel Glover and Samuel Topliff. She was distinguished for piety and other rare gifts. For the remainder of her life, after her second widowhood, she became a teacher of youth in Dorchester, and devoted herself to that employment. She was a member of the Church at Dorchester, and had her children presented for baptism, as shown by the following extracts from the Church Records:

"19 : 9 : 1682. Baptized the children of John Smith, Deceased, and Miriam, afterwards the wife of Ellis Wood, viz.: James and Mary, Anna, Miriam, Sarah and David." "10 : 14 : 1683. James and Mary, the son and daughter of John Smith, Deceased; but their mother, the Wife of Ellis Wood, being in full communion, James and Mary being adults, this same day owned the Covenant."

Mrs. Miriam (Smith) Wood, the mother of Miriam, wife of John Glover, died in Dorchester, and her death is thus recorded on the Church Records: — "Died Oct. 29, 1706, the Ancient and pious Widow Wood." She was buried in Dorchester, and has a grave-stone at the Northwesterly part of the old burying yard, with the following inscription:

"In Memory of Mrs. Miriam Wood, Widow of Ellis Wood, and formerly Wife of John Smith, Deceased; died in Dorchester, Oct. 29, 1706. Aged 73 years.

> A Woman well beloved of all her neighbours
> From her care of small folks education,
> Their number being great,
> That when she died she scarcely left her Mate.
> So wise, discreet was her behaviours,
> That she was well esteemed by all her neighbours.
> She lived in love with all, to dye
> So let her rest to Eternaty."

Her age at death, as nearly as can be deciphered from the grave-stone, was 73 years, which seems to confirm the conjecture that before marriage she was Miriam Deane, daughter of Stephen Deane, of Plymouth.

Thus it appears that Miriam Smith was presented for baptism by her mother about six years after the death of her father. The precise date of her marriage with John Glover has not been ascertained by any record, but the following notice appears on the records of the Dorchester Church. "20 (3) 1688. Miriam, the wife of John Glover and daughter of John Smith, Dec⁴, owned the Covenant." Their only son, "John, the son of John Glover, was baptized May 12, 1689, not in full communion."

19*

(3) ANNE GLOVER, only daughter of Mr. Nathaniel and Mary (Smith) Glover, was born in Dorchester in the year 1656, and died in Braintree at the Rawson homestead about 1730, aged 74 years. The place of her burial is supposed to be in the ancient cemetery at Quincy. At the age of four years, in 1660, her mother, being married to Gov. Thomas Hinckley, went to Barnstable to live, leaving her children in Boston under the care of Mrs. Anna Glover, their grandmother, and under their duly appointed guardians, Mr. Habackuk Glover and Mr. John Gurnell, who had the care of their education. After the decease of her grandmother in 1670, she went to reside in the family of her uncle Habackuk Glover, where she remained until her marriage. In 1673, at the age of eighteen years, she was married, at the house of her uncle and guardian, to Mr. William Rawson, a wealthy merchant of Boston, of distinguished family and connections. The following is a copy of the record of her marriage, as taken from the ancient family Bible, now in the possession of one of the Rawson descendants.

"This may certify all whomsoever it may concern, that on y* 11th day of July, 1673, on a certificate 'I received that William Rawson and Anne Glover y* daughter of the late Mr. Nathaniel Glover had been duly and legally published, I joined them in marriage, at the house and in the presence of Mr. Habackuk Glover, his wife, Mr. Edward Rawson, father of the said William, and other friends ; as witness my hand, this 31st day of July, 1673.   EDWARD TYNG, Ass'tt."

"27 (6) 1676, was Anne, the daughter of Mr. Nathaniel Glover, now wife unto William Rawson, dismissed unto the third Church in Boston, though not in full communion, but by her father's Covenant." — *Dorchester Church Records.*

It appears from the records of the first Church in Boston, that William and Anne Rawson were received and admitted to that Church, 27 (2) 1676.

Dorcas, her negro, being a member of the Church in Dorchester, was dismissed 27 (6) 1676, to join the first Church at Boston ; and 24 (4) 1677, was received and admitted to the latter Church.

The inherited estate of Anne Glover was one fourth part of the Dorchester homestead, which formerly belonged to her father, Mr. Nathaniel Glover, deceased, and which was settled on her by an order of Court in 1674, one year after her marriage ; one twelfth part of Newbury farm, which formerly belonged to her grandfather,

John Glover, Esq., of Boston; also a share in the Common and Undivided Lands in Dorchester New Grant and elsewhere.

In 1684, William Rawson, and Anne Rawson in her own right, by deed of sale bearing date the 30th day of April, 1684, conveyed and sold to John Harwood, Esq., of Boston, "Thirty-six acres and one half and fifteen Rods of land in the Township of Dorchester in the County of Suffolk, &c., said land being in the 65th lot in the Third Division of the Cow Walk. Bounded on the North by the lott formerly owned by Edward Bullock, which is the 64th lott; on the South by the lott now owned by Thomas Millett, being the 66th lott, the Westerly end butting on the five hundred acres belonging to ——; the Easterly end butting on the other Divisions, together with all the privileges, appurtenances, &c., with any former and after Rights in any former and after divisions."* Signed by William Rawson and Anne Rawson.

In 1689, William and Anne Rawson, in consideration of two hundred pounds in money paid to them by her uncle "John Glover, of Boston, Gentleman," sold to him their dwelling house, barn, &c., as shown by the following extract from the original deed, written on parchment and signed by them.

"Dwelling house and Barn in Boston, at the Southerly End, near Capt. Samuel Sewall's house; said house containing three lower rooms, two chambers and a cellar, one wood-house and a Brewhouse, with all the land on which it standeth; likewise all the garden on the South-westerly side of the said house, and all the land at the South-Easterly End of it. Butted and bounded as follows: At the South-Easterly end on the Street to the Widow Morse's Land, on the land of Capt. Samuel Sewall; Southwesterly by the land of the Widow Morse; Northwesterly by the land of William Rawson, and North Easterly by the Street leading to the Waterside. And measures at said South Easterly side Sixty seven feet and three inches from the corner of the street aforesaid to the Widow Morse's house; thence on a straight line all along the Widow Morse's land Eighty two feet; thence to the street on a straight line is Sixty four feet and three inches or thereabouts; thence along the street (beginning three feet

---

* "May 16, 1723. Jonathan Barnard, of Boston in New England, Merchant, lawful Attorney of Elizabeth Harwood of the Parish of St. Butolph, without Bishop's Gate, in the County of Middlesex, England, Widow, and William Harwood of Talgate in Bishops Gate Street, in the County aforesaid, by virtue of a power of Attorney well executed and proved, dated the 20th day of September, 1722, and recorded in the Notary public's office for Suffolk County, sold to Samuel Capen, junior, of Dorchester, for One hundred and twenty seven pounds, and confirmed unto him the above described premises, which were purchased by the said John Harwood of William and Anne Rawson, April 30, 1684." Recorded in Vol. 37, fol. 103.

westward of the woodhouse or Brewhouse aforesaid) Eighty-four feet to the South East End thereof. Together with all the privileges and appurtenances, &c. To have and to hold, &c., unto him the said John Glover, his heirs and assigns forever.

(Signed)   WILLIAM RAWSON,
ANNE RAWSON.

Signed, sealed and delivered in presence of us,
> James Green,
> Joseph Webb.

    This Instrument was acknowledged by William Rawson and Anne Rawson, the 14th day of Oct. 1689, before me,

SIMON BRADSTREET, *Just.*

    Rec. of Deeds for Suff. Co., Lib. 15, fol. 108.

Attest :   JOSEPH WEBB, *Clerk.*

    WILLIAM RAWSON, the husband of Anne Glover, was born in Boston, May 21, 1651; was baptized " 26 (3) 1651," and died in Braintree, September 20, 1726, in his 75th year. He was the third son of Edward and Rachael (Perne) Rawson, who came from Gillingham in Dorsetshire, England, and settled in Newbury in the Colony of Massachusetts in New England, in the year 1636 or '37. His father was a lineal descendant of Sir Edward Rawson of that County, and was born at the village of Gillingham, upon the River Stour, April 16, 1615. On his arrival at Newbury he was first made freeman in March, 1637–8, and in April of the same year was invested with the office of Public Notary and Registrar for the town of Newbury. He was elected Representative, and served the town in that capacity from 1639 to 1643. He was seven years a Deputy to the General Court at Boston, from 1643 to 1650, and held at the same time the office of Clerk of the Deputies from 1645. May 22, 1650, he was elected to the office of Secretary of the Massachusetts Colony in New England, and served in that capacity until his decease. He removed to Boston in 1650, and died there August 27th, 1693, at the age of 78 years.

    The mother of William Rawson was a granddaughter of Rev. John Hooker, whose wife was Rachael Grindall, a sister of Dr. Edmund Grindall, Archbishop of Canterbury in the reign of Queen Elizabeth. His paternal grandmother was a sister of the Rev. John Wilson. Thus he was descended from two of New England's greatest divines, and collaterally connected with the distinguished Archbishop of Canterbury.

William Rawson was educated to a mercantile life, and became a prominent merchant and an importer of foreign goods. He resided with his father, at the time of his marriage, in Rawson's lane, now Bromfield Street, Boston, where he kept a dry goods store. At the age of twenty-two years he was married to Anne Glover, and subsequently purchased a house of Mr. John Glover, of Boston, uncle to his wife. In 1689 he sold his estate in Boston to Mr. Glover of whom he purchased, and removed with his family to Dorchester, residing on a portion of Newbury farm, the inheritance of his wife. He afterwards purchased a tract of land, for a homestead estate, of the heirs of his great uncle, the Rev. John Wilson — "being a portion of the Grant made to that distinguished Divine by the General Court of the Colony."

This estate was situated in Braintree, adjoining the homestead of the Hon. Josiah Quincy, and extending to the lands of the Newbury farm estate on the north. It has passed down to the succeeding generations of his descendants until the present time. It was first settled on his son David Rawson, who left it to his son Jonathan Rawson in 1760. Jonathan Rawson, Jr., in 1782, succeeded to his father in the possession and occupation, and left it at his decease, in 1819, to his son Samuel Rawson, who resided there until his death in 1858. He died unmarried. His sisters still occupy and possess it. They are of the fifth generation from William and Anne (Glover) Rawson, and the seventh from the Hon. John Glover, of Boston, by direct descent. The Family Bible of Secretary Rawson descended to his son William, together with his portrait and other relics, all of which have been carefully preserved by his descendants. A Rawson Memorial has been gathered and published by a descendant.*

* Mr. Reuben Rawson Dodge — who is a lineal descendant of Secretary Rawson, by the line of his son, the Rev. Grindell Rawson, of Mendon, a brother of William, whose history is given above — has gathered and published the "Rawson Memorials." The work is of much interest, and contains two original portraits — one of Secretary Rawson, the other of his daughter Rebecca, whose unfortunate history he has given in detail. The following is the description of the Family Bible of Edward Rawson, his first American ancestor, as it appeared in the Worcester Daily Spy: "The Bible is in folio, but the title page and the books of Genesis and Exodus are wanting. It is of the Geneva version, translated and published by the English reformers who fled to that city during the persecution in Queen Mary's time, and which was the favorite version of the Puritans long after the translation made by order of King James was published. Mr. George Livermore, a very competent judge, believes it to have been printed as early as 1520, or before." It contains the birth of Edward Rawson, in 1615; the date of his death, in 1693; the births of all his children, twelve in number; the marriage certificate given of Wellcom Rawson, with the births of his twenty children, deaths, and other items.

Children of WILLIAM and ANNE (GLOVER) RAWSON, born in Boston, Dorchester and Braintree — twenty in number — as follows:

14. Anne,   b. April 11, 1674,   (Boston); died in infancy.
15. Wilson,   b. ——   1675,   "   "   "
16. Margaret, b. Aug.   1, 1676,   "   "   "
17. Edward,   b. Sept.   6, 1677,   "   "   "
18. Edward,   b. Aug. 29, 1678,   "   "   "
19. Rachael,   b. Oct. 16, 1679,   "   "   "
20. Dorothea, b. Aug.   8, 1681; d. in Boston, Sept. 20, 1689, aged 8 years.
+21. William,   b. Dec. 2, 1682; H. C. 1703; m. Sarah Crosby, of Braintree.
+22. David,   b. Dec. 13, 1683 ; m. Mary Gulliver, of Milton.
23. Dorothea, b. June 19, 1686; d. in Boston, in infancy.
24. Ebenezer, b. Dec. 1, 1687 (Dorchester); d. Aug. 28, 1696, aged 9 years.
25. Thankful, b. Aug. 6, 1688 (Dorchester); d. Aug. 21, 1688, aged 15 days.
+26. Nathaniel, b. Dec. 3, 1689 (Braintree) ; m. Hannah Thompson, of Braintree.
27. Ebenezer, b. July 25, 1691 (Braintree) ; d. in infancy.
+28. Edward, b. Jan. 27, 1692; m. Preserved Baily, of Boston.
29. Ann,   b. Aug. 28, 1693 ; d. in infancy.
30. Patience, b. Nov.   8, 1694 ; d. young.
+31. Pelatiah, b. July   2, 1696 ; m. Hannah Hall, of Dorchester.
32. Grindal,   b. Aug. 24, 1697 ; d. young.
33. Mary,   b. Dec. 16, 1698 ; d. in infancy.

June 13, 1701. ANNE RAWSON to her brother NATHANIEL GLOVER. A Release of Title and Inheritance in the One Twelfth of Newbury Farm.

To all People unto whom these Presents shall come. I William Rawson, of Braintree, in the County of Suffolk, within his Majesty's Province of Massachusetts Bay in New England, Yeoman, formerly of Boston, within the said County, Shopkeeper, who married with Anne the daughter of Mrs. Nathaniel Glover, sometime of Dorchester aforesaid, Deceased, Sends Greeting. Know Ye, that Roger Billings, late of Dorchester aforesaid, Yeoman, Dec^d, did, in or about the year 1677, for and in consideration and behalf of my Uncle Mr. John Glover of Sudbury, in the County of Middlesex and in the Bay of New England aforesaid, Gentleman, now Deceased, treat and bargain to and with the said John Glover my Uncle,   *   *   *   *   * and with and of the before named William Rawson, A Third part of a quarter or One Twelfth part of that Farm commonly called Newberry Farm, situate and lying in the Township of Dorchester, heretofore in the possession of John Glover, Esq. late of Boston, Deceased, father of the said John Glover before named. And Whereas The said John Glover of Sudbury, Gentleman, Deceased, in consideration of the love and affection which he had for his nephew Nathaniel Glover, Senior, aforesaid, Tanner, and brother of the said me Anne Rawson, being the Eldest son of Mr. Nathaniel Glover of Dorchester, Deceased,

and for divers other good causes and considerations, and by a certain
Deed or Instrument bearing date December 7th, 1686, did Give, grant,
convey and confirm unto my said brother Nathaniel Glover, his heirs
and Assigns forever, All that One Third part of a Quarter of said
Newberry Farm, purchased of my Husband, William Rawson, with
arable pasture and woodland, as well as Meadows and Marsh Ground
Thereto belonging or appertaining thereto, and of all Housings, Barns,
Edifices and Timber thereon, or aught thereof, standing, lying or
growing; and Interest, use, property, possession, claim or demand
whatsoever, of, in, and unto said Lands, Housing, Fences, woods,
trees, commonages, pastures, feedings, waters, springs, profits, privileges, Commodities and Appurtenances herewith appertaining thereto, with One Twelfth part of all the other lands Situate in Milton or
on Squantum Rock thereto belonging, As by the said Deeds reference
thereto being had more at large. Now Know Ye, that I Anne Rawson, for and in Consideration of the sum of Ten pounds Currant money of New England, and for other good causes and Considerations me
thereto moving, have ratified and confirmed the sale of my said Husband, William Rawson, of One Third part of a Quarter or One Twelfth
part of All that farm called and known by the name of Newbury farm.
And by these Presents for myself and my Heirs, do fully and absolutely remiss, release and forever Quitclaim unto my said brother
Nathaniel Glover, his heirs and assigns forever, all the Estate, Right,
Title, Interest, Inheritance, use, property, or Dower, possession,
claim or demand which I ever had or can have in time to come, or
shall by any manner of ways or means whatsoever, of, in, to, or out
of the said One Third part of a Quarter or One Twelfth of all the said
farm, Lands and Hereditaments and premises granted and sold as
aforesaid by my said husband William Rawson to the said John Glover, and by him given and granted as above mentioned unto my said
brother Nathaniel Glover, in whose possession the same now are,
and of, in, and unto every part and parcel of the same. To Have and
to Hold the said One Twelfth part of all the said farm, with all and
singular the hereof and hereby released premises, unto my said brother
Nathaniel Glover, his heirs and Assigns, to his and their only proper
use, benefit and behoof forever, freely, fully and absolutely of consideration, redemption, revocation in any wise and without let or hindrance, suit, trouble, claim or demand whatsoever of Me the said Anne
Rawson or my heirs, or any other person or persons whatsoever from,
by or under Me.

In witness whereof, I have hereunto set my hand and seale this
13th day of June, 1701, Annoq R.R. Guil. tertii.

(WILLIAM RAWSON.)   ANNE RAWSON.

Signed, sealed and delivered in presence of us,
          Roger Billings,
          Joseph Billings.

June 13, 1701, Anne Rawson personally appeared before me the
Subscriber, One of His Majesty's Justices of the Peace, and did
acknowledge the within written Instrument to be her free Act and
Deed.   As attest,   JOHN WILSON, *Justice of the Peace.*

          Boston, February 20, 1718.

Received and Recorded with the Records of Deeds for the County
of Suffolk, Lib. 33, fol. 212.

Bay Field conveyed.   William and Anne Rawson to Nathaniel Glover.

To All People unto whom these Presents shall come.   William Rawson of Braintree, in the County of Suffolk in New England, Gentleman, and Anne his wife, send Greeting.

Know Ye, That I William Rawson and Anne his said wife, for and in consideration of the Sum of Two Hundred Pounds Current Money of New England, well and truly to him in hand paid before the ensealing and delivery of these Presents, by Nathaniel Glover of Dorchester, in the County of Suffolk, aforesaid, Tanner, the Receipt whereof to full content and satisfaction he doth hereby acknowledge, and thereof and of every part thereof doth hereby acquit, Exonerate and discharge the said Nathaniel Glover, his heirs, Executors, Administrators and Assigns, and every of them forever, and by these Presents and for Divers other good causes and considerations them hereunto moving; they the said William Rawson and Anne his wife have given, granted, bargained, sold, aliened, enfeoffed, conveyed and confirmed, and by these Presents for themselves and their heirs do give, grant, sell and convey, &c., unto the said Nathaniel Glover, his heirs and Assigns forever, viz., A Certain Tract or parcel of land called the Bay-field, containing by estimation Twenty Acres, Be the same more or less, lying and being in the Township of Dorchester—

Butted and bounded as follows: Westerly upon the Highway, and Northerly with the land of Roger Billings; Easterly upon the Sea or Salt Water; and Southerly upon the Land of the said Nathaniel Glover, or however otherwise bounded or reputed to be bounded. Together with all the privileges thereunto belonging, to him the said Nathaniel Glover, his heirs and Assigns forever.

To Have and to Hold unto him the said Nathaniel Glover, his heirs and Assigns forever, the aforegranted and bargained premises, with all their privileges and Appurtenances, for their own sole and proper use and behoof forever.

In witness whereof, they the said William Rawson and Anne his wife have hereunto set their hands and seals this Twentieth day of July, 1706.   WILLIAM RAWSON,
                                                                  ANNE RAWSON.

Signed, sealed and delivered in presence of us,
          Samuel Shepard,
          William Rawson, Junʳ.

August 7th, 1706.   William Rawson and Anne Rawson personally Appearing, acknowledged the above Deed to be their free Will, Act and Deed.   JOHN WILSON, *Just. Peace.*

Entered and Recorded with the Records of Deeds for the County of Suffolk, Liber 23, folio 32.   ADDINGTON DAVENPORT, *Recorder.*

*Land in Braintree.   William and Anne Rawson to John Glover and
                              Thomas Glover.*

To all Christian People to whom these Presents shall come.   William Rawson of Braintree in the County of Suffolk, &c., Gentᵐⁿ, For and in Consideration of the Sum of Two Hundred and Fourteen Pounds to him in hand paid in silver money before the ensealing and delivery of these Presents, to John Glover and Thomas Glover, both of Dorchester in the County aforesaid, Yeomen, Have Given, granted, &c., A Certain Tract or Parcel of Land in Braintree aforesaid, adjacent to Capt. Wilson's farm, Containing Thirty-two Acres, Be the same more or Less, Said land being Wood Land, Arable and Swamp.

Bounded Easterly on Land of Capt. John Wilson aforesaid, the line running from the Town Way which leads to Milton ; Southerly Fifty-Two Rods to a Walnut Tree newly marked, there being a Rail fence now standing on said line ; Southerly on the Lands of the said William Rawson ; the line running from said Walnut-tree Westerly Fifty-Six Rods to a stake and heap of Stones ; Westwardly on Lands of Capt. Jonathan Gulliver ; the line running on the top or middle of the ridge (so called) One Hundred and Nine Rods from the Stake and Stones aforesaid ; or however otherwise bounded or reputed to be bounded :

To Have and to Hold, &c., the above granted, &c., with all the privileges and Appurtenances, unto them the said John Glover and Thomas Glover, their heirs and Assigns forever.

In Witness whereof, I the said William Rawson, with Anne my wife, have set our hands and seals This Sixth day of May, 1715, and in the first year of our Sovereign Lord George the 1st, King of Great Britain, France and Ireland, Defender of the Faith.

WILLIAM RAWSON,

In presence of
ANNE RAWSON.
David Rawson,
Edward Rawson.

May 27, 1715. Acknowledged in person by the said William and Anne Rawson, before   EDMUND QUINCY, *Just. Peace.*

Received, Entered and Recorded with the Records of Deeds for the County of Suffolk, Liber 29, fol. 202.   JOHN BALLANTINE, *Reg.*

Mrs. Rawson was in Barnstable a short time before her marriage, and with her mother, in the family of Gov. Hinckley. Her name appears as a witness to a deed, from John Flecker to Jedediah Lombard, of a tract of land in that County, dated January 20, 1671, and acknowledged before Gov. Hinckley, August 17, 1672. "Signed, sealed and delivered in presence of us, Mary Hinckley, Anne Glover."

Mrs. Rawson is said to have been a lady of rare gifts and accomplishments, and inherited a portion of her mother's comeliness and grace. She had the advantages of a superior education, under the care of her grandmother, Mrs. Anna Glover, of Boston. Very interesting letters written by her in 1681–82, addressed to her mother, have been preserved among a collection of "Hinckley Papers," Vols. 1 and 2, and may be seen at the Library of the Massachusetts Historical Society, in her own hand-writing.

20

[*Fourth Generation.*]

(6) NATHANIEL GLOVER, eldest son of Nathaniel and Hannah (Hinckley) Glover, was born at the Dorchester homestead, November 10, 1676, baptized the 13th of the same month, and died in London, England, on the 13th of March, 1726, in his fiftieth year. He left a widow and six children. He is said to have been remarkable for his early piety. At the age of ten years he voluntarily gave himself to the watch and care of the Church in Dorchester, and was admitted as a member in full communion at the age of twenty years. "Since August," say the Church Records, "unto this instant, Dec. 1696, the following persons, having been proved by the pastor as to their knowledge and experience, and by the congregation as to conversation, publicly took hold on the covenant, viz., young Nathaniel Glover (jun.), Mary Glover," and others. During his minority, he was engaged in the tanning business, carried on by his father on the Glover estate. At the age of twenty-four years, Nov. 13, 1701, he was married to Rachael Marsh, of Braintree, by the Worshipful Mr. Wilson. She was the daughter of Alexander and Martha Marsh, of Braintree, and was born there 12 : 2 : 1673. Soon after her marriage, she was admitted to join the Church at Dorchester. The Records inform us — "Among those names of such as were examined, allowed and propounded before the Church for laying hold on the Covenant, Feb. 3, 1701–2, were Nathaniel Glover's wife Rachael, Elizabeth and Hannah Glover." She died April 10, 1752, aged 79 years. They had seven children, all baptized at the Church with which they were in full communion.

Children of NATHANIEL, Jr. and RACHAEL (MARSH) GLOVER, born at the homestead in Dorchester:

    34. Rachael, b. Aug. 23, bap. Aug. 28, 1702–3 ; d. in her 4th year.
+35. Nathaniel, b. May 16, 1704 ; m. Anne Simpson, of Boston.
+36. Rachael, b. July 30, 1707 ; m. { 1st, Ebenezer Clough,of Boston; 2d, Richard Salter, Esq.   "
+37. Hannah, b. Feb. 24, 1708–9 ; m. Joseph Bass,Esq., Dorchester.
+38. Alexander, b. Nov. 13, 1710 ; m. Sarah White, of Dorchester.
+39. Mary,   b. Nov. 17, 1713 ; d. unm. May 20, 1772, aged 59.
+40. Pelatiah, b. April 2, 1716 ; m. Mary Cochrane, of Boston.

Nathaniel Glover, Jr., was, like his progenitors, an extensive landholder, and belonged to the class of Joint Stock and Landed Proprietors. In 1700 he came in possession of the Dorchester homestead, which had come down to him in a direct line from the Hon. John Glover, his first American ancestor. He received it from his father, Nathaniel Glover, Sen., by a deed of gift, as recorded among the acts of the latter, page 185. In addition to the homestead, he came in possession, in right of his wife Rachael, of land in Braintree, and a house and land in Boston. He also purchased several other tracts of land, and was a shareholder in the Common and Undivided Lands in Dorchester New Grant. The homestead estate contained one hundred and eighty acres. Feb. 16, 1713–14, he purchased a piece of land, adjoining his estate, of Hannah Hix, relict widow of Samuel Hix — consideration, twenty pounds — containing two and a half acres.

In 1715, Nathaniel Glover, Jr., at the age of thirty-five years, was chosen one of the Selectmen for the town of Dorchester, and was again chosen the two succeeding years. It has been said of him that he fulfilled the duties of that office with ability and honor, and retired from it, having the entire approbation of the inhabitants of the town. In 1715, he made a donation or gift to the Proprietors of the new Church in Summer Street, Boston, towards the building of that Church.

Being largely interested in the Common and Undivided Lands in Dorchester New Grant, he was a constant attendant on the meetings of the Proprietors. Another survey of these lands was commenced in the winter of 1714. In 1716, Nathaniel Glover, Sen., and Nathaniel Glover, Jr., were appointed, with others, a committee for examining and apportioning the lots; for making laws, calling meetings, and securing their rights from innovators. He was one of every committee, elected by the Proprietors, and sometimes acted as Proprietors' Clerk. At a meeting of the Proprietors in Dorchester, December 21, 1719, already referred to, a Committee was chosen, who in June following reported that "they find by computation that there is land sufficient in the township of Dorchester, that never has been divided, to make one hundred and fifty divisions to every proprietor." Therefore they proceeded to choose a Committee to lay out "to every such proprietor that can prove his right and propriety in every division of land yet undivided throughout the township of Dorchester to Plymouth bounds, the whole of his right together, or in as many parts as he sees cause; he giving into the hands of the Committee in writing the place where, and the bounds, and the number of acres he would have laid out, and the said Committee shall be obliged to lay out on the very spot to the man who first desires it in writing."

In 1718, Nathaniel Glover, Jr., quit-claimed rights in the Common and Undivided Lands in the Township of Dorchester, as follows:

To Nathaniel Glover, Sen.

To all Christian People to whom these Presents shall come, Greeting. Know Ye, that I Nathaniel Glover, Junior, of Dorchester, Tanner, in the County of Suffolk in New England, Being one of the Proprietors of the Common and Undivided Lands in Dorchester aforesaid, Have given, granted, and by these Presents for certain reasons and considerations me thereunto moving, do freely, clearly and absolutely give, grant, quit-claim and confirm unto my Honored Father, Mr. Nathaniel Glover, of said Dorchester, Husbandman, Six hundred and sixty eight acres of my (as yet) Common and Undivided Lands in the New Grant in the Township of Dorchester aforesaid. The said land hereby given him the said Nathaniel Glover, to be sett off to him in such places as by lott it may happen to fall in the subdivision that shall hereafter be made betwixt us, when that my own Rights shall be set off to me at the division of the whole Undivided lands in the Township of said Dorchester. To have and to hold the said Six hundred and Sixty Eight Acres, to him (my father), his heirs and assigns, to his and their own and proper use forever.

In witness whereof, I have hereunto set my hand and seal this tenth day of September, 1718.   (Signed)   NATHANIEL GLOVER, Jr.

In presence of us,
    Thomas Glover,
    Charles King.

Sept. 10, 1718. Nathaniel Glover Junior personally appeared and acknowledged the above instrument to be his free Will, Act and Deed, before me,   ELIJAH DANFORTH, Just. of Peace.

June 6, 1720, at a meeting of the Proprietors, Nathaniel Brewer, Joseph Hall and Nathaniel Glover, Jr., were chosen a Committee for the purpose of laying out to every such proprietor that can prove his right and propriety, his true and proper apportionment. It was also ordered that every man should bear the charges of laying out his own land.

December 17, 1720, Nathaniel Glover, Jr., Nathaniel Brewer and Jonathan Blake were appointed a Committee, and empowered to sell land, or timber, or ore, on any part of Dorchester New Grant. Mr. Glover was continued on the Committee until the close of their labors.

The work of surveying and apportioning these lands progressed slowly; the first and second generations, and very many of the third, had passed to their rest, with no other benefit arising from their ownership and inheritance than that derived from the anticipation that at some time in the future they or their descendants would come in possession of extensive and valuable lands, which could be by them possessed and improved as Manorial estates. That such hopes were entertained and cherished by many of the Joint Stock Company, has been settled by writers of that time who had opportunity to become acquainted with their motives and lofty aims. These hopes and visions were never realized. When apportioned and entered upon, in cases where the claimants possessed sufficient courage to occupy and become inhabitants of such a wilderness as was that sterile and uninviting region between Blue Hills on the North and the Colony line on the South, their visions vanished like "castles in the air." Very many of them were dissatisfied with their allotments, and not without reason, probably, as new proprietors had come in and taken the places of the original ones, and many were displaced and dispossessed entirely by persons who had taken up lands and settled on them without any inheritance or title. This was the case with the Glovers, much of the land allotted to them being claimed by usurpers, and could never be recovered except by a suit at law, to which they had an hereditary aversion, unless driven to it on the defensive. Nathaniel Glover, Jr., aside from his propriety, or inheritance from his father, became also a proprietor in his own right of nearly one thousand acres, very little of which was ever recovered. In the Twenty-five Divisions, now situated in Stoughton, in the allotment he received just one fourth of what was laid out originally to Mr. Glover, and one half of what was apportioned to his father. In Dead Swamp, 48th lot, he was to have two acres two quarters in every division. In 9th lot, in Burnt Swamp and Iron Mine Meadow, three acres of meadow bottom; and so in all the other divisions, wherever the names of his father and grandfather occur.

In 1722–3, Nathaniel Glover, Jr., as committee with Nathaniel Brewer and Jonathan Blake, sold a tract of land in Dorchester New Grant, called Iron Mine Meadow, or Burnt Swamp, to James Leonard, of Taunton, in the County of Bristol; witnessed by Joseph Bass and Rachael Glover.

20*

In 1722, January 9, Nathaniel Glover, Jr., tanner, sold a tract of upland to Joshua Fairbanks, situated in Dorchester New Grant.

January 16, 1723, he sold to Ephraim Tucker, of Milton, eighty-eight acres of land in Dorchester New Grant. Bounds described as beginning at a white oak tree at the easterly end of Dorchester Swamp, in Stoughton. Acknówledged in person, Feb. 26, 1723.

May 3, 1723, he sold Nathaniel Blake and James Blake, of Milton, yeomen, two hundred acres of land, situated in Dorchester New Grant, aforesaid, bounded westerly by marked trees. Considera-tion, one hundred pounds current money of New England. Ac-knowledged in person before Elijah Davenport, Justice of the Peace, May 13, 1723.

November 8, 1723, he sold a tract of land to William Sumner, of Milton; said tract containing one hundred and sixty-two acres, lying near Dorchester Swamp, in Stoughton.

December 3, 1723, he sold to Ralph Freeman two acres of land in every division of Dorchester New Grant.

March 3, 1724–5, he, with his wife, sold to Ebenezer Clough, of Boston, their "Messuage, Dwelling House, Shop, Barn, Yard, Gar-dens, and all the land belonging to them, under, about and around the premises, at the southerly end of Boston."

June 17, 1724, he sold a tract of land in Dorchester New Grant to Eleazer Carver.

March 31, 1725, appears to be the last date in which his signature can be found in relation to the sale of any land. The following extract from an original deed of conveyance, of that date, of land belonging to the heirs of Nathaniel Glover, Sen., and in which they all join, is here given:

We Nathaniel Glover, Tanner. John Glover and Thomas Glover, Yeomen, sons of Mr. Nathaniel Glover Sen. of Dorchester Deceased, with Mary Glover, Hannah Glover and Elizabeth Glover, Spinsters, daughters of Mr. Nathaniel Glover Sen. deceased, with our Honour-ed Mother, widow and relict of the said Nathaniel Glover Sen. afore-said, Quitclaim unto Oxenbridge Thacher Esq. of Milton, ten acres of Woodland belonging to our Honoured father, said land lying in the Town of Milton.
Signed by Nathaniel Glover, John Glover, Thomas Glover, Hannah Glover Senior, Mary Glover, Hannah Glover Junior, Elizabeth Glover.

Nathaniel Glover, Jr., continued to act as Committee and in defence of his rights and the rights of the original Proprietors against the new ones, and the conflict was continued. The judgment obtained at his Majesty's Superior Court begun and holden at Boston on the first Tuesday in May, 1719, was not accepted. An appeal was made through the Governor and Assistants, to the General Court at Boston. A hearing was obtained before that body, but without success. It was proposed by the original Proprietors, who claimed under the apportionment of 1636, '37 and '38, as recorded on the Records of the Company's lands, that Nathaniel Glover, Jr., should be appointed, in case of a failure before this Court of the Colony, to proceed to England and plead their case before the King in Council. The reigning King at this time was George I., and it was finally determined by the injured claimants to lay their case before his Majesty and obtain a decision from the Courts of Great Britain. Nathaniel Glover was accordingly chosen as their agent. The following account was related to the writer by a distinguished and venerable great grandson of his, now deceased. It describes his appearance and characteristics at the final decision before the Superior Court, previous to his departure for England.

"Nathaniel Glover, Jr.," says the narrator, "was present, and received it with becoming coolness and self-control. He arose and addressed the Court, making a collected statement of the great wrong which had been done, not only to himself, in his own personal rights, but to his ancestors, and announced his intention of appealing to the Court of Great Britain, where he expressed himself fully assured of having justice granted him." It is said, also, that his personal appearance was majestic, and awed the Court, causing some of his enemies to tremble. "He was dressed in the full style of gentlemen at that time, with Coat of scarlet Broadcloth, the skirts plaited and wadded, reaching below the knee; full sleeves, with cuffs reaching below the elbow, and wristbands fringed with lace; an embroidered band lay around the top with tassels in front. The trimmings which adorned the garment were of gold and silver, wrought in fringe or lace, and spread over it. Small Clothes or breeches of buff colour, with points of Ribbon at the knee; the Vest of buff colour, fringed with lace. Buckles of Silver on the knees and on the Shoes." A powdered wig and three-cornered hat completed the dress, as it has been graphically described by the descendant alluded to.

After making all necessary arrangements for his family, and collecting the requisite documents and copies of Court proceedings, he sailed for England in the month of April, 1725. He arrived safely in England and proceeded to London, where he obtained a hearing of his case before the King in Council. He was soon attacked, however, with a fatal disease, and died before the consummation of his object. Thus closed the pursuit which had occupied his attention for seven years, and thus ended the controversy with the Dorchester Proprietors. The descendants of Glover and heirs at law were obliged to accept the apportionment of the new Proprietors, being, according to the statement, less by one thousand acres in the Twenty-Five Divisions, than had been allotted them in the original laying out, and to which they believed themselves justly entitled.

In 1727, there was another list made out by the so-called new Proprietors, allowing only the former proportion which was assigned them by the grant of 1713; being eight acres to Mr. Glover, four acres to Nathaniel Glover, Sen., and two to Nathaniel Glover, Jr., in every single division of land in the Twenty-Five Divisions, and amounting to less by several hundred acres than their shares claimed.

The plan printed on the next page represents the apportionment to the Glovers and others, according to the survey of 1713, and the decision of the new Proprietors. It relates only to the twenty-first and twenty-second lots in the Twenty-five Divisions, and shows the names of the persons owning in common, and with whom the Glovers were to divide. After the death of Nathaniel Glover, Jr., it appears no further effort was made to obtain the original claim of thirty-six acres, two quarters and twenty-five rods, out of every single Division in the Twenty-five Divisions, and there were set off to Mr. Glover two hundred acres, with one hundred and twelve to Nathaniel Glover, and fifty to Nathaniel Glover, Jr., and the land was accepted and entered upon. The portion of Mr. Glover remains to this day in the possession of a descendant; that of Nathaniel Glover was sold and became afterwards the Paul estate, but of whom purchased is not known; and it is said the portion belonging to Nathaniel Glover, Jr., was taken up and settled upon by usurpers, and never sold by his heirs, by any legal conveyance.

A List of the Lotts in the Twenty-Five Divisions of Land, so called, late in the Township of Dorchester and now in Stoughton, containing the names of the Proprietors in every Lott, and what quantity belongeth to Every Man. Proprietors' Right and propriety in a single Division, so called, and as it was laid out; and being doubled Twenty-Five times, and the place where each lot was laid out. Which List was ordered to be made at a Proprietors' Meeting, on the Eighth day of December, 1727.

No. of Lot.	NAMES.	Single. A. Q.	Doubled 25 T. A. Q. R.		Places where the Lots lye.
	Mr. Glover, ...	8	200		These two Lotts were laid out together, partly in the 6th Range on the East side of Dorchester Swamp, all of the 7th Range on the South of the before said Swamp, and part in the 8th Range next to the Colony line.
21st,	Nathaniel Glover, . .	4 2	112	2	
	Nicholas Allen, . . .	3	75		
	Ralph Pope, ...	3	75		
	Sherebiah Butt, . . .	1	25		
	Samuel Rigbee, . . .	2	50		Except Ebenezer Billings, Jun., whose Right was laid out in two places in the West Land among the Twelve Divisions, adjacent to the said Billings's own Land.
	Samuel Butt, . . .	3	18	3	
	Nathaniel Glover, Jun.	2	50		
22d,	Roger Billings, Sen., his Right, & the other belong'g to the 4 Lott	2 2	62	2	After the said Ebenezer Billings Jun. his Right is deducted of the 22 Lot, is to have 45 acres aforesaid allowance with the Rest. There was half an Acre in a single Division mistaken in the 21 Lot, which was afterwards supplied in Iron Mine Meadow. See page 81 of this Book.
	Ebenezer Billings, . .	5	125		
	Ebenezer Billings, Jun.	1	25		

A true Copy from the Proprietors' Records.

JAMES BLAKE, *Proprietors' Clerk.*

The following account of Nathaniel Glover, Jr., appeared in a Boston newspaper, under date of Dorchester, June 6th, 1726.

"This day we have the afflicting news, that on March 13th last past, died of the Small Pox, in London, Mr. Nathaniel Glover of this Town, in the 49th year of his age. He was a great grandson of the Honble John Glover, Esq., one of the first Planters of Massachusetts, and one of the Magistrates or Assistants of the Colony, chosen in 1652. This descendant of his of late fell into an unhappy Controversy with a great part of the inhabitants of the Town about the Right of the Undivided Lands; and in April of last year went over as an Agent of the Aboriginal Proprietors, to the Court

of Great Britain; where he died just as he was expecting an audience of his cause before the King in Council. 'Till this unhappy
Contest began, he was greatly and universally respected and valued
in the Town; and his adversaries will yet generally own that he
was a Gentleman of a sober life, strong natural powers, great penetration, and a kind and obliging neighbour; and of such admirable
command of temper, that no abuse of his enemies could either disturb him in his public argument, or move him to reflect upon them.
He has left a virtuous and most sorrowful widow and six young children. May God be a Father of the Fatherless, and a Judge of the
Widow in His Holy Habitation. (Psalm 68: 5.)"

Rachael Glover, his widow, survived him about twenty-six years,
and died April 10, 1752. She made her will, which bears date
March 19, 1749. She is buried in the ancient burial place in Dorchester, and has a gravestone.

Rachael Glover, widow, is taxed in the List of Province Taxes,
for estate real, personal, and one female slave, from 1726 to 1752.

Will of Rachael Glover (Widow).

In the name of God, Amen. This Nineteenth day of March, Anno
Domⁿ One Thousand Seven Hundred and Forty-Nine, and in the
Twenty-Third year of his Majesties Reign, King George the Second
of Great Britain.

I Rachael Glover of Dorchester, in the County of Suffolk, in the
Province of Massachusetts Bay in New England, widow. Being at
this present writing hereof, of a sound and disposing mind and memory, do therefore make this my Last Will and Testament in manner and
form as followeth.

Impr. And first of all I recommend my precious Soul into the
hands of God who gave it; and my Body I commit to the Dust by a
decent Christian burial, in the hope of the Resurrection of the Just.
And as for my Worldly Good with which God hath seen fit to bless
me, I give and dispose of it in the following manner.

Imprimis. That all my just debts and funeral charges be paid first
out of my estate. Secondly. I then give unto my two daughters
Hannah and Mary Glover all my Wearing Apparel, and all my Household Furniture of every sort, with all the Provisions that may be in
the House at the time of my decease. And to the above named Mary
Glover I give my negro boy Richard. And to my Grandson Richard
Salter, son to my daughter Rachael, I give One Hundred Pounds Old
Tenor, or money equivalent thereunto, to be paid him by my Executors when he arrives at the age of Twenty One Years of age; but if
he die before, the said sum is to be equally divided among my children.

The remaining part of my Real and Personal estate I give to my
Five Children, viz.: Nathaniel Glover, Alexander Glover, Pelatiah
Glover, Hannah Glover, and Mary Glover, equally to be divided
among them.

And I appoint my Two eldest sons Nathaniel Glover and Alexander Glover sole Executors of this my last Will and Testament. And that this is my last Will, exclusive of all others, I have, in Testimony hereof, set my hand and seale, this 19th day of March, 1749.

RACHAEL + GLOVER, and scale.
Her mark.

Signed, sealed, published and declared to be my Last Will and Testament, in presence of

      Joseph Bass,
      Ruth Trott,   } *Witnesses.*
      Christian Trott,

Letters of administration, with the will annexed, were granted to the executors named in her will, but the administration was not finished. Nathaniel Glover, eldest son and senior executor, of Boston, died in 1773. Alexander Glover, the second son, also died before the execution of the will. The estate was finally settled in 1785, about thirty-three years after her death, by her eldest grandson, Alexander Glover, jun.

Suffolk ss. Nov. 8, 1785. The Second Account of Alexander Glover, Administrator with the Will annexed, of the Estate of his late Grandmother Rachael Glover, Late of Dorchester, in said County, Widow, Deceased.

Said Accomptant prays Allowance as follows.

For the foot of the Debit of Account exhibited May 31, 1785, ...	£4	16	
To ditto paid the Dividers and Appraisers . .	1	10	
To ditto Expenses of Dividers and Appraisers .	0	9	
To ditto for Exam⁵ Allow⁵ and Record⁵ This Acct. and Copy thereof	6	8 0	
To ditto for Drawing out this Account . . .	1		
To Allowance to the Administrator for his time and trouble in Administering, &c.	5 00	00 0	
	12 02	8 0	

November 8, 1785.   ALEXANDER GLOVER.

Suffolk ss. Alexander Glover, Administrator cum Testamentis annexis, presented the aforegoing Account, produced Vouchers, and was sworn.

Examined and Allowed by Me this 8th day of November, 1785.

O. WENDELL, *Judge of Probate.*

Attest: WILLIAM COOPER, *Register.*

(7) MARY GLOVER, the eldest daughter of Nathaniel and Hannah (Hinckley) Glover, was born at the homestead in Dorchester, April 12, 1679, and baptized at the Dorchester Church 20 (2) 1679,

by Rev. Josiah Flint. The date of her death has not been ascertained.

In December, 1696, her name was enrolled among those who were examined and owned the covenant, and in 1701–2 she was admitted to join the Church in full communion.

In 1723 the name of Mary Glover appears as a witness to a deed from Nathaniel Glover, senior, to Thomas and Hannah Glover.

July 17, 1724, she appeared before the magistrate and acknowledged the above deed, her father having deceased a short time before.

Mary Glover, at her father's decease in 1723–4, came in possession of one-third of the twenty-six acres of land which she, with her sisters Hannah and Elizabeth, received by a deed of gift from her father, bearing date Nov. 20, 1723.

In 1724 her name appears among a list of those who were shareholders in the Common and Undivided Lands. In 1725, May 31, her name appears on a deed confirming the sale of ten acres of woodland, in Milton, to Oxenbridge Thacher. (See page 222.)

In 1725, at the decease of her sister Elizabeth, she came in possession of one half of her share; and in 1729 the following indenture was executed between Mary Glover and her sister Hannah Glover.

Indenture between Hannah Glover and her sister Mary Glover.

This Indenture, made the Fifth of March, 1729, and in the Second Year of Our Sovereign Lord George the Second, King of Great Britain, &c., between Mary Glover of Dorchester, in the County of Suffolk and in the Province of Massachusetts Bay in New England, Spinster, on the one part, and Hannah Glover of the same Dorchester, &c., on the other part.

Whereas There are Certain Pieces or Parcels of Land and Meadow in Dorchester aforesaid, now in the possession of the said Mary and Hannah Glover, holden by them in joint or equal shares, under and by virtue of a Deed from their father Mr. Nathaniel Glover sen', now Deceased, bearing date the 20th day of November, 1723, as by reference to said Deed of Gift may more fully and at large appear.

Now the said Mary and Hannah Glover have mutually agreed and consented, and also acknowledged, made and finished a Division of said Land, to the end, intent and purpose that each other of them the said Mary and Hannah Glover, their heirs and assigns, may know, have, hold, use, possess and enjoy each their proper part and proportion thereof Forever, in manner and form following.

That is to say, That the said Mary Glover, her Heirs and Assigns, shall have, hold, use, possess and enjoy that part which is called the Little Pasture or Second Division, about Twelve Acres more or less, in full for her part, Bounded North on the Way leading to Damm Meadow ; West, partly on the Land of Hannah Glover and partly on

Land of Moses Billings ; South on Rye Field Hill ; and Easterly on the Land of said Moses Billings.

Now this Indenture Witnesseth for a further confirmation of the aforesaid Division and Partition, that the said Hannah Glover, for herself and her Heirs, Executors, Administrators and Assigns, do fully, freely and absolutely grant, release, assign, enfeoffe and confirm unto the said Mary Glover, her Heirs and Assigns forever, all that before mentioned Little Pasture or Second Division as it is before described and bounded, together with all the appurtenances thereof, against the lawful claims of all persons claiming any Right, title or interest thereto or therein, from or under me the said Hannah Glover.

In witness whereof, the said Hannah Glover hath to this Indenture put her hand and seale, the day and year first above written, in presence of Us,

David Rawson,   HANNAH GLOVER.
Thomas Glover.

A duplicate was drawn the same day, conveying the remaining portion of the land to Hannah Glover, and signed by Mary Glover, in presence of David Rawson and Thomas Glover.

In 1733 Mary Glover went to reside with her sister in Boston, who was married and had removed there.

In 1737 she made a transfer of all her estate of inheritance, both real and personal, as expressed in the following deed of gift to her sister Hannah Laws.

Deed of Gift from Mary Glover, of Boston, to Hannah Laws.

To all people before whom these Presents may come. Know ye, That I Mary Glover of Boston, in the County of Suffolk in New England, send Greeting.

Know ye, That I the said Mary Glover, for and in consideration of the sum of Ten Shillings to me in hand paid at and before the delivery of these Presents by my sister Hannah Laws, of Boston, aforesaid, widow, the receipt whereof I do hereby acknowledge, but more especially for the love, good will and affection which I have and do bear unto her ; I have given, granted, enfeoffed and confirmed, and do by these Presents give, grant, enfeoffe and confirm unto her the said Hannah Laws, All my share, Right, Title and Interest of and in a certain parcel of Land in Dorchester, in the County and Province aforesaid, containing Twenty Six Acres ; and also a piece of Salt Marsh lying on the South side of Pine Neck, with all the privileges and appurtenances thereof ; which Lands are particularly described and bounded in and by a certain Deed of Gift from my Honored father Mr. Nathaniel Glover of Dorchester (Deceased), Yeoman, made to me and my two sisters the said Hannah and Elizabeth Glover, bearing date the Twentieth day of November, 1723, and recorded the Twenty Seventh day of November, 1724, with the Records of Deeds for Suffolk County, by John Ballantine, Register ; relation thereto or the record thereof being had, will more fully appear.

21

And also 2 Feather beds and 2 Feather bolsters, a Coverlet, 2 Blankets, 3 large Pewter Platters, One small Pewter Platter, 6 Pewter Plates, One Iron Porridge pot, One Iron Kettle, 6 Leather Chairs, Great Brass Kettle, 2 Turkey Worked Stools, 6 Three-backed Chairs, a parcel of Linen and Woolen, and all my Wearing Apparel, together with half a Silver Tankard.

And also I give to my said sister Hannah Laws a Certain Bond from under the hand and seale of my brother Thomas Glover, dated the 15 day of July, 1736, of the penalty of Two Hundred Pounds, conditional for the payment of One Hundred Pounds with Lawful interest thereon for the same on or before the 15th day of July, 1737, which remains due and the Bond fair and Uncancelled. To Have and to Hold all the above given and granted Lands and personal Estate, and the whole of the aforesaid Bond, unto her the said Hannah Laws (Widow), her heirs, Executors, Administrators and assigns forever. And I the said Mary Glover do avouch myself to be the sole, true and Lawful owner of the said Land and Premises, and have in myself full power and Lawful authority to give, grant and dispose thereof in manner as aforesaid.

And I the said Mary Glover do hereby Covenant to and with the said Hannah Laws, her Heirs, Executors, Administrators and Assigns, by these Presents, to Warrant and defend the said granted and given Land and Premises, Personal Estate and Bond, unto her the said Hannah Laws, her Heirs, Executors, Administrators and Assigns, Forever, Against Myself, My Heirs, and all persons claiming any Right or Interest therein from, by or under Me.

In Witness whereof, I the said Mary Glover have hereunto put my hand and seale this 14 day of September, 1737, and in the Eleventh Year of Our Sovereign Lord George the Second, Anno Domini 1737.

MARY GLOVER, and a Seale.

Signed, sealed and delivered in presence of us,
John Beard,
Mary Hanover.

Memorandum.

This 23d day of September, 1737, The said Mary Glover delivered to the said Hannah Laws, and the said Hannah Laws accepted and received, One of the Six Pewter Plates granted and conveyed by the above written Instrument, in the name of the whole, in presence of us,
John Beard,
Mary Hanover.

Boston, September 28, 1737. Mrs. Mary Glover personally appeared before me, William Tyng, Justice of the Peace, and acknowledged the foregoing Instrument to be her free Act and Deed.
Attest: WILLIAM TYNG.

January 10, 1743, Mary Glover with others conveys her right in a tract of land in Stoughton to her brother Thomas Glover, of Dorchester, as follows:

To all People to whom these Presents shall come. We Mary Glover of Boston, Spinster; and Hannah Glover and Mary Glover junior, both of Dorchester, Spinsters; All in the County of Suffolk and Province of the Massachusetts Bay in New England, send Greeting. Know Ye, that We the said Mary Glover, Hannah Glover and Mary Glover junior, for and in consideration of the sum of Fifty Pounds to Us in hand paid before the enleasing and delivery of these Presents, by Thomas Glover of Dorchester aforesaid, Gentleman; We the said Mary Glover, Hannah Glover and Mary Glover junior, have given, granted, sold, aliened, enleased, conveyed and confirmed unto him the said Thomas Glover, his heirs and assigns forever, all the Right, Title, Interest, Use, Possession and Property, claim or demand whatsoever, of, in or to a certain Parcel or Tract of Land Lying in Stoughton, in the County and Province aforesaid, Containing Two Hundred Acres, Laid out to Mr. Glover in the year A.D. 1716, in the Twenty-five Divisions in Dorchester New Grant (so called), as by the Proprietors Records of Dorchester may more fully appear.

Said Land is bounded Southerly on the Nineteenth and Twentieth Lotts; Northerly on Land laid out to Nathaniel Glover;* Westerly on Land laid out to Samuel Rigbee and Sherebiah Butt partly, and partly on Dorchester Swamp;† or however otherwise bounded or reputed to be bounded. To Have and to Hold, all and singular the afore granted Premises, with all the Privileges and Appurtenances belonging to the aforesaid Premises, Unto the said Thomas Glover, Sen', his heirs and assigns forever, without the Least let or hindrance, suit or molestation from Us, or any Persons claiming by, from, or under Us, the said Mary Glover, Hannah Glover and Mary Glover junior.

In Testimony whereof, We have hereunto set our hands and seals, This Tenth day of January, One Thousand Seven Hundred and Forty three, and in the Seventeenth Year of his Majesty's Reign, King George the Second, &c.

MARY GLOVER of Boston.
HANNAH GLOVER, } of Dorchester.
MARY GLOVER jun.

Signed, sealed and delivered in presence of us,
Alexander Glover,
Hannah Laws.

Dorchester, February 22, 1743. Then the above named Mary Glover, Hannah Glover and Mary Glover jun' appeared before me personally and acknowledged the above written Instrument to be their free Will, Act and Deed.

THOMAS TILESTON, *Justice of the Peace.*

The above date of Feb. 22, 1743, is the last found of Mary Glover, that can be identified with any certainty. There have been many conjectures concerning her. She had at this date attained the age of 66 years, and was residing in Boston with her sister Mrs.

---

* The son of Mr. Glover who died in 1657.
† In Stoughton.

Hannah Laws. From what has been gathered she seems fully to have disposed of all her property, both real and personal. It is not known that she ever married. There is a marriage entered on the Boston Records, March 1, 1743, of a Mary Glover, of Boston, with Zebulon Hastings, of Watertown, which is only a few days after the date of her acknowledgment of the above conveyed land; but circumstances render it extremely doubtful as to its relating to the Mary Glover whose brief history has been here given. The most reasonable conjecture is, that she died unmarried, and in Boston; but the time when, or the place where, is shrouded in obscurity. Some persons have supposed that she went to England, and died there; and there is some plausibility in the suggestion, but no proof, not even by tradition. She had relations there, as cousins and others, who might have entertained her; but, with no further evidence, we must leave her in Boston.

(8) HANNAH GLOVER, the second daughter of Nathaniel and Hannah (Hinckley) Glover, was born at the homestead in Dorchester, July 26, 1681, and baptized 10 (5) 1681, at the Dorchester Church. In 1701–2 she was examined and owned the covenant before the Church. March 2, 1706–7, at the age of twenty-five years, she was admitted to the Church in full communion. In 1723 she received from her father, by deed of gift, conjointly with her brother Thomas Glover, a portion or right which might come to him in the distribution of the estate of his uncle John Glover. (See p. 187.)

Nov. 20, 1723, she received a portion of Newbury farm by another deed of gift from her father.

Her name appears on the agreement of the heirs, in 1724, at the final settlement of the estate of John Glover, Esq., of Boston, who was her great grandfather. (See page 77.)

In 1725, after the decease of her father, she joins in the sale of a tract of woodland in Milton to Oxenbridge Thacher, as Hannah Glover junior.

In 1729 she makes a division of land with her sister Mary Glover.

Hannah Glover was married to Thomas Laws, Esq., of Marblehead, March 10, 1733, at the age of 51 years, and removed to Boston. Thomas Laws died in Boston in 1736. She lived a widow thirteen years, and died in Boston July 1, 1749, in her 68th year, and was buried in the ancient burial yard at Dorchester.

About one year previous to her death, she made transfers of her property: the first, June 2, 1748, to her brother John Glover, of Dorchester; and June 20, 1748, to her brother Thomas Glover, of Newbury farm, Dorchester.

Hannah Laws to her brother John Glover.

Know All Men by these Presents, that I Hannah Laws of Boston, in the County of Suffolk and Province of the Massachusetts Bay in New England, Widow, for and in consideration of the sum of Ten Pounds lawful money, and for the love and affection which I have and do bear towards my brother John Glover, and to his heirs and Assigns forever, of Dorchester, in the County and Province aforesaid, Yeoman. Have given, granted, bargained, sold, conveyed and confirmed unto him the said John Glover and to his heirs and Assigns forever, A Certain piece of Land in Dorchester aforesaid, containing about Eight Acres, more or less, and is bounded Northerly on Land belonging to Moses Billings; Westerly on said Glover's Land; Southerly on a fence; Easterly on Land in the possession of my brother Thomas Glover.

And Also a piece of Salt Marsh in the aforesaid Dorchester, containing four Acres More, on the South side of Pine Neck (so called), both pieces being in the possession and improvement of the said John Glover. To Have and to Hold the land and Salt Marsh above mentioned unto him the said John Glover and to his heirs and Assigns forever, by virtue of these presents.

In witness whereof, I the said Hannah Laws have set my hand and seal, this 20ᵗʰ day of June, 1748.

(Signed)   HANNAH LAWS.

Signed, sealed and delivered in presence of us,
     Sarah + Triches,
       Her mark.
     Abijah Hart.

Suffolk ss. At His Majesties Court of Common Pleas, held at Boston, for said County, the first Tuesday of July, 1749. Then appeared Sarah Triches and Abijah Hart and made Oath that they saw Hannah Laws, the Above Grantor, sign and deliver the above Instrument as her free Act and Deed, and that they set their hands as Witnesses to the Execution thereof at the same time.

Attest: MIDDLECOTT COOKE.

[Received July 13, 1749.]

Hannah Laws to Thomas Glover.

Know all men by these Presents, that I Hannah Laws of Boston, in the County of Suffolk and Province of Massachusetts Bay in New England, Widow, for and in consideration of the sum of ten pounds lawful money, and for the love and affection which I have and do bear to my brother Thomas Glover of Dorchester, in the County and Province aforesaid, Gentleman, have given, granted, bargained, sold, conveyed and confirmed unto him the said Thomas Glover and to his heirs

21* .

and assigns forever, a certain piece or Parcel of land in Dorchester
aforesaid, containing about twelve acres, more or less ; and is bounded Easterly and Northerly on land belonging to Moses Billings ; Westerly and Southerly as the fence now stands ; which land is in the possession and improvement of my brother Thomas Glover. To have
and to hold the said land above mentioned, with the privileges and
appurtenances unto him the said Thomas Glover, his heirs and assigns forever, by virtue of these Presents.
    In witness whereof, I the said Hannah Laws have hereunto set my
hand and seal this 20 day of June, 1648.
                                            HANNAH LAWS.
Signed, sealed and delivered in presence of us,
        Sarah + Triches,
            Her mark.
        Abijah Hart.
    At His Majesty's Court of Common Pleas, held at Boston for said
County of Suffolk, on the first Tuesday of July, 1749, then appeared
Sarah Triches and Abijah Hart, and made Oath that they saw Hannah
Laws, the above Grantor, sign, seal and deliver the above Instrument
as her act and deed, and that they set their names as Witnesses to
the Execution thereof at the same time.
                        Attest :   MIDDLECOTT COOKE.

    (9) ELIZABETH GLOVER, the third and youngest daughter
of Nathaniel and Hannah (Hinckley) Glover, was born at the homestead in Dorchester, July 26, 1683, baptized 29 (5) 1683, by Rev.
John Danforth at the Dorchester Church, and died in Dorchester
April 11, 1725, in her 42d year, unmarried. In 1701–2, she was
examined before the Church and owned the covenant, and was admitted to full communion April 2, 1706.
    We have a date of her in 1724, at the final settlement of the estate
of John Glover, Esq., who was her great grandfather. Another,
Nov. 7, 1723, as a witness to a deed from her father to Hannah
Glover and Thomas Glover, and also in acknowledgment of his act
in 1724.
    Nov. 20, 1723, she received a portion of the Newbury farm es-
tate by a deed of gift from her father; and the last time her name
appears on any writing, is in the transaction of Glovers to Oxenbridge Thacher, of Milton, after the decease of her father, as a signer
to that document, March 31, 1725. There appears to have been no
settlement to her estate. Her sisters Mary and Hannah shared her
property between them.

    (10) JOHN GLOVER, the fourth son of Nathaniel and Hannah
(Hinckley) Glover, was born at the homestead in Dorchester, Sept.

18, 1687, was baptized at the Dorchester Church 2 (8) 1687, by Rev. John Danforth, and died in Braintree (now Quincy), July 6, 1768, in his 81st year. He was twice married. First, to Susannah Ellison, of Boston, January 1, 1714, by the Rev. Peter Thacher, of Milton. She was born in Boston in 1690, and died at Dorchester in January, 1724, in her 35th year. The names of her parents have not been ascertained. At the time of her marriage she resided in the family of Rev. Peter Thacher, of Milton, and was a cousin of his wife. She was also a near relative of the Oxenbridge family of Boston. Second, he was married Dec. 22, 1724, by Samuel Checkley, Esq., of Boston, to Mary Horton, of Milton, who survived him and died in Braintree Dec. 19, 1775, aged 71 years.

His first wife was a member of the Church at Milton before her marriage. Their four eldest children were baptized there by the Rev. Peter Thacher, their father owning the covenant. In 1729 John Glover and Mary his wife were admitted to join that Church in full communion, and had four more children baptized there.

John Glover was a landholder by inheritance; and by purchase he made extensive additions to his landed estate.

We have the following dates of him on record: the first in 1724, as one of the heirs of John Glover, Esq., of Boston, to the Common and Undivided Lands (page 77); and in March, 1725, in the sale of a wood-lot in Milton by the heirs of Nathaniel Glover, Sen. John Glover's bond to John George and John Trail bears date March 1, 1738; witnessed by Thomas Glover and Thomas Maccarty. Oct 5, 1739, he purchased of John George a tract of land situated in Braintree; witnessed by Thomas Glover and Rachel Hinckley. In 1741 John Glover and Mary his wife sold a tract of land to Robert Auchmuty, Esq., and others. The deed represents the land to have been in Braintree, County of Suffolk, containing thirty-four acres, and the consideration one hundred pounds. The names of the purchasers were Robert Auchmuty, Esq., of Boston; Samuel Adams and William Stoddard, Esqs., of Boston; Peter Chardon, of Boston, merchant; Samuel Watts, of Chelsea, County of Suffolk; George Leonard, of Norton, County of Bristol; Robert Hall, of Beverly, County of Essex; John Choate, of Ipswich, County of Essex; and Thomas Cheever, of Lynn, County of Essex. The land is described as adjoining land of Moses Belcher, John Glover, and William Rawson.

Children of JOHN and SUSANNAH (ELLISON) GLOVER, born in Dorchester:

+41. Susannah, b. Jan. 8, 1715 ; m. Lazarus Pope, of Stoughton.
+42. John, b. April 4, 1717 ; m. { 1st, Elizabeth Bill ;
                                   { 2d, Mary ——, of Bristol, R. I.
+43. Joseph,   b. June 6, 1720 ; m. Elizabeth Bass, of Boston.
+44. Jerusha,   b. Dec. 3, 1722 ; m. Col. Wm. Burbeck, of Boston.

By wife MARY HORTON:

45. Nathaniel, b. Sept. 30, 1725 ; d. Dec. 5, 1725.
+46. Nathaniel, b. Dec. 12, 1731 ;
                              m. { 1st, Mary Field, of Braintree ;
                                 { 2d, Abigail Copeland, of Braintree.
+47. Josiah,   b. Dec. 2, 1726 ; m. Mary Blackman, of Dorchester.
+48. Elisha,   b. Jan. 9, 1729 ;
                              m. { 1st, Elizabeth Glover, of Dorchester ;
                                 { 2d, Jerusha Billings, of Dorchester.
+49. Ezra,   b. Jan. 25, 1732 ; m. Elizabeth Belcher, of Chelsea.
+50. Enoch,   b. May 14, 1734 ; m. Susannah Bird, of Dorchester.
+51. Mary,   b. April 21, 1736 ; m. Elijah Belcher, of Braintree.
52. Jacob,   b. July 29, 1737 ; d. in infancy.

In 1734 he was elected Constable, but declined to serve, and paid his fine. He served for several years as a Grand Juror for the County of Suffolk.

Glovers' Conveyance to John Glover.

To All People to whom these Presents shall Come. Thomas Glover of Dorchester, Gentleman ; Nathaniel Glover of Boston, Gentleman ; Alexander Glover of Dorchester, Tanner ; and Pelatiah Glover of Boston, Innholder ; All in the County of Suffolk and in the Province of Massachusetts Bay in New England, send Greeting.
Know Ye, That We the aforesaid Thomas Glover, Nathaniel Glover, Alexander Glover and Pelatiah Glover, for and in consideration of Two Hundred Pounds in Money to them in hand paid before the ensealing and delivery of these Presents, by John Glover of Dorchester, in the County and Province aforesaid, Yeoman ; have given, granted, Bargained, Sold, Aliened, Enfeoffed, Conveyed and Confirmed unto the said John Glover and to his Heirs and Assigns Forever, All the Right, Title, Interest, Inheritance, Use, Property and Possession, Claim or Demand Whatsoever, of, in and to a Certain Tract or Parcel of Land in Stoughton in the County and Province aforesaid. Said Land containing about Three Hundred Acres, be the same more or less ; situate and lying within the Twelve Divisions of Land (so called) in Dorchester New Grant, and which was sold to Nathaniel Stearns, as by Deed upon Record may more fully appear.
To Have and to Hold, All and Singular the above bargained Premises, with their Appurtenances, to him the said John Glover, his

Heirs and Assigns Forever, and all the Right, Title, Interest, Inheritance, Claim or Demand whatsoever, without the Least Lett or hindrance, suit or denial, from us, or any person by, from or under us the aforesaid Thomas Glover, Nathaniel Glover, Alexander Glover and Pelatiah Glover. In Testimony whereof, We have hereunto set our hands and seals, this Tenth day of July, 1742, and in the Sixteenth Year of His Majesty's reign King George the Second.

THOMAS GLOVER, and seal.

NATHANIEL GLOVER, and seal.

ALEXANDER GLOVER, and seal.

PELATIAH GLOVER, and seal.

Signed, sealed and delivered in presence of us,

    William Bowen,

    Thomas Paine.

Boston, Aug. 18, 1743. Thomas Glover, Nathaniel Glover, Alexander Glover and Pelatiah Glover personally appeared, and each acknowledged the above written Instrument to be their free Act and Deed.   HABIJAH SAVAGE.

In Vol. 80, pp. 273–4, Suffolk Registry of Deeds, dated Boston, Aug. 18, 1743, is a quit-claim deed wherein " John Glover, of Dorchester, Yeoman, and Thomas Glover, of Dorchester, Gentleman, in the County of Suffolk, and in His Majesty's Province of Massachusetts Bay in New England, sold to Nathaniel Glover, of Boston, Gent., in the County and Province aforesaid, in consideration of two hundred pounds in Money, All their Right, Title, Interest and Inheritance, Use, Property and Possession of, in and to a Certain Tract of Land Lying in Stoughton in the same County and Province; Said Tract containing five hundred acres, with allowance for bad land, which said land Mr. Nathaniel Glover recovered by a judgment of the Supreme Court in the year 1719 or 20." It is represented to be bounded as follows: " Southerly on the Colony Line; Westerly, partly on the School-farm and partly on the 60th Lott; Northerly, partly on Bray Wilkins, partly on the Road, and partly on the School-farm; Easterly, partly on the 51st and 52d Lotts, partly on a One hundred Acre lott belonging to James Barber, and partly on a Two hundred and Eighty acre lott belonging to a Mr. Pool," &c. Signed by John Glover and Thomas Glover, in presence of William Bowen and Thomas Caine, and acknowledged in person by the parties.*

---

* The above or another tract of five hundred acres of land is referred to in a conveyance of a tract from Samuel Fayerweather and Abigail Fayerweather, of South Kingston, Rhode Island, to John Commee, of Stoughton, said land being in Common and Undivided, and lying in the town of Stoughton, bounded on Mr. Glover's five hundred acres, &c. Signed at Bristol County, Taunton, Aug. 12, 1765, by Samuel Fayerweather and Abigail Fayerweather.

Will of John Glover.

In the name of God, Amen. This Twenty Seventh day of March, and in the year of our Lord One Thousand Seven Hundred and Fifty One, and in the Thirty first year of His Majestie's Reign, King George the Second, I John Glover of Dorchester, in the County of Suffolk in New England, Yeoman ; considering the Uncertainty of Life, and being now in sound disposing mind and Memory, do make and declare this my last Will and Testament in the manner and form following, That is to say—

Imp. First and principally I resign my precious and immortal soul into the hands of Almighty God my Heavenly Father, trusting through the merits of His free grace and the merits and intercession of the Lord Jesus Christ the only Saviour of Mankind, to obtain the forgiveness of my sins and justification to Eternal Life.

My body I commit to the Earth, to be decently buried according to the discretion of my Executors, hereinafter named.

2dly. After my just debts and funeral expenses are well and truly paid out of my Estate by my Executors, I will, devise and bequeath my Temporal Estate as followeth, viz.

I give to my beloved wife Mary Glover One third part of my Estate during her natural Life, as the Law directs.

Item. I give to my son John Glover the sum of One Hundred and ten pounds lawful money, to be paid out of my Estate by my Executors hereinafter named within one year after my decease.

Item. I give to my son Joseph Glover the sum of One Hundred Pounds, to be paid out of my Estate by my Executors within one year after my decease.

Item. I give to my daughter Susanna Pope the sum of Forty Pounds, to be paid by my Executors within Two Years after My Decease.

Item. I give to my daughter Jerusha Burbeck the sum of Forty Pounds, besides what I have already given her, to be paid by my Executors within one year after my Decease.

Item. I give to my Grand-daughter Mary Belcher, besides what I have already given her mother (now deceased), the sum of Thirty Pounds if she shall live to the age of Twenty One Years, or be married ; but in case she shall not live, then it is not to be paid, but to remain to my Executors.

Item. I give to my sons Josiah, Elisha, Nathaniel, Ezra and Enoch Glover, to be equally divided between them, My Two Dwelling Houses adjoining together, my Barn, Corn House, also all my Farm both Upland and Meadow in Dorchester and Braintree. Bounded Easterly, partly on Jonathan Rawson's Land, and partly on Edmund Billings' Land, and partly on Moses Billings' Land, and partly on Thomas Glover's Land. Southerly, partly on Edmund Billings's Land, and partly on Moses Billings, Enoch Horton, Nathan Babcock and Thomas Lyon's Salt Marsh, and partly on Sagamore Creek. Westerly, on a Salt Marsh belonging to Joseph Billings partly, and on Sagamore Creek, or however otherwise bounded or reputed to be bounded. Also, my Twenty Acres of Woodland in said Braintree. Bounded Easterly on Land of Andrew Belcher, Esq. ; Northerly, on the land of Enoch

Horton; Westerly, on Land of Nathan Babcock; and Southerly, on Land formerly belonging to Edmund Quincy, Esq.

Further, that the aforesaid sums are to be paid out of my Whole Estate if there be occasion for it by my said sons, viz., Josiah, Elisha, Nathaniel, Ezra and Enoch Glover.

And Lastly, I do hereby appoint my two sons Josiah and Elisha Executors of this my Last Will and Testament. Hereby revoking all former Wills by me made, in Witness whereof I the said John Glover have hereunto set my hand and seale, in the presence of these Witnesses, the day and year first above written (March 27, 1751).

JOHN GLOVER, and a seal.

Moses Billings,
John Billings,   } *Witnesses.*
Edmund Billings.

Inventory of this Estate taken February 14, 1769.

(11) THOMAS GLOVER, the third and youngest son of Mr. Nathaniel and Hannah (Hinckley) Glover, was born at the homestead in Dorchester, Dec. 26, 1690; was baptized 28 (10) 1690, by Rev. John Danforth, and died at Newbury farm, in that town, June 16, 1758, in his 68th year. He was buried in the ancient cemetery at Quincy, and has a gravestone.

June 7, 1722, at the age of 32 years, he was married to Elizabeth Clough, of Boston, by Rev. Thomas Prince, of the Old South Church, Boston. He resided at Newbury farm from the time of his father's removal there, and succeeded to it in 1723–4, at the time of his father's decease.

June 9, 1717, he was admitted to the Dorchester Church in full communion. April 12, 1728, Elizabeth, the wife of Thomas Glover, was admitted to full communion. In 1729 he received the commission of Deputy Sheriff for the County of Suffolk, from under the hand and seal of Edward Winslow, Esq., which service he performed with great faithfulness and ability for several years, and until his health required him to relinquish it.

In 1734 he was chosen to be one of the Selectmen, and he served a few years in that office. He also served as Grand Juror at several times.

In 1741 a commission of " Lieutenant of a Troop of Horse, under the command of Estes Hatch, Esq., of the First Regiment of Horse in the Province of Massachusetts Bay in New England," was granted " to Thomas Glover, Esq., of Dorchester, by Jonathan Belcher, Esq., Governor of his Majesty's Province, in the 15th year of his Majesty's reign, King George II.," &c.

Children of THOMAS and ELIZABETH (CLOUGH) GLOVER, born in Boston and Dorchester:

+53. Thomas, b. Sept. 1, 1723 ; m. Rebeckah Pope, of Stoughton.
+54. Elijah, b. July, 20, 1725 ;
        d July 1, 770   m. { 1st, Abigail Kingsley, of Milton ;
                                   { 2d, Elizabeth Tucker, of Milton.
  55. Elizabeth, b. Oct. 7, 1727 ; d. Aug. 28, 1729, in her 2d year.
  56. Anna,   b. Feb. 15, 1729 ; d. March 4, 1730, in her 2d year.
+57. William, b. Aug. 1, 1731 ; m. Mary Capen, of Dorchester.
+58. James,   b. June 5, 1734 ;
                          m. { 1st, Lois Bent, of Framingham ;
                             { 2d, Mary Hill Metcalf, of Franklin.
+59. Ebenezer, b. June 27, 1736 ;
                          m. { 1st, Sarah Wadsworth, of Milton ;
                             { 2d, Mary Davenport, of Milton.
  60. Elizabeth, b. Sept. 6, 1733 ; m. (48) Elisha Glover, of Dorchester.
  61. Dorothy, b. Dec. 20, 1739 ; d. March 19, 1740, aged 4 months 21 days.
  62. John Clough, b. Nov. 19, 1743 ; d. Sept. 26, 1744, aged 10 months 4 days.
+63. Jerusha, b. May 20, 1745 ; m. { 1st, Daniel Arnold, of Braintree;
                                    { 2d, Capt. Joseph Baxter.
+64. Anna,   b. Aug. 3, 1749 ; m. Jason Bent, of Sudbury.

In 1755 Thomas Glover, of Dorchester, Gentleman, with Elizabeth his wife, appealed from the judgment of the Inferior Court, begun and holden at Boston in 1752 and '53, to the Superior Court, in the case of a lot of land belonging to Mary Clough, daughter of James Clough, and niece of said Elizabeth Glover. The said lot of land, according to an original writ in a plea of ejectment against Arthur Savage and Rachel his wife, comprised

" A Messuage in Boston aforesaid, situate Northerly upon Walker Street, there measuring one hundred and twenty one feet : Easterly upon Orange Street, there measuring seventy five feet ; Southerly upon Land of John Blake, there measuring fifty feet ; Easterly upon land of said Blake, there measuring thirty one feet ; Southerly upon land of Rebeckah Potter, there measuring one hundred feet ; Easterly on said Potter's land, measuring three feet ; and Southerly on said Potter's land, fifteen feet ; Easterly on her land, twenty one feet, and Southerly on Land of John Allen, twenty five feet ; North Westerly on land of William Butler, ninety seven feet. And whereas Mary Clough, the daughter of the said James Clough, died childless, seized in her desmesne as of fee thereof, whereupon the premises descended to the said Elizabeth Glover and John Clough as co-heirs, viz.: To the said Elizabeth as sister of the said James Clough, and to the said John as the son of John Clough Deceased, the brother of the said James

Clough, Dec⁴ ; and whereas the said nephew John Clough and co-heir
has since died, and his said right to the said premises descended to the
said Elizabeth. And the said John Blake and William Blake unjustly
entered upon the premises and disseized them thereof, and the said
John Blake and William Blake unjustly hold the said Thomas and
Elizabeth Glover out of them, to the damage, as they say, of one
hundred pounds, Therefore the said Thomas and Elizabeth Glover, who
was Elizabeth Clough, bring this suit.

THOMAS GLOVER,
ELIZABETH GLOVER.

Witness, STEPHEN SEWALL, Esq., of Boston, this
17ᵗʰ day of April, 1755.

Judgment of the Inferior Court which led to the above appeal, was
as follows :

In the case depending between Thomas Glover and Elizabeth his
wife as demandants against Arthur Savage and Rachel his wife, The
Jurors upon their Oaths say, that the said Mary Clough, about the
10ᵗʰ day of May, 1751, died seized in fee of the Messuage aforesaid
and its appurtenances, without issue and intestate ; and that the said
Elizabeth was the sister of the said James Clough* then deceased,
and the said John the son of the said John Clough Dec⁴, brother of
the said James ; and after the said Mary, as the said demandants have
alleged ; and they further upon their oaths say, that the said Mary
was the daughter of the said Rachel, who at the time of the death of
the said Mary and before, was, and still is, the wife of the said James
Clough, and that the said Arthur and Rachel in her right upon the
death of the said Mary, her daughter, entered upon and into the said
Messuage with its Appurtenances, drawing the same in Right of the
said Rachel as Mother of the said Mary, and next of kin by force of
laws.

In 1757, Elizabeth, the wife of Thomas Glover, was made a legatee to the property of her aunt Elizabeth (Beard) Wheeler, of
Boston, by the following Deed of Gift:

To All People unto whom these Presents shall come, I Elizabeth
Wheeler of Boston, in the County of Suffolk and in the Province of
Massachusetts Bay in New England, Widow, one of the Sisters of
James Beard late of Boston, Mariner, Deceased, in the County and
Province aforesaid, Sendeth Greeting. Know ye, that I the said
Elizabeth Wheeler, for and in consideration of the sum of Four Pounds,
lawful money, to me in hand well and truly paid, before the ensealing
and delivery of these Presents, by Thomas Glover of Dorchester, in the

---

* James Clough was married to Rachel Ruggles the 2d day of March, 1737. He died,
leaving a widow and one daughter, and his widow was married again to Arthur Savage, of
Boston, July 25, 1746. She was married, third, to James Noble, Esq., of Boston, March
14, 1768. He died, and she was married to her fourth husband,———— Packard. She survived him, and died in 1794, leaving a will.

County and Province aforesaid, Gentleman, and Elizabeth his wife,
but more especially for the love and good will and affection which I
have and do bear unto the said Elizabeth, as she is the daughter of
Mary Clough late of Boston Deceased ; I do hereby give, grant and
convey, and absolutely confirm unto the said Elizabeth Glover, her
heirs and assigns forever, One full Third part of the Real Estate of
my Brother James Beard, more especially that which was coming to
him after his decease, in a Messuage or Tenement, with its appurtenances ; being One Seventh part which was the inheritance of Thomas
Beard, and whereof he died seized in his own Proper Right, Situate
and lying at the end of the Town of Boston aforesaid ; bounded with
two highways meeting or coming into the other Eastward and Southward, and with the land formerly Theodore Atkinson's Sen., Northward ; and with the land of the Widow Deming, formerly, and since
has been in the tenure and possession of Edward Wright of said Boston, Shoemaker, Westward ; or however otherwise bounded or reputed to be bounded.

To have and to hold the said third part of one seventh part of said
Messuage, with the appurtenances thereof, unto the said Elizabeth
Glover, her heirs and assigns forever, against the lawful claims and
demands of all and every person and persons whatsoever.

In witness whereof, I have hereunto set my hand and seal, this
thirtieth day of June, 1757.

ELIZABETH + WHEELER.
Her mark.

Signed, sealed and delivered in presence of us,
    Ebenezer Downes,
    Henry Hills.

Will of Thomas Glover.

In the name of God, Amen. This Thirty-first day of [——] Anno
Dom One Thousand Seven Hundred and Fifty Eight, and in the Thirty
first year of His Majesty's reign, King George the Second.

I Thomas Glover of Dorchester, in the County of Suffolk and Province of Massachusetts Bay in New England, Gentleman, considering
the uncertainty of Life, and being now of sound disposing mind and
memory, do make and declare this to be my last Will and Testament
in manner following. That is to say, First and principally I resign
my precious and immortal soul into the hands of Almighty God my
Heavenly Father, trusting through his free grace, and the merits and
intercession of the Lord Jesus Christ the only Saviour and Redeemer
of Mankind, to obtain the forgiveness of my sins and justification to
Eternal Life. My body I commit to the Earth, to be decently buried
according to the discretion of my loving wife and the Executors hereinafter named.

And after my just debts and funeral expenses are paid by them out
of my Estate, I Will, devise and bequeathe the residue of my Temporal Estate as follows :

Item. I give to my beloved wife Elizabeth Glover, to be improved
by her for her comfort and support and for the Use and benefit of my
children, My Whole Real and Personal Estate in Dorchester and
Braintree, so long as she shall remain my widow, and One Third part

during her natural Life in my Houses and Lands ; and One Third part of my Personal Estate forever.

Item. I give, devise and bequeathe unto Two of my sons—That is, to Thomas Glover and James Glover, and to their heirs and assigns forever—All my Right, Title and Interest in a Lot of Land lying in Stoughton, where the said Thomas Glover and James Glover now dwell, in the Twenty-five Divisions (so called—laid out in the year One Thousand Seven Hundred and Sixteen [1716], to Mr. John Glover, one of the first Proprietors of Dorchester and Boston). Said Land containing about Two Hundred Acres, in equal halves. The said Thomas Glover to have his part on the North side of said Lot, with the Buildings thereon standing ; and the said James Glover to have his part on the South side of said Lot.

Item. I give to my son Elijah Glover, the sum of Twenty six pounds Thirteen shillings and Four pence, lawful money, besides what I have already given him, to be paid him or his heirs in one year after the Decease of my said wife, by my Executors hereinafter named.

Item. I further give to my son James Glover the sum of Twenty Six Pounds Thirteen Shillings and Four Pence lawful money, to be paid him or his heirs in One Year after the Decease of my said wife, by my Executors hereafter named.

Item. I give to my grandson Elisha Glover, the sum of Forty Pounds lawful money, besides what I have already given his mother, if he shall live while he shall come to the age of Twenty One Years old, to be paid by my Executors hereafter named ; and in case the said Elisha should die before the time aforesaid, then the said sum is not to be paid at all, but to go equally to my Executors hereafter named.

And it is to be understood that my Will is that the foregoing sums are all to be paid out of what I give my Executors hereafter named, as I give them the more of my Estate for that purpose.

Item. I give and bequeathe unto my two sons William Glover and Ebenezer Glover and to their heirs and Assigns forever, immediately after the decease of my said wife, or in case she should marry then to come into actual possession at that time—her Dower excepted—and all the aforesaid sums to be paid as they are afore described in case of her Decease. That is to say, I give to William Glover and Ebenezer Glover, to be equally divided between them, as follows, viz.: My Dwelling House and Barn and Corn House and all the Homestead belonging thereunto, called the Bayfield, containing about Fifty Two Acres. And also Four Acres of Salt Marsh on the North side of Horse Hammocks Hill. And one piece of Land containing about One Acre, called the Three Cornered piece, on the West side of the Way leading to the Old Spring so called. And one piece of Land containing about an Acre, on the East side of the Way leading to the said Spring. And also Six Acres of Salt Marsh or thereabouts, called Squantum Marsh—all in the Township of Dorchester.

And also I give to the aforesaid William and Ebenezer Glover about Twenty-two acres of Land in the Township of Braintree, called Ridgehill Pasture. And also Twenty-five acres of Woodland in said Braintree, which I bought of Edmund Quincy, Esq., Deceased. And also I give to my said Two sons William Glover and Ebenezer Glover, Two feather beds which they usually lye upon, and all my living stock of creatures, and all my outdoor moveables, that shall be left not disposed of before the Decease of my said wife. And also all my said wife's Thirds or Dower in my Real Estate, to be equally divided between the said William and Ebenezer Glover, after her Decease.

And in case the said William and Ebenezer either of them die without Lawful Issue, then his portion to be equally divided among my surviving children, unless he or they should sell or dispose of it in their Lifetime.

Item. I give to my Two daughters Jerusha Glover and Anna Glover, and to their heirs and assigns forever, a certain piece of land in Dorchester aforesaid, containing about Fourteen Acres, called the Further Pasture, Bounded on all parts on John Glover and Moses Billing's Land. And I also give unto the said Jerusha and Anna Glover the sum of Twenty Pounds Lawful Money, to be divided equally between them, and to be paid them by my Executors hereafter named within Two Years after the Decease of my said wife, and to pay them Lawful Interest for the same from the Decease of her till the whole sum is paid.

Item. I further give to my two daughters Jerusha Glover and Anna Glover aforesaid, equally to be divided between them, All my In-door Moveables that shall not be disposed of before the Decease of my wife, Excepting my Silver Plate. And my Will is that the said Jerusha and Anna Glover shall have liberty from my Executors to live in the West Chamber and Back Chamber of my Dwelling House, rent free, until they are of age or are married.

Item. I give my Silver Plate, after the Decease of my wife, to All my children—to wit: To Thomas Glover, Elijah Glover, James Glover, William Glover, Ebenezer Glover, Jerusha Glover, and Anna Glover, to be equally divided between them.

And Lastly, I do hereby nominate and appoint my two sons William Glover and Ebenezer Glover aforesaid, to be my Executors of this my Last Will and Testament.

THOMAS GLOVER, and a seal.

   Moses Billings, }
   Oliver Billings, } *Witnesses.*
   Ebenezer Crosby, }

Suffolk ss. By the Honorable Thomas Hutchinson, Esq., Judge of Probate. The above written Will being presented for Probate by the Executors therein named, the Witnesses above named made oath that they saw Mr. Thomas Glover, the subscriber to this Instrument, sign the same, and heard him publish and declare it to be his Last Will and Testament, and that when he did so he was of sound disposing mind and memory, according to these Deponents best discerning, and that they set their hands as Witnesses thereof in the presence of the said Testator.   Boston, July 1, 1758.

  Attest: WILLIAM COOPER.   JONATHAN COTTON, Register.

The above Will was presented for Probate by the Executors, viz., William Glover and Ebenezer Glover, and approved.

August 6, 1763, Elizabeth Glover, of Dorchester, widow of Thomas Glover, Esq., deceased, sold a house and land in Boston bordering on

Orange street, to Joseph Jackson, of Boston. She lived a widow forty years, and was deprived of her sight for the last thirty years of her life.

ELIZABETH CLOUGH, the wife of Mr. Thomas Glover, was born in Boston, May 20, 1706; baptized at the Third Church (Old South), May 23, 1706; married at the age of sixteen years, and died at Newbury farm, in Dorchester, Jan. 10, 1798, aged 92 years, and was buried in the ancient cemetery at Quincy. She has a gravestone.

She was the daughter of Deacon John and Mary (Beard) Clough, who was an extensive landed proprietor in Boston and vicinity, and also in the Colony of Connecticut. He is said to have been of Welch origin, and a lineal descendant of Richard Clough, of Denbigh, in the County of Flintshire in Wales, who is noticed among Fuller's Worthies as a distinguished benefactor.* His first American ancestor was John Clough, who came early to New England and settled in Watertown, where he became a Freeman in 1642. He owned a house and land there, the latter bounded South by Pond Road and East by William Paine; West by Highway and William Perry; North by Joseph Morse. He removed to Salisbury, in Essex County, and died there in 1691; left children: John, Samuel and Thomas, Sarah Morrell, Elizabeth Horne and Martha George, and wife Martha (second wife probably).

John Clough, the eldest son, removed to Charlestown; was admitted to the Church there, with wife Elizabeth, in 1652, and in 1657 was received or transferred to the First Church in Boston. He died in 1668, in Boston.

---

* ("Flintshire in Wales.") "Benefactors to the Public.—Richard Clough was born at Denbigh in this County, whence he went to be a chorister in the City of Chester. Some were so affected with his singing therein that they were loath he should lose himself in their employ (Church music beginning then to be discountenanced), and persuaded, yea, procured his removal to London, where he became apprenticed to and afterwards partner with Sir Thomas Gresham. He lived some years at Antwerp, and afterwards travelled as far as Jerusalem, where he was made Knight of the Sepulchre, though not owning it after his return, under Queen Elizabeth, who disdained that her subjects should accept foreign honors. He afterwards, by God's blessing, grew very rich; and there wants not those who will avouch that some thousands of Pounds were disbursed by him for the building of the Royal Exchange; such numbers that it was agreed betwixt him and Sir Thomas Gresham that the survivor should be chief heir to both; on which account they say the Knight carried away the bulk of the estate. How much the new Church at Denbigh was beholden to his bounty, I am not yet certainly informed. But this is true, that he gave the impropriation of Kilken in Flintshire, worth a hundred pounds per annum, to the free schools in Denbigh. He died in 1600."

"Richard Clough, High Sheriff of Surry. Coat of Arms, &c."—*Fuller's Worthies of England.*

22*

John Clough, junior, the father of Elizabeth, was born in 1669, and was baptized at the First Church in Boston, June 6, 1669–70, by Rev. John Davenport. He was married to Mary, daughter of Thomas and Mary (Andrews) Beard, of Boston, April 12, 1693. Jan. 31, 1696, John Clough and Mary his wife were admitted to join the Third Church in Boston. They had children: John, James, Mary and Elizabeth, who were baptized at that Church by the Rev. Samuel Willard. He was chosen a Deacon of the Third Church, and was in that office at the time of his decease.

In 1715, when the New South Church was organized, John Clough was present at the first meeting of members, signed the covenant, and entered into relations with that Church from the Third or " Old South" Church. He assisted in the building of the New South Church in Summer street (Church Green), by liberal donations, and worshipped there with his family. His pew in the new meeting house was No. 16—value, £38. In 1744 he gave a silver cup to the Church for the Communion service. It is thus acknowledged on the records of the New South Church: " August 13, 1644. At a meeting of the Church in the Meeting House, it was voted that the Deacons give the Thanks of the Church to Mr. John Clough for a Silver Cup given by him to the Church." In 1744 he owned a pew in the Hollis Street Meeting House, of which Rev. Mather Byles, Sen., was Pastor, and gave it to his daughter Elizabeth Glover. (See deed.)

John Clough owned a house and land in Boston in 1693. In 1700 he received permission of the Selectmen of Boston to erect a wooden house, twenty-six feet long and twenty-five feet wide, and nineteen feet stud, with a flat roof, on his own land, between the land of Joseph Simpson and the house of Daniel Epes, abutting on Orange Street.

In 1700 Thomas Chamberlain agrees to erect a house for Mr. John Clough, next to Mr. Atkinson's land.

In 1702 he was appointed attorney to his brother-in-law, James Beard, who was on a voyage at sea.

In 1703 he purchased land in Boston of Thomas Powell.

In 1704 he bought a negro boy, named Manuel, of Samuel Phillips, of Boston.

In 1715 he bought land of Dorcas Pollard and William Pollard.

In 1718 he bought, conjointly with Thomas Downes, two tracts of land in the townships of Windham and Ashford, in the County of Windham and Colony of Connecticut —about seven hundred acres.

In 1721 he bought land in Boston of Benjamin Sanderson.

In 1726 he bought a piece of land in Boston of Robert Sanders, of the Colony of Connecticut, goldsmith.

In 1730 he bought a house and land in Boston, at the Southerly end, of his Excellency Jonathan Belcher.

In 1736 he bought an estate, with house and garden, on Middle street, of Abigail Dilloway.

In 1737, March 23, John Clough and Thomas Childs, distillers, agreed to open or run two lines between their premises, wide enough for a street; now called Essex street.

In 1740, April 18, John Clough and Zachariah Johonnet agreed to lay out a street, each yielding seventeen feet, to run the whole length of their land, extending six hundred and seventy-four feet, to Benjamin Elliot's land.

John Clough carried on the business of felt-making and leather-dressing. His residence was on the Southerly corner of what is now Washington street, where the large book store stands. He was twice married. His first wife, Mary, died in 1736. Oct. 14, 1737, he was married to Abigail Stacy, who survived him. He died in Boston, Sept. 17, 1744, aged 75 years, and was buried in the Stone Chapel yard. He died intestate.

A few months previous to his decease, he made disposals of his estates which had not already been disposed of by deeds of gift. His house and land, and other estate on Middle street, April 2, 1744, he gave to his son James Clough, of Boston, who was married to Rachel Ruggles, and died in 1743, leaving a large estate. To his grandson John Clough, Jun., of Middletown, Conn., he gave his Negro man Manuel, which he bought of Samuel Phillips with one other Negro. Also a silver tankard marked I. C. M., two silver spoons, and other silver plate.

About one month before his decease he gave to his daughter Elizabeth Glover the following articles, by Deed of Gift:

To all People to whom this Present Deed of Gift shall come. John Clough of Boston, in the County of Suffolk and Province of the Massachusetts Bay in New England, Leather-dresser, Sendeth Greeting. Know ye, that for and in consideration of the sum of fifty Pounds by me received of my Son-in-law Thomas Glover, of Dorchester, in the County and Province aforesaid, Gent", and Elizabeth his wife, but more especially for the Parental love and affection I have and do bear to and for her support and comfort, have given, granted, bargained and sold and delivered, and by these presents do fully, freely, and absolutely give, grant, bargain, sell and convey unto the said Elizabeth Glover, her heirs and assigns forever, my new bed, under bed and bedstead, and Curtains belonging to it, One Green Rugg and two pair of Sheets, Six Cain Chairs and one great Cain Chair, a pair of brass andirons which were my first wife's, my largest Black-trunk, my Best Looking-Glass, Six of my largest Pewter Plates, and six Smaller ones, my middle Brass Kettle, my largest and best Silver Tankard, my largest and best Scolloped Silver Basin, two silver spoons marked I. C., and also a Pew in the South Meetinghouse in Boston where Mr. Byles is Pastor, The second pew at the left hand from the East door. To have and to hold the above said premises, with the appurtenances belonging thereunto. And also two blankets, my clock and Teakettle and my Lignumvitæ mortar. To have and to hold, all and singular the aforementioned premises, to the said Elizabeth Glover, her heirs and assigns forever, freely, peaceably and quietly, without any reclaim, challenge or demand of me the said John Clough, my heirs or assigns forever, at any time to come. And I the said John Clough, my heirs or assigns, do promise to warrant and defend the same from any person or persons whatsoever, and have hereunto set my hand and seal this twelfth day of August, 1744, and in the Seventeenth year of his Majesty's Reign King George the Second.   JOHN CLOUGH.

Signed, sealed and delivered in presence of
Samuel Wheeler,
John Goff.

August 12, 1744. This day I delivered the within mentioned premises with their appurtenances to my daughter Elizabeth Glover, as witness my hand,   JOHN CLOUGH.

Suffolk ss. Boston, August 14, 1744. John Clough acknowledged the within written instrument to be his free act and deed, before me,   SAMUEL SWIFT, *Just. Peace.*

August 15, 1744. This certifies that I Elizabeth Glover have left the within mentioned premises with my honored father, Mr. John Clough, during his natural life, to improve as he sees cause, as witness my hand,   ELIZABETH GLOVER.

To Elizabeth Glover his daughter he also gave his silver-headed cane, marked I. C., his stuffed easy chair, and other articles of furniture and plate.

Deed of Deacon John Clough to Thomas and Elijah Glover.

I John Clough of Boston, in the County of Suffolk in New England, Leather-dresser, for and in consideration of Fifty Pounds to me in hand paid by Thomas Glover junior, and Elijah Glover of Dorchester, Husbandmen, two of the children of my daughter Elizabeth Glover, have sold and conveyed unto them the said Thomas Glover Junior and Elijah Glover, my Grandsons, and to their heirs and assigns forever, my Negro boy named George, to their use, benefit and be-

hoof forever. And I the said John Clough, for myself, my heirs, &c., do promise hereby to warrant and defend said Negro boy to the aforesaid Thomas and Elijah Glover from the demands of all persons whatsoever. (Signed) JOHN CLOUGH.

In presence of April 2, 1744.
  Samuel Wheeler,
  John Goffe.

The maternal grandmother of Elizabeth Clough was Mary Andrews, the third daughter of Joseph and Elizabeth Andrews, of Hingham, who was a son of Thomas Andrews, of Devonshire, England, born there about 1596, and died in Hingham Aug. 11, 1662. He had been much interested in the settlement of the Plymouth Colony, and was one of those merchants and gentlemen whom, it is said, sold their effects and accompanied their minister to Holland with the intention of emigrating to New England, and who were prevented from embarking by an order from the Council of England, and compelled to return.

In 1642, Thomas Andrews was elected High Sheriff of London, and one of the four Treasurers who were appointed by Parliament to grant receipts to contributors of money and plate.

In 1649 he was made Lord Mayor of the City of London, in the place of Abraham Reynardson, who had refused to proclaim the act of abolishing the Kingly Government. He immediately, on being inducted into office, proclaimed the act in person, as is shown by the following record: "In 1649 Sir Thomas Andrews, Lord Mayor of London, assisted by Alderman Bateman and others, publicly proclaimed the abolition of the Kingly Government under King Charles I. of England," &c. The same year he was made one of the Judges at the King's trial,* but refusing to sign the death warrant, he was afterwards attainted.

In 1651 he is said to have been a merchant in London, and lived in Rowe Lane; also to have been Lord Mayor of the city. After his arrest, he made his escape to New England, and settled in Hingham, where he soon died.

His son Joseph was at that time an inhabitant of Hingham, having preceded his father and established himself there in 1635. He received his freedom March 3, 1635–36, and was the same year chosen Constable. Joseph Andrews was the first Town Clerk of Hingham,

---

* King Charles was beheaded January 30, 1649.

and was chosen to represent the town at the General Court at Boston
for the years 1636, 1637 and 1638. He was married to Elizabeth
—— before he came to New England. She died in Hingham in
1688. The will of Joseph Andrews was dated Sept. 27, 1679.
He died Jan. 1, 1679–80, in his 83d year. The following children
are named in his will: Hannah, wife of Rehoboth Gannett; Mary,
wife of Thomas Beard, of Boston; Joseph, Jun.; Ephraim, who was
a physician and went to New Jersey; Thomas, and wife Ruth; Hepzibah, wife of Jeffrey Manning; Elizabeth, wife of —— Eames.

The above extracts confirm the lineage of Elizabeth Clough (who
afterwards married Thomas Glover, of Dorchester) by a direct line
of descent from Thomas Andrews of Devonshire and London, by his
eldest son Joseph Andrews, whose second daughter Mary Andrews
married with Thomas Beard, of Boston, and were the grandparents
of Elizabeth, wife of Thomas Glover, of Dorchester. Her mother,
Mary Beard, inherited a competent estate from her father Thomas
Beard. She was also a legatee to the will of her brother James
Beard, who died in 1707, leaving one-third of all his estate to his
sister Elizabeth Beard, one-third to his sister Mary, the wife of John
Clough, and the other third to two of his kinswomen, Mary Wybourne and Elizabeth Wybourne; and appoints his eldest sister
Elizabeth Beard, and his brother-in-law Deacon John Clough, his
Executors. Will approved and executed in 1707. Witnessed in
1702, by Thomas Salter, Mary Salter and Joseph Deane, who testified before the Probate Court that they saw James Beard sign and
heard him declare it to be his last will and testament.

Will of Elizabeth Glover, Widow of Thomas.
In the name of God, Amen.
   This Eighteenth day of September, In the Year of our Lord One
Thousand Seven Hundred and Ninety-four, and in the Eighteenth year
of the American Independence, I Elizabeth Glover, of Quincy, in the
County of Norfolk and Commonwealth of Massachusetts, Widow,
Considering the Uncertainty of Life, and being now of perfect health
and of sound mind and memory, yet by God's Providence I have been
deprived of the sight of my eyes, do make and declare this to be my
Last Will and Testament, in manner following, that is to say. First
and principally I resign my precious and immortal soul into the hands
of Almighty God my Heavenly Father, trusting through his free Grace
and the merits and intercession of the Lord Jesus Christ to obtain the
forgiveness of my sins and Justification to Eternal Life. My body I
commit to the Earth, to be decently buried according to the discretion of my Executor, hereafter named.

And after all my Just debts and funeral expenses are paid out of my Estate, I will, devise and bequeath the Residue of my Estate as follows:

Item. I give to my Son Thomas Glover One shilling and sixpence, to be paid him at my Decease.

Item. I give to the Children of my son Elijah Glover, viz., Samuel Kinsley Glover and Susanna Glover, the some of Three shillings, to be paid them at my Decease.

Item. I give to my son William Glover, the sum of One shilling and sixpence, to be paid him at my Decease.

Item. I give to my son James Glover the sum of One shilling and sixpence, to be paid him at my Decease.

And it is to be understood that my Will is that the foregoing sums are to be paid by my Executor hereafter named.

Item. I give to my Grandson, Benjamin Wadsworth Glover, my Silver Headed Cane.

Item. I give to my two daughters, Jerusha Baxter and Anna Bent, all my in-door moveables (Except my Silver Plate), to be equally divided between them, and to their heirs forever.

Item. I give to my son Ebenezer Glover, to him and his heirs forever, All my Money, Notes, Bonds, Accompts and Securities, and all my other Estate of every description, whether Real or Personal, not already given away. And lastly I do hereby appoint my son Ebenezer Glover aforesaid sole Executor of this my last Will and Testament, hereby revoking all former Wills by me made.

In witness whereof I have hereunto set my hand and seale the day and year first above written.   ELIZABETH + GLOVER, and a Seale.
her mark.

Sept. 18, 1794.

Signed, sealed, published, pronounced and declared by the said Elizabeth Glover to be her last Will and Testament,

In presence of us,
John Billings,
Samuel Billings,   } *Witnesses.*
Mary Billings,

(12) ROBERT GLOVER, eldest son of John and Mary (——) Glover, was born in Boston in 1673, and removed with his parents to Barnstable. It is said that in early life he went to sea with some of his relatives. He studied navigation, and acquired the art with so much readiness that he soon became a skilful mariner, and master of a ship. In 1694, at the age of twenty-one years, he was in command of the sloop Dragon, a privateer.* In July, 1695, Capt. Robert

* Richard Hart, one of his seamen, died in January, 1694-5. Feb. 14, of that year, Letters of Administration were granted on his estate, by William Stoughton, Esq., Commissioner, to Patrick Keen, his kinsman, as follows:

"To Patrick Keen, of Newport, on Rhode Island, kinsman of Richard Hart, Seaman,

Glover, of the sloop Dragon, sailed along the Atlantic coast as far as the St. Lawrence, and at the mouth captured a French ship called the St. Joseph, containing a valuable cargo, prized at about fifteen hundred pounds sterling. He brought the prize to Boston.

In the Massachusetts Archives, Vol. 62, folio 45–48, there are notices of Capt. Robert Glover, commander of a privateer — dragged in 1696.

Robert Glover is also recorded as a citizen of Boston in 1695. He paid taxes there in 1695 and 1696. After leaving the Dragon it is supposed he sailed to England in the subsequent years, and was lost at sea in one of his return voyages, and may have been the one who by tradition was cast away on Lovell's Rock, which afterwards and to this day has been called Glover's Rock.

Children of Capt. ROBERT and ——— GLOVER:

+65. Robert,   m. Mary ——, of Boston.
+66. Thomas,   m. Sarah Bonney, of Pembroke.
+67. Hannah,   m. Henry Nicholson, of Boston, Feb. 10, 1728.
+68. Anna,   m. Charles Grimes, of Boston, Dec. 9, 1729.

(13)   JOHN GLOVER, only son of John and Miriam (Smith) Glover, was born in Dorchester, May 6, 1689; and baptized at the Dorchester Church May 12, 1689, by Rev. John Danforth. The date of his death has not been ascertained. He lived in Dorchester until he attained the age of manhood, but it does not appear that he ever owned any real estate there. His name is no where enrolled on the tax lists. He was a cordwainer, and worked at his trade when not engaged in military life. His name is enrolled among those who served at Castle William, from 1710 to 1744; also among a list in

<hr/>

(late belonging to the Sloop Dragon, Robert Glover Commander), Deceased, Intestate, and also Creditor to the estate of said Deceased, Greeting: Trusting in your care and Fidelity, I do by these Presents commit unto you full power of Administration of all and singular the goods, chattels, Rights and Credits of the said deceased, and well and faithfully to dispose of the same according to law; and to receive all whatsoever credits of the said Deceased, which to him while he lived and at the time of his death did appertain, and to pay all debts in which the deceased stood bound, so far as his goods, chattels, &c. shall extend, and to exhibit the same to the Register's office of the aforesaid County of Suffolk at or before the 14th day of May next ensuing, and to render a true and perfect Account of your administration upon Oath at or before the 14th day of February, which will be in the year of our Lord 1695-6. And I do by these Presents ordain, constitute and appoint you administrator as aforesaid, This 14th day of February, 1694-5, In Testimony whereof I have hereunto set my hand and seal of the said office. Dated at Boston in the County aforesaid, Feb. 14, 1694-5.   WILLIAM STOUGHTON.

ISAAC ADDINGTON, *Register.*

1744, "of all those who were capable of bearing arms and liable to appear at the alarm and living within the limits of the first Independent Company in the town of Dorchester, whereof Col. Estes Hatch is Captain."

He was at one time the owner of a tract of land in Braintree, and sold it in 1720 to Samuel Jones. Deed signed by John Glover and Lydia Glover.

John Glover was twice married, as follows:

Feb. 15, 1713–14, when he was twenty-four years old, he was married to Hannah Capen, daughter of Samuel and Anne (——) Capen, of Dorchester. She was born there March 1, 1696, baptized by Rev. John Danforth, and died in Dorchester Feb. 25, 1717–18. She was a member of the Dorchester Church, in full communion. Her grandparents were John Capen, Jr. (son of Capt. John Capen, of Dorchester), and wife Susanna Barsham, of Watertown.

John Glover was married a second time, Dec. 12, 1718, to Lydia Norcott, of Roxbury. Her origin has not been ascertained, or the place and date of her death. She was living in 1752, and signed her name as witness to a transaction—the discharge of a mortgage from Thomas Glover, Esq., of Dorchester, to Rachael, widow of Nathaniel Glover, deceased.

Children of JOHN and HANNAH (CAPEN) GLOVER, born in Dorchester:

+69. John,   b. Oct. 17, 1715.
 70. Benjamin,   b. Feb. 18, 1717–18; d. next day.

        By wife LYDIA NORCOTT:

 71. Miriam,   b. Feb. 1, 1720, bap. Feb. 21, 1720; m. Thomas Partridge, of Weston, July 10, 1755.
+72. William,   b. Sept. 27, 1724; m. Mary Coye, of Brookline.
 73. Hannah,   b. Feb. 10, 1725–6; died same year.
 74. Abigail,   b. July 1, 1728; d. May 15, 1730.
+75. Samuel,   b. July 28, 1730; m. Ruth Wheat, of Needham.
 76. Experience, b. Oct. 18, 1732; d. unmarried, Oct., 1756.

In 1724 John Glover, cordwainer, signed the compact at the final settlement of the estate of the Hon. John Glover. (See page 77)

He was an heir at law to the estate of John Glover, A.M., of Boston, whose remaining estate was ordered to be distributed in 1724, and made the following disposal of his share, before he received it, to Benjamin Neale, of Braintree:

23

In consideration of such part of the estate of my Uncle John Glover, late of Boston, Gentleman, Deceased, as the Judge of Probate of
Wills, &c., for the County of Suffolk shall or may order to be paid to
me as my part or share of my said Uncle John Glover's estate, I John
Glover (Cordwainer) do hereby release and quit-claim unto Benjamin
Neale, Junior, of Braintree, All my Right, Title or Inheritance in the
estate of my Uncle John Glover, or his wife Elizabeth Glover, alias
Elizabeth Cleverly, alias Elizabeth Mosman, of said Boston, Deceased,
or either of their heirs, &c. &c., more particularly all my Right in
the Dwelling house and land which was my Uncle John Glover's
aforesaid, and of which he died seized, from the beginning of the
world to the date hereof, April 3ᵈ, 1724.

(Signed)   JOHN GLOVER.

In presence of
    Simon Rogers,
    Joseph Stephens.

Acknowledged in person by John Glover, April 6, 1724.

Suffolk Registry of Deeds, Vol. 37, folio 206.

He was at this time said to be of Braintree, and probably he resided there at some time, as his first wife Hannah, with her youngest
child, are buried in the ancient cemetery at Quincy, and also two
daughters by his last wife are buried there and have gravestones. It
is supposed that he removed from Braintree to some other place
before he died.

(21) WILLIAM RAWSON, eighth child and eldest surviving
son of William and Anne (Glover) Rawson, was born in Boston,
Dec. 2, baptized Dec. 8, 1682, and died in Mendon, Oct. 1769, in his
87th year. He graduated at Harvard College in the class of 1703,
and settled himself as a farmer at Mendon. He was married to
Sarah Crosby, of Billerica, in 1710.

Children of Capt. WILLIAM and SARAH (CROSBY) RAWSON, born
at Mendon:

+77. William, b. Feb. 20, 1711 ; m. Margaret Cook, of Uxbridge.
 78. Perne,   b. Oct. 3, 1713 ; d. young.
+79. Sarah,   b. Jan. 3, 1715 ; m. —— Saunders, of Upton.
 80. Rachael, b. Sept. 19, 1716 ; m. Capt. Torrey, of Weymouth.
 81. Anna,   b. in 1720 ; m. Isaac Walton, of Mendon.
 82. Perne,   b. June 1, 1727 ; d. April 19, 1741, aged 14 years.

Mr. William Rawson, Jr., was admitted to join the Church at Milton, Feb. 28, 1719.

(22) DAVID RAWSON, ninth child and second son of William and Anne (Glover) Rawson, was born in Boston, Dec. 13, 1683, and died in Braintree, April 20, 1752, in his 69th year. He lived on the Rawson homestead farm, and is said to have been a man of uncommon energy and perseverance. He left a valuable estate. He was married to Mary Gulliver, daughter of Capt. John Gulliver, of Milton.

Children of DAVID and MARY (GULLIVER) RAWSON, born in Braintree:

+83. David,   b. Sept. 14, 1714 ; m. Mary Dyer, of Weymouth.
+84. Jonathan, b. Dec. 26, 1715 ;·m. Susanna Stone, of Roxbury.
+85. Elijah,   b. Feb.   5, 1717 ; m. Mary Paddock, of Swansey.
+86. Mary,   b. May 20, 1718 ; m. Joseph Winchester, of Roxbury.
 87. Hannah, b. April 2, 1720 ; d. July 24, 1726, in her 6th year.
 88. Silence,   b. June 12, 1721 ; d. Aug. 17, 1721.
 89. Anne,   b. July 30, 1722 ; m. Samuel Bass, of Braintree.
+90. Elizabeth, b. Nov. 30, 1723 ; m. Peter Adams, of Braintree.
+91. Josiah,   b. Jan. 31, 1727 ; m. Hannah Bass, of Braintree.
+92. Jerusha, b. Sept. 21, 1729 ; m. Israel Eaton, of Boston.
 93. Lydia,   b. Jan. 17, 1731 ; m. Samuel Baxter, of Braintree.
+94. Ebenezer, b. May 31, 1734 ; m. Sarah Chase, of Cheshire, N. H.

(26) NATHANIEL RAWSON, son of William and Anne (Glover) Rawson, was born in Braintree, 1689, and died there, date not ascertained. He was married in 1712 to Hannah Tompson, daughter of Samuel and Sarah (Shepard) Tompson, and granddaughter of the Rev. William and Abigail Tompson, of Braintree. He was born in England about 1597; was admitted at the University of Oxford, January 28, 1619, at the age of 22 years; graduated there, and became a preacher at Winwick; married in the latter place, and came to New England about 1637, and was installed as first pastor of the Church at Braintree, now Quincy.

Children of NATHANIEL and HANNAH (TOMPSON) RAWSON, born in Braintree:

 95. Samuel,   b. June, 1714 ; died young.
+96. Nathaniel, b. May 27, 1716 ; m. { 1st, Mary Thwing ;
                                       { 2d, Rachael Daniels.
 97. Barnabas, b. Aug. 11, 1721 ; m. Mary ——.
+98. Edward,   b. April 19, 1724 ; m. Deborah Warren, of Upton.
 99. Rachael,   b. May 20, 1721.

(28) EDWARD RAWSON, ninth son and fourth surviving child
of William and Anne (Glover) Rawson, was born in Braintree, June
27, 1692, and died there in 1721, aged 29 years.

He was a mariner in early life, and resided in Boston. He afterwards removed to Braintree, and settled on a farm. He married, in
1718, Sarah ——, of Milton, and had one daughter, who died in
infancy, and his wife Sarah died soon after. He married, second,
Preserved Bailey, of Boston, and had one more child, who also died
young, and his line became extinct. His wife Preserved survived
him, and died in Boston.

Children of EDWARD and SARAH (——) RAWSON :

100. Anna, b. June 17, 1719 ; died in a few months.

By wife PRESERVED BAILEY :

101. Preserved, b. 1720 ; died young.

(31) PELATIAH RAWSON, tenth son and fifth surviving child
of William and Anne (Glover) Rawson, was born in Braintree, July
2, 1696, and died in Milton in 1769, aged 73 years. He was buried
in the ancient burying yard in Milton.

In 1720 he was married to Hannah Hall, of Dorchester, daughter
of Samuel and Bathshua (Hinckley) Hall, who was born in Dorchester in 1792. She died in Milton, August 1, 1775, aged 83 years, and
was buried in Milton.

Children of PELATIAH and HANNAH (HALL) RAWSON, born in
Milton :

+102. Grindal,   b. July 29, 1721 ; m. Desire Thacher, of Yarmouth.
  103. Edward,   b. May 27, 1723 ; d. young.
+104. Elliot,   b. June 23, 1724 ;
                   m. { 1st, Sarah Russell, of Middletown, Conn.
                        { 2d, Anne Cushing, of Providence, R. I.
  105. Elizabeth, b. March 26, 1726 ; d. Jan. 3, 1735–6.
  106. Sarah,   b. March 2, 1727–8.
  107. Jonathan, b. July 10, 1730 ; d. June 23, 1733, aged 3 years.
  108. Experience, b. Dec. 13, 1734 ; d. March 18, 1739.
  109. Lydia, b. June 24, 1736 ; m. Dr. John Cleverly, of Braintree.
  110. Jonathan, b. July 1, 1738.

[*Fifth Generation.*]

(35) NATHANIEL GLOVER, the eldest son of Nathaniel, Jr., and Rachael (Marsh) Glover, and the fourth in succession who bore the name, was born at the Dorchester homestead, May 16, 1704, baptized at the Dorchester Church, 19 (3) 1704, by Rev. John Danforth, and died in Boston in December, 1773, in his 69th year.

In 1719, at the age of fifteen years, he was prepared and entered Harvard College at Cambridge, and at the age of nineteen graduated there in the class of 1723. He never studied any profession. Soon after leaving college he became a clerk in the store of Mr. Thomas Hancock, and applied himself to mercantile pursuits. At the age of twenty-one years he was accepted as a co-partner in the business of Mr. Hancock, and became a merchant of considerable celebrity. He continued in that occupation nearly fifty years. Mr. Thomas Hancock died in 1769, and was succeeded by his nephew Mr. John Hancock, and the business of the firm was continued without interruption until Mr. Glover resigned it and withdrew to a more quiet life.

In 1726 Mr. Nathaniel Glover became a shareholder in the Common and Undivided Lands in Dorchester, as an estate of inheritance, in right of his father Mr. Nathaniel Glover, Jr., who died in London while prosecuting the original claims of the proprietors. (See page 224.) He also purchased other rights in those lands of other proprietors.

In 1743 he purchased a tract of five hundred acres of land of John Glover and Thomas Glover, of Dorchester. (See page 237.)

In 1744 he was made a residuary legatee by the will of Mrs. Mary Cursette, and, in connection with Mr. Thomas Hancock, his partner in business, was appointed co-executor of her will. In 1747 he presented the above will for probate, and came in possession of a good estate, of which he died seized, as may be seen by his will made in 1773. The following is the will of Mrs. Cursette:

In the name of God, Amen. I Mary Cursette, now resident in Boston, in the County of Suffolk, and in the Province of Massachusetts Bay in New England, Widow; Being at this present writing hereof of a sound, disposing mind and memory, do therefore make and ordain this my last Will and Testament, in manner and form following, to wit: And first of all, I commend my precious Soul into the hands of God who gave it; And my Body I commit to the dust, by a decent

23*

christain burial, in hope of the resurrection of the just. And as to
my Worldly Goods God has seen fit to bless me with, I dispose in the
following manner.

Imprim[ls]. My Will is that all my just debts and funeral charges
be defrayed. Item. I give unto Lydia Scott, daughter to Mr. Josiah
Franklin, of Boston, Twenty-five Pounds, Old Tenor. Item. I give
unto Mary Franklin, granddaughter to the said Josiah Franklin by his
first Wife, Twenty-five Pounds. Item. I give Three hundred Pounds
towards finishing the Church of England now building at Hebron, in
the Colony of Connecticut, to be paid out of the produce of a certain
tract of land lying in Canterbury in the Colony of Connecticut. It
being the fourth part of William Johnson's Outlands, of said Canterbury, Dec[d]., Being the 2[d] Lott of said Outlands in the distribution of
those Lotts. Item. I give unto Nathaniel Glover of Boston, after the
above said Legacies have been paid out, All my Real and Personal
Estate in the Province of Massachusetts, or in any other Province
wheresoever it may be found, to him and his heirs forever. And I
constitute and appoint Mr. Thomas Hancock and Mr. Nathaniel Glover of Boston, Merchants, sole executors of this my last Will and
Testament, hereby revoking all other Wills by me made.

In Testimony whereof, I the said Mary Cursette have hereunto set
my hand and seal, this 29th day of October, A.D. 1744, in the Eighteenth year of the Reign of His Majesty King George the 2[d].

(Signed)   MARY + CURSETTE.
                                          Her mark.

Signed, sealed and delivered in presence of us,
        Jonathan Lowder,
        Nathaniel Phillips,
        Benjamin Wheeler.

Mary Cursette* died in Boston in July, 1747. Her will was
proved as follows:

Suffolk ss.   By the Hon. Edward Hutchinson, Esq., Judge of Probate of Wills.   Whereas the within written Will being presented for
Probate by Nathaniel Glover, one of the Executors of those within
named (Thomas Hancock, the other Executor, at the same time re-
nouncing his Executorship), Jonathan Lowder, Nathaniel Phillips and

---

* Mrs. Mary Cursette is stated to have been from England, and is introduced thus: " In
1740, Mrs. Mary Cursette, an English lady, travelling to Boston, was obliged to stop some
days at Hebron, in the Colony of Connecticut, where seeing the Church (Episcopal) not
finished, and the people suffering great persecutions, she told them to persevere in their good
work and she would send them a present when she got to Boston. Soon after her arrival
in Boston, Mrs. Cursette fell sick and died. In her Will she gave a legacy of three hundred
pounds old tenor, then equal to one hundred pounds sterling, for their benefit." The
above account is all that has been gathered of this lady. She was in some way connected
with the family of Josiah Franklin, but it is not known that she was connected with Glover,
or the Glover family; but certain it is that she distinguished Nathaniel Glover with her fa-
vors, and placed in him her unbounded confidence and trust. It would be gratifying to learn
more of her history, and the circumstances which influenced her in the above transactions.

Benjamin Wheeler made oath that they saw Mary Cursette, the subscriber to this Instrument, sign and seal, and heard her publish the same to be her last Will and Testament, and that when she did so, she was of sound disposing mind and memory, according to these deponents' best discerning ; and that they set their names as witnesses thereof, in the presence of said Testatrix.

Boston, July 14, 1747.   EDWARD HUTCHINSON.

At the age of forty-six years, Nathaniel Glover was married to Anne Simpson, of Boston, Dec. 17, 1750, by Rev. Joseph Sewall, D.D., of the Old South Church. She was the daughter of Deacon Jonathan and Anne (Agon) Simpson, of Boston, born there about 1725, and died in May, 1776. She was buried in the Granary burial ground, in Simpson's tomb. They had seven children, four of whom died in infancy. She inherited a competent estate from her father, a portion of which was sold in 1763 to John Hancock, Esq., of Boston. The following is an extract from the conveyance :

May 19th, 1763. Nathaniel Glover, Merchant, and Anne his wife in her right, John Simpson, all of Boston in the County of Suffolk and in the Province of Massachusetts Bay in New England ; and Edward Augustus Holyoke of Salem, in the County of Essex and Province aforesaid, Physician, and Mary his wife, Jonathan Simpson, Esq., which said Jonathan and Anne are the children, and Mary the grandchild of Jonathan Simpson, Esq., late of Boston, Shopkeeper, decd, for and in consideration of six hundred and forty Pounds, sold to John Hancock, Esq., of Boston, Merchant, all that portion of land in the Southerly part of Boston aforesaid, bounded and measuring as follows : Easterly on Newbury Street, measuring forty feet and three inches ; South on land of William Fleet, there measuring eighty-seven feet ; then turning and is bounded again on said Fleet's land, seventy-nine feet ; then Westerly on said Fleet's land, measuring thirteen feet ; then South on said Fleet's land, measuring seventeen feet, eight inches ; and Northerly on land of said Fleet, &c., together with the dwelling house and buildings thereon.

(Signed)   NATHANIEL GLOVER,
              ANNE GLOVER,
              EDWARD AUGUSTUS HOLYOKE,
              MARY HOLYOKE,
              JOHN SIMPSON,
              JONATHAN SIMPSON,
              MARGARET SIMPSON.

Mr. Nathaniel Glover was admitted to join the Third Church in Boston, January 25, 1756.

Children of NATHANIEL and ANNE (SIMPSON) GLOVER, born in Boston, and baptized at the Old South Church :

111. Nathaniel, bap. Oct. 20, 1751 ; died young.
+112. Anne, bap. April 1, 1753 ; m. Samuel Whitwell, of Boston.
113. Nathaniel, bap. July 13, 1755 ; died young.
+114. Nathaniel, bap. June 20, 1756 ; d. in Philadelphia, 1790.
115. Jonathan, bap. Oct. 20, 1757 ; died in infancy.
+116. Mary,   bap. Oct. 15, 1758 ; m. Deacon James Morrell, of
       Wilmington.
117. Hannah,   bap. June 8, 1760 ; died in infancy.

Will of Mr. Nathaniel Glover, of Boston.

In the name of God, Amen. I Nathaniel Glover, of Boston, in the
County of Suffolk, Gentleman, Being of sound mind and memory,
God be praised therefor : do make and ordain this my last Will and
Testament, as follows, To Wit, (Vizgt.)

I will that all my just debts and funeral charges be paid as soon
as conveniently after my decease.

Item. I give and bequeathe unto my son Nathaniel Glover, the
sum of One hundred and thirty-three Pounds, six Shillings and Eight
Pence in Lawful Money ; which sum is to remain at interest in the
hands of my Executors until he attain the age of Twenty One Years,
and then to be paid to him. The income of said sum, until that
time, to go towards his support.

Item. My mind and will is, and I do hereby order and direct, that
my Executors, in case of the marriage of my daughters Anne and
Mary, or either of them, in the lifetime of my said Wife, and with
her consent if she be then living, to pay unto each of them the sum
of One hundred and Thirty three Pounds, Six Shillings and Eight
pence, Lawful Money, upon or immediately after their said marriage.

Item. I give and bequeathe unto my Well-beloved Wife the Improvement of all my Estate, both real and Personal, during the term
of her natural life. And I give and bequeathe all the remainder of
my Estate unto my three children aforenamed, that is to say, to each
of them One part thereof.

Item. I do hereby authorize and empower my Executors hereafter
named to bargain and sell my Real estate in Canterbury, in the Colony
of Connecticut ; and in case my said Executors should be of opinion,
that for the comfortable support of my son, Wife and Children, it be
necessary to sell my house and land where I now dwell, I do hereby
authorize and empower my said Executors to sell the same House and
land and to execute legal Deeds thereof, of bargain and sale, to the
purchaser or purchasers of my said Estate. Lastly, I do hereby constitute and appoint my said Wife and John Hancock, Esq., and Mr.
John Soley, to be Executors of this my last Will and Testament.

In Witness whereof, I do hereby set my hand and Seale this Seventh day of January, 1773, and in the Thirteenth year of the Reign
of His Majesty George the III., King of Great Britain, &c.

                    NATHANIEL GLOVER, and a Seale.

Signed, sealed, published and declared by Nathaniel
Glover to be his last Will and Testament,

In presence of us,
       Benjamin Church,
       Daniel Crosby,
       Samuel Savage.

Codicil.

As an additional token of regard to my beloved son Nathaniel Glover, I do furthermore bequeathe, and by this Codicil annexed to my will hereby give and bequeathe and devise to my said son Nathaniel Glover, the sum of One hundred Pounds Lawful Money, to be by him received at the decease of his Mother, before the division of the Estate that shall remain at her decease. And it is my express meaning and intention that this receipt shall in no wise act as a bar to his receiving his proportion of the remaining Estate, as directed above in my Will.

In Witness whereof, I do hereunto set my hand and seale, this 11th day of May, 1773, in the 13th year of His Majesty's Reign, &c.

NATHANIEL GLOVER.

Attest: Mary Read,
Benjamin Church, Jun.
William Chaloner.

Boston, June 11th, 1773.

(36) RACHAEL GLOVER, the eldest daughter of Nathaniel, Jr., and Rachael (Marsh) Glover, was born at the Dorchester homestead, July 30th, 1707, baptized at the Dorchester Church by the Rev. John Danforth, 4 (6) 1707, died in Boston, Oct. 16, 1749, aged 42 years, and was buried in the ancient cemetery at Dorchester. She was twice married. First, May 20, 1725, to Ebenezer Clough, of Boston, by the Rev. Jonathan Bowman. He was the son of Ebenezer and Martha (Goodwin) Clough, who were married in Boston, March 28, 1693, and was born in Boston, Dec. 9, 1697, and baptized at the First Church there, Dec. 12, 1697, his parents being members of that Church in full communion. Oct. 27, 1723, he was admitted to join the New South Church in Summer Street, Rev. Samuel Checkley, pastor. Dec. 28, 1725, Rachael his wife was admitted to join the same Church. They had five children, who were all baptized at that Church by Rev. Mr. Checkley.

Children of EBENEZER and RACHAEL (GLOVER) CLOUGH, born in Boston :

118. Rachael, b. May 27, 1727 ; died in infancy.
119. Mary, b. June 5, 1728.
120. Susannah, b. April 12, 1730.
121. Nathaniel, b. Aug. 1, 1731.
122. John, b. Oct. 2, 1732.

Ebenezer Clough died in Boston in 1734, and left an estate valued at £3792.

Nov. 10, 1736, Rachael (Glover) Clough was married the second time, to Richard Salter, Esq., of Boston. She survived him, and died a widow. He was the son of Rev. Richard and (——) Salter, of Boston, was a merchant, and died in Boston in October, 1747. They had three children, as follows:

+123. Richard, b. in 1738 ; was a merchant in Boston in 1785.
  124. Rachael, b. in 1739 ; died young, unmarried.
  125. William, b. in 1742 ; died young.

The will of Richard Salter, Sen., merchant, was made April 4, 1747, and proved November 3, of the same year. By this will, after the payment of his just debts and funeral charges, he bequeaths to his wife Rachael one third of all his estate personal, and the other two thirds of such estate to his son Richard Salter. Also, he bequeaths one third of all his real estate to his wife Rachael during her widowhood; the remaining two thirds to his son Richard Salter. If it please God to remove his son by death, the whole estate, real and personal, to go to his wife until her intermarriage or death and in that event to his brother John Salter, son of the Rev. Richard Salter. Signed by Richard Salter, in presence of Henry Atkins, Joseph Clarke and John Proctor.

(37) HANNAH GLOVER, third daughter of Nathaniel, Jr., and Rachael (Marsh) Glover, was born in Dorchester at the home-stead, Feb. 24, 1708, and was baptized at the Dorchester Church, March 6, 1708–9, by Rev. John Danforth. She died in Dorchester, Nov. 3, 1766, aged 57 years, and was buried there. She was married to Joseph Bass, Esq., Nov. 14, 1751, and was his second wife. His first was Elizabeth Breck, of Dorchester, by whom he had several children—Sarah, Joseph, Susanna, Edward, and others. Edward was born in Dorchester, Nov. 23, 1726, graduated at Harvard College in the class of 1744, was a schoolmaster in Dorchester, and in 1751, after completing his studies for the ministry in the Episcopal Church, and being chosen assistant minister of St. Paul's Church in Newburyport, went to England for ordination, which took place there May 24, 1752. In 1796 he was elected the first Bishop of the dio-cese of Massachusetts. He died on the 10th of September, 1803, aged 77 years. His mother, Elizabeth Bass, died June 21, 1751, and Capt. Joseph Bass married, second, Hannah Glover, who sur-vived him. He died January 9, 1752. There was no issue by the second marriage.

(38) ALEXANDER GLOVER, the second son of Nathaniel, Jr., and Rachael (Marsh) Glover, was born at the homestead in Dorchester, Nov. 13, 1710, baptized Nov. 26, 1710, by the Rev. John Danforth, died in Dorchester, March 15, 1770, in his 60th year, and was buried in the ancient burial yard; he has a grave-stone. Feb. 5, 1732, he was married to Sarah White, daughter of Edward and Patience (Bird) White, by Rev. Jonathan Bowman. She was born in Dorchester, April 3, 1711, and died there Dec. 3, 1790, in her 80th year. He occupied the homestead with his mother, and at her decease succeeded to his inheritance. (See p. 54.) It has been said of him that he possessed in a remarkable degree those admirable and desirable traits of character and habits of life which distinguished his father, although not called to so public and active a life. He was a member of the Dorchester Church, and adorned his profession by a quiet, sober, and useful life. He occasionally served in town offices. May 13, 1746, his name is enrolled among a list of elderly persons qualified to serve as Grand Jurors for the County of Suffolk. In 1744 he is enrolled among those capable of bearing arms and liable to appear at alarm, " and living within the limits of the First Independent Company in the Town of Dorchester, whereof Col. Estes Hatch is Captain."

Children of ALEXANDER and SARAH (WHITE) GLOVER, born at the homestead in Dorchester (see p. 54):

126. Sarah,   b. Oct. 18, 1732 ; d. Nov. 29, 1733, in her 2d year.
+127. Nathaniel, b. March 15, 1735 ; m. Mehitable Hill, Dorchester.
+128. Sarah,   b. March 4, 1737 ; m. Ephraim Mann, of Boston.
+129. Patience, b. Jan. 23, 1739 ; m. Jonathan Leeds, Dorchester.
+130. Alexander, Jr., b. Feb. 1, 1741 ; m. Hannah Pope, Stoughton.
+131. Edward,   b. May 21, 1743 ; m. Hannah Fifield, of Boston.
+132. Rachael, b. Oct. 8, 1745 ; m. John Howe, Esq., of Dorchester.
133. Hannah,   b. Feb. 15, 1747 ; d. Jan. 20, 1752, in her 4th year.
+134. Abigail,   b. Oct. 14, 1750; m. Joseph Clap, of Dorchester.
+135. Mary,   b. June 24, 1753 ; m. Jonathan Pierce, Dorchester.

Alexander Glover served at Castle William as a soldier, and was discharged in 1748.

(40) PELATIAH GLOVER, the third son of Nathaniel, Jr., and Rachael (Marsh) Glover, was born at the homestead in Dorchester, April 2, and baptized April 5, 1716, by the Rev. John Danforth. He died in Dorchester, April 3, 1770, aged 54 years, and was buried in the ancient burial yard. He has a gravestone.

In June, 1740, he was married to Mary Cochrane, daughter of Samuel Cochrane, of Boston, born there about 1718. It is supposed she died in Dorchester, but no record of her death has been found, and if buried there she has no gravestone.

He resided in Boston for several years after his marriage, and kept a school there. He inherited a portion of the Dorchester homestead conjointly with his brothers Nathaniel and Alexander.

In 1753, and previous, his name is enrolled among a list of soldiers in the "First Independent Company in the Town of Dorchester, whereof Estes Hatch, Esq., is Captain, James Foster Lieutenant, Edward Hillon Second Lieutenant, Nathaniel Langley Ensign, Thomas Pimer, Humphrey Atherton and Zebulon Pierce Sergeants, William Marion Drummer, Samuel Blake Clerk."

In 1756, Pelatiah Glover was appointed by the town of Dorchester to "keep school for Squantum and the Farms." He probably remained in that employment but a short time. At some time during the French and Indian war he went as sutler to the army, and it is said of him that he furnished provisions for the soldiers from his own store. After his return from the army he kept a provision store in Boston, and also opened a public house, and was at one time known as "Pelatiah Glover, Innkeeper of Boston." After his decease, in 1770, his widow continued the business. A widow Glover died in Boston, February, 1772, no age mentioned, who may have been the widow of Pelatiah, the date of whose death has not been found in Dorchester.

Children of PELATIAH and MARY (COCHRANE) GLOVER, born in Boston:

+136. Rachael, b. Aug. 14, 1741; m. William Blake, of Boston.
+137. Elizabeth, b. Oct. 19, 1742; d. Aug. 12, 1827, aged 85 years, unmarried.

(41) SUSANNAH GLOVER, eldest daughter of John and Susannah (Ellison) Glover, was born in Dorchester, Jan. 8, 1715, and died in Stoughton, Nov. 3, 1803, aged 89 years. She was buried in Stoughton, and has a gravestone.

Jan. 19, 1740, she was married to Lazarus Pope, of Dorchester and Stoughton, by Rev. William Walker. They removed to Stoughton, where Mr. Pope inherited a large tract of land, and owned a house and sawmill. He was the son of Ralph and Rachael (Neale)

Pope, of Dorchester, born there Nov. 1, 1714, and died in Stoughton April 1, 1752, aged 37 years. He·was buried in Stoughton in the old burying yard, and has a gravestone. He was a brother of Dr. Ralph Pope, of Stoughton, and they resided near each other, in the South Precinct, about one mile from the Plymouth Colony line." They were members of the Church in Stoughton North Precinct, Rev. Samuel Dunbar, pastor.

Children of LAZARUS and SUSANNAH (GLOVER) POPE, born in Stoughton:

+138. Micajah,   b. June 6, 1741; m. Sarah Whitney, of Braintree.
+139. Ralph,   b. Oct. 1, 1742; m. Hannah Gay, of Stoughton.
+140. Susannah, b. Dec. 27, 1744;

         m. { 1st, Capt. Joseph Farrington ;
             { 2d, Dr. Peter St. Medord, U. S. Navy.

+141. Lazarus,   b. Jan. 19, 1747 ; m. Mary Swan, widow of Rufus
        Spurr.
+142. Jerusha,   b. April 18, 1749 ;

         m. { 1st, Philip Marchant ;
             { 2d, Samuel Bisbee, of Stoughton.

(42) JOHN GLOVER, the eldest son of John and Susannah (Ellison) Glover, was born in Dorchester, April 4, 1717, baptized in Milton by the Rev. Peter Thacher, and died in Bristol, R. I., Nov. 1, 1784, aged 67 years. He was twice married, as appears from what has been gathered from records and other sources. In 1741, March 15, he was married to Elizabeth Bill, of Bristol, R. I., by Rev. John Burt, Pastor of the Catholic Congregational Church at Bristol. The date of her death has not been ascertained, or of his second marriage with Mary ——, whose death, as recorded in the family Bible, took place Dec. 10, 1782, aged 76 years. His children were all by the first marriage. He settled in that part of Bristol known by the name of Poppasqua. He left a good estate, both real and personal.

Children of JOHN and ELIZABETH (BILL) GLOVER, born in Bristol, R. I.:

+143. Mary,   b. in 1743 ; m. Caleb Turner.
+144. Rebecca,   b. in 1745 ; m. James Nooning, of Bristol, R. I.
+145. Jonathan, b. in 1746 ; d. unm. in Amenia, N. Y., in his 42d year.

(43) JOSEPH GLOVER, the second son of John and Susannah (Ellison) Glover, was born in Dorchester, June 6, 1720, baptized at
24

Milton by the Rev. Peter Thacher, June 5, 1720, and died in Charleston, S. C., of yellow fever, Aug. 25, 1769, in his 49th year. He left a widow and seven children. At the age of twenty-eight years, Dec. 8, 1748, he was married to Elizabeth Bass. She was the daughter of Deacon Joseph Bass, formerly of Braintree, and afterwards of Boston, and was born in the former place in 1720. She died in Boston, May 18, 1804, aged 84 years. Capt. Joseph Glover was a mariner and shipmaster, and lived mostly at sea. He left a good estate, which was administered on by Elizabeth Glover his wife. James Bracket, Oliver Billings and William Glover, of Dorchester, were appointed guardians to his minor children.

Children of Capt. JOSEPH and ELIZABETH (BASS) GLOVER, born in Braintree:

+146. Elizabeth, b. April 2, 1749–50;
  m. { 1st, Benjamin Greenwood, of Boston;
      { 2d, Thomas Caldwell, of Ipswich.
+147. Susannah, b. Oct. 8, 1750–51; m. Gershom Thomas, of Boston.
+148. Catharine, b. Oct. 14, 1752–3; m. Benjamin Wardwell, Esq.,
       of Bristol, R. I.
+149. Hannah, b. Jan. 1, 1755; m. James Brown, of Killingly, Ct.
+150.· Mary, b. Dec. 4, 1757; m. Ebenezer Hemenway, of Boston.
+151. Margaret, b. Jan. 20, 1760; m. William May, of Roxbury.
+152. Jane, b. Oct. 16, 1762; m. Bryant Newcomb, of Braintree.

(44) JERUSHA GLOVER, the second daughter of John and Susannah (Ellison) Glover, was born in Dorchester, Dec. 3, 1722, baptized in Milton by the Rev. Peter Thacher, Dec. 29, 1722, and died in Boston, July 27, 1777, in her 55th year. She was buried at Copp's Hill, and has a gravestone. At the age of twenty-five years, Oct. 7, 1748, she was married to Col. William Burbeck, and was his second wife. They had nine children.

Col. William Burbeck was of English parentage, but born in Boston, in 1715, and died there July 22, 1785, aged 69 years. He was buried at Copp's Hill, and has a gravestone. He was twice married; the first time to Abigail Shute, of Boston, by whom he had two children, Edward and Abigail. Edward married a Little, was settled in Newburyport, and was killed there by lightning, June 23, 1782. He had children born there. Has descendants, who settled in Littleton, N. H. Abigail married Peter King, of Boston, who left a daughter Abigail, married to Benjamin Coates,

Esq., of Boston. Col. Burbeck had a brother Edward, the only one of the name cotemporary with himself, who was married to Hannah Loring, of Hull, April 3, 1729, by the Rev. Ezra Carpenter, of Hull.

Children of Col. WILLIAM and JERUSHA (GLOVER) BURBECK, born in Boston, and baptized at the Old North or Christ Church:

153. William, bap. March 15, 1749; died young.
+154. Jerusha, bap. June 16, 1751; m. Capt. John Cathcart, Boston.
155. Mary, bap. April 15, 1752; died in infancy.
+156. Henry, bap. June 9, 1754;
                 m. { 1st, Abigail Webb, of Bath, Maine; 2d, Lucy E. Rudd, of New London.
+157. John, bap. Aug. 1, 1755; m. Jerusha Baker, of Boston.
+158. Joseph, bap. Nov. 21, 1756; m. Elizabeth ——, Marblehead.
+159. Thomas, bap. Aug. 27, 1758; m. Sally Coverly, of Boston.
160. Mary, 2d, bap. July 11, 1762; died unmarried, before 1785.
161. Susannah, bap. April 18, 1765; died unmarried, in 1812.

In 1749 Col. William Burbeck, and Mrs. Jerusha Burbeck his wife, were admitted to Christ Church (Episcopalian) in Boston.

The following incidents in the life and character of Col. William Burbeck have been gathered from a letter, furnished by his son Gen. Henry Burbeck, and other family letters, and also from personal interviews with his descendants.

Col. William Burbeck was by trade a carver, and worked successfully in that employment for several years. There are many specimens of his genius in that art still to be seen in Boston. The carving of the Corinthian pillars in King's Chapel, and other elaborate work, were done under his direction. While employing himself at his trade, he occupied his leisure moments in reading and close study, particularly in the science of mathematics. The arts of Gunnery and Artillery next engrossed his attention, and having furnished himself with a competent library, he advanced rapidly in those studies, and soon became master of every branch of them. He also devoted a portion of his time to the art of Pyrotechnics, and soon became competent to prepare fireworks, equal if not superior to any which were ever made in his time. He prepared those which were used for the celebration of the repeal of the Stamp Act in 1765, and which were considered to be equal to any ever produced. He passed many years at Castle William. In 1769 he was appointed to fill a vacancy there as second officer, or gunner, in which art he had acquired great

skill and efficiency.   Old Castle William was at that time garrisoned
and supported by the Colony, as its chief fortress of defence.
Very soon after, in the autumn of 1770, Castle William was taken
possession of by Great Britain.   He still remained there, and was
appointed Ordinance Storekeeper.

He was uneasy under British control, and sought means to escape
from their jurisdiction and honors of office as soon as possible.   It
required a little strategic manœuvring to enable him to escape; but
having friends to aid him, he was able to accomplish his passage
to Boston without being discovered or even suspected.   He selected
a time when all the mechanics were at dinner, and passing down to
the boat which was awaiting him, rowed himself over to Noddle's
Island, now East Boston, passed thence to Chelsea, thence to Cambridge, and landed without interruption.   He hired a carpenter's
shop in Cambridge on the northeast side of the Common, and employed himself in preparing ammunition.

In 1774 he received an appointment, through his friend Dr. Joseph
Warren, to superintend the laboratory and artillery belonging to the
Colony, and to see that everything was prepared for service.   He
had proved himself fully competent for that office.   When the conflict
with Great Britain commenced, he joined the standard of the American colonies, and distinguished himself for his patriotism and ardent
attachment to the cause.   He had made a previous agreement, that
in case the United Colonies obtained their independence, his pay
should continue the same for life.   The contract was fulfilled, and he
received his pay during his life.

At the close of the year 1775 he was appointed to succeed Col.
Gridley in the command of the Massachusetts artillery.   But although
skilled in military tactics, he was not fond of a military life.   He
declined the acceptance, and strongly recommended Gen. Knox, who
was appointed.   He filled the office of Lieutenant Colonel in the army
while it remained at Cambridge; but when, in 1776, the army march-
ed away to engage in active service, he remained under the contract
which he had previously entered into with the colony.   As an officer
it is said he was highly valued by Gen. Washington, who, it has been
stated, received his resignation with much disappointment and regret.
After the peace of 1783, " Old Castle William " was again in possession of the State, and Col. Burbeck was reappointed to the command,
and continued in that office until his decease.

Will of Col. William Burbeck.

In the name of God, Amen. This 20th day of July, 1785, I William Burbeck, Esq., of Boston, in the County of Suffolk and State of Massachusetts Bay, being sick in body but of a sound disposing mind and thanks be to God therefor, do make and ordain this my Last Will and Testament.

That is to say, principally and first of all, I commit my precious and immortal soul into the hands of God my Creator and Redeemer, relying solely on his grace in and through the merits and satisfaction of my Lord Jesus Christ for pardon with him. And my body I commit to the earth, to be decently buried at the discretion of my Executors hereinafter named.

And as touching my worldly Goods and Estate, after my just debts and funeral expenses are discharged, which I would have done with all convenient speed after my decease, I give, bequeath and devise the same as followeth.

Imprimis. To my Grandchildren, James Burbeck, Jenny Burbeck, Abigail Burbeck, Elizabeth, Mary, William and Joseph Burbeck, the children and heirs of my eldest son, Capt. Edward Burbeck, Decd, I give, bequeath and devise to them my said grandchildren, One single share of my Estate Real and Personal, equal to my sons and no more ; to be divided amongst them my said grandchildren, each share and share alike, to them and their heirs and assigns forever.

Item. I give to my granddaughter Abigail King and daughter to Peter and Abigail King, Deceased, I bequeath to her One share of my Real and Personal Estate, and to her heirs and assigns forever.

Item. To my son John Burbeck I give, bequeath and devise my case of Instruments, over and above his single share in my Estate and magazine that came in Capt Scott.

Item. To my son Capt. Henry Burbeck I give, bequeath and devise the cash or money that I lent him, over and above his single share in my Estate.

Item. To my children Jerusha Cathcart, Captn Henry Burbeck, John Burbeck, Joseph, Thomas, and Susannah Burbeck, I give, bequeath and devise all the remainder and residue of my Estate, Real and Personal, to be equally divided to and among them, share and share alike, to them and to each of them and to their heirs and assigns forever.

And, lastly, I do hereby nominate, constitute and appoint my loving sons Captn Henry Burbeck and John Burbeck, in the State of Massachusetts Bay, to be my Executors to this my last Will and Testament, revoking all former Wills by me at any time heretofore made.

In witness whereof, I have herewith set my hand and seal, the day and year first within written.

WILLIAM BURBECK, and a seal.

Signed, sealed, published, pronounced and declared by the said William Burbeck the Testator, to be his last Will and Testament.

In the presence of us,
Giles Harris,
William Salisbury,
Sukey Cathcart.

24*

Boston, Aug. 9, 1785. The afore written will being presented for Probate by the Executors therein named, Giles Harris, William Salisbury and Sukey Cathcart made oath that they saw William Burbeck, the subscriber to this Instrument, sign, and heard him declare the same to be his last Will and Testament; and that he was, when he did so, of sound disposing mind and memory, according to these deponents' best discerning; and that they set their hands as witnesses thereof in the Testator's presence.   OLIVER WENDELL,
Judge of Probate.

Inventory of his Estate.

LIBRARY.

	£ s d
Dictionary of the Arts and Sciences, ...	£00 08 0
Langley's Architecture, 8s.; Principles and Art of Military, 3s., ...	00 11 0
An old book upon Fortifications, with cuts, . . .	00 06 0
Remarkable Providences, ...	00 02 0
Sharp's Sermons, 3 vols., ...	00 06 6
Mutho on Philosophy and Astronomy, ...	00 03 0
De la Martin's Travels, 2s.; Surveying, 5s., .	00 07 0
Anderson's Art of War, 4s.; Dic. of the Arts and Scien., 12s.	00 16 0
Royce's Dictionary, 8s.; The Field Engineer, 4s., .	00 12 0
Burnet's Ministry, 1s.; Prayers and Meditations, 2s.,	00 03 0
Complete French Master, 1s.; Flavel's Works, 5s., .	00 06 0
Old books on different subjects, some one hundred and fifty years old, ...	00 07 0
Gibbs's descriptions on Architecture, 20s., . . .	01 00 0
Treatise on Shipbuilding, folio, ...	00 18 0
London Art of Building, quarto, ...	00 05 0
Method of Representing Natural Objects, folio, . .	00 08 0
Somes's Medley of Military Discipline, . . .	00 05 0
Halfpenny Architecture, quarto, ...	00 05 0
Practical Surveying Art, 14s.; Military Engineer, 2 vols., 6s.,	01 00 0
Bland's Treatise of Military Discipline, . . .	00 02 0
Mechanical Principles, folio, ...	00 10 0
Müller's Engineer, 5 vols., ...	01 00 0
Buchanan's Family Physician, ...	00 05 0
Robinson on Mathematical Instruments, . . .	00 03 0
Hudibras, 1 vol., 4s 6d.; Wilson's Navigation, 8s., .	00 12 6
Langley's Architecture, 2 vols., ...	00 08 0
Bisset's Theory of Fortifications, ...	00 09 0
Cook's Voyages, 2 vol., ...	00 10 0
Robertson's Treatise of Mathematics, . . .	00 01 4
Euclid's Elements of Mathematics, . . .	00 04 0
Modern Fortifications in 1673, 3s. 6d.; 3 old pictures, 3s.,	00 06 6
	£12 12 10
HOUSEHOLD FURNITURE, ...	£149 07 11
Mansion House and Land under it belonging to the same, at the North part of Boston, in Battery Alley,	280 00 00
Total	£442 00 09

Boston, Aug. 23, 1785.

Henry Burbeck, one of the Executors, presented the foregoing inventory, and made oath that it contained a true and perfect Inventory of the Estate of William Burbeck, late of Boston, Decᵈ, so far as has come to his knowledge, and that if more hereafter do appear, he will cause it to be added and render account thereof when required.

Boston, Aug. 23, 1785. OLIVER WENDELL, *Judge of Probate.*

Examined by
William Cooper.

(46) NATHANIEL GLOVER, the fourth son of John and Mary (Horton) Glover, was born in Dorchester, Dec. 12, 1731, was baptized at the Milton Church by the Rev. Peter Thacher, and died in Milton, Dec. 14, 1801, aged 70 years. He was buried at Quincy in the ancient cemetery.

He owned an estate at Milton, and another in Braintree, and lived at Milton towards the close of his life. His funeral was attended by the Rev. Joseph McKean, of Milton, and his burial service is recorded on the records of the First Church there. He was a member of the Church at Braintree.

He was twice married. Jan. 9, 1753, by Rev. Mr. Niles, to Mary Field, of Braintree, by whom he had four children. She died July 21, 1779, aged 45 years; and he married, for a second wife, Abigail Copeland, of Braintree, Nov. 15, 1783, by whom he had four more children. She was admitted to join the Church in Braintree, Nov. 7, 1784, and died there since 1825.

Nathaniel Glover's will was probated at Dedham, in the County of Norfolk, in January, 1802.

Children of NATHANIEL and MARY (FIELD) GLOVER, born in Braintree:

162. Eunice,   b. June 11, 1763; d. April 8, 1790, aged 26, unm.
+163. Mary,   b. May 27, 1766 ; m. Lemuel Allen, of Braintree.
+164. John,   b. Aug. 13, 1769 ; m. Phebe Curtis, of Braintree.
+165. Nathaniel, b. July 23, 1772 ; m. Esther Glover, of Dorchester.

By wife ABIGAIL COPELAND:

+166. Josiah, b. Aug. 15, 1784 ;
        m. { 1st, Sophia I. Sorrelle, of Braintree ;
             { 2d, Mary P. Adams (widow), of Quincy.
+167. Abigail, b. Oct. 3d, 1785 ; m. Stephen Veazie, of Quincy.
+168. Delight, b. Sept. 2, 1787 ; m. Joseph Nightingale, of Quincy.
+169. Elisha, b. Nov. 25, 1789 ;
        m. { 1st, Mary Veazie, of Quincy ;
             { 2d, Elizabeth Seward, of Ipswich.

(47) JOSIAH GLOVER, the fifth son of John and Mary (Horton) Glover, was born in Dorchester, Dec. 2d, 1726, baptized at Milton by the Rev. Peter Thacher, Dec. 11, 1726, died in Dorchester, Dec. 14, 1803, aged 77 years, and was buried in the ancient cemetery in Quincy. He left a widow, but no issue. He was a landholder by inheritance, and by purchase he acquired a competent estate, both real and personal. His house is said to have been situated about half way between the Newbury farm homestead and the farm of Mr. Billings on the Squantum road. It has been since sold and removed. He made a will, and bequeathed all his personal estate to his wife. His lands he ordered to be equally divided among his surviving brothers.

Aug. 24, 1758, he was married to Mary Blackman, of Dorchester, who was born there Jan. 12, 1739, died in Chelsea, Dec. 20, 1820, and was buried in the ancient cemetery in Quincy. Her will, proved Feb. 18, 1821, bequeaths all her property to Mrs. Elisha Hayden, of Jay, Me. No relationship has been traced between Mrs. Hayden and the Glover family. Lewis Glover Hayden, son of Elisha Hayden, was baptized in Quincy, Nov. 5, 1797, and the name is supposed to be from courtesy.

(48) ELISHA GLOVER, the sixth son of John and Mary (Horton) Glover, was born in Dorchester, Jan. 9, 1729, baptized at Milton by the Rev. Peter Thacher, Jan. 31, 1729, and died in Quincy, Oct. 18, 1811, in his 83d year. He was a mariner and navigator, passed many years at sea, and went on several foreign voyages.

Capt. Elisha Glover was twice married. First, Dec. 26, 1754, to Elizabeth, the daughter of Thomas and Elizabeth (Clough) Glover (60), of Newbury farm, a first cousin. She was born Sept. 6, 1738, and was sixteen years old when married. She died in Quincy, May 10, 1757, in her 19th year. She left a son. He married, a second time, Oct. 15, 1759, Jerusha Billings, daughter of John and Miriam (Davenport) Billings, of Dorchester. She was born in Dorchester, Sept. 22, 1743, and died in Quincy, April 2, 1807, in her 64th year.

Capt. Glover left a good estate. He was an extensive landholder, both by purchase and inheritance. He purchased the Hinckley estate of the heirs of Ebenezer Hinckley, and left it to his son Ezra at his decease.

Children of Capt. ELISHA and ELIZABETH GLOVER, born in Dorchester:

170. Elisha, b. March 29, 1756 ; d. Sept. 12, 1783, at Providence, R. I., in his 28th year, unm. He was a merchant, and lived for a time at Dorchester Village.

By second wife, JERUSHA BILLINGS:

+171. Elizabeth, b. Feb. 21, 1761 ; d. March 13, 1847, unm., aged 86.
172. Lewis, b. Sept. 20, 1763 ; d. at Guinea, in Africa, Nov. 10, 1787, aged 25 years.
173. Josiah, b. Nov. 6, 1765 ; d. Aug. 1, 1782, at N. York, aged 16.
174. Joseph, b. Nov. 1, 1767 ; d. Jan. 11, 1792, at Richmond, Va.
+175. Ezra, b. June 22, 1770 ; m. Eunice Minot, of Dorchester.
+176. Mehitable, b. Nov. 8, 1773 ; m. Samuel Kinsley Spurr, Milton.
+177. Russell, b. June 15, 1776 ; d. June 10, at New York city, unmarried, aged 64 years.
+178. Stephen, b. Jan. 9, 1778 ;

m. { 1st, Mary Woodward, of Boston ;
{ 2d, Rebecca Payne Gore, of Boston.

179. Elijah, b. Aug. 2, 1780 ; d. Dec. 8, 1781, in his second year.

(49) EZRA GLOVER, seventh son of John and Mary (Horton) Glover, was born in Dorchester, Jan. 5, 1732, baptized at Braintree, Feb. 25, 1732–3, and died in Chelsea, Jan. 11, 1792, aged 60 years. He inherited from his father a portion of the land which was at Quincy, belonging to John Glover's estate. He also owned an estate in Chelsea, and resided there, after his marriage until his decease. No issue. He was married to Elizabeth Belcher, daughter of Jonathan and Elizabeth (Tuttle) Belcher, of Chelsea, June 1, 1786, by Rev. Phillips Payson, of Chelsea. Her parents were married in Chelsea, May 13, 1742, and had a permanent residence there, owning an estate. After the decease of Mr. Glover, his widow Elizabeth was married a second time to William Barrows, of Boston, March 27, 1797, by Rev. Phillips Payson, of Chelsea. She removed to Boston, and died there, Nov. 25, 1797. The Boston Records say : "Mrs. Barrows, that was the widow Glover, died, aged 53 years." She was born, therefore, in 1744.

Ezra Glover made a will, and left his income to his wife Elizabeth — proved in Feb., 1792. His lands in Dorchester and Quincy to be equally divided among his surviving brothers. " The estate of Ezra Glover was divided by order of Court, in 1798, according to the purport and true intent of his Will."

(50) ENOCH GLOVER, the eighth son of John and Mary
(Horton) Glover, was born in Dorchester, May 14, 1734, and baptized in Braintree at the First Church there, May 19, 1734. He
died in Dorchester, Nov. 21, 1801, in his 68th year. He was an innkeeper, and owned a competent landed estate. His mansion house was
situated on the Upper Road leading from Dorchester to Boston, about
one mile from Dorchester "Four Corners," and is now owned by
Edmund Wright, Esq., of Boston. Some of his descendants own
and occupy portions of his land.

Nov. 23, 1756, he married Susannah Bird, daughter of Benjamin
and Johannah (Harris) Bird, of Dorchester, and born there in 1736.
She died in Dorchester, Oct. 26, 1802, in her 66th year.

Children of ENOCH and SUSANNAH (BIRD) GLOVER, born in Dorchester :

+180. Johannah, b. Feb. 3, 1758 ; m. Aaron Bird, of Dorchester.
+181. Susannah, b. April 2, 1759 ; m. Ebenezer Baker, Dorchester.
+182. Mary, b. Oct. 18, 1760 ; m. Ebenezer Clap, Esq., Dorchester.
  183. Enoch,   b. Nov. 5, 1762 ; never married ; d. in Dorchester,
        Feb. 13, 1817, in his 55th year.
+184. Elizabeth, b. Nov. 1, 1764 ; m. Benjamin Lyon, of Dorchester.
  185. Benjamin, b. April 29, 1766 ; d. March 17, 1833, aged 67 yrs.
        Unmarried.
+186. Anna, b. Jan. 17, 1768 ; m. Stephen Wales, Esq., Dorchester.
+187. Samuel, b. March 29, 1770 ; m. Martha Holden, Dorchester.

(51) MARY GLOVER, the third daughter of John and Mary
(Horton) Glover, was born in Dorchester, April 21, 1735–6, baptized at the First Church in Braintree, May 23, 1735–6, and died
in Braintree, Nov. 2, 1754, in her 18th year.

Feb. 4, 1753, she was married to Elijah Belcher, of Braintree.
They had one daughter born there, viz.:

  188. Mary, b. Nov. 1, 1754 ; d. young, unmarried.

By the will of her grandfather, Mr. John Glover, she was to receive the sum of thirty pounds if she lived to attain the age of twenty-
one years ; if not, the sum bequeathed to her was to be retained in
the estate.

Elijah Belcher died in Braintree, June 1, 1800, aged 71 years.
He was married a second time, and had other children.

(53) THOMAS GLOVER, Jr., the eldest son of Thomas and Elizabeth (Clough) Glover, was born in Boston, Sept. 1, 1723, at the house of his maternal grandfather, Deacon John Clough, who resided on the corner of Main and Essex Streets. He received the ordinance of baptism, Sept. 3, 1723, at the New South Church, Summer Street, by Rev. Samuel Checkley, pastor, and died in Stoughton, Jan. 11, 1811, in his 89th year. In the spring of 1723–4, his parents removed from Boston to Dorchester, and resided on the Newbury farm, which had become the inheritance of his father (see page 80). He resided here until the year 1748. From 1731 to 1748, he served as a soldier and an officer on Castle William, in Boston harbor, and was chosen Lieutenant of the militia, and served in that capacity a short time. In 1744, the name of Thomas Glover, Jr., is enrolled among a list of persons "capable of bearing arms and liable to appear at the alarm, and living within the limits of the first Independent Company in the Town of Dorchester, whereof Col. Estes Hatch is Captain, and Samuel Blake Clerk. He obtained his discharge from the Castle in 1748, as is shown by the following order: — "Dorchester, April 12, 1748. Mr. Samuel Blake: Sir — Please pay to Mr. Thomas Welles, the bearer hereof, what is due to us the subscribers for our training at the Castle William in the year 1746, in the time of the Alarm, and this receipt shall be your discharge." Signed by Thomas Glover, Jr., Elijah Glover, Elisha Glover, and John Billings, Jr.

Thomas Glover, Jr., became an extensive landed proprietor by inheritance from his father, and his maternal grandfather, Dea. John Clough, of Boston.

Lands in Ashford and Windsor, Conn.

In 1744, Thomas Glover, Jr., and Elijah Glover his next brother, received, by deed of gift from their grandfather, Dea. John Clough, of Boston, the following described tracts of land, containing by estimation about six hundred acres. The following is copied from the original deed:

To all People unto whom these Presents shall come. I John Clough of Boston, in the County of Suffolk, in the Province of Massachusetts Bay in New England, Leather Dresser, send Greeting. Know ye, That I the said John Clough, for and in Consideration of the love and affection that I have and do bear towards two of my grandchildren, Thomas Glover, Jun', and Elijah Glover, both of Dorchester in the

County and Province aforesaid, Have Given, Granted, Conveyed and
Confirmed, and by these Presents do fully, freely, clearly and abso-
lutely give, grant, convey and confirm unto them the said Thomas
Glover and Elijah Glover, and to their heirs and assigns forever, in
equal halves, All my Right, Title and Interest in several tracts or
Parcels of Land lying in the Township of Ashford and in the Colony
of Connecticut, on the North side of the Township, commonly called
the North Half-mile, which I with Mr. Thomas Downes purchased of
Nathaniel Fuller and Philip Eastman (an. 1718), as upon Record in
Ashford may fully appear, viz., One Tract containing Two hundred
and ninety-five acres, Butted and bounded as follows.   Beginning at
a Chestnut Tree marked, standing in the North Part of said Ashford
Township; from thence running on the Town line across the East
Branch of Roaring Brook 295 Perch to a Red Oak, standing on a
Great Rock on the East side of a Hill; and from thence running South
One Hundred and Sixty Perch to a Black Oak Tree marked; and
from thence running East two hundred and ninety-five Rods to a great
White Oak Tree marked; and from thence the line runs North One
Hundred and Sixty Perch to the bounds first mentioned.   Another
Tract or Parcel of Land containing by estimation Three Hundred and
Twenty Six acres, more or less; Beginning at a Rock with Stones
about it; from thence running West three hundred and twenty six
Perch upon the Town line, to a Great Rock with Stones upon it, it
being in the Town line—then running South 160 Perch to a Stake and
Stones; From thence running South 160 Perch to a Chestnut Tree;
Then Running East 326 Perch to a Stake and Stones; From thence
running North 160 Perch to the first mentioned Corner.   Also another
Tract of land containing about forty two Acres.   Beginning at a Red
Oak standing on a Great Rock, on the East side of a Hill; from thence
running West on the Town line 42 Perch to a Chestnut Tree; From
thence running South 160 Perch to a Black Birch tree marked; thence
running East 42 Perch to a Black Oak Tree marked; thence running
North to the first mentioned Bounds.   Also another Tract or Parcel
of Land situate and lying and being in the County of Windham, in
the Township of Windsor, in the Colony of Connecticut, lying between Union and Stafford, bounded as follows.   Beginning at a Stake
and Stones standing in a line, commonly called and known by the
name of Farrar's line; and in the South line of land belonging to
Uriah Loomis of Windsor, and from thence runs Southerly on the said
line 52 Rods to a leaning White Oak marked, with Stones about it;
and from thence the line runs Easterly 209 Rods to a Stake and heap
of Stones in the North line of Land belonging to James Eanos of Windsor, Thirty nine Rods from the North West Corner of said Eanos's
Land; and from thence the line runs North Westerly 104 Rods to a
Stake and heap of Stones in the aforesaid line of said Loomis Land;
and from thence the Line runs Westerly rounding on the said Loomis
Line to the first mentioned Bounds.   Or however otherways bounded
or reputed to be bounded, either of the said parcels of land may be.
And all the Estate, Right, Title, Interest and Inheritance, Claim or
demand whatsoever of Me the said John Clough, of, in and to each
and every Parcel of the aforesaid Tracts of land with the Privileges
and Appurtenances thereof.   To Have and to Hold all and singular
of the aforementioned and granted Premises, with all the Privileges

and Appurtenances thereof, unto the said Thomas Glover and Elijah Glover and to their heirs and assigns forever as their own proper Estate in Fee simple, from henceforth forever, absolutely, without any manner of Condition whatsoever. And Further I do hereby Promise, Bind and oblige myself, my heirs, Executors and Administrators, from henceforth and forever, to warrant and defend all the above granted Premises and Appurtenances thereof unto the said Thomas Glover and Elijah Glover and their heirs and assigns forever, against the lawful claims and demands of all Persons.

In Witness whereof, I the said John Clough have hereunto set my hand and Seale this 1 day of January, 1744, &c.

JOHN CLOUGH, and a seal.

Witnessed by
  John Goffe,
  Samuel Wheeler.   Acknowledged before

SAMUEL WELLES,
Justice of the Peace.

In 1744, Thomas Glover, Jr., also received by deed of his grandfather, Dea. John Clough, of Boston, a negro boy named George, which he owned conjointly with his brother Elijah for several years; and they subsequently, in about 1770, disposed of him to their brother William Glover, who lived in Dorchester, and the boy died and was buried on Mr. Glover's estate. (See page 248.)

In 1748, soon after obtaining his discharge from Castle William, Thomas Glover, Jr., went to Stoughton, and made arrangements to settle there on a tract of land belonging to his father, Thomas Glover, Esq., who guaranteed to two of his sons the inheritance of the two hundred acres of land which had been assigned to "Mr. John Glover" in the Twenty-five Divisions of Land in Dorchester New Grant, as specified in a deed of quitclaim from Glovers to Thomas Glover, bearing date 1743. This land was situated in the South Precinct of Stoughton, and at the most southerly portion of it, adjoining the estates of Dr. Ralph and Lazarus Pope. He commenced building a house, which was finished about 1750. The public road was hardly passable farther than the North Precinct (now Canton), and those who intended to settle in that wilderness had to find their way by marked trees to the South Precinct (now Stoughton), where were a few families living who had commenced a settlement near the Colony line, reaching there by the old Plymouth and Taunton roads. He made his journeys on foot or on horseback, and resided alternately at Dorchester (Newbury farm), and at Stoughton, while his house was building.

25

In the war of the French and Indians, Thomas Glover was conscripted or drafted to serve in the expedition against the French. He procured a substitute in William Monk,* and conveyed to him forty acres of his land on the homestead farm in Stoughton as an equivalent and compensation to serve for him in that war. Subsequently Thomas Glover, Jr., by purchase added to his acres thus reduced; he bought land in the Twelve Divisions of Henry Leadbetter and Increase Leadbetter, Standfast Foster, Benjamin Lynde, Esq., and others.

April 19, 1775, he served in a company marching from Stoughton on the alarm. (Vol. 13, p. 104, Army Rec.: "Lieut. Thomas Glover, of Stoughton, 58 miles travel.") Officers, Capt. Peter Talbot and Col. Frederick Pope, of Stoughton. Capt. James Pope and Ralph Pope went in the same company.

Thomas Glover was married in Stoughton, Feb. 20, 1752, to Rebeckah Pope, eldest daughter of Dr. Ralph and Rebeckah (Stubbs) Pope, of Stoughton (South Precinct), by Rev. Jedediah Adams, pastor of the First Church there. She was born in that town, Dec. 29, 1730, and baptized at the North Precinct by Rev. Joseph Morse, Jan. 2, 1731, her parents being members of that Church, and she was carried thither on horseback to receive the ordinance only a few days from her birth. She removed from her father's to her new house at the time of her marriage, and died there Aug. 12, 1812, in the 82d year of her age. She was buried in the old burying ground in Stoughton, by the side of her husband, and has a gravestone.

Children of Thomas and Rebeckah (Pope) Glover, born in Stoughton:

+189. Elizabeth, b. Sept. 25, 1752 ; m. Samuel Bird, of Sharon.
  190. Rebeckah, b. May 16, 1754 ; d. unm. May 1, 1785, aged 28.
+191. Hannah, b. June 3, 1756 ; m. Jonathan Capen, Jr., Stoughton.
+192. Thomas, b. Dec. 29, 1757 ; m. { 1st, Eunice Bent, of Sudbury ; 2d, Abigail Hewins, of Sharon.
+193. William, b. July 17, 1759 ; m. Content Porter, of Stoughton.
+194. Rachael, b. Jan. 15, 1761; m. { 1st, Benj. Homes, Esq., Norton ; 2d, Solomon Hall, Dorchester.
+195. Samuel, b. Feb. 5, 1763 : m. Eleanor Hawes, of Sharon.
+196. Ebenezer, b. Feb. 2, 1765 ; m. Mary Trescott, widow of Isaac Fenno, of Dorchester.

---

* William Monk returned home, having been in the battles of Louisburg and Fort William Henry, and was present at the taking of Quebec. He built a house and married, and passed his life on his homestead thus acquired.

+197. Jerusha, b. April 28, 1766 ; m. Unite Blackman, Dorchester.
+198. Anna, b. Nov. 13, 1768 ; m. Josiah Leeds, of Dorchester.
+199. Elijah, b. April 20, 1770 ; m. { 1st, Martha Pope, Dorchester ; 2d, Sarah Howe, Dorchester.

Thomas Glover and Rebeckah his wife became members of the First Church in Stoughton, South Precinct, in 1752, and their children were all baptized there within a few days of their birth. His will bears date July 26, 1796; probated the first Tuesday in May, 1811. He gave portions of land to his sons; and to his daughters, who were all married and had received their marriage portions, he gave a balance of money as their full share in his estate, and settled the homestead on his youngest son, Elijah Glover (see p. 80). The house built in 1750 is still standing; the land is in possession of his heirs.

In the life and character of Thomas Glover the Christian graces were developed and shone with admirable lustre. Of strict integrity, of mild and amiable temperament, of sound and discretionary judgment, he was a kind husband, a tender parent, a friendly and obliging neighbor, a patriotic and law-abiding man, of whom it was once remarked by a prominent citizen and officer of the town of Stoughton, that "if all people were like Mr. Thomas Glover, there would be no need to make laws." Of the Church to which he belonged he was an exemplary and worthy member, and observed the ordinances with great veneration and strict adherence, both in public and in the family, continuing the worship of God at the family altar until nearly the close of his life, a period of almost sixty years. He was an honorable and worthy citizen and member of society, and is remembered as such by all survivors who ever knew him. In his deportment he was gentlemanly, and was possessed of a degree of manly grace and beauty.

(54) ELIJAH GLOVER, the second son of Thomas and Elizabeth (Clough) Glover, was born at Newbury farm, in Dorchester, July 20, 1725, baptized at the Church in Dorchester, Rev. John Danforth, pastor, July 25, 1725, and died in Milton at his residence on Milton Hill, July 1, 1770, aged 45 years. He was buried in Milton in the ancient burial yard, and has a gravestone. His death was caused by an internal injury received by wrestling at a match or ring, formed for that exercise, on Election day the May previous. It is said that he had carried the ring by his agility and superior

strength, and while enjoying his victory received a challenge from a new champion who had come on the ground. He accepted, and triumphed, but the contest caused the rupture of a blood-vessel, which resulted in death in a few months. He made his will, appointing wife Elizabeth executor; Elijah Glover, of Pembroke, was one of the witnesses. In 1744 his name is enrolled upon the alarm list, and also at Castle William on the list of soldiers who had served there in 1747 and previous, under the command of Col. Estes Hatch.

Elijah was an extensive landholder in Dorchester and Milton. He inherited a competent estate from his father, and was an owner, conjointly with his elder brother Thomas Glover, in lands received from their grandfather, Dea. John Clough, at Ashford and Windsor, in the Colony of Connecticut. He also came in possession of valuable lands in right of his wife Abigail. His homestead estate was situated in Milton, on the Milton Hill road leading to Quincy meetinghouse, nearly opposite the estates of Gov. Belcher and Gov. Hutchinson, who lived at one time on Milton Hill, and whose estates have passed to Joseph Rowe, Esq., and the Hon. Jonathan Russell. The house built by Elijah Glover has been taken down and a new one built on the same spot, and the location of his estate may be identified at the present time by two large elm trees which once adorned the premises and still remain to mark the spot.

He was twice married. First, on Dec. 21, 1751, to Abigail Kingsley, daughter of Samuel and Mary (Gulliver) Kingsley, of Milton, born there Oct. 16, 1727, and died Feb. 8, 1761, in her 35th year. Her earliest American ancestor was John Kingsley, who came from England and settled in Milton, and was married there June 25, 1669, to Susannah Daniell. By his first marriage Elijah Glover had one son. He was married, second, Jan. 1, 1762, to Elizabeth Tucker, of Milton. They had one daughter.

Only child of ELIJAH and ABIGAIL (KINGSLEY) GLOVER, born in Milton:

200.　Samuel Kingsley, b. June 28, 1753; m. Eunice Babcock, Milton.

　　　By wife ELIZABETH TUCKER:
201.　Susannah, b. April 21, 1765; m. Charles Pierce, of Milton.

Elizabeth Tucker, the widow of Elijah Glover, married, a second time, Nov. 2, 1776, George Clark, of Milton. He died, and she married, a third time, Deacon Moses Carey, of North Bridgewater, and died there in 1825. She had two children by George Clark. Eleanor, born in 1790, married Deacon Daniel Noyes, of Boston.

(57) WILLIAM GLOVER, the third son of Thomas and Elizabeth (Clough) Glover, was born at the Newbury farm homestead, in Dorchester, Aug. 1, 1731, and was baptized at the First Church in Quincy, Aug. 8, 1731. He died in Dorchester, March 7, 1797, in his 67th year, and was buried in Quincy, in the ancient burial yard; he has a gravestone. He inherited a portion of Newbury farm, was co-executor to his father's will, and joint heir to his homestead estate. He also came in possession of extensive and valuable lands in right of his wife, and built a house and settled on her estate. It is still owned and occupied by his descendants. Dr. William B. Duggan is the present possessor, in right of his wife, who is a grandchild.

Oct. 15, 1772, William Glover was married to Mary Capen, daughter of John Capen, of Dorchester, born there in 1738, and died Nov. 11, 1813, aged 75 years; buried in Quincy, and has a gravestone. At the age of 16 years, in 1747, his name is enrolled among those who served at Castle William under the command of Col. Estes Hatch.

Children of WILLIAM and MARY (CAPEN) GLOVER, born in Dorchester:

202. William, b. Aug. 9, 1775 ; d. Aug. 9, 1779, aged 4 years.
203. Edward, b. March 13, 1778 ; d. May 26, 1843, unm. aged 65.
204. William, b. Oct. 3, 1780 ; m. Mary Billings, of Quincy.
205. Mary, b. Nov. 12, 1784 ; d. Nov. 12, 1800, aged 16 years.

(58) JAMES GLOVER, the fourth son of Thomas and Elizabeth (Clough) Glover, was born at the Newbury farm homestead, in Dorchester, June 5, 1734, baptized at the Church in Braintree, June 9, 1733–4, and died in Vinalhaven, at Fox Islands, Lincoln County, Maine, April 22, 1806, in the 72d year of his age. He resided in Dorchester until he arrived at the age of manhood. His name is enrolled among a list of officers and soldiers in Col. Estes Hatch's first Independent Company in the town of Dorchester, dated Oct. 11, 1753, when he was at the age of twenty years. He also served at Castle William, and was discharged in 1748. In that year he went to Stoughton, and made preparations to settle on a tract of

25*

land there, belonging to his father, in the Twenty-five Divisions in
Dorchester New Grant. In 1758 the portion of his inheritance was
confirmed to him by his father's will. While in Stoughton, he resided at Dr. Ralph Pope's, and after the marriage of his brother
Thomas Glover became an inmate of his house, making alternate
excursions and visits to the Newbury farm homestead in Dorchester.

Four years after the decease of his father, in 1761, he sold his
estate in Stoughton to Thomas Shepard, of the North Precinct (now
Canton). He had broken up and cleared the land, and made other
improvements. Date of deed, March 24, 1761. Consideration, two
hundred and ten pounds. Description and location are as follows:

A certain Tract or Parcel of land lying in the Third Precinct in
Stoughton, containing One hundred Acres, be the same more or less.
And is the one half of a lot formerly laid out by the Dorchester Proprietors to " Mr. Glover." Butted and Bounded as follows. Beginning at a Stake and heap of Stones at a Corner in the Division line
between Thomas Glover's land and the said Hundred Acres, then runs
in a strait line till it comes to the corner bounds of said " Mr. Glover's" line ; and is bounded Westerly partly on Judge Lynde and
partly on David Thompson ; then running in the line between said
land and George Monks's land till it comes to the corner bounds between the said Lot and Thomas Crane's land ; and is bounded Easterly partly on Thomas Crane's land and partly on Johnson Tolman's
Lot, till it comes to a Stake and heap of Stones in the Division line
between said land and Thomas Glover's ; and is bounded Northerly
on Thomas Glover, till it comes to a stake and heap of stones by the
Way (road), then the Way as it is now improved is the bounds till it
comes to a fence in the Division line on the Contrary side of the Way ;
and from thence in a strait line to the Stake first mentioned.

                                              JAMES GLOVER.
Signed, sealed and delivered in presence of us,
          Thomas Glover,
          William Pope.

This estate has passed down in the Shepard family, and is now
(1866) in possession of Samuel Shepard Stetson, a great-grandson
of Thomas Shepard.

June 2, 1762, James Glover purchased a tract of land in Framingham, of Mr. John Haven, administrator on the estate of Nathaniel
Stacey. He owned a house and land there in that part of the town
known by the name of "Salem End." Also he owned land in East
Sudbury.

June 9, 1790, he sold his estate at Framingham and removed to
Fox Islands, in Maine. He took a farm in Vinalhaven, on a lease or

shares, of Eleazer Crabtree. The indenture was signed by Eleazer
Crabtree and James Glover, and witnessed by Samuel Train, Jr., and
Enoch Train. He subsequently purchased the estate, and resided
there at his decease.

He was twice married. First, Feb. 3, 1762, to Lois Bent, of Sudbury, who was the eldest daughter of Thomas and Mary (Stone)
Bent. She was born in Sudbury, Dec. 3, 1740, and died at Framingham in 1783. Her earliest American ancestor was Hopestill Bent,
who came from England with his parents in the early settlement of
New England, settled at Bent's Point, now in the precinct of South
Boston, and was married to Elizabeth Brown, Nov. 27, 1701. Thomas
their son, and father of Lois Bent, was born in Sudbury, July 27,
1706, married Mary Stone, May 28, 1733, and had eight children.
James Glover married, a second time, Sept. 23, 1784, Mrs. Mary
(Hill) Metcalf, widow of —— Metcalf, of Franklin, Mass. They
had six children. She died at Vinalhaven, Feb. 15, 1842.

Children of JAMES and LOIS (BENT) GLOVER, born at "Salem End,"
Framingham:

+206. Lois Bent, b. Nov. 30, 1762; m. Asa Nourse, of Framingham.
+207. Mary, b. Aug. 10, 1764; m. { 1st, Ezra Haven, Framingham; 2d, Asa Nourse, "
208. Anna, b. May 13, 1766; d. Sept. 8, 1779, aged 14 years.
+209. Elizabeth, b. June 5, 1768; m. Isaac Fisher, of Framingham.
+210. Sarah, b. July 9, 1770; m. Sam'l Thomas, of Vinalhaven, Me.
+211. Martha, b. Nov. 3, 1772; m. Jonathan Rugg, of Framingham.
212. James, b. Dec. 4, 1774; d. Feb. 15, 1778, in his 4th year.
213. Eunice, b. June 20, 1777; d. July 22, 1825, in her 49th year.

By MARY HILL (METCALF) GLOVER, born in Vinalhaven, Fox
Islands, Me.:

+214. Jerusha, b. Nov. 29, 1785; m. Thomas Verille, of Vinalhaven.
+215. Julia, b. April 20, 1787; m. Benjamin Crabtree, of Vinalhaven.
+216. John Clough, b. Oct. 21, 1788; m. Martha White, of Camden.
+217. Elijah, b. Aug. 27, 1792; m. Nancy Crabtree, of Vinalhaven.
218. Susannah, b. Dec. 13, 1795; d. Jan. 8, 1853, aged 58 years.
+219. Willard, b. July 29, 1796; m. Emeline Packard.

Mr. James Glover and his first wife were members of the Church
at East Sudbury. His second wife, Mary, was a member of the
Church at Franklin, Mass. The above children were all baptized.

(59) EBENEZER GLOVER, the fifth son of Thomas and Elizabeth (Clough) Glover, was born at Newbury farm, in Dorchester,

June 27, 1736, baptized at the First Church in Braintree (now Quincy), July 4, 1736, and died in Dorchester at the homestead, Dec. 26, 1807, in his 72d year.   He was buried in the ancient cemetery in Quincy, and has a gravestone.

In 1758, at the age of twenty-two years, he succeeded to the possession and occupancy of the homestead of Newbury farm (see p. 74), and continued there until his decease.   He was co-executor to the will of his father, with his brother William, in that year.   He was an extensive landed proprietor, by inheritance and by purchase; was the owner of lands in Braintree, Dorchester and Milton, and paid taxes in those towns.   His name is enrolled in the army list of those who composed the alarm men in the war of the Revolution in 1776; was among those who were called out on the 19th of April, 1775, to meet the enemy at Lexington, and was active and patriotic in his country's cause throughout the conflict.   It is said, also, that he was one of the memorable Boston " Tea Party," and assisted in the removal and destruction of that article in Boston harbor in the year 1774.

Ebenezer Glover was twice married.   First, in 1772, to Sarah Wadsworth, who was a daughter of Deacon Benjamin and Esther (Tucker) Wadsworth, of Milton, born there Oct. 29, 1747, and died at Newbury farm, January 8, 1783, in her 35th year.   Her first American ancestor was Christopher Wadsworth, one of the early Plymouth Pilgrims, who settled at Duxbury, and had, by wife Grace, Samuel and others: second, Capt. Samuel Wadsworth, born about 1630, married Abigail Lindall, daughter of James Lindall, of Marshfield, in 1656; killed at Sudbury in 1676, in a battle with the Indians, for whom and his compatriots the Wadsworth monument was erected in 1852: third, Dea. John Wadsworth, his son, born in 1674, died 1733–4, married Elizabeth Vose, and had eleven children, of whom was Dea. Benjamin Wadsworth, born 1707, died 1771, and by wife Esther Tucker had Sarah, who became the first wife of Ebenezer Glover, Esq.   They had two children.   Mr. Glover married, second, June 23, 1785, Mary Davenport, daughter of Stephen and Thankful (Bent) Davenport, of Milton, born there in 1751, died in Quincy at the house of her daughter, Mrs. Adams, June 7, 1833, aged 82 years, and was buried in Quincy.   They had one daughter.

Children of EBENEZER and SARAH (WADSWORTH) GLOVER, born at Newbury farm, Dorchester:

+220. Benjamin Wadsworth, b. Dec. 14, 1774; m. Mehetable Willard Baxter, of Quincy.

221. Esther, b. Sept. 4, 1778; m. (165) Nathaniel Glover, of Quincy.

By wife MARY DAVENPORT:

+222. Hannah, b. Sept. 4, 1789; m. Thomas Adams, Esq., Quincy.

(63) JERUSHA GLOVER, the fourth daughter of Thomas and Elizabeth (Clough) Glover, was born at Newbury farm, in Dorchester, May 20, 1745, and died in Quincy, Sept. 17, 1817, in her 73d year.

She was twice married. First, June 30, 1763, to Daniel Arnold, of Braintree. He died in 1780, and she was married, a second time, June 5, 1785, to Capt. Joseph Baxter, of Quincy, who was born there in 1740, and died May 7, 1829, aged 89 years. Capt. Baxter was twice married. First, to Anna Adams, Dec. 27, 1764, who died Sept. 5, 1784; and he married, a second time, Mrs. Jerusha (Glover) Arnold.

Children of DANIEL and JERUSHA (GLOVER) ARNOLD, born in Braintree:

+223. Joseph Neale, b. Oct. 10, 1764; m. Mehetable Adams, of Braintree.

+224. Daniel, b. Oct. 21, 1766; m. Charlotte Cleverly, of Braintree.

+225. Elizabeth, b. Sept. 16, 1770; m. Jesse Fenno, of Milton.

+226. Jerusha, b. July 27, 1774; m. { 1st, John Pierce, of Milton; 2d, Caleb Thayer, Braintree.

+227. Elisha, b. March 28, 1778; m. Catharine Sherman.

By Capt. JOSEPH BAXTER, born in Braintree:

+228. James, b. June 28, 1787; m. Mary Phipps, of Braintree.

(64) ANNA GLOVER, sixth and youngest daughter of Mr. Thomas and Elizabeth (Clough) Glover, was born at Newbury farm, in Dorchester, Aug. 3, 1749, and died in Sudbury, Nov. 10, 1837, in her 89th year. She was buried in Sudbury.

She was married to Jason Bent, of Sudbury, Aug. 17, 1773, and removed there to live. His house was about one mile from the centre of the town. In the autumn of 1773, Jason Bent and Anna his wife were admitted to join the First Congregational Church there. He was the son of Thomas and Mary (Stone) Bent, of Sudbury; was born there in 1734, and died Oct. 1, 1786, very suddenly, aged 52 years. He left a widow and seven children. The homestead passed into the possession and occupancy of his eldest son Thomas Bent, who died there March 28, 1848, leaving a widow.

Children of JASON and ANNA (GLOVER) BENT, born in Sudbury:

+229. Elizabeth Clough, b. July 18, 1774 ; m. Jabez Maynard, of Sudbury.
+230. Thomas,   b. Sept. 4, 1776 ; m. Sarah Patch, of Stowe.
+231. Sewell,   b. Oct. 9, 1778 ; m. Lydia Patch, of Stowe.
+232. Nancy,   b. Oct. 9, 1780 ; m. Moody Tenney, of Stowe.
+233. Jerusha,   b. May 26, 1783 ; m. Samuel Browne, of Sudbury.
+234. Jason,   b. Sept. 12, 1785 ;
                         m. { 1st, Asaneck Fairbank, of Framingham ;
                              { 2d, Martha Plympton, of Sudbury.

(65) ROBERT GLOVER, the eldest son of Capt. Robert Glover. The date of his birth has not been ascertained, but it is presumed he was born about 1697 or '98. He resided at one time in Boston, and was associated with the merchants of that time. He also resided for some time in the ancient Piscataqua country, near Portsmouth, N. H. He served in Queen Anne's war, under Sir William Pepperell, was in service at the taking of Cape Breton, and, as it appears, died or was killed about that time, or in 1745. He was married, and the name of his wife was Mary — whom, it seems, was a relative of the Fayerweathers of Boston, and of the Apthorps. At the time of Mr. Glover's death, or soon after, she was residing on the Island of Antigua, in the British West Indies. They had one son, viz.:

235. Robert, b. in 1720 ; went to the Island of Antigua. Was a merchant, and, it is supposed, died there.

The following letters, written from the Island of Antigua by Mrs. Mary Glover, and her son Mr. Robert Glover, in 1745–6, to Thomas Fayerweather, Esq., of Boston, comprise nearly all that has been gathered of them:

Mrs. MARY GLOVER, residing at Antigua, West Indies, to Mr. THOMAS FAYERWEATHER, merchant, at Boston, N. E.

Antigua, Feb. 5, 1745–6.

SIR,—I received your favor by my sister Frances Fayerweather, and by her recommendation have taken the liberty to write to you and enclose a power of attorney, requesting the favor of you to act for me in all my affairs, which my husband Mr. Robert Glover was concerned in ; and to take in to your hands a negro, and what other things he might have left in Boston or any other place. I likewise beg the favor of you to make enquiry of the officers which went against Cape Breton, and of the company at home, and if the same came over before the death of Mr. Glover. I understand that Mr. Glover left two negroes in hands of Mr. Sherborne, a native of Piscataqua, which he carried from home, besides the above mentioned negro he carried to wait on him at Cape Breton, which boy I understand was left in the hands of Samuel Baker, which if you get, please send to this Island. I have also been informed that one Mr. Price, a Tailor, was indebted to Mr. Glover a considerable sum, for Gold and Silver buttons, which I hope you inquired about; for Mr. Glover carried with him a large quantity. He also bought a horse in Cape Breton. Mr. Samuel Fayerweather was present when he paid the money for him. If you send the negro or Mr. Glover's effects, please have them insured. Your favor in this will infinitely oblige, Sir,

  I am your most humble and obedient Servant,

MARY GLOVER.

P. S. To Mr. Thomas Fayerweather,—Your Cousin Fanny desires you to ask Mr. Samuel Fayerweather, who can inform you about the horse which Mr. Glover paid the money for while at Cape Breton. Please to dispose of it to the best advantage. Your Cousin Fanny desires you to remember her love to her Cousin Fayerweather and family, and Miss Apthorp and Cousin Allen, and likewise Miss Tyng and family, and all acquaintances who inquire for her.

MARY GLOVER.

From ROBERT GLOVER, of Antigua, to Mr. THOMAS FAYERWEATHER, merchant, of Boston.

Antigua, March 25, 1747–8.

SIR,—My mother received yours some time ago, acquainting her that you could not receive my father's effects without Letters of Administration, which she never thought of before, and now it is too late: But as it is left between my Mother and myself, I dont suppose but the copy of the Will will be sufficient, as I have given my mother Power to act in my behalf, and desire that you would forward it as soon as possible, for lying out of the money so long is a great detriment to us both. I hope you will excuse the trouble we give you in this affair. But hope it will be in my power in a little time to serve you more largely in the mercantile way. My Mother presents her love and service to your father and family, as doth your sincere friend and servant,   ROBERT GLOVER.

P. S. I shall be glad to have a line from you by all opportunity. If you will direct to Mr. Robert Glover, living with Mr. Michael Lovell, Merchant, in Antigua. Please to send me a copy of my father's papers by the first opportunity. There is an account of two Negroes left with Mr. Sherborne, of Piscataqua.   ROBERT GLOVER.

(66) THOMAS GLOVER, the second son of Capt. Robert Glover, was born about 1700. He settled in Pembroke, Mass., and died

there in 1761, in his 61st year. Very little has been gathered of
him. His name is enrolled among a list of those who served in
Queen Anne's war, in 1745–6; but it appears he was absent from
his home in Pembroke but a short time, and was residing there at
the time of his decease in 1761.

He was married, Jan. 23, 1723, to Sarah Bonney, of Pembroke,
who was the daughter of Elisha Bonney, of that place.

Children of THOMAS and SARAH (BONNEY) GLOVER, born in Pembroke :

   236. Martha, b. July 7, 1724.
+237. Robert, b. Nov. 2, 1726 ; m. { 1st, Bethiah Tubbs, Plymouth ;
                                    { 2d, Alice Standish, Pembroke.
   238. James, b. June 15, 1728.
   239. Thomas, b. Jan. 1, 1730 ; d. Jan. 9, 1731.
+240. Thomas, b. Aug. 30, 1732.
+241. George, b. in 1735 ; m. Mary Fisher, of Plymouth.

January 11, 1758, Thomas Glover purchased twenty-eight acres
of land in Pembroke, of Thomas Little, Esq., of that place. Consideration, eleven pounds. It was bounded, according to the Plymouth Records of Deeds, " by the way leading from the Street where
John Bishop dwelt, to Jonathan Crooker's; and Northerly by the
land sold to John Bishop; South East by land of Robert Glover
which I sold to John Cunningham."

March 2, 1761, letters of administration were granted " on the
estate of Thomas Glover, late of Pembroke, deceased, to Robert
Glover, his eldest son." March 31, 1761, an inventory of the estate
was taken by Elisha Bonney, Joshua Weston and John Stetson,
which was presented by Robert Glover, April 8, of the same year,
who made oath that it was a true inventory, and that if more should
appear he would make known the same. The estate was rendered
insolvent. List of creditors notified — William Sever, Jacob Dingley, Elisha West, Ichabod Bonney, Isaac Tubbs, Percy Tilson, Micah
Lowden, widow Desire Witherell, Robert Glover, widow Abigail
Bears. Dated at Plymouth, April 5, 1762.

(69) JOHN GLOVER, Jr., eldest son of John Glover (cordwainer) and Hannah (Capen) Glover, was born in Dorchester, Oct.
17, 1715. There is no record of his baptism, his marriage or his
death. It is presumed that he was brought up with his mother's

relatives, who lived in Roxbury. He was made a legatee to the will of his aunt Sarah Capen, whom it is stated was "late of Roxbury, and who died unmarried."

Feb. 8, 1732, he chose John Capen, of Dorchester, to be his guardian, as appears by the following document. Mr. Capen accepted the trust.

Know all men by these Presents, That I John Glover, a Minor, aged about 17 years, son of John Glover, Soldier, belonging to his Majesties Castle William, in the County of Suffolk and in his Majesties Province of Massachusetts Bay in New England, have named, ordained and made, and do by these Presents put and constitute John Capen of Dorchester in the County of Suffolk, Cordwainer, to be my Guardian, with full power and authority for me and in my name and for my use, to ask, demand and sue for, recover and receive and take into his possession and custody, all and singular such part and portion of an estate accrueing to Me in Right of my Aunt Sarah Capen, late of Roxbury, Spinster, Dec^d, or which by any other way or means whatsoever belonging to me, and to manage, employ and improve the same for my best advantage and profit during my Minority. And to do all whatsoever may be necessary in and about the Premises as fully and effectually, to all intents and purposes, as I myself might or could do personally, and being of full age. Praying that he may be accordingly accepted in the same Trust and Power.

In Testimony whereof, I have hereunto set my hand and seal this 28th day of February, 1732, and in the Sixth year of his Majesty's Reign, Our Sovereign Lord George the 2d, King over Great Britain, &c. (Signed) JOHN GLOVER, and a seal.

Signed, sealed and delivered in presence of us,
      Ebenezer Williams,
      John Payne.

Feb. 28, 1732. The within named John Glover personally appearing before me, acknowledged this Instrument or Letter of Guardianship to be his free will, act and Deed, which I allow and approve.
      JOSIAH WILLARD, *Judge of Probate.*

John Capen's Guardianship Account.

The account of John Capen, late Guardian to the said John Glover a Minor, was presented to the Probate Court, Dec. 6, 1737, and is as follows :

He the accountant charges himself with a Legacy left to the said John Glover by Sarah Capen his Aunt, which he received from her Executor, amounting to Thirty-six pounds. And the said Accountant prays allowance as follows, viz. :

Paid for Letters of Guardianship,	.	.	.	.	£00 10 00 0
To the Bondsmen,	.	.	.	.	00 10 00 0
For my time and expenses in coming to Boston to take out Letters of Guardianship,		.	.	.	00 19 00 0

For my care and trouble and expenses for Four years
   more than he earned, at Five Pounds a year,   .   20 00 00 0
For drawing and allowing and recording this Account,   00 15 00 0

                                     £22 14 00 0

    Dec. 6, 1737. John Capen, Guardian, presented the foregoing
Account, and made oath that it contains a just and true account of
his Guardianship to John Glover, which I allow and approve, and
hereby order him to pay the Overplus to Mr. Samuel Lyon, of Roxbury, Uncle to the said John Glover.

    The next date which can be found of him is also in 1737, when he
was twenty-two years old. It appears he had resided in Roxbury, with
his mother's relatives, and had never become an inhabitant of Dorchester. In 1739, two years later, and when he had arrived at the
age of twenty-four years, he was residing in the latter place, and was
thus requested to give security for his permanent residence, or depart
the town:

    Suffolk ss. To Samuel Blake, one of the Constables of the Town
of Dorchester, Greeting. In his Majesty's name you are required
to give warning unto John Glover, Junior, now residing in this Town,
but is no inhabitant of this Town, that he depart out of the Town of
Dorchester within the space of fourteen days, or give security for his
longer continuance as the law directs. Hereof fail not, and make
return of this warrant and of your doings therein unto myself or to
the Selectmen as soon as convenient you may. Dated at Dorchester,
in the Thirteenth year of his Majesty's Reign, on the 14th day of
February, 1739. By the order of the Selectmen.
                                             JAMES BLAKE, *Town Clerk*.

    It is presumed he gave the required guarantee, as his name is en-
rolled among those who served at Castle William on the alarm list
of 1744, and also of 1747, and was discharged from there in 1748.
Alexander Glover received the amount due for his services, and gave
the following receipt:

    We the Subscribers do respectfully acknowledge to have received
of Samuel Blake the full amount of Our Wages and Subsistence,
money allowed us for our Service at Castle William in the time of the
Alarm in the Year 1746.   (Signed)   ALEXANDER GLOVER, for
                                        JOHN GLOVER, Jr.

    The above is the last date that has been gathered of him. At
this period he was 33 years of age. No record has been found relating to his subsequent life. There is a traditional rumor or anec-

dote, which has been passed down among the Glovers at Dorchester, that "a John Glover was residing at Newbury farm in the time of the Revolutionary War, and that during the great excitement occasioned by the Lexington alarm in 1775, he took his gun and went out to find a place of safety in the woods, but soon returned and provided himself with a ' bag of salt,' intending to subsist on game until he could get beyond the reach of the enemy; and that afterwards he went to Rhode Island and never returned." He was at that time, if living, aged 60 years, and there seems to have been then no other John Glover to whom this story could possibly relate.

(72) WILLIAM GLOVER, the third son of John and Lydia (Norcott) Glover, was born in Dorchester, Sept. 24, 1724, baptized at the Church there, Sept. 27, 1724, and died in Brookline, April 1, 1757, in his 33d year. Letters of administration were granted " on the estate of William Glover, late of Brookline, deceased, intestate," to Jonathan Davis, April 15, 1757. Inventory taken Oct. 14, 1757, by Samuel Crafts and Jonathan Winchester, Appraisers, as follows: "Bed and bed-clothes, half Dozen chairs, a child's chair, Square Table, Chest and Joynt Stools, Household Furniture and Pictures. Whole amount, Seven Pounds Eighteen Shillings (£7 18s.)."

William Glover was married in Brookline, as certified by B. F. Baker, Town Clerk in that place, to Mary Coye, Nov. 24, 1748. She survived him, and there is reason to suppose that she was married again to Isaac Harper, Feb. 12, 1769, and nothing further is known of her.

The records of the First Congregational Church in Brookline, the Rev. Cotton Brown, pastor, furnish the following baptisms of two children of William Glover:

242. Samuel, bap. May 13, 1750.
243. Anne,   bap. July 18, 1756.

No other children appear there, and Mr. Baker certifies that none are to be found recorded on the Town Records of Brookline. The above children are recorded as of William and Mary Glover. No marriages or deaths are recorded previous to 1760, and until the ministry of Rev. Joseph Jackson.

July 22, 1811, the death of a Samuel Glover is recorded thus: "Samuel Glover, at Mrs. Partridges, 24 years old, *felo-de-se.*" He was probably a son of the Samuel baptized in 1750, and grandson of William and Mary (Coye) Glover.*

(75) SAMUEL GLOVER, fourth son of John and Lydia (Norcott) Glover, was born in Dorchester, July 28, 1730, baptized Aug. 2, 1730, by Rev. John Danforth, and died at or near Albany, N. Y., in 1756. He was married to Ruth Wheat, of Needham, Sept. 28, 1752. He bought a farm in Needham, and went there to live in September, 1755, at the age of 26 years. He enlisted as a volunteer in the French and Indian war, and served in the army under Capt. Kingsbury and Col. Brinley. In the return of men's names, made July 26, 1756, page 496, Army Records, we find "Samuel Glover sick at Albany." Company mustered Oct. 11, 1756, under Capt. Stebbins and Col. Ruggles; and again on page 511, "Samuel Glover sick at Albany." In an alphabetical list of men's names in Col. Timothy Ruggles's company, is "Samuel Glover, born at Dorchester, lived last at Needham; farmer; 26 yrs old; volunteer, served at Fort Edward." His name was not reported after 1756. It is supposed by some of his descendants that he was murdered by the Indians at Greenbush, near Albany.

Children of SAMUEL and RUTH (WHEAT) GLOVER, born in Needham, Mass.

244. Thomas, b. in 1753; died in infancy.
245. Anna, b. June 26, 1755; d. Sept. 20, 1755.
+246. Samuel, b. April 25, 1756; m. Miriam Clarke, of Sturbridge.

RUTH WHEAT, the wife of Samuel Glover, was the daughter of Moses Wheat, of Needham, was born there, and died in Belchertown, Mass. She was twice married. After the death of Samuel Glover, she married Joseph Mason, of Sturbridge. Intention dated, on Town Records, Jan. 9, 1761. They were not married until April of that year. It is not known how long after their marriage they remained in Sturbridge, but they subsequently removed to Belchertown, taking with them her only son, Samuel Glover, to reside in their family.

---

* Mrs. Partridge was his patron, but whether related or not, has not been ascertained. She was Elizabeth, the daughter of John Hubbard, Esq., and widow of Capt. Samuel Partridge, and had not always resided in Brookline. In her last years she went to board with the Gooch family, and died there Jan. 6, 1814, aged 86 years.

Copy of a Marriage Contract made and signed in relation to her son, previous to the marriage of Capt. Joseph Mason with Ruth Glover.

Sturbridge, March 17, 1761. Whereas Marriage is intended between Joseph Mason and Ruth Glover, both of Sturbridge, in the County of Worcester and Province of Massachusetts Bay in New England, This may Certify that I Joseph Mason, Yeoman, do covenant, promise and engage to and with the said Ruth Glover, that after marriage, as she has therefore a desire to bring her son Samuel Glover, who is about five years of age, into my family until he be fourteen years of age, I therefore do grant her request, and do promise and engage if she the said Ruth will earnestly engage to do her endeavor of putting him out as soon as she can find a place to please her mind. And I therefore do promise and engage that I the said Joseph Mason will not act or do any thing to disturb or vex her the said Ruth Glover about disposing of this her said son while he is under my protection. And I do therefore promise and engage to allow him the necessaries of Life as I do one of my other Children, so long as he shall live with me while he is under fourteen. And if there be no great or heavy expenses, sickness or lameness, or any unforeseen accidents happen to make a great change while he the said Samuel Glover shall live with me, I do therefore promise that I will not expect any thing that belongs to him the said Samuel Glover, of his portion nor Estate, neither myself nor my heirs. And may the Good God enable us to live and maintain Love, peace and Unity.

Witness my hand,   JOSEPH MASON.

Signed, sealed and delivered in presence of
> Ebenezer Fay,
> Thankful Fay.

(77) WILLIAM RAWSON, eldest son of Capt. William and Sarah (Crosby) Rawson, and grandson of William, Esq., and Anne (Glover) Rawson, was born at Mendon, Feb. 20, 1711, and died there in 1790, aged 79 years.

May 13, 1731, he was married to Margaret, daughter of Thomas Cook, of Uxbridge. He studied Law, settled in Mendon as a lawyer, and became eminent in his profession. He had eight children.

Children of WILLIAM and MARGARET (COOK) RAWSON, born in Mendon:

247. Thomas, b. May, 1732; m. Miss Read, of Uxbridge.
248. William, b. in 1734; d. at Crown Point in 1756; was a sutler in the army there.
249. John,   b. in 1736; m. Elizabeth Bruce, of Mendon.
250. Perne,   b. Oct. 24, 1741; m. Mary Aldrich, of Mendon.
251. Edward,   b. July 25, 1744; m. Sarah Sadler, of Upton.
252. Margaret, b. May 14, 1745; d. in 1748.
253. Jonathan, b. March 16, 1749; m. Bathsheba Tracy, of Preston, Ct.
254. Margaret, b. in 1751.

26*

(79) SARAH RAWSON, the eldest daughter of Capt. William and Sarah (Crosby) Rawson, and granddaughter of William, Esq., and Anne (Glover) Rawson, of Boston and Braintree, was born in Mendon, Jan. 15, 1715, and died in Upton about 1760. She was married to a Mr. Saunders, of Upton, about 1740. They had four children, two sons and two daughters, viz.:

255. Elijah,   b. in 1741 ; m. and left children.
256. William, b. in 1743 ; m. and had a family of children.
257. Sarah,   b. in 1745 ; m. Capt. William French, of Mendon.
258. Anna,   b. in 1749 ; died young.

(83) DAVID RAWSON, the eldest son and child of David and Mary (Gulliver) Rawson, and grandson of William and Anna (Glover) Rawson, was born in Braintree, at the homestead farm of William Rawson, Esq., Sept. 14, 1714. He died in Milton, June 17, 1790, as recorded on Milton Records, aged 76 years.

He was married, about 1740, to Mary Dyer, of Weymouth, daughter of Benjamin Dyer, Esq. She died in Milton, March 19, 1780. He was a farmer, settled in Milton, and owned a homestead estate there. He was a Justice of the Peace, and served in several offices of honor in the town.

Children of DAVID, Jr., and MARY (DYER) RAWSON, born in Milton:

259. Hannah, b. May 28, 1742 ; m. John Ruggles, of Milton.
260. Eunice,   b. Dec. 3, 1743 ; m. Abner Packard, of Milton.
261. Sarah,   b. Sept. 25, 1745 ; m. James Blake, of Milton.
262. Dyer,   b. March 17, 1747 ;
                     m. { 1st, Susannah Webb, of Weymouth ;
                         { 2d, Abigail Pope, of Dorchester.
263. Rebecca, b. May 6, 1749 ; d. March 28, 1802, aged 53, unm.
264. Mary,   b. Feb. 1, 1754 ; m. Daniel French, of Milton.
265. Nathaniel, b. Feb. 7, 1757 ; d. in New York city, Dec. 11, 1780, aged 23 years.
266. Anna,   b. Aug. 21, 1758 ; m. John Young, of Milton.
267. Esther,   b. March 6, 1761 ; d. Oct. 27, 1792.

(84) JONATHAN RAWSON, the second son of David and Mary (Gulliver) Rawson, and grandson of William, Esq., and Anne (Glover) Rawson, was born at the Rawson homestead, in Braintree, Dec. 26, 1715, and died there in November, 1782, aged 67 years.

Jan. 10, 1760, he was married to Susanna Stone, of Roxbury. He settled on the homestead. His wife died in 1773.

Children of JONATHAN and SUSANNAH (STONE) RAWSON, born in Braintree:

268. Jonathan, b. Aug. 7, 1762; m. widow Mary (Pope) Houghton.
269. Stephen, b. Aug. 26, 1766; d. in Gibraltar, unm.
270. Susannah, b. Sept. 1, 1768; d. Sept. 11, 1840, aged 72.
271. Mary, b. in 1770; m. Lemuel Billings, of Quincy.
272. Hannah, b. in 1772; m. Israel Cook, of Watertown.

(85) ELIJAH RAWSON, the third son of David and Mary (Gulliver) Rawson, and grandson of William, Esq., and Anne (Glover) Rawson, of Boston and Braintree, was born at the Rawson homestead, Feb. 5, 1717, and died in Pittstown, N. Y., in 1798.

He married Mary Paddock, of Swansey, and lived a number of years in Warren, R. I. He afterwards removed to Pittstown, N. Y., and resided there until his decease. He had eight children.

Children of ELIJAH and MARY (PADDOCK) RAWSON, born in Warren, R. I.:

273. Jonathan.
274. Ann; married a Stone.
275. James.
276. Samuel; married.
277. Edward.
278. David.
279. Elijah.
280. Mary; married a Smith.

(86) MARY RAWSON, the eldest daughter of David, Esq., and Mary (Gulliver) Rawson, and granddaughter of William, Esq., and Anne (Glover) Rawson, of Boston and Braintree, was born at the Rawson homestead, in Braintree, May 20, 1718, and died in Roxbury.

In September, 1745, she was married to Joseph Winchester, of Roxbury. The names of their children were:

281. Mary.
282. William.

(90) ELIZABETH RAWSON, the fourth daughter of David, Esq., and Mary (Gulliver) Rawson, and granddaughter of William,

Esq., and Anne Glover Rawson, was born at the Rawson homestead, in Braintree, Nov. 30, 1723, and died in Braintree, now Quincy.

She was married, in 17—, to Peter Adams, of Braintree, a brother of the Rev. Jedediah Adams, of Stoughton. They had two children:

283. Peter.
284. Jedediah.

(91) JOSIAH RAWSON, fourth son of David, Esq., and Mary (Gulliver) Rawson, and grandson of William, Esq., and Anne (Glover) Rawson, was born at the Rawson homestead, Jan. 31, 1727, and died in Warwick, in 1811, aged 84 years.

Aug. 28, 1750, he was married to Hannah Bass, of Braintree, and removed to Grafton and resided there for a few years. He subsequently removed to Warwick, Mass., and lived there the remainder of his days. He was a man distinguished for his good sense and superior judgment.

Children of JOSIAH and HANNAH (BASS) RAWSON:

285. Josiah,   b. in Grafton, in 1752; lived in Richmond, Mass.
286. Simeon,   b. in   "   in 1754; died in New York.
287. Jonathan B., b. in   "   in 1755; settled in Alstead, N. H.
288. Lemuel,   b. in 1756; settled in Richfield, Ohio.
289. Anna B.,   b. in 1757; m. Thomas Leland, and went to Guilford, Ohio.
290. Abigail,   b. in 1758; m. Joshua Garfield.
291. Mary,   b. in 1759; m. David W. Leland.
292. Lydia,   b. in 1761; died in 1779, aged 18 years.
293. Betsey,   b. in 1763.
294. Hannah,   b. in 1764; died in Warwick, unmarried.
295. Amelia,   b. in 1766; m. —— Ellis, and went to Orange.
296. Secretary,   b. Sept. 19, 1773; m. Lucy Russell.

(92) JERUSHA RAWSON, the sixth daughter of David, Esq., and Mary (Gulliver) Rawson, and granddaughter of William, Esq., and Anne (Glover) Rawson, was born at the Rawson homestead, in Braintree, Sept. 21, 1729, and died in Boston.

She married Israel Eaton, of Boston, and went there to live. They had two daughters:

297. Jerusha.
298. Mercy; m. Nathaniel Glover, of Dorchester.

(94) EBENEZER RAWSON, youngest son and child of David, Esq., and Mary (Gulliver) Rawson, and grandson of William, Esq.,

and Anne (Glover) Rawson, was born at the Rawson homestead, in Braintree, May 31, 1734. The date of his death has not been ascertained. He was a farmer, and settled in Sutton, N. H.

In 1756, he married Sarah, daughter of the Hon. Samuel Chase, of Cheshire, N. H. It has been recorded of him that he was a man of "genius and of extensive historical attainments, gifted with remarkable powers of conversation, and endowed with a vein of acute irony and good humor. The peculiar bias of his mind was antiquarian, which was aided by a memory inexhaustible and retentive." He had fourteen children.

Children of EBENEZER and SARAH (CHASE) RAWSON:

299. Prudence,   b. Dec.   24, 1758.
300. Lydia,   b. April 28, 1760.
301. Ebenezer,   b. Dec.   22, 1761.
302. Sarah,   b. March 16, 1763.
303. Abner,   b. March 2, 1765.
304. John,   b. June   13, 1767.
305. Jerusha,   b. Oct.   13, 1769.
306. Samuel,   b. Sept. 4, 1771.
307. Elizabeth, b. June   5, 1774.
308. Marmaduke, }
309. Nigulia,   } b. April 18, 1777.
310. Mary,   b. July   5, 1779.
311. Clarissa,   b. Feb.   26, 1782.
312. Abigail,   b. May   11, 1786.

(96) NATHANIEL RAWSON, the second son of Nathaniel and Hannah (Tompson) Rawson, and grandson of William, Esq., and Anne (Glover) Rawson, was born in Braintree, May 27, 1716, and died in West Stockbridge, in 1803, aged 88 years.

He was twice married. First, March 17, 1737-8, to Mary Thwing; and second, to Rachael Daniels, about 1740, by whom he had eleven children, and by his first wife one, as follows:

313. Silas,   b. Nov. 17, 1739 ; settled in Palmyra, N. Y.
314. Rachael,   b. May 20, 1741 ; settled in Conway, Mass.
315. Nathaniel, b. Feb. 19, 1745 ; m. Miss Woodruff, Baker, N. Y.
316. Mary,   b. Jan. 18, 1749 ; m. —— Thwing, Conway, Mass.
317. Jonathan, b. March 17, 1751 ; m. Miss Baldwin, Victor, N. Y.
318. Moses,   b. April 26, 1753 ; m. Miss Bussey.
319. Anna,   b. Aug. 21, 1755 ; m. —— Parmely, West Stockbridge, Mass.
320. Mary,   b. Aug. 13, 1757 ; m. J. Wheeler, Grafton, Mass.
321. Elias,   b. Sept. 4, 1760 ; m.

322. Grindal, b. Jan. 22, 1762 ; m. Martha Grover, Windsor, Mass.
323. Abner,   b. Nov. 11, 1764 ; m. Mrs. Jeffards.
324. ———,   b. 1765 ; died soon.

(97) BARNABAS RAWSON, the third son of Nathaniel and
Hannah (Tompson) Rawson, was born in Mendon, Aug. 11, 1721,
and died in Woodstock, Conn.

He was married, in 1743, to Mary ———. After the birth of his
fourth child he removed to Woodstock, Conn. He had eight children,
as follows:

325. Lois,   b. Aug. 24, 1744 ; died young.
326. David,   b. Dec. 18, 1745 ; m. and settled in Woodstock, Ct.
327. Asa,   b. Nov. 10, 1748.
328. Ruth,   b. in 1749.
329. Elizabeth, b. in 1750 ; died young.
330. Lois,   b. in 1751.
331. Elizabeth, b. in 1752.
332. Josiah,   b. Dec. 18, 1753.

(98) EDWARD RAWSON, the fourth son of Nathaniel and
Hannah (Tompson) Rawson, and grandson of William, Esq., and
Anne (Glover) Rawson, was born in Mendon, April 19, 1724, and
died there.

He was married, about 1746, to Deborah Warren, of Upton. She
died in Mendon, Feb. 11, 1802. They had eight children, as follows:

333. Levi,   b. March 27, 1748 ; m. Thankful ———.
334. Olive,   b. Aug. 13, 1749 ; d. Oct. 9, 1774, aged 25 years.
335. Hannah,   b. June 22, 1751.
336. Eunice,   b. July 25, 1753.
337. Mark,   b. Jan. 31, 1757 ; d. Oct. 26, 1761.
338. Luke, } b. July   6, 1759. { d. Nov. 9, 1759.
339. Oliver, }   { d. Oct. 26, 1759. ·
340. Tompson,   b. Feb. 22, 1764 ; m. Lucy Baker Fisher, of
         Brookfield, Mass. He died in New Orleans, March 24, 1848.

(102) GRINDAL RAWSON, eldest son and child of Pelatiah
and Hannah (Hall) Rawson, and grandson of William, Esq., and
Anne (Glover) Rawson, was born in Milton, July 29, 1721; graduated at Harvard College, in Cambridge, in the class of 1741; was
installed as the first pastor of the Church in Ware, Mass., May 9,
1751, remained there about three years, and was dismissed from his
charge June 19, 1754. In 1755 he was installed at Yarmouth as the
successor of the Rev. Thomas Smith, and continued there until 1760,

when he was again dismissed. He died in Sutton, at the house of a relative, Ebenezer Rawson, in 1795.

He was married about 1756, to Desire Thacher, daughter of Col. Joseph Thacher, of Yarmouth. They had four children;

341. Ruth,   bap. Aug. 14, 1757; died in infancy.
342. Jonathan,   bap. in 1759; m. Miss Gage, Dover, N. H.
343. Jonathan Augustus, b. in 1760; d. May 17, 1794.
344. Hannah, b. May 25, 1761; m. Paul Thurston, of Medway.

[*Sixth Generation.*]

(112) ANNE GLOVER, the eldest daughter of Mr. Nathaniel and Anne (Simpson) Glover, was born in Boston, March 28, 1753, was baptized there, at the Old South Church, April 1, 1753, Rev. Thomas Prince, pastor, and died in Roxbury, August, 1797, in her 45th year.

July 11, 1776, she was married to Samuel Whitwell, Jr., of Boston, son of Samuel Whitwell, of that place. He was a merchant, and died in August, 1828.

Children of SAMUEL and ANNE (GLOVER) WHITWELL, born in Boston:

345. Nancy,   b. Feb., 1778;
               m. { 1st, Jonathan Stone, of Brunswick, Me.;
                     { 2d, Thomas K. Thomas, of Boston.
      She died in Boston, Dec., 1859, in her 82d year. No issue.
346. Catharine, b. May, 1779; d. in Roxbury, June 20, 1851, unm., aged 71 years.
347. Samuel,   b. April, 1780; d. Oct., 1781.
+348. Lucy,   b. Aug., 1781; m. Dr. Isaac Rand, of Boston.
349. Mary,   b. Feb., 1783; d. July, 1856, aged 73 years, unm.
350. Sarah,   b. Sept., 1785; d. ——, 1861, aged 77 years, unm.
351. Eliza,   b. Sept., 1787; is in her 80th year; resides in Dor.
352. William,   b. Sept., 1788; d. May, 1790.

(114) NATHANIEL GLOVER, the third son of Mr. Nathaniel and Anne (Simpson) Glover, was born in Boston, June 17, 1756, and baptized at the Old South Church, Rev. Thomas Prince, pastor, June 20, 1756. He died of yellow fever at Philadelphia, about 1790, aged 34 years, and was buried in a place called Potter's Field. He is said to have been a gentleman of rare and ingenious powers of mind, but of too delicate an organization to allow of close or continued application; of refined and cultivated taste, united with much

elegance of manners.   His father died when he was at the age of
seventeen years, and he was placed under the guardianship of John
Hancock, Esq.   He was for a time in the store with Gov. Hancock,
and engaged in mercantile pursuits.   At the age of twenty-one years
he came in possession of a competent estate, left him by the will of
his father.   Subsequently he retired from that occupation, and devoted himself to literary pursuits, wrote essays and poetry, travelled,
and became distinguished for his natural and acquired accomplishments.   In belles lettres he excelled, and in all other learning to which
he gave his attention.   He was generally admired and greatly beloved by all his relatives and friends to whom he was personally
known.   He was the fifth of the name in a direct line from Mr. Nathaniel Glover, the fourth son of the Hon. John Glover, of Boston,
and with him the name of Nathaniel Glover ceases and becomes extinct in this male line of succession.

(116) MARY GLOVER, the second daughter of Mr. Nathaniel
and Anne (Simpson) Glover, was born in Boston, Oct. 12, 1758, and
died there, April 3, 1842, aged 84 years.
     April 23, 1778, she was married to James Morrell, of Wilmington,
by Rev. Dr. Sewall, of the Old South Church.   He removed to Boston, was a member of the Chauncy Place Church, was elected a
Deacon there and officiated in that service over forty years.   He died
in Boston, April 3, 1833, aged 82 years.

     Children of Deacon JAMES and MARY (GLOVER) MORRELL, born
in Boston:

+353. Mary,   b. Feb. 20, 1779 ; m. Rev. Wilkes Allen, Chelmsford.
 354. James,   b. Aug. 30, 1780 ; d. in Boston, March 24, 1783.
+355. Anne,   b. Sept. 10, 1784 ; m. Rufus Wyman, M.D., Roxbury.
 356. Sarah,   b. Jan. 23, 1793 ; d. March 29, 1802, aged 8 years.
+357. Elizabeth, b. Jan. 20, 1796 ; m. Joseph Neal Howe, Cambridge.
 358. James,   b. Nov. 13, 1800 ; m. Pamela Smith, Ellsworth, Me.

(123) RICHARD SALTER, Jr., the eldest son of Richard and
Rachael (Glover) Salter, was born in Boston, in January, 1738, and
died there, June 14, 1803, aged 65 years.   At the age of twenty-one
years, in 1759, he succeeded to his father's homestead estate, and
became a successful and eminent merchant.   By the will of his grandmother, Mrs. Rachael Glover, he was to receive the sum of one hun-

dred pounds, old tenor, when he had attained the age of twenty-one years, and, as it appears, he was sole heir to his father's estate. He died intestate, and his estate was administered on by John Heard, Esq. Rufus G. Amory, Esq., and James Morrell, merchant, both of Boston, became bound with the administrator for the faithful performance of said trust, as attested on the Probate Records by Perkins Nichols, Register. Inventory taken and appraised by Azor G. Archibald, Samuel H. Flagg, and Stephen Howe. Amount of property, $806.85.

April 13, 1762, at the age of twenty-four years, he was married to Jane Carnes, of Boston, by Rev. Charles Chauncy, D.D. Their children were as follows:

+359. Jane, b. Aug. 7, 1763 ; m. Joseph Ingraham, of Boston.
  360. Rachel, b. 1768 ; married.
+361. John, b. April 13, 1770 ; m. Elizabeth Rice, of Boston, June 24, 1798.
  362. Richard, b. Sept. 21, 1779 ; m. Sarah Appleton, Nov. 29, 1801, by Rev. Samuel Stillman, D.D.

(127) NATHANIEL GLOVER, the eldest son of Alexander and Sarah (White) Glover, was born at the Dorchester homestead, March 15, 1735, baptized March 20, 1735, by Rev. Jonathan Bowman, and died in Dorchester, of lung fever, March 7, 1770, in his 34th year. He was buried in the ancient cemetery there, and has a gravestone.

In 1755 he was married to Mehetable Hill, daughter of John and Mehetable Hill. They lived on the upper road, near the spot now occupied as a tin shop by Mr. Charles P. Tolman. They were members of the Church—admitted to full communion, Dec. 21, 1756. Their children were all baptized in Dorchester.

Nathaniel Glover was a landholder. He owned a homestead, woodland, and other lands. He died intestate. Letters of administration were granted to Mehetable Glover, his widow, May 18, 1770.

Mrs. Mehetable Glover was married a second time, January 10, 1774, to Ezekiel Tilestone, Esq., of Dorchester, by Joseph Williams, Esq., of Roxbury, and removed to Boston. There were two children by this marriage. She died in Boston, September 17, 1720, and was buried there, in the Tilestone tomb. He was the second son of Timothy Tilestone, Esq., of Dorchester, and was born there. He was thrice married. First, to Sarah ——, who died Jan. 9,

27

and was buried Jan. 12, 1766. He was married, second, to Anna
Evans. Intention, Aug. 23, 1767. She died in Dorchester, and was
buried Feb. 4, 1772. He was married the third time, Jan. 10, 1774,
to Mrs. Mehetable (Hill) Glover, widow of Mr. Nathaniel Glover, of
Dorchester, who survived him. He died in Boston. The Boston
Centinel says of him: "Died in Boston, on Sunday morning, April
26, 1799, Mr. Ezekiel Tilestone, formerly of Dorchester. The funeral will be from his house in Middle street." There were two children by this last marriage: Jane Hill, baptized at Dorchester Church,
Dec. 11, 1774, married a Whittemore, and went to New York to live;
William, baptized 1778, also at Dorchester, lives in Boston.

Children of NATHANIEL and MEHETABLE (HILL) GLOVER, born in
Dorchester:

+363. Nathaniel, b. Jan. 2, bap. Jan. 4, 1756; m. Mercy Eaton.
+364. John Hill, b. Feb. 25, bap. Feb. 27, 1757; m. Mary Osborne,
   of Danvers.
+365. Mary,   b. March 5, bap. March 11, 1759; m. George Vose,
   of Dorchester.
+366. Sarah,   b. June 6, bap. June 9, 1760; m. Richard Jenkins,
   of Boston.
+367. Alexander, b. Nov. 11, bap. Nov. 15, 1761; m. Nancy Sprung,
   of New York.
+368. William, b. May 3, bap. May 6, 1763; d. Jan. 25, 1774, in
   Boston, and brought to Dorchester to be buried.
 369. Edward, b. Nov. 1, bap. Nov. 8, 1765; d. Nov. 16, 1766.
 370. Jane Hill, b. April 1, bap. April 24, 1768; d. in Boston, and
   brought to Dorchester to be buried, Sept. 3, 1769.

(128) SARAH GLOVER, the second daughter of Alexander
and Sarah (White) Glover, was born at the Dorchester homestead,
March 4, 1737, baptized at the Dorchester Church, March 8, 1737,
Rev. Jonathan Bowman, pastor, and died in Dorchester, Oct. 16,
1796, in her 60th year.

Dec. 3, 1760, she was married to Ephraim Mann, of Boston, and
removed there. He died at Dorchester Neck, Sept. 23, 1803. He
served in the French and Indian War. His named is enrolled on a
list dated May 20, 1756—Jonathan Fessenden, Lieut.; Edward Glover, of Milton, Ensign. They had four children:

 371. Sarah,   b. June 4, 1761; m. Aaron Spear.
 372. Mary,   b. Jan. 6, 1763; m. Moses Marshall.
 373. Ephraim, b. Dec., 1764.
 374. William, b. Jan. 11, 1766; m. Sarah ———.

(129) PATIENCE GLOVER, the third daughter of Alexander and Sarah (White) Glover, was born in Dorchester, Jan. 23, 1739, and died there April 4, 1804, in her 66th year.

She married Jonathan Leeds, of Dorchester, Dec. 15, 1763.

Children of JONATHAN and PATIENCE (GLOVER) LEEDS, born in Dorchester :

+375. Elizabeth, b. in 1765 ; m. Dea. Nathaniel Topliff, Dorchester.
376. Patience, b. in 1768 ; d. Jan. 9, 1770.
377. Edward,   b. in 1769 ; d. Jan. 11, 1771.
378. Patience, b. in 1770 ; m. { 1st, Thomas White ; 2d, Enos Withington.
379. Hopestill, b. Dec. 22, 1773 ; d. Jan. 12, 1774.
380. Alexander, b. Jan. 19, 1775 ; went West, and died unmarried.
+381. James,   b. June 27, 1777 ; m. Anna Corey, of Brookline.
382. Jonathan, b. in 1778 ; went to the State of New York, and died there, unmarried.
+383. Mary,   b. in 1780 ; m. Elijah Corey, of Brookline.

(130) ALEXANDER GLOVER, the second son of Alexander and Sarah (White) Glover, was born in Dorchester, Feb. 1, 1741, and died there, July 13, 1813, in his 73d year. He succeeded his father in the possession of the Dorchester homestead, formerly belonging to John Glover, Esq., of Dorchester and Boston; and was the fifth in the direct line of succession from him. He was engaged in the lumber trade for many years. He was an honorable and worthy citizen, inheriting the virtues and noble traits which characterized his ancestors; was of a mild and genial temperament, upright and honest.

He was married to Hannah Pope, of Stoughton, Dec. 28, 1769, by Rev. Jedediah Adams. She was the daughter of Dr. Ralph and Rebeckah (Stubbs) Pope, of Stoughton, and was born there June 1, 1744; she died in Dorchester, Sept. 28, 1825, in her 82d year. Her Pope lineage was, first, John Pope, of Dorchester, who by his wife Margaret had Ralph, who married Rachel Neale, of Braintree, and was her second American ancestor. Dr. Ralph Pope was their son. (See Pope Genealogy.)

Children of ALEXANDER and HANNAH (POPE) GLOVER, born in Dorchester :

+384. Alexander, b. Nov. 19, 1770 ; m. Jemima Tolman, Dorchester.

385. Hannah,   b. Aug. 23, 1772; d. unm., Aug. 22, 1794, aged 22.
386. Rebekah,   b. March 23, 1775; d. Feb. 22, 1776, aged 10 years
     and 11 months.
+387. Oliver,   b. June 15, 1777; m. Lydia Barrett Lewis, of
     Marblehead.
+388. Abigail,   b. June 21, 1781; m. Joseph Lemmon Lewis, of
     Marblehead.
+389. James,   b. Jan. 21, 1785; m. Jane Beale, of Dorchester.

(131) EDWARD GLOVER, the third son of Alexander and
Sarah (White) Glover, was born in Dorchester, May 21, 1743, and
died there Sept. 13, 1804, in his 62d year.

He was married to Hannah Fifield, Aug. 11, 1767, and succeeded
his father in the occupation of a portion of the homestead.

Children of EDWARD and HANNAH (FIFIELD) GLOVER, born in Dorchester:

+390. Edward,   b. Dec. 8, 1767; m. Hannah Howe, of Dorchester.
+391. Hannah,   b. Aug. 13, 1771; m. Nathaniel Clap, Dorchester.
+392. Mary,   b. Dec. 1, 1773; m. Bela Hearsey, of Dorchester.
+393. Lewis,   b. June 26, 1776; m. Anne Brazer, of Boston.
+394. Elizabeth, b. Jan. 6, 1781; m. Zerubbabel Hearsey, Dorchester.
+395. Samuel,   b. Nov. 6, 1785; died, unm., in New York; was a
     merchant there.

(132) RACHAEL GLOVER, the fourth daughter of Alexander
and Sarah (White) Glover, was born in Dorchester, Oct. 8, 1745,
and died there June 1, 1811, aged 65 years.

She was married to John Howe, Esq., of Dorchester, Nov. 29,
1764, and resided, after her marriage, near what is now called Savin
Hill in that town. They had seven children. He was the son of
Samuel and Elizabeth (Clap) Howe, of Dorchester, and was born
there Jan. 30, 1739–40. He was elected and served as a Representative of the town of Dorchester to the General Court, in the years
1790, 1791, and some years after. Hon. John Howe died in Dorchester, Sept. 22, 1818, aged 77 years.

Children of JOHN and RACHAEL (GLOVER) HOWE, born in Dorchester:

+396. John, b. Sept. 4, 1765; m. { 1st, Martha Bird;
                                   { 2d, Elizabeth Heath, Brookline.
397. Elizabeth, b. May 20, 1767; d. July 27, 1845, aged 78 yrs., unm.

+398. George,   b. July 6, 1769; m. Mary Anne Holden, Dorchester.
  399. Rachel,   b. Aug. 25, 1771; died in infancy.
+400. Rachel,   b. Aug. 19, 1773; m. James Robinson, Dorchester.
+401. Joseph,   b. Sept. 23, 1776; m. Lucy Hunt, of Weymouth.
+402. James,   b. Jan. 28, 1781; m. Elizabeth Clap, Dorchester.

(134) ABIGAIL GLOVER, the sixth daughter of Alexander and Sarah (White) Glover, was born in Dorchester, Oct. 14, 1750, and died there Oct. 3, 1775, in her 25th year.

She was married Oct. 3, 1772, to Joseph Clap, Jr., of Dorchester, son of Joseph and Abigail Clap, and was born in Dorchester. They had two children:

  403. Joseph, b. Aug. 10, 1774; m. Betsey Tilestone, Dorchester.
  404. Abigail Glover, b. Sept. 26, 1775; m. Ebenezer Clap, Jr.

Joseph Clap married the second time, Nov. 14, 1776, Abigail Humphreys, and had nine more children.

(135) MARY GLOVER, the seventh daughter of Alexander and Sarah (White) Glover, was born in Dorchester, June 24, 1753, and died there Jan. 18, 1830, aged 77 years.

Sept. 10, 1776, she was married to Jonathan Pierce, of Dorchester, who died there Dec. 21, 1830. They had seven children, born in Dorchester:

+405. Jonathan, b. Oct. 11, 1777; m. { 1st, Eunice Tolman; 2d, Clarissa Blake, Dorch.
  406. Jerusha,   b. Oct. 11, 1777, twin to the above; d. in infancy.
+407. Daniel,   b. Aug. 4, 1779; m. Lydia Davenport, Dorchester.
+408. Mary, b. Nov. 2, 1781; m. Stephen Tolman, of Dorchester.
+409. Alexander, b. Aug. 7, 1783; m. Margaret C. H. Spear, Dorch.
  410. Sarah, b. Oct. 2, 1787; d. June 6, 1828, aged 58 years, unm.
  411. Elisha, b. Sept. 11, 1792; d. June 8, 1839, aged 52 years, unm.

(136) RACHAEL GLOVER, the eldest daughter of Pelatiah and Mary (Cochrane) Glover, was born in Boston, Aug. 14, 1741, and died in Boston, Sept. 17, 1797, aged 56 years.

She was married to William Blake, merchant, of Boston, Nov. 29, 1767. They resided in Orange street. He was lineally descended from the first William Blake, of Dorchester, and was born there in 1740. He died in Boston, and is thus noticed in the Independent Chronicle: "William Blake, Esq., died on Saturday morning, June

27*

20, 1797, aged 52 years; funeral from his late dwelling house in Orange street."

Children of WILLIAM, Esq., and RACHAEL (GLOVER) BLAKE, born in Boston:

412. William Pynson, b. Jan. 9, 1769; d. at New York, June 5, 1820, aged 51 years, unmarried.
+413. Elizabeth, b. Sept. 15, 1771; d. Nov. 25, 1835, in her 65th year, unmarried.
414. Henry, b. Feb. 17, 1774; d. June 8, 1776.
+415. Lemuel, b. Aug. 9, 1775; d. in Boston, March 4, 1861, aged 86 years, unmarried.
416. Henry, b. Jan. 18, 1777; d. Nov. 4, 1777.

(137) ELIZABETH GLOVER, the second daughter of Pelatiah and Mary (Cochrane) Glover, was born in Boston, Oct. 19, 1742, and died in Dorchester, Aug. 12, 1827, aged 85 years. She was unmarried. After the decease of her father, she boarded in the family of the Hon. John Howe, in Dorchester, and kept, for several years, a private school. Later in life she boarded with Mrs. Cyrus Bolkum, in whose family she died. She was a member of the First Church in Dorchester, Rev. T. M. Harris, pastor, and was highly esteemed by him as an upright, truthful and conscientious christian woman, of whom he always spoke in terms of regard.

(138) MICAJAH POPE, the eldest son of Lazarus and Susannah (Glover) Pope, was born in Stoughton, June 6, 1741, and died in Quincy, about the year 1800.

April 4, 1767, he was married to Sarah Whitney, of Braintree.

Children of MICAJAH and SARAH (WHITNEY) POPE, born in Quincy:

417. John.
418. Martha Fletcher, b. Nov. 1, 1787; m. Anthony Hunt, of Weymouth.

(139) RALPH POPE, the second son of Lazarus and Susannah (Glover) Pope, was born in Stoughton, Oct. 1, 1742, and died there in 1790, aged 48 years.

Jan. 1, 1771, he was married to Hannah Gay, of Stoughton, daughter of David and Hannah (Talbot) Gay. He succeeded to the homestead estate of his father, which at his decease was sold by his heirs to Capt. Roger Sumner, who owned and occupied it until his decease, when it was passed to his heirs.

Children of RALPH and HANNAH (GAY) POPE, born in Stoughton:

419. Joseph, b. Oct. 4, 1771 ; m. Elizabeth Tower, of Randolph.
420. Micajah, b. May 5, 1774; m. widow Lucinda Howard.
421. Nancy, b. June 12, 1776 ; m. Joshua Wilder, of Randolph.
422. Ralph, b. Feb. 18, 1779 ; m. Ruth Tower, of Randolph.
423. Lemuel, b. Oct. 12, 1781 ; m. Elizabeth Clark, of Quincy.

(140) SUSANNAH POPE, the eldest daughter of Lazarus and Susannah (Glover) Pope, was born in Stoughton, Dec. 27, 1744, and died in Boston, April 13, 1822, in her 78th year.

She was twice married. First, Oct. 5, 1767, to Capt. Joseph Farrington, of Boston. They had two daughters. May 30, 1781, she was married, a second time, to Dr. Peter St. Medard, a French physician. He was born in Rochelle, in France, in 1755, and died in Boston, March 28, 1822, aged 66 years. He came to Boston in the early part of the War of the Revolution, and was employed as a Surgeon in the United States Navy. After the war he settled in Boston, attended to his profession as physician and surgeon, and had a successful practice. He held a high rank among the profession of that time, as a distinguished physician and surgeon.

Children of Capt. JOSEPH and SUSANNAH (POPE) FARRINGTON, born in Boston:

424. Susannah, b. in 1768 ; d. Dec. 7, 1824, aged 56 years.
+425. Sarah, b. June 4, 1770 ; m. Mammy Masson, of Dijon, France.

Children by Dr. PETER ST. MEDARD, born in Boston:

426. Peter, b. May 21, 1782 ; d. Dec. 24, 1813, aged 31 years ;
      Lieut. U. S. Artillery.
427. George, b. April 23, 1784 ; d. Aug. 12, 1788.
428. Samuel, b. Sept. 18, 1785 ; d. April 13, 1787

(141) LAZARUS POPE, Jr., the third son of Lazarus and Susannah (Glover) Pope, was born in Stoughton, Jan. 19, 1747, and died there March 10, 1802, aged 55 years. He was buried in the ancient burial ground, and has a gravestone.

He was married about 1778, to Mary Swan, widow of Rufus Spurr.

She survived him, and died Sept. 28, 1808, aged 60 years.   He lived on a farm at the southerly part of Stoughton, adjoining Easton. The house is now removed, and the farm owned by Mr. Marshall.

Children of LAZARUS and MARY (SWAN) POPE, born in Stoughton:

429. Mary,   b. in 1778 ; d. Dec. 25, 1846, unmarried.
430. Susannah, b. in 1780 ; d. in Dorchester, April 12, 1812, unm.
431. Lazarus,   b. in 1782 ; m. Elizabeth Talbot, of Stoughton.
432. Ebenezer,   b. in 1784 ; died young.
433. Sarah,   b. in 1787 ; d. March 15, 1812, aged 25 years, unm.
434. Abigail,   b. in 1788 ; m. Isaac Washburn, No. Bridgewater.
435. Jerusha,   b. in 1789 ; m. Ichabod Holbrook, of Randolph.
436. Thomas,   b. in 1792 ; m. Tiley Holmes, of Stoughton.
437. Otis,   b. in 1794 ; m. Eliza Hutchins, of Maine.

(142)   JERUSHA POPE, the second daughter of Lazarus, Sen., and Susannah (Glover) Pope, was born in Stoughton, April 18, 1749, and died in Canton in 1840.

She was twice married.   First, Dec. 11, 1773, to Philip Marchant, of Boston, and went there to live.   She was a member of the Church in Stoughton, Rev. Jedediah Adams, pastor, and was received by letter from that Church and admitted to join the First Church in Boston, March 26, 1775.   They had one son born in Boston, and baptized there at the First Church, viz.:

438. John, b. in 1775 ; m. widow Mary (Remington) Skinner.

After the death of Mr. Philip Marchant, she removed to Stoughton, and was married, a second time, to Samuel Bisbee, in 1783.   They had six children, born in Bridgewater:

439. Elisha,   b. in 1784 ; m. Eliza Wade, of Easton.
440. Mary,   b. in 1786 ; m. Lewis Drake, of Canton.
441. Jerusha,   b. in 1791 ; m. Zenas Gardiner, of Canton.
442. Nancy,   b. in 1792 ; died in Canton, unmarried.
443. Susannah, b. in 1796 ; died young, unmarried.
444. Hannah,   b. in 1800 ; m. Solomon Drake, of Canton.

SAMUEL BISBEE, the second husband of Jerusha Pope, was born in West Bridgewater, March 29, 1757, and died in Canton, May 28, 1845 ; he was buried in Stoughton, and has a gravestone.

He served in the Revolutionary War, and was enrolled under Gen. Washington's command at Long Island, White Plains, Trenton and Germantown.

(143) MARY GLOVER, the eldest daughter of John and Elizabeth (Bill) Glover, was born in Bristol, R. I., about 1743. The date
of her death has not been ascertained.

She was married, about 1770, to Caleb Turner, and nothing further
has been reported of her or her family.

(144) REBECKAH GLOVER, the second daughter of John
and Elizabeth (Bill) Glover, was born in Bristol, R. I., in 1745, and
died there Jan. 19, 1819, aged 74 years.

Oct. 20, 1771, she was married to James Nooning, of Bristol, by
the Rev. James Burt, pastor of the Catholic Congregational Church
in that town. They had six children, as follows:

445. Timothy, b. April 25, 1772 ; lost at sea, Dec., 1811, aged 39.
446. Sarah, b. Aug. 22, 1775 ; d. Sept. 10, 1854, aged 79 yrs., unm.
447. Mary,   b. July 15, 1779 ; d. Nov. 28, 1828, aged 44 years.
448. Rebecca, b. Oct. 26, 1781 ; d. April 27, 1794, aged 13 years.
+449. Jonathan, b. Aug. 1, 1784 ; m. Hannah Talbee, of Bristol.
450. James,   b. Oct. 22, 1785 ; d. March 28, 1856, aged 71 years,
        unmarried.

(145) JONATHAN GLOVER, only son of John and Elizabeth
(Bill) Glover, was born in Bristol, R. I., in 1746, and died in Amenia, N. Y., in 1788, aged 42 years.

A letter received from Charles M. Benjamin, Esq., of Amenia,
states that Jonathan Glover came to that place from Bristol, R. I.,
and resided in the family of a Mr. Peck. He was in delicate health ;
he labored on Mr. Peck's farm ; was never married ; was never taxed
or elected to any office while a resident there. He died in the family
of Mr. Peck, leaving no property, and was buried in that town.

(146) ELIZABETH GLOVER, daughter of Joseph and Elizabeth (Bass) Glover, was born in Quincy, Sept. 7,* 1750, and died in
Boston, Nov. 25, 1825, aged 75 years.

She was twice married. First, to Benjamin Greenwood, of Boston, who died soon after, leaving no children. She was married,
second, to Thomas Caldwell, of Ipswich, May 1, 1787, and went there
to live. They had two daughters.

Children of THOMAS and ELIZABETH (GLOVER) CALDWELL, born in
Ipswich :

* Family Bible of Dr. Simeon Palmer. Town Records say April 2, 1749–50.

451. Susannah, b. June 16, 1788 ; m. Ezra Palmer, of Boston.
452. Mary,   b. Sept. 19, 1790 ; m. Simeon Palmer, of Boston.

(147) SUSANNAH GLOVER, daughter of Joseph and Elizabeth (Bass) Glover, was born in Braintree (now Quincy), Oct. 8,
1750–1, and died in Boston.

She was married to Gershom Thomas, of Boston, Jan. 3, 1771, by
Rev. Dr. Lathrop.   She resided, after her marriage, in what was then
Back street, now Salem street, Boston.

Children of GERSHOM and SUSANNAH (GLOVER) THOMAS, born in
Boston:

453. Mary, b. in 1772 ; m. Capt. Edward Tyler, of Boston; died
     in Boston.
454. Susan, b. in 1774 ; m. Capt. Edward Tyler, Boston ; no issue.
455. Elizabeth, b. in 1775 ; m. Benjamin Russell, Boston, printer.
456. Joseph Glover, b. in 1776 ; mariner ; killed by Indians ; unm.

(148) CATHARINE GLOVER, the third daughter of Capt.
Joseph and Elizabeth (Bass) Glover, was born in Braintree, and baptized there Oct. 16, 1752–3.   She died in Bristol, R. I., Jan. 14,
1803, aged 51 years.

Nov. 19, 1780, she was married to Benjamin Wardwell, Esq., of
Bristol, and went there to reside.   He was the son of Benjamin
Wardwell, Esq., of that place, who was born there in 1758, and died
Feb. 28, 1830, aged 72 years.

Children of BENJAMIN and CATHARINE (GLOVER) WARDWELL, born
in Bristol, R. I. :

457. Mary,   b. Oct.   4, 1781 ; d. Oct. 12, 1781.
458. Mary,   b. Aug. 30, 1783 ; d. Sept. 23, 1783.
+459. Benjamin, b. Aug. 24, 1784 ; m. Elizabeth Manchester, Bristol.
460. Mary,   b. Aug. 13, 1785 ; d. Aug. 7, 1787.
461. William,   b. Oct.   4, 1786 ; d. Sept. 22, 1787.
462. Henry,   b. April 7, 1789 ; d. Oct. 12, 1789.
463. Mary,   b. Oct. 24, 1791 ; m.
464. Catharine, b. July   8, 1793 ; d. April 1, 1863 ; aged 70 years.

(149) HANNAH GLOVER, fourth daughter of Capt. Joseph
and Elizabeth (Bass) Glover, was born in Braintree (now Quincy),
and baptized at the Church there in 1755.   She died in Killingly,
Conn., since 1800.

In 1780 she was married to James Brown, of Killingly, and went there to reside. Before her marriage she resided in the family of Mr. Oliver Billings, of Dorchester, who was her guardian. She had two children, a son and daughter:

465. Jeremiah, b. in 1782; d. in 1804, at Swansey, aged 22 years.
466. Ann Dorinda, b. in 1784; m. George Larned, of Killingly, Ct.

(150) MARY GLOVER, the fifth daughter of Capt. Joseph and Elizabeth (Bass) Glover, was born in Braintree, Dec. 4, 1757, baptized there Dec. 5, 1757, and died in Roxbury, at the house of her brother-in-law, Mr. William May.

July 9, 1787, she was married to Ebenezer Hemenway, of Boston. They had no children.

(151) MARGARET GLOVER, the sixth daughter of Capt. Joseph and Elizabeth (Bass) Glover, was born in Braintree, Jan. 20, baptized Oct. 26, 1760, and died in Roxbury, in 1819, aged 58 years.

Oct. 16, 1788, she was married to William May, born in England. He came to the United States soon after the close of the Revolutionary War, in 1783, and settled in Roxbury. He was the first person who set up the business of manufacturing house paper in New England. Among those to whom he communicated the art, was Josiah Bumstead, of Boston, who succeeded Mr. May, at his decease, in carrying on the business of paper manufacturing. He owned a house and land in Roxbury, and died possessed of a competent estate. The house is still standing. A portion of the land bears the name of "May's Woods." He died in Roxbury, March 3, 1859, aged 69 years.

Children of WILLIAM and MARGARET (GLOVER) MAY, born in Roxbury:

+467. Maria, b. Jan. 1, 1790; m. Charles Carroll, of Roxbury.
+468. Joseph, b. May 10, 1791; m. Harriet Bird, of Dorchester.
469. William, b. in 1794.
470. John Glover, b. Dec. 4, 1796; d. Feb. 15, 1798.
471. Henry Burbeck, b. Dec. 29, 1799.

(152) JANE GLOVER, seventh daughter of Capt. Joseph and Elizabeth (Bass) Glover, was born in Braintree, Oct. 16, 1762, and died at Quincy Point, at the house of her son, James Newcomb, March 22, 1845, aged 83 years.

Aug. 2, 1783, she was married to Bryant Newcomb, who was born in Braintree, in 1762, and died there. He served in the War of the Revolution; was taken prisoner by the British and carried to Dartmoor prison, with several others from Quincy. They were confined there until they obtained their release through the influence of Mrs. Adams, the wife of President John Adams, he being at that time Minister to the Court of St. James.

Children of BRYANT and JANE (GLOVER) NEWCOMB, born in Quincy or Braintree:

472. Charlotte,   b. Jan.   4, 1785.
473. James,   b. Nov.   6, 1786; m.   { 1st, —— Baxter;
                                             { 2d, —— Baxter.
474. George,   b. Dec.   10, 1787.
475. Jesse,   b. Nov.   2, 1789.
476. Louisa,   b. Sept. 17, 1791.
477. Isaac, b. March 15, 1794; m. Caroline (Glover) Dwelle, a cousin.
478. Bryant Bass, b. Jan. 22, 1796; m. Louisa Hardwick.
479. Jane,   b. April 17, 1798; m. Elisha Turner, of Quincy.
480. Lewis,   b. July 17, 1800.

(154) JERUSHA BURBECK, eldest daughter of Col. William and Jerusha (Glover) Burbeck, was born in Boston, June 12, 1751, baptized at Christ Church, June 16, 1751, and died in Boston.

April 30, 1780, she was married to Capt. John Cathcart. They had no children. His father was a Scotchman, and resided in Boston. He was a shipmaster, and made foreign voyages. The following account is gathered from a letter addressed to Mr. John Adams, Minister to the Court of Great Britain, written by his wife, under date of Dec. 9, 1781, and is copied from vol. i., page 166, of her published letters:

"Capt. Cathcart, Commander of the Privateer Essex, from Salem, went out on a cruise last April, and was on the 10th of June so unfortunate as to be taken while cruising in the English Channel, and carried to Ireland. The officers were all confined there, but the sailors were sent prisoners to Plymouth jail, twelve of whom were from this town (Quincy), a list of whom I enclose. The friends of these people have received intelligence, by way of an officer who belonged to the Protector, and who escaped from the jail, that in August last they were all alive, but several of them were very destitute of clothing, having taken out few with them, and those for summer—particularly Ned Saville and Job Field, Josiah Bass and Bryant Newcomb. Their request is that you would render them assistance. Capt. Cathcart got home about three months ago, by escaping to France."

Dated at Quincy, Dec. 9, 1781, and endorsed by Mrs. Adams.

He died at sea. The Boston Record says—May, 1776, "Capt. John Cathcart died on a voyage to the East Indies, suddenly."

He was twice married. After the decease of Jerusha Burbeck he married, second, a Miss Sigourney, of Boston. There were no children by this marriage. After the death of Capt. Cathcart, his widow married Judge Hammatt.

(156) **HENRY BURBECK,** son of Col. William and Jerusha (Glover) Burbeck, was born in Boston, June 8, and baptized at Christ Church (Episcopal), June 9, 1754. He died in New London, Conn., Oct. 2, 1848, in his 95th year; he was buried there, with military honors.

He was twice married. First, in 1790, to Abigail Webb, of Bath, Maine, who lived but a few months, and died July 9, 1790. He married, a second time, Lucy E. Rudd, widow of Capt. Henry Caldwell, of the U. S. Marine Corps, and had the following children :

481. Susan Henrietta, b. Sept. 23, 1815 ; m. Lieut. Epaphras Kibby, of U. S. A., June 9, 1835, and died Sept. 15, 1839, aged 24 years. He died Sept. 30, 1840 ; buried with military honors.
482. Charlotte Augusta, b. March 8, 1818 ; resides in New London.
483. Henry William, b. May 31, 1819 ; d. Feb. 19, 1840, aged 21.
484. Mary Elizabeth, b. March 7, 1821 ; m. Chandler Smith, N. Y.
485. William Henry, b. Oct. 3, 1823 : resides in New York.
486. John Cathcart, b. Feb. 1, 1826 ; resides in New London, Ct.

The following account of incidents connected with the life and death of Gen. Burbeck, appeared in the Daily Chronicle, of New London, Ct., Oct. 28, 1848:

"The funeral of this venerable and distinguished officer was attended yesterday afternoon by a deputation from the Cincinnati of Massachusetts, of which the deceased was President, by the Mayor and Common Council of this city, by several officers of the Army, Judge Wayne of the Supreme Court, and by a large concourse of our citizens. The body was borne from the residence of the late General, by a detachment of the 3d Artillery from Fort Trumbull, and half hour guns were fired at that Post from 12 o'clock to the time of interment. The services in the Church were performed by the Rev. Mr. Hallam, Rector, assisted by the Rev. Mr. Baury, of Massachusetts, who was one of the committee of the Cincinnati, deputed to attend the funeral."

" At a meeting of the Society of the Cincinnati of Massachusetts, at the United States Hotel, Boston, on the 3d day of October, 1848, the melancholy tidings having been received of the decease of Gen. Burbeck, their President, which took place yesterday morning at his residence in New London, Ct., at the advanced age of nearly ninety-five years, the following resolutions were unanimously adopted :

" *Whereas*, The meritorious military services of General Burbeck during the War of the Revolution, and during a large portion of his life, are held in high estimation, while his honorable and exemplary conduct, as a citizen, has won the eminent regard and attachment of those who have enjoyed his acquaintance ; gratefully acknowledging the kind and merciful Providence by which his life has been extended to the latest term allotted to mortality, and deeply deploring the loss which this Society has sustained in its cherished and honored President, and anxious to evince the respect it entertains for his virtues—

" *Resolved*, That Gen. Henry A. S. Dearborn, Robert G. Shaw, Thomas Jackson, Elijah Vose, Charles S. Davies, Adams Bailey, Henry K. Hancock, Rev. Alfred S. Baury, Rev. Eleazer M. P. Wells and William Perkins, be a Committee to visit New London to attend the funeral of General Burbeck to-morrow afternoon, and at the same time to communicate to his bereaved family its expression of the deep and sincere sympathy of this Society in an event which has brought grief and sorrow into his mourning household.

" *Resolved*, That this expression be communicated to the family of the deceased by the hands of the Secretary.

" THOMAS JACKSON, Secretary.   H. A. S. DEARBORN, Chairman."

" Much of the early part of Gen. Burbeck's life was spent at Castle William, now Fort Independence, in Boston Harbor, his father being an officer of the Ordnance Department in the service of Great Britain.   His father promptly took part with the popular cause, and entered into the service of his country at the breaking out of the War of the Revolution.   He also, having just attained his majority, joined the American army ; and his first commission as Lieutenant in a company of which his father had command, is dated at Cambridge, 10th of May, 1775, and is signed by Gen. Joseph Warren.   This commission ranks among the earliest in the American service.   He received the commission of Captain in the Regiment of Artillery of the Massachusetts line, the 11th of September, 1777, and continued in that regiment and line until the close of the war.   In the toils and sufferings of the Revolution, Gen. Burbeck bore a full share.   In 1775, he was with the army at Cambridge, Mass.   In 1776, he was employed in the vicinity of New York, until the evacuation of the city in September; and in 1777 he joined the army in Pennsylvania under Gen. Washington ; was in the battles of Brandywine and Germantown, and in the terrible deprivations and sufferings of the winter at Valley Forge. He shared the perils of the memorable retreat through New Jersey, and was present at the battle of Monmouth.   He continued in active service until the close of the war in 1783 ; and when the army was disbanded, he returned to private life with the brevet rank of Major.

" Three years subsequently he again entered the service of his country with the rank of Captain, and was for several years actively engaged in the Indian Wars along the Western frontier under General

Anthony Wayne. His death has left Gen. Solomon Van Rensselaer the only surviving officer of Wayne's army. Four years he held the command of Fort Mackinaw, then a solitary Post, almost entirely cut off from all communication with the civilized world.

"In the war with Great Britain, which commenced in 1812, he commanded at New York, Newport, New London and Greenbush, with the rank of Brigadier General; and, on the declaration of peace, in 1815, he retired from public service to spend the evening of his days in the tranquillity of domestic life, having spent thirty-eight years, almost incessantly, in active military service.

"Gen. Burbeck was one of the original members of the Society of Cincinnati, and was the last survivor of those whose names were first subscribed to the articles of that Association. At the time of his decease he was President of the Cincinnati of Massachusetts.

"Few men live so long as Gen. Burbeck, and to still fewer is long life so great a blessing. Blessed with a sound mind in a sound body, with an attentive and affectionate family, and the respect and confidence of his fellow citizens, his years glided calmly and happily away. A man of war from his youth, he was characterized by a soldier's sincerity and freedom. He had a heart without malice and without guile. All who knew him, knew a man of sterling honesty and openhearted truth, without disguise and without pretension. A shrewd observer of men and things, he uttered his opinion of them without reserve or ceremony; yet in a spirit so devoid of acrimony or unkindness, as seldom to give pain or excite displeasure. His mental faculties knew no decay, but remained, till within a short time of his death, as fresh, sprightly and active as they were in the days of his youth. With a memory remarkably retentive and minute, looking back upon a past rich in materials of uncommon interest and variety, he was an amusing and instructive companion, entirely free from the asperities and repetitions which are the usual infirmities of age. Indeed, he kept pace with the course of events, and ever lived in the present that was around him, and not after the manner of old age, in the past that had faded away. No second childhood overtook him, but at the end of his almost century of years on earth, he came to his death-bed with no sign or symptom of childishness in his mind and character. In his last sickness he expressed his firm belief in the Christian Revelation, his faith in the Redeemer, and his reliance on the mercy of God, and calmly and cheerfully obeyed the summons that called him from earthly scenes to the world of spirits, missed and mourned by many who knew and esteemed him in his walks among men."

(157)   JOHN GLOVER BURBECK, the second son of Col. William and Jerusha (Glover) Burbeck, was born in Boston, baptized August 1, 1755, and died Feb. 1, 1819, in his 64th year.

Capt. John Burbeck died intestate, and his widow resigned the trust as administratrix, as follows:—"March 15, 1819. To the Hon. Thomas Dawes, Judge of Probate for Suffolk County. It being inconvenient for me to administer on the estate of John Burbeck, late of Boston, Gentleman, deceased, I hereby signify to your honor, and request that William Henry Burbeck, of said Boston, Trader, may be appointed to that trust.   JERUSHA BURBECK."

Nov. 1, 1784, he was married to Jerusha Baker, daughter of Thomas and Sarah (Lash) Baker, of Boston, by Rev. John Elliot, D.D. Jerusha (Baker) Burbeck died March 7, 1830, aged 70 years. Their children were as follows:

487. Jerusha Cathcart, b. Feb. 12, 1786; m. Gedney King, Salem.
488. Sarah,   b. July 20, 1788; m. Heman Fay, Westborough.
489. Elizabeth,   b. May 11, 1790; d. in 1820, aged 30 years, unm.
490. John,   b. May 12, 1792; d. Sept., 1816, unmarried.
491. William,   b. May 12, 1794; m. Caroline Prince, of Boston.
492. Abigail Coates, b. in 1796; died unmarried.

(158) JOSEPH BURBECK, son of Col. William and Jerusha (Glover) Burbeck, was born in Boston, Nov. 18, 1756, and died there in September, 1820, in his 64th year.

Feb. 1, 1784, he was married to Elizabeth Saunders, by Rev. Dr. John Elliot. She died in Boston, Dec. 10, 1816, suddenly, aged 53 years. Their children were:

493. Joseph,   b. Jan., 1785; died at sea.
494. Robert,   b. in 1797; married; died.
495. Elizabeth,   b. in 1789; died in 1824, aged 35 years.
496. Edward,   b. in 1792; married; died.
497. William Henry, b. in 1794; died in 1820, aged 26 years.
498. Sylvia,   b. in 1800; d. in 1824, aged 24 years.

(159) THOMAS BURBECK, son of Col. William and Jerusha (Glover) Burbeck, was born in Boston, Aug. 25, 1758, and baptized there, at the Old North or Christ Church, Aug. 27, 1758. He died in Boston, May 8, 1846, in his 88th year.

Oct. 8, 1787, he was married to Sarah Coverly, by Rev. John Elliot.

Children of THOMAS and SARAH (COVERLY) BURBECK, born in Boston:

499. Sarah,   b. in 1788; resides in New York.
500. Susan,   b. in 1790; m. Ebenezer W. Hayward, Uxbridge.
501. Thomas,   b. in 1792; married; died.
502. Henry,   b. in 1794; married; died.
503. Mary Glover, b. in 1796; resides in Uxbridge.
504. William,   b. in 1798; married; resides in Amesbury.

(163) MARY GLOVER, second daughter of Nathaniel and Mary (Field) Glover, was born in Braintree, May 27, 1766, and died there before 1801.

Aug. 18, 1787, she was married to Lemuel Allen, of Braintree. They had one daughter:

505. Abigail Glover, b. in Braintree, in 1788 ; d. unmarried, at the house of her half sister in Randolph.

LEMUEL ALLEN was born in Braintree, in 1768, and died there Jan. 24, 1805, aged 37 years. He was twice married. After the death of Mary Glover he married, a second time, ——— Faxon, and had other children.

(164) JOHN GLOVER, eldest son of Nathaniel and Mary (Field) Glover, was born in Braintree, Aug. 13, 1769, and died there in October, 1855, in his 87th year.

He was married to Phebe Curtis, June 14, 1798. She was the daughter of Noah Curtis, and born in Braintree in 1772. She died there April 1, 1852, aged 80 years.

Children of JOHN and PHEBE (CURTIS) GLOVER, born in Braintree:

+506. Elizabeth Curtis, b. Jan. 2, 1799 ; m. Augustus Field, Boston.
  507. Mary Field,   b. Dec. 14, 1800 ; d. July 23, 1802.
+508. John,   b. Nov. 27, 1803 ; m. Margaret N. Field.
  509. Anne Curtis,   b. March 22, 1806 ; d. Jan. 12, 1829, aged 23 years, unmarried.
  510. Mary Field,   b. Feb. 14, 1808 ; d. Jan. 19, 1829, aged 20 years, unmarried.
+511. Phebe Neale, b. Feb. 6, 1811 ; m. Horatio N. Faxon, Quincy.
  512. Samuel,   b. Jan. 27, 1813 ; d. Oct. 11, 1814.
  513. Samuel Curtis,   b. July 22, 1815 ; d. May 1, 1824.
+514. Noah A.,   b. June 21, 1818 ; m. Elizabeth Bevlee.
  515. Adam,   b. Jan. 27, 1821 ; lives single, in Quincy.

(165) NATHANIEL GLOVER, the second son of Nathaniel and Mary (Field) Glover, was born in Braintree, July 23, 1772, baptized Aug. 2, 1772, and died there March 27, 1853, in his 81st year. He resided in Quincy, and owned a farm there.

Dec. 1, 1796, he was married to Esther Glover (221), a first cousin. She was the eldest daughter of Ebenezer and Sarah (Wadsworth) Glover, of Dorchester, and was born at the Newbury farm homestead, Jan. 15, 1778, and died March 22, 1845.

Children of NATHANIEL and ESTHER GLOVER, born in Quincy:

516. Sarah Wadsworth, b. Sept. 1, 1797; d. May 26, 1800.
517. Esther Wadsworth, b. July 16, 1800; died young.
+518. John Bass, b. June 16, 1803; m. Margaretta N. Reid, Boston.
+519. Nathaniel Ebenezer, b. Oct. 4, 1805; resides in Quincy.
+520. Caroline Sarah Wadsworth, b. Sept. 25, 1808;
m. { 1st, William Dwelley;
    { 2d, Isaac Newcomb.
521. George Warren, b. Dec. 20, 1812; d. July 9, 1835, aged 22.

(166) JOSIAH GLOVER, son of Nathaniel and Abigail (Copeland) Glover (2d wife), was born in Braintree, Aug. 15, 1784, and died in Quincy, of paralysis, Nov. 17, 1863, in his 80th year.

He was twice married. First, to Sophia I. Sorrelle, Feb. 5, 1809. She died Aug. 20, 1830, aged 46 years. He was married, second, Nov. 1, 1832, by Rev. Peter Whitney, to Mrs. Mary P. Brackett, widow, and daughter of Jedediah Adams, of Quincy. She died in Quincy, Dec. 17, 1862.

Children of JOSIAH and SOPHIA I. (SORRELLE) GLOVER, born in Quincy:

522. Harriet E.,   b. Oct.   31, 1810; m. Freeman Moore.
523. Mactaelle,   b. March   7, 1811; m. Gridley Totman.
524. Eliza,   b. April   30, 1813; d. March 23, 1814.
525. Josiah,   b. Dec.   18, 1815; d. Oct. 22, 1839, aged 24.
526. Eliza Miller,   b. Jan.   10, 1817; d. Nov. 16, 1817.
527. Ingersoll,   b. May   22, 1819; d. Dec. 11, 1819.
+528. William Sullivan, b. Nov. 5, 1820; m. Harriet M. A. Fisher.
529. Nathaniel,   b. May   22, 1822; d. Dec. 11, 1822.

By 2d wife, Mrs. MARY P. (ADAMS) BRACKETT:

+530. Erastus Miller, b. April 24, 1834; resides in Quincy.

(167) ABIGAIL GLOVER, daughter of Nathaniel and Abigail (Copeland) Glover, was born in Braintree, Oct. 3, 1785, and resides in Quincy.

She was married to Stephen Veazie, of Quincy, Dec. 15, 1803.

Children of STEPHEN and ABIGAIL (GLOVER) VEAZIE, born in Quincy:

531. Stephen.
532. Abigail.
533. John Glover,   } bap. June 6, 1813.
534. Edward Augustus, }

(168) DELIGHT GLOVER, daughter of Nathaniel and Abigail (Copeland) Glover, was born Sept. 2, 1787, in Quincy, and died there, Aug. 17, 1829.

She was married to Joseph Nightingale, Nov. 19, 1804.

Children of JOSEPH and DELIGHT (GLOVER) NIGHTINGALE, born and baptized in Quincy:

535. Mary,   b. in 1806.
536. Jerusha,   b. in 1808.
537. Nathaniel Glover, b. in 1810.
538. Harriet Delight,   baptized June 6, 1813.

(169) ELISHA GLOVER, son of Nathaniel and Abigail (Copeland) Glover, was born in Braintree, Nov. 25, 1789, and died in Ipswich, Nov. 17, 1757, aged 68 years.

He was twice married. First, to Mary Veazie, of Quincy, Jan. 15, 1815. She died June 11, 1823, aged 28 years. He then removed to Ipswich, and married, in 1828, for his second wife, Elizabeth Seward, of that place. He was a carpenter, and worked at his trade there.

Children of ELISHA and MARY (VEAZIE) GLOVER, born in Quincy:

+539. Mary D., b. Dec., 1815, bap. Aug. 4, 1816 ; d. Dec. 17, 1816.
+540. Esther Hallett, bap. June 6, 1818 ; m. Eben. G. Green, Boston.
+541. James Francis, b. April 2, 1820 ; m. Susan Thayer, of Braintree.
+542. Winslow Brigham, b. in 1822 ; m. Harriet D. Copeland.

By second wife, ELIZABETH SEWARD, born in Ipswich:

543. Albert Henry,   b. in 1829 ; m. Mary A. Wilson, of Salem.
544. Mary Elizabeth,   b. in 1831 ; m. Albert Roundy, of Beverly.
545. Edward,   b. in 1832.
546. William Wood,   b. in 1834 ; d. Oct., 1857, aged 23 years.
547. Caroline,   b. in 1836 ; m. George Roundy, of Beverly.
548. Otis Kimball,   b. in 1838 ; went to sea.
549. Susan Cogswell,   b. in 1840.
550. John,   b. in 1843.

(175) EZRA GLOVER, son of Elisha and Jerusha (Billings) Glover, was born in Dorchester, June 22, 1770, and died in Quincy, July 14, 1847, aged 77 years.

He was married, Jan. 1, 1807, to Eunice Minot, of Dorchester, daughter of George and Eunice (Billings)' Minot. They had three children. She was born in Dorchester, Sept. 28, 1781, and died in Quincy, Dec. 31, 1863, aged 82 years.

Children of EZRA and EUNICE (MINOT) GLOVER, born in Quincy:

+551. Lewis Joseph, } b. Feb. 26, 1807 ; { d. June 24, 1856, unm.
   552. Earlmira,   { d. Jan. 9, 1833, unm.
+553. John Jefferson, b. June 13, 1828 ; resides in Quincy.

(176) MEHETABLE GLOVER, daughter of Elisha and Jerusha (Billings) Glover, was born in Dorchester, Nov. 8, 1773, and died there, March 25, 1839, aged 66 years.

She was married to Samuel Kinsley Spurr, of Milton, Sept. 27, 1800. They lived in Dorchester.

Children of SAMUEL KINSLEY and MEHETABLE (GLOVER) SPURR, born in Dorchester :

   554. Stephen Elisha, } b. Nov. 10, 1801 ; { married.
   555. Russell Glover,   { married.
   556. Mary Glover,   b. in 1803 ; d. Nov. 22, 1822, aged 19, unm.
   557. Ezra Glover,   b. May 25, 1804 ; d. Oct. 8, 1833, in Randolph, unmarried.
   558. Jerusha Elizabeth Glover, bap. May 22, 1815 ; died young.

(178) STEPHEN GLOVER, son of Elisha and Jerusha (Billings) Glover, was born in Dorchester, Jan. 9, 1778, and died on his estate at Mount Pleasant, Nov. 21, 1843, of enlargement of the liver; he was buried at Mount Auburn. He was a shipmaster and navigator, and followed that profession for many years.

He was twice married. First, to Mary Woodward, daughter of Joseph and ——— Woodward. She died Sept. 21, 1817, aged 24 years, and is buried at Mt. Auburn. Capt. Glover married, for his second wife, March 10, 1818, Rebecca Payne Gore, daughter of Samuel and Rebecca (Payne) Gore. She died Dec. 13, 1846, aged 56 years, and was buried at Mt. Auburn.

Children of Capt. STEPHEN and MARY (WOODWARD) GLOVER, born in Dorchester :

   559. Joseph Stephen, b. Feb. 26, 1815 ; d. on board ship in Boston harbor, in 1840.
+560. George Stephen, b. in 1817 ; m. Ellen Paul, of Shrewsbury.

By second wife, REBECCA PAYNE GORE :

561. Samuel Gore, b. in 1820 ; m. Rebecca Page, of Salem, and d. July 17, 1856 ; no issue.
562. Fanny, m. Samuel F. Train, of Boston.
563. Theodore Russell, m. Mary Malbone, Hingham ; no children.

(180) JOHANNAH GLOVER, daughter of Enoch and Susannah (Bird) Glover, was born in Dorchester, Feb. 3, 1758, and died in Minot, Me., about 1826.

She was married to Aaron Bird, of Dorchester, Nov. 23, 1775. He was the son of Aaron Bird, and was born in Dorchester. He removed to Minot, and died there.

Children of AARON and JOHANNAH (GLOVER) BIRD, born in Dorchester :

564. William,   b. May 11, 1779 ; d. Nov. 27, 1794, aged 15 years.
+565. Johannah, b. Feb. 9, 1781 ; m. Samuel Ward, of Roxbury.
566. Enoch Glover, b. April 14, 1784 ; married.
567. Anna, b. March 29, 1786 ; m. Samuel Hancock, of Roxbury.
568. Rachel Robinson, b. Jan. 1, 1788 ; m. ——— Holbrook.
569. Grace, b. Sept. 12, 1789 ; m. Dr. Joseph Keith, of Elliot, Me., Sept. 5, 1810, and died April 15, 1814.
570. Benjamin Glover, b. Feb. 24, 1793 ; d. Sept. 9, 1793.
571. William,   b. Aug. 17, 1796 ; died the next day.
572. Charles Jarvis,   b. Feb. 14, 1798 ; died in infancy.
573. Susannah Baker,   b. in 1800 ; m. Solomon Hancock.

(181) SUSANNAH GLOVER, daughter of Enoch and Susannah (Bird) Glover, was born in Dorchester, April 2, 1759, and died at Evansville, Kentucky, Oct. 7, 1820, aged 61 years.

She was married to Ebenezer Baker, of Dorchester, June 1, 1786. They had two children :

574. Ebenezer, b. in 1788 ; m. William Adams.
575. Hannah, b. in 1790 ; m. Charles Adams, of Dorchester.

(182) MARY GLOVER, the third daughter of Enoch and Susannah (Bird) Glover, was born in Dorchester, Oct. 18, 1760, and died there in 1817, in her 57th year.

She was married, May 13, 1779, to Ebenezer Clap, Esq., of Dorchester, who was born there, April 23, 1732, and died Jan. 29, 1802. It is said that his estate was the largest, at that date, that had ever been rendered in Norfolk county to the Probate Court.

Children of Col. Ebenezer and Mary (Glover) Clap, born in Dorchester:

576. Polly,   b. Feb. 20, 1780; d. Dec. 10, 1799.
577. Ebenezer, b. Aug. 20, 1781; d. May 18, 1821, at the island of
        St. Thomas, in the West Indies, aged 40 years, unmarried.
578. Elizabeth, b. Sept. 10, 1782; m. James Howe, of Dorchester.
579. Lemuel,   b. June 2, 1784; d. unm., June 11, 1866, aged 82.
580. Eleazer, b. Aug. 18, 1786; H. C. 1807; physician; d. Aug.
        27, 1817, aged 31 years, unmarried.
581. Benjamin, b. July 17, 1788; d. Oct. 12, 1789.
582. Enoch Glover, b. Aug. 6, 1790; m. Mary Tyson, of Baltimore.
583. Anne, b. Dec. 8, 1792; m. { 1st, Alexander Balch, Dorchester;
                                 { 2d, John Wheeler, of Dorchester.
        Alexander Balch died July 5, 1812, aged 26 years.
584. Benjamin, b. Jan. 16, 1795; m. Elizabeth Pierce, Dorchester.
585. Elisha Glover, b. Oct. 22, 1796; d. Aug. 8, 1823, aged 27, unm.
586. Amasa,   b. Jan. 14, 1799; resides in Dorchester.

(184) ELIZABETH GLOVER, the fourth daughter of Enoch and Susannah (Bird) Glover, was born in Dorchester, Nov. 1, 1764, and died in New Orleans, La., when on a visit to her son and daughter.

Nov. 24, 1780, she was married to Benjamin Lyon, of Dorchester. They had six children, born in Dorchester:

587. Benjamin Glover, b. Aug. 4, 1781; m. Eliza Babcock, Milton.
588. Susannah Glover, b. March 26, 1783; d. March 26, 1783.
589. Susannah,   b. in 1784; d. in 1814, aged 30 years.
                                    { 1st, Ichabod Frost;
590. Mary,   b. in 1786; m. { 2d, Capt. —— Pierce;
                                    { 3d, Capt. —— Nichols.
591. Asa,   b. in 1788; d., unm., 1839, aged 51 years.
592. Samuel,   b. in 1790; d., unm., at New Orleans.

(186) ANNA GLOVER, the youngest daughter of Enoch and Susannah (Bird) Glover, was born in Dorchester, Jan. 17, 1768, and died there, Nov. 20, 1849, in her 82d year.

Oct. 10, 1792, she was married to Stephen Wales, Esq., son of Timothy and Hannah Wales, of Dorchester, born there June 14, 1769, and died in that town Feb. 6, 1842, in his 74th year.

Children of Stephen and Anna (Glover) Wales, born in Dorchester:

593. Charlotte, b. March 1, 1794; d. April 19, 1813, aged 19 years.
594. Harriet,   b. Jan. 24, 1797; d. Nov. 18, 1798.

595. Stephen, b. April 5, 1798 ; m. Lydia Vose Read, of Milton.
596. Harriet Gorham, b. June 28, 1800 ;

m. { 1st, Benjamin Sherborn, of Nashua, N. H. ;
{ 2d, Heman Bassett, of Boston.

Benjamin Sherborn died June 4, 1826 ; Heman Bassett died
March 24, 1851.
597. Nancy Glover, b. Oct. 10, 1802 ; m. Joseph Warren Parker,
of Brimfield.
598. Mary, b. Aug. 30, 1807 ; resides in Roxbury.
599. Amasa, b. Feb. 9, 1809 ; m. Martha E. Ward, of Roxbury ;
died in Genesce, Ill., in 1865.

(187) SAMUEL GLOVER, the third son of Enoch and Susannah (Bird) Glover, was born in Dorchester, March 29, 1770, and
died in South Boston, suddenly, Dec. 13, 1837, in his 68th year. He
was buried in the ancient burying ground in Dorchester. He resided
in Dorchester, near the homestead of his father, and his house stood
on a portion of the land belonging to the homestead estate. He employed himself in the cultivation of choice fruit, and succeeded in
producing some of the richest and rarest kinds, which he carried or
sent regularly to the Boston market.

At the age of twenty-five years, June 1, 1796, he was married to
Martha Holden, daughter of Dr. Phinehas Holden, of Dorchester,
born there Nov. 28, 1776, and died in 1864. He was the
son of Dr. William Holden, a native of Cambridge, born there
March 4, 1713; studied medicine, took his degree, and became
the immediate successor of Dr. Danforth in Dorchester. Phinehas
was born in Dorchester, Jan. 31, 1744, studied medicine with his
father, and continued in the practice of his profession until his decease in 1819.

Children of SAMUEL and MARTHA (HOLDEN) GLOVER, born in Dorchester :

600. Martha Holden, } b. Aug. 11, 1797; { m. Sam'l Davis, Brighton.
+601. A daughter, } { d. Aug. 18, 1797.
602. Phinehas Holden, b. Oct. 16, 1807 ; m. Mary Carlton, Portland.

Mrs. Martha (Holden) Glover married, a second time, Ezekiel
Holden, Esq., of Dorchester, May 1, 1838, who died soon, and she
married, a third time, Deacon Ebenezer Clap, of Dorchester, who
died March 6, 1860, in his 89th year. She survived him, and died
in Dorchester, April 5, 1864, in her 87th year.

(189) ELIZABETH GLOVER, the eldest daughter of Thomas and Rebeckah (Pope) Glover, was born in Stoughton, Sept. 25, 1752, and died there June 3, 1838, in her 86th year.

Dec. 16, 1773, she was married to Samuel Bird, of Sharon, son of Deacon Samuel and Anna (Atherton) Bird, born there July 4, 1743, and died in Stoughton, July 2, 1816. His homestead was situated at the westerly side of Mashapoag Pond, in Sharon. The house is still standing in which he was born and which he occupied during his residence in Sharon. He resided on his estate of inheritance twenty-three years after his marriage, and all but one of his children were born there. In 1794, they removed to Stoughton, and resided there the remainder of their lives. They were members of the Church at Sharon, Rev. Philip Curtis, pastor.

Children of SAMUEL and ELIZABETH (GLOVER) BIRD, born in Sharon and Stoughton:

603. Rebeckah, b. May 7, 1775; d. July 31, 1785, aged 10 years.
+604. Samuel, b. March 12, 1777; m. Betsey Trask, of Boston.
+605. Elizabeth, b. Nov. 24, 1779; m. John Taylor, of Boston.
+606. James, b. Oct. 6, 1781; m. Abigail Hobart, Braintree.
607. Anna, b. Feb. 14, 1783; d. Aug. 13, 1785, aged 2 years.
608. Hannah, b. Dec. 4, 1787; d. Aug. 20, 1813, in Stoughton, unm.
+609. Jenner, b. Oct. 3, 1794; m. Elizabeth Cook, of Westford.
+610. Rebeckah, b. Sept. 13, 1799; m. Ansel Capen, of Stoughton.

(191) HANNAH GLOVER, the third daughter of Thomas and Rebeckah (Pope) Glover, was born in Stoughton, June 3, 1756, and died there Nov. 18, 1821, in her 65th year.

Sept. 21, 1780, she was married to Jonathan Capen, of Stoughton, by the Rev. Jedediah Adams. He was the son of Deacon Jonathan and Jerusha (Talbot) Capen, and was born in Stoughton, Sept. 22, 1752, and died there Jan. 1, 1841, in his 89th year.

Children of Lieut. JONATHAN and HANNAH (GLOVER) CAPEN, born in Stoughton:

611. Louis, b. Dec. 1, 1781; d. March 13, 1782.
612. Hannah, b. Dec. 19, 1782; d. July 5, 1796, in her 14th year.
+613. Eleanor, b. July 11, 1784; m. Joseph S. Andrews, of Boston; d. July 20, 1839, aged 55 years.
614. Betsey, b. Dec. 10, 1785; resides in Stoughton, unmarried.
+615. Melatiah, b. Oct. 21, 1787;
m. { 1st, Otis Billings, of Canton;
{ 2d, Ephraim Capen, of Dorchester.

+616. Rachel,   b. March 18, 1789; m. Stephen Blake, of Canton.
+617. Azubah,   b. Nov. 17, 1790; m. Levi Hawes, New Bedford.
+618. Jane,   b. July 12, 1792; m. David Cobb, of Taunton.
 619. Jerusha,   b. April 30, 1794; m. Levi Melcher, of Boston.
 620. Jonathan, b. Sept. 27, 1796; d. Nov. 11, 1800, in his 9th yr.
+621. Thomas,   b. Aug.   1, 1798; m. Hannah Melcher, of Hampton Falls, N. H.
 622. Hannah,   b. May 24, 1801; d. Aug. 24, 1825, in her 25th yr.

(192) THOMAS GLOVER, eldest son of Thomas and Rebeckah (Pope) Glover, was born in Stoughton, Dec. 29, 1757, and died in Sharon, July 11, 1845, aged 88 years.

He was twice married, and had thirteen children. Aug. 8, 1782, he was married to Eunice Bent, of Sudbury. She was the daughter of Thomas and Mary (Stone) Bent, and was born in Sudbury, Feb. 11, 1763. She died in Sharon, Jan. 1, 1806, aged 42 years. Aug. 30, 1806, Thomas Glover married, for a second wife, Abigail Hewins, daughter of Deacon Jacob and Abigail (Everett) Hewins, of Sharon. She was born there in 1777, and died Dec. 8, 1844, aged 67 years. Thomas Glover purchased a farm, at the time of his first marriage, of Mr. Thomas Wormell, a Frenchman, and lived upon it until his death. It has since been sold.

Children of THOMAS and EUNICE (BENT) GLOVER, born in Sharon:

 623. Eunice, b. Aug. 26, 1783; d. at Jamaica Plain, March 16, 1848, aged 68 years.
+624. Lois, b. Sept. 29, 1785; m. Samuel Blackman, of Dorchester.
 625. Susannah, b. Sept. 5, 1790; d. Feb. 23, 1823, unmarried.
+626. Thomas,   b. July 21, 1792;
                m. { 1st, Mary Damon, of Dedham.
                   { 2d, Bethiah Thompson, of Roxbury.
 627. Mary,   b. Sept. 16, 1794; d. Feb. 12, 1827, aged 32, unm.
 628. Elijah,   b. April 29, 1797; m. Maria Pettee, of Sharon, in 1820; died April 3, 1838, in Sharon. No issue. She died Feb. 9, 1834, in Sharon.
+629. Elizabeth, b. May 6, 1801; m. Willard Morse, of Sharon.

Children by second wife, ABIGAIL HEWINS:

+630. William, b. Sept. 30, 1807; m. Anne Maria Fuller, Dedham.
 631. Hannah, b. July 12, 1809; d. in April, 1852, unm., aged 41.
 632. Nancy, b. April 17, 1813; m. Billings Fisher, of Dedham, May 4, 1846; d. in Stoughton, March 14, 1852.
 633. James, b. March 22, 1815; d. May 2, 1830, aged 15 years.
 634. John,   b. May 28, 1817; lives in Canton.
 635. Davis, b. Jan.   6, 1822; d. unmarried, at Ashland, Aug. 11, 1848, aged 26 years.

29

(193) WILLIAM GLOVER, the second son of Thomas and Rebeckah (Pope) Glover, was born in Stoughton, July 17, 1759, and died there, March 23, 1788, in his 29th year. He left a widow and one son. In 1781, at the age of 21 years, he purchased, conjointly with two of his brothers, Samuel and Ebenezer Glover, a tract of land of David Thompson, of Easton, adjoining the homestead estate of his father, Mr. Thomas Glover. In 1786, he received, by deed of gift, a portion of the homestead farm on the north side of Mr. Thomas Glover's house, and separated from the remaining portion by a brook.

July 1, 1786, he was married to Content Porter, daughter of Joseph and Elizabeth (Burrill) Porter, of East Stoughton, born there in 1767, and died in Canton, April 26, 1816, in her 50th year. She was married, a second time, to Benjamin Gill, of Canton, about two years after Mr. Glover's decease, or in 1790. She had one son by her first marriage, born in Stoughton, viz.:

636. William, b. Jan. 1, 1787 ; d. in Canton, at the house of his
     father-in-law, Aug. 28, 1802, in his 16th year.

(194) RACHAEL GLOVER, the fourth daughter of Thomas and Rebeckah (Pope) Glover, was born in Stoughton, Jan. 15, 1761, and died in Dorchester, Jan. 8, 1852, aged 91 years.

She was twice married. First, Jan. 1, 1785, at the age of twenty-four years, to Benjamin Homes, Esq., of Norton, by the Rev. Jedediah Adams, of Stoughton. He was of distinguished family and ancestry, was the second son of William and Rebecca (Dawes) Homes, of Boston, and was born there in 1763. At the time of his marriage he was twenty-two years of age, and had already been elected to various town and county offices, and was Justice of the Peace for the County of Bristol. His father, William Homes, was born in Boston, March 9, 1717, and was married, April 24, 1790, by the Rev. Dr. Sewall, of the Old South Church, to Rebecca, the eleventh child and fifth daughter of Thomas Dawes, Esq., of Boston, and his wife Sarah. They were eminently religious and worthy members of that Church. They had fifteen children, born in Boston, and baptized there. He was by trade a goldsmith, and was employed for many years in the manufactory of gold and silver ware, jewelry, &c., and kept a store in Ann street, where Oak Hall now stands. By industrious habits and strict integrity, he acquired a competent estate, and was known by the name of the " honest silversmith." In the year 1770 he retired from business, and was succeeded by his eldest son William, who carried on the business in Boston extensively for many years. William Homes, senior, purchased a farm in Norton, Bristol county, removed there with his family, and became a prominent and active member of the Church and of the town.* He was elected to many town offices, which he filled with dignity and honor, was chosen Representative and Councillor, and served in those offices. He died in Boston, at the house of his son William, in the month of July, 1783. He left a good estate, which was administered on by his eldest son. His widow removed to Boston, and passed the remainder of her days with her son William, and died there in July or August, 1788. She was buried with her husband, in the Chapel burying yard on Tremont street.

The grandparents of Benjamin Homes were—Captain Robert Homes, who went to sea in early life, became a shipmaster, and emigrated with his father to New England in 1700; and Mary Franklin, daughter of Josiah and Abiah (Folger) Franklin, sister of Dr. Benjamin Franklin, of Boston. She was born there, Sept. 26, 1694, and died about 1730. Capt. Robert Homes was lost at sea. They had two children: William, the father of Benjamin, and Abiah, a daughter, who soon died.

The earliest American ancestor of Benjamin Homes was the Rev. William Homes, who was his great-grandfather. He was a clergyman of the Scotch Presbyterian order, of distinguished piety and talents, and was at first settled at Strabane, near Londonderry, in Ireland. He was married there to Miss Craghead, and came with his family to New England in 1700; was installed pastor of the Church in Chilmark, near Martha's Vineyard, in 1716, and continued there until his decease in 1745.

The immediate collateral relatives of Benjamin Homes were: his sisters, Mrs. Benjamin Tappan, of Northampton; Mrs. Barnabas Webb, of Thomaston, Me., died there in 1833, aged 93 years; Elizabeth Homes, who died unmarried, in 1790, while on a visit to Boston aged 33 years; and his only brother William, who married Miss Whitwell, first, and, second, Miss Greenough, of Boston, and was the father of Henry Homes, of the recent firm of Homes & Homer, and Nathaniel B. Homes, lately deceased, unmarried.

---

* See Clark's History of Norton.

BENJAMIN and RACHAEL (GLOVER) HOMES had issue—a son born in Stoughton, viz.:

+637. William, b. Oct. 3, 1785 ;
    m. { 1st, Elizabeth Blackman, of Dorchester ;
      { 2d, Eliza Glover Wheelock, of Dorchester.

Mrs. Rachael (Glover) Homes (widow) was married, a second time, Jan. 9, 1792, to Solomon Hall, of Dorchester. He was the son of Solomon and Mary (Nash) Hall, of Dorchester, born there Feb. 12. 1768, and died March 3, 1806, aged 39 years. He was lineally descended from Richard Hall, one of the early settlers of Dorchester, who belonged to the landed class of Joint Stock Proprietors in the town of Dorchester, and in Dorchester New Grant.

Children of SOLOMON and RACHAEL (GLOVER-HOMES) HALL, born in Dorchester :

+638. Luther, } b. July 28, 1792 ; { m. Phebe Foster, Machias, Me.
+639. Elijah, }   { m. Joanna Sevey, Machias, Me.
+640. Mary Nash, b. April 1, 1794 ; m. Josiah Myles, Machias, Me.,
    April, 1826, and had one son, Henry, who died in infancy.
+641. Rebeckah, b. Feb. 29, 1796 ; m. Jonathan Collier, Dorchester.
+642. Stephen, b. Feb. 1, 1798 ; m. Elizabeth Tolman, Dorchester.
+643. Oliver, b. Feb. 16, 1800 ;
       { 1st, Laura Richards, of Dorchester ;
     m. { 2d, Eunice Lyon, of Dorchester ;
       { 3d, Caroline Laughton, of Brookline.
644. Abigail, b. May 18, 1802 ; d. March 29, 1804.

(195) SAMUEL GLOVER, the third son of Thomas and Rebeckah (Pope) Glover, was born in Stoughton, Feb. 5, 1763, and died there, April 23, 1855, in his 93d year. He was a landholder by inheritance, and by purchase he came in possession of several other tracts of land. His homestead estate he purchased in 1795, of Samuel Bird, 2d, of Stoughton, and occupied it until his decease, a period of sixty years. It has since been sold to Dr. E. G. Leach, who is the present possessor.

Jan. 17, 1787, he was married to Eleanor Hawes, of Sharon, by the Rev. Joseph Palmer. She was the second daughter of Elijah and Abigail (Everett) Hawes, and was born in Sharon, July 19, 1766, and died in Stoughton, May 11, 1846, in her 80th year. Her father was lineally descended from Richard Hawes, of the early settlers of Dorchester, and of the Joint Stock Company of Dorchester New

Grant, and by his mother Mary Belcher from the Hon. Andrew Belcher, of Boston and Sudbury. Her lineage from the Everett family was by, first, Richard Everett, of the first settlers of Dedham; second, Capt. John Everett and Elizabeth Pepper, married in 1662, died in Dedham in 1715; third, Deacon John Everett, of Dedham, born June 9, 1676, married to Mercy Brown, Jan. 3, 1700, and died March 20, 1751; fourth, Joseph Everett, second son of John and Mercy (Brown) Everett, born July 31, 1703, married Hannah Richards, of Dedham, Feb. 1, 1727, and died Feb. 17, 1774, whose second daughter, Abigail Everett, was born in Sharon, Dec. 25, 1740, married to Elijah Hawes, son of Eleazer and Mary (Belcher) Hawes, Oct. 9, 1760, and died June 26, 1781, and were the parents of Eleanor Hawes.

Children of SAMUEL and ELEANOR (HAWES) GLOVER, born and baptized in Stoughton, Rev. Jedediah Adams, pastor:

+645. Eleanor, b. Oct. 7, 1788; resides in Stoughton.
  646. Thomas, b. March 26, 1790; d. Aug. 4, 1790 (baptized in private, Aug. 2, 1790).
+647. Jarvis, b. June 21, 1792; m. Fanny Fuller, of Dalton.
  648. Anna, b. Jan. 27, 1801; bap. May 3, 1801, by Rev. Pitt Clark, of Norton.

(196) EBENEZER GLOVER, the fourth son of Thomas and Rebeckah (Pope) Glover, was born in Stoughton, Feb. 2, 1765, and died in Dorchester, June 28, 1818, in his 54th year. He was a merchant, kept a store, and traded successfully. He owned a house, opposite his father's, conjointly with his brother Samuel, and inherited a considerable portion of land. He also acquired more land by purchase. He resided in Stoughton until 1796, then removed to Dorchester, and continued his business of shopkeeping and mercantile pursuits.

He was married in Dorchester, by the Rev. T. M. Harris, Sept. 21, 1797, to Mary Trescott, widow of Isaac Fenno. They had three children. She was the daughter of Joseph and Mary (Payson) Trescott, of Dorchester, and was born there, Feb. 18, 1765. She died in Dorchester, Feb. 18, 1826, aged 61 years.

Children of EBENEZER and MARY (TRESCOTT-FENNO) GLOVER, born in Dorchester:

649. Charlotte, b. April 27, 1799; d. in infancy.
+650. Mary,   b. June   7, 1800; m. James Lewis, Jr., of Roxbury.
651. Ebenezer, b. March 21, 1803; m. Thankful Hopkins, of Truro.
      He died June 22, 1834, aged 31 years, no issue. She died
      in Boston, Dec. 3, 1837.

(197) JERUSHA GLOVER, the fifth daughter of Thomas and
Rebeckah (Pope) Glover, was born in Stoughton, April 28, 1766, and
died in Dorchester, April 30, 1833, in her 67th year. She was distinguished for rare personal beauty, which seemed not impaired by
time or trouble.

March 4, 1793, she was married, by the Rev. Jedediah Adams, of
Stoughton, to Unite Blackman, of Dorchester. He was the son of
Samuel and Waitstill (Tolman) Blackman, born in Dorchester, Feb.
17, 1772, and died there, Nov. 8, 1806, in his 35th year, leaving a
widow and seven children, another son being born a few months after
his decease. He was a merchant, and owned and occupied the house
near the estate of Gov. James Bowdoin, at the Four Corners, on the
Dorchester Upper Road leading to Boston.

Children of UNITE and JERUSHA (GLOVER) BLACKMAN, born in
Dorchester, and baptized at the Church there, Rev. T. M. Harris,
pastor—parents being in full communion :

652. Eliakim, b. Jan. 2, 1794 ; d. July 24, 1807, in his 13th year.
653. Thomas Glover, b. May 21, 1795 ; d. March 3, 1833, aged 38.
654. William, b. Oct. 3, 1796 ; d. May 9, 1827, aged 30 years, unm.
655. Warren, b. July 19, 1799 ; d. July 19, 1819, aged 20 years.
+656. Jerusha, b. Aug. 3, 1800 ; m. Joseph Bugbee, of Roxbury.
+657. Lucy,   b. Jan. 1, 1803 ; m. Robert Gilmore Babcock, Milton.
658. Unite,   b. Nov. 8, 1805 ; d. Sept. 8, 1829, aged 24 years,
      unmarried ; buried with military honors by the Dorchester
      Artillery Company.
659. Eliakim, b. Jan. 1, 1807, posthumous ; d. in Ohio, date of
      death not ascertained.

The last named child was born about two months after the decease
of his father, and bore the name of Eliakim at the request of his
eldest brother, of the same name, who was, at the time of his birth,
in the last stages of consumption. A family meeting was therefore
called, with a few members of the Church to which Mrs. Blackman
belonged, and her minister, the Rev. T. M. Harris, and the little
orphan was baptized in the presence of his elder brother, who was
expecting soon to pass away, being fully sensible of his condition.

The early death of Mr. Blackman, the birth of this last child, and the death of the elder son a few months after, were the commencement of a series of heart-rending troubles, which terminated her life at the age of sixty-six years.

(198) ANNA GLOVER, the sixth and youngest daughter of Thomas and Rebeckah (Pope) Glover, was born in Stoughton, Nov. 13, 1768, and died in Dorchester, Aug. 26, 1840, aged 72 years.

She was married, March 28, 1796, to Josiah Leeds, of Dorchester, by the Rev. Edward Richmond, of Stoughton, and went to Dorchester to reside. Josiah Leeds was born Dec. 4, 1771, and inherited a homestead estate on what is now called Savin Hill Avenue, formerly "Leeds's Lane," leading to Savin Hill. He died there, June 25, 1828, aged 57 years.

Children of JOSIAH and ANNA (GLOVER) LEEDS, born in Dorchester:

+660. Lewis,   b. March 29, 1798 ; m. Pedy Thompson, of Rockingham, Vt.
+661. Joseph, b. Nov. 12, 1799 ; m. { 1st, Eliza Gerry, Stoneham ; 2d, Eliza Lynde, Stoneham.
 662. William, b. Sept. 18, 1801 ; d. Oct. 8, 1838 ; aged 37, unm.
+663. Anna,   b. Aug.   21, 1803 ; m. William Parker, Brimfield.
+664. Thomas, b. Feb.   3, 1806 ; m. —— Lynde, of Stoneham.
 665. Mary,   b. Feb.   21, 1808 ; d. June 22, 1849, aged 41 years.
 666. Rebeckah, b. April 6, 1812 ; d. June 26, 1841, aged 29 years.

(199) ELIJAH GLOVER, the fifth son and youngest child of Thomas and Rebeckah (Pope) Glover, was born in Stoughton, April 20, 1770, and died there, March 9, 1855, in his 85th year. In 1801 he built a house on Dorchester Meeting-house Hill; was a merchant, and resided there ten years.

He was twice married. First, February 13, 1805, by Rev. T. M. Harris, to Martha Pope, daughter of Elijah and Martha (White) Pope, of Dorchester. She was born there, Dec. 12, 1780, and died in Stoughton, July 16, 1813, aged 33 years. They had three children, the two eldest born and baptized in Dorchester. He was married, the second time, to Sarah Howe, Dec. 2, 1814. She was the eldest daughter of Isaac and Sarah (Wiswall) Howe, of Dorchester, born there May 21, 1786, and died Oct. 21, 1859, in her 74th year. He removed to Stoughton in 1810, and occupied the homestead estate of his father, which was his inheritance, and resided there until his decease.

Children of ELIJAH and MARTHA (POPE) GLOVER, born in Dorchester and Stoughton:

+667. Louisa, b. Aug. 5, 1808; m. Joseph Parshley, of Braintree.
+668. Martha Harriet, b. May 22, 1810; m. Isaac T. Dyer, Braintree.
 669. Mary Smith, b. May 25, 1813, in Stoughton; d. July 6, 1813.

By wife SARAH HOWE:

+670. Asahel Howe, b. March 30, 1816; m. Sarah Elizabeth Homes, of Dorchester.
 671. Isaac Howe, b. July 28, 1817; m. Caroline A. Arnold, of Braintree, May 6, 1846; died Aug. 2, 1849; no issue. His widow died in January, 1853.
+672. John Clough, b. March 14, 1819;
                        m. { 1st, Ann W. Monk, of Stoughton;
                             { 2d, Mary F. Horton, of Milton.
+673. Rebeckah, b. Jan. 14, 1821; m. Edmund Packard, of North Bridgewater.
+674. Elijah, b. March 14, 1824; m. Eunice P. Swan, of Stoughton.
+675. Frederick Pope, b. Dec. 28, 1825; m. Emeline Morton, of Needham.
 676. Nathaniel, b. Oct. 20, 1827; resides in Janesville, Wisconsin.

(200) SAMUEL KINGSLEY GLOVER, only son of Elijah and Abigail (Kingsley) Glover, was born in Milton, June 28, 1753, and died there, July 1, 1839, aged 86 years. At the age of 18 years he entered Harvard College, at Cambridge, and left there at the time instruction was suspended in the War of the Revolution. He applied himself to the study of medicine and surgery, under the instruction of Dr. John Warren, and served his country as Surgeon to the army until peace was restored in 1783. He was employed as Surgeon of several armed vessels until 1778. He then was elected as superintendent of a smallpox hospital on Prospect Hill, where the troops of Gen. Burgoyne were stationed as prisoners of war. In 1783, on relinquishing military life, he also retired from the practice of medicine and surgery generally, excepting that he devoted a portion of his time to a private smallpox hospital. He inherited a competent landed estate from his father and from his maternal grandfather, and owned and occupied a homestead estate on Milton Hill, which has descended to his grandchildren. He received a pension from government for several years.

He was married, April 21, 1781, to Eunice Babcock, of Milton. Nothing further of her origin has been ascertained. She died at Milton Hill, Dec. 1, 1826, and left three sons.

Children of SAMUEL KINGSLEY and EUNICE (BABCOCK) GLOVER, born at Milton Hill:

677. Samuel, b. May 6, 1783 ; d. July 22, 1831, aged 48 yrs., unm.
678. Elijah Anson, b. July 19, 1785 ; d. Sept. 22, 1819, in his 35th year, unmarried.
+679. William, b. July 26, 1788 ; m. Eliza Gleason, of Wrentham.

(201) SUSANNAH GLOVER, daughter of Elijah and Elizabeth (Tucker) Glover, was born in Milton, April 21, 1765, and died there, Aug. 31, 1845, aged 80 years.

She was married, Nov. 4, 1790, to Charles Pierce, of Milton, son of John Pierce, of that place.

Children of CHARLES and SUSANNAH (GLOVER) PIERCE, born in Milton:

680. Charles,   b. Feb. 11, 1792 ; resides in Milton, unmarried.
681. Elizabeth, b. Oct. 31, 1793 ; resides in Milton, unmarried.
682. Elijah,   b. Nov. 4, 1795 ; m. —— White, of Weymouth.
683. Isaac,   b. Feb. 9, 1799 ; d. Oct., 1860, unmarried.

(204) WILLIAM GLOVER, second son of William and Mary (Capen) Glover, was born in Dorchester, Oct. 3, 1780, and died there, Sept. 27, 1822, in his 43d year.

He was married to Mary Billings, of Quincy, Jan. 14, 1804. He succeeded to the homestead of his father, conjointly with his brother Edward Glover, who was never married, and dying without issue his line became extinct.

Children of WILLIAM and MARY (BILLINGS) GLOVER, born in Dorchester:

+684. Eunice Billings, b. Sept. 5, 1805 ; m. William Brazer Duggan, of Boston.
+685. James Madison, b. Aug. 9, 1809 ; m. Harriet Louisa Gibbs, of Sandwich.

(206) LOIS BENT GLOVER, daughter of James and Lois (Bent) Glover, was born in Framingham, Nov. 30, 1762, and died there, Feb. 14, 1800, aged 37 years and 10 months.

She was married, May 3, 1781, to Asa Nourse, of Framingham.

Children of ASA and LOIS BENT (GLOVER) NOURSE, born in Framingham:

686. Lois,   b. May 3, 1782 ; died the same day.
687. James,   b. July 6, 1783 ; died young.
688. Mary, b. May 7, 1785 ; m. Rufus Brewer, Esq., Framingham.
689. Charlotte, b. June 12, 1787 ; m. Aaron Hadley.
690. Lois,   b. Feb. 10, 1789 ; died young.
691. Millicent,   b. Feb. 3, 1791 ; m. { 1st, Aaron Eames ;
                                         { 2d, Edward Childs.
692. Newell,   · b. March 21, 1792 ; m. Harriet Bullard, Holliston.
693. Olive,   b. Dec.   3, 1793 ; m. David Brewer, Framingham.
694. Sarah,   b. Sept. 9, 1795 ; m. Nathan Fairbanks, of Hol-
     liston ; died in 1819.
695. Susannah, b. May 11, 1797 ; m. Henry Brewer, Framingham.
696. Asa,   b. Feb. 14, 1800 ; died young.

(207) MARY GLOVER, daughter of James and Lois (Bent)
Glover, was born in Framingham, Aug. 10, 1764, and died there, Jan.
31, 1322, aged 57 years.

She was twice married. First, to Ezra Haven, in April, 1782.
He was the son of Jesse Haven, of Framingham, and lived on the
homestead of his father, dying there Oct. 00, 1794, and leaving a widow
and eight children. She was married, second, to her brother-in-law,
the husband of her sister Lois, Dec. 29, 1800, and had one daughter
by this last marriage.

Children of Ezra and Mary (Glover) Haven, born in Framingham :

697. William, graduated at Brown University ; died, unmarried.
698. Joseph, d. unmarried, in 1845.   •
699. Anna,   m. Alexander Edwards.
700. John,   m. Martha F. Smith, of Needham.
701. Jason,   m. Esther Tucker.
702. Olive,   m. Seth Drury, of Natick.
703. Milly,   m. Willard Haven.
704. Sally,   died, unmarried.

     By Asa Nourse :

705. Elizabeth, m. Charles Haven.

(209) ELIZABETH GLOVER, daughter of James and Lois
(Bent) Glover, was born in Framingham, June 5, 1768.

She was married to Isaac Fisher, of Framingham, about Dec. 1,
1786, and removed to Springfield, Coos Co., New Hampshire. No
children reported.

(210) SARAH GLOVER, daughter of James and Lois (Bent) Glover, was born in Framingham, July 9, 1770, and died in Vinalhaven, Fox Islands, Maine, Feb. 13, 1859.

She was married, in 1791, to Samuel Thomas, of Vinalhaven, Me.

Children of SAMUEL and SARAH (GLOVER) THOMAS, born in Vinalhaven, Me.:

706. Samuel,   b. in 1792; died, unmarried.
707. Sarah,   b. in 1793.
708. Josiah,   b. in 1794.
709. Stephen,   b. in 1796; died.
710. Alvan,   b. in 1798.
711. James Glover, b. in 1799; died.
712. Nathaniel,   b. in 1801.
713. Zilpah,   b. in 1803; m. Asa M. Glover, of Fox Islands.
714. Harriet,   b. in 1805; m. Zilpah Beveridge.

(211) MARTHA GLOVER, daughter of James and Lois (Bent) Glover, was born in Framingham, Nov. 3, 1772, and died there, Aug. 1, 1824.

She was married to Jonathan Rugg, of Framingham, Dec. 29, 1800.

Children of JONATHAN and MARTHA (GLOVER) RUGG, born in Framingham:

715. Eliza,   b. Dec. 19, 1801; d. July 27, 1821, aged 20 years.
716. Caroline,   b. Dec. 9, 1803; d. July 2, 1810, aged 7 years.
717. Glover,   b. July 3, 1805; d. June 3, 1825, aged 20 years.
+718. Emeline,   b. Sept. 22, 1807; m. Seymour Gates.
719. Jerusha,   b. Nov. 29, 1809; d. June 30, 1814.
+720. Martha,   b. Jan. 2, 1819; d. at Niagara Falls, Aug. 24, 1844.

JONATHAN RUGG was married, a second time, in 1826, to Lucinda Marsh, of Holliston, Mass., and died July 1, 1843. His widow survived him, and is now (1866) living, at the age of 87 years.

(214) JERUSHA GLOVER, daughter of James and Mary (Hill-Metcalf) Glover, was born in Framingham, Nov. 29, 1785, and died there, July 21, 1865, aged 80 years.

She was married to Thomas Verille, in April, 1828.

Children of THOMAS and JERUSHA (GLOVER) VERILLE, born in Vinalhaven:

721. James, b. in 1830.
722. Lucy, b. in 1832.
723. Mary, b. in 1835.

(215)   JULIA GLOVER, daughter of James and Mary (Hill-Metcalf) Glover, was born in Framingham, April 20, 1787; resides in Camden, Me.

(216)   JOHN CLOUGH GLOVER, son of James and Mary (Hill-Metcalf) Glover, was born in Framingham, Oct. 21, 1788, and died in Belfast, Me., March 5, 1865. He was a shipmaster and mariner for several years. He retired from his sea-faring life in 1853, and lived on his farm, situated in Camden, on the banks of the Penobscot river. He resided with his daughter, Mrs. Winthrop O. Thomas, at the time of his death.

He was married, Sept. 28, 1810, to Martha White, daughter of George and Sarah (Oliver) White, of Camden, Me., and was born there, Jan. 12, 1791; died in September, 1854.

Children of JOHN CLOUGH and MARTHA (WHITE) GLOVER, born in Vinalhaven, Me.:

+724. Thomas, b. Feb. 20, 1812 ;
                                    m. { 1st, Lucy Jane Eaton ;
                                         { 2d, Lucy B. Stetson, of Camden.
+725. Mary Hill, b. Sept. 15, 1815 ; m. Rev. Winthrop O. Thomas, of Marshfield, Mass.
+726. Sarah White, b. March 4, 1818 ; m. Benjamin Cushing, Esq., Camden, Me.
+727. John White,   } b. Nov. 5, 1821 ; { m. Sarah C. Stetson ;
+728. Martha White, }   { m. Hosea B. Eaton, M.D.
                                            Both of Camden.
+729. James Russell, b. April 4, 1824 ; m. Nancy Palmer, Camden.
+730. George White, b. April 29, 1827 ; m. Philena Hartford, "
+731. Clara Fisher, b. Dec. 28, 1829 ; d. Oct. 9, 1848, aged 18 years.

(217)   ELIJAH GLOVER, son of James and Mary (Hill-Metcalf) Glover, was born in Vinalhaven, Me., Aug. 27, 1792; resides in Camden, Me., near the steamboat landing. He was for many years a shipmaster; has acquired a competent estate, and retired from business.

He was married to Nancy Crabtree, of Vinalhaven, daughter of Eleazer and Lucy (Train) Crabtree, March 20, 1822. She was born in Vinalhaven, April 15, 1796, and is now living.

Children of Capt. ELIJAH and NANCY (CRABTREE) GLOVER, born in Vinalhaven:

+732. Susannah, b. Feb. 11, 1823; m. Rev. Edward Freeman.
+733. Benjamin Franklin, b. Dec. 24, 1824; d. Oct. 6, 1849, aged 25.
+734. Rachel Crabtree, b. April 28, 1827; m. Charles R. Pottle.
+735. Marshall Parks,   b. June 20, 1830; m. Mary Daggett.
 736. Adelaide Harriet, b. July 29, 1832; d. May 11, 1851, aged 18.
+737. Lucy Hill, b. June 3, 1835; m. Orris Starrett Andrews, of
       Warren, Me.

(219) WILLARD GLOVER, fourth and youngest son of James and Mary (Hill-Metcalf) Glover, was born in Vinalhaven, Me., July 29, 1796, and died in Swanville, Waldo Co., Me., Sept. 18, 1865, in his 70th year. He graduated at Waterville College, Maine, in 1825, studied Divinity, and became a preacher of the Baptist denomination; was ordained, about 1828, over the Baptist Church in Lyndeborough, N. H.; resigned about 1838, and was installed in Swanville, about 1840. He remained there until his decease. He was an earnest and successful clergyman.

He was married to Emeline Pickard.

Children of Rev. WILLARD and EMELINE (PICKARD) GLOVER:

738. Emeline.
739. Mary Anne.
740. Harriet.
741. Julia.
742. Susan.
743. Lucy.

(220) BENJAMIN WADSWORTH GLOVER, son of Ebenezer and Sarah (Wadsworth) Glover, was born at Newbury farm, Dorchester, now Quincy, Dec. 14, 1774, and died in Reading, May 21, 1815, in his 42d year, leaving a widow and two children. He succeeded to the inheritance of the homestead at Newbury farm, on the decease of his father, and left it, at his decease, to his heirs.

Jan. 6, 1799, he was married to Mehetable Willard Baxter, of Quincy. She was the daughter of Capt. Joseph Baxter and his first wife Anna Adams, of Quincy, and was born there. She died at the homestead in Quincy, Dec. 4, 1858.

Children of BENJAMIN WADSWORTH and MEHETABLE WILLARD (BAXTER) GLOVER, born at Newbury farm, Quincy:

+744. Horatio N., b. March 6, 1801 ; m. Martha Turpin Hovey, of
        Brighton.
+745. Benjamin F., b. June 3, 1803 ; m. Josephine Baxter, Boston.

(222) HANNAH GLOVER, daughter of Ebenezer and Mary
(Davenport) Glover, was born at the Newbury farm homestead, in
Dorchester, Sept. 4, 1789, and died in Quincy, Jan. 31, 1861, in her
72d year.

Jan. 1, 1810, she was married to Thomas Adams, Esq., of Quincy.
They had one son, born in Quincy:

746. Francis, b. in Nov., 1810 ; m. Sarah Beale, of Boston.

(223) JOSEPH NEALE ARNOLD, eldest son of Daniel and
Jerusha (Glover) Arnold, was born in Quincy, Oct. 10, 1764, and died
there, Oct. 24, 1816, in his 53d year.

June 16, 1785, he was married to Mehetable Adams, of Quincy,
where they continued to live until his decease.

Children of JOSEPH NEALE and MEHETABLE (ADAMS) ARNOLD, born
in Quincy :

+747. Joseph,   b. Feb. 5, 1786 ; m. Elizabeth Briesler, of Quincy.
+748. Mehetable, b. Feb. 16, 1787 ; m. Dr. Thomas Phipps, Jr., "
 749. Ebenezer,   b. Nov. 5, 1789 ; m. Patience Mann, of Quincy.
 750. Louisa,   b. Feb. 24, 1793 ; m. James Arnold, of Quincy.
 751. Elihu Adams, b. Oct. 11, 1795 ; m. Mary Ann Turner, Quincy.
 752. Jerusha Glover, b. Nov. 16, 1797 ; m. George A. Thayer.
 753. Charles, b. March 27, 1800 ; m. Elizabeth Wayland, Boston.
 754. Lemuel, b. March 13, 1802 ;
                    m. { 1st, Susan Smith, of Charleston, S. C. ;
                         { 2d, Caroline Gilbert, of New York.
        Lives in New York.

(224) DANIEL ARNOLD, second son of Daniel and Jerusha
(Glover) Arnold, was born in Quincy, Oct. 21, 1766, and died there.
He was married to Charlotte Cleverly, of Quincy, Sept. 3, 1789.

Children of DANIEL and CHARLOTTE (CLEVERLY) ARNOLD, born in
Quincy :

755. James,   b. Aug. 21, 1794.
756. Daniel,   b. Dec. 5, 1798.
757. Elizabeth, b. May 13, 1797 ; m. William Baxter, of Quincy,
        Feb. 17, 1821, removed to Quincy, and lives there at the
        present time.

(225) ELIZABETH ARNOLD, eldest daughter of Daniel and Jerusha (Glover) Arnold, was born in Quincy, Sept. 16, 1770, and died there, Dec. 5, 1858, aged 88 years.

Oct. 10, 1793, she was married to Jesse Fenno, of Milton. He died in Quincy, July 19, 1827, aged 68 years.

Children of JESSE and ELIZABETH (ARNOLD) FENNO, born in Quincy:

758. Elizabeth Clough, b. in 1794 ; m. Thomas Weld, of Roxbury.
759. Jerusha Glover, m. Samuel Curtis, of Quincy.
760. Maria D., m. Nathaniel Mann, of Quincy.
761. Charlotte, m. John Carr, of Quincy.
+762. Thomas Glover, m. Elizabeth R. Adams, of Quincy.
763. Jesse, died young, aged 20 years.
764. Isaac, lives single, in Quincy.

(226) JERUSHA ARNOLD, second and youngest daughter of Daniel and Jerusha (Glover) Arnold, was born in Quincy, July 27, 1774, and is now living in Quincy.

She was twice married. First, to John Pierce, of Milton, March 3, 1799 ; they lived in Milton, and he died there. She married, second, Caleb Thayer, of Braintree, Oct. 30, 1834. No issue by last marriage. By her first marriage she had one son :

765. John, b. in 1807 ; died young.

(228) JAMES BAXTER, son of Capt. Joseph and Jerusha (Glover-Arnold) Baxter, was born in Quincy, June 28, 1787.

In 1807 he was married to Mary Phipps, daughter of Dr. Thomas Phipps, Sen. She was born in Quincy in 1789, and died there, June 2, 1862, in her 74th year. Her father was the son of Samuel and Eleanor (Danforth) Phipps, of Cambridge ; born there, March 15, 1737-8 ; graduated at Harvard College in 1757 ; studied medicine, and commenced the practice of his profession in Quincy, and died there, Nov. 3, 1817, aged 80 years.

Children of JAMES and MARY (PHIPPS) BAXTER, born in Quincy:

766. Samuel Danforth, b. Oct. 12, 1809.
767. Charles Francis, b. July 15, 1811 ; m. Elizabeth Brigham, of Quincy.
768. James, b. July 23, 1813 ; m.
769. Eleanor, b. July 31, 1815 ; m. Clift Rogers, of Marshfield.

770. Mary Jerusha,   b. Oct. 28, 1819; died young.
771. Joseph,   b. Jan. 4, 1822.
772. George Washington, b. Feb. 14, 1824.
773. John Adams,   } b. July 12, 1827.
774. Thomas Phipps,   }
775. Rebecca Phipps,   b. Nov. 24, 1833; m. Horace Eaton.

(229) ELIZABETH CLOUGH BENT, daughter of Jason and Anna (Glover) Bent, was born in Sudbury, July 13, 1774, and died in Stowe, Nov. 30, 1810, aged 36 years.

She was married to Jabez Maynard, May 28, 1794, and removed to Stowe.

Children of JABEZ and ELIZABETH CLOUGH (BENT) MAYNARD, born in Stowe:

776. Anna Glover, m. —— Smith.
777. Jason.
778. John Clough.
779. Mary Stone, m. Abner Everett, of Brighton.

(230) THOMAS BENT, son of Jason and Anna (Glover) Bent, was born in Sudbury, Sept. 4, 1776, and died there, March 28th, 1848, aged 72 years.

He was married to Sarah Patch, of Stowe, Jan. 29, 1807. He was a farmer, and inherited the Bent homestead in Sudbury, residing on it at his decease.

Children of THOMAS and SARAH (PATCH) BENT, born in Sudbury:

780. Newell, b. Nov. 15, 1807; m. Sarah Goodman, of Sudbury.
781. Isabella Jane, b. March 7, 1809; m. Jesse Shattuck, Pepperell.
782. William Glover, b. Nov. 21, 1810; m. Matilda Lunt, Orono, Me.
783. Thomas E.,   b. June 18, 1812; m. Matilda Louisa Phelps, of Lowell.
784. John H., b. May 28, 1814; m. Sally Woodman, Portsmouth.
785. Jonathan C., b. Feb. 26, 1817; m. Clarissa Ann Smith, of Sudbury.
786. Rufus H., b. May 3, 1820; m. { 1st, Eliza M. Colburn; { 2d, Mary N. Rice, Brighton.
787. Sarah Ann, b. July 4, 1826; d. March 21, 1847, in her 21st yr.
788. Lucy Jane, b. May 15, 1828; d. Dec. 13, 1846, in her 19th year.

(232) NANCY BENT, daughter of Jason and Anna (Glover) Bent, was born in Sudbury, Oct. 9, 1780, and died in Stowe. Date of death not ascertained.

Sept. 1, 1806, she was married to Moody Tenney, of Stowe.

Children of MOODY and NANCY (BENT) TENNEY:

789. Eliphalet.
790. Lewis.
791. David.
792. Jason.
793. Anna Glover, died in infancy.
794. Elbridge.
795. Anna Glover.

(233) JERUSHA BENT, daughter of Jason and Anna (Glover) Bent, was born in Sudbury, May 26, 1783.
She was married to Samuel Browne, of Sudbury, in 1803.

Children of SAMUEL and JERUSHA (BENT) BROWNE, born in Sudbury:

796. Elbridge Gerry.
797. Jerusha.
798. Emeline Augusta.
799. Samuel.
800. Sewell, died in 1830.

(234) JASON BENT, son of Jason and Anna (Glover) Bent, was born in Sudbury, Sept. 12, 1785, and is still living.
He was twice married. First, April 10, 1810, to Asonick Fairbank, of Framingham. She died; and he married, second, in May, 1835, Martha Plimpton, of Sudbury.

Children of JASON and ASONICK (FAIRBANK) BENT, born in Sudbury:

801. Elizabeth Clough.
802. Daniel, died in infancy.
803. Daniel.
804. Asahel.
805. Harriet Sophia.
806. Mary Anne.

(237) ROBERT GLOVER, eldest son of Thomas and Sarah (Bonney) Glover, was born in Pembroke, Mass., Nov. 2, 1726, and died there, Aug. 20, 1787, in his 61st year. He left a widow.

30*

He was twice married. First, in 1746, to Bethiah Tubbs; and by her he had six children. She died in 1780, and he married, second, Jan. 23, 1783, Alice Standish. There was no issue by the last marriage.

Children of ROBERT and BETHIAH (TUBBS) GLOVER, born in Pembroke:

+807. James,   b. Sept. 22, 1748 ; m. Rachel Bonney, of Pembroke.
+808. Lydia,   b. Dec. 15, 1750 ; m. Josiah Witherell, Pembroke.
 809. Sarah,   b. May 6, 1753 ; m. Thomas Bore, of Boston.
+810. Thomas,   b. March 24,1757 ; m. —— Rollins, St. George, Me.
+811. Bethiah,   b. March 24,1760 ; m. Foster McFarland, Scituate.
+812. Robert,   b. March 27,1763 ; m. Kezia Barrows, Hebron, Me.
+813. Jonathan,b. Oct. 8,1767 ; m. —— Smith, of Rehoboth.

Robert Glover purchased a tract of land in Pembroke, of Isaac Little, in 1772.

The will of Robert Glover, of Pembroke, July 18, 1787, County of Plymouth, Commonwealth of Massachusetts, bequeaths to beloved wife Alice one-third part of his personal estate. To well-beloved daughter Bethiah all his estate, both real and personal, she paying all his just debts and legacies. To his five children—James, Thomas, Robert, Jonathan, and Lydia Witherell—ten shillings each. Appoints John Turner, Jr., sole executor. Witnessed by John Stetson, Nathan Stetson, and Miles Standish. Daniel Bonney, Samuel Stetson and Nathan Stetson, were appraisers. In 1788, warrant of inventory; his estate rendered insolvent. Warrant and list of claims; executor's account, 1789 ; warrant and dower.

(240) THOMAS GLOVER, fourth son of Thomas and Sarah (Bonney) Glover, was born in Pembroke, Aug. 30, 1732. He lived in Duxbury, and was enrolled in the company of Capt. Abel Keene —Col. Joseph Thacher's regiment—the 24th of July, 1756, when 23 years old. He went in the expedition to Crown Point, and served under Capt. Thomas Clap in the French and Indian War. "Oct. 11, 1756—Thomas Glover sick at Albany."—(P. 516, Army Rec.) No record appears there of his return or of his death.

He was married, previous to 1756, and had a son:

+814. "June 12, 1756. Thomas, the son of Thomas Glover, was baptized."—*Pembroke Church Record.*

(241) GEORGE GLOVER, the fifth son of Thomas and Sarah (Bonney) Glover, was born in Pembroke, in 1735. He resided in Plymouth; no date of death recorded.

He was married, April 27, 1753, to Mary Fisher, of Plymouth, by Rev. Dr. Bacon, of that place.

He was enrolled in Capt. Stephen Churchill's company, Col. Hyde's regiment, in 1780. In February, 1781, enrolled again in Capt. Stephen Churchill's company, Col. Thomas Cotton's regiment, which did duty at Newport, R. I., Feb. 28, 1781.

Children of GEORGE and MARY (FISHER) GLOVER, born in Plymouth:

+815. Mary, b. July 16, 1758; perhaps m. Nath. Prentice Peabody.
  816. George, b. Feb. 23, 1761; d. in Milton, May 11, 1799, aged 38.
+817. Margaret, b. April 10, 1763; m. Nathaniel Cooper, Kingston.
  818. Samuel, b. Aug. 1, 1764.

(246) SAMUEL GLOVER, second son of Samuel and Ruth (Wheat) Glover, was born in Needham, April 24, 1756, and died in Greenwich, N. Y., Jan. 17, 1808, aged 52 years. When 14 years of age, he was bound to an apprenticeship with Aaron Martin, of Sturbridge, and learned a trade. He was a soldier in the War of the Revolution; he enlisted when 21 years of age, while living in Sturbridge. ("Samuel Glover, of Sturbridge, 5 months service, Col. Eben Larned, Capt. Marden's company.") He was sick at Albany, and discharged. He was again enrolled in the service of his country, 15th regiment, Capt. Martin's command (Sturbridge), and served 36 months and 8 days.

April 5, 1781, he was married to Miriam Clarke, daughter of Moses Clarke, of Sturbridge, and born there in 1766. She died in Greenwich, N. Y., in 1814, aged 48 years.

Children of SAMUEL and MIRIAM (CLARKE) GLOVER, born in Sturbridge:

+819. Elizabeth Dickerson, b. Nov. 9, 1781; m. Artemas Martin, of Jackson, N. Y.
+820. Samuel, b. Jan. 23, 1783; m. Mary Stone, of Boston.
+821. Henry, b. Dec. 6, 1785; m. Isabella Hutchins.
  822. Lucy, b. Jan. 17, 1788; m. { 1st, John Martin; 2d, —— Clark.
  823. Moses, } b. Feb. 20, 1790; { died in infancy.
  824. Aaron, } { died in infancy.

+825. Jeremiah,   b. April 24, 1791 ; m. Nancy Gilchrist.
826. Miriam,   b. Aug. 25, 1793 ; died in infancy.
827. Dilly,   b. Sept. 25, 1794 ; died in infancy.
+828. Anna,   b. Dec. 18, 1796 ; m. David Barton, ——, N. Y.
829. Sarah,   b. Dec. 28, 1798 : m. Jeremiah Wheeler.
830. Moses Clarke, b. June 25, 1802 ; living, in 1858, with his bro-
        ther Jeremiah Glover.
+831. Reuben,   b. Aug. 30, 1804 ; m. Calista Clarke, Southbridge.

[*Seventh Generation.*]

(348) LUCY WHITWELL, the third daughter of Samuel and
Anne (Glover) Whitwell, was born in Boston, August, 1781, and died
there in October, 1846, aged 65 years.

She was married to Dr. Isaac Rand, then residing at St. Christopher's. They had one daughter, viz.:

+832. Elizabeth Malcolm, m. Dr. Alexander Thomas ; died in Sept.,
        1863, leaving a son.

Dr. ISAAC RAND, the husband of Lucy Whitwell, was a son of
Isaac Rand, who graduated at Harvard College in 1761, and was
himself a graduate at Harvard College in 1787.

(353) MARY MORRELL, eldest daughter of Deacon James
and Mary (Glover) Morrell, was born in Boston, Feb. 20, 1779, and
died in Cambridge, at the residence of Dr. Wilkes Allen, Jan. 8,
1864, aged 85 years.

She was married, Nov. 13, 1805, to Rev. Wilkes Allen, of Chelmsford, Mass. They had eight children, born to them there. He was
the son of Elnathan and Thankful (Hastings) Allen ; born in
Shrewsbury, July 10, 1775 ; graduated at Harvard College, in Cambridge, in the class of 1801 ; was the first teacher in School District
No. 1, in Dorchester ; ordained as a Minister at Chelmsford, Nov.
16, 1803, and dismissed at his own request, Oct. 21, 1832 ; removed
to Andover, and died there, Dec. 2, 1845, aged 70 years.

Children of Rev. WILKES and MARY (MORRELL) ALLEN :

+833. James Morrell,   b. Oct. 5, 1807 ; m. Mary Dauby Robins.
+834. Charles Hastings, b. March 11, 1809 ; m. Sarah Adams.
+835. Wilkes,   b. Dec. 30, 1810 ; m. Jane Munroe.
836. John Clarke, b. Nov. 15, 1812 ; H. C. 1833 ; d. in 1834, aged 22.
837. Israel,   b. Nov. 27, 1814 ; d. Jan. 16, 1815.

+838. Nathaniel Glover,　b. Jan.　22, 1816 ; m. Catharine Parker.
　839. Mary,　　　　　　b. Feb.　26, 1818 ; d. Sept.　9, 1821.
　840. Sarah,　　　　　　b. March 17, 1820 ; d. Sept. 18, 1821.

(355)　ANNE MORRELL, the second daughter of Deacon James and Mary (Glover) Morrell, was born in Boston, Sept. 10, 1784, and died in Roxbury, May 22, 1843, in her 60th year.

She was married, Jan. 24, 1810, to Rufus Wyman, M.D.　He was the son of Zebediah and Eunice Wyman, of Woburn, and was born there July 16, 1778; graduated at Harvard College in 1799; attended the study of medicine and surgery under the instruction of Dr. John Jeffries, Sen.; and subsequently, when he had acquired a competent knowledge of the profession, commenced the practice of medicine in Chelmsford, where he was highly esteemed for his professional skill, integrity of character, and usefulness as a citizen. In 1818 he was chosen Physician and Superintendent of the McLean Asylum for the Insane, then just commencing its operations, the whole management of which he organized, and where he remained in active service seventeen years.　Of his success, Dr. Luther V. Bell, twenty-four years later, speaks in these words: "The weight of responsibility and difficulty which necessarily fell upon him, must have been far greater than any of his successors in such trusts, who had the aids of his ingenuity and labors, can have experienced.　Indeed, to this day, scarce any institution can be visited in the land where evidence of the operations of his mind do not present themselves on every hand, not only in details of architectural and mechanical arrangements, but in the moral regimen and internal system."　"There was a moral beauty in his character, a sterling, uncompromising integrity in him, as a medical director of a public institution, and which may well serve as a model to all who may be called upon to discharge such functions."　Dr. Wyman left the Asylum in 1834, on account of the failure of his health, and the remainder of his life was passed in Roxbury.　During his retirement he manifested the same untiring activity and the same interest in all good works that marked his public career in previous years.　In a sermon preached after his death, Dr. George Putnam used the following words in relation to him: "I cannot now, I could not in his life-time, gather any words concerning him, but words of commendation and admiring respect. He was not one of those who are prized only after death.　His character was of that positive sort, so obviously and constantly ruled by high principle, that men noted it while he lived, as they only note those who are really above the level of common excellence, who live not by exponents but by principle, not to appearances but to fulfil righteousness for righteousness sake." He was appointed and served in various offices of trust and honor in the town where he lived; was a member of the American Academy of Arts and Sciences; and, for two years previous to his decease, was President of the Massachusetts Medical Society. He died in Roxbury, June 22, 1842, aged 64 years. His death is alluded to in one of the daily newspapers, as that of one "long and extensively known and respected as the Superintendent of the McLean Hospital for the Insane at Charlestown."

Children of Dr. RUFUS and ANNE (MORRELL) WYMAN, born in Chelmsford, Mass.:

841. Rufus,   b. Dec. 15, 1810; resides in Cambridge, unmarried.
+842. Morrill,   b. Jan. 25, 1812; m. Elizabeth Aspinwall Pulsifer.
+843. Jeffries, b. Aug. 11, 1814;
        m. { 1st, Adaline Wheelwright, Roxbury;
             2d, Anna Williams Whitney, Boston.
844. Edward,   b. July 18, 1816; d. Nov. 7, 1817.
+845. Edward,   b. Aug. 1, 1818; m. Margaret Curry Boyd, Boston.
+846. Elizabeth, b. May 1, 1820; resides in Cambridge, unmarried.
847. Hamilton, b. Dec. 10, 1827; died April 8, 1828.

(357) ELIZABETH MORRELL, fourth daughter of Deacon James and Mary (Glover) Morrell, was born in Boston, Jan. 20, 1796, and still resides there.

She was married, June 17, 1831, to Joseph Neal Howe, of Cambridge, and was his second wife. He was the son of —— Howe, of Cambridge, and died in Boston in 1865. Aug. 23, 1822, he was married to Elizabeth Kneeland Harris, of Cambridge, by whom he had children. He was engaged extensively in commercial pursuits.

Children of JOSEPH NEAL and ELIZABETH (MORRELL) HOWE, born in Boston:

848. Anne Janette, b. in 1832.
849. Eliza,   b. in 1834.
850. Maria Louise, b. in 1837; married.

(358) JAMES MORRELL, second son and youngest child of Deacon James and Mary (Glover) Morrell, was born in Boston, Nov. 13, 1800, and died in Dorchester, Oct. 11, 1846, aged 46 years.

In 1820, he was married to Pamela Smith, of Ellsworth, Maine. They had six children.

Children of JAMES and PAMELA (SMITH) MORRELL, born in Boston:

851. Charles James,   b. Feb. 29, 1821 ; m.
852. Sarah Cecelia,   b. May 26, 1827.
853. Mary Glover,   b. Aug. 28, 1829.
854. Anne Wyman,   b. Feb. 8, 1833.
855. Pamelia,   b. Oct. 20, 1837.
856. Frances Elizabeth, b. Jan. 13, 1839.

(359) JANE SALTER, the eldest daughter of Richard and Jane (Carnes) Salter, was born in Boston, Aug. 7, 1763, and died before 1795.

Oct. 11, 1785, she was married to Joseph Ingraham, by the Rev. Simeon Howard.

Children of JOSEPH and JANE (SALTER) INGRAHAM:

857. Joseph,   b. Sept. 13, 1787.
858. Frederick William, b. April 4, 1788.
859. Daniel Greenleaf, b. June 11, 1791 ; graduated at Harvard
       College in 1809 ; has been a teacher in Boston and other
       places, and is now living in Weymouth, Mass.

(361) JOHN SALTER, eldest son of Richard and Jane (Carnes) Salter, and grandson of Richard and Rachel Glover (Clough) Salter, was born in Boston, April 13, 1770, and died, it is supposed, in Mansfield, Conn.

June 24, 1798, he was married to Elizabeth Rice, of Boston. They had one daughter, born there:

860. Elizabeth, b. Sept. 15, 1801 ; d. Nov. 15, 1802.

ELIZABETH SALTER, wife of Capt. John Salter, died Dec. 2, 1801. He removed to Connecticut, and married, a second time, Mary Williams, and had other children.

(363) NATHANIEL GLOVER, eldest son of Nathaniel and Mehetable (Hill) Glover, was born in Dorchester, Jan. 2, 1756, and died in Boston, July 10, 1804. He was buried in Dorchester; funeral from the Parish Meeting House, sermon by Rev. Dr. Harris. He was in his 49th year, and left a widow and seven child-

ren. He was employed as Custom House bargeman, and followed that business for many years.

Dec. 7, 1778, he was married to (298) Mercy Eaton, of Boston, daughter of Israel and Jerusha (Rawson) Eaton. The date of her birth has not been ascertained. Her mother was sixth daughter of David and Mary (Gulliver) Rawson, and granddaughter of William, Esq., and Anne (Glover) Rawson. She was twice married. After the death of Mr. Nathaniel Glover she was married, a second time, to Nathaniel Hayden, of Quincy, Sept. 1, 1807. There was no issue by the last marriage. She died Dec. 25, 1810, and was buried in Dorchester.

Children of NATHANIEL and MERCY (EATON) GLOVER, born in Dorchester and South Boston:

861. Jerusha Eaton, b. Nov. 12, 1779; resides at the " Old Ladies' Home," Boston; a member of Dr. Neale's Church since 1804.
862. Mercy Eaton, b. March 10, 1782; resides with her sister, as above, and also a member of Dr. Neale's Church since 1804.
863. Nathaniel, b. July 1, 1786; d. July 16, 1811, aged 25 years, killed by the falling of a tree on his head.
+864. Abigail, b. in 1788; m. Ambrose Hayden, of Brookline.
865. Mary, b. in 1790; d. in South Boston, Dec. 11, 1845, unm.; buried at Copp's Hill.
866. William, b. in 1792; resides in the family of Dr. William B. Duggan, in Quincy.
+867. Israel Eaton, b. in 1794; m. Harriet Burditt, of Roxbury.

(364) JOHN HILL GLOVER, second son of Nathaniel and Mehetable (Hill) Glover, was born in Dorchester, Feb. 25, 1757, and died in Salem, June, 1812, aged 55 years. He was by trade a baker, and supplied bread to the army in the War of the Revolution.

In 1777 he was married to Mary Osborne, daughter of John and Mary (Cooke) Osborne, of Danvers, born there in 1760, and died in Salem, March 20, 1832, aged 72 years. She continued to carry on the bakery business after her husband's decease, and was noted for her nice " Election cakes," and other fancy breads.

Children of JOHN HILL and MARY (OSBORNE) GLOVER, born in Salem:

+868. John Hill, b. Oct. 22, 1779;
m. { 1st, Lucy Trafton;
     { 2d, Nancy Phippen (Smith), widow.

869. Mary Osborne, b. Jan. 1, 1781 ; d. Aug. 22, 1782.
870. Mary Osborne, b. Aug., 1783 ; d. Aug. 10, 1810, aged 27.
871. Daniel, b. March 17, 1787 ; lost at sea, Aug. 10, 1815, aged 28.
+872. Cooke Osborne, b. Sept. 19, 1797 ; m. Deborah Foss, of Tamworth, N. H.

(365) MARY GLOVER, eldest daughter of Nathaniel and Mehetable (Hill) Glover, was born in Dorchester, March 5, 1759, and
died Sept. 25, 1819, aged 60 years; buried in Hon. John Howe's
tomb.

Oct. 22, 1778, she was married to George Vose, of Dorchester,
born there Feb. 29, 1754.

Children of GEORGE and MARY (GLOVER) VOSE, born in Dorchester:

+873. Mary Glover, b. May 25, 1779 ; m. Capt. Thomas Munroe.
+874. George, b. May 5, 1781 ; m. { 1st, Susan Lewis ;
                                   { 2d, Sarah Glover, Dorchester.
875. Mehetable, b. Jan.   4, 1783 ; m. Joseph Howe, Dorchester.
876. William,   b. Sept. 24, 1784 ; d. in 1802, aged 18 years.
877. Edward,   b. Sept. 24, 1786 ; drowned at sea.
878. John,   b. Dec. 24, 1787 ; m. Elizabeth Lord, Ipswich.
+879. Thomas,   b. Aug. 25, 1789 ; m. Abigail Glover Howe, Dor.
880. Ezekiel,   b. Nov. 25, 1792 ; m. Eliza Farlee, E. Turner, Me.
881. Jacob,   b. Feb.   3, 1793 ; died when five or six years old.
+882. Elizabeth Glover, b. Jan. 6, 1796 ; m. John Hawes, Roxbury.

(366) SARAH GLOVER, second daughter of Nathaniel and
Mehetable (Hill) Glover, was born in Dorchester, June 6, 1760, baptized there June 9, 1760, and died in Boston since 1800.

She was married to Richard Jenkins, about 1790. They had no
children.

(367) ALEXANDER GLOVER, third son of Nathaniel and
Mehetable (Hill) Glover, was born in Dorchester, Nov. 11, 1761,
baptized there Nov. 15, 1761, and died Aug. 4, 1821, in his 60th
year. At the age of twelve years he went to New York, and in
1775 enlisted in the regular army, at that time recruiting to serve in
the War of the Revolution. He served his country faithfully during
the war, and was honorably discharged.

Jan. 1, 1782, he was married, by Rev. Mr. Graham, to Nancy
Sprung, of New York, daughter of Peter Sprung, Esq., of that city,
born there in 1766, and then but sixteen years of age. She died in

Dorchester, Sept. 21, 1848, aged 82 years.   They had ten children: five born in New York, and five after their removal to Dorchester.

In January, 1786, Alexander Glover had the misfortune to lose his right hand.   The following account is given in a Boston newspaper of Jan. 30, 1786: "An unhappy accident occurred at Dorchester on the 19th inst.   The company of artillery in that town, having turned out to fire a salute on the celebration of a wedding, in loading one of the pieces which was not sufficiently cleansed, the cartridge took fire, by which one of the company, Mr. Alexander Glover, in the act of loading, unfortunately had his right hand shot off, and was otherwise much hurt."   He never enjoyed good health after his return from the war.

Children of ALEXANDER and NANCY (SPRUNG) GLOVER, born in New York and Dorchester:

883. Jane Brower, b. Aug. 28, 1782 ; d. March 23, 1804, aged 22.
+884. Sarah, b. July 19, 1784 ; m. George Vose, of Dorchester, a
         first cousin.
885. Daniel Oliver, b. April 14, 1786 ; d. at sea.
+886. Elizabeth, b. Sept. 12, 1787 ;
                         m. { 1st, Eleazer Norcutt, of Roxbury ;
                              { 2d, Robert Honors, of Charlestown.
887. Nancy Jenkins, b. Jan. 1, 1792 ; d. in 1803, in Dorchester.
+888. William,   b. June 1, 1794 ; m. Sarah Sylvester.
+889. Peter Sprung, b. May 1, 1797 ; m. Eliza Robinson, Barnard,Vt.
890. James Gilmore Nichols, b. Oct. 15, 1800 ; d. in Salem, May
         16, 1835, aged 35 years.
891. Anne Jenkins, b. July 27, 1803 ; d. July 27, 1808, aged 4 yrs.
892. Rachel, b. Jan. 19, 1805 ; m. Samuel Thompson, of Boston,
         May 20, 1852 ; d. in March, 1861, aged 56 years.

(368)   WILLIAM GLOVER, fourth son of Nathaniel and Mehetable (Hill) Glover, was born in Dorchester, May 3, 1763, baptized May 6, 1763, and died in Boston, Jan. 25, 1774, at the residence of Ezekiel Tilestone, Esq., aged 11 years. He was buried in Dorchester.

(375)   ELIZABETH LEEDS, eldest daughter of Jonathan and Patience (Glover) Leeds, was born in Dorchester, April 18, 1765, and died there.

She was married, in 1790, to Nathaniel Topliff, son of Deacon Samuel Topliff, of Dorchester, who was chosen to that office in Sept, 1764, and died Sept. 18, 1807, aged 79 years.

Children of NATHANIEL and ELIZABETH (LEEDS) TOPLIFF:

893. Nathaniel.
894. Samuel Glover.
895. Mary, m. —— Nichols.
896. Sarah, m. —— Cutler.

(381) JAMES LEEDS, fourth son of Jonathan and Patience (Glover) Leeds, was born in Dorchester, June 27, 1777, and died in Brookline, May 4, 1846, aged 69 years.

He was married, Oct. 27, 1803, to Anna Corey, fifth child of Timothy and Elizabeth (Griggs) Corey, of Brookline, born there March 19, 1778, and died there after 1814.

May 4, 1806, James Leeds and Anna his wife were admitted to join the Congregational Church in Brookline, Rev. Dr. Pierce, pastor.

Children of JAMES and ANNA (COREY) LEEDS, born in Brookline, baptized by Rev. Dr. Pierce:

897. James,   bap. May 4, 1806.
898. Timothy Corey, bap. March 1, 1807.
899. Anna Elizabeth, bap. Oct. 4, 1812.

(383) MARY LEEDS, fourth daughter and youngest child of Jonathan and Patience (Glover) Leeds, was born in Dorchester, in 1780, and died in Brookline, Oct. 21, 1827, aged 47 years.

She was married, Nov. 17, 1797, to Elijah Corey, of Brookline third son of Timothy Corey, of Groton, by his wife Elizabeth Griggs, of Roxbury, and was born Nov. 7, 1773, and died in 1860. He was Deacon of the Baptist Church in Brookline, a trustee of the Theological Seminary at Newton, and filled many other offices of trust and honor.

He was twice married; the second time, Jan. 19, 1829, to Lucy (Stearns) Davis, widow. There was no issue by the last marriage.

Children of ELIJAH and MARY (LEEDS) COREY, born in Brookline:

900. Aaron, b. Oct. 23, 1798; m. Amelia Brown, a cousin, of Cambridgeport. They resided in Cambridgeport a few years, and removed to Alton, Illinois.
+901. Elijah,   b. Aug. 14, 1800; m. Mary Richards, of Brookline.
902. Timothy, b. June 21, 1803; d. Feb. 21, 1807.
+903. Mary Glover,   b. March 20, 1806; m. Rev. John Pratt.
+904. Elizabeth Griggs, b. Nov. 21, 1809; m. Rev. Barnas Sears.
905. Timothy,   b. April 21, 1811; d. Oct. 22, 1816.

(384) ALEXANDER GLOVER, eldest son of Alexander, Jr., and Hannah (Pope) Glover, was born at the Dorchester homestead, in Dorchester, Nov. 19, 1770, and died there, Oct. 24, 1842, aged 72 years.

He was married, July 21, 1794, to Jemima Tolman, daughter of John and Elizabeth (Baker) Tolman, of Dorchester, born there Nov. 3, 1774, and died in South Boston, August, 1854, aged 80 years. At the decease of his father in 1813, he succeeded to a portion of the ancient Glover homestead, and was the fifth possessor of it in a direct line of succession of male heirs from the Hon. John Glover, of Dorchester, his first American ancestor.

· Children of ALEXANDER and JEMIMA (TOLMAN) GLOVER, born in Dorchester:

+906. Hannah, b. Sept. 27, 1794 ;
               m. { 1st, Charles Fiske, of Boston :
                   { 2d, Samuel Blake, of South Boston.
 907. Charles, b. Sept. 4, 1796 ; died in 1799, aged 3 years.
+908. Andrew, b. March 26, 1798 ;
               m. { 1st, Mary Anne Holden, of Dorchester;
                   { 2d, Sarah White, Weymouth.
+909. Eliza,   b. July 1, 1800 ;
               m. { 1st, Silas Wheelock, of Westborough;
                   { 2d, William Homes, of Dorchester.
 910. Charles, b. Nov. 10, 1802 ; d. Dec. 19, 1821, aged 19 years.
+911. John,   b. Sept. 28, 1804 ; m. Abigail Pope, of Dorchester.
+912. Alexander, b. Feb. 28, 1807 ; m. Mary Anne Ogle, Baltimore.
 913. Sarah, b. Sept. 3, 1809 : m. Albert A. Bent, South Boston.
 914. Mary Anne, b. Aug. 8, 1814 : m. John Pike, South Boston.
+915. Amasa Stetson, b. July 15, 1817 ; m. Sophia Packard, North Bridgewater.

(387) OLIVER GLOVER, second son of Alexander and Hannah (Pope) Glover, was born at the ancient Dorchester homestead June 15, 1777. He is now living, at the age of 89 years, and resides on a portion of the Glover estate. He was at one time extensively engaged in the lumber business, and traded at Machias, Lubec and other places.

Nov. 10, 1800, he was married to Lydia Barrett Lewis, daughter of Thomas and Elizabeth (Barrett) Lewis, of Marblehead, born there, July 7, 1780, and died in Dorchester, Feb. 2, 1855, in her 75th year.

Children of OLIVER and LYDIA BARRETT (LEWIS) GLOVER, born in Dorchester:

+916. Elizabeth Lemmon, b. April 11, 1802 ; m. Willard Felt.
+917. Mary Lemmon, b. April 24, 1804 ; m. John Pearson, Roxbury.
+918. Thomas Oliver, b. July 5, 1806 : m. Elizabeth Burns, Lubec, Me.
+919. George,   b. May 29, 1808 ; m. Emily Lyon, Dorchester.
920. Rebecca,   b. Aug. 18, 1811 ; resides at the homestead.
+921. Lucretia,   b. Dec. 20, 1814 ; m. John Whittemore.
922. Azor, b. Aug. 18, 1817 ; m. Eliza Lewis Austin, of Marble-
    head, July 13, 1841. He engaged in business in New Jersey,
    and died there, May 20, 1847, aged 30 years.

(388) ABIGAIL GLOVER, third daughter of Alexander and Hannah (Pope) Glover, was born at the ancient Glover homestead, June 21, 1781, and died in Boston, May, 1860, aged 79 years.

Nov. 22, 1800, she was married to Capt. Joseph Lemmon Lewis, of Marblehead, born there, and died in Dorchester, May 31, 1815. He was the son of Thomas and Elizabeth (Barrett) Lewis; was a shipmaster and navigator, and lived mostly at sea until about the time of his decease. After his death, Mrs. Lewis removed, with her family, to Boston. She kept the Hancock House at one time, resided several years in Boylston street, opposite the Boston Common, removed in 1849 to 21 Franklin place, and in 1857 to Union Park street, where she remained until her decease. She was an estimable woman ; discreet, of sound judgment, of enlarged benevolence; of deep and strong attachments, which extended beyond her own family and im-mediate collateral relatives, to far off and remotest kindred; of vigor-ous mental powers, and great penetration; of a strong and inherent love of ancestry and genealogical investigations.

Children of Capt. Joseph Lemmon and Abigail (Glover) Lewis, born in Dorchester:

923. Hannah, b. Nov. 21, 1802; d. Oct. 29, 1822, aged 20 years.
924. Joseph Lemmon,   b. in 1804; died soon.
925. Joseph Alexander, b. in 1806 ; resides at Cincinnati, Ohio.
+926. Thomas May, b. July 22, 1810; m. Mary Harris, New York.
927. Caroline, b. March 4, 1808 ; resides at Union Park street,
    Boston.

(389) JAMES GLOVER, third and youngest son of Alexander and Hannah (Pope) Glover, was born at the ancient Glover home-stead in Dorchester, and now resides at 66 Boylston street, Boston. He has been an eminent and successful merchant.

Dec. 14, 1807, he was married to Jane Beale, daughter of Joseph

31*

and Lillie (Davis) Beale, of Dorchester, born there, and died in Boston, April 15, 1862.

Children of JAMES and JANE (BEALE) GLOVER, born in Dorchester:

+928. Henry,   b. Sept. 7, 1808 ; m. Susan Dana Flintham.
 929. Augusta, b. Dec. 25, 1810 ; resides with her father in Boston.
+930. James,   b. Feb. 19, 1813 ; m. Lydia Elizabeth Holden, Dor.
+931. Joseph Beale, b. May 5, 1815 ; resides at 66 Boylston street, Boston.
+932. Albert, b. May 14, 1817 ; resides at 66 Boylston street, Boston.
 933. Caroline Lewis, b. Nov. 10, 1819 ; resides at 66 Boylston street, Boston.

(390)   EDWARD GLOVER, eldest son of Edward and Hannah (Fifield) Glover, was born in Dorchester, Dec. 8, 1767, and died in Langdon, N. H., Oct. 17, 1825, aged 58 years.

He was married, Aug. 14, 1788, to Hannah Howe, daughter of Samuel and Margaret (Preston) Howe, of Dorchester.   They resided there, after their marriage, twenty-one years.   In December, 1809, they left their native place, and settled in Alstead, N. H.   They arrived in Walpole, N. H., the first day of January, 1810 ; removed the next April to Alstead, where they remained seven years.   In April, 1817, they removed again, to Langdon, N. H., and remained there during his life.   She subsequently returned to Alstead, and resided with her eldest son, and died there, Oct. 15, 1851.

Children of EDWARD and HANNAH (HOWE) GLOVER, born in Dorchester :

+934. Margaret Preston Howe, b. Mch 13, 1789 ; m. Lemuel Babcock.
+935. Lydia,   b. Dec. 17, 1790 ; m. Joseph Field, Rochester, N. Y.
+936. Edward, b. Oct. 19, 1793 ; m. { 1st, Polly Blake ;
                                     { 2d, Sarah E. Studley.
 937. Anson,   b. Oct. 14, 1795 ; d. Sept. 1, 1798, aged 3 years.
+938. Ansel,   b. March 12, 1799 ; m. Nancy Elwell, Alstead, N. H.
+939. Charles, b. Sept. 23, 1802 ; m. Maria Frink, Walpole, N. H.

(391)   HANNAH GLOVER, eldest daughter of Edward and Hannah (Fifield) Glover, was born in Dorchester, Aug. 13, 1771, and died there, Feb. 28, 1829, aged 58 years.   She had been in a state of mental derangement thirty years.

Nov. 24, 1791, at the age of twenty years, she was married to Nathaniel Clapp, son of Roger and Susannah (Wales) Clapp, of

Dorchester; born there, July 13, 1761, and died March 27, 1826, aged 65.

Children of NATHANIEL and HANNAH (GLOVER) CLAPP, born in Dorchester:

+940. Lewis,   b. Aug. 17, 1792 ; m. Lucy Humphreys Clapp.
 941. Enos,   b. May 31, 1794 ; m. Adaline Cassell, July 13, 1834.
 942. Moses,   b. Feb. 15, 1796.
 943. Johanna, b. Feb. 15, 1797 ; d. Sep. 9, 1832, aged 35 yrs., unm.
 944. Hannah, b. Aug. 15, 1798.
 945. Nancy,   b. in 1800.

(392) MARY GLOVER, second daughter of Edward and Hannah (Fifield) Glover, was born in Dorchester, Dec. 1, 1773, baptized Dec. 9, 1773, and died in Roxbury, Nov. 1, 1832, aged 59 years.

Jan. 13, 1793, she was married to Bela Hearsey, of Hingham; born there in 1765, and died in Dorchester, April 1, 1813, aged 48 years.

Children of BELA and MARY (GLOVER) HEARSEY, born in Dorchester :

 946. Edward,   b. May 1, 1794.
+947. Mary Glover,   b. in 1795 ; m. Samuel Coolidge Bird.
+948. Lewis Glover,   b. in 1798 ; m. Hannah S. H. Bryant.
 949. Hannah Fifield,   b. March 21, 1799 ; d. March 31, 1799.
 950. Joseph,   b. in 1802 ; m. Sarah Ann B. Hearsey.
 951. Hannah Matilda,   b. June 1, 1807 ; m. Lemuel Collyer.

(393) LEWIS GLOVER, second son of Edward and Hannah (Fifield) Glover, was born in Dorchester, June 26, 1776, and died in Boston, June, 1810, aged 34 years. He was a merchant.
– In 1800, he was married to Nancy Brazer, daughter of Major John Brazer, of Boston, born there, and died in 1814.

Children of LEWIS and NANCY (BRAZER) GLOVER, born in Boston :

 952. Mary Anne,   b. in 1800 ; d. March 1, 1831, aged 31, unm.
 953. Anne Brazer, b. in 1802 ; m. Benjamin Leeds, of Dorchester.
+954. Lewis,   m. Elizabeth E. Kearney, of Berrysville, Va.
+955. John Brazer, m. { 1st, Charlotte Elizabeth Lyon ;
                       { 2d, Caroline Lincoln, of New Bedford.
 956. Jane Brimmer, b. July 28, 1806 ; m. William H. Montague, of Dedham.
 957. Sarah, b. in 1808 ; m. William H. Guild, of Dedham.

(394) ELIZABETH GLOVER, the third daughter of Edward
and Hannah (Fifield) Glover, was born in Dorchester, Jan. 6, 1781,
and died in Roxbury, Nov. 24, 1819, aged 38 years. "An amiable
and exemplary woman," as styled in the Boston Centinel for Nov.
24, 1819.

March 12, 1799, she was married to Zerubbabel Hearsey, of
Hingham, and removed to Roxbury.

Children of ZERUBBABEL and ELIZABETH (GLOVER) HEARSEY, born
in Roxbury :

958. Elizabeth,   b. June   30, 1799 ; d. Nov. 30, 1802.
959. Charles,   b. May   8, 1801 ; d. Nov. 30, 1801.
960. Mary Glover,   b. in 1803 ; d. in 1805.
961. Margaret Glover, b. March 5, 1805.
962. Samuel May,   b. Aug.   12, 1807.
963. Mary Anne Glover, b. Aug.   10, 1809.
964. Sarah Ann Brazer, b. Nov.   17, 1810 ; m. Joseph Hearsey.
+965. Hannah W., b. in 1812 ; m. Frederick Thayer, of Gloucester.
+966. Elizabeth,   b. in 1814 ; m. Samuel Hatch, of Abington.
967. Harriet,   b. in 1816 ; resides in Boston, unmarried.

(395) SAMUEL GLOVER, third son of Edward and Hannah
(Fifield) Glover, was born in Dorchester, Nov. 6, 1785, and resided
there until he attained the age of his majority. He went to New
York, was a merchant, and died there since 1810.

(396) JOHN HOWE, eldest son of Hon. John and Rachael
(Glover) Howe, was born in Dorchester, Sept. 4, 1765, and died
there, May 25, 1825, aged 59 years.

He was twice married. First, in January, 1788, to Martha Bird,
of Dorchester ; second, Oct. 13, 1813, he was married, by Rev. Dr.
Pierce, to Elizabeth Heath, of Brookline, daughter of John Heath,
born Nov. 21, baptized Nov. 26, 1769. She was admitted to join
the Congregational Church in Brookline, April 15, 1798. After his
marriage, John Howe removed to Brookline, and lived there until
after the death of his second wife, when he returned to Dorchester
and passed the remainder of his days there.

Children of JOHN and MARTHA (BIRD) HOWE, born in Brookline :

968. Rachael Glover, b. Jan. 4, 1789 ; m. William Worthington.
+969. John, b. March 14, 1792 ; m. { 1st, Hannah Williams, Heath ;
                                     { 2d, Louisa Goddard, Brookline.

970. Martha, b. Feb. 1, bap. Feb. 15, 1795 ; d. Aug. 22, 1795.
No record of other children has been found, and none have been
reported.

(398) GEORGE HOWE, son of Hon. John and Rachael (Glover)
Howe, was born in Dorchester, July 6, 1769, and died there, Aug.
16, 1828, aged 59 years.

He was married to Mary Anne Holden, in 1788, and had one
child, born in Dorchester, viz. :

971. Abigail Glover, b. March 19, 1790 ; m. Thomas Vose, of
Boston, Aug. 23, 1812.

(400) RACHEL HOWE, third daughter of Hon. John and
Rachael (Glover) Howe, was born in Dorchester, Aug. 19, 1773, and
died there, Dec. 17, 1847, aged 74 years.

She was married in Roxbury, Dec. 6, 1792, to Major Edward
Robinson, of Dorchester ; born there in 1756, and died Feb. 13,
1823, aged 64 years. He was twice married. First, Dec. 11, 1787,
to Rachel Bird, by whom he had one son, James Robinson, who was
born in Dorchester, May 10, 1789. Mrs. Rachel Robinson died June
3, 1789, and he married, a second time, Rachel Howe, by whom he
had four children.

Children of JAMES and RACHEL (HOWE) ROBINSON, born in Dorchester :

972. Rachel Bird,   b. Jan.,   1794.
973. Edward,   b. March,   1796.
974. Rachel Bird Howe, b. Jan. 2, 1801 ; d. May 14, 1802.
+975. John Howe, b. Nov. 21, 1809 ; m. Elizabeth Clapp, of Dorchester.

(401) JOSEPH HOWE, son of Hon. John and Rachael (Glover)
Howe, was born in Dorchester, Sept. 23, 1776, and died there in 1858.

He was married to Lucy Hunt, of Braintree, Dec. 31, 1811. She
was the daughter of Anthony and (418) Martha Fletcher (Pope)
Hunt, was born in Braintree, July 12, 1772, and is now living.

Children of JOSEPH and LUCY (HUNT) HOWE, born in Dorchester :

+976. Theodore Lyman, b. Oct. 9, 1815 ; m. Louisa Field, Dorchester.
977. Joseph Henry,   b. Nov. 20, 1816 ; d. Sept. 13, 1822.
078. Francis Augustus, b. Jan. 2, 1818 ; d. Jan. 28, 1821.

+979. Elizabeth, b. June 18, 1819; m. Lyman Willard, Cambridge.
980. Lucy Anne Robinson, b. July 12, 1822 ; m. George Woodman, of Dorchester, May 2, 1849.
981. Joseph Francis, b. Aug. 3, 1824 ; d. Sept. 14, 1842, aged 18.

(402) JAMES HOWE, son of Hon. John and Rachael (Glover) Howe, was born in Dorchester, Jan. 28, 1781, and died there, Aug. 27, 1830, aged 49 years.

He was married to Elizabeth Clap, June 30, 1803. She was the daughter of Ebenezer, Esq., and Mary (Glover) Clap, of Dorchester, was born Sept. 10, 1782, and is still living in that town.

Children of JAMES and ELIZABETH (CLAP) HOWE, born in Dorchester :

982. Eliza Ann, m. Edward Pierce, of Dorchester.
983. James Theodore, m. Martha Jenkins, of Dorchester.

(405) JONATHAN PIERCE, son of Jonathan and Mary (Glover) Pierce, was born in Dorchester, Oct. 11, 1777, and died in Boston, Feb. 10, 1831, aged 54 years.

He was twice married. First, to Eunice Tolman, Dec. 6, 1804. She was the daughter of John and Elizabeth (Baker) Tolman, and was born in Dorchester, Jan. 16, 1782; died in Boston, Feb. 10, 1831. He was married, second, to Clarissa Blake, born in Dorchester, Jan. 12, 1784.

Children of JONATHAN and EUNICE (TOLMAN) PIERCE, born in Dorchester and Boston :

984. John, b. Sept. 21, 1805 ; d. in Mobile, Alabama, Nov. 29, 1847.
985. Amasa, b. April 11, 1807 ; lives in Hollis, N. H. ;
m. { 1st, Hannah Cummings ; 2d, ———— Emerson.
986. Henry, b. March 8, 1809 ; drowned at the Balize, New Orleans, by the upsetting of a boat, June 5, 1827.
987. Eunice, b. Jan. 27, 1811 ; d. in Boston, April 12, 1822, aged 11.

Children born in Boston :

988. Hannah Preston, b. May 1, 1813 ; d. Sept. 3, 1852, aged 39 years, unmarried.
989. Lucy Inglee, b. June 15, 1815 ; m. Edwin Pronk, June 18, 1844, son of J. D. V. Pronk ; resides in Dorchester.
990. Mary, b. Dec. 6, 1818 ; d. Nov. 3, 1844, in her 26th year, unm.
991. Martha, b. Feb. 26, 1821 ; d. May 26, 1846, aged 25 years.
992. Charles, b. Oct. 23, 1823 ; d. Sept. 8, 1826, aged 3 years.
993. Martha Eunice, b. Nov. 12, 1828.

(407) DANIEL PIERCE, son of Jonathan and Mary (Glover) Pierce, was born in Dorchester, Aug. 4, 1779, and died there, Nov. 1, 1848. He was a cabinet maker.

He was married to Lydia Davenport, May 10, 1803.

Children of DANIEL and LYDIA (DAVENPORT) PIERCE, born in Dorchester:

994. Elisha Davenport, b. March 15, 1804; d. Aug. 8, 1843, aged 39.
995. Daniel, b. Sept. 16, 1805 ;
         m. { 1st, Maria A. Howe, Sept. 16, 1835 ;
            { 2d, Sarah Gay, Jan. 1, 1850.
+996. Samuel Stillman, b. March 27, 1807 ; m. Ellen M. T. Wallis, February, 1836.
997. Elizabeth Glover, b. March 18, 1809; d. May 23, 1848, aged 39.
998. Lydia Holden,   b. Jan. 31, 1811.
999. Mary Glover,   b. Sept. 6, 1812; d. Sept. 1, 1825, aged 13.
1000. Harriet,   b. Dec. 2, 1813.

(408) MARY PIERCE, daughter of Jonathan and Mary (Glover) Pierce, was born in Dorchester, Nov. 2, 1781, and died in that town.

She married Capt. Stephen Tolman, Oct. 16, 1806. He was the son of John and Hannah Tolman, and was born in Dorchester, Jan. 4, 1777. He is a farmer, and lives in Dorchester. In the War of 1812 he commanded a company of militia, and was stationed at Fort Independence, Boston harbor.

Children of STEPHEN and MARY (PIERCE) TOLMAN, born in Dorchester:

1001. Hannah, b. July 18, 1807 ; m. Ebenezer Pope, April 5, 1832.
1002. Mary,   b. Dec. 13, 1808 ; m. Enos Howe, Dec. 24, 1829.
1003. Stephen, b. Jan. 19, 1810 ;
         m. { 1st, Hannah C. Foster, Nov. 19, 1840 ;
            { 2d, Caroline Sumner Sawyer, Nov. 26, 1846.
1004. Rachel, b. Nov. 5, 1812.
1005. John,   b. July 14, 1814 ; d. Sept. 5, 1838, aged 24 years.
1006. Clarissa, b. Dec. 18, 1815 ; m. Rev. William Wakefield, Jr.
1007. Richard, b. Sept. 30, 1817 ; m. Olivia Sweetser, Dec. 1, 1845.
1008. Albert, b. Feb. 13, 1824 : grad. at Amherst Coll., 1845 ; was a tutor in 1848 ; in 1850 a teacher in the Young Ladies' Institute at Pittsfield.
1009. Anne, b. Nov. 23, 1826 ; lives with her father, in Dorchester.

(409) ALEXANDER PIERCE, third son of Jonathan and Mary (Glover) Pierce, was born in Dorchester, Aug. 7, 1783, and died there, Oct. 8, 1820, in his 37th year.

Sept. 9, 1807, he was married to Margaret Cunningham Hall
Spear. They had a son, who went West and died there—name not
reported.

(415) LEMUEL BLAKE, the third son of William and Rachel
(Glover) Blake, was born in Boston, Aug. 9, 1775, and died there,
March 4, 1861, in his 86th year. He was never married. With his
decease, the line of Pelatiah Glover, Jr., the youngest son of Nathaniel Glover, Jr., became extinct. He used often to say that
"he was the last of his line." He always took a lively interest
in whatever related to the history and genealogy of his family, of
both Blake and Glover descents, and has from time to time communicated to the writer his recollections of family incidents and relationships. Of his business relations and occupations he gave in substance the following: In early life he was placed in a bookstore kept
by Gould & Blake, known as the Boston Book Store, on the corner
of Spring Lane and Cornhill. In 1797, at the age of 22 years, he
commenced business with his brother William Pynson Blake, and
carried on the book and publishing business, under the firm of William P. & Lemuel Blake. He was subsequently connected with
David West, in the same business, as West & Blake. At another
time, after discontinuing the book and publishing business, he connected himself with Joseph L. Cunningham, as Auctioneers and Commission Merchants, under the firm and name of Blake & Cunningham. He read much, and was intellectually agreeable and well informed on present and past literature and histrionic lore. He prepared a few works for publication, among which was Webster's
Speeches on the Constitution. Of Mr. Webster he was an ardent
admirer. His last employment, and to which he devoted much of his
time, was the construction of a Portable Map of the World, which
was never issued, on account of the failure of the publishers into
whose hands he had committed it. He was enthusiastic in view of
the great good to be accomplished by it, and spent much of his time
and money to render it acceptable to the public. Its failure was the
cause of a bitter disappointment, occurring as it did towards the
close of his life. He took a great interest in military affairs, belonged to two independent companies, and was an officer in each. He
was first a member of the Independent Cadet company, and was
elected Sergeant; second, was chosen Ensign, and subsequently

Lieutenant, in the New England Guards, and received from them a valuable piece of silver plate as a token of their regard for him and gratitude for his services. He was elected to various offices of trust and honor in civil life. He was treasurer and secretary of the Washington Benevolent Society; was an efficient and active member, and was a regular attendant at its meetings. He was forward and energetic in procuring the statue of Washington, which now stands in the State House, and was present at the first meeting for the consideration of that subject. He is said, by all who had the honor of his acquaintance, to have been a gentleman of strict integrity, the soul of honor, with noble and generous aspirations, strong affections, and appreciated in the fullest sense the kindness of the many friends who gathered around him in the decline of life to show their high estimation of his worth.

(425) SARAH FARRINGTON, second daughter of Capt. Joseph and Susannah (Pope) Farrington, and granddaughter of Lazarus and Susannah (Glover) Pope, was born in Boston, June 4, 1768, and died there, Jan 26, 1846.

Dec. 25, 1793, she was married to Mammy Masson, who came from Dijon, in France, resided in Boston; was a baker, and carried on the business to a considerable extent. He died in Boston, April 7, 1797. They had one daughter:

+1010. Susan, b. Nov. 8, 1795; m. John Andrews, of Boston.

(449) JONATHAN NOONING, second son of James and Rebeckah (Glover) Nooning, was born in Bristol, R. I., Aug. 1, 1784, and died there, July 9, 1855, in his 71st year.

He was twice married. First, March 18, 1805, to Hannah Talbee, who was born in Bristol in 1784, and died there, Nov. 27, 1827, in her 43d year. He was married, a second time, Aug. 13, 1833, to Widow Hall, of Londonderry, N. H.

Children of JONATHAN and HANNAH (TALBEE) NOONING, born in Bristol, R. I.:

1011. Edward Talbee, b. Aug. 12, 1805.
1012. Rebecca Glover, b. Oct. 28, 1806; m. William P. Bradford, of Bristol.
1013. Mary S., b. July 30, 1808.
1014. Adalaide W., b. Mch. 27, 1810; m. Jonathan Brownell.

1015. Jonathan,   b. Jan. 12, 1812 ; m. Eliza Bowler.
1016. Hannah Talbee, b. Sept. 17, 1813.
1017. Anne W., b. Dec. 30, 1815 ; m. William Bradford, of Bristol.
1018. Emeline M.,   b. Dec. 6, 1817 ; m. George W. Dimon.
1019. Isabella F.,   b. May 27, 1825.

By second wife, ABIGAIL HALL :

1020. Mary J.,   b. Oct. 6, 1834.
1021. Harriet L., b. Oct. 27, 1836.

(451) SUSANNAH CALDWELL, daughter of Thomas and
Elizabeth (Glover) Caldwell, was born in Ipswich, June 16, 1788,
and died in Boston, Dec. 5, 1852, aged 64 years.

She was married to Ezra Palmer, of Ipswich, Aug. 5, 1822.

Children of EZRA and SUSANNAH (CALDWELL) PALMER, born in
Boston :

1022. Martha Caroline, b. in 1824.
1023. Almira Glover,   b. in 1826.

(452) MARY CALDWELL, daughter of Thomas and Elizabeth
(Glover) Caldwell, was born in Ipswich, Sept. 19, 1790, and died in
Boston.

She was married to Simeon Palmer, of Boston.

Children of SIMEON and MARY (CALDWELL) PALMER, born in Boston :

1024. Simeon, b. in 1818 ; was graduated at Harvard College in
        1837 ; is a physician, and resides in Milton.
1025. Maria, m. Rev. Henry M. Dexter, of Boston.

(453) MARY THOMAS, daughter of Gershom and Susannah
(Glover) Thomas, was born in Boston in 1772, and died there.

She was married to Capt. Edward Tyler, of Boston, about 1792.
After her death, Capt. Tyler married her sister, Susannah Thomas.
There were no children by the last marriage.   He removed with his
family to New York.

Children of Capt. EDWARD and MARY (THOMAS) TYLER, born in
Boston :

1026. Mary.
1027. Edward.

(459) BENJAMIN WARDWELL, eldest son of Benjamin, Esq., and Catharine (Glover) Wardwell, was born in Bristol, R. I., Aug. 24, 1784, and is now living there, at the age of 82 years.

He was married, Jan. 14, 1807, by Rev. Amasa Shepard, to Elizabeth Manchester, of Little Compton, R. I., daughter of Zebedee and Deborah Manchester, of that place.

Children of BENJAMIN and ELIZABETH (MANCHESTER) WARDWELL, born in Bristol, R. I.:

+1028. Henry, b. March 17, 1808; m. Sarah L. Lindsey, of Bristol.
+1029. Benjamin, b. Aug. 9, 1809; m. Eliza Cook, of Fall River.
 1030. George M., b. Sept. 2, 1810; d. Oct. 2, 1811.
 1031. A son,⎫ b. Sept. 12, 1812; ⎧ d. same day.
 1032. A daughter,⎭   ⎩ d. same day.
+1033. Jeremiah M., b. Dec. 7, 1813; m. Mary Jane Sturgis, N. Y.
 1034. Elizabeth M., b. March 7, 1816; d. Jan. 18, 1826, aged 10.
 1035. Twin daughters, b. Sept. 2, 1817; d. Sept. 4 and 12, 1817.
 1036. Adam M., b. Nov. 6, 1818; d. Jan. 23, 1827, aged 9 years.
 1037. George W., b. March 14, 1821; d. Aug. 16, 1821.
 1038. Catharine Glover, b. May 28, 1822; resides with her father.
 1039. Mary A., b. Oct. 6, 1825.
 1040. Elizabeth M., b. Nov. 6, 1827; m. Ramon Guiteras, Esq.

(467) MARIA MAY, only daughter of William, Esq., and Margaret (Glover) May, was born in Roxbury, March 1, 1790, and died there, March 11, 1855, aged 65 years.

In 1810, she was married to Charles Carroll, of Roxbury. They had one son:

 1041. Charles, b. in 1812, resides in Roxbury.

(468) JOSEPH GLOVER MAY, son of William and Margaret (Glover) May, was born in Roxbury, May 10, 1792, and died there, Oct. 19, 1831, aged 39 years.

He was married to Harriet Bird, of Dorchester, Aug. 17, 1815. She was the daughter of William Bird, of Dorchester, and was born there, Jan. 31, 1792. She resides with her son William B. May, in Roxbury.

Children of JOSEPH GLOVER and HARRIET (BIRD) MAY, born in Roxbury:

+1042. Maria, b. April 13, 1816; m. ⎧ 1st, James Green;
                                    ⎩ 2d, Henry S. Bird, Dorchester.

+1043. Henry Burbeck, b. Aug. 18, 1818; m. Susan Simmons, of Hingham.
+1044. William Bird, b. Nov. 16, 1819; m. Susan Johnson Warren, of Brookfield, N. H.
+1045. John Glover, b. Feb. 2, 1821; m. Syrelda Lowler, of Virginia.
+1046. Margaret Glover, b. Jan. 31, 1824; a Sister of Charity at St. Joseph's, Emmetsburg, Maryland.
+1047. Samuel Joseph, b. Dec. 4, 1827; m. Caroline Elizabeth Davis, of Boston, in 1851.
1048. Charles Thayer, b. Feb. 12, 1829; d. May, 1830.

(506) ELIZABETH CURTIS GLOVER, daughter of John and Phebe (Curtis) Glover, was born in Braintree, Jan. 2, 1799; lives in West Canton street, Boston.

She was married, May 19, 1816, to William Augustus Field, born in Braintree, June 21, 1794, and died in Boston, June 23, 1856. He was a musician in Boston for many years; lived at 122 West Canton street.

Children of WILLIAM AUGUSTUS and ELIZABETH CURTIS (GLOVER) FIELD, born in Braintree, Quincy and Boston:

1049. Phebe Anne, b. Aug. 27, 1817; m. —— Sawyer, Nov. 30, 1840; Mr. Sawyer died Jan. 18, 1842.
1050. Elizabeth Curtis, b. Oct. 16, 1819; d. Feb. 28, 1820.
1051. Mary Augusta, b. March 27, 1821; m. Willis Ross, April 4, 1840.
1052. Samuel Augustus, b. Nov. 6, 1827; m. Mary Nason, May 19, 1851.
1053. William Mears, b. March 5, 1833; d. Aug. 8, 1833, in Boston.
1054. William Americus, b. July 5, 1834; m. Eliza Armstrong, May 5, 1859.
1055. Elizabeth,   b. June 19, 1836; d. Aug. 8, 1836.
1056. Francis Curtis, b. July 30, 1837.
1057. Henry,   b. Oct. 3, 1842.

(508) JOHN GLOVER, son of John and Phebe (Curtis) Glover, was born in Braintree, Nov. 27, 1803; lives in Braintree; is a boot-maker.

He was married to Margaret N. Field, of Quincy, Nov. 5, 1826.

Children of JOHN and MARGARET N. (FIELD) GLOVER, born in Braintree:

1058. John,   b. April 8, 1827; d. same year.
+1059. William Henry, b. April 25, 1829; m. Elvira Rideout, Quincy.
1060. John,   b. March 8, 1832; m. Laura Beard, Quincy.

1061. Joseph Mears, b. April 11, 1834; m. Frances A. Dodge, of Quincy.

(511) PHEBE NEALE GLOVER, daughter of John and Phebe (Curtis) Glover, was born in Braintree, Feb. 6, 1811, and died in Quincy, in 1847.

She was married to Horatio N. Faxon, of Quincy, May 21, 1838. They lived in Quincy, and had one son:

1062. George, b. Sept. 8, 1848.

(514) NOAH A. GLOVER, son of John and Phebe (Curtis) Glover, was born in Braintree, Jan. 21, 1818. He lives in Braintree (Penn's Hill), and is a bootmaker.

He was married to Elizabeth Beals, in 1841. She was the daughter of —— Beals, of Weymouth, and was born there, Sept 27, 1823.

Children of NOAH A. and ELIZABETH (BEALS) GLOVER, born in Braintree:

1063. Samuel Curtis,   b. July   6, 1842.
1064. Elizabeth Anna,   b. Sept.   8, 1844.
1065. Phebe Augusta,   b. Jan.   30, 1847.
1066. Charles Gideon,   b. Nov.   11, 1849.
1067. John,   b. March   19, 1851.
1068. Winfield Scott,   b. July   25, 1853.
1069. Anne,   b. Nov.   12, 1855.
1070. Rufus Gardiner,   b. April   24, 1857.
1071. George Wilson Ellsworth, b. in 1862.

(518) JOHN BASS GLOVER, son of Nathaniel, Jr., and Esther (Wadsworth) Glover, was born in Quincy, June 16, 1803; lives there, and is a bootmaker.

He was married to Margaretta Frances Garaux Reed, of Boston, May 6, 1830. She was the daughter of John Reed, for many years a well-known constable in Boston, and was born there, May 8, 1812.

Children of JOHN BASS and MARGARETTA F. G. (REED) GLOVER, born in Quincy:

+1072. John Francis Garaux, b. March 7, 1831; m. Laura Jane Hunt, March 30, 1856.
 1073. Benjamin Wadsworth, b. Oct. 4, 1832; d. June 20, 1835.
 1074. William Dwelley, b. Dec. 10, 1833; m. Adelaide Whitney, July 27, 1859.

+1075. Nathaniel Ebenezer, b. Feb. 20, 1836 ; m. Elizabeth Albena
   Packard, July 27, 1859.
1076. George Church Reed, b. July 28, 1838 ; d. Jan. 2, 1843.
1077. Margaret Esther Rebecca, b. Sept. 6, 1840 ; m. William
   Henry Derry, Jan. 21, 1857.
1078. Julianna Clementina, b. Aug. 16, 1842 ; m. Leonard Brigham
   Harrington, Sept. 22, 1859.
1079. Elizabeth Georgianna,   b. Aug. 18, 1844 ; married.
1080. Caroline Sarah Wadsworth, b. July 17, 1847.

(520) CAROLINE SARAH WADSWORTH GLOVER, daughter of Nathaniel and Esther (Wadsworth) Glover, was born in Quincy, Sept. 25, 1808.

She was twice married. First, to William Dwelley, of Quincy; second, Sept. 25, 1833, to Isaac Newcomb, of Braintree, son of Bryant Newcomb.

Children of WILLIAM and CAROLINE SARAH WADSWORTH (GLOVER) DWELLEY, born in Quincy :

1081. Caroline.
1082. Jane.

(528) WILLIAM SULLIVAN GLOVER, son of Capt. Josiah and Sophia I. (Sorrelle) Glover, was born in Quincy, Nov. 5, 1820; lives in Quincy.

He was twice married. First, to Harriet M. A. Fisher, July 30, 1845. She was the daughter of Richard and Hannah B. Fisher, of Quincy, formerly of Nova Scotia, was born there in 1824, and died in Quincy, Nov. 4, 1853, aged 29 years. He married, second, Fayette Villa Gordon, of Augusta, Me., Dec. 24, 1854. She was the daughter of William and Mary J. Gordon, of Augusta, and was born there.

Children of WILLIAM SULLIVAN and HARRIET M. A. (FISHER) GLOVER, born in Quincy :

1083. William Edward, b. April 18, 1846 ; d. July 8, 1847.
1084. William Earl,   b. July 21, 1848.
1085. Lucy Upham,   b. Aug. 12, 1852 ; d. Oct. 30, 1853.

 By second wife, FAYETTE VILLA GORDON :

1086. Lucy Fayette, b. Dec. 21, 1856.
1087. Josiah,   b. Dec. 27, 1858.

(530) ERASTUS MILLER GLOVER, fifth son and youngest child of Capt. Josiah and (second wife) Mary P. (Adams) Glover, was born in Quincy, April 24, 1834; is a boot finisher.

Nov. 25, 1861, was enrolled in the 32d regiment, Co. A, for three years; discharged Nov. 29, 1862; enrolled again in the 60th regiment, Co. B, for 100 days, July 16, 1864; mustered out Nov. 30, 1864. He was never married.

(540) ESTHER HALLETT GLOVER, daughter of Elisha and Mary (Veazie) Glover, was born in Quincy, baptized June 6, 1818, and died in Germantown (Quincy Point), in 1853, aged 35 years.

She was married to Ebenezer G. Green, of Boston, Feb. 15, 1837. He died in Quincy, June 1, 1863.

Children of EBENEZER G. and ESTHER H. (GLOVER) GREEN, born in Quincy (Germantown):

1088. Georgiana,   b. in 1839; m. —— Webster.
1089. Mary Francis, b. in 1841; m. —— Clarke.
1090. Ellen,   b. in 1843; m.
1091. George,   b. in 1845.
1092. William Wood, b. in 1851.

(541) JAMES FRANCIS GLOVER, son of Elisha and Mary (Veazie) Glover, was born in Quincy, April 2, 1820; lived in Braintree, in 1862; has lived in Gloucester.

He was married to Susan Thayer, of Braintree, Jan. 1, 1848.

Children of JAMES FRANCIS and SUSAN (THAYER) GLOVER, born in Braintree:

1093. George Parker, b. Nov., 1848.
1094. Jennie Francis, b. Sept., 1857.

(542) WINSLOW BRIGHAM GLOVER, son of Elisha and Mary (Veazie) Glover, was born in Quincy, April 7, 1822, and lived in Boston. He is a carpenter. Went west, but returned to Boston in the Spring of 1860, and lived in Metropolitan place. He lives now (1864) at Newton Corner.

He was married, May 18, 1848, to Harriet D. Copeland, and has five children.

Children of WINSLOW BRIGHAM and HARRIET D. (COPELAND) GLOVER:

1095. Henry Winslow, } b. Aug. 12, 1851.
1096. Charles Howard,
1097. Frank Herbert,   b. June 23, 1853.
1098. Anna Curry,   b. July 7, 1855.
1099. William Copeland, b. Jan. 10, 1858.

(551) LEWIS JOSEPH GLOVER, eldest and twin son of Ezra
and Eunice (Minot) Glover, was born in Quincy, Feb. 26, 1807, and
died in Pepperell, Mass., June 24, 1856. He commenced his preparatory studies for college at Lexington Academy, where he remained one year. The instruction in that institution being interrupted
and suspended, he completed his studies at Milton Academy. He
entered Harvard College, passed through the regular course of study,
and graduated there in the class of 1832. He commenced the study
of medicine under the instruction of Dr. James Jackson (H. U. 1796),
and at the end of three years received his medical diploma, and
began the practice of his profession in Boston, where he was in successful practice about twelve years. He attained a high rank as a
physician and surgeon, and was much esteemed by his acquaintance
and professional brethren. He was distinguished for his uprightness,
integrity, and faithfulness to his patients. Being in affluent pecu-
niary circumstances, he had great consideration for the poor. After
the decease of his father, in 1847, he left Boston and his practice
there, and resided at the homestead in Quincy, employing himself in
taking care of his estates. About two years previous to his decease
he had a slight attack of paralysis, followed by mental alienation,
which continued, with occasional lucid intervals, until his death. He
was never married.

(553) JOHN JEFFERSON GLOVER, second and youngest son
of Ezra and Eunice (Minot) Glover, was born in Quincy, June 13,
1828, on the estate and in the mansion house where he now resides
(Nov., 1866), and which has passed down to him as an estate of inheritance from his ancestors. At an early age he attended private
schools at Neponset and Quincy, and subsequently studied a preparatory course of three years at Milton Academy. In 1845, at the age
of seventeen years, he entered Harvard College at Cambridge, and
was graduated there, in the class of 1849. He was intended for the
profession of law, but delicate health and peculiar domestic relations
compelling a change from the original plan, he turned his attention

to agricultural pursuits. The decease of his father before his collegiate course was completed; the disease which had attacked his only brother; the sole care and comfort of a beloved mother devolving at once on him, threw around him circumstances, which, added to the care and management of their estates, rendered it imperative on him to remain at home and relinquish the pursuit of a profession. The estate which he possesses was originally a portion of the farm called Newbury farm, formerly belonging to the Hon. John Glover, of Dorchester, his first American ancestor, and which was the portion of the fifth son, Rev. Pelatiah Glover, of Springfield, and sold by his heirs in 1699 to William Rawson and Nathaniel Glover, who divided in 1702. The half part belonging to William Rawson was sold by him in 1716, and by his eldest son Capt. William Rawson, for sums of sixty, and four hundred pounds, to Ebenezer Hinckley, youngest son of Gov. Thomas Hinckley, of Barnstable. After the decease of Mr. Hinckley in 1721, a portion of it was in possession of his widow, who married John George in 1722, and the remainder was the inheritance of his son Ebenezer and daughter Rachel Hinckley. In 1739 John George sold the widow's dower to John Glover, the great-grandfather of the present incumbent, including the mansion house and lands belonging to it, for a homestead estate, who left it at his decease to his son Elisha Glover, who subsequently purchased the rights of the Hinckley heirs, bringing the whole estate together, and left it (the mansion house and a portion of the land), in 1811, to his son Ezra Glover, who owned and occupied it until his decease in 1847, when it passed to his heirs, viz., his widow and two sons. At the decease of Lewis Joseph, the eldest son, who died intestate, his portion passed to his mother, who deceased in 1863, leaving the youngest son sole heir, and who is the present possessor and occupant.

John Jefferson Glover has been for many years connected with the management of the Granite Bridge Corporation, and was one of the original projectors and grantees of the Quincy Railroad, of which he was a Director, and in August, 1865, was elected its President.

(560) GEORGE STEPHEN GLOVER, second son of Capt. Stephen and Mary (Woodward) Glover, was born in 1817, and is now living in Boston, at 131 Boylston street.

He was married, about 1840, to Ellen Paul, of Shrewsbury—resided for a time in Dorchester; built a house on Columbia street, which has since been sold to C. C. Holbrook. On account of impaired health he left Dorchester, and afterwards resided in Hingham. His family at present reside in Boston. They have one daughter:

1100. Mary Woodward, b. in 1842.

(565) JOHANNAH BIRD, eldest daughter of Aaron and Johannah (Glover) Bird, was born in Dorchester, Feb. 9, 1781, and died in Roxbury, after 1830.

Oct. 27, 1799, she was married to Samuel Ward, of Roxbury; born there in 1771, and died, Jan. 3, 1830, aged 59 years.

Children of SAMUEL and JOHANNAH (BIRD) WARD, born in Roxbury:

1101. Edward,   b. Sept. 11, 1800 ; m. Mary Dunn.
1102. Mary Clapp,   b. Jan. 6, 1802 ; m. Calvin Heald.
1103. James, b. July 13, 1803 ; m. Martha Dame, of Boston.
1104. Henry S.,   b. Jan. 1, 1805 ; m. Hannah G. Parker.
1105. Preble,   b. Dec. 1, 1807 ; died unmarried.
1106. John Jackson,   b. Sept. 12, 1810 ; died young.
1107. Martha Elizabeth, b. Sept. 12, 1812 ; m. Amasa Wales.
1108. Joanna Bird,   b. Jan. 20, 1815 ; m. Franklin Dyer.
1109. Harriet Curtis, b. May 10, 1819 ; m. Dr. Stone.
1110. Judith Bussey, b. Feb. 21, 1820 ; m. Warren Hollis, Brighton.
1111. Sarah Moore,   b. May 1, 1821 ; m. Oliver Cousins.
1112. John,   b. Feb. 21, 1825 ; m. Margaret Smith.

(587) BENJAMIN GLOVER LYON, eldest son of Benjamin and Elizabeth (Glover) Lyon, was born in Dorchester, Aug. 4, 1781, and died there.

Dec. 28, 1804, he was married to Eliza Babcock, of Milton, daughter of Samuel and Sarah (Howe) Babcock. She died in Boston, in August, 1858. They had two children, and perhaps others. The two reported are as follows:

1113. Charlotte Elizabeth, b. Nov., 1805 ; m. John Brazer Glover.
1114. Benjamin, married.

(600) MARTHA HOLDEN GLOVER, eldest daughter of Samuel and Martha (Holden) Glover, was born in Dorchester, Aug. 11, 1797, and died in Cincinnati, Ohio, Feb. 12, 1855, in her 58th year.

She was married, Sept. 12, 1824, to Samuel Davis, Jr., son of Samuel Davis, Esq., of Brighton. They had children—one only reported:

1115. Samuel, b. in (1826); resides in Boston.

(602) PHINEHAS HOLDEN GLOVER, only son of Samuel and Martha (Holden) Glover, was born in Dorchester, Oct. 16, 1807; resides in Calais, Maine.

March 31, 1833, he was married to Mary Carlton, of Portland.

Children of PHINEHAS HOLDEN and MARY (CARLTON) GLOVER born in Portland and Calais, Me.:

1116. Mary Lizzie,   b. March 9, 1834; d. April 1, 1835.
1117. Mary Abbott,   b. Jan.   10, 1836.
1118. Phinehas Holden, } b. Oct.   12, 1837.
1119. Edward Kent,   }
1120. Martha Holden,   b. Nov. 19, 1838.
1121. Russell,   b. Oct.   12, 1841.
1122. John Abbot,   b. March 21, 1849.

(604) SAMUEL BIRD, eldest son of Samuel and Elizabeth (Glover) Bird, was born in Sharon, March 12, 1777, and died in Stoughton, May 23, 1826, in his 50th year.

July 31, 1796, he was married to Betsey Trask, daughter of Abraham Trask, of Boston, born there in 1780. At the age of eighteen years he went to Boston, and engaged in the business of trucking—was truckmaster for many years.

Children of SAMUEL and BETSEY (TRASK) BIRD, born in Boston:

1123. Abraham Brown, b. May 1, 1797; m. Susan Allen.
+1124. Eliza Trask, b. Feb. 1, 1799; m. Nathaniel Frothingham, of Boston.
1125. Ebenezer Glover, b. in 1800; lost at sea.
1126. Edwin L.,   b. in 1815;
               (1st, Catharine Kurtz, of Boston;
        m. { 2d, Laura ———;
              (3d, Jane Kurtz, March 5, 1853;
by trade a carriage maker; has devoted much time to the cultivation of his eminent musical talents.

(605) ELIZABETH BIRD, second daughter of Samuel and Elizabeth (Glover) Bird, was born in Sharon, Nov. 24, 1779, and died in Stoughton, Nov. 5, 1807, in her 29th year.

March 23, 1800,* she was married, by Rev. T. M. Harris (at the
house of her Aunt Blackman, in Dorchester), to John Taylor, of
Boston, of the firm of Taylor & Trull, distillers, of the Essex Street
Distillery. He was the son of John Taylor, of Billerica, Mass.;
born there, May 11, 1777, and died in Boston, Sept. 5, 1807, leaving
a widow and four children.

Children of JOHN and ELIZABETH (BIRD) TAYLOR, born in Boston:

+1127. John, b. Jan. 16, 1801 ; m. Maria Sumner, of Stoughton.
  1128. Elizabeth, b. March 31, 1802 ; m. Moses Bullard, Medfield.
  1129. Edward, b. Feb. 10, 1804 ; m. Mary Briggs, Pompey, N. Y.
+1130. Samuel Bird, b. Oct. 20, 1806 ; m. Mary Shepard, of Canton.

(606) JAMES BIRD, second son of Samuel and Elizabeth (Glover) Bird, was born in Sharon, Oct. 6, 1781, and died in Stoughton,
Feb. 14, 1821, in his 41st year. He went early to Boston, and
engaged in the business of trucking; he was truckmaster, was a
member of several societies there, and an officer in the military company of U. S. Light Dragoons.

He was married to Abigail Hobart, in 1804, daughter of ——
and Mary (Copeland) Hobart, of Braintree.

They had three children, born in Boston :

  1131. James, b. in 1806 ; lost at sea.
  1132. Fanny, b. in 1808 ; died young.
  1133. William, b. in 1810 ; m. Mary Thayer, of Braintree, and died
      there in July, 1866.

(609) JENNER BIRD, third son of Samuel and Elizabeth (Glover) Bird, was born in Sharon, Oct. 3, 1794, and died in Brighton,
April 15, 1830, in his 36th year.

He was married, Nov. 3, 1817, by Rev. Thomas Grey, of Roxbury,
to Elizabeth Cook, daughter of Enoch and Abigail (Pitts) Cook,†
of Groton, Mass.; born there, April 26, 1791. They had seven
children, born in Brighton, as follows :

+1134. Elizabeth, b. Nov. 21, 1819 ; m. { 1st, Moses Sanderson ;
                                { 2d, Samuel Deering.

* The date of Elizabeth Bird's marriage is given as found recorded on Dorchester records.
In family records, since produced, the date is written March 3, 1799.
† The mother of Elizabeth Cook married a second time, and at the time of her daughter's
marriage with Jenner Bird, was the widow of Samuel Butterfield, of Townsend, Mass.

1135. Charles,   b. March 19, 1821 ; d. Feb. 20, 1822.
+1136. Mary Fiske, b. Nov. 29, 1823 ;

m. { 1st, Joel Franklin Willis ;
{ 2d, Amos J. Dean, of Roxbury.

+1137. Hannah, b. April 12, 1825 ;

m. { 1st, Francis Morey, of Roxbury ;
{ 2d, Francis Jones.

1138. Catharine, b. Feb. 6, 1827 ; d. March 20, 1827.
+1139. Geo. Washington, }
+1140. Jenner Warren,   } b. Mch 6, 1830 ; { m. Harriet S. Deering :
{ m. Emily Peabody, of
Cambridge.

(610) REBECKAH BIRD, the fifth daughter and youngest child
of Samuel and Elizabeth (Glover) Bird, was born in Stoughton,
Sept. 13, 1799, and now resides there.

Sept. 19, 1841, she was married to Ansel Capen, Esq., of Stoughton, son of James and Elizabeth (Cummings) Capen, of that place.
He was, for a period of twenty-five years, employed as a teacher of
youth in public and private schools in his native town, and by his
original and thorough manner of imparting instruction, attained to
eminent success in that profession. In 1821, he was admitted to
join the Rising Star Lodge of Free Masons. In 1825, he was admitted to the Royal Arch Chapter of Free and Accepted Masons,
which was organized in July of that year, in Stoughton. He was
elected to the offices of Secretary of the Rising Star and Grand
Scribe to the Chapter, and served in those offices thirty-one years.
He was elected also, and served, as Master of the Lodge, and High
Priest of the Chapter, during the constitutional period. At the expiration of his office he was presented by the brethren with a valuable
gold pen and pencil, as a testimonial of his services.

(613) ELEANOR CAPEN, the third daughter of Lieut. Jonathan and Hannah (Glover) Capen, was born in Stoughton, July 11,
1784, died in Boston, July 20, 1839, aged 55 years, and was buried
in Stoughton. She was industrious and ingenious. She kept a private school in Stoughton in 1807–8, in the house then owned and
occupied by Lewis Johnson, Sen.; and subsequently and for several
years resided in the family of Dr. John Jeffries, and was employed
there in delicate needlework and embroidery, and as decorator to
the house of Mrs. Jeffries, who was her friend and patron. After
the decease of Madam Jeffries she opened a store for dry goods and

33

millinery in Boston, in company with two of her sisters, which business she continued for many years.

In 1824 she married Joseph S. Andrews, formerly of Warren, Me. They resided in Boston, and continued the business of storekeeping some years longer. Mr. Andrews died in Boston, a few years after their marriage. They had no issue.

(615) MELATIAH CAPEN, the fifth daughter of Jonathan and Hannah (Glover) Capen, was born in Stoughton, Oct. 21, 1787, and now lives in Canton.

She has been twice married. First, to Otis Billings, of Canton; and second, to Ephraim Capen, of Dorchester, who removed to Canton, and lived there the remainder of his life.

Children of EPHRAIM and MELATIAH CAPEN, born in Canton:

1141. Ida Jerusha, died in infancy.
1142. George,   m. Susan Hill, of Canton.
1143. Edwin,   died young.
1144. Thomas,   died in infancy.

(616) RACHEL CAPEN, the sixth daughter of Jonathan and Hannah (Glover) Capen, was born in Stoughton, March 18, 1789; lives in New Bedford.

Sept. 7, 1809, she was married to Stephen Blake, Jr., of Canton, the second son of Stephen, Sen., and Chloe (Wentworth) Blake; born in Canton, June 21, 1783, and died in Stoughton, Sept. 25, 1860, in his 78th year. He owned a house and land in Stoughton Centre. He was by trade a hatter, but soon after his marriage discontinued that employment, and occupied himself with the cultivation of his land. Stephen Blake, Sen., the father of Stephen Blake, Jr., was born probably in the town of Milton, in 1740. His marriage with Chloe Wentworth, by Rev. Samuel Dunbar, Dec. 1, 1768, is the first notice of the name on the Stoughton records. His death is recorded, also, in the North Precinct, now Canton, as having taken place April 4, 1823, aged 83 years.

Children of STEPHEN, Jr., and RACHEL (CAPEN) BLAKE, born in Stoughton:

+1145. Aaron, b. June 18, 1810; m. Elizabeth R. Wright, Hope, Me.
+1146. Jane, b. Dec. 31, 1811; m. Theophilus C. Clapp, Dorchester.

+1147. Elijah, b. June 19, 1814; m. Hannah B. Morrell, Newton, L. I.
  1148. Jonathan, b. Feb. 19, 1817; d. Sept. 13, 1825, in his 9th year.
+1149. Edmund, b. July 24, 1819; m. Caroline S. Fay, Marlborough.
  1150. Rachel,   b. Oct. 10, 1823; d. Jan. 17, 1825.
  1151. Jerusha C., b. July 4, 1826; m. Jonathan C. Hawes, of New
        Bedford.
  1152. Phinehas,   b. June 24, 1828; d. April 9, 1829.
  1153. Caroline,   b. Oct. 15, 1830; d. July 25, 1844.

(617) AZUBAH CAPEN, seventh daughter of Jonathan and
Hannah (Glover) Capen, was born in Stoughton, Nov. 17, 1790;
lives in New Bedford.

She was married to Levi Hawes, July 16, 1820, being his second
wife. He was born in Canton, May 25, 1792, and has been twice
married. First, in 1813, to Harriet, daughter of Seth and Alice
(Gay) Pierce, of Stoughton, by whom he had four children. She was
born in Stoughton, June 16, 1796, and died in New Bedford, Feb.
20, 1820. Their children were: Levi, born May 15, 1815, died
July 13, 1815; Harriet N., born April 25, 1816, married Calvin
Marshall; Simeon, born Aug. 14, 1817; Jason, born Nov. 19, 1818,
died March 23, 1825.

Children of LEVI and AZUBAH (CAPEN) HAWES, born in New Bedford:

  1154. Eleanor, b. Nov. 23, 1821; m. James Webb, New Bedford.
  1155. Azubah, b. May   7, 1823; m. Elphinstone M. Smith, of New
        Bedford.
  1156. Levi, b. Dec. 4, 1824: m. Abby Macomber, of Providence.
+1157. Jonathan C., b. May 8, 1826; m. Jerusha C. Blake, Stoughton.
  1158. Thomas C., b. March 2, 1828; m. Elizabeth (Sisson) Ward
        (widow).
  1159. Elisha, b. Oct. 6, 1829; m. Abby (Macomber) Hawes, widow
        of Levi Hawes.
  1160. David Cobb, b. June 15, 1832; Mary Hannah Sanborn, of
        Hampton Falls, N. H.

(618) JANE CAPEN, the eighth daughter of Jonathan and
Hannah (Glover) Capen, was born in Stoughton, July 12, 1792, and
died there, Oct. 21, 1824, in her 33d year.

Aug. 12, 1810, she was married to David Cobb, of Taunton; born
there in 1781, and died in Stoughton, Sept. 25, 1811, aged 29 years.
He was a merchant, and resided in Stoughton. They had one son:

  1161. David, b. in 1812; d. Nov. 19, 1833, in Boston, aged 21
        years; buried in Stoughton.

(621)   THOMAS CAPEN, the second and youngest son of Lieut. Jonathan and Hannah (Glover) Capen, was born in Stoughton, Aug. 1, 1798, and resides there at the present time (1866). He succeeded to the homestead of his father, which he still owns and occupies.

July 1, 1832, he was married to Hannah Melcher, of Hampton Falls, N. H., daughter of Joseph and Mary (Rowell) Melcher; born there, March 6, 1805. They have no children. He possesses a competent estate, is industrious and frugal, a promoter of education, and has contributed a considerable amount to Tufts College at Medford, to Dean Academy in Franklin, and other institutions of learning. In the late civil war, although too far advanced to bear arms in his country's defence, he assisted with his means in furnishing bounties for men who could serve, and by word and deed encouraged the government during the rebellion. In his christian character he is upright and sincere; temperate in all things, and exemplary; is a member of the Universalist Church. He is not a sceptic, bigot or fanatic, but strongly devoted to Universalism and the extension of Christianity. The temperance reform, and all reforms of the age, engage his cheerful coöperation.

(624)   LOIS GLOVER, second daughter of Thomas and Eunice (Bent) Glover, was born in Sharon, Sept. 29, 1785, is now (Nov. 1866) living, at the age of 81 years, and resides in Dorchester.

Dec. 7, 1810, she was married to Samuel Blackman, son of Samuel and ———— Blackman, of Dorchester; born there in 1780, and lives in Dorchester. They have had two children, as follows:

1162. Augustus Lawrence, b. July 7, 1814; m. Eliza Cole, Jan. 16, 1838; died in 1858—no issue.
1163. Eliza Anne, b. Nov. 27, 1820; m. Jedediah Rich.

(626)   THOMAS GLOVER, eldest son of Thomas and Eunice (Bent) Glover, was born in Sharon, July 21, 1792, resides at Jamaica Plain (Roxbury).

He has been twice married. First, May 28, 1822, to Mary Damon, daughter of David and Anna (Paul) Damon, of Dedham; born there in Sept., 1800, and died in Roxbury, Sept. 3, 1838, aged 38 years. He was married, the second time, April 1, 1842, to Bethia Thompson. There was no issue by this marriage. By first wife Mary Damon there were two children:

+1164. Thomas, b. Jan. 2, 1833; d. May 16, 1851, aged 18 years.
1165. Anna, b. April 12, 1837; resides at Jamaica Plain, with her parents.

(629) ELIZABETH GLOVER, fifth daughter of Thomas and Eunice (Bent) Glover, was born in Sharon, May 6, 1801, and resides in that town.

July 3, 1827, she was married to Willard Morse, son of Capt. John and Lucy (Fisher) Morse, of Sharon; born there in 1799. He inherited the Morse homestead in Sharon, and still owns and occupies it. They have had six children, born in Sharon:

1166. Esrom, b. April 25, 1828.
1167. Willard, b. June 16, 1829.
1168. Elizabeth, b. Oct. 11, 1830.
1169. Bushrod, b. Oct. 24, 1832; a lawyer in Boston.
1170. Guilford, b. June 5, 1835.
1171. Elijah Glover, b. May 6, 1838; married.

(630) WILLIAM GLOVER, third son of Thomas and Abigail (Hewins) Glover, was born in Sharon, Sept. 30, 1807; resides in Dorchester, at the Upper Mills, now called Mattapan; owns an estate there. He is engaged in the manufacture of paper, in the employ of Tileston & Hollingsworth; is an honorable and worthy member of the Village Church, and an upright and honest man.

Sept. 12, 1832, he was married, in Dedham, by the Rev. Harrison G. Park, to Anne Maria Fuller, daughter of Elisha and Sarah (Bartlett) Fuller, of Newton; born in Phillipstown, Worcester Co., Feb. 21, 1811.

Children of WILLIAM and ANNE MARIA (FULLER) GLOVER, born in Boston and Dorchester:

1172. William Franklin, b. April 3, 1833; d. Oct. 2, 1856, aged 23.
1173. George Grenville, b. May 29, 1829. In 1862, he was enrolled in the 42d Regiment of Vols., destined to Newbern, N. C., and served three years in the army.

(637) WILLIAM HOMES, only son of Benjamin and Rachel (Glover) Homes, was born in Stoughton, Nov. 3, 1785, and died in Dorchester, Dec. 25, 1858, aged 73 years. He resided in Stoughton with his grandparents, at the Glover homestead, until he arrived at the age of twenty-one years. In 1796 he went to Dorchester, and

33*

was clerk in the store of Mr. Unite Blackman. He continued ther until about 1810, and transacted business for Mrs. Blackman aer the decease of her husband. He subsequently opened a store on Meeting-house Hill, in that town, and traded there successfully for several years, when he relinquished the business, purchased an estate on the eastern slope of Mount Ida, and turned his attention to agricultural pursuits. The estate is now in the possession of his heirs, and occupied by his widow.

He was twice married. First, Dec. 8, 1811, to Elizabeth Blackman, daughter of Eliakim and Sarah (Wiswall) Blackman, of Dorchester; born there, Dec. 6, 1791, and died in Dorchester, March 21, 1830. By her he had eight children. April 13, 1833, he was married, a second time, to (909) Eliza Glover, daughter of Alexander and Jemima (Tolman) Glover, and widow of Silas Wheelock, of Westborough, to whom she was married May 4, 1830, and he died Oct. 16, 1831, at Thomaston, Me., aged 33 years. There was no issue by this marriage.

Children of WILLIAM and ELIZABETH (BLACKMAN) HOMES, born in Dorchester:

    1174. George Ellis,   b. Nov. 12, 1812; thrice married, no issue.
+1175. Luther, b. May 11, 1814; m. Hannette Bridge Currier.
    1176. Sarah Elizabeth, b. Feb. 25, 1816; m. Asahel Howe Glover.
+1177. Warren,   b. Aug. 5, 1818; m. Julia Adelaide Snow.
    1178. Martha,   b. Feb. 28, 1820; d. Oct. 22, 1822.
+1179. William Henry, b. Sept. 7, 1823; m. Anna Winchester.
    1180. Caroline,   b. July 29, 1825; d. Oct. 6, 1834, aged 9.
+1181. Anne Mary,   b. Mch 14, 1830; m. William Jacobs.

(638) LUTHER HALL, a twin son of Solomon and Rachael (Glover-Homes) Hall, was born in Dorchester, July 28, 1792; lives in Machias, Maine, and is a lumber dealer.

He was married, Feb. 3, 1820, to Phebe Foster, born Jan. 4, 1798.

Children of LUTHER and PHEBE (FOSTER) HALL, born at Machias, Me.:

    1182. Albert,   b. Sept. 28, 1821
    1183. Warren,   b. Aug. 9, 1823; d. Sept. 5, 1823.
    1184. Elizabeth A., b. July 13, 1825.
    1185. Miranda T., b. Dec. 2, 1826.
    1186. Augustus,   b. Jan. 19, 1829; d. Feb. 14, 1829.
    1187. Oliver L.,   b. Jan. 9, 1830; d. May 2, 1831.

1188. George L.,   b. Feb.   4, 1832.
1189. Mary A.,   b. Dec.   6, 1834.
1190. Orrin A.,   b. April 12, 1836.
1191. James A.,   b. May   31, 1838.
1192. Julien B.,   b. Sept.   8, 1840.
1193. Inez S.,   b. May   20, 1844.

(639) ELIJAH HALL, a twin son of Solomon and Rachael (Glover-Homes) Hall, was born in Dorchester, July 28, 1792; lives in Machias, Me., and is engaged in the lumber business.

He was married, Aug. 3, 1821, to Joanna Sevey.

Children of ELIJAH and JOANNA (SEVEY) HALL, born in Machias, Me.:

1194. Lucinda R., b. March 5, 1823; m. John S. Sevey, Machias.
1195. Solomon,   b. April 29, 1827.
1196. Stephen,   b. May   6, 1830; m. Harriet E. Simpson.
1197. Oliver,   b. May   5, 1833.
1198. Joshua A. L., b. Oct. 21, 1837.
1199. Sylvanus S., b. March 17, 1841.
1200. Elijah G.,   b. Aug. 19, 1846.

(640) MARY NASH HALL, eldest daughter of Solomon and Rachael (Glover-Homes) Hall, was born in Dorchester, April 1, 1794, and died in Machias, Me.

She was married, April, 1826, to Josiah Myles, of Machias, and went there to reside.   They had one son:

1201. Henry, b. in 1827; died in infancy.

(641) REBECKAH HALL, second daughter of Solomon and Rachael (Glover-Homes) Hall, was born in Dorchester, Feb. 29, 1796, and died there, Nov. 23, 1858, in her 63d year.

She was married, June 11, 1821, to Jonathan Collier.   He died in Nov., 1863.   They had three children:

1202. Rachel, b. Sept. 4, 1822; d. May 13, 1845, in her 23d year.
1203. Mary,   b. June 19, 1828; resides in Dorchester.
1204. Luther, b. Aug. 23, 1837; m. Sarah Ann Hunt.

(642) STEPHEN HALL, third son of Solomon and Rachael (Glover-Homes) Hall, was born in Dorchester, Feb. 1, 1798, and died there, about 1840.

He was married, Dec. 19, 1822, to Elizabeth Tolman, daughter of Stephen Tolman.   They had four children, born in Dorchester:

1205. Elizabeth Tolman, b. in 1823 ; m. Joseph Howe, Jr.
1206. Mary,   b. in 1825 ; died.
1207. Stephen,   b. in 1827 ; died.
1208. Caroline,   b. in 1837.

(643) OLIVER HALL, fourth and youngest son of Solomon
and Rachael (Glover-Homes) Hall, was born in Dorchester, Feb. 16,
1800; resides there on his estate, near Meeting-house Hill.   He is·
by trade a cabinet-maker, and continues the business under the name
and firm of Oliver Hall & Son.   He has been elected to various
offices in the town of Dorchester; has served as Selectman, Assessor
and Town Treasurer, has gained an honorable name by his faithfulness and trustworthy conduct, and has the esteem and confidence of
his fellow citizens.   He is President of the Mattapan Bank, at Harrison Square.

He has been thrice married.   First, Sept. 14, 1826, to Laura
Richards, daughter of Samuel Richards, Esq., of Dorchester; born
there in 1803, died Nov. 20, 1832, aged 29 years, leaving two daughters.   He married, second, Eunice Lyon, of Brookline, daughter of
Samuel Lyon, by whom he had five children.   She died Dec. 14,
1843; and Nov. 28, 1844, he was married, by Rev. Dr. Pierce, of
Brookline, to Caroline Laughton, of that place.   No issue by the last
marriage.

Children of OLIVER and LAURA (RICHARDS) HALL, born in Dorchester :

1209. Oliver Lyman, b. in 1827 ; died in infancy.
1210. Maria, b. in 1829 ; m. Frederick Pierce, in 1850 ; died April
        12, 1854, no issue.
1211. Laura, b. in 1830 ; resides in Dorchester.

    By second wife, EUNICE LYON :

1212. Oliver,   b. in 1835 ; d. Nov. 6, 1843, aged 9 years.
1213. Emily,   b. in 1837 ; died young.
1214. Henry,   b. in 1838 ; resides in Dorchester.
1215. Oliver,   b. in 1839 ; died young—aged 3 years.
1216. Adalaide, b. Jan., 1840.

(645) ELEANOR GLOVER, eldest daughter and child of
Samuel and Eleanor (Hawes) Glover, was born in Stoughton, Oct. 7,
1788, baptized there by Rev. Jedediah Adams, her parents being in
full communion with the Church in Stoughton.   In 1811 she attend-

ed Day's Academy, at Wrentham, under the instruction of Rev. Martin
Moore.   In 1812 she commenced teaching a public school in Stoughton, and continued there five years.   In 1818, she engaged in a
school at Mansfield, and continued there eight years.   In 1826, she
went to Milton, and gave instruction in the "Scotch Woods" school,
four years.   In 1830 and '31 she was employed in the school district
in Stoughton village.   In 1834 she opened a boarding and day school
for young ladies on the homestead estate, and continued, with very
little interruption, until 1854.   She resides in Stoughton, and still
receives pupils for private study.   She is a member of the Female
Benevolent Society, organized in 1818; was elected a teacher in the
first organized Sabbath school in Stoughton, in the same year, and
still continues a teacher in the school; has been a member of the
Orthodox Church in her native town, since Dec. 11, 1825.

(647)   JARVIS GLOVER, the second son of Samuel and Eleanor (Hawes) Glover, was born in Stoughton, June 21, 1792, baptized
at the Church in Stoughton, Rev. Jedediah Adams, pastor, and died
in Springfield, Aug. 13, 1864, aged 72 years.

Jan. 2, 1820, he was married to Fanny Fuller, of Dalton, in Berkshire County, Mass.   She was the daughter of Lemuel and Fanny
(Briggs) Fuller, and was born in Mansfield, Aug. 8, 1796.   She is a
widow, and resides in Springfield.

Jarvis Glover resided in Stoughton until 1822; was an active and
energetic citizen, of noble and generous impulses, and unselfish in all
his acts for the promotion of education and the maintenance of good
order in the town.   In 1810, at the age of 18 years, he was enrolled
in the militia; in 1813, at the age of 21 years, he was enrolled in
the troop of horse, and continued in that company until 1820.   He
invariably declined accepting any political or military office, although
eminently endowed by nature for distinction in public life.

In 1822 he removed to Canton, and resided there until the Spring
of 1825.   He removed to Springfield in May, 1825, and resided
there until his decease, a period of nearly forty years.

Children of JARVIS and FANNY (FULLER) GLOVER, born in Canton
and Springfield :

1217. Martha, b. July 3, 1821 ; d. in Springfield, Dec. 21, 1846, in
        her 26th year.   She was a teacher, and a much esteemed
        member of the South Church.

1218. Mary Elizabeth, b. May 15, 1823 ; m. John Jacob Simmons,
    of Troy, N. Y., Oct. 19, 1846 ; resides in Chicago, Ill.
1219. Fannie Maria, b. April 18, 1826 ; resides in Springfield.
+1220. George Henry, b. June 28, 1830 ; resides in Chicago, Ill.
+1221. Samuel Jarvis, b. Jan. 8, 1832 ; resides in Chicago, Ill.
+1222. Frank W. Thomas, b. Sept. 28, 1838 ; resides in Hartford, Ct.

(650) MARY GLOVER, second daughter of Ebenezer and
Mary (Trescott-Fenno) Glover, was born in Dorchester, June 7,
1800, and died in Roxbury, Oct. 10, 1826, aged 26 years.

Dec. 9, 1821, she was married to James Lewis, Jr., son of James
and Hannah (Seaver) Lewis, of Roxbury; born there in 1798, and
resides in Dorchester.   They had three children, born in Dorchester:

1223. Mary Glover, b. Aug. 30, 1822 ; resides in Dorchester.
+1224. Hannah Seaver, b. Dec. 13, 1823 ; m. { 1st, Josiah Goss ;
                                             { 2d, Benj. F. Bartlett.
1225. Ebenezer Glover, b. July 20, 1825 ; d. Oct. 26, 1826.

(656) JERUSHA BLACKMAN, eldest daughter of Unite and
Jerusha (Glover) Blackman, was born in Dorchester, Aug. 3, 1800;
resides in Roxbury.

She was married, May 26, 1821, to Joseph Bugbee, Esq., son of
Ebenezer and Mary (White) Bugbee, of Roxbury; born there, Nov.
23, 1795, and died July 22, 1859.   They had four children, born in
Roxbury :

+1226. Mary White,   b. June   3, 1822 ; m. Daniel C. Bates.
1227. Caroline Maria,   b. May   11, 1828 ; m. Luther D. Styles.
1228. Josephine Augusta, b. April 22, 1834 ; resides in Roxbury.
1229. Anne Elizabeth Coffin, b. March 31, 1839 ; resides in Roxbury.

(657) LUCY BLACKMAN, second daughter of Unite and
Jerusha (Glover) Blackman, was born in Dorchester, June 1, 1803;
lives in South Boston.

She was married to Robert Gilmore Babcock, April 25, 1822, and
removed to Roxbury; has lived in New London, Conn., in Milton,
Mass., and several other places.

Children of ROBERT GILMORE and LUCY (BLACKMAN) BABCOCK,
born in Roxbury and New London, Conn.:

1230. Jerusha Glover,   b. Nov. 27, 1822 ; d. Aug. 20, 1826.
1231. George La Fayette, b. May 22, 1824 ; d. Jan. 25, 1848.

1232. Louisa Gilmore, b. Oct. 27, 1827 ; m. George W. Bolton, April 4, 1855.
1233. Andrew Jackson, b. July 12, 1830 ; m. Harriet A. Palmer, Jan., 1852.
1234. Lucy Blackman, b. Sept. 8, 1832 ; m. Henry Fobes, of Dorchester, Dec. 14, 1851.
1235. Sarah Otis, b. June 22, 1834 ; teacher in the Bigelow School, South Boston.
1236. Josephine Augusta, b. March 11, 1836 ; d. March 1, 1850, aged 14 years.
1237. Robert Gilmore, b. June 27, 1838 ; m.
1238. Elizabeth Averill, b. April 12, 1840 ; d. Nov. 1, 1841.
1239. John Reed, b. July 6, 1842 ; died in 1865.
1240. Solomon Willard, b. Dec. 13, 1844.

(660) LEWIS LEEDS, eldest son of Josiah and Anna (Glover) Leeds, was born in Dorchester, March 29, 1798; lives in Savin Hill Avenue, Dorchester, on a portion of the Leeds estate.

He was married to Pedy Thompson, of Rockingham, Vt., April 23, 1826.

Children of LEWIS and PEDY (THOMPSON) LEEDS, born in Dorchester:

1241. Elizabeth, b. Feb. 27, 1827 ; m. Isaac Field, Jan. 23, 1848.
1242. Mary Anne, b. Oct. 16, 1829 ; resides in Dorchester.
1243. Ellen, b. April 16, 1832 ; resides in Dorchester.
1244. Louisa Burnham, b. March 12, 1835 ; m. Joseph A. Arnold, of South Braintree, July, 1860.
1245. Josiah, b. June 13, 1837 ; d. Dec., 1860, unm., aged 23 years.
1246. John, b. Dec. 29, 1839 ; d. Sept. 26, 1843, aged 7 years.
1247. Anna Frances, b. Sept. 16, 1843 ; resides in Dorchester.
1248. Frederick, b. Aug. 21, 1845 ; resides in Dorchester.

(661) JOSEPH LEEDS, son of Josiah and Anna (Glover) Leeds, was born in Dorchester, Nov. 12, 1799; lives in Stoneham; is a blacksmith; Deacon of the Universalist Church in Stoneham.

He has been thrice married. First, June 5, 1823, to Eliza Gerry, daughter of Capt. David and Sarah (Richardson) Gerry, of Stoneham; born there, July 5, 1801, and died Jan. 19, 1824, in her 23d year. No issue. He married, second, Betsey Lynde, daughter of Stephen and Hannah (Willey) Lynde, of Stoneham; born there, March 1, 1806; died March 22, 1826, aged 20 years. His third wife was Eliza Lynde, daughter of Benjamin Lynde, Esq., of Malden; married March 10, 1827. There were two children by this marriage:

1249. Eliza Anne, m. —— Washburn.
1250. Mary,	m. —— Stevens.

(663) ANNA LEEDS, eldest daughter of Josiah and Anna (Glover) Leeds, was born in Dorchester, Aug. 21, 1803, and lives in Savin Hill Avenue. She inherited the mansion house, with a portion of the land belonging to the estate, from her father, and resides on it.

She was married, Feb. 8, 1826, to William Parker, son of Capt. Nathaniel and Rebecca (Dudley) Parker, of Roxbury, who was lineally descended from Gov. Joseph Dudley, by his mother Rebecca Dudley, who was a granddaughter of the Governor. He was born in Brimfield, Jan. 28, 1798, and died in Dorchester, March 17, 1865, in his 68th year.

Children of WILLIAM and ANNA (LEEDS) PARKER, born in Dorchester:

1251. Mary Anne, b. July 14, 1827 ; resides in Dorchester.
1252. William,	b. May 11, 1829 ; m. Fidelia French, Callao, S. A.
1253. Caroline Augusta, b. June 11, 1831 ; resides in Dorchester.
1254. Thomas Leeds, b. July 27, 1834 ; m. Sarah Daniels, Boston.
1255. Charles Davis,	b. Oct. 10, 1836 ; resides in Callao, S. A.
1256. George Henry,	b. April 11, 1838 ; resides in Dorchester.
1257. Rebecca Leeds, b. Sept. 29, 1840 ; m. Eleazer Bullard, Sept. 13, 1864.
1258. Edward,	b. July 29, 1843 ; resides in Callao, S. A.
1259. Dudley,	b. March 7, 1846 ; d. July 24, 1849.

(664) THOMAS LEEDS, third son of Josiah and Anna (Glover) Leeds, was born in Dorchester, Feb. 3, 1806, and died in Stoneham, Aug. 7, 1834, aged 28 years. He was a blacksmith, and lived in Stoneham.

He was married to —— Lynde, of Stoneham. They had one daughter:

1260. Rebecca Glover, date of birth not reported.

(667) LOUISA GLOVER, eldest daughter of Elijah and Martha (Pope) Glover, was born in Dorchester, Aug. 5, 1808, baptized by Rev. Dr. Harris, Aug. 10, 1808, and resides in Braintree.

She was married, June 4, 1835, by Rev. Dr. Park, of Stoughton, to Joseph Parshley, of Braintree. They have had three children born in Braintree:

1261. Isaac Glover,   b. in 1839 ; died in infancy.
1262. Harriet Rebeckah, b. July 20, 1848.
1263. Louisa Harriet,   b. May 25, 1850.

(668) MARTHA HARRIET GLOVER, second daughter of Elijah and Martha (Pope) Glover, was born in Dorchester, May 22, 1810, and resides in Brighton.

April 13, 1836, she was married to Isaac Thayer Dyer, son of Capt. Isaac and Sarah (Thayer) Dyer, of Braintree; born there, May 28, 1809. Owns an estate in Brighton, near the cattle market.

Children of ISAAC THAYER and MARTHA HARRIET (GLOVER) DYER, born in Brighton:

   1264. Louisa Harriet, b. Dec. 7, 1837 ; resides in Brighton.
+1265. Almeda, b. June 24, 1839 ; m. Henry C. Foster, Dorchester.
+1266. Isaac Henry,   b. Nov. 20, 1840 ; resides in Brighton.
+1267. Nehemiah Franklin, b. Feb. 10, 1844; d. April 5, 1866, a. 22.
   1268. Sarah Jane,   b. Sept. 1, 1848; resides in Brighton.
   1269. Katie Adalaide, b. Jan. 21, 1854; d. Feb. 10, 1862.

(670) ASAHEL HOWE GLOVER, eldest son of Elijah and Sarah (Howe) Glover, was born in Stoughton, March 30, 1816; resides in Dorchester, is the owner of several estates there. His homestead is situated on a portion of the ancient estate which formerly belonged to the Hon. John Glover, of Dorchester, described on page 53.

Nov. 8, 1842, he was married to (1176) Sarah Elizabeth Homes, eldest daughter of (637) William and Elizabeth (Blackman) Homes, of Dorchester; born there, Feb. 25, 1816.

Children of ASAHEL HOWE and SARAH ELIZABETH (HOMES) GLOVER, born in Dorchester:

1270. Sarah Elizabeth, b. Aug. 20, 1843.
1271. Caroline Luthera, b. Sept.   1, 1844 ; m. Frederick Beck.
1272. Edmund Walter, b. March 18, 1846 ; d. Jan 18, 1847.
1273. Anne Augusta,   b. Dec. 29, 1847.
1274. Rebecca,   b. March 28, 1850.
1275. Herbert Hinckley, b. Aug.   6, 1853.
1276. Ella,   b. June 25, 1856.

(672) JOHN CLOUGH GLOVER, third son of Elijah and Sarah (Howe) Glover, was born in Stoughton, March 14, 1819; resides in Stoughton, on a portion of the Glover homestead.

He has been twice married. First, Nov. 10, 1842, to Ann Wads-worth Monk, daughter of Elijah Wadsworth and Abigail (Morton) Monk, of Stoughton; born there in 1822, and died Nov. 6, 1861, aged 39 years. He was married, second, Aug. 25, 1864, to Mary (Farrington) Horton (widow), of Milton.

Children of JOHN CLOUGH and ANN W. (MONK) GLOVER, born in Stoughton :

1277. Annis Crane,   b. Aug. 25, 1843.
1278. Ellis Morton,   b. Dec. 19, 1845 ; d. Aug. 28, 1855, aged 10.
1279. Sarah Hannah, b. in   1850.
1280. Frederick Pope, b. May 2, 1852 ; d. Nov. 5, 1853.
1281. Thomas,   b. July 28, 1855 ; d. Aug. 31, 1855.
1282. Frederick,   b. Aug. 28, 1856.
1283. Abby Anne,   b. Aug. 20, 1861.

By second wife, MARY (FARRINGTON) HORTON :

1284. Ellis Horton, b. Oct. 4, 1866.

(673) REBECKAH GLOVER, daughter of Elijah and Sarah (Howe) Glover, was born in Stoughton, Jan. 14, 1821, and died in North Bridgewater, March 26, 1846, in her 23d year. The first Sabbath in July, 1842, she was admitted to join the First Congrega-tional Church in Stoughton, Rev. Henry Eddy, pastor. She was an active member of the Juvenile Society, from its organization until her decease.

Oct. 3, 1844, she was married to Edmund Packard, of North Bridgewater, and went there to reside. They had one son :

1285. Edmund, b. March 14, 1846 ; died in a few days.

(674) ELIJAH GLOVER, the fourth son of Elijah and Sarah (Howe) Glover, was born in Stoughton, March 14, 1824, and died in that town, Oct. 7, 1849, in his 26th year, leaving a widow and one child.

Oct. 29, 1846, he was married, by Rev. William M. Cornell, to Eunice Packard Swan, daughter of James and Betsey (Capen) Swan; born in Stoughton, Feb. 2, 1823. They had one daughter :

1286. Mary Rebecca, b. Oct. 11, 1848.

March 1, 1855, the widow of Elijah Glover was married, a second time, to Elisha Hawes, by Rev. J. W. Dennis.

(675) FREDERICK POPE GLOVER, the fourth son of Elijah and Sarah (Howe) Glover, was born in Stoughton, Dec. 28, 1825; baptized there by Rev. Dr. Park; resides in Boston.

Nov. 14, 1861, he was married to Emeline Morton, daughter of Otis and Persis (Coolidge) Morton, of Boston; born there, April 14, 1832. They have one son:

1287. Frederick Morton, b. Feb. 23, 1863.

(679) WILLIAM GLOVER, third son of Dr. Samuel Kingsley and Eunice (Babcock) Glover, was born at Milton Hill, July 26, 1788, and died there, June 15, 1856, aged 68 years. He was a goldsmith by trade, and kept a shop of jewelry and silver plate in Boston for several years. After he removed to Milton Hill, he occupied the homestead estate, and succeeded to it at the decease of his father. Subsequently he opened a store of the same kind near the bridge at Dorchester and Milton Lower Mills.

He was married, Jan. 2, 1816, to Eliza Gleason, daughter of Joseph and Elizabeth (Bacon) Gleason, of Wrentham; born there, Oct. 10, 1795, and resides (in 1866) with her daughter in Brooklyn, N. Y.

Children of WILLIAM and ELIZA (GLEASON) GLOVER, born in Boston and at Milton Hill:

1288. William Joseph Gleason, b. May 17, 1817 ; d. Oct. 25, 1817.
+1289. Eliza Rebecca, b. June 26, 1818 ; m. Joseph Emerson Payne, of New York.
1290. Sarah Maria, b. Dec. 1, 1819 ; resides in Brooklyn, N. Y.
1291. William,   b. Oct. 1, 1821 ; d. Oct. 9, 1821.
1292. Caroline Josephine, b. Jan. 12, 1823 ; d. Aug. 9, 1824.
1293. William Anson,   b. Oct. 2, 1824 : d. Oct. 10, 1824.
1294. Mary Lebaron, b. Dec. 12, 1825 ; m. William Davis, of Salem, June 7, 1850 ; went to Illinois, and died there in 1863.
+1295. Alfred Richardson, b. July 18, 1828 ; m. Mary Louisa Bodge, of Roxbury.
1296. William Charles,   b. Aug. 6, 1830 ; d. June 26, 1832.
+1297. Harriet Wood, b. May 18, 1833 ; m. Lucius Parker Starr, of New York.
1298. William,   b. March 18, 1838 ; resides in New York.

(684) EUNICE BILLINGS GLOVER, only daughter of William and Mary (Billings) Glover, was born in Quincy, Sept. 5, 1805; resides in Quincy, on her inheritance from the estate of William

Glover, which was passed to him from his father, William Glover, Sen. (See page 281.)

Nov. 4, 1827, she was married to William Brazer Duggan, of Boston, a graduate of Harvard College in the class of 1824. They have had six children, born in Quincy:

1299. James Glover,   b. in 1829 ; d. April 4, 1839.
1300. Eunice Angelina, m. Robert B. Barsham, Oct. 19, 1865.
1301. Anne E.,   b. in 1846.
1302. Rowland,   b. in 1848.
1303. Emma.
1304. William.

(685) JAMES MADISON GLOVER, only son of William and Mary (Billings) Glover, was born in Quincy, Aug. 9, 1809 ; resides in Quincy ; owns an estate there, near Neponset Bridge.

He was married, Dec. 25, 1831, to Harriet Louisa Gibbs, daughter of Capt. Nathan Gibbs, of Sandwich.

Children of JAMES MADISON and HARRIET LOUISA (GIBBS) GLOVER, born in Quincy:

1305. Thomas Jefferson, b. Nov. 29, 1834 ; m. Anna Pope, Dorches.
1306. Nathan Gibbs,   b. May 8, 1835 ; m. Mary A. French, Quincy.
1307. Harriet Louisa, b. in March, 1837.
1308. Ripley,   b. Jan. 27, 1838 ; d. April 29, 1838.
1309. Hannah Gibbs, b. June 17, 1843 ; m. John Stedman Williams, of Quincy.

(718) EMELINE RUGG, third daughter of Jonathan and Martha (Glover) Rugg, was born in Framingham, Sept. 22, 1807, and died in Holyoke, Mass., May 17, 1842, in her 34th year.

She was married, April 9, 1835, to Seymour Gates, son of Stephen and Ruth (Worden) Gates, of Holyoke; born there in March, 1811, and is now living, in his 56th year. They had two children, born there, as follows :

1310. Jonathan Rugg, b. Aug. 20, 1841 ; m. Sophia Durgin, April 14, 1859 ; no issue.
1311. Lucinda Marsh, b. Aug. 20, 1841 ; m. Morris Ely, and has one son, Henry Morris, b. March 13, 1860.

(720) MARTHA RUGG, youngest daughter of Jonathan and Martha (Glover) Rugg, was born in Framingham, Jan. 2, 1819, and died at Niagara Falls, Aug. 24, 1844, aged 24 years. She was edu-

389

cated in Boston, under the instruction of Professor Felton, and was distinguished for her natural and acquired accomplishments, and her attainments in science. She early manifested a love for the science of botany, and devoted a great portion of her time to its study. In the summer of 1844, she visited Niagara Falls for the purpose of making botanical investigations, and adding to her knowledge in that department. She was eagerly pursuing her favorite study, when she fell from a precipice and lost her life. The spot from which she fell is graphically described by Grace Greenwood, in her "Greenwood Leaves," and the following allusion made to the sad event: "Miss Martha Rugg lost her life by falling from a precipice of one hundred and sixty-seven feet, while plucking a flower, Aug. 24, 1844. This young lady resided in Lancaster, Mass.; she was educated in Boston, by Professor C. C. Felton, and was remarkable for her acquirements in botany."

(724) Capt. THOMAS GLOVER, eldest son of Capt. John Clough and Martha (White) Glover, was born at Vinalhaven (Fox Islands), Maine, Feb. 20, 1812, and died in Camden, Nov. 15, 1860, in his 48th year. He went early to sea with his father, became a shipmaster, made many foreign voyages, and, it is said, was an able and accomplished commander.

He was twice married. First, July 28, 1838, to Lucy Jane Eaton, daughter of William and Lucy (White) Eaton, of Camden; born there, July 10, 1815, and died Oct. 25, 1851, aged 35 years. He was married, second, Dec. 18, 1853, to Lucy B. Stetson, daughter of Deacon Joseph and Mary (Eaton) Stetson, of Camden; born there, Dec. 19, 1827. She is a widow, and resides in Camden. There were no children by this marriage.

Children of Capt. THOMAS and LUCY JANE (EATON) GLOVER, born in Camden:

1312. Julia Antoinette, b. April 18, 1842; m. Wilfred B. Glover, April 28, 1861.
1313. Horatio Herbert, b. Sept. 18, 1845.
1314. Mary Selina,   b. July 15, 1847.
1315. Clara Fisher,   b. April 25, 1851.

(725) MARY HILL GLOVER, eldest daughter of Capt. John Clough and Martha (White) Glover, was born at Vinalhaven, Me., Sept. 15, 1815; resides now in Belfast, Me.

She was married, Nov. 24, 1836, to Rev. Winthrop O. Thomas, of Marshfield, Mass. He is of the Baptist denomination, and has been settled in the City of Rockland, and now (1866) is preaching at Belfast. There was no issue.

(726) SARAH WHITE GLOVER, second daughter of Capt. John Clough and Martha (White) Glover, was born in Vinalhaven, Me., March 4, 1818, and died there, March 22, 1853, aged 35 years. She was married, Feb. 9, 1843, to Benjamin Cushing, 2d, Esq.; there was no issue.

(727) Capt. JOHN WHITE GLOVER, second son of Capt. John Clough and Martha (White) Glover, was born at Vinalhaven, Me., Nov. 5, 1821, and died at Calcutta, of cholera, Sept. 1, 1863. He went early to sea with his father, and after passing through the regular grades of office, was for many years first mate under his father's command. Subsequently he became a shipmaster, and continued such until his decease.

He was married, in New York City, Dec. 1, 1847, to Sarah C. Stetson, eldest daughter of Deacon Joseph and Mary (Eaton) Stetson, of Camden; born there, Aug. 15, 1823. Her earliest American ancestors, of her mother's lineage, were, first, William and Martha (Abercrombie) Thorn, who came from England and settled on the coast of Maine; second, Major George and Lucy (Thorn) White; her mother, Mary Eaton, was their granddaughter, and married Deacon Joseph Stetson, of Massachusetts ancestors.

Children of Capt. JOHN WHITE and SARAH C. (STETSON) GLOVER, born in Camden, Me.:

1316. William Franklin, b. Nov. 26, 1850.
1317. Joseph Stetson,   b. Nov. 24, 1852.
1318. Charles Brooks,   b. Aug. 15, 1856.

(728) MARTHA WHITE GLOVER, third daughter of Capt. John Clough and Martha (White) Glover, twin sister to (727) Capt. John White Glover, was born at Vinalhaven, Me., Nov. 5, 1821; resides in Rockport, Me.   .

She was married, Jan. 16, 1848, to Hosea Ballou Eaton, M.D., son of Parker and Mary Seymour (Manson) Eaton, of Plymouth,

Me., and a descendant, in a direct line, from Gov. Joseph Dudley, of Roxbury, Mass. They had four children, born in Rockport:

1319. John Parker, b. Nov. 21, 1849; d. Feb. 20, 1852.
1320. Martha Verenna, b. Jan. 8, 1853.
1321. Hosea Ballou, b. Sept. 17, 1855.
1322. Thomas Glover, b. Feb. 17, 1858.

Parker Eaton, Esq., the father of Dr. H. B. Eaton, was born in Fitchburg, Mass., in 1786. March 19, 1807, he was married, by Rev. Dr. Baldwin, to Mary Seymour Manson, of Boston; born there in 1788; died in Plymouth, Me., July 11, 1848, aged 60 years. In 1821, they removed to Plymouth, where he now resides.

(729) JAMES RUSSELL GLOVER, third son of Capt. John Clough and Martha (White) Glover, was born in Vinalhaven, Me., April 4, 1824, and is now (1866) in California.

He was married, May 12, 1850, to Nancy Palmer, daughter of Nathaniel and Theresa (Pinkham) Palmer, of Boothbay; born in Camden, Me., in 1826. They had two children, born in Camden:

1323. Clara Ella, b. Dec. 17, 1851.
1324. Lulie Eva, b. Sept. 11, 1856.

(730) GEORGE WHITE GLOVER, fourth son of Capt. John Clough and Martha (White) Glover, was born at Vinalhaven, Me., April 29, 1827; resides in Camden. Is a shipbuilder, owns a shipyard at the mouth of the Penobscot river, and carries on the business of shipbuilding extensively, in company with his brother, James Russell Glover.

He was married to Philena Hartford, of Camden, July 31, 1852.

Children of GEORGE WHITE and PHILENA (HARTFORD) GLOVER, born in Camden:

1325. Frederick Russell, b. Jan. 18, 1856.
1326. Maria Ada, b. Sept. 26, 1862.
1327. Georgie Eva, b. July 15, 1864.

(732) SUSANNAH GLOVER, eldest daughter of Capt. Elijah and Nancy (Crabtree) Glover, was born in Vinalhaven, Me., Feb. 11, 1823, and died in Camden, Feb. 26, 1865, aged 42 years.

She was married, March 23, 1853, to Rev. Edward Freeman, of Camden. They had four children—names not reported.

(733) Capt. BENJAMIN FRANKLIN GLOVER, eldest son of Capt. Elijah and Nancy (Crabtree) Glover, was born in Vinalhaven, Me., Dec. 24, 1824. He went to sea in the "Levi Woodbury," and was lost from on board Oct. 6, 1849, aged 25 years. He was held in high estimation by all who knew him. He was a beloved and honored member of the Masonic Fraternity. The Portland Advertiser of March 5, 1850, has the following notice of him, written by a brother of the Lodge: "Capt. Benjamin Franklin Glover, son of Elijah Glover, Esq., of Camden, perished in the ill-fated schooner Levi Woodbury, on the 6th day of October last (1849). His body is deposited in the great deep, over which no monument can be erected, and over his remains the storm will beat, the sun will shine, and the waves of old ocean will roll on, leaving no traces to mark his lone grave, until the sound of the last trump, when the sea shall give up its dead. But his memory still survives, and is written on the hearts of his brethren, and, we trust, is also written on the trestle board of the Great Architect of the universe, where it will be noticed and receive ample justice in the great day of accounts."

At a regular meeting of Amity Lodge, at their hall in Camden, Me., Jan. 25, 1850, the following preamble and resolutions were unanimously adopted:

" *Whereas* it has pleased the Great Architect above to remove from among us an esteemed brother and member of our Order, Brother Benjamin Franklin Glover, therefore

" *Resolved*, That we are deeply affected by this intelligence of Brother Glover's death, and view it as a solemn admonition to us to 'be also ready.' And although he was but a short time member of our Order, yet the high estimation in which he was held for his amiable deportment and good moral character, will embalm his memory in our hearts.

" *Resolved*, That we tender to the bereaved parents and relatives of the deceased our sincere condolence for the overwhelming bereavement visited upon them in the loss of a beloved son and affectionate friend."

(734) RACHEL CRABTREE GLOVER, second daughter of Capt. Elijah and Nancy (Crabtree) Glover, was born in Vinalhaven, Me., April 28, 1827.

She was married, July 4, 1854, to Charles R. Pottle, of Camden, and removed first to East Boston, thence to Belmont, where they now reside. They have two daughters, names not reported.

(735) MARSHALL PARKS GLOVER, second and only son living of Capt. Elijah and Nancy (Crabtree) Glover, was born in Vinalhaven, Me., June 20, 1830; resides now in Chelsea, Mass. In 1850 he went to California, and resided there until 1856, when he returned and established himself as a shipbuilder. He owns a ship-yard and carries on the business extensively in Chelsea.

He was married to Mary Daggett, in 1860. No children reported.

(737) LUCY HILL GLOVER, youngest and fourth daughter of Capt. Elijah and Nancy (Crabtree) Glover, was born in Vinal-haven, Me., June 3, 1835, and lives now in the City of Rockland, Me.

She was married, May 1, 1854, to Orris Starrett Andrews, of Warren, Me. He is an eminent merchant. They removed to Rock-land; have had three daughters.

(744) HORATIO NELSON GLOVER, eldest son of Benjamin Wadsworth and Mehetable Willard (Baxter) Glover, was born at the Newbury farm homestead, Quincy, March 6, 1801, and died there, Dec. 28, 1863, in his 62d year.

He succeeded to the Newbury farm homestead in 1823, and was in possession there forty years, leaving it to his heirs. He was the seventh possessor, and of the seventh generation, in a direct male line of succession, from his first American ancestor, the Hon. John Glover. (See page 74.) He was distinguished for his uprightness and great moral worth, enjoyed the confidence and high esteem of his fellow citizens and townsmen, and was honored by them in being elected to various offices of trust and honor for a series of years, and in which he served them faithfully until his failing health compelled him to retire. In the domestic circle, and in his daily life, he imparted joy and happiness to all with whom he was connected; and in his neighborhood relations he was always kind, prompt and obliging. After he had retired from public service and honors, he devoted his attention to agricultural pursuits; was an active and prominent member of the Norfolk County Agricultural Society, and made great improvements on his own estate, which he held in high veneration from having received it through a long line of honored and worthy ancestors. He was an active promoter of education and educational interests; the habit of his thoughts, also, had a genealo-gical tendency, and a strong and inherent love of ancestry inspired and gàve an impulse to the pursuit and completion of these "Memorials and Genealogies " of his family name.

He was married, Dec. 14, 1826, by Rev. Bela Jacobs, to Martha Turpin Hovey, second daughter of James and Anna (Wilson) Hovey, of Brighton ; born in Cambridge, Oct. 3, 1804. She is a widow, and resides at the homestead in Quincy.

Children of HORATIO N. and MARTHA T. (HOVEY) GLOVER, born in Quincy :

+1328. Horatio N., b. Sept. 14, 1827 ; m. Anne Augusta Holbrook.
  1329. James Hovey, b. May 9, 1829 ; drowned in Quincy Bay by
      the upsetting of a boat, Oct. 8, 1850, in his 22d year.
  1330. Anna Hovey, b. May 25, 1831 ; d. Feb. 16, 1863, in 31st yr.
  1331. Martha Maria,   b. July 8, 1833 ; d. March 16, 1835.
+1332. William Bowles,   b. Sept. 20, 1835.
  1333. Abby Caroline,   b. Feb. 16, 1838 ; d. May 25, 1839.
  1334. Harriet Lincoln, b. July 5, 1840.
  1335. Julia Elizabeth, b. Feb. 14, 1843.
  1336. Emily Lincoln,   b. July 9, 1845.
  1337. Sarah Wadsworth, b. Oct. 5, 1847.

(745)   BENJAMIN FRANKLIN GLOVER, second and youngest son of Benjamin Wadsworth and Mehetable Willard (Baxter) Glover, was born at the Newbury farm homestead in Quincy, June 3, 1803, and resides in Dorchester.

He was married, Oct. 29, 1826, by Rev. John G. Palfrey, to Josephine Baxter, daughter of Joseph and Anna (Dashwood) Baxter, of Boston ; born there in 1803, and now living in Dorchester.

Children of BENJAMIN FRANKLIN and JOSEPHINE (BAXTER) GLOVER, born in Dorchester :

+1338. Benjamin F., b. Aug. 4, 1827 ; m. Mary Valentine, Weymouth.
  1339. Evelina,   b. Jan. 27, 1829 ; d. Oct., 1858, in her 30th year.
  1340. John Henderson, b. July 15, 1830 ; resides in San Francisco.
  1341. Albert Baxter, b. Nov. 2, 1832 ; resides in San Francisco.
  1342. Josephine Maria, b. Oct. 20, 1833.
  1343. Samuel Woodward, b. March 31, 1843 ; d. May 9, 1849.
  1344. Henrietta Dashwood, b. Nov. 7, 1844 ; resides in S. Francisco.

(747)   JOSEPH ARNOLD, eldest son of Capt. Joseph Neale and Mehetable (Adams) Arnold, and grandson of Daniel and Jerusha (Glover) Arnold, was born in Quincy, Feb. 5, 1786, and died at Cranston, R. I., Aug. 19, 1836, aged 50 years.

He was married to Elizabeth Briesler, about 1806.

Children of JOSEPH and ELIZABETH (BRIESLER) ARNOLD, born in Quincy:

1345. Elizabeth, b. March 25, 1808 ; m. John Fowle ; resides in Brighton.
1346. Joseph Neale, b. June 29, 1809 ; died young.
1347. John,   b. in   1811 ; died young.
1348. Caroline,   b. Feb. 6, 1813 ; m. James Newcomb, Quincy.
1349. Harriet,   b. Aug. 4, 1815 ;
              m. { 1st, William Simpson, of Boston ;
                   { 2d, Samuel O. Robinson, of Boston.
1350. Edward, b. Sept. 18, 1816 ; m. Mary Ann Magoon, of Salem.
1351. Abigail, b. May 16, 1819 ; died in infancy.
1352. Abigail B.,   b. Dec. 2, 1820 ; m. Owen Huff, of Boston.
1353. Anne Maria, b. in   1822 ; m. Henry L. Christian, Boston.

(748) MEHETABLE ARNOLD, the eldest daughter of Capt. Joseph Neale and Mehetable (Adams) Arnold, was born in Quincy, Feb. 16, 1787; resides in Quincy.

Oct. 9, 1807, she was married to Dr. Thomas Phipps, Jr. He died in Quincy, Aug. 29, 1832. They had six children, born in Quincy, viz. :

1354. Thomas Glover,   b. May 21, 1808.
1355. Emeline Mehetable Adams, b. Nov. 2, 1809.
1356. Harrison Gray Otis, b. Dec. 13, 1811 ; H. C. 1832; pastor of the Unitarian Church at Cohasset; died in Boston, Dec. 27, 1841, aged 30 years.
1357. Eliza,   b. Sept. 13, 1814.
1358. James Lawrence, b. Aug. 1, 1816.
1359. Helen Louisa,   b. July 11, 1818.

(762) THOMAS GLOVER FENNO, eldest son of Jesse and Elizabeth (Arnold) Fenno, grandson of Daniel and Jerusha (Glover) Arnold, was born in Quincy, in 1813, and died there, Jan. 12, 1865, aged 52 years.

He was married, July 29, 1839, to Elizabeth R. Adams, of Quincy; no children reported.

(807) JAMES GLOVER, eldest son of Robert and Bethiah (Tubbs) Glover, was born in Pembroke, Sept. 22, 1748, and died there, Feb. 6, 1819, aged 71 years, leaving a widow. Letters of administration were granted in 1820; warrant and inventory same

year. April 20, 1775, he was enrolled in the militia under command of Capt. Thomas Turner, Col. Anthony Thomas's regiment.

July 27, 1765, he was married to Rachel Bonney, daughter of Elisha Bonney, of Pembroke; born there in 1752. She removed to Sumner, Me., and died there, June 10, 1833, aged 81 years.

Children of JAMES and RACHEL (BONNEY) GLOVER, born in Pembroke:

+1360. James, b. Oct. 28, 1768 ; m. Ruth Stetson, of Pembroke.
1361. David, b. March 2, 1771 ; m. { 1st, Lydia Crocker, Pembroke; 2d, Lydia Lapham, Pembroke.
1362. Elisha, b. July 8, 1773 ; d. in 1782, aged 9 years.
+1363. Sarah, b. May 30, 1776 ; m. James Bonney, of Pembroke.
1364. Lydia, b. Oct. 24, 1778 ; m. Edmund Warren, Buckfield, Me.
+1365. Bethiah, b. July 14, 1781 ; m. Calvin Bisbee, Sumner, Me.
+1366. Joshua Sonney, b. Sept. 18, 1784 ; m. Susan Ames, Hartford, Me.
+1367. Elijah,   b. Sept. 18, 1786 ; m. Mary Walker, of Pembroke.
+1368. John,   b. Sept. 14, 1789 ; m. Mary Gullifer, Pembroke.
1369. Thomas,   b. in   1791 ; d. in 1793.
+1370. Charles,   b. Aug. 12, 1795 ; m. Almira Sayward, Rockland.

(808) LYDIA GLOVER, eldest daughter of Robert and Bethiah (Tubbs) Glover, was born in Pembroke, Dec. 15, 1750.

She was married to Josiah Witherell, of Pembroke, in 1768. They had two daughters:

1371. Lydia, b. in 1770 ; m. ——— Sampson.
1372. Ruth, b. in 1772 ; died unmarried.

(810) THOMAS GLOVER, second son of Robert and Bethiah (Tubbs) Glover, was born in Pembroke, March 24, 1757, and died at St. George, a part of Old Thomaston, Me.

He was married and had four sons:

1373. Joseph.
1374. Ezra.
1375. Thomas.
1376. Edmund.

(811) BETHIAH GLOVER, third daughter of Robert and Bethiah (Tubbs) Glover, was born in Pembroke, March 24, 1760, and died there, date of death not ascertained.

She was married to Foster MacFarland, of Scituate, June 2, 1787; no children reported.

(812) ROBERT GLOVER, Jr., third son of Robert and Bethiah (Tubbs) Glover, was born in Pembroke, March 27, 1763, and died in Hebron, Oxford County, Me., Feb. 21, 1820.

He was married, in 1782, to Kezia Barrows, of Hebron. She died there, July 9, 1820.

Children of ROBERT, Jr., and KEZIAH (BARROWS) GLOVER, born in Hebron, Me.:

1377. Zillah,   b. Dec. 12, 1783; died the same year.
+1378. Joseph,   b. May 20, 1787; m. Sarah Whittemore, Hebron.
+1379. Jonathan,   b. Dec. 10, 1789; m. Rebecca Chipman, Hebron.
1380. Olive,   b. Sept. 8, 1791; died, unmarried.
1381. Hannah,   b. June 28, 1793; d. Nov. 7, 1820, aged 27, unm.
1382. Bethiah,   b. May 27, 1795; d. Nov. 7, 1820, unm.
1383. Harriet,   b. April 10, 1798; d. Aug. 26, 1813, aged 15 yrs.
+1384. Erving,   b. Jan. 10, 1801; m. Orilla Reckord.
1385. Rebeckah,   b. May 18, 1804; died, unmarried.

(813) JONATHAN GLOVER, fourth son of Robert and Bethiah (Tubbs) Glover, was born in Pembroke, Oct. 8, 1767, and, it is said, died in Quebec, Lower Canada.

He was married to ——— Smith, of Rehoboth, in 1791; no children reported.

(814) THOMAS GLOVER, the eldest son of Thomas and ——— Glover, was born in Pembroke, June 8, 1756, and baptized at the Church in Pembroke, June 12, 1756. He was enrolled, in 1775, to serve in the Army of the Revolutionary War. Nothing further has been ascertained of him.

(815) MARY GLOVER, eldest daughter of George and Mary (Fisher) Glover, was born in Plymouth, July 16, 1758, and died in Norwich, Conn., Dec. 3, 1822, aged 64 years.

She was married, May 12, 1782, to Capt. Nathaniel Prentice Peabody, son of Asa and Mary (Prentice) Peabody, of Boxford, Mass.; born there, Dec. 26, 1746, and died at Norwich, Conn., Jan. 12, 1805, aged 59 years. They had children—not reported. The mother of Capt. Peabody was a native of Windham, Conn.

— (817) MARGARET GLOVER, second daughter of George and Mary (Fisher) Glover, was born in Plymouth, Mass., April 10, 1763, and died in Kingston, Dec. 1, 1836, in her 74th year.

She was twice married. First, March 8, 1788, to Nathaniel Cooper, of Plymouth; born there, July 17, 1745, and died in Kingston, May 3, 1802, aged 57 years. She was married, second, to ———— Cobb, of Kingston.

Children of NATHANIEL and MARGARET (GLOVER) COOPER, born in Kingston, Mass.:

1386. Hannah Ryder, b. Nov. 12, 1789; m. Zenas Sampson, of
      Duxbury.
+1387. George Glover, b. Feb. 21, 1791; m. Nancy Kimball, of
      Waltham.
1388. Sarah, b. May 7, 1793; d. Sept. 11, 1846, in 54th year, unm.
1389. Jane Fisher, b. April 15, 1795; m. Edward Winslow, of
      Duxbury.
1390. Nancy, b. Jan. 26, 1797; d. Dec. 17, 1820, in 24th year, unm.
1391. Thomas, b. Jan. 10, 1799; m. Mary Roundy, Blue Hill, Me.;
      d. at sea.
+1392. Nathaniel, b. Feb. 11, 1801; m. Elizabeth Andrews Heard, of
      Newton Lower Falls.

(819) ELIZABETH DICKERSON GLOVER, eldest daughter of Samuel and Miriam (Clarke) Glover, was born in Sturbridge, Nov. 9, 1781; resides in East Greenwich, in the State of New York.

She was married, March 3, 1807, to Artemas Martin, of Jackson, N. Y. They have had six children, born in East Greenwich:

1393. Geo. Clinton, b. Oct. 22, 1808; m. Mary Leigh, Feb. 28, 1833.
1394. Miriam Clarke, b. Aug. 10, 1810; resides in East Greenwich.
1395. James Madison, b. July 7, 1813; m. Orinda Bradley, 1834.
1396. William Henry, b. Jan. 3, 1816.
1397. Olive,   b. Dec. 9, 1819; d. Jan. 13, 1820.
1398. Aaron,   b. Sept. 3, 1821.

(820) SAMUEL GLOVER, eldest son of Samuel and Miriam (Clarke) Glover, was born in Sturbridge, Mass., Jan. 23, 1783, and died at Cambridgeport, Nov. 13, 1851, in his 68th year. He was admitted to join the First Baptist Church in Boston, April 7, 1805; was graduated at Brown University, in Providence, R. I., in the class of 1808; studied Divinity, and was first settled over the Baptist Church in Kingston, in 1808, and remained as pastor there nearly twenty years. In 1838, he was settled over the Baptist Church in Leominster, Mass., and subsequently in Marshfield and Carver. The greater portion of his life was passed in Plymouth County.

He was married, May 10, 1810, to Mary Stone, daughter of Ebenezer and Hannah ——— Stone, of Boston; born there in 1786. She resides in Cambridge, and is in her 81st year.

Children of Rev. SAMUEL and MARY (STONE) GLOVER, born in Kingston, Mass.:

1399. Samuel Stillman, b. in 1812; d. in 1815.
+1400. Henry R., b. in 1814; m. Lydia B. Manning, Boston.
1401. Samuel, b. in 1819; grad. Brown Univ. 1839; d. Aug. 21, 1842, in his 23d year; buried at Mount Auburn. A stone erected there by his classmates bears this inscription: "In affectionate remembrance of the virtues of their departed brother. 'He being dead, yet speaketh.'"

(821) HENRY GLOVER, second son of Samuel and Miriam (Clarke) Glover, was born in Sturbridge, Mass., Dec. 6, 1785, and died at Mount Gilead, Ohio, Jan. 17, 1852, in his 68th year. He served his country in the army in 1812, in the second war with England; was absent forty-five days; was entitled to a pension, but lost it by being one year too late in his application. His widow has since received a land warrant for two hundred and sixty acres of land in Ohio.

He was married, May 29, 1823, to Isabella Hutchins, of Hebron, N. Y. They resided several years in East Greenwich, N. Y., and removed to Mount Gilead, Ohio, in the autumn of 1835.

Children of HENRY and ISABELLA (HUTCHINS) GLOVER, born in East Greenwich:

+1402. Elizabeth, b. Feb. 18, 1825; m. Finley Gillis, E. Greenwich.
1403. Miriam, b. Aug. 22, 1826; d. May 16, 1830, in her 4th yr.
1404. Hugh, b. Dec. 23, 1828; d. May 18, 1830.
+1405. Henry, b. Feb. 8, 1831; m. Hannah Leggett, Mt. Gilead.
1406. John, b. June 23, 1833.

(825) JEREMIAH GLOVER, fifth son of Samuel and Miriam (Clarke) Glover, was born in Sturbridge, April 24, 1791, and died in Howard, Steuben Co., N. Y., Oct. 1, 1855, in his 64th year. He owned a large tract of land there, on which was his homestead estate, and employed himself successfully in agricultural pursuits.

He was married, Dec. 17, 1818, to Nancy Gilchrist, of Howard, N. Y., daughter of Alexander Gilchrist, of that place.

Children of JEREMIAH and NANCY (GILCHRIST) GLOVER, born in Howard, N. Y.:

+1407. Alexander, b. June 9, 1821; m. Julia Adalaide Stewart.
1408. Margaret Anne, b. Nov. 14, 1824.
1409. Louisa Miriam, b. May 28, 1829.
1410. Lucy Jane, b. May 19, 1831.
1411. Gratia, b. July 11, 1835.

(828) ANNA GLOVER, fifth daughter of Samuel and Miriam (Clarke) Glover, was born in Sturbridge, Dec. 18, 1796; resides in East Greenwich, N. Y.

She was married, July 1, 1823, to David Barton, of East Green-wich. He is still living; is a landholder, and cultivates a portion of his land for a homestead estate.

Children of DAVID and ANNA (GLOVER) BARTON, born in East Greenwich, N. Y.:

1412. Daniel Nelson, b. April 30, 1824; m. Aurilla Sibley, Oct., 1848(?).
1413. Louisa, b. Jan. 2, 1826; a teacher in New York City in 1860.
1414. William King, b. Dec. 11, 1827; m. Arvilla Sibley, July, 1852.
1415. Hollis Gilbert, b. Aug. 29, 1830.
1416. Heman Ferris, b. Feb. 10, 1832.
1417. Marvin Freeman, b. Oct. 28, 1833.
1418. Earl Glover, b. Dec. 8, 1836.
1419. Timothy Stowe, b. Feb. 17, 1839; d. May 6, 1842.

(831) REUBEN GLOVER, the seventh and youngest son of Samuel and Miriam (Clarke) Glover, was born in Sturbridge, Aug. 30, 1804; resides in Providence, R. I.; is a merchant tailor.

He was married, in 1824, to Calista Clarke, daughter of Lemuel Clarke, of Sturbridge; born there in 1806. They have had no children.

[*Eighth Generation.*]

(832) ELIZABETH MALCOLM RAND, only daughter of Dr. Isaac and Lucy (Whitwell) Rand, and granddaughter of Samuel and Anne (Glover) Whitwell, was born in Boston in 1805, and died there in September, 1863, aged 58 years.

She* was married, in 1829, to Alexander Thomas, M.D., of Boston, son of Thomas K. Thomas (page 299), by his first wife, and a graduate of Harvard College in the class of 1822. They had one son, born in Boston, as follows:

1420. Arthur Malcolm, b. in 1847; resides in Dorchester.

(833) JAMES MORRELL ALLEN, eldest son of Rev. Wilkes and Mary (Morrell) Allen, grandson of Deacon James and Mary (Glover) Morrell, was born in Chelmsford, Oct. 5, 1807; is a merchant, and resides (1866) in New York City. He was for several years a merchant of Boston.

He was married, May 11, 1830, to Mary Dorby Robins, daughter of Jonathan Dorby Robins, Esq., of Boston. They have had six children:

1421. James Morrell,   b. in 1831; m. Eliza Jane Stanton.
1422. Catharine Robins, b. in 1833.
1423. Mary Dorby,   b. May, 1835; d. April 3, 1836.
1424. Jonathan Robins, b. in 1837; d. in Brooklyn, N. Y., June 8,
                            1862, aged 25 years.
1425. Julia Gorham,   b. in 1839; m. Henry Larr, Brooklyn, N. Y.
1426. Mary Anne,   b. in 1841; m. Anson C. Allen.

(834) CHARLES HASTINGS ALLEN, M.D., the second son of Rev. Wilkes and Mary (Morrell) Allen, and grandson of Deacon James and Mary (Glover) Morrell, was born in Chelmsford, March 11, 1809; was graduated at Harvard College in the class of 1831; studied medicine, and is a physician in the successful practice of his profession in Cambridgeport.

He was married, Aug. 10, 1836, to Sarah Adams, of Chelmsford, who is lineally descended from the first Henry Adams who came to

---

* The following additional items in relation to the father and grandfather of Elizabeth Malcolm Rand have been communicated in a letter from her husband, Dr. Thomas:—" Dr. Isaac Rand, Sen., was of Charlestown. Among his sons was one who went to sea, became a distinguished master mariner, and took up his abode in St. Christopher's, British West Indies. He married there a Scotch lady, Miss Malcolm, and their son Isaac Rand (born there in 1769) was the father of the above. He was sent, at a very early age, to Charlestown to be educated under the care of his grandfather; entered Harvard College, and graduated in the class of 1787, at the age of 18 years; studied medicine, and practised his profession in Boston; married there, in 1804, to Lucy Whitwell (see page 344). In 1819 he went to St. Christopher's to attend to the settlement of an estate of a deceased brother, and died there in June of the same year."

The above account differs from the one before gathered, as it is stated on page 344 that the husband of Lucy Whitwell was a son of Dr. Isaac Rand; by the last account, we learn that he was a grandson, and that his father was a sea captain instead of a physician.

35*

New England in 1630 and settled in Braintree, and is of the sixth generation. They have had three children, born in Cambridgeport, as follows:

1427. Charles Adams, b. Aug. 17, 1837; H. C. 1858; studied divinity at Meadville, Penn.; is a settled minister at Montpelier, Vt.
1428. William Adams, b. Oct. 4, 1839; was educated to mercantile pursuits, and engaged in business in Boston; is now (1866) a wool merchant in Chicago, Illinois.
1429. Mary R. P., b. July 17, 1842; m., Dec. 26, 1865, to Capt. Richard Robins, of Boston, now (1866) an officer in the U. S. Infantry.

(835)   Dr. WILKES ALLEN, third son of Rev. Wilkes and Mary (Morrell) Allen, and grandson of Deacon James and Mary (Glover) Morrell, was born in Chelmsford, Dec. 30, 1810; resides in Cambridge. He was educated to the profession of dental surgery, and is now (1866) in successful practice.

He was married, Nov. 21, 1850, to Jane Munroe, of Boston. They have no children.

(838)   Rev. NATHANIEL GLOVER ALLEN, the sixth son of Rev. Wilkes and Mary (Morrell) Allen, and grandson of Deacon James and Mary (Glover) Morrell, was born in Chelmsford, Jan. 22, 1816. In 1832, when in his seventeenth year, he went to Boston, and was, for a short time, in a store with his brother James. He attended St. Paul's Church while there, and was confirmed at that Church, Dec. 25, 1834, by Bishop Griswold. He remained with his brother until 1837, and then began a preparatory course for entering college, at Phillips Academy in Andover. He entered Harvard College in 1838, and was a member of the two hundredth class for the first graduation; was graduated in the class of 1842. In his senior year he commenced a mission among the poor in Broad street, Boston. It was attended with so much success that a Church was built in Purchase street, and endowed by the Hon. William Appleton, at a cost of twenty thousand dollars, which is the present Church of St. Stephen's, now under the care of Rev. E. M. P. Wells. He studied for the ministry with the Rt. Rev. Bishop Griswold, and passed one year in New York City as General Serviceman. In 1845, he was ordained Deacon by Rt. Rev. Bishop Eastburn, of Boston; and to the Priesthood, by the same, in 1846. He was for

a time in Hopkinton, Mass. From 1848 to 1850 he had charge of the Episcopal Church in East Boston; has since founded a Church in Baltimore, Md., and also in Perry, N. Y., in Somerville, Mass., and has organized and revived several other parishes. Now, in 1866, is the editor of "Devotions of the Ages," and also of the "Churchman's Daily Quickener."

He was married, Oct. 15, 1844, to Catharine Durant Parker, of Newton. 'Her Durant lineage was from the noted Italian "Dante," originally written Durand. Her maternal grandfather, —— Dehon, Esq., was a French refugee in 1788. She is also a niece of William Dehon, D.D., Bishop of South Carolina. No issue.

(842) MORRILL WYMAN, second son of Dr. Rufus and Anne (Morrell) Wyman, and grandson of Deacon James and Mary (Glover) Morrell, was born at Chelmsford, Mass., July 25, 1812; graduated at Harvard University in 1833; studied engineering, and was an assistant under Col. John M. Fessenden, Chief Engineer of the Boston and Worcester Railroad, in 1834; subsequently studied medicine; was appointed House Physician of the Massachusetts General Hospital in May, 1836; was graduated in medicine in 1837, and settled that year in Cambridge, where he has since remained in the successful practice of his profession. In 1853 he received the appointment of Adjunct Professor of the Theory and Practice of Medicine at Harvard University; resigned in 1856. He is a member of the Massachusetts Medical Society; of the American Academy of Arts and Sciences; and one of the Vice Presidents of the Institute of Technology.

He was married, Aug. 14, 1839, to Elizabeth Aspinwall Pulsifer, daughter of Capt. Robert S. Pulsifer, of Boston. They have had four children, born in Cambridge:

1430. Elizabeth Aspinwall, ⎫ b. July 23, 1840 ; ⎰ d. March 2, 1862.
1431. Anne Morrill, ⎭   ⎱ m. Gen. Charles
                                                    F. Wolcott, Oct. 7, 1863.
1432. Morrill, b. July 10, 1855.
1433. Jeffries, b. June 15, 1859.

(843) JEFFRIES WYMAN, third son of Dr. Rufus and Anne (Morrell) Wyman, and grandson of Deacon James and Mary (Glover) Morrell, was born in Chelmsford, Mass., Aug. 11, 1814; was graduated at Harvard University in 1833, and in Medicine in 1837.

In the years 1841 and 1842 he attended the medical schools in Paris, France, and studied Natural History there at the "Jardin des Plantes." In 1843 he received the appointment of Professor of Anatomy and Physiology in Hampden-Sidney College, in Virginia. In 1847 he was appointed Hersey Professor of Comparative Anatomy and Physiology in Harvard College, which office he still (1866) holds. He is also Bigelow Professor of Comparative Anatomy in the Lawrence Scientific School; President of the Boston Society of Natural History; Member of the American Academy of Arts and Sciences, and Corresponding Member of the Academy of Natural Sciences in Philadelphia. He resides in Cambridge.

He has been twice married. First, Dec. 19, 1850, to Adaline Wheelwright, eldest daughter of William and Susan C. Wheelwright. She died June 15, 1855, leaving two children:

1434. Susan,   b. Sept. 15, 1851.
1435. Mary Morrill, b. May 15, 1855.

He was married, second, Aug. 15, 1861, to Annie Williams Whitney, eldest daughter of Benjamin D. and Elizabeth (Williams) Whitney. She died in Cambridge, Feb. 20, 1864, leaving one child:

1436. Jeffries, b. Feb. 3, 1864.

(845) EDWARD WYMAN, fourth son of Dr. Rufus and Anne (Morrell) Wyman, and grandson of Deacon James and Mary (Glover) Morrell, was born in Charlestown, Mass., Aug. 1, 1818; resides in Roxbury.

He has been twice married. First, Sept. 23, 1845, to Margaret Curry Boyd, daughter of James Boyd, Esq., of Boston. She died at Roxbury, March 22, 1854. They had three children, born in Roxbury:

1437. James Edward, b. Jan. 22, 1847 ; d. in Switzerland, June 28, 1853.
1438. Edward, b. April 27, 1851 ; d. in Roxbury, Sept. 4, 1852.
1439. Margaret Curry, b. March 13, 1854.

Edward Wyman married, a second time, Sept. 22, 1865, Caroline K. Hooper, daughter of Henry N. Hooper, Esq., of Boston.

(864) ABIGAIL GLOVER, third daughter of Nathaniel and Mercy (Eaton) Glover, was born in South Boston, in 1788, and died in Boston in 1852, aged 64 years.

She was married, Nov. 20, 1817, to Ambrose Hayden, son of Nathaniel Hayden, of Brookline. He lives in Cohasset—keeps a hotel there. They have had six children, born in Boston:

1440. Nathaniel, b. in 1818; resides at Cohasset.
1441. James S., b. in 1820.
1442. Lydia Anne, b. in 1822; gone West.
1443. George, b. in 1824; died young.
1444. William, b. in 1826; died young.
1445. John, b. in 1828; died young.

(867) ISRAEL EATON GLOVER, third and youngest son of Nathaniel and Mercy (Eaton) Glover, was born in South Boston, in 1792, and died in New Orleans, about 1828. He was an umbrella maker; he kept a store in 1819, and carried on the business extensively at one time with Mr. Binney in Court street.

He was married, Aug. 16, 1820, to Harriet Burditt; born in Boston, June 14, 1797, and died there, June 1, 1825, in her 28th year. No issue.

(868) Capt. JOHN HILL GLOVER, eldest son of John Hill and Mary (Osborne) Glover, was born in Salem, Oct. 22, 1779, and died there, March 29, 1859, in his 80th year. He went to sea at the age of sixteen years, studied navigation, and became a skilful navigator and shipmaster. He was for several years commander of his own ship, visited foreign ports, and traded successfully. The brig *Dr. Rogers* was owned by him, and he made his last voyage in her in 1852. After his return, he sold her and retired from business. He was admitted a member of the Masonic Brotherhood, Essex Lodge, Salem, Sept. 5, 1813.

He was twice married. First, to Lucy Trafton, Aug. 2, 1802; born in Salem, Oct. 20, 1780, and died there, Oct. 22, 1830, at the age of 50 years. He married, a second time, June 11, 1832, Mrs. Nancy Phippen Smith (widow), who died in Salem, Jan. 4, 1863.

Children of Capt. JOHN HILL and LUCY (TRAFTON) GLOVER, born in Salem:

1446. Mary Glover, b. April 18, 1803; d. in infancy.
1447. Mary Glover, 2d, b. April 18, 1805; d. young.
+1448. Lucy Anne, b. Feb. 3, 1809; m. Samuel Robinson.
1449. John Hill, b. Oct. 16, 1812; d. Sept. 3, 1824.
1450. Daniel, b. Feb. 19, 1814; d. Oct. 1, 1814.

+1451. Mary Osborne,   b. March 14, 1816; m. William Archer.
+1452. Elizabeth Barnard, b. Dec.   17, 1818; m. John Chapman.
+1453. Sarah Anne,   b. Nov.   23, 1820; m. William Phipps.

By second wife, NANCY PHIPPEN SMITH:

1454. Sophronia Chadbourne, b. June 24, 1834; d. June 21, 1840.

(872)   COOKE OSBORNE GLOVER, third and youngest son of John Hill and Mary (Osborne) Glover, was born in Salem, Sept. 19, 1797, and died there, May 27, 1839, in his 42d year.

He was married, in 1822, to Deborah Foss, daughter of William and Deborah (Dockham) Foss, of Tamworth, N. H.   They had one son, born in Salem:

+1455. George Dodge, b. April 30, 1823; m. Mary Anne Dan, Salem.

(873)   MARY GLOVER VOSE, eldest daughter of George and Mary (Glover) Vose, was born in Dorchester, May 25, 1779, and died there, July 19, 1855, in her 77th year.

She was married, in 1810, to Capt. Thomas Munroe, of Dorchester. He died there, Aug. 26, 1821, aged 44 years.

Children of THOMAS and MARY GLOVER (VOSE) MUNROE:

1456. Thomas,   b. in   1811.
1457. Mary Glover, b. Oct. 24, 1813; d. at Worcester, Sept. 1,
        1846, aged 33 years.
1458. Nancy Glover, b. April 15, 1815; m. Stephen Hersey.
1459. Edward Vose.
1460. William.

(874)   GEORGE VOSE, eldest son of George, Sen., and Mary (Glover) Vose, was born in Dorchester, May 5, 1781, and died there, May 27, 1834, in his 54th year.

He was twice married.   First, to Susan Lewis.   She died, and he married, second, (884) Sarah Glover, a first cousin, who survived him and died in Boston in 1858.   No issue by the second marriage.

Children of GEORGE and SUSAN (LEWIS) VOSE:

1461. George.
1462. Mary.
1463. Thomas.

(879) THOMAS VOSE, the fourth son of George and Mary (Glover) Vose, was born in Dorchester, Aug. 25, 1789, and died there, date of death not ascertained.

He was married, Aug. 23, 1812, to (971) Abigail Glover Howe, daughter of (398) George and Mary Anne (Holden) Howe, of Dorchester; born there, March 19, 1790.

(882) ELIZABETH GLOVER VOSE, the third and youngest daughter of George and Mary (Glover) Vose, was born in Dorchester, Jan. 6, 1796; resides in Roxbury.

She was married to John Hawes, of Roxbury, Int. Jan. 22, 1813. They had five children, as follows:

1464. Mary Glover, b. May 12, 1815.
1465. Catharine, b. Sept., 1816; died in 1816.
1466. Catharine R., b. in 1817.
1467. Elizabeth, b. in 1818.
1468. John, b. in 1820.

(886) ELIZABETH GLOVER, third daughter of Alexander, 3d, and Nancy (Sprung) Glover, was born in Dorchester, Sept. 12, 1787, and died in Charlestown, Mass., in 1860.

She was twice married. First, Sept. 28, 1809, to Eleazer Norcutt. He was enrolled in the army in 1812, and served in the second war with England. He died at Greenbush, in the vicinity of Albany, near the close of the war, in 1815. They had three children, born in Dorchester:

1469. Nancy Sprung, b. July 30, 1810.
1470. Eleazer, b. Dec. 31, 1811.
1471. Elizabeth, b. Dec. 1, 1812.

She was married, second, to Robert Honors, of Charlestown, who died there, since 1860.

(888) WILLIAM GLOVER, second son of Alexander, 3d, and Nancy (Sprung) Glover, was born in New York, June 1, 1794, and died, it is supposed, on an island in the South Sea. He went early to sea, and followed the business until, in 1848, he was taken by Cannibals and carried to the South Sea Islands. He wrote to his mother in Dorchester, in 1848, since which time no one has heard from him, and his fate is known only by conjecture.

He was married, May 28, 1816, to Sarah Sylvester, of Boston. They had four children, born in Boston:

1472. Mary Anne, b. March,   1817 ; m. —— Fuller.
1473. Sarah,   b. August,   1818 ; m. —— Jones.
1474. William,   b. December, 1819 ; d. in 1821 ; male line extinct.
1475. Elizabeth, b. in   1821 ; m. —— McIntire.

(889) PETER SPRUNG GLOVER, third son of Alexander, 3d, and Nancy (Sprung) Glover, was born in New York City, May 1, 1797, and died in Barnard, Vt., in 1837, aged 40 years. He resided in Dorchester until he attained the age of manhood; then went to Vermont, purchased a farm, and was married to Eliza Robinson. They had seven children, born in Barnard:

1476. Ezra.
1477. Peter.
1478. Elizabeth.
1479. Ellen.
1480. Gilmore.
1481. Nancy Sprung.

(901) ELIJAH COREY, Jr., eldest son of Elijah and Mary (Leeds) Corey, and grandson of Jonathan and Patience (Glover) Leeds, was born in Brookline, Aug. 14, 1800, and died there, June 28, 1843, aged 43 years.

He was married, in 1821, to Mary Richards, of Brookline; born there, March 10, 1800, and died Sept. 15, 1848, in her 48th year. They had six children, born in Brookline:

[cester.
1482. Charles Richards, b. Nov. 4, 1822 ; m. Eliza Witherell, Wor-
1483. Amanda Maria, b. Oct. 28, 1824 ; m. Jas. Edmands, Portland.
1484. Francis Henry, b. Jan. 27, 1827 ; m. Lucy Stevens, Brookline.
1485. Mary Cornelia,   b. Jan. 15, 1831.
1486. Frederick Adolphus, b. June 20, 1833.
1487. Theodore Franklin,   b. Oct. 17, 1836.

(903) MARY GLOVER COREY, eldest daughter of Elijah and Mary (Leeds) Corey, and granddaughter of Jonathan and Patience (Glover) Leeds, was born in Brookline, March 20, 1806, and now resides in Granville, Ohio.

She was married, in 1830, to Rev. John Pratt, of Thompson, Conn., who was graduated at Brown University in 1827, and is now (1866) Professor of Divinity in Granville College, Ohio.

(904) ELIZABETH GRIGGS COREY, second and youngest daughter of Elijah and Mary (Leeds) Corey, and granddaughter of Jonathan and Patience (Glover) Leeds, was born in Brookline, Nov. 21, 1809, and now resides at Providence, R. I.

She was married, in February, 1830, to Rev. Barnas Sears, who was graduated at Brown University in 1825; received the degree of Doctor of Divinity at Harvard College in 1841; was for a time Professor in the Theological Seminary at Newton; subsequently was elected and filled the office of President of that Seminary. In 1852, was chosen Superintendent of the Public Schools of Massachusetts; was President of the Board of Education at the same time, and was elected to the office of President of Brown University in 1855, as successor to Rev. Francis Wayland, D.D.

(906) HANNAH GLOVER, eldest daughter of Alexander and Jemima (Tolman) Glover, was born at the ancient Glover homestead, Sept. 27, 1794, and resides at South Boston. She was educated at the celebrated school of Mrs Saunders and Beach, in Dorchester, and was herself a successful teacher of a young ladies' school, and continued it until about the time of her marriage.

She has been twice married. First, to Charles Fiske, of Boston, Dec. 3, 1819. They had one son, born in Boston:

> 1488. Theodore, b. Sept. 11, 1820; bap. by Rev. T. M. Harris, April 7, 1821, and died in New Orleans, Sept. 4, 1847, in his 27th year.

She married, second, Samuel Blake, of South Boston, Nov. 25, 1830. He was born in Boston, Sept. 13, 1788, was a merchant there, settled in South Boston in 1835, and died there, Jan. 17, 1853, aged 64 years. They had one son, born in Boston:

> 1489. Warren Henry, b. Oct. 17, 1831; resides in South Boston.

(908) ANDREW GLOVER, second son of Alexander and Jemima (Tolman) Glover, was born at the ancient Glover homestead, in Dorchester, March 26, 1798, and resides in Dorchester at the present time. He has been a merchant, but has retired from business. For many years he owned and occupied the stone store on "Glover's Corner," which is now occupied by Deacon Foster.

He has been twice married. First, May 15, 1832, to Mary Anne Baker Holden, of Dorchester, who died there, June 25, 1833, aged

36

37 years.   They had one child, born and died June 22, 1833.   He married, second, Sarah White, of Weymouth, Dec. 24, 1836; no issue.

(911) JOHN GLOVER, fourth son of Alexander and Jemima (Tolman) Glover, was born at the ancient Glover homestead, Sept. 28, 1804.   In the year 1850 he went to California; has acquired a competent estate, and has fixed his homestead residence in Sacramento City.   He visited Dorchester in the summer of 1866, and returned to California in November.

He was married, March 27, 1832, to Abigail Pope, only daughter of Edmund and Susannah (Rawson) Pope; lineally descended from William, Esq., and Anne (Glover) Rawson, and from John Pope, 2d, and Margaret his wife, who settled early in Dorchester.   She was born there on the ancient Pope homestead estate, May 21, 1810.   No issue.

(912) ALEXANDER GLOVER, fifth son of Alexander and Jemima (Tolman) Glover, was born at the ancient Glover homestead, in Dorchester, Feb. 28, 1807, and resides on Meeting-house Hill in Dorchester.   He is the owner of several estates in that town.

He was married, June 23, 1832, at Baltimore, Md., to Mary Anne Ogle, daughter of William and Sarah Ogle, of Wilmington, N. C.; born there, May 15, 1811.

Children of ALEXANDER and MARY ANNE (OGLE) GLOVER, born in Baltimore and Dorchester:

```
1490.  William,          b. June 23, 1833 ; m.                    [more.
1491.  Silas Wheelock, b. Aug. 13, 1836 ; d. Oct. 4, 1839, at Balti-
+1492. Robert,   b. July 25, 1839 ; m. Mary E. Ormond, New York.
1493.  Andrew, b. July 25, 1841 ; d. in Callao, S. A., Sept., 1865,
           aged 24 years.
1494.  Alexander,   b. July   9, 1847.
1495.  Eliza Homes, b. April   4, 1850 ; d. May 25, 1853.
1496.  Mary Anne,  b. May  25, 1853.
```

(915) AMASA STETSON GLOVER, sixth and youngest son of Alexander and Jemima (Tolman) Glover, was born at the ancient homestead in Dorchester, July 25, 1817.   He is a cabinet maker, and resides in North Bridgewater.

He was married, Nov. 29, 1838, to Sophia Packard, daughter of

———— Packard, of North Bridgewater; born there, May 4, 1818. In 1861 he was enrolled as a volunteer in the 33d Regiment, Co. M, as a Musician, and served one year.

Children of AMASA STETSON and SOPHIA (PACKARD) GLOVER, born in North Bridgewater:

1497. Sarah Bent,   b. Oct. 30, 1839 ; m.
1498. Amanda Stetson, b. Nov. 12, 1843 ; m.
1499. Hannah Blake,   b. Sept. 25, 1848; m.
1500. Walter,   b. Sept. 1, 1850.

(916) ELIZABETH LEMMON GLOVER, eldest daughter of Oliver and Lydia Barrett (Lewis) Glover, was born on the ancient Glover homestead estate, in Dorchester, April 11, 1802, and resides at West Farms, Westchester County, N. Y.

She was married, Jan. 27, 1825, to Willard Felt, son of Benjamin and Waitstill (Capen) Felt, of Canton, Mass.; born there, May 7, 1796, and died at West Farms, N. Y., March 2, 1862, in his 66th year.

Children of WILLARD and ELIZABETH LEMMON (GLOVER) FELT:

+1501. Willard Lemmon, b. Dec. 10, 1825 ; m. Maria Louisa Austin.
+1502. David Wells,   b. May 20, 1828 ; m. Mary C. Farrar.
+1503. George Henry,   b. Sept. 21, 1831 ; m. Mary Anne Fruin.
+1504. Edwin Mead, . b. Oct. 17, 1835 ; m. Lydia Thayer Wheel-
           wright.

(917) MARY L. GLOVER, the second daughter of Oliver, Esq., and Lydia Barrett (Lewis) Glover, was born at the Dorchester homestead, April 24, 1804, and resides in Roxbury.

Nov. 11, 1820, she was married to John Pearson. They have had seven children.

Children of JOHN and MARY L. (GLOVER) PEARSON, born in Roxbury:

1505. Thomas Oliver, b. Dec.   2, 1822 ; m. Celia Belcher.
1506. Mary Elizabeth, b. Nov. 26, 1824 ; m. Edwin Litchfield.
1507. Sarah L.,   b. Oct. 15, 1829 ; m. Isaac Nott.
1508. Charles C.,   b. March 1, 1832 ; d. in 1841, aged 19 yrs.
1509. Emily L.,   b. Aug. 20, 1837 ; m. Gorham S. Hendricks.
1510. Hannah L.,   b. Sept. 19, 1840 ; resides in Roxbury.
1511. Lucretia E.,   b. Dec.   9, 1846 ; resides in Roxbury.

(918)   THOMAS OLIVER GLOVER, eldest son of Oliver and Lydia Barrett (Lewis) Glover, was born in Dorchester, on the homestead estate, July 5, 1806; resides in Roxbury; is a commission merchant.

He was married, in 1829, to Elizabeth Burns, of Lubec, Maine; born there, Jan. 19, 1807.

Children of THOMAS and ELIZABETH (BURNS) GLOVER, born in Roxbury:

+1512. Joseph Lemmon,   b. March   6, 1830; m. Hannah Dill.
 1513. Lydia Elizabeth, b. March 14, 1832; m.
+1514. Oliver,   b. May   5, 1835; m. Lucretia Chadbourne.
 1515. George Henry,   b. July   5, 1837; m.
 1516. Emeline Fuller,   b. Dec. 29, 1839.
 1517. Adalaide,   b. May 13, 1842.
 1518. Harrison,   b. Sept. 11, 1848.
 1519. Sarah Anne Hunt, b. Jan.   2, 1847.
 1520. Lucy Maria,   b. Sept. 4, 1849.

(919)   GEORGE GLOVER, second son of Oliver and Lydia Barrett (Lewis) Glover, was born on the homestead estate, in Dorchester, May 29, 1808, and resides on the Upper Road in that town; has lived in Rome, N. Y.

He was married, Feb. 25, 1826, to Emily Lyon, daughter of Samuel Lyon, Esq., of Dorchester.

Children of GEORGE and EMILY (LYON) GLOVER, born in Dorchester and Rome, N. Y.:

+1521. George,   b. Sept. 4, 1837 ; m. Margaret A. Gould.
 1522. Rebecca Jones, b. May 17, 1842; resides with her parents.

(921)   LUCRETIA GLOVER, fourth daughter of Oliver and Lydia Barrett (Lewis) Glover, was born in Dorchester, on the ancient homestead estate, Dec. 20, 1814, and resides in Rome, N. Y.

She was married, Jan. 21, 1834, by the Rev. Benjamin Whittemore, to John Whittemore, of Peterborough, N. H.

Children of JOHN and LUCRETIA (GLOVER) WHITTEMORE, born in Rome, N. Y.:

1523. Edward Oliver,   b. March 6, 1835; d. Sept. 21, 1835.
1524. Mary Lodge,   b. Jan.   13, 1837.

1525. Seraphine,	b. Nov.	18, 1839; d. Feb. 13, 1840.
1526. Henry,	b. Jan.	4, 1841; d Jan. 28, 1841.
1527. Annette Madeline,	b. Jan.	21, 1842; d. May 13, 1844.
1528. Willard Felt,	b. Jan.	1, 1844.
1529. Charlotte,	b. May	23, 1851.
1530. Joseph Phinney,	b. July	31, 1854.

(926) THOMAS MAY LEWIS, the third and youngest son of Capt. Joseph and Abigail (Glover) Lewis, was born in Dorchester, July 22, 1810. He is a merchant, residing in the City of New York.

In 1842, he was married to Mary Harris, of that city. They have had two children :

1531. John Saxton ; d. in New York in 1859.
1532. Caroline.

(928) HENRY GLOVER, eldest son of James and Jane (Beale) Glover, was born on the Glover homestead estate in Dorchester, Sept. 7, 1808 ; has resided in Cincinnati, Ohio, and was at one time extensively engaged in the flour business. Resides now (1866) in St. Louis, Mo.; was a member of the Old Guard which was organized there for the defence of the city in 1861.

He was married, Nov. 24, 1833, to Susan Dana Flintham, daughter of William and Mary (Bradford) Flintham, of Philadelphia, Penn.; born there in 1811.

Children of HENRY and SUSAN DANA (FLINTHAM) GLOVER, born in Cincinnati and Columbus, Ohio :

1533. Eliza Lee,	b. in Cincinnati.
1534. Henry,	b. in Cincinnati.
1535. Jennie Beale,	b. in Columbus.
1536. William Flintham,	b. in Columbus.

(930) JAMES GLOVER, Jr., second son of James and Jane (Beale) Glover, was born on the ancient homestead estate in Dorchester, Feb. 19, 1813 ; resides in Dorchester, on Humphrey street.

He was married, March 15, 1835, to Lydia Elizabeth Holden, daughter of John and Rhoda (Sumner) Holden, of Dorchester.

Children of JAMES, Jr., and LYDIA ELIZABETH (HOLDEN) GLOVER :

| +1537. Albert Holden, b. Dec. 31, 1835. |
1538. James,	b. in	1837.
1539. Gustavus,	b. in	1839.
1540. Louisa,	b. in	1840.

36*

(931) JOSEPH BEALE GLOVER, third son of James and
Jane (Beale) Glover, was born on the Glover homestead estate, May
5, 1815.   He is an industrious and enterprising Boston merchant, in
which business he has been actively engaged for the last twenty-five
years.

(932) ALBERT GLOVER, the fourth son of James and Jane
(Beale) Glover, was born in Boston, May 14, 1817.   He was educated to mercantile pursuits, and was for many years actively
engaged as a merchant in Boston ; has recently retired from business.

(934) MARGARET PRESTON HOWE GLOVER, eldest
daughter of Edward and Hannah (Howe) Glover, was born in
Dorchester, March 13, 1789, and died at Windsor, Vt., Sept. 20,
1830, aged 41 years.
  She was twice married.   First, January 1, 1807, to Lemuel Babcock, of Milton.   They removed to Walpole, N. H., and lived there
till 1817.   He then went South, and was never again heard from.
They had five children, born in Walpole.   She was married, second,
Jan. 15, 1828, to Alvah Houghton.

  Children of LEMUEL and MARGARET PRESTON HOWE (GLOVER)
BABCOCK, born in Walpole, N. H.:

1541. Margaret Preston, b. Jan 1, 1808 ; died in Langdon, N. H.,
       June 30, 1823.
1542. Lemuel Ebenezer, b. June 1, 1809 ; lives in Ottawa, Canada.
1543. Edward Glover,   b. March 10, 1812.
1544. Hannah Howe,   b. Feb.   5, 1814.
1545. Emily Field, b. Feb. 18, 1817 ; m. Dr. Ira Prouty, of Lang-
       don, in 1838, and died there Oct. 25, 1849, aged 32 years,
       leaving one child, a daughter, who lives with her father in
       Ogdensburg, N. Y.

  By second husband, ALVAH HOUGHTON :

1546. George Alvah, b. Nov. 16, 1828 ; residence unknown.
1547. Margaret A., b. July 29, 1830 ; d. Sept. 17, 1830.

(935) LYDIA GLOVER, second daughter of Edward and
Hannah (Howe) Glover, was born in Dorchester, Dec. 17, 1790, and
died in the City of Rochester, N. Y., May 23, 1865.
  She was married, May 23, 1808, to Joseph Field, Esq., of Dor-

chester; removed to Walpole, N. H., in 1811; removed to Rochester, in 1827. They have had five children:

1548. Lydia Emily, d. young, in Walpole.
+1549. Eliza Anne, m. Rev. Dr. Stanton, of Pottsdam, N. Y.
+1550. Emeline, m. Charles Cobb, of Buffalo.
+1551. Caroline, b. in 1818: m. Alfred Ely, of Rochester.
+1552. Almira, m. Lewis P. Beers, of New York.

(936) EDWARD GLOVER, eldest son of Edward and Hannah (Howe) Glover, was born in Dorchester, Oct. 19, 1793; resides in Alstead, N. H., owns a farm there, and is engaged in agricultural pursuits.

He has been twice married. First, to Polly Blake, Jan. 28, 1813, who died in May, 1836, leaving five children; second, Nov. 28, 1836, to Sarah E. Studley. They had two daughters.

Children of EDWARD and POLLY (BLAKE) GLOVER, born in Alstead, N. H.:

1553. Charles Edward, b. March 1, 1814; d. Aug. 12, 1814.
1554. Mary Anne Ely, b. Nov. 2, 1815; m. Lyman Chandler.
1555. Ansel Edward, b. May 1, 1819; m. Annah Willard.
1556. Margaret Babcock, b. Feb. 11, 1823; m. Ira Slade; d. at Detroit, Michigan, May 22, 1855.
1557. Charles Baker, b. June 22, 1825.

By second wife, SARAH E. STUDLEY:

1558. Julia Anne Sophia, b. April 23, 1838; d. Oct. 4, 1838.
1559. Sarah Elizabeth, b. March 4, 1841.

(938) ANSEL GLOVER, third son of Edward and Hannah (Howe) Glover, was born in Dorchester, March 12, 1799, and resides at Alstead, N. H.

He was married, Feb. 10, 1824, to Nancy Elwell, of Alstead, N. H., daughter of Benjamin and Betsey (Kendall) Elwell. Her father was born at Cape Ann, April 26, 1768; her mother was born at Fitzwilliam, N. H., Jan. 31, 1774: they were married in 1794, and died within seven hours of each other, of influenza, in Alstead, March 18, 1855, having lived together over 60 years, and were buried in the same grave. Ansell, by wife Nancy Elwell, had:

1560. George Ansel, b. Aug. 28, 1827; died in infancy.

(939)   CHARLES GLOVER, fourth son of Edward and Hannah (Howe) Glover, was born in Dorchester, Sept. 23, 1802 ; resides in the City of Rochester, N. Y.   At the age of seven years he removed, with his parents, to Walpole, N. H. ; removed again, the next spring, to Alstead, N. H., and lived there until 1817.   He then removed with them to Langdon, N. H., and remained there until 1827, ten years, and in 1827 removed to his present residence in Rochester.

He was married, May 26, 1825, to Maria Frink, of Walpole, N. H.   They have had two children :

1561. George Anson, b. June 24, 1833 ; m. Lizzie W. Stewart, Oct. 7, 1856.
1562. Edward Augustus, b. Jan. 19, 1837.

(940)   LEWIS CLAPP, eldest son of Nathaniel and Hannah (Glover) Clapp, was born in Dorchester, Aug. 17, 1792, and died there, Jan. 18, 1854, aged 62 years.

He was married, May 7, 1835, to Lucy Humphreys Clapp, second daughter of Stephen and Hannah White (Humphreys) Clapp, of Dorchester, born there in 1812.   They had six children, born in Dorchester, as follows :

1563. Lydia.
1564. Fanny.
1565. Cornelia.
1566. Clara Humphreys.
1567. Antoinette.
1568. Lucy.

(947)   MARY GLOVER HEARSEY, daughter of Bela and Mary (Glover) Hearsey, was born in Dorchester in 1795, and resides there at the present time (1866).

She was married, May 19, 1823, to Samuel Coolidge Bird, of Dorchester.   He died there in 1860.   No children reported.

(948)   LEWIS GLOVER HEARSEY, second son of Bela and Mary (Glover) Hearsey, was born in Dorchester in 1798, and died there in November, 1855, aged 57 years.

He was married, Nov. 20, 1823, to Hannah Studley Harris Bryant, of Dorchester.   He kept a store in Dorchester, near Meeting-house Hill.   They had two children :

1569. Lewis Glover,   b. Sept. 22, 1824 ; d. Jan. 11, 1825.
1570. Hannah Frances, b. May 11, 1826.

(954) LEWIS GLOVER, eldest son of Capt. Lewis and Nancy (Brazer) Glover, was born in Boston, in 1802, and died at Berrysville, Clarke County, Virginia, Oct. 6, 1839, aged 37 years. He was graduated at Harvard University in 1822, studied law; went to Virginia and commenced the practice of his profession at Berrysville.

He was married there, in 1834, to Elizabeth Elliott Kearney, of Berrysville, and had three children:

1571. Catharine Kearney, b. in 1834.
1572. John.
1573. Kirkland.

(955) JOHN BRAZER GLOVER, second son of Capt. Lewis and Nancy (Brazer) Glover, was born in Boston, and died in the harbor of San Francisco, California, in November, 1849. He was a merchant, and traded in Boston for several years; subsequently he went to New Bedford and was engaged in commercial pursuits; thence to California, where he died before commencing business.

He was twice married. First, Sept. 20, 1827, to Charlotte Elizabeth Lyon, eldest daughter of Benjamin and Eliza (Babcock) Lyon, of Dorchester; born there, Nov. 1, 1805, and died Dec. 7, 1832, aged 27 years. He was married, second, to Caroline Lincoln, daughter of Gen. Lincoln, of New Bedford, who was married a second time, in 1861, to William C. Whittredge, Esq., of New Bedford. She is still living, and residing there.

Children of JOHN BRAZER and CHARLOTTE ELIZABETH (LYON) GLOVER, born in Boston:

1574. Lewis, b. in 1830 ; d. at San Francisco in 1852, aged 22 yrs.
1575. John Brazer, b. in Nov., 1832 ; d. in 1853, in New York City.

(965) HANNAH W. HEARSEY, sixth daughter of Zerubbabel and Elizabeth (Glover) Hearsey, was born in Roxbury, and is at present living in Gloucester, Mass.

She was married, Dec. 23, 1842, to Frederick Thayer, of Gloucester. No children reported.

(966) ELIZABETH HEARSEY, seventh daughter of Zerubbabel and Elizabeth (Glover) Hearsey, was born in Roxbury, and lives now in East Abington.

She was married to Samuel Hatch, of Abington.   One child reported :

1576. Samuel.

(969)   JOHN HOWE, eldest son of John and Martha (Bird) Howe, and grandson of the Hon. John and Rachael (Glover) Howe, was born in Brookline, March 14, 1792; baptized March 25, 1792.

He was twice married.   First, Dec. 10, 1818, to Hannah Williams Heath, of Brookline; second, March 9, 1842, to Louisa Goddard, born in England.   Joined the Congregational Church in Brookline, Sept. 3, 1847, from the South Congregational Church in Boston. No children reported by first marriage.

By wife LOUISA GODDARD:

1577. Annie Louisa, b. April 1, and baptized Sept. 12, 1843, by Rev. Dr. Pierce.

(975)   JOHN HOWE ROBINSON, youngest son of Major Edward and Rachael (Howe) Robinson, and grandson of the Hon. John and Rachael (Glover) Howe, was born in Dorchester, Nov. 21, 1809.   He is now living in Adams street, Dorchester.   He succeeded to the homestead estate of his father, and occupies the mansion house formerly possessed by him; he is extensively engaged in agricultural pursuits.

He was married, May 14, 1835, to Elizabeth Clapp, fourth daughter of Deacon Ebenezer and Eunice (Pierce) Clapp; born in Dorchester, July 14, 1814.   They have had eight children, as follows:

1578. Ellen Elizabeth,   b. April   6, 1836 ; d.
1579. Mary Caroline,   b. Sept.   26, 1838.
1580. John Howe,   b. Dec.   19, 1840.
1581. Edward Francis,   b. May   11, 1843 ; d. Oct. 17, 1844.
1582. Emma Frances,   b. Jan.   11, 1846 ; d. Oct. 6, 1847.
1583. Lucy Ann,   b. March   5, 1848.
1584. Emily Pierce,   b. Aug.   20, 1850.
1585. Isabella Howe,   b. Sept.   2, 1854.

(976)   THEODORE LYMAN HOWE, eldest son of Joseph and Lucy (Hunt) Howe, and grandson of the Hon. John and Rachael (Glover) Howe, was born in Dorchester, Oct. 9, 1815, and resides at the corner of Park Street and Dorchester Avenue.   He is a merchant, and transacts business in Boston.

He married Louisa Field, of Dorchester. No children reported.

(979) ELIZABETH HOWE, eldest daughter of Joseph and Lucy (Hunt) Howe, and granddaughter of the Hon. John and Rachael (Glover) Howe, was born in Dorchester, June 18, 1819. Resides in Cambridge.

She was married, Dec. 19, 1844, to Lyman Willard, son of Lyman and ———— Willard, of Cambridge; born there in 1816, and died May 11, 1860, aged 50 years. They had one child:

    1586. George Willard, b. in 1846; drowned in Fresh Pond, Aug. 1, 1858.

(996) SAMUEL STILLMAN PIERCE, third son of Daniel and Lydia (Davenport) Pierce, and grandson of Jonathan and Mary (Glover) Pierce, was born in Dorchester, March 27, 1807. He is a grocer, and resides in Boston.

He was married, Feb. 17, 1836, to Ellen Maria T. Wallis, daughter of Mordecai L. and Ellen B. Wallis, of Boston; born there, Feb. 22, 1812. They have had five children:

    1587. Charles Hudson,   b. Jan. 3, 1837; d. Sept. 10, 1837.
    1588. Mary E.,   b. Nov. 20, 1838.
    1589. Samuel Stillman,   b. Nov. 7, 1840.
    1580. H. Maria,   b. Aug. 27, 1842.
    1591. Harriet E.,   b. Oct. 13, 1848.

(1010) SUSAN MASSON, only daughter and child of Mammy and Sarah (Farrington) Masson, granddaughter of Capt. Joseph and Susannah (Pope) Farrington, and great-granddaughter of Lazarus and Susannah (Glover) Pope, was born in Boston, Nov. 8, 1795; resides at Newtonville.

She was married, May 12, 1816, to John Andrews, Esq., of Boston. They have had four children:

    1592. Peter St. Medard, b. Feb. 28, 1819.
    1593. Sarah Elizabeth, b. Feb. 23, 1821.
    1594. Charles Joseph,   b. Nov. 23, 1830.
    1595. Daniel Webster, b. Aug. 13, 1835.

(1028) HENRY WARDWELL, eldest son of Benjamin and Elizabeth (Manchester) Wardwell, and grandson of Benjamin, Esq., and Catharine (Glover) Wardwell, was born in Bristol, R. I., March 17, 1808, and (1866) resides there.

He was married, May 11, 1835, by Rev. J. Hascall, to Sarah L. Lindsay, of Bristol. They have had eight children, born there, as follows:

1596. Benjamin,   b. May 16, 1836 ; d. same day.
1597. Sophia Lindsay, b. May   3, 1838.
1598. Anna Elizabeth, b. Aug.   9, 1840.
1599. Sarah Frances, b. Jan. 25, 1843.
1600. Harriet Parker, b. July   4, 1845.
1601. Isabella Maine, b. Jan. 12, 1848.
1602. Henry Adam,   b. Aug. 26, 1850 ; d. Feb. 18, 1853.
1603. Henry Irenias,   b. July 15, 1853.

(1029) BENJAMIN WARDWELL, the second son of Benjamin and Elizabeth (Manchester) Wardwell, and grandson of Benjamin, Esq., and Catharine (Glover) Wardwell, was born in Bristol, R. I., Aug. 9, 1809 ; resides in Bristol.

He was married, Feb. 2, 1836, to Eliza Cook, of Fall River· They have had three children:

1604. A son,   b. Jan. 1, 1837 ; died same day.
1605. George Henry, b. June 11, 1838 ; d. August, 1839.
1606. Ellen Cook,   b. Dec.,   1840.

(1033) JEREMIAH M. WARDWELL, the fifth son of Benjamin and Elizabeth (Manchester) Wardwell, and grandson of Benjamin, Esq., and Catharine (Glover) Wardwell, was born in Bristol, Dec. 7, 1813, and resides there at the present time (1866).

He has been twice married. First, June 19, 1844, to Mary Jane Sturgis, daughter of Lathrop L. Sturgis, of New York City. She died Oct. 3, 1860. He was married, second, Nov. 18, 1865, to Mrs. Eliza B. Ingraham, daughter of William Fellowes, Esq., of Staten Island, N. Y.

By the first marriage there were six children, as follows:

1607. William Henry,   b. March 29, 1846.
1608. Theodore Sturgis, b. June 13, 1848.
1609. Richard Patrick,   b. April 17, 1852.
1610. Mary Sturgis,   b. April 16, 1855 ; d. July 22, 1855.
1611. Helen,   b. Sept.   6, 1857.
1612. Jane Elizabeth,   b. Aug.   17, 1859.

(1040) ELIZABETH M. WARDWELL, seventh daughter and youngest child of Benjamin and Elizabeth (Manchester) Wardwell, and granddaughter of Benjamin, Esq., and Catharine (Glover) Ward-

well, was born in Bristol, R. I., Nov. 6, 1827, and resides at Ma-
tanzas, Cuba.

She was married, Sept. 27, 1853, to Ramon Guiteras, of that
place. They have had two children, born there, as follows:

1613. Gertrude Elizabeth, b. March 2, 1855.
1614. Ramon Benjamin, b. Aug. 17, 1858.

(1042) MARIA MAY, the eldest daughter of Joseph Glover
and Harriet (Bird) May, and granddaughter of William and Margaret (Glover) May, was born in Roxbury, April 13, 1816, and now
resides at Melrose.

She has been twice married. In 1842, she was married to James
Green; he died soon, and she married, second, Henry S. Bird, of
Dorchester, Nov. 12, 1858. By James Green she had one daughter:

1615. Margaret

(1043) HENRY BURBECK MAY, eldest son of Joseph Glover
and Harriet (Bird) May, and grandson of William and Margaret
(Glover) May, was born in Roxbury, Aug. 18, 1818, and died at
Marysville, California, July 20, 1859, in his 41st year. He kept a
shoe store in Boston. In March, 1849, he went to California;
studied medicine, and was employed as a physician there, until his
decease.

April 8, 1850, he was married to Susan Simmons, of Hingham.
They had three children, born in California, as follows:

1616. Henry, b. Jan., 1851; d. the same year.
1617. Harriet Elizabeth, b. Sept., 1853.
1618. Henry, b. Aug. 6, 1856.

The widow of Henry B. May returned to Boston, and resides in
Hingham with her mother.

(1044) WILLIAM BIRD MAY, the second son of Joseph
Glover and Harriet (Bird) May, and grandson of William and Margaret (Glover) May, was born in Roxbury, Nov. 16, 1819, and
resides in St. James street, Roxbury. He is a broker, and transacts
business in Boston.

He was married, April 7, 1842, to Susan Johnson Warren, daughter of Josiah and Submit (Neale) Warren, of Brookfield, N. H.;

born there, April 27, 1822.   They have had four children, born in
Roxbury, as follows:

1619. Sarah Ellen,   b. Aug.   5, 1843.
1620. William Bird,   b. Feb. 14, 1846; d. Dec. 12, 1848.
1621. Anna Odlin,   b. Sept. 30, 1849.
1622. George Warren, b. Aug. 24, 1851.

(1045) JOHN GLOVER MAY, the third son of Joseph Glover
and Harriet (Bird) May, and grandson of William and Margaret
(Glover) May, was born in Roxbury, Feb. 2, 1821, and resides in
Clayton, Adams County, Illinois.

He was married in January, 1848, to Syrelda Lowler, of ———,
Virginia.   They have had four children, born in Clayton, Illinois, as
follows:

1623. Henry,   b. January,   1849.
1624. Harriet, b. September, 1851.
1625. Anna,   b. September, 1853.
1626. William, b. August 8,   1855.
1627. John,   b. August 5,   1860.

(1046) MARGARET GLOVER MAY, the second daughter of
Joseph Glover and Harriet (Bird) May, and granddaughter of William and Margaret (Glover) May, was born in Roxbury, Jan. 31,
1824, and resides at St. Joseph's, Emmetsburg, Maryland.   She was
educated in Boston by the Sisters of Charity, until she had passed
her sixteenth year; she then went to Emmetsburg, and was in the
Academy of St. Joseph's one year, and in the year 1841 became,
from choice, one of the Sisters of Charity belonging to that institution.   She makes occasional visits to her relatives in Roxbury—the
last one in 1862, and returned soon to attend to her duties at St.
Joseph's.

(1047) SAMUEL JOSEPH MAY, fourth son of Joseph Glover
and Harriet (Bird) May, and grandson of William and Margaret
(Glover) May, was born in Roxbury, Dec. 4, 1827, and died in Sacramento City, California, Dec. 29, 1859.   He went to California in
1849; came to Boston in 1851, and was married to Caroline E.
Davis, of Boston.   He returned to California the same year, and
settled in Sacramento City.   They had one child born to them there:

1628. Caroline, b. in 1853.

The widow of Samuel Joseph May has returned to Boston, and resides there with her parents.

(1059) WILLIAM HENRY GLOVER, the second son of John and Margaret N. (Field) Glover, was born in Braintree, April 25, 1829, and resides there at the present time (1866).

He was married, Sept. 9, 1851, to Elvira Rideout. They have had three children:

1629. Elizabeth Blanchard, b. January, 1853.
1630. William Stanley, b. in 1855.
1631. Walter Seymour, b. in 1857.

(1060) JOHN GLOVER, Jr., the third son of John and Margaret N. (Field) Glover, was born in Braintree, March 8, 1832; resides in Quincy.

He was married, Sept. 8, 1861, to Laura Beard. They have children, not reported.

He was enrolled in the 60th Regiment, Co. B, July 16, 1864, for 100 days; mustered out Nov. 30, 1864.

(1061) JOSEPH MEARS GLOVER, fourth son of John and Margaret N. (Field) Glover, was born in Braintree, April 11, 1834, and resides there at the present time.

He was married, Jan. 3, 1861, to Frances A. Dodge, of Quincy. They have had children, not reported.

He was enrolled, for the United States service, in the 60th Regiment, Co. B, for 100 days, July 16, 1864; mustered out Nov. 30, 1864.

(1063) SAMUEL CURTIS GLOVER, eldest son of Noah A. and Elizabeth (Beals) Glover, was born in Quincy, July 6, 1842.

He was enrolled in the United States service, 9th Battery, Heavy Artillery, Aug. 1, 1862, for three years, in the Malden quota. Mustered out June 6, 1865, returned to Quincy, and resides there (1866).

(1072) JOHN FRANCIS GARAUX GLOVER, eldest son of John Bass and Margaretta F. G. (Reed) Glover, was born in Quincy, March 7, 1831, and now resides there. He is a boot manufacturer.

He was married, March 30, 1856, to Laura Jane Hunt, of Quincy. They have had two children:

1632. William Francis Adams, b. Nov. 31, 1856.
1633. Elizabeth Justina, b. Nov. 8, 1858; d. July 28, 1865, aged 7.

(1075)   NATHANIEL EBENEZER GLOVER, fourth son of
John Bass and Margaretta F. G. (Reed) Glover, was born in Quincy,
Feb. 20, 1836; resides there in 1866.

He was married, July 27, 1859, to Elizabeth Albena Packard.
He was enrolled in the 4th Regiment, Co. H, April 22, 1861; served
three months, and was mustered out July 22, 1861.   They have had
one child:

1634. Minnie Lizzie, b. April 24, 1860.

(1124)   ELIZA TRASK BIRD, eldest daughter of Samuel and
Betsey (Trask) Bird, and granddaughter of Samuel and Elizabeth
(Glover) Bird, was born in Boston, Feb. 1, 1799, and died there,
Feb. 10, 1851, aged 52 years.

She was married, in 1820, to Nathaniel Frothingham, son of Nathaniel Frothingham, of Boston; born there in 1797, and died in
Boston, June 24, 1852, aged 54 years.   They had three children,
born in Boston:

1635. Caroline Eliza T., b. Dec., 1822; m. William B. Fowle, Jr.,
         of Boston.
1636. Eliza,   died in infancy.
1637. Nathaniel,   m.; is a merchant in Boston.

(1127)   JOHN TAYLOR, eldest son of John and Elizabeth
(Bird) Taylor, and grandson of Samuel and Elizabeth (Glover) Bird,
was born in Boston, Jan. 16, 1801; resides in Stoughton.

He was married, in 1826, to Maria Sumner, daughter of Ebenezer
Billings and Sarah (Swan) Sumner; born in 1808, and died in 1860.
They have had three children:

1638. John Henry, b. Jan., 1830; m. Azubah Drake, of Stoughton.
1639. Lewis Sumner,   b. Feb. 12, 1835.
1640. Ebenezer Sumner, b. in 1840, in Easton; d. there in 1842.

(1130)   SAMUEL BIRD TAYLOR, the third and youngest son
of John and Elizabeth (Bird) Taylor, and grandson of Samuel and
Elizabeth (Glover) Bird, was born in Boston, Oct. 20, 1806; resides
in Stoughton.

He was married, April 3, 1831, by Rev. Dr. Park, of Stoughton,

to Mary Shepard, daughter of John and ———— Shepard, of Canton;
born there, May 9, 1807. They have had ten children:

1641. Eliza,   b. Oct. 20, 1831; d. Dec. 30, 1831.
1642. Mary,   b. July 10, 1833; m. Franklin French, of Easton.
1643. Elizabeth, b. Feb. 25, 1836; m. ———— Hall, N. Bridgewater.
1644. Charles,   b. Feb. 5, 1838; served 3 mos. from April 16,
        1861, also from Sept. 17, 1862, to Aug. 28, 1863, in 4th
        Reg. M. V. M.; and in 14th Mass. Light Battery, from
        Feb. 12, 1864—killed in action before Petersburg, Va.,
        Aug. 21, 1864.
1645. Henry, b. Jan. 18, 1840; served 3 mos. from April 16, 1861,
        also from Sept. 17, 1862, to Aug. 28, 1863, in 4th Reg. M.
        V. M.
1646. Samuel J. B., b. Aug. 21, 1842; enrolled in 4th Reg. M. V.
        M., Sept. 16, 1862; died in the hospital in New Orleans,
        Aug. 15, 1863.
1647. Ansel Capen,   b. May 18, 1845.
1648. Edward,   b. Oct. 3, 1846.
1649. Rebekah Bird, b. Nov. 15, 1849; d. Feb. 15, 1852.
1650. George Shepard, b. April 9, 1851; d. March 21, 1852.

(1134) ELIZABETH BIRD, the eldest daughter of Jenner and
Elizabeth (Cook) Bird, and granddaughter of Samuel and Elizabeth
(Glover) Bird, was born in Brighton, Nov. 21, 1819, and resides
there.

. She was married, in 1838, to Moses Sanderson. They have had
two children:

1651. Mary E., b. January, 1840; m. Edward Marstens.
1652. Anna,   b. February, 1845; m. George Lamson.

MOSES SANDERSON died soon after the birth of the last child, and
she was married a second time, in 1850, to Samuel Deering, of Bath,
Me. They have had one son:

1653. Charles, b. Jan. 14, 1852.

(1136) MARY FISKE BIRD, the second daughter of Jenner
and Elizabeth (Cook) Bird, and granddaughter of Samuel and Elizabeth (Glover) Bird, was born in Brighton, Nov. 29, 1823, and resides
in Roxbury.

She has been twice married. First, Sept. 1, 1847, to Joel Franklin Willis, a native of Concord, Mass.; born there, in 1805, and died
at Detroit, Mich., Aug. 3, 1855, aged 50 years. They had one
daughter, born in Syracuse, N. Y.:

1654. Florence, b. June 9, 1852.

37*

Mrs. Mary F. Willis was married, a second time, Aug. 13, 1856, to Amos John Dean, of Roxbury. He was the son of William and Sarah Amos Dean, and was born in Faversham (near London), in the County of Kent, England, Feb. 27, 1809. His mother was a native of Wye, in Kent, and was married there, Dec. 26, 1804, by Rev. W. Flacks, Rector of Faversham Church (Episcopal). His parents came to New England in 1816, and settled in Roxbury, Mass. His father, William Dean, was a merchant tailor, and kept a clothing and furnishing store in Roxbury street. After his death the business was continued by his widow, and son Amos J. Dean, who was educated to the business, and at the present time keeps a clothing store in Dean's Block, 83 Washington street, Roxbury, and has an extensive and successful trade. They have had one son, born in Roxbury:

1655. George Frederick, b. June 30, 1857; d. July 12, 1864, aged 8.

(1137) HANNAH BIRD, third daughter of Jenner and Elizabeth (Cook) Bird, and granddaughter of Samuel and Elizabeth (Glover) Bird, was born April 12, 1825, and resides in Roxbury.

She has been twice married. First, in 1849, to Francis Morey. They had three children:

1656. Adelaide, b. April 26, 1850.
1657. Frances, b. Nov. 1, 1853.
1658. Frederick, b. April 7, 1856.

FRANCIS MOREY died in Roxbury, and, Feb. 19, 1860, Mrs. Morey was married, a second time, to Francis Jones, of New Bedford. They have one son:

1659. Albert Henry, b. September, 1865.

(1139) GEORGE WASHINGTON BIRD, the second son of Jenner and Elizabeth (Cook) Bird, and grandson of Samuel and Elizabeth (Glover) Bird. was born in Brighton, March 6, 1830, and resides in Brookline; is a druggist and apothecary.

He was married, Jan. 25, 1855, to Harriet Susan Deering, daughter of Rev. John and Anne (Webb) Deering. of Bath, Me.; born there, March 31, 1837. They have had three children, born in Brookline, as follows:

1660. Carrie A., b. Dec. 1, 1855.
1661. George H., b. Feb. 19, 1857.
1662. Stella, b. Aug. 10, 1859.

(1140) JENNER WARREN, twin brother to the above, and
third son of Jenner and Elizabeth (Cook) Bird, was born in Brighton,
March 6, 1830, and resides in Roxbury.

He was married, Aug. 14, 1857, to Emily Peabody, of Cambridge.
They have had two children:

1663. Charles Bird, b. Oct. 3, 1858.
1664. A son,   b. in 1862.

(1145) AARON BLAKE, D.D.S., the eldest son of Stephen, Jr.,
and Rachel (Capen) Blake, and grandson of Lieut. Jonathan and
Hannah (Glover) Capen, was born in Stoughton, June 18, 1810, and
now resides in St. Louis, Mo. He lived in Stoughton until he attained the age of manhood. He then applied himself to the study
of Dental science, commenced the practice of Dentistry, and soon
became eminent in his profession.

Oct. 20, 1842, he was married to Elizabeth Robbins Wright, of
Hope, Me. They have no children. In 1845 he removed to St.
Louis, where he engaged in the successful practice of his profession,
and labored earnestly to advance the cause of Dental education in
the West. In 1860 he was elected, by the Western Dental Society,
a delegate to attend the annual meeting of the American Dental
Association in Washington City, D. C. He attended, and read a
paper in relation to the Present and Future Progress of Dental
Science, which tended to give a favorable impulse to the object of
the meeting. In 1861 he received the honorary degree of Doctor of
Dental Surgery from the Ohio Dental College. In the late rebellion
he took an active part in the cause of his country. He volunteered,
and did service in a company of Old Guards in St. Louis, of which
the Rev. Dr. W. G. Elliot was Chaplain.

Elizabeth Robbins Wright, the wife of Dr. Aaron Blake, is the
youngest daughter of John C. and Elivenai Robbins Wright, of Hope,
Waldo County, Maine; born there, July 9, 1820. She is endowed
with superior gifts and graces. Her exalted aspirations and faith in
God shed the beauty of holiness over her daily life. When, in times
of secession and rebellion, she was surrounded by the conflicting
strifes of war, she remained unchanged in her devotion and loyalty
to her country, being borne up by her strong and overcoming faith,
which is with her a living principle.

(1146)   JANE BLAKE, eldest daughter of Stephen, Jr., and
Rachel (Capen) Blake, and granddaughter of Lieut. Jonathan and
Hannah (Glover) Capen, was born in Stoughton, Dec. 31, 1811, and
died there, July 12, 1853.

She was married, Oct. 16, 1834, to Theophilus C. Clapp, of Dorchester; born there, Dec. 1, 1803, and now residing in Needham.
They had six children, as follows:

1665. David, b. Aug. 23, 1836 ; m. Abby Elizabeth Otis, Barnstable,
      Nov. 20, 1862.   She died July 8, 1865, leaving one son,
      William Stephen, b. Dec. 30, 1864.
1666. Susannah Humphreys, b. Sept. 7, 1838 ; d. June 27, 1857.
1667. Stephen Blake,   b. April 2, 1841.
1668. Elijah Blake,   b. April 5, 1844 ; d. July 25, 1846.
1669. Jonathan Capen,   b. June 19, 1847.
1670: Mary Jane,   b. July   7, 1850.

(1147)   ELIJAH BLAKE, second son of Stephen and Rachel
(Capen) Blake, and grandson of Lieut. Jonathan and Hannah (Glover)
Capen, was born in Stoughton, June 19, 1814, and died at Newton,
Long Island, N. Y., Dec. 16, 1843, in his 29th year.   He studied
and prepared himself for the profession of teaching, and in 1838
went to Long Island and engaged as a teacher.   He was eminently
successful, and remained in that employment until within a few weeks
of his decease.

He was married, March 25, 1841, to Hannah B. Morrell, of Newton, L. I.; no issue.

(1149)   EDMUND BLAKE, the fourth son of Stephen, Jr., and
Rachel (Capen) Blake, and grandson of Lieut. Jonathan and Hannah
(Glover) Capen, was born in Stoughton, July 24, 1819, and resides
there at the present time.   He is a dentist, and in the successful
practice of his profession.   He studied the science of Dentistry with
Dr. D. S. Stocking, of Boston, commenced practice in Stoughton, and
travelled and gained practice in other towns in Massachusetts.   He
has an office at his present residence, and also in Boston, where he
has had an uninterrupted practice for the last twenty-three years.
He has acquired distinction in his profession, and is actively engaged
in promoting and extending the knowledge of Dental science.   He
assisted in the organization of the Massachusetts Dental Association,
and has been a member from its commencement; has held offices in

it, read essays at its meetings, and is held in high estimation by the members of that body.

He was married, May 27, 1850, to Caroline S. Fay, daughter of Mark and Sophia (Brigham) Fay, of Marlborough, Mass. They have had four children:

1671. Walter Raymond, b. March 23, 1852.
1672. Lelia Corey,   b. Oct.   3, 1853; d. Feb. 21, 1855.
1673. Fannie Eliza, b. Sept. 26, 1855.
1674. Stella Fay,   b. Aug.   2, 1858.

(1157) JONATHAN CAPEN HAWES, the second son of Levi and Azubah (Capen) Hawes, and grandson of Lieut. Jonathan and Hannah (Glover) Capen, was born in New Bedford, May 8, 1826. He is a shipmaster, and is now on a whaling voyage in the Arctic Ocean.

He was married to (1151) Jerusha C. Blake, June 19, 1854. They have had three children:

1675. Addie R.,   b. Feb. 23, 1858.
1676. Ellsworth L., b. Aug. 15, 1861.
1677. Frederick B., b. April 8, 1863.

Capt. HAWES has passed most of his life at sea. In 1841, at the age of 15 years, he sailed before the mast in the ship Roman, on a whaling voyage of three years, and returned to New Bedford in the autumn of 1844. He sailed again in the same ship, as Boat Steerer, in Nov., 1844, on a whaling voyage of three years, and in the second year of the voyage was promoted to Third Mate. He returned in 1847, and sailed on his third voyage, as Second Mate, in the ship Liverpool 2d, Capt. Charles West, Oct. 1, of that year. He returned in 1851, and sailed again the fourth time, on Nov. 15, 1851, as First Mate, in the ship Liverpool 2d, Capt. Weston J. Swift. The ship was lost the second season, and Mr. Hawes went on board a ship bound to California, and passed the winter of 1853 at San Francisco. He returned to New Bedford, May 1, 1854, was married in July, and sailed again, Oct. 20, 1854, as Captain of the ship Eliza Adams. He returned home, May 1, 1857, after nearly a three years voyage and successful cruise. He sailed again August 10, 1858, as Captain of the ship Emma, taking with him his wife and child five months old. They cruised for whales off the coast of the Rio de la Plata, on the coast of South America. They crossed the Atlantic to

the coast of Africa in the month of June, and went into port at Little
Fish, a Portuguese settlement. On their return voyage they stopped
at St. Helena, and visited Napoleon's tomb, and Longwood, his last
residence. They arrived home Aug. 28, 1860. Of his five voyages,
all but one had been successful. He remained at home about three
years, built a house in New Bedford, and after arranging his home
comforts, he sailed again as Captain of the ship Milo, Nov. 26, 1863,
and was captured by the rebel cruiser Shenandoah, while cruising in
the North Pacific Ocean, June 22, 1865. After signing bonds for
the ship, the rebel Captain·put him on board the Milo again, with the
officers and crews of four vessels which had been burned, in all about
one hundred and fifty men, and gave them provision enough to last
until they could arrive at San Francisco. They arrived safely at
that port, July 7, 1865, and he was soon refitted by the owners of the
ship for another voyage of three years to cruise in the Arctic Ocean.

(1164) THOMAS GLOVER, only son of Thomas and Mary
(Damon) Glover, was born at Jamaica Plain, Roxbury, Jan. 2, 1833,
and died there, May 16, 1851, aged 18 years. He was the fifth who
bore the name of Thomas Glover in a direct male line, from (11)
Thomas and Elizabeth (Clough) Glover, by their eldest son (53)
Thomas and Rebeckah (Pope) Glover, by their eldest son (192)
Thomas and Eunice (Bent) Glover, and lastly by (626) Thomas and
Mary (Damon) Glover; and with his decease the perpetuation of the
name in that line becomes extinct. He was a remarkable boy; eminently precocious and intelligent, and endowed with many natural
gifts and accomplishments. His death was caused by a fall from a
pile of lumber while actively engaged in play. He was confined
to his bed for six years, during which time he manifested great amia-
bility of temper, and was an example of trust and patience. He
beguiled the hours of sickness and suffering by various expedients—
kept a diary, wrote poetry, embroidered, crochetted, and left, at his
death, many specimens of his industry and ingenuity. He also
sketched admirably from nature and from imagination, painted in
water colors, and read much and profitably. He had numerous
visitors and patrons, among whom was Mrs. Thomas Motley, who
purchased and has preserved many relics of him. As he came near
the close of life, his mind seemed to open to the enjoyment of
heavenly things, and holy aspirations beckoned him on to the

other world. He had the assurance of faith, by which he was cheered and guided to his celestial home, and passed quietly away.

(1175) LUTHER HOMES, the second son of William and Elizabeth (Blackman) Homes, and grandson of Benjamin and Rachel (Glover) Homes, was born in Dorchester, May 11, 1814, and resides in New Orleans, La.

He was married, Jan. 8, 1842, to Hannette Bridge Currier, a native of Boston. They have had three children, born in New Orleans:

    1678. Anne Elizabeth, b. in   1845; m.
    1679. Ella,   b. in Dec., 1848.
    1680. Warren,   b. in   1849.

(1177) WARREN HOMES, the third son of William and Elizabeth (Blackman) Homes, and grandson of Benjamin and Rachel (Glover) Homes, was born in Dorchester, Aug. 5, 1818; resides in Dorchester, and is a cabinet maker.

He was married, April 6, 1841, to Julia Adelaide Snow, daughter of Martin and Anna (Wilbur) Snow, of Easton; born in North Bridgewater, Feb. 19, 1822. They have had three children:

    1681. Julia Adelaide, b. April 14, 1842.
    1682. William,   b. Sept. 13, 1849.
    1683. Florence Wilbur, b. Aug. 1, 1859.

(1179) WILLIAM HENRY HOMES, fourth and youngest son of William and Elizabeth (Blackman) Homes, was born in Dorchester, Sept. 7, 1823; and resides on St. James street, Roxbury.

He was married, Oct. 17, 1860, to Anna Fuller Winchester, daughter of William and Mary (Scaverns) Winchester, of Jamaica Plain, Roxbury; born there, Aug. 10, 1832. They have one child:

    1684. Frank Winchester, b. Feb. 8, 1863.

(1181) ANNE MARY HOMES, youngest daughter of William and Elizabeth (Blackman) Homes, was born in Dorchester, March 14, 1830; now residing in Boston.

She was married, Nov. 29, 1849, to William Jacobs, son of William and Eliza (Howe) Jacobs. They have one son, born in Dorchester:

    1685. George, b. in 1852.

(1220)   GEORGE HENRY GLOVER, eldest son of Jarvis and Fanny (Fuller) Glover, was born in Springfield, June 28, 1830; is a merchant in Chicago, Illinois.   He was educated in Springfield to mercantile pursuits.   At the age of seventeen years he went to New York City, and engaged in the clothing and furnishing store of Brooks Brothers, corner of Cherry and Catharine streets; was there five years.   When their new store was completed and opened on Broadway, he was appointed salesman there, and remained in the establishment until 1865 (twelve years)—making a period of seventeen years of active business for that firm.   In the spring of 1865 he went to Chicago; passed one year in travelling, and has again commenced business in a clothing and furnishing house in Chicago, with King, Kellogg & Co., the largest wholesale dealers in clothing in the Northwest.   He is endowed with excellent business qualifications.

(1221)   SAMUEL JARVIS GLOVER, the second son of Jarvis and Fanny (Fuller) Glover, was born in Springfield, Jan. 8, 1832; resides in Chicago.   He was brought up to mercantile pursuits; was a few years engaged in the dry goods business in New York; subsequently, in 1855, he went to Chicago, and was appointed Cashier of the P., F. W. & C. R. R. Co., which position he still occupies.   He also holds the offices of Director of a Transportation Company, and President of a Joint Stock Company; and has been Director of a Library Association since 1863.   He has filled other positions of trust and honor since his residence in Chicago.   He unites with excellent business habits a taste for literature and science, and devotes a portion of his time to those pursuits.

(1222)   FRANK W. T. GLOVER, third and youngest son of Jarvis and Fanny (Fuller) Glover, was born in Springfield, Sept. 28, 1838.   In 1860 he went to Hartford, Ct., and engaged in the dry goods business in the house of Talcott & Post.   He has excellent business habits, and has filled his position with satisfaction to his employers, for the last six years.

(1224)   HANNAH SEAVER LEWIS, second and youngest daughter of James and Mary (Glover) Lewis, was born in Dorchester, Dec. 13, 1823; resides in Dorchester; is a widow.

She has been twice married. First, Jan. 5, 1847, to Josiah Goss, of Bolton, Mass. He was accidentally killed in a sporting excursion in Boston Harbor, Oct. 17, 1847. They had one son, born in Dorchester (posthumous):

1686. Josiah, b. Dec. 17, 1847.

She was married, second, March 10, 1855, to Benjamin F. Bartlett, a native of Bethel, Me. He was enrolled in the U. S. service, 42d Regiment, Co. H, as Lieutenant in command, in the summer of 1862; sailed in November, 1862, under Gen. Banks's command, destined to Galveston, Texas. He was taken prisoner immediately after his arrival there; was sent, with the other officers who were captured with him, to the Penitentiary in the interior of Texas, and died there in the summer of 1863. They had one daughter, born in Dorchester:

1687. Hannah Lizzie, b. in 1860.

(1226) MARY WHITE BUGBEE, eldest daughter of Joseph and Jerusha (Blackman) Bugbee, and granddaughter of Unite and Jerusha (Glover) Blackman, was born in Roxbury, June 3, 1822; resides there at the present time (1866).

She was married, Feb. 4, 1841, by Rev. C. H. Fay, to Daniel C. Bates, of Roxbury, formerly of Connecticut. They have had four children, as follows:

1688. Mary Elizabeth, b. Sept. 22, 1841 ; m. Robert Draper Gould.
1689. Joseph Bugbee, b. Mch 17, 1843 ; d. Jan., 1863, aged 20.
1690. Helen Augusta, b. Oct.   7, 1847.
1691. Daniel Webster, b. Sept. 16, 1850.

(1234) LUCY BLACKMAN BABCOCK, third daughter of Robert Gilmore and Lucy (Blackman) Babcock, and granddaughter of Unite and Jerusha (Glover) Blackman, was born in Roxbury, Sept. 8, 1832, and resides in Dorchester.

She was married, Dec. 14, 1851, to Henry Fobes, of Dorchester. They have had three children, as follows:

1692. Frank Pierce, b. Oct.   14, 1852 ; d. May, 1853.
1693. Lucy Otis,   b. Aug. 23, 1854.
1694. Henry,   b. in   1856.

(1265) ALMEDA DYER, the second daughter of Isaac Thayer and Martha Harriet (Glover) Dyer, was born in Brighton, June 24, 1839, and now resides there.

38

She was married, Sept. 7, 1862, to Henry C. Foster, son of Jacob and ——— Foster, of Dorchester; born there in 1835, and died at New Orleans, Sept. 31, 1863. He was enrolled as a private in the U. S. service, 42d Regiment, Gen. Banks's expedition to Texas, and was taken prisoner of war on his first arrival there; was parolled and returned to New Orleans to await the exchange of prisoners, and died a few days before the Dorchester company was ready to start for home.

(1266) ISAAC HENRY DYER, eldest son of Isaac Thayer and Martha Harriet (Glover) Dyer, was born in Brighton, Nov. 20, 1840. He was enrolled as a private in the U. S. service, on the 8th day of Jan., 1862, Co. B, of the 99th Regiment of New York Volunteers, Capt. Charles E. Cartwright; served at Newbern, N. C., three years; discharged Jan. 9, 1865. He returned to Brighton, and resides there.

(1267) NEHEMIAH FRANKLIN DYER, the second son of Isaac Thayer and Martha Harriet (Glover) Dyer, was born in Brighton, Feb. 10, 1844. He was enrolled in the U. S. service as a private, Dec. 30, 1861, Co. B, Capt. Charles E. Cartwright, 99th Regiment of N. Y. Volunteers; was discharged Jan. 27, 1865, at Newbern, N. C. He returned to Brighton, and died there, April 5, 1866.

(1289) ELIZA REBECCA GLOVER, eldest daughter of William and Eliza (Gleason) Glover, was born in Boston, June 26, 1818; now resides in Brooklyn, N. Y.

She was married, Nov. 23, 1852, to Joseph Emerson Payne, of New York. They have had two children, as follows:

1695. Rosalia,   b. Jan. 3, 1854.
1696. Mary Eliza, b. Dec. 17, 1859.

(1294) MARY LEBARON GLOVER, the fourth daughter of William and Eliza (Gleason) Glover, was born in Boston, Dec. 12, 1825, and died in Illinois, in 1858.

She was married, June 7, 1850, to William Davis, of Salem, and they went West. They had one child:

1697. Albert Day, b. Nov. 1, 1851.

(1295) ALFRED RICHARDSON GLOVER, fourth son of William and Eliza (Gleason) Glover, was born in Boston, July 18, 1828. He was enrolled in Leominster, in 1861, as First Lieutenant in the U. S. service, 53d Massachusetts Regiment, Co. C; served, and was in many battles; was killed at the battle of Port Hudson, according to one account, July 14, 1863. The officers under whom he served were Col. Kimball and Capt. Joel Stratton.

He was married, Dec. 11, 1855, to Mary Louisa Bodge, daughter of John Bodge, Esq., of Roxbury. They had one son, born in Roxbury:

1698. Alfred Kingsley, b. Jan. 4, 1861.

(1297) HARRIET WOOD GLOVER, the fifth and youngest daughter of William and Eliza (Gleason) Glover, was born in Milton, at the Milton Hill homestead, May 18, 1833; resides in Brooklyn, N. Y.

She was married, Feb. 7, 1856, to Lucius Parker Starr, of New York. He was a merchant, and died in New York, in September, 1866; accidentally killed by explosion of a foundry. They had bree children:

1699. Florence,   b. Jan. 5, 1857.
1700. Helen Maria,   b. Jan. 24, 1858.
1701. William Glover, b. Jan. 7, 1860.

(1305) THOMAS JEFFERSON GLOVER, eldest son of James M. and Harriet Louisa (Gibbs) Glover, was born in Quincy, Nov. 29, 1834; resides in Milton.

He was married, Oct. 27, 1859, to Anna F. Pope, daughter of Edmund and Anne (Walker) Pope, of Dorchester. They have had two children:

1702. Edmund T., b. July 25, 1860.
1703. Herbert,   b. April 18, 1864.

(1306) Capt. NATHAN GIBBS GLOVER, the second son of James M. and Harriet Louisa (Gibbs) Glover, was born in Quincy, May 8, 1835. He is a master mariner.

He was married, July 24, 1863, to Mary A. French, daughter of Washington French, Esq., of Quincy. They have had one child:

1704. Mary Louisa, b. Nov. 19, 1864; d. Aug. 10, 1865.

(1328)   HORATIO N. GLOVER, Jr., the eldest son of Horatio
N. and Martha Turpin (Hovey) Glover, was born in Quincy, Sept.
14, 1827; resides at Neponset Village, Dorchester.   He is a
merchant, and one of the trustees of the Newbury farm estate since
Jan., 1864.   (See page 74.)   Owns an estate in Marshfield, Mass.

He was married, Aug. 2, 1855, to Anne Augusta Holbrook, daughter of Nathan and ——— Holbrook, of Dorchester, formerly of
Weymouth.   They have had three children:

1705. Nathan Holbrook, b. Aug.   2, 1856.
1706. Horatio Nelson,   b. Dec.   23, 1862.
1707. Willie Augustus, b. March 6, 1865 ; d. March 31, 1865.

(1332)   WILLIAM BOWLES GLOVER, the third son of Horatio N. and Martha Turpin (Hovey) Glover, was born at the Newbury farm homestead, Sept. 20, 1835, and resides there (1866).   He
is a merchant, and transacts business daily in Boston; has been one
of the trustees of the Newbury farm estate since 1864.   (See page 74.)

(1338)   BENJAMIN F. GLOVER, eldest son of Benjamin
Franklin and Josephine (Baxter) Glover, was born in Dorchester,
Aug. 4, 1827; resides in Weymouth.   He is by trade a baker, and
carries on the business there.

He was married, April 30, 1854, to Mary Valentine, of Weymouth.
They have had three children:

1708. Emily Frances,   b. Aug. 2, 1856 ; d. Oct. 26, 1856.
1709. Benjamin Franklin, b. Feb. 25, 1858.
1710. ——— ———,   b. in   1865.

(1360)   JAMES GLOVER, the eldest son of James and Rachel
(Bonney) Glover, was born in Pembroke, Mass., Oct. 28, 1768, and
died in Sumner, Me., Dec. 12, 1846, aged 78 years.

He was married, Nov. 20, 1791, to Ruth Stetson, daughter of
Robert Stetson, of Pembroke; born there, Sept. 29, 1772, and died
in Sumner, July 22, 1837, aged 65 years.

Another account, which may be the true one, says that Ruth
Stetson was a daughter of Nathaniel and Sarah (Bishop) Stetson.
She was a descendant of Robert, the sixth son of Cornet Robert
Stetson, the earliest of the name who settled in Pembroke.

Children of JAMES and RUTH (STETSON) GLOVER, born in Pembroke, Mass., and in Hartford and Sumner, Me.:

+1711. Nathaniel S., b. Mch. 30, 1793; m. Ruth Thompson, Sumner.
+1712. James,   b. Sept. 27, 1796; m. Anna Bonney,   "
+1713. Joshua S.,   b. Nov. 29, 1806;
          m. { 1st, Mrs. Ruth (Thompson) Glover;
              { 2d, Eliza Raynolds, of Canton, Me.
+1714. Caroline, b. Dec. 11, 1813;
          m. { 1st, Alanson Young, of Hartford, Me.;
             { 2d, Winslow Richardson.

(1361) DAVID GLOVER, the second son of James and Rachel (Bonney) Glover, was born in Pembroke, Mass., March 2, 1771, and died there, at an advanced age, leaving no issue.

He was twice married. First, Nov. 16, 1794, to Lydia Crooker, of Pembroke. She died soon, and he married a second time to Lydia Lapham, of the same town. Soon after his second marriage, he removed to Sumner, in Maine; resided there a few years, then returned to his native town and died there. His wife Lydia remained, and died in Sumner.

(1363) SARAH GLOVER, the eldest daughter of James and Rachel (Bonney) Glover, was born in Pembroke, May 30, 1776, and died in Buckfield, Me., Jan. 15, 1859, aged 83 years.

She was married in 1800 to James Bonney, of Pembroke; born there in 1764, and died in Buckfield, March 18, 1836, aged 72 years. They had three children:

1715. James, b. in Buckfield; is Colonel of the Militia there.
1716. Sarah.
1717. ———, died in infancy.

(1364) LYDIA GLOVER, the second daughter of James and Rachel (Bonney) Glover, was born in Pembroke, Oct. 24, 1779, and died in Buckfield.

She was married there in 1806, to Edmund Warren, of that town. They had four children, as follows:

1718. Cyrus.
1719. Dominicus.
1720. Lydia.
1721. Jennette.

(1365) BETHIAH GLOVER, the third daughter of James and Rachel (Bonney) Glover, was born in Pembroke, July 14, 1781, and died in Sumner, Me., Oct. 18, 1858, aged 77 years.

She was married to Calvin Bisbee, of Sumner, Me.; born in Pembroke, Oct. 14, 1774, and died in Sumner, Nov. 28, 1857, aged 83 years.   They had eight children, as follows:

1722. Volney.
1723. David.
1724. Charles.
1725. Lewis.
1726. Mahala.
1727. Chloe.
1728. Cecelia.
1729. Hosea.

(1366)   JOSHUA BONNEY GLOVER, fourth son of James and Rachel (Bonney) Glover, was born in Pembroke, Mass., Sept. 18, 1784, and died in Hartford, Me., Feb. 27, 1850, aged 66 years. He fell from his chair and died instantly.

He was married, in 1809, to Susan Ames, of Hartford, who is still living.   He was for a time a resident in Boston.

Children of JOSHUA B. and SUSAN (AMES) GLOVER, born at Hartford, Me.:

+1730. Leviston,   m. Abigail Bartlett.
+1731. David,   m. { 1st, Harriet Larrabee, of Hartford;
                     { 2d. Belinda C. Bisbee,   "
1732. Charles,   m. Cordelia Linfield, of Stoughton.
1733. Jesse C.,   m. Mary Anne Linfield, of Stoughton.
1734. Sarah.
1735. Francis A., m. Ruth E. Allen.
1736. Anne L.
1737. Cyrus W.

(1367)   ELIJAH GLOVER, the fifth son of James and Rachel (Bonney) Glover, was born in Pembroke, Sept. 18, 1786, and died there, Dec. 17, 1858, aged 72 years.   He went early to sea, and followed it for several years, making coasting voyages; subsequently he worked on a farm in Quincy.   At the age of thirty years he lost the use of his limbs, and this was followed by mental imbecility, which rendered him incapable of attending to his business, and in 1812 he had a guardian appointed to take charge of him.

He was married, in 1807, to Mary Walker, of Pembroke.

Children of ELIJAH and MARY (WALKER) GLOVER, born in Pembroke:

1738. Elijah, b. March 8, 1808; d. Sept. 12, 1826, aged 18.
+1739. George Clarke, b. March 12, 1810; m. Sarah K. Nash.
+1740. John James, b. Sept. 21, 1812; m. Anna Drew Bryant.

(1368) JOHN GLOVER, the sixth son of James and Rachel (Bonney) Glover, was born in Pembroke, Sept. 14, 1789, and died in Duxbury, Nov. 6,* 1855.

He was married, March 28, 1815, to Mary Gullifer, of Duxbury, and removed there.

Children of JOHN and MARY (GULLIFER) GLOVER, born in Duxbury:

+1741. Mary, b. Sept. 6, 1815; m. Esaias Peterson, of Duxbury.
+1742. Sarah, b. Oct. 16, 1817; m. Alvah Remick, of Elliot, Me.
+1743. Anne, b. Sept. 18, 1819; m. Elisha Peterson, of Duxbury.
+1744. John, b. April 23, 1823; m. Jane F. Sampson, Duxbury.
+1745. Bethiah, b. Dec. 5, 1825; m. Francis H. Drake, Duxbury.

(1370) CHARLES GLOVER, the seventh son of James and Rachel (Bonney) Glover, was born in Pembroke, Aug. 12, 1795, and resides in the City of Rockland, Me.

He was married, March 21, 1821, to Almira Sayward, of Thomaston, Me.

Children of CHARLES and ALMIRA (SAYWARD) GLOVER, born in Rockland:

1746. George S., b. March 23, 1822; d. July 6, 1845, aged 23 yrs.
1747. Sarah, b. Oct. 9, 1823; d. March 13, 1837, aged 14.
1748. Bethiah, b. Oct. 2, 1825; m. Alden T. Sherman.
1749. Marcey G., b. Dec. 20, 1827; m. William B. Staples.
1750. Thomas B., b. Dec. 18, 1829; m. Elvira S. Wheeler.
1751. Charles C., b. Feb. 3, 1833; m.
1752. William H., b. Dec. 13, 1834; m.
1753. Eliza T., b. Nov. 13, 1836; m. Samuel L. Clarke.
1754. Edward, b. Nov. 14, 1839; m. Sarah C. Fernald.
1755. Lucy A., b. March 11, 1842.
1756. Abba Almira, b. Nov. 17, 1844.

(1378) JOSEPH GLOVER, eldest son of Robert and Kezia (Barrows) Glover, was born in Hebron, Me., May 20, 1787, and died there, March 17, 1832, aged 45 years.

---

* Another account says Nov. 13, 1855.

He was married to Sarah Whittemore, May 21, 1812. She died there, Sept. 10, 1852.

Children of JOSEPH and SARAH (WHITTEMORE) GLOVER, born in Hebron, Me.:

+1757. Joseph S., b. March 17, 1813 ; m. Anne Weston, Fryeburg.
1758. Harriet,   b. Oct.   22, 1814 ; d. Nov. 14, 1860, aged 46.
+1759. Robert,   b. Sept.   2, 1817 ; m. Miranda Marshall.
1160. Isaac B.,   b. Nov.   15, 1820 ; d. in Illinois, unm., in 1845.
1761. Sarah,   b. April   7, 1823 ; d. June 4, 1823.
1762. Sarah, b. June 23, 1825 ; m. Ezra Mitchell, Grovestown, N. H.
1763. Nancy J.,   b. May 10, 1827 ; m. Josiah Bucknam, Minot, Me.
1764. Keziah,   b. Jan. 27, 1830 ; m. Jerome Bates, Paris, Me.

(1379) JONATHAN GLOVER, second son of Robert and Keziah (Barrows) Glover, was born in Hebron, Me., Dec. 10, 1789, and died there, May 3, 1823, aged 34 years, leaving a widow.

March 30, 1820, he was married to Rebeckah Chipman. They had one child, viz.:

1765. Hannah, b. Sept. 11, 1821.

(1384) ERVING GLOVER, third son of Robert and Keziah (Barrows) Glover, was born in Hebron, Me., Jan. 10, 1801.

Dec. 2, 1824, he was married to Orilla Reckord, of Hebron.

Children of ERVING and ORILLA (RECKORD) GLOVER, born in Hebron, Me.:

1766. Jonathan,   b. April 25, 1825.
1767. Frederic W.,   b. March 13, 1827.
1768. Augustus E.,   b. April 18, 1829.

(1387) GEORGE GLOVER COOPER, eldest son of Nathaniel and Margaret (Glover) Cooper, was born in Kingston, Mass., Feb. 21, 1791, and died in Berwick, Me., May 10, 1826, aged 35 years, leaving a widow and one child. He was a stage proprietor, and at one time resided in Waltham.

He was married, May 19, 1822, to Nancy Kimball, daughter of Henry and Elizabeth (Wellington) Kimball, of Waltham ; born there, Nov. 5, 1803. They had one son, born in Waltham:

+1769. George Glover, b. April 2, 1824 ; m. Theodosia Aurelia Banta.

After the death of Mr. Cooper, his widow married, March 10,

1830, Dr. Newell Sherman, of Wayland; born there, Nov. 22, 1806, son of Reuben and Elizabeth (Rice) Sherman. He is a dentist, and practices his profession in Boston—is postmaster of Waltham, and resides there. They have had several children.

(1392) NATHANIEL COOPER, third and youngest son of Nathaniel and Margaret (Glover) Cooper, was born in Kingston, Feb. 11, 1801, and died in Saxonville, June 20, 1849, in his 49th year.

He was married, Nov. 28, 1826, to Elizabeth Andrews Heard, daughter of Capt. Samuel and Miriam (Gibbs) Heard, of Berlin, Mass. Capt. Heard was a native of Worcester, Mass.; removed, after his marriage, to Newport, Lower Canada. Elizabeth, his daughter, was born there in 1803, and died in Saxonville, Sept. 8, 1844.

Children of NATHANIEL and ELIZABETH ANDREWS (HEARD) COOPER, born at Newton Lower Falls:

    1770. Margaret Elizabeth Miriam, b. Nov. 7, 1828; m. Darius S. Wiley, of Elmwood, Peoria, Illinois.
    1771. Martha Jane, b. Jan. 14, 1831; m. William Evans, Cambridge.
    1772. George Thomas, b. May 9, 1832; d. Feb. 21, 1833.

(1400) HENRY R. GLOVER, second son of Rev. Samuel and Mary (Stone) Glover, was born in Kingston, in 1814, and now resides in Cambridge. He is a merchant, and is connected in business with his brother-in-law, under the firm of "Manning & Glover," for many years of Dock Square, in Boston, and subsequently at 100 Hanover street. They have had an extensive business.

He was married, in 1836, to Lydia Brown Manning, daughter of William and Lydia (Brown) Manning, of Boston. They have had three children—one of whom, a daughter, is now living. The male line is here extinct in this branch:

    1773. Henry R.,   b. in May, 1838; d. in Jan., 1839.
    1774. Mary Abby,   b. in Oct., 1842.
    1775. Josephine Robinson, b. in May, 1848.

(1402) ELIZABETH GLOVER, eldest daughter of Henry and Isabella (Hutchins) Glover, was born in Mount Gilead, Ohio, Feb. 18, 1825, and is now living there.

She was married, Jan. 2, 1845, to Finley Gillis; born Dec. 25, 1811, in Harrison County, Ohio. They have had five children:

1776. Elizabeth,   b. Oct. 21, 1845 ; d. same day.
1777. James,   b. Nov. 17, 1846.
1778. Isabella,   b. Oct. 29, 1849.
1779. Thomas C.,   b. Feb. 2, 1854.
1780. John H.,   b. Nov. 2, 1856.

(1405)   HENRY GLOVER, second son of Henry and Isabella (Hutchins) Glover, was born in Mount Gilead, Ohio, Feb. 8, 1831; is now residing there.

He was married, July 20, 1854, to Hannah Leggett, born in Mount Gilead, Oct. 1, 1830.

Children of HENRY and HANNAH (LEGGETT) GLOVER, of Mount Gilead :

1781. Thomas Hutchins, b. Aug. 9, 1855.
1782. Isabella,   b. Nov. 2, 1856 ; d. in 1860.

(1407)   ALEXANDER GLOVER, son of Jeremiah and Nancy (Gilchrist) Glover, was born in New York, Jan. 9, 1821 ; resides in Howard, N. Y.

He was married, May 20, 1850, to Julia Adalaide Stewart, daughter of Andrew Stewart, Esq., and his wife Lydia, of Howard; born there, March 15, 1834.

Children of ALEXANDER and JULIA ADALAIDE (STEWART) GLOVER, born in Howard, N. Y.:

1783. Cynthia, b. April 3, 1851.   *Mary*
1784. Lydia,   b. June 12, 1852.   *Jennie*
1785. Miriam, b. Jan. 19, 1854. *Myron   Maud*
1786. Anna,   b. June 23, 1857. *Nancy*

[Ninth Generation.]

(1448)   LUCY ANNE GLOVER, the third daughter of Capt. John Hill and Lucy (Trafton) Glover, was born in Salem, Feb. 3, 1809, and died there, Sept. 11, 1865, in her 57th year.

She was married, May 22, 1837, to Samuel Robinson, son of Benjamin and Anna (Wooldridge) Robinson, of Marblehead ; born there, Feb. 5, 1809, and died in Salem, Sept. 27, 1847. He kept a shoe store there. They had three children, born in Salem :

1787. Lucy Trafton, b. Jan. 24, 1838; resides in Salem (1866).
1788. John Glover, b. Oct. 27, 1840; was enrolled in the U. S.
service, Sept., 1862, as Quartermaster Sergeant in the 48th
Reg't., M.V. M., Col. Stone, and served nine months under
Gen. Banks's command, at Baton Rouge, La.; mustered
out in 1863.
1789. Annie E. Wooldridge, b. Jan. 24, 1843; m. in Charlestown,
July 18, 1866, to Capt. George C. Gray, of Salem, U. S. A.

(1451) MARY OSBORNE GLOVER, the fourth daughter of
Capt. John Hill and Lucy (Trafton) Glover, was born in Salem,
March 14, 1816, and died there, Sept. 9, 1860, in her 45th year.

She was married, Aug. 9, 1842, to William Archer, Esq., son of
William and Elizabeth (Daniels) Archer, of Salem; born there, July
27, 1816. He was an auctioneer and commission merchant in Salem
in 1862; was admitted a member of the Essex Lodge of Freemasons, April 3, 1855. They have had three children, born in Salem,
as follows:

1790. William Augustus, b. Aug. 21, 1843; d. Dec. 31, 1845.
1791. Mary Elizabeth,   b. Feb. 22, 1846.
1792. Sarah Sluman,   b. May 28, 1849; d. April 13, 1857.

Mr. ARCHER has been twice married; the second time, June 19,
1862, to Mary Jane Brown, daughter of Oliver and Mary Brown, of
Charlestown; born there, Feb. 8, 1830. He is in possession of the
records of the Archer family from the earliest date of their settlement in Salem in 1630, and is a lineal descendant of the first William
Archer, of the seventh generation.

(1452) ELIZABETH BARNARD GLOVER, the fifth daughter
of Capt. John Hill and Lucy (Trafton) Glover, was born in Salem,
Dec. 17, 1818, and died there, May 1, 1843, aged 25 years.

She was married, June 4, 1839, to John Oliver Chapman, son of
John and Abigail (Roundy) Chapman, of Salem. He resides in
Salem; is a printer. They had one child, born in Salem, viz.:

1793. Rebecca Roundy, b. June 9, 1840; d. Oct. 26, 1859.

(1453) SARAH ANNE GLOVER, the sixth daughter of Capt.
John Hill and Lucy (Trafton) Glover, was born in Salem, Nov. 23,
1820, and resides in Charlestown.

She was married, May 22, 1851, to William S. Phipps, son of

William S. and Mary S. Phipps, of Charlestown, Mass.; born there, Feb. 14, 1814. He was educated in Charlestown, studied the profession of dental surgery in Boston, and commenced the practice of his profession in 1843, in the town of Marlborough; subsequently he removed to his native city, where he now resides and continues his practice. They have no children.

(1455) GEORGE DODGE GLOVER, only son of Cooke and Deborah (Foss) Glover, was born in Salem, April 30, 1823. He resides in Salem, and keeps a boot and shoe store. He was mustered into the U. S. service May 27, 1862, served four months, and was mustered out Oct. 17, 1862. He was Sergeant in the Salem Independent Cadets, and was stationed at Fort Warren. Since the close of the war he has returned to his business in Salem. By the death of his son the male line of descendants of Capt. John Hill Glover becomes extinct.

He was married, Oct. 2, 1848, to Mary Anne Dane.

Children of GEORGE DODGE and MARY ANNE (DANE) GLOVER, born in Salem:

1794. Horace Osborne, b. June   11, 1849; d. May 9, 1850.
1795. Alice Williams, b. March   9, 1851.
1796. Grace Austin,   b. April   10, 1859.

(1492) ROBERT GLOVER, third son of Alexander and Mary Anne (Ogle) Glover, was born in Baltimore, July 25, 1839, and resides in Dorchester.

He was married, April 17, 1862, by Rev. S. G. Bulfinch, to Mary Elizabeth Ormond, of New York. They have had one child, born in Dorchester:

1797. Robert, b. June 19, 1863.

(1501) WILLARD LEMMON FELT, eldest son of Willard and Elizabeth L. (Glover) Felt, was born in Milton, Mass., Dec. 10, 1825; resides in New York City. He was graduated at the University of the City of New York in the class of 1844, studied law with Horace Holden, Esq., and admitted to the Bar in 1849.

He was married, Oct. 11, 1854, to Maria Louisa Austin, of New York. They have had two children, born in New York, as follows:

1798. Louisa Austin, b. April 13, 1861.
1799. Walter Lewis, b. in   1864.

(1502) DAVID WELLS FELT, the second son of Willard and
Elizabeth L. (Glover) Felt, was born in Milton, Mass., May 20, 1828;
resides in New York.

He was married, in 1849, to Mary C. Farrar, who died in Mel-
bourne, Australia, April 22, 1853. They had two children:

1800. Mary Elizabeth, b. June 7, 1851; d. Aug. 7, 1852.
1801. Elizabeth Maria, b. Jan. 18, 1853, at sea, in barque Syracuse,
        and died at Collingwood, Australia, May 14, 1853.

(1503) GEORGE HENRY FELT, third son of Willard and
Elizabeth L. (Glover) Felt, was born in Boston, Sept. 21, 1831;
resides at West Farms, N. Y.

He was married, in 1854, to Mary Anne Train, of New York.
They have had four children:

1802. Willard Oliver,   b. Jan. 13, 1858.
1803. Henry Leighton, b. April 7, 1859, at Harlem, N. Y.
1804. Mary Elizabeth, b. April 20, 1861, at Plainfield, N. J.
1805. Anna Rebecca,   b. Aug. 4, 1864, at Harlem, N. Y.

(1504) EDWIN MEAD FELT, fourth son of Willard and
Elizabeth L. (Glover) Felt, was born in New York City, Oct. 17,
1835. He is a lawyer, and resides in New York. He was graduated at the University of the City of New York in the class of 1856,
studied the profession of law with Messrs. Smith & Martin, and was
admitted to the New York Bar in 1858.

He was married, April 20, 1864, to Lydia Thayer Wheelwright,
of New York, who died there, Sept. 20, 1866; no issue.

(1512) JOSEPH LEMMON GLOVER, eldest son of Thomas
Oliver and Elizabeth (Burns) Glover, was born in Lubec, Me., March
6, 1830. Resided for a time in Roxbury, afterwards went to the West.

He was married, in 1854, to Harriet Dill, born in 1836. They
have had four children, but only one reported:

1806. Azor Lewis, b. June 25, 1855.

(1514) OLIVER GLOVER, the second son of Thomas Oliver
and Elizabeth (Burns) Glover, was born May 5, 1835; is a cabinet-
maker, and resides in Dorchester.

39

He was married, May 28, 1861, to Lucretia Chadbourne, daughter of John, Esq., and Anne (Myers) Chadbourne, of Dorchester. They have had one child:

1807. Anna Felt, b. Feb. 25, 1863.

(1521) GEORGE GLOVER, 3d, only son of George and Emily (Lyon) Glover, was born in Dorchester, Sept. 4, 1837, and now (1866) resides there. He was enrolled in the 42d Mass. Regiment in the U. S. service in 1862, and went in Gen. Banks's expedition to Texas; was taken prisoner of war, on his first arrival there, was parolled, returned to New Orleans and remained there until an exchange of prisoners; returned to Dorchester in June, 1865.

He was married, Sept. 14, 1862, to Margaret Gould, of Dorchester. They have had two children:

1808. Jennie, b. in 1863.
1809. Albert.

(1537) ALBERT HOLDEN GLOVER, eldest son of James, Jr., and Lydia Elizabeth (Holden) Glover, was born in Dorchester, Dec. 31, 1835. He was enrolled in the U. S. service in May, 1861, for three years, 33d Regiment, Co. M, Mass. Volunteers, and returned with that company in June, 1864.

(1549) ELIZA ANNE FIELD, eldest daughter of the Hon. Joseph and Lydia (Glover) Field, was born in the City of Rochester, N. Y., about the year 1811, and resides (1866) in the City of New York.

She married Rev. Dr. Stanton, of Pottsdam, St. Lawrence County, N. Y. They have had seven children, as follows:

1810. Eliza Anne,   m. William W. Green.
1811. John Armitage.
1812. Mary Frances.
1813. William Field, m. Mary Gray, of Hartford.
1814. Caroline Lydia.
1815. Joseph Field.
1816. George Edward.

(1550) EMELINE FIELD, third daughter of the Hon. Joseph and Lydia (Glover) Field, was born in Rochester, N. Y., and now resides in Buffalo, N. Y.

She was married to Charles Cobb. They have had three children, as follows:

1817. Emeline.
1818. Sarah.
1819. Josephine.

(1551) CAROLINE LYDIA FIELD, daughter of the Hon. Joseph and Lydia (Glover) Field, was born in Rochester, N. Y., about the year 1818, and still resides there.

She was married, May 31, 1842, to Alfred Ely, twin and seventh son of Charles and Elizabeth Ely, of Lyme, Conn.; born there, at the ancient Ely homestead, Feb. 19, 1815. He is a lawyer by profession, an eminent statesman, and has been a member of Congress. In 1861 he was enrolled and served as a volunteer in the Army of the Potomac, and was taken prisoner of war at the battle of Bull Run in July of that year. He published a small volume on the subject of his imprisonment after his release.

Children of ALFRED and CAROLINE LYDIA (FIELD) ELY, born in the City of Rochester, N. Y.:

1820. Joseph Field,   b. March 5, 1843.
1821. Charles Alfred, b. Nov.   6, 1845.
1822. Caroline Lydia, b. Sept. 7, 1847.
1823. Elizabeth,   b. July   6, 1850.

(1552) ALMIRA FIELD, the fifth and youngest daughter of Hon. Joseph and Lydia (Glover) Field, was born in Walpole, N. H., and is now residing in the City of New York.

She was married to Lewis P. Beers, and has had three children, born in New York, as follows:

1824. Lewis Villeroy.
1825. Joseph Field.
1826. Francis.

(1711) NATHANIEL S. GLOVER, eldest son of James and Ruth (Stetson) Glover, was born in Pembroke, Mass., March 30, 1793, and died in Hartford, Me., Aug. 7, 1823, aged 30 years.

He was married, about 1812, to Ruth Thompson, of Sumner, Me.; born there, March 25, 1793.

Children of NATHANIEL S. and RUTH (THOMPSON) GLOVER, born in Hartford, Me.:

1827. Sarah S.,   b. May 10, 1813; m. John B. Bosworth.
1828. John Stetson, b. Aug. 28, 1815; m. Cynthia Drew, Stoughton.
1829. Charles,   b. June 1, 1817; d. young.
1830. Harriet,   b. in   1819; d. young.
1831. Nathaniel S., b. June 1, 1822; m. Abigail Raynolds.

(1712) JAMES GLOVER, the second son of James and Ruth (Stetson) Glover, was born in Pembroke, Mass., Sept. 27, 1796; resides in Hartford, Me. He is an extensive landholder, and an active business man. He attested the above record of his family, and has ever manifested an especial interest in obtaining and communicating a knowledge of his ancestry and relatives.

He was married, in 1818, to Anna Bonney, of Sumner; born there, April 16, 1797.

Children of JAMES and ANNA (BONNEY) GLOVER, born in Hartford, Me.:

1832. Susan S., b. Jan. 29, 1820; m. Joseph W. Rowe, of Sumner.
1833. Charles, b. Feb. 27, 1822; m. Betsey Jane Russell, Hartford.
1834. Benjamin F., b. March 30, 1825; m. Anne W. Ellis, Canton.
1835. James,   b. July 19, 1827; m. Cynthia E. Crockett.
1836. John,   }   { m. Mary F. Bartlett.
1837. Ruth S.,   } b. March 7, 1832; { d. in 1837.
1838. Sewall S.,   b. April 10, 1835; m. Sarah M. Buck.
1839. George Quimby, b. in   1837; d. in 1841.

(1713) JOSHUA S. GLOVER, third son of James and Ruth (Stetson) Glover, was born in Pembroke, Mass., Nov. 29, 1806.

He has been twice married. First, in 1827, to Ruth Thompson, widow of his brother Nathaniel S. Glover. By her he had no children. He was married, second, to Eliza Raynolds, of Canton, Me. There were two children by this marriage, as follows:

1840. Chloe, d. young.
1841. Charles.

(1714) CAROLINE GLOVER, only daughter and youngest child of James and Ruth (Stetson) Glover, was born in Hartford, Me., Dec. 11, 1813, and resides in Turner, Me.

She has been twice married. First, about 1824, to Alanson Young, of Hartford. They had two children, born in Hartford, viz.:

1842. Alanson.
1843. Fanny.

After the death of Mr. Young she married, second, Winslow Richardson; they reside in Turner. They have had one child:

1844. Margaret Luellen.

(1730) LEVISTON GLOVER, eldest son of Joshua Bonney and Susan (Ames) Glover, was born in Hartford, Me.
He was married to Abigail Bartlett.

Children of LEVISTON and ABIGAIL (BARTLETT) GLOVER, born in Hartford, Me.:

1845. Loren,   m. Dorcas Goddard.
1846. Amelia,   m. Loren Swain.
1847. Susan.
1848. Salome.
1849. Lucius.
1850. Harriet.
1851. Cordelia.
1852. Ernest.

(1731) DAVID GLOVER, second son of Joshua Bonney and Susan (Ames) Glover, was born in Hartford, Me., and still resides there.
He has been twice married. First, to Harriet B. Larrabee, who died soon, and he married, second, Belinda C. Bisbee. They have one daughter, viz.:

1853. Mary Anne.

(1739) GEORGE CLARKE GLOVER, the second son of Elijah and Mary (Walker) Glover, was born in Pembroke, Mass., March 12, 1810, and resides in Medford, Mass.
He was married, Feb. 12, 1836, by Rev. Morrell Allen, to Sarah Keene Nash, daughter of Zebulon and Sarah (Keene) Nash, of Pembroke; born there in 1815.

Children of GEORGE CLARKE and SARAH KEENE (NASH) GLOVER, born in Medford:

1854. Sarah Lamaine, b. Dec. 14, 1836; m. Edwin Gordon Johnson, of Medford.
1855. George Francis Marion, b. Jan. 29, 1841; m. Fanny Elizabeth Mitchell.
1856. Andrew Warren, b. Sept. 29, 1843.
1857. Mary Helen,   b. Aug. 14, 1847; d. July 20, 1848.
1858. James Otis,   b. Jan. 1, 1849; d. June 4, 1849.

(1740) JOHN JAMES GLOVER, the third and youngest son of Elijah and Mary (Walker) Glover, was born in Pembroke, Mass., Sept. 22, 1812, and is now residing in Hartford, Me.

He was married, in 1839, to Anna Drew Bryant, of Turner, Me.; born there, May 20, 1819, daughter of Nehemiah and Mary (Bisbee) Bryant.

Children of JOHN JAMES and ANNA DREW (BRYANT) GLOVER, born in Waterford, Me.:

1859. Huldah Reed, b. Jan. 27, 1841 ; m. Henry Fuller, of Sumner.
1860. George Bates, b. Feb. 5, 1843 ; m. Marilla Kingsbury. He was enrolled in the U. S. service, in 1862, for nine months, in the 23d Regiment of Maine Volunteers.
1861. Mary Anna,   b. May 7, 1847.
1862. John Nelson, b. Feb. 13, 1851 ; d. Jan. 31, 1854.
1863. Annis Turner, b. Nov. 16, 1853.

(1741) MARY GLOVER, eldest daughter of John and Mary (Gullifer) Glover, was born in Duxbury, Sept. 6, 1815, and resides there at the present time.

She was married, Aug. 3, 1845, to Esaias Peterson, of Duxbury. They have had five children :

1864. Henry R.,   b. June 15, 1846.
1865. Andrew H.,   b. May 22, 1848.
1866. Melvin E.,   b. May 1, 1850.
1867. Herman J.,   b. June 15, 1852.
1868. Albert O.,   b. Feb. 7, 1854.

(1742) SARAH GLOVER, second daughter of John and Mary (Gullifer) Glover, was born in Duxbury, Oct. 16, 1817, and resides in Elliot, Me.

She was married, Jan. 28, 1835, to Alvah Remick, of Boston, by Rev. Mr. Himes. They have had nine children, born in Elliot, Me.:

1869. Granville A., b. May 12, 1836 ; m. Eveline Simmons.
1870. Mary E.,   b. Jan. 28, 1838 ; m. Jan. 28, 1857.
1871. Lucy J.,   b. July 15, 1839 ; d. Oct. 1, 1840.
1872. James A. D., b. Sept. 5, 1842.
1873. Sarah A.,   b. Dec.   7, 1843.
1874. Frank,   b. March,   1846.
1875. Frederick,   b. June,   1848.
1876. John H.,   b. Nov. 10, 1852.
1877. Helen F.,   b. May   21, 1858.

(1743) ANNE GLOVER, third daughter of John and Mary (Gullifer) Glover, was born in Duxbury, Sept. 13, 1819, and now (1866) resides there.

She was married to Elisha Peterson, of Duxbury, Oct. 8, 1837. They have had six children, born in Duxbury:

1878. Laura A.,   b. Dec.   9, 1839.
1879. Luella,   b. May   16, 1840; d. March 1, 1842.
1880. Alonzo F.,   b. March 12, 1844.
1881. Isabella M., b. July   3, 1849; d. Oct.   3, 1850.
1882. Lucy J.,   b. Dec.   17, 1852; d. Dec. 20, 1857.

(1744) JOHN GLOVER, fourth child and only son of John and Mary (Gullifer) Glover, was born in Duxbury, April 23, 1823, and still resides there.

He was married, Nov. 30, 1845, to Jane F. Sampson, of Duxbury. They have had eight children:

1883. Louisa M., b. April 28, 1846; m. George W. Whiting, April 28, 1864.
1884. Nahum,   b. April   1, 1848.
1885. Caroline F.,   b. Nov.   23, 1850.
1886. Clara F.,   b. Aug.   22, 1855; d. Nov. 15, 1856.
1887. John H.,   b. June   24, 1858.
1888. Clarence W.,   b. March 25, 1861; d. Oct. 8, 1861.
1889. Theodore W., b. June   2, 1863.

(1745) BETHIAH B. GLOVER, fourth daughter and youngest child of John and Mary (Gullifer) Glover, was born in Duxbury, Dec. 5, 1825, and resides in Pembroke.

She was married, April 20, 1845, to Francis H. Drake, of Pembroke. They have had eight children, born in Pembroke:

1890. Luella A., b. Jan. 16, 1846; m. Frank Hill, Hanson, May, 1864.
1891. Melissa,   b. April 23, 1848.
1892. Josephine A.,   b. May 30, 1850.
1893. Bethia J.,   b. Sept. 26, 1852.
1894. James J.,   b. Oct.   25, 1854.
1895. Susan L.,   b. Nov. 15, 1856.
1896. Frederick L.,   b. Feb.   22, 1858; d. Oct. 14, 1858.
1897. Marshall M.,   b. April 23, 1862.

(1757) JOSEPH S. GLOVER, eldest son of Joseph and Sarah (Whittemore) Glover, was born in Hebron, Me., May 17, 1813, and died in Illinois, in 1843, aged 30 years.

He was married, in 1838, to Anne Weston, of Fryeburg, Me. They had two children, born in Joliet, Illinois:

1898. Edward Weston, b. in 1840; graduated at Harvard College in the class of 1866; is a lawyer in New York City.
1899. Charles J., b. in 1842; enrolled in the U. S. service in 1862, was a prisoner at Andersonville, and exchanged with other surviving prisoners; has since engaged in business at Wilbraham, Mass.

(1759) ROBERT GLOVER, Esq., the second son of Joseph and Sarah (Whittemore) Glover, was born in Hebron, Me., September, 1817, and now (1866) resides there, and is postmaster of that town.

He was married, June 23, 1841, to Miranda Marshall, daughter of Moses and Ruth Marshall, of Paris, Me.; born there, Jan. 18, 1818.

Children of ROBERT and MIRANDA (MARSHALL) GLOVER, born in Hebron, Me.:

1900. Emma J.,   b. May   17, 1843; d. April 14, 1866, aged 23.
1901. Isaac S.,   b. Jan. 15, 1845.
1902. Anne W.,   b. July   3, 1849.
1903. Charles H., b. Nov. 23, 1850.
1904. Frank R.,   b. Nov. 15, 1852.
1905. Carrie S.,   b. Jan.   5, 1855.
1906. Eddie M.,   b. Feb. 14, 1857.
1907. Bertie T.,   b. March 21, 1859.
1908. Nellie M.,   b. Dec.   5, 1862.

(1769) GEORGE GLOVER COOPER, only son of George Glover and Nancy (Kimball) Cooper, and grandson of Nathaniel and Margaret (Glover) Cooper, of Kingston, was born in Waltham, Mass., April 2, 1824, and is now residing in the City of Rochester, N. Y. He is co-editor and publisher of the Rochester Daily Times and Advertiser, and has been for sixteen consecutive years in charge of the local department of that journal.

He was married, Oct. 6, 1848, to Theodosia Aurelia Banta, daughter of William and Mary Banta, of Coburg, Upper Canada; born there June 20, 1830. They have had three children, as follows:

1909. George Glover, b. Sept. 20, 1849.
1910. Nathaniel,   b. in   1852.
1911. Aurelia Banta, b. in   1854.

[*Second Generation.*]

PELATIAH GLOVER.

V. Rev. Pelatiah Glover, the fifth son and youngest child of John Glover, Esq., and Anna his wife, was born in Dorchester, N. E., in November, 1636–7, and baptized there by Rev. Richard Mather, pastor of the Church in Dorchester. He died at Springfield, March 29, 1692, aged 55 years. He resided during his youth in Dorchester, as appears by the list of names of those who attained the age of twenty-one years previous to 1700,* and was prepared for college under the instruction of Rev. Mr. Mather. We have no means of ascertaining the date of his entrance at Harvard College but by conjecture. At the time of his father's decease he had attained the age of seventeen years. By a codicil to his father's will, bearing date April 11, 1653, he was to receive the sum of two hundred pounds in money in addition to what had been provided for his education, and one-fourth part of his two farms in Dorchester, which had been reserved as the widow's dower, at the decease of his mother. His father died in 1653, and it is not probable he had entered Harvard at that date. Farmer writes of him, that he was educated at Harvard College, but did not receive a degree. Another writer says he entered Harvard College and passed through a regular course of three years, but did not graduate, without assigning any reason. The following notice of him, on the Dorchester Church Records, shows he was a student there in 1658, and at the age of twenty-one years: "26: 7: 1658. Mr. Pelatiah Glover united with the Church at Dorchester, he being then at Harvard College:" There is no record of the time he left there, but it is probable that, at that date, his course of three years was nearly completed, and that he left soon after. We learn from the College records, that about this time another year was added to the course of collegiate study, requiring four years instead of three before conferring a degree, and that seventeen students, having completed a course of three years, left Harvard and commenced the study of Divinity under private teachers. Only a few names of these are mentioned on the records, viz., William Brinsmaid, Ichabod Wiswall, &c.; but there can be little doubt that Mr. Pelatiah Glover was one of the seventeen who left at

* History of Dorchester, page 145.

that time and commenced the study of their profession with clergy-men. He studied Divinity with the Rev. Richard Mather, and it is recorded of him that he preached at Dorchester, June 15, 1659, about one year from the date when he is stated to be of Harvard College. An extract from the Church Records is as follows: "June 15, 1659, this year, was a day of fasting, humiliation and prayer in all the jurisdiction in behalf of our native country; the fears, com-motions and troubles in the country and in Parliament; rents and divisions in many of the Churches, especially at Hartford (N. E.); the hand of God against us in the unseasonable wet and rain of last spring; and the face of things in regard to the rising generation. Mr. Pelatiah Glover preached in the morning from Second Chronicles 7th chapter, 14, 15, 16 verses; Mr. Mather in the afternoon, from Hosea, 6th chapter, 1st verse."

July 3, 1659, he preached at Springfield, which is noted in the records of that town as his first sermon there. June 10, 1660, there was another day of fasting and prayer at Dorchester. "Mr. Pelatiah Glover preached in the morning from Zechariah 1 chap. 3 verse; Mr. Mather in the afternoon, from Ezekiel 21 chap. 27 verse."

"9: 4: 1661. Mr. Pelatiah Glover was appointed by the Church at Dorchester to the settlement of the Rev. Eleazer Mather at North-hamton." He preached the sermon on that occasion. "13: 8: 1661. Mr. Pelatiah Glover was dismissed from the Church at Dorchester to the Church in Springfield, they intending shortly to call him to office there."—(Dor. Ch. Rec.)

June 18, 1661, he was ordained at Springfield over the First Church there, as its second minister and the successor of the Rev. George Moxon.* He was furnished with a parsonage, and eighty

---

* Rev. George Moxon was the first minister of the Church at Springfield. He was a native of Yorkshire, England, and was graduated at the University of Cambridge. After due preparation he gave himself to the ministry. The date of his coming to New England has not been ascertained; but he was in Dorchester as early as 1636, and was admitted to the Church there under that date, soon after its gathering. On the fourth page of the first volume of the Dorchester Church Records it is said of him: "Mr. George Moxon, Mr. William Tompson, and Mr. Samuel Newman, Ministers, were admitted to join the Church this day, August 30, 1636." He was called to preach at Springfield, and was ordained there in the year 1637; and in that year he was made freeman at Boston and sent as a Deputy to the General Court at Hartford, from Springfield. His house was built in 1639. He con-tinued in the ministry at Springfield fifteen years. The date of his marriage, and his wife's name, have not been ascertained. The births of three of his children are found in the early records at Springfield, as follows: "Union Moxon, son of Rev. George Moxon, was born 12: 16: 1641; Samuel Moxon was born 3: 10: 1645; —— Moxon was born 3: 10: 1647, baptized the 23 of the same month." The christian name of the last child has been torn off

pounds a year salary, which was subsequently, in 1678, increased by twenty pounds more, making it equal to one hundred pounds annually. The parsonage mansion was built for Mr. Moxon by voluntary assessment. It was 35 by 15 feet, with a porch and study in it. The roof was thatched, and the cellar walls were planked. The following extract from an historical discourse by Rev. William B. Sprague, pastor of the First Church in West Springfield, delivered there Dec. 2, 1824, gives an account of the contract and the conditions of his settlement:

"The town of Springfield purchased Mr. Moxon's estate for seventy pounds. Although it seems to have been their original purpose to appropriate it for the benefit of the ministry, it does not appear that this was expressly done until 1665. At the time of Mr. Glover's settlement, in 1661, the town voted that he should have the use of the house and land belonging to it while he continued with them in the ministry, on condition that he should leave it in as good a state as he found it. But in 1665 they voted to give the aforesaid estate to Mr. Glover, provided he should continue to be their teacher during his life, or that he should remove by mutual consent; and in case of his thus removing, or in case that after his death his wife and children should choose to leave the place, the town should then have the refusal of the property. It was during Mr. Glover's ministry, in the year 1675, that the town was scourged by the Indians. The conflagration of the town immediately ensued, and about thirty dwelling houses and thirty-five barns were destroyed. Among them was the house occupied by the Rev. Mr. Glover, together with his library, which is said to have been extensive and valuable.

"In 1677, shortly after the destruction of the town by the Indians, in which Mr. Glover's house was burned, they voted to rebuild it; but having determined that they had no right to transfer to him the property which had been appropriated to the use of the ministry forever, they voted that the building, with the land connected with it, should be improved according to the original appropriation, it being

---

or worn out, so that it cannot be read. In 1652 Rev. Mr. Moxon resigned his charge and returned to England, in company with Mr. Pyncheon and others. He never returned. The cause of his departure is not certainly known, but supposed to be on account of two of his children having been accused of witchcraft, and the unpleasant circumstances which were connected with this trouble. He died Sept. 15, 1687, aged 87 years—and, as it is said, "poor and out of the ministry." A further notice of Mr. Moxon may be found in Calamy's "Ejected Ministers." Some of his manuscript sermons are still in existence.

no longer considered as private property; but inasmuch as they had
once been given to Mr. Glover, in order to recompense him the town
agreed to allow him one hundred pounds in addition to his stated
salary, provided he should continue to be their minister during his
life.   In 1681 there was an agreement between Mr. Glover and the
town to refer to the General Court the question, 'whether the donation which the town had made to him, of the house and land purchased for the ministry, was legal and consistent with right.' The
General Court decided that the town had no right to dispose of the
property after the original appropriation; but that they were nevertheless bound to make up the loss to Mr. Glover in some other way.
In 1682 they endeavored to bargain with him by an exchange of
property; but the controversy was never finally settled until after his
decease. In 1692 there was an agreement between the town and
Mr. Pelatiah Glover, son of the deceased clergyman, to refer the
matters to arbitrators, and their decision was that the town should pay
to Mr. Glover the sum of three hundred and fifty pounds, and the land
on that condition should revert back to its original use. This decision ended the controversy."

The following is the deed of transfer of the estate in question to
Mr. Glover:

Here ffolloweth the coppy of a deed whereby certayne persons of
the Town of Springfield who were appoynted by the said Town of
Springfield to make an agreement wth Mr. Pelatiah Glover have in the
name and by the appoyntment of ye said Town made over to the said
Mr. Glover those lauds in Springfield which were Mr. Moxons. These
presents certify that it is agreed by and between Capt. John Pyncheon, George Colton, Benjamin Cooley, Nathaniel Ely, Samuel Marshfield, Rowland Thomas and Lawrence Bliss, in the name and by the
appoyntment, and with ye full consent of the Town of Springfield on
the one p'te, and Mr. Pelatiah Glover Minister of the Word and
Teacher to this Plantation and Congregation of Springfield aforesaid
on ye other pte, for the more comfortable accommodation and Subsistence of the said Mr. Glover and for his settlement in this plantation, through the favour of God a Minister of the Word to this people,
that the said Mr. Glover shall have, hold, and enjoy for himself as his
own property and for his heirs and assigns forever, that Dwelling
house where he now dwelleth, together with the outhouse and barn
thereunto belonging, and all the land thereunto belonging which was
Mr. Moxon's.   That is to say, ye house lott contayning seven acres
more or less in breadth ffourteen rod and extending from the Street to
ye Great River.*   Also ffoure acres more or less of Wet Meadow and

_____

* Connecticut River.

a Wood lott at the end thereof of seven acres, more or less, being both of the same breadth wth the house lott. Also seven acres more or less on the West side of the great River opposite to the house lott above mentioned which is also ffourteen rod broad, & ffourscore rod long from the River. Also ffive acres more or less in the second division in breadth ten rod and in length fourscore rod from ye River. Also in ye third division sixteen acres more or less the breadth whereof is sixteen rod and in length one hundred & sixty rod. Also in the playne above end brooke sixteen acres more or less being in breadth ffoure & twenty rod & in length extending from ye place where ye fence stood at ye Easterly end thereof to ye great River, in length one hundred and twenty rod. Also nine acres more or less of meddow in the houst meddow. Also ffoure acres more or less of meddow wth some addition extending from the Indian ffeilds by Agawam River one hundred & ffourteen rod Northward. Also two acres more or less on the East branch of the Mill River. All which parcells of land are Registered in the Towne booke of Records under M^r. Moxons name & are now given & granted unto the above named M^r. Pelatiah Glover on ye tearmes hereafter mentioned. That is to say, that the said M^r. Pelatiah Glover shall & will continue & abide with this people as a Minister of the Word during his life, except he shall by mutual consent & agreement between himselfe and the people of this Plantation remoove himselfe otherwhere; which housing & land soe granted him, together with ffourescore pounds pr annum to be given unto him by the People of this Plantation the said M^r. Glover doth accept of as competent mayntenance. And it is aggreed by and between the partyes to this p'sents that if the s^d M^r. Glover shall remoove from this Plantation by mutual consent as above said, or y^t after his decease his wife and children chuse to leave this towne & shall, their house or housing and lands above mentioned, then the towne shall have the refusall of it vizt to buy it or not to buy it as this towne shall see cause. And it is the intent of these presents that this grant is not to be to the p'judice of any highways that pass thorow or at the ends of any of the said lands, nor shall the towne be liable to make good full measure of any prcll of lands where the River may have eaten in uppon any of them. Also the said M^r. Glover is henseforth to take the charge & care of makinge & repayring all ye fences belonginge to the said parcells of land or any of them. And it is further aggreed that these p'sents shalbe Recorded in some Publike Record of the towne as well for ye use and behoofe of the Plantation as also for the use and behoofe of the said M^r. Glover.

And in witness to these p'sents & the counterpart thereof the partyes hereto aggreeing have interchangeably sett their hands this 24th day of Aprill Anno D^mo 1665.

Subscribed and delivered in ye p'sence of   PELATIAH GLOVER.

Elizur Holyoke.   John Holyoke.

     John Pyncheon, Jr.

The counterpart of these presents was subscribed and delivered to Mr. Glover in the name of the Towne of Springfield, the day and year above written, by Capt. John Pyncheon, George Colton, Benjamin

40

Cooley, Nathaniel Ely, Samuel Marshfield, Rowland Thomas and Lawrence Bliss, and recorded June 29, 1665.

                          per Me   ELIZUR HOLYOKE, *Recorder.*

The foregoing is a copy of a deed recorded in Hampden Registry of Deeds, Book A, page 52.   J. E. RUSSELL, *Register,*

Springfield, August 27, 1862.   by   WELLS BRIDGE.

The same writer, Rev. Mr. Sprague, says, " He continued his labors among them until they were terminated by death, the record of which is as follows, under date of March 29, 1692: ' The Rev. Pelatiah Glover fell asleep in Jesus.' " He also adds the following: " He is represented as having been a diligent student, an energetic preacher, and a faithful pastor."

Another writer says, " Mr. Glover was an able man and of high attainments as a scholar."

All writers of his time who have noticed him, represent him as a man of distinguished talents, of great dignity and suavity of manners, united with the graces of christian accomplishments, which rendered his address that of the polished gentleman, as well as of the dignified clergyman; and also as having attained to a high degree of scholarship and literary distinction. He received students in Divinity, and prepared for the ministry many who became eminent in their time for learning and ability; among whom was the Rev. Timothy Edwards, of East Windsor, Conn. His " large and elegant library has been noticed by many of his cotemporaries as containing rare and valuable books, such as could never be replaced. It was destroyed with his house at the time the Indians ravaged and burned Springfield, in the year 1675. His house was replaced by a new and more commodious one, built of brick and fortified, at a cost of £108 15 shillings; but his library, which it is stated he valued and cherished above all his other household goods, could never be restored."

An extract from the Narrative of Indian Wars, page 111, shows the high value he placed upon his library. It appears that some time previous to the burning of his house, he had removed the treasures contained in his library to a neighboring garrison, to secure them from the dangers which were then apparent; and the extract describes the destruction and irreparable loss as follows:

" Among the ruins of said dwellings, the saddest to behold was the house of Mr. Pelatiah Glover, the minister of the town. It was furnished with a brave library, which he had newly brought back from the garrison wherein it had been for some time before secured; but as if the danger had been past and over with them, the said minister, a great student, *helluo librarum*, being impatient for want of his books, brought them back, to his great sorrow, fit for a bonfire to the proud insulting enemy. Of all the mischiefs done by the said enemy, the burning of the Town of Springfield did more than any other to discover the said actors to be the children of the Devil, full of all subtlety and malice; there having been for above forty years a good correspondence between the English of .that Town and the neighboring Indians. But in them is made good what is said in the 55th Psalm, verse 21, 'Though their words were smoother than butter, yet war was in their hearts; and though their words were softer than oil, yet were they drawn swords.' "

Trumbull, the historian, in his account of the burning of the town of Springfield by the Indians, adds the following: "The Rev. Mr. Pelatiah Glover, minister of the town, had his house burned, with a large and elegant library."

A late writer, Dr. Holland, thus notices him in his History of Western Massachusetts, Volume I.: " Nine years after the discharge of the Rev. George Moxon, they settled the Rev. Pelatiah Glover, a man of fine talents, high attainments and ardent piety. He lost one of the most valuable private libraries that New England then contained, which was burned with his mansion house by the Indians in 1675;" and refers to Hubbard's account in his Indian Narratives.

Mr. Glover was often called to sit in judgment at Ecclesiastical Councils, both in Connecticut and Massachusetts; and invariably attended—his presence, it has been stated, " being indispensable among them, on account of his sound and discriminating judgment." The Church over which he presided was, according to some writers, the fourteenth in order of time, of the New England Churches. Mr. Savage, in Winthrop's Journal, makes it the twenty-sixth, postponing its foundation until 1645. His cotemporaries in the ministry were, first, the Rev. Eleazer Mather, of Northampton, whom he assisted to ordain—a graduate of Harvard College in 1656. Between them there was a great intimacy. They were admitted to the Church on the same day, and were fellow students in Divinity. Mr. Glover survived him, and was a cotemporary with his successor, the Rev. Solomon Stoddard: also with Rev. Samuel Hooker, of Farmington, Conn.; Rev. Joseph Elliot, of Guilford; Rev. Edward Taylor, of Westfield, Mass., whom he assisted to ordain. The letters missive, calling a Council to organize the Church at Westfield, and ordain the first pastor, were dated July 1, 1679. The Council was requested to convene on the last 4th day of the 6th month, 1679, which was Aug. 27th, O. S.—the year at that time commencing with March. The Council consisted of the Rev. Solomon Stoddard, of Northampton—Mr. Strong, Ruling Elder, and Capt. Aaron Cook and Lieut. Clark, Messengers; Rev. John Russell, of Hadley, Pastor—Lieut. Smith and Mr. Younglough, Messengers; Rev. Pelatiah Glover, of Springfield, Pastor and Teaching Elder—Mr. John Holyoke, Dea. Burt and Mr. Parsons, Messengers; and one Messenger from Windsor, Ct., the pastor being detained by sickness in his family. There were present as guests, the Rev. Samuel Hooker, of Farmington, Ct., and the worshipful Major John Pyncheon, of Springfield. After the Church was organized, Mr. Taylor signified his acceptance, and the Rev. Mr. Russell offered the introductory prayer, and Mr. Glover the ordaining prayer.

Trumbull gives the following notice of Mr. Glover in the acts of the Synod of Connecticut, under date of Oct. 11, 1666: "It is ordered that all the presiding Elders who are or shall be settled in this colony at the time appointed for the meeting of this Synod, be sent to." It was also ordered by the Legislature that Mr. Mitchell, Mr. Brown, Mr. Skinner and Mr. Glover of Massachusetts should be invited to assist as members of the Synod.

From the journal of Rev. William Adams, dated Nov. 10, 1671: "This day, at evening, I received a letter from the inhabitants of Westfield, inviting me thither to preach, with one from Major Pyncheon and another from Mr. Glover, both in their behalf."

Rev. Pelatiah Glover was married, May 20, 1660, to Hannah Cullick, daughter of Capt. John Cullick, of Boston, by his first wife; born about 1640, and died in Springfield, Dec. 20, 1689. Nothing further in relation to her mother has been ascertained, as to her origin, the time of her marriage, or the date of her death, which latter was previous to 1648. It is probable that she was a native of England, and came over after her marriage. Her father, Capt. John Cullick, was at one time a prominent man in Boston, was largely engaged in commercial pursuits, and ranked among the wealthy merchants of the place. He was a member of the Ancient and Honorable Artillery Company in England, a branch of which was organized in Boston, N. E., in 1637. He was also a member of the Masonic Brotherhood before coming to New England. Capt. Cullick was married to his second wife, Elizabeth Fenwick, May 20, 1648. She was the daughter of Col. George Fenwick, of Saybrook, Ct., by his wife the Lady Alice Apsley, who died and was buried in Lyme, Ct. A monument for her has been erected there. She retained her title after her union with Col. Fenwick, and it is borne on the inscription engraved on her monument, which was designed by her husband. Col. Fenwick afterwards returned to England, and died there in 1657.

Capt. Cullick was early in Boston. Farmer says he died there, Jan. 23, 1663. His will bears date 1662, and is in substance as follows: " I John Cullick of Boston being sick, &c., I give unto my son John Cullick 150 pounds Lawful Money of New England to be payed him at the age of twenty one years; unto my daughter Mary Cullick, and to my daughter Elizabeth Cullick, 150 pounds each to be payed them at the age of twenty one years or on the day of their marriage. To my wife Elizabeth Cullick, my sole Executrix, the rest of my estate. My loving friends Capt. John Leverett and James Penn, both of Boston, Overseers of this my disposition of my estate by my Last Will and Testament."

Witnessed by John Leverett, James Penn, and Increase Mather, who deposed Jan. 27, 1662-3.

An inventory of the estate, taken Feb. 10, 1662-3, by Edward Huchinson and Thomas Brattle, mentions in the schedule a quarter part of " a vessell at sea, whereof Capt. Samuel Gallop is master." Mrs. Elizabeth Cullick, Executrix and relict widow of Capt. John Cullick, deposed 19 March, 1662-3.

There is no mention in all this of any daughter Hannah. The date of the will and his death, according to Farmer, is about one year after her marriage with Mr. Glover; which leads to the supposition that he must have been twice married, and that his daughter Hannah, as there appears to be no record of her birth here, may have been born in England. The year 1648 seems to be the first date found of him, which was the time of his marriage to Elizabeth Fenwick, of New London. He must have resided there, or at Hartford, a short time after his marriage, and the births of two of his children are found in the Hartford Town Records as follows: " John, son of Capt. John Cullick, was born May 4, 1649;" and "Elizabeth, daughter of Capt. John Cullick, was born July 15, 1652." Among the admissions to the First Church in Boston, there is recorded of him—"Capt. John Cullick and his wife were admitted this day; and two children, John and Elizabeth, were baptized 27:9: 1659."

There is nothing irreconcilable in all this, but in the will of Edward Hopkins there is found this bequest: "To the eldest child of Capt. John Cullick, by Elizabeth his first wife, who was a daughter of Col. George Fenwick." This, if true, raises an objection to the first statement or supposition that the wife of Mr. Glover was by a former wife of Capt. Cullick; but that she was his daughter and the same of whom the above items are recorded, is beyond a doubt. It is distinctly stated thus on the Boston Records by the recorder of her marriage, and no further testimony has been found in relation to it. Twelve years after her father's marriage to Elizabeth Fenwick, in 1648, as it is recorded, Hannah was married, which renders it indisputable that Elizabeth Fenwick was his second wife, and not the mother of the wife of Mr. Glover. And the presumption is also as undisputable that Mrs. Glover was a daughter by a former wife.

Children of the Rev. PELATIAH and HANNAH (CULLICK) GLOVER, born in Springfield:

+1. Samuel,   b. Nov. 28, 1661; d. July 24, 1689, in his 28th year.
 2. John,   b. July   1, 1663; d Jan. 14, 1664–5.
+3. Pelatiah,   b. Jan. 27, 1665–6; m. Hannah Parsons.
 4. Anna,   b. Aug. 21, 1668; d. June 6, 1690.
+5. Mary,   b. April 17, 1672; m. John Haynes, Esq., Hartford.

Rev. Mr. Glover, his wife, and all but one of his children, were buried in the ancient burial ground in Springfield, and the bodies remained there many years. In 1838, the Western Railroad, from Worcester to the State line of New York, was located to pass directly through this consecrated spot, where the founders of the town had laid out a final resting-place for themselves and their descendants; and in 1848 the remains of all who had been buried there were exhumed and removed to a new cemetery which was purchased and dedicated to the purpose. When this took place there was much interest manifested, and a deep and reverent sensation pervaded the minds of the inhabitants then living there. Many assembled to witness the solemn spectacle, and to observe the state in which the bodies might be found, as well as to show their profound reverence and veneration for their ancestors. It is stated, by persons who were present, that the form of the Rev. Pelatiah Glover remained perfect. It had become petrified in the long time it had been buried—a period of one hundred and fifty-six years. The grave, from which it was taken, was submerged with water. His gravestone had gone entirely to decay, as well as those of all but one of his family. Yet the body was fully identified. The inscription on the headstone of his son John was imperfectly deciphered, and was as follows:

" Here lyeth ye bodye of John ye son of Mr. Pelatiah Glover, who died ye 14 of January 1664.

> My Bodye sleeps—my soule hath quiet rest
> In Arms of God in Christ who makes us blest;
> The time draws on apace when God ye Son
> To see his face shall both unite in one."

The following account, in relation to the state in which the remains of this child, not two years old when buried, were found, appeared in the Springfield Gazette: " We witnessed this afternoon the disinterment of the remains of John Glover, a son of the Rev. Pelatiah Glover, second minister of Springfield. He was buried in Jan., 1664, one hundred and eighty-four years ago. Notwithstanding the lapse of this long period, pieces of the decayed coffin, and all the larger bones of the body, with the skull and portions of the hair yet remaining upon it, were found and removed. This is the oldest grave, save one, the identity of which is known."

The spot on which the ancient burial ground was laid out is now covered with buildings of various kinds—a commodious depot and other edifices, stores, machine shops, &c., to accommodate the Western Railroad Company.

Mr. Glover was wealthy, and it is stated that his house was the seat of hospitality; that to all of his numerous friends and acquaintances he always gave a courteous and elegant reception. His house was well supplied with servants, and he was in every respect possessed of ample means and facilities for the entertainment of distinguished strangers; and the neighboring clergy, as well as those more distant and in adjoining States, have added their testimony to the freedom and grace with which they were made participants of the bounties of his hospitable mansion.

In addition to his settlement and salary which have been noticed, as also his father's bequest of two hundred pounds in money, and other distinguished privileges, in 1670–1 he came in possession of lands in Dorchester, which were still his at the time of his decease and sold by his executor, as will be further noticed. He often visited the " Bay," as it is designated, and his estates there. He was entitled to one-fourth part of Newbury farm after the decease of his mother in 1670, and his name occurs in the quadripartite partition, called Glover's agreement (described on page 71), which was made and signed by them in 1680. An orchard on a portion of that estate bears the name of " Pelatiah's Orchard."

In a lease dated Nov. 1, 1682, and signed by Rev. Pelatiah Glover with Hannah his wife, he confirms, for two hundred pounds current money of New England, to Thomas Vose all his fourth part of the farm in Milton with a tenement thereon, known as the Newbury farm; together with one-fourth part of all his division of land in Milton which was devised to him by his father, John Glover; it being the reversion of Mrs. Anna Glover's right of dower, which at her decease in 1670–1 was divided, according to the will of her late husband, among her four sons, viz.: Mr. Habackuk Glover, Mr. Nathaniel Glover, Mr. John Glover, and Mr. Pelatiah Glover. Bounded in a deed of sale to Robert Vose from Mrs. Anna Glover and her four sons above named, and bearing date 13th July, 1654 (see page 65). Signed, sealed and delivered in presence of Habackuk Glover, and Nathaniel Glover, Sen.

Nov. 1, 1682, the same day, witnesses an obligation or bond from Thomas Vose, of Milton, to Rev. Pelatiah Glover, wherein the former " agrees to pay Mr. Pelatiah Glover, clergyman, of Springfield, four hundred pounds and restore to him the fourth part of Newbury farm, or pay to him two hundred pounds within the year."

Will of Rev. Pelatiah Glover, made March 11, 1691–2.

From Probate Records for the County of Hampshire.

I Pelatiah Glover of Springfield, in the County of Hampshire and Commonwealth of Massachusetts (Clergyman), being weak in body, but blessed be God of sound mind and understanding: to the end I may settle peace among my relations after my decease, and that Righteousness may be attended with those with whom I am concerned, I do make, ordain and constitute this my last Will and Testament, in manner and form following. Imprimis—

I give my soul into the arms of a tender hearted heavenly Father, trusting only in the Merits and Redemption of Jesus Christ for life and salvation, yielding my body to a comely and decent burial according to the discretion of friends or executors. And for the outward estate with which the Lord hath graciously blessed me, I do dispose of that as followeth.

And first to my son Pelatiah Glover I give and bequeathe all my Housing and lands in Springfield of what sort, nature or quality soever, both that which was Mr. Moxon's, stated me and given me by the Town of Springfield upon my settling among them as their Minister, which having done both of right belong to me, as also all other quantities or parcels of land whatsoever I am possessed of in Springfield, whether by purchase, grant from the Town or otherwise, all to be, and belong to my said son Pelatiah Glover and to his heirs forever.

As also I give to my son Pelatiah all my cattle of whatsoever kind with all the implements of husbandry and military implements whatsoever.

Item. I give and bequeathe to my daughter Mary Glover seventy pounds in money, which is in the hands of Richard Burke, payable by obligation from him to my heirs and assigns which sum I now assign to my daughter Mary. Moreover I give to my daughter Mary what flax I have and the wool of my sheep and all my household stuff, excepting one piece of Plate, viz., the standing silver cup and the bed I lye on, with the furniture to it whatsoever; and likewise that bed which Crowfoot* had, and lay on, as also all my books, all which before mentioned and excepted I give unto my son Pelatiah : Only two books, viz. Mr. Shepard's Works, I give unto my daughter Mary.

My Lands in the Bay of New England I order to be sold for the payment of all just debts of my sons Samuel and Pelatiah, by such as I herein appoint and confide in for that end, viz. my brother Habackuk Glover and Mr. Peter Sargent, whom I request that office of love and service from, unless my said son Pelatiah by the help and assistance of his Uncles shall be able to redeem said land from what I now appoint it for the payment of just debts. In that case I then give said land also to my son Pelatiah, or however and whatever remainder of it is, or surplusage in money may or shall be, I give that to Pelatiah.

And for what money I have lodged in Boston, or is due to me there, after all my just debts and funeral expenses are paid, I give it between my son and daughter, I say to be equally divided between Pelatiah and Mary.

Further as to what other debts are due to me, by arrears of accounts, Rents, Rates, or any other lawful wages, I hereby give the same to my son Pelatiah, whom I hereby make and constitute my sole executor: and expect his faithful attendance in performing of this which I hereby declare to be my last Will and Testament; revoking and making void and null any former Will whatsover by me intended. Adding further that if in law any dispute arise referring to anything herein mentioned and declared, I direct my son Pelatiah to take the advice and direction of my Overseers Mr. Habackuk Glover and Mr. Peter Sargent aforesaid, and to act thereby for the continuance of peace and love accordingly.

---

* Negro servant, probably.

In confirmation of this as my last Will and Testament, I do hereunto set my hand and scale, this Eleventh day of March, one thousand
six hundred and ninety-one–two.
    Before us,   PELATIAH GLOVER (with his seal).
      John Pyncheon,
      John Holyoke,
      John Pyncheon, Jr.

Mr. Pelatiah Glover hereto subscribed and affixed his hand and
scale, and declared this to be his last Will and Testament, this 11th
day of March, 1691–2. Before me at Springfield, at a meeting of the
worshipful Peter Tilton, the worshipful Major Jonathan Pyncheon,
and to the undernamed County Clerk, April 9th, 1692.

Mr. Glover declaring also, that it is his mind that his daughter
Mary, as long as she continues single and unmarried, shall have the
use of one-half the dwelling house; further, "if Mary die unmarried,
that all whatsoever I have given her shall return and be my son Pelatiah's."

April 29th, 1692. Mr. Pelatiah Glover presented the above will in
the presence of the abovesaid gentn as the last Will and Testament of
the Revd Pelatiah Glover deceased, and the witnesses to the said Will
being all present, did make oath to the truth of the subscription as
witnesses to the said Will, and that the Revd Mr. Pelatiah Glover was
of sound mind and perfect memory to their understanding, when he
signed the aforesaid as his last Will and Testament.

April 23, 1692. This last Will and Testament is here recorded by
John Holyoke, Clerke.   Attest, JOHN HOLYOKE, *Clerke.*

Springfield, in the County of Hampshire in the Province of Massachusetts. Mr. Peletiah Glover presented this Inventory of the Estate
of the Revd Mr. Pelatiah Glover, his late father deceased, and made
oath to the truth thereof, and that if more Estate appear he will readily reveal it to the Court, as attest,   JOHN HOLYOKE, *Clerke.*

April 26, 1692. This Inventory of the Estate of the Revd Mr. Pelatiah Glover, deceased, is hereby recorded,
                by JOHN HOLYOKE, *Clerke.*

Co. Hampshire, Liber 15, fol. 408.

An Inventory of the Estate of the Revd Mr. Pelatiah Glover, of
    Springfield, lately deceased, taken at Springfield, the 2d day of
    April, 1692, by John Pyncheon, John Hitchcock, and James War-
    riner, Appr.
Imp. Purse and Wearing Apparel at   .   .   .   £6 10 00 0
Viz. House, Housing and the ministry land which the
    Town gave Mr. Glover, viz. the Home lot and
    Meadow with Woodlot of about Fifteen Acres in the
    Plaine, and one on the West side of the great River
    about five or six acres.
Sixteen acres in the 3d Division.
Fifteen acres in the 2d Division.
Four acres of Meadow towards Agawam River.

Eight acres over Agawam River. Two acres at Mill
River. Land which was William Branche's. House
Home lot and that at Crooked point .   .   . £75 00 00 0
Forty acres upon the Hill over Agawam, some by the
Pond and that at Skipmuck granted by the Town of
Springfield 30 00 00 0
Books in Library 25 00 00 0
Silver bowl or standing cup 03 00 00 0
Gun and Ammunition 02 00 00 0
Bed which Mr. Glover lay on, with the Coverlet and
Curtains, Sheets and Furniture .   .   . 06 10 00 0
Also that which Crowfoot lodges on, with the Furni-
ture—2 pr of Sheets 03 10 00 0
Meat, besides what was left for Miss Mary Glover . 1 10 00 0
Corn, what Indian, &c. 10 00 00 0
1 pr Steel Yards 1 00 00 0
Scythe tackling, Rubstones, Beetle, Pease, Hooks . 8 00 00 0
Plough Irons, Cart Tackling, Collars, Chains and Spade
Paddles 6 00 00 0
5 Cows, 15 Pounds ; 2 Horses, £10 ; 11 Sheep, £5 . 30 00 00 0
3 New Castors 5 00 00 0
4 Swine, 3 Grindstones, 3 Axes, Plow Chains .   . 5 03 00 0
Rakes, Forks, Hoes and Cradles .   .   . 0 12 00 0
Plate, viz. Tankard, Spoons, &c. 11 00 00 0
Brass, Iron, Pots, Kettles, Pans, Tongs, Andirons,
Gridirons, and a (·   ) 8 00 00 0
Pewter Candlesticks, Earthen Ware, and a (   ) 24 00 00 0

In the Hall.
6 Chairs, 1 Forme, 6 more Chairs and a Tobacco Knife 2 10 00 0

In the Parlor.
Chairs, Table Forme and Carpet, Bedstead and Bed
Curtains 18 05 00 0

In the Hall Chamber.
Bed Curtains and Vallence and other Furniture . 16 00 00 0
Truckle Bed and Furniture, Table and Box of Drawers 12 00 00 0
Frame Box, Little Trunk and 2 Great Trunks .   . 3 02 00 0
A Chest. 2 Small silk Wrought Cushions. Stand and
Cushion, Wrought cover for Cushion, Silk Cushions
and small one 12 00 00 0
2 Carpets, Cupboard Cloth, Table Cloths, another Car-
pet. Broadcloth and Ticking, 4 yds Holland, 2 pr
Holland Sheets 6 17 00 0
Pillows and Pillow Beers 13 14 00 0
A Wrought Holland Bag and Diaper, Table Cloths, 3,
and other Linen 39 00 00 0
1 doz. Diaper Napkins, 1 doz. Holland Napkins, 6
Cotton Napkins, Table Cloth, doz. Towels .   . 18 11 00 0
A Cupboard Cloth, Scarlet Blanket, Demi Castors,
another Scarlet Blanket, Hat, Linen Yarn .   . 10 14 00 0
3 Books, Box and Brush and 6 Cushions .   .   . 3 18 00 0

In the Kitchen Chamber.

Old Bed and Bolster, Old Wheels and Feathers .	£2 10 00 0
Chest, another Box, an Old Trunk	1 03 00 0
13 lbs. Woolen Yarn, 46 lbs. linen Yarn, 2 pieces Linen	
Cloth, India Trays	6 13 00 0
Brass Scales and Weights, 2 small pair; 20 lbs. Flax	
and 28 lbs. Wool ; Glass Bottles	3 07 00 0

In the Garret.

Box, Rug, Blanket, Bolster, Pillows, Silk Grass .	3 10 00 0
More Wool, 4 old Bottles, a Chest, a little meal, 3 sieves	1 16 00 0

In the Kitchen Chamber.

Books and Wooden Trays, 2 Baskets, Tubs, Bowls,	
Churn, Can Cheese Moulds	2 03 00 0
Barrels, Tubs, and several things in the Cellar .	1 14 00 0
Salt, Flax in the Barn	0 17 00 0
	£441 19 00 0

An Obligation from Burke for 70 Pounds in money for
the House and Land in place of money   .   .   70 00 00 0

Land in the Bay of New England, we know not what,
which is to be added.

The money at Boston.

Debts due to the Estate, we understand of but know
them not, so leave them.

Apprized by us,   JOHN PYNCHEON.
JOHN HITCHCOCK.
JAMES WARRINER.

At a meeting of the Worshipful Peter Tilton, Esq. and the Worshipful Jonathan Pyncheon, Esq. with the County Clerk undernamed at Springfield, Mr. Pelatiah Glover presented this inventory of the estate of the Rev. Mr. Pelatiah Glover, his father Deceased, and made Oath to the truth thereof, and that if more estate do appear he will readily reveal it to the Court, as   Attest,   JOHN HOLYOKE, *Clerke.*

April 26, 1692.   This inventory of the estate of the Rev. Mr. Pelatiah Glover deceased is here recorded.   JOHN HOLYOKE, *Clerke.*

[*Third Generation.*]

(1)   Capt. SAMUEL GLOVER, the eldest son of Rev. Pelatiah and Hannah (Cullick) Glover, was born in Springfield, Nov. 28, 1661, died there, July 24, 1689, in his 28th year, and was buried in the ancient burial ground in that town.   It appears, from what is found recorded of him, that he owned an estate and had fixed his abode in Suffield, Conn.   There is no evidence that he was ever married or had children, and by his decease may be ranked among the lines which have become extinct.   His father, Rev. Pelatiah Glover, was appointed administrator to his estate, which is represented to be as follows:

An Inventory of the Estate of Capt. SAMUEL GLOVER, son of the Rev^d Mr. Pelatiah Glover, of Springfield, who departed this life July 24, Anno Domⁿ, 1689; taken by John Barber and James Warriner.

All his Lands at Suffield, Connecticut	.	.	.	£80	00	00 0
His Clothing	.	.	.	30	00	00 0
Guns and Sword and Belt	.	.	.	08	00	00 0
A Chest	.	.	.	00	12	00 0
				118	12	00 0

Also there is a debt due by arbitration from Captⁿ.

Maudsley, viz. in current pay	.	.	.	10	00	00 0
And in Cash	.	.	.	5	00	00 0
				£133	12	00 0

Mr. Pelatiah Glover, Junior, presented to the Court at Springfield September 29th, 1691, this Inventory of the Estate of his brother, Captⁿ Samuel Glover deceased, and made oath, to the best of his knowledge that it is a true and just Inventory, and if more Estate do appear it shall be revealed to the Court.

And in as much as the said deceased died intestate, this Court do grant Power of Adminstration to the Rev^d Mr. Pelatiah Glover, his father, he giving bonds in the sum of 200 pounds for security of said Estate and to give an account of his Adminstration thereon.

From the original file at Northampton, Hampshire County.
December, 1691. Attest, JOHN HOLYOKE, Clerke.

This Inventory of the Estate of Captⁿ Samuel Glover is here recorded. JOHN HOLYOKE, Clerke.

Millington to Glover.

Know all men by these Presents, that I John Millington, of Southfield (alias Suffield), in the County of Hampshire, in the Colony of Massachusetts, New England, for and in consideration of the Sum of Twenty Six Pounds to me in hand paid by Samuel Glover of Springfield, in the County of Hampshire, in the Colony aforesaid, &c. &c. Grant and sell, &c. two parcels of Land lying and being in said Southfield, as followeth. That is to say, a parcel of land containing Forty acres, more or less, being upland and low land, and in length two hundred and forty Rods, and in breadth Twenty Nine Rods; and is bounded on the North by Timothy Hale Sen.; on the South by James Rysend, on the East by land of George Norton, and on the West by the Street called High Street. The other parcel of Land is Meadow, containing Four Acres more or less, lying upon Muddy Brooke, and is bounded by Joshua Willis Eastward, down the said Brooke; Westward up the Brooke by Major John Pynchoon, which said parcels of Land hereby sold, viz. the Forty Acres more or less, and the Four Acres of Meadow more or less, together with all the buildings, wood, timber, fences, trees, woods, waters, profits and commodities, and also all the Appurtenances thereof, &c. To Have and to Hold, &c., unto him the said Samuel Glover, &c. In witness

41

whereof, I the said John Millington have hereunto set my hand and seal this 16ᵗʰ day of March, Anno Dom. 1681 or 82.

Signed, sealed and delivered in presence of us,   JOHN MILLINGTON.
    John Holyoke,
    Joseph Ashley,
    Samuel Marshall.

This witnesseth that the wife of the said John Millington doth hereby consent to the act and Deed of the bargain and sale of her said Husband.   The—S—mark of Sarah Millington.

By the above deed, made and executed nine years previous to his decease, it appears probable that Capt. Glover had resided that portion of his time in Suffield.

(3)   PELATIAH GLOVER, the third son of Rev. Pelatiah and Hannah (Cullick) Glover, was born in Springfield, Jan. 27, 1665–6, and died there, Aug. 22, 1737, in his 72d year.

He was an extensive landholder, and ranked with the wealthy landed class of his time. He was principal legatee to the will of his father, and also sole executor. He inherited with his lands the prefix of Mr., and was thus designated on records and notices of him. The first notice of him on the Probate Records is in 1691, when he presented the inventory of his deceased brother Samuel's estate. In 1692 he was called to settle the estate of his father. In 1699, Feb. 14, he sold, by the following deed, his lands in the Bay of New England to his cousins Nathaniel Glover, Sen., and William Rawson, to be possessed by them in equal halves. (See page 182.) It is copied from the original document, which is written on parchment, and is now (1866) in a good state of preservation.

To All People unto whom this present Deed of Sale shall come, Pelatiah Glover of Springfield, in the County of Hampshire within his Majesties Province of Massachusetts Bay in New England, Yeoman, only surviving son and heir of Pelatiah Glover late of Springfield aforesaid, Decᵈ, sendeth Greeting : Whereas the said Deceased Pelatiah Glover, in and by his last Will and Testament bearing date the 11ᵗʰ day of March, 1691, duly proved, approved and on Record in the County of Hampshire aforesaid, did devise and order in the words following, To Wit. "My Lands in the Bay of New England I order to be sold for the payment of all my just debts ; of my sons Samuel Glover and Pelatiah Glover by such as I here confide in for that end, and I put my brother Habackuk and Peter Sargeant of Boston, whom I request that office, love and service from, unless Pelatiah by the help and assistance of his Uncles shall be able to redeem said land from what I now appoint it for the payment of my just debts, and then I give said land also to Pelatiah, however or whatever remaineth of it or of surplusage I give that to Pelatiah."

And Whereas the said Habackuk Glover, brother of the said Deceased Pelatiah Glover and one of the persons entrusted by him as aforesaid to make sale of his said lands, is also deceased, and no sale of said lands by him and the said Peter Sargeant, pursuant to the power and trust to them committed, as abovementioned.

Therefore Know Ye : That I the said Pelatiah Glover, son and Heir as aforesaid of the said Deceased Pelatiah Glover, for and in consideration of the sum of Two Hundred and Thirteen Pounds and Ten Shillings current money of New England to me in hand paid, before the ensealing and delivery of these Presents, by Nathaniel Glover of Dorchester in the County of Suffolk within his Majesties Province aforesaid, Farmer ; and William Rawson of Brantry, within the County and Province aforesaid, Yeoman, well and truly paid, to enable me to pay out and discharge the just debts of the said Deceased Pelatiah Glover and of my brother Samuel Glover (who is also deceased) according to the mind and will of my said father as above expressed. The receipt whereof of which sum for that end and use, so far as shall be necessary for the same and of the surplusage or remainder to my own proper use and behoof (being so given unto me as aforesaid). Therefore I the said Pelatiah Glover do hereby acknowledge myself to be therewith fully satisfied, contented and paid, and thereof and of every part thereof, do acquit, exonerate and discharge the said Nathaniel Glover and William Rawson, each of them and each of their Heirs, Executors, and Administrators, forever by these Presents have given, granted, bargained, sold, aliened, enfeoffed, released, conveyed and confirmed ; and by these Presents do fully, freely and clearly and absolutely give, grant, bargain, sell, alien, enfeoffe, release, convey and confirm unto the said Nathaniel Glover and William Rawson, their Heirs and Assigns forever, All that One fourth part of a Certain Farm called Newbury Farm, said Farm lying and being within the Township of Dorchester aforesaid, which upon the division of the said Farm between Habackuk Glover, John Glover, Nathaniel Glover and my said father Pelatiah Glover, Dec^d, sons of Mr. John Glover, formerly of Boston, Esq. Deceased, was set forth and assigned unto my father Pelatiah Glover, Dec^d. (The said farm being devised by the last Will and Testament of the said Mr. John Glover last named to his four sons before mentioned.) Be the quantity of the said fourth part of the said Farm more or less. However the same may be bounded or reputed to be bounded. Together with all and singular the Houses, Edifices, Buildings, Fences, Woods, Underwoods, Trees, Timber, Waters, Watercourses, Pastures, Meadows, Fields, Titles, Rights, members, profits, privileges, commodities, advantages, hereditaments, emoluments and appurtenances whatsoever, to his said Fourth part of the said Farm belonging to or in any wise appertaining to, or upon the same, or aught thereof, standing, growing or being or therewith used, occupied or enjoyed.

Also One Fourth part of the lands belonging to the said Farm within the Township of Milton, in the County of Suffolk aforesaid, and of all Wood, Timber, members, appertaining to or belonging to the same, and of all the Estate, Right, Title, Interest, Inheritance, Use, profits, privileges and demands whatsoever of me the said Pelatiah Glover and my Heirs and Assigns of, in, or out of the hereinbefore granted Premises and every part and parcel thereof, and the Reversion and Reversions, Remainder and Remainders, Rents, issues, and Profits of the same.

To Have and to Hold the said Fourth part of the aforesaid Farm. and all and singular the Premises herein before granted, bargained and sold, with the Rights, Members and appurtenances thereof, Unto the said Nathaniel Glover and William Rawson, their heirs and assigns in equal halves, as aforesaid forever. The same in two equal parts to be divided to the only proper use, benefit, and behoof of the said Nathaniel Glover and William Rawson, their heirs and assigns forever. And I the said Pelatiah Glover, for myself and my heirs, executors and administrators, do hereby covenant, grant, and agree, to and with the said Nathaniel Glover and William Rawson, their heirs and assigns, in manner and form following, That is to say: that I the said Pelatiah Glover at and until the ensealing and delivery of these presents, am the true, sole and lawful owner of all in the lands and Premises herein and hereby granted, bargained, and sold; and have in myself full power, good right and lawful authority, in manner as aforesaid; and that the said granted Premises are free and clear, and thereby acquitted, exonerated and discharged of, and from all and all manner of former and other gifts, grants, bargains, sales, leases, releases, Mortgages, Joyntures, Dowers, Titles of Dowers, Wills, Entails, Judgments, Executions, Titles, Troubles and encumbrances whatsoever. And further that I the said Pelatiah, my Heirs and Assigns, Executors and Administrators, shall and will warrant and defend the said Fourth part of the aforesaid Farm and all and singular the Title of the Premises herein and hereof granted, bargained, sold, with the appurtenances hereof, unto the said Nathaniel Glover and William Rawson, their Heirs and Assigns forever, in equal halves as aforesaid, against the lawful claims and demands of all and every Person or Persons who should at any time or times hereafter, at the request of the said Nathaniel Glover and William Rawson, their Heirs and Assigns, at his or their cost and charges at the law, shall and will make, pass and operate under them, such further Act or Instrument, for the better confirmation or sure making of the herein above-granted and bargained Premises, and of every part thereof, unto the said Nathaniel Glover and William Rawson, their Heirs and Assigns, according to the true intent and meaning of these Presents, as by their Council Learned in the Law shall be lawfully or reasonably devised, advised or requested.

In Witness whereof, I the said Pelatiah Glover have hereunto set my hand and seale this Fourteenth Day of February, 1699. Annoq RR William Tertii England Duodecimo. PELATIAH GLOVER.

In presence of Us,
Robert Howard,
William Clark.

The Within Written Deed was signed, Sealed and Delivered by Pelatiah Glover, the grantor therein named, as also the Postscript by Peter Sargeant, Esq., in presence of Us, ROBERT HOWARD.
WILLIAM CLARK.

Pelatiah Glover's Receipt.

Received on the day of the date of the within written Deed, of the within named Nathaniel Glover and William Rawson, the sum of Two Hundred and Thirteen Pounds and Ten Shillings currant money of New England, in full payment and satisfaction and discharge of the purchase within mentioned. PELATIAH GLOVER.
£213 10s.

Entered and Recorded with the Records of Deeds for the County of Suffolk, Lib. 19, fol. 261. ADDINGTON DAVENPORT, *Register.*

Confirmation of Peter Sargeant to the Deed of Pelatiah Glover to Nathaniel Glover and William Rawson.

Know all Men by these Presents, That I Peter Sargeant of Boston, in New England aforesaid, do hereby approve of and consent unto the above mentioned and bargained Premises and the bargain and sale made as above said by Pelatiah Glover, Son and Heir of Pelatiah Glover late of Springfield deceased. And so far as I am by the said Pelatiah Glover's last will and Testament any ways empowered or entrusted to make sale of his lands above granted (his brother Habackuk Glover, who was joyned with me in that Trust, being Deceased), I do by these Presents Ratify and confirm unto the said Nathaniel Glover and William Rawson, the above named Grantees, their Heirs and Assigns forever, in equal halves, all and singular the lands herein to them granted and sold in and by the above written Deed.

In Witness whereof, I have hereunto set my hand and scale on the day of the date of the above written Deed. PETER SARGEANT.
February 14, 1699.

The within named Pelatiah Glover personally appearing before me the Subscriber, one of the Council and Justice of the Peace within His Majesties Province of Massachusetts Bay in New England, acknowledged the within written Instrument to be his free Will, Act and Deed, and Peter Sargeant, Esq. also appearing at the same time acknowledged the within written Postscript to be his Voluntary Act and Deed. JAMES ADDINGTON, *Justice of the Peace.*
Boston, February 16, 1699.

Mr. Pelatiah Glover was married Jan. 7, 1686, to Hannah Parsons, of Northampton, County of Old Hampshire; born there in 1663, and died in Springfield, April 1, 1739, aged 76 years. She was the daughter of Joseph and Mary (Bliss) Parsons, who were married in Northampton, Nov. 26, 1646. Her father, it is related, with a younger brother, Benjamin Parsons, were brought by their parents to New England at a very early age, from Torrington, a town in the northwest part of the County of Devonshire, England. (It is supposed they came with Mr. Pyncheon.) He lived first in Springfield —was witness to a deed there, in 1636, from the Indians to Mr.

41*

Pynchcon.   He removed to Northampton after 1655, and lived there until 1679, when he removed back to Springfield, where he died, Oct. 9, 1683.   He was elected to serve in several town offices, which he filled with great acceptance to the inhabitants; was Cornet to the Horse Company there, and is said to have been one of the richest men in Springfield at the time of his decease.   Freeman in 1669.

Her mother, Mary Bliss, was the daughter of Thomas and Margaret Bliss, and was born in England.   She was brought to New England by her parents, with four of her brothers and sisters, and died in Northampton, Mass., Jan. 29, 1712.*

Children of Mr. PELATIAH and HANNAH (PARSONS) GLOVER, born in Springfield:

+ 6. Pelatiah, b. Aug. 27, 1687 ; m. $\begin{cases} \text{1st, Mary Wright;} \\ \text{2d, Martha Ould;} \\ \text{3d, Hannah Burt (widow).} \end{cases}$

+ 7. Thomas, b. Nov. 16, 1688 ; d. in Wilbraham, Dec. 30, 1775, aged 87 years.
+ 8. John, b. Sept. 12, 1690 ; d. in Springfield, Mch 27, 1733, aged 43.
+ 9. Hannah, b. Dec. 27, 1693 ; m. John Ashley, of Westfield.
+10. Mary,   b. Aug. 25, 1695 ; m. Benjamin Horton, of Springfield.
  11. Samuel, b. April 1, 1698 ; d. April 21, 1698.
+12. Abigail, b. July   9, 1702 ; m. Jonathan Mills, of Brookfield.
+13. Samuel, b. Dec. 16, 1706 ; m. Joyce (Newcomb) Jones (widow).

In addition to his inherited estate, Pelatiah Glover was the owner of large tracts of land by purchase.   In 1696 he bought of Jonathan Ashley and Sarah his wife, " of the Town of Hartford in Connecticut in New England," several tracts of land in Springfield, for £165.

---

* Thomas Bliss, the grandfather of Hannah Parsons, by her mother's lineage, was an early but not an original settler of New England. The time of his arrival here is not certainly known, but it appears that his first residence was at Braintree (now Quincy), in that part of the town called the " Mount," probably Merry Mount—Mount Wollaston. He is first mentioned in Connecticut in 1639 or 1640. The date of his death has not been ascertained, but it is known that he died in Hartford, Ct. He had a wife Margaret, who survived him and removed to Springfield after his decease, taking with her all her children except Thomas and Anne. They had in all ten children ; five they brought over with them, and five more were born to them after their emigration. Mrs. Margaret Bliss purchased a tract of land in Springfield, as is stated by her descendants, one mile square, situated in the south part of the town, on what is now Main street, and bordering on the Connecticut River. Her descendants are numerous in that part of the town (which has become a city), and of high respectability ; they have built houses, and laid out streets on the Manor Tract, one of which, leading from Main street to the river, bears her name, " Margaret street," and another " Bliss street," on which is the South Congregational Church. There are still a few of the ancient houses remaining, two or three of which look as if they might have been built by her immediate descendants. Mrs. Margaret Bliss died in Springfield, Aug. 28, 1684, and was buried there. It has been said of her that she was a lady of superior abilities, great resolution and uncommon enterprise.

In 1715 is recorded a deed from Benjamin Braman, to Pelatiah Glover, of Springfield, of several other tracts of land. He was allotted lands in Brimfield and Plainfield, in the western part of Massachusetts.

In 1717 he conveyed, by deed of gift, to his third son John Glover, "four acres of land called a Homestead, situated at the Northerly end of the Town of Springfield, Plot street, and on the East side of the Great River, as an absolute estate of inheritance." Deed dated July 3, 1717, and signed by Pelatiah Glover and Hannah Glover.

In 1724 he conveyed a tract of land to his eldest son, Pelatiah Glover, Jr.

In 1726, Dec. 24, is recorded a deed of gift from Pelatiah Glover, Sen., to his four sons, viz.: Pelatiah Glover, Jr., his eldest son; Thomas Glover, his second son; John Glover, his third son; and Samuel Glover, his fourth son, by which he conveys to them all his lands in Springfield, to be entered upon after his decease.

In 1728, Dec. 10, a deed of gift was given by Pelatiah Glover, Sen., to his son Thomas Glover—reference being made to deed bearing date Dec. 24, 1726, as above.

In 1736, one year before his death, is recorded another deed of gift to his fourth son, Samuel Glover, in which the income of this estate or tract is reserved until after the decease of himself and his wife Hannah.

Thus it will be seen that he died intestate, and that his estate and lands were mostly conveyed to his sons, from time to time, previous to his decease.

Estate of Pelatiah Glover, 2d.

Power of Administration of All and singular of the Goods, Chattels, Rights and Credits of Pelatiah Glover, late of Springfield, in the County of Hampshire, deceased, Sen., Gent[n], is granted to his Two sons, viz., Pelatiah Glover and Samuel Glover, both of said Springfield, and Bond taken for their true and faithful performance of said trust, Y[e] Mother declining said office.

Sept. 13, 1737.

Hampden, ss. Springfield, Nov. 23[d], 1737. These may certify, that Messrs. John Worthington, Obadiah Cooley and Luke Hitchcock, 2[d], all of Springfield, being freeholders, were appointed and sworn to make a Just and Indifferent apprizement of the Estate of Mr. Pelatiah Glover, late of Springfield, deceased, as should be presented to them by the Administrators on Said Estate.

Pr WILLIAM PYNCHEON, Jun[r], *Just. Peace.*

An Inventory of the Estate of Mr. Pelatiah Glover, late of Spring-field, deceased, taken by the subscribers, Nov. 25, 1737.

	£ s d
Imp. His Clothes, viz. Coat and Jacket, 5 Pounds	£5 00 00 0
One Loose Coat, 40s.; One Beaver Hat, 50s.; one do., 8s.	4 18 00 0
2 pair Stockings, 18s. ; 2 fine Shirts, 32s. . . .	2 10 00 0
Item. His books. The English Annotation, 80s. .	4 00 00 0
Great Bible, 15s. ; London Dispensatory, 3s. ; other sm'l Books	2 10 00 0
One small Table, 4s. ; a small Trunk, 20s. . . .	1 04 00 0
One Large Table, 10s. ; Five Covered Chairs, 45 shill.	2 15 00 0
One small Looking Glass, 4s. ; a small Box, 4s. . .	0 08 00 0
One Chest, 3s. ; One small Trunk, 11s. ; Branding Iron, 3s.	0 17 00 0
One Old Saddle and Stirrups-Irons, 14s. ; One Cane, 30	2 04 00 0
Two small Branding Irons, 2s. ; Half bush⁴ Plated, 5s.	0 07 00 0
Old Tubs and Barrels, 22s. ; Bowl and Keeler, 5s.	1 07 00 0
One Churn, 7s. ; Wooden Tunnel, 4s. ; Two Suet Tubs, 1–6	0 12 06 0
Eight Old Cider Barrels, 24s. ; Three small Tables, 7–6	1 11 06 0
Three Great Chairs, Six Small ones	0 18 00 0
Two Mortars, 2–6 ; Two wooden bowls, Three Knots, Dishes, Two Cheese-fatts	0 14 00 0
Three pails, 7s. ; One Cupboard, 7s.	0 14 00 0
One large Chest, 15s. ; One Chest, 3s. ; One Box, 4s. ; One Looking Glass, 15	1 17 00 0
Two Large Glass Bottles, 8s. ; Two Glass Cafes size, 6s. Five Small Glass Bottles, 5s. ; Spade, 8s. . .	1 07 00 0
Plow Irons, 20s. ; half bush¹ and Pecks, 4s. each ; Wheel Boxes and Bands, 36s. ; Axletree, Pins, Cl. pin .	3 06 00 0
A Bush Hoe, half to be prized, 4s. ; Handsaw, 4s. ; Two augers, 8s ; Two drawing Knives, 5s., and Hammers, 3	1 04 00 0
Old Broad Axe, Old Adze and Hatchet, 5s. ; Cow bell, 8s. ; Fetters, 4s. ; One pr Addze	1 07 00 0
One Cart Rope, 7s. ; A Large pair Steelyards, 12s. ; small ones	1 17 00 0
One Large Brass Kettle, £9 ; One small, 32s. . .	11 12 00 0
One smaller, 60s. ; One smaller, 25s. ; One smaller, 15s.	5 00 00 0
Old Brass Skillet, 12s. ; smaller do., 10s. ; Brass pan, 20	2 02 00 0
One large Iron Pot, 40s. ; One smaller do., 6s. ; Iron Kettle, 10s. ; Bellmettle Posnet, 7s. . . .	3 03 00 0
One Brass Candlestick, 5s. ; One pewter do., 4s. ; One pair Hand Irons, 20s. ; Slice and Tongs, 10s. . .	1 19 00 0
Warming pan, 38s. ; Gridiron, 4s. ; Frying pan, 2s. .	3 04 00 0
One Large Stone Jug, 9s. ; One smaller, 3s. ; 6 large Pewter Platters, the weight 21 pounds and ½ at 6s. pr. Plaʳ	6 09 00 0
One Pewter Tankard, 10s. ; One small Pewter Platter, 3s.	0 13 00 0
Four Pewter plates, 10s. ; One large Basin, 5s. . .	0 15 00 0
One Pewter Salt cellar, 3s. ; Bason, Saucer, Ponger .	0 07 00 0
One Great Cup, 7s. ; Tin Tunnel, 2s. ; Earthen Quart Cups, 3s. ; 2 Drinking Glasses	0 14 00 0
One Feather Bed, Bolster, Pillows, Under Bed Rug and Old Blanket, 35s.	10 15 00 0
Curtains, 60s. ; Bedstead and Rope, 18s. ; Old Bed and Bolster, 20s. ; The Coverlets, £2	6 18 00 0

An Old Bed and Bolster, 35s. ; Two Coverlets, 20s. ; Two
   old Bedsteads and Bed Ropes   .   .   .   3 05 00 0
One Feather Bed, 85s. ; Shagg Rugg, 35–6 ; One Coverlet,
   15s. 6 15 00 0
Two Augers and a Gouge, 2s. ; One Pistol, 20s. ; a Gun, 40s. 3 03 00 0
One Cow, £6 15s. ; Smaller one, £5   .   .   11 15 00 0
One Horse and Mare, 40s. ; half a timber Chain, 16s. ;
   Half a fan, 7s. ; An Old file, 2s.   .   .   .   3 05 00 0

Homestead, House and Barn at the upper end of the
   Town Plot 200 00 00 0
Four Acres and Twenty Seven Rods of Land in the
   Plainfield, Forty Acres at Poor Brook, £5   .   .   27 00 00 0
Ten Acres of Land at Swan Pond, 2–10   .   .   7 10 00 0
Fifteen Acres of Land bounded Southwesterly on the
   corner of Mr. Joseph Pyncheons, Mr. Willistons
   . and Mr. Worthingtons on the Hill against the upper
   end of the Town Plot 15 00 00 0
Ten Acres of Land known by the name of the Ten Acre
   Lot, on the East side of the Great River   .   1 00 00 0
Twenty Seven Rods, three feet and four inches of Land
   in the Outward Common in the middle Division of the
   East side of the Great River 60 00 00 0
Eight Rods and Twelve feet more in said Division in the
   Aforesaid Commons 17 00 00 0
Twenty-three Rods and a half of Land in the Upper
   Division in the aforesaid Commons   .   .   12 00 00 0
Three Rods and five feet of land in the aforesaid Mid-
   dle Division of said Commons   .   .   .   7 00 00 0
                                                ————————
                                           £472 11 00 0

The Above Inventory taken by Us, Nov. 25, 1737.

                     PELATIAH GLOVER, } *Administrators.*
                     SAMUEL GLOVER, }

JOHN WORTHINGTON, }
LUKE HITCHCOCK, } *Apprizers.*
OBADIAH COOLEY. }

    At a Court of Probate holden at Northampton within the County of
Hampshire, on the Second Tuesday of December, being the Tenth
day of said month, Anno Dom". 1737, John Stoddard, Esq., Judge of
said Court, Pelatiah Glover and Samuel Glover, Administrators on the
Estate of Mr. Pelatiah Glover, late of Springfield in the County of Hampshire, Gentleman, Deceased, presenting the aforesaid Inventory, made
Oath that it is a true and perfect Inventory of the Estate of their late
Father, as far as has come to their knowledge ; and if anything more
of said Estate afterwards appear, they will readily make discovery of
the same to the Judge or his successor in office from time to time.
                                          Cor^m JOHN STODDARD.

A List of Debts due from the Estate of Mr. Pelatiah Glover, Deceased.

To John Pyncheon, Esq.	£8 12 07 0
A note to Mr. Brewer	15 00 00 0
A Bond to Capt. Smith	14 00 00 0
To Peletiah Hitchcock	00 15 00 0
Note to Lt. Worthington	10 00 00 0
To Joseph Warriner	1 00 00 0
Doct' Eben' Terry	0 08 00 0
Samuel Bliss	0 06 00 0
To Abigail Glover for her service in doing the Household business, and for extraordinary trouble for One year and Eight months	30 00 00 0
To Peletiah Glover for Glassing his House . .	12 00 00 0
To a Debt due Abigail Glover on a Bond given her by John Glover, with Interest Eight years .	50 00 00 0
Ebenezer Warriner, Deceased, 6s. ; Joseph Ashley, 3s.	00 09 00 0
	£142 10 07 0

A List of Debts due to the Estate.

Moses Merick, 26 ; Mr. Robert Breck, 20s. . .	2 06 00 0

PELATIAH GLOVER,
SAMUEL GLOVER.

Hampshire, ss. May 18th, 1738. The Administrators on the Estate of Mr. Pelatiah Glover, Deceased, personally appearing, made Oath that the foregoing accounts of Debts and Credits of the Estate of the said Deceased is a true account as far as has come to their knowledge, and if more Estate afterwards appear they will readily discover the same to the Judge of Probate for said County or his successor in office, from time to time.   Cor^m JOHN STODDARD, *Judge of Probate.*

The Estate of Mr. Pelatiah Glover, late of Springfield, Deceased, To Pelatiah Glover and Samuel Glover, his sons and Administrators on his Estate, is . . . . Dr.

November, 1737, To a Journey to Northampton and expenses for Letter of Administration and fees, paid all by Pelatiah only	£1 16 00 0
To the Justices for appointing and swearing the Appraisers, 3s. To 25s. Paid the Appraisers and for taking the Inventory and expenses . . .	1 08 00 0
Dec. To a Journey to Northampton to exhibit the Inventory and expenses with fees . . .	2 04 00 0
Funeral expenses, to making Coffin and digging Grave	1 12 00 0
To a Journey to Northampton, 30s.	1 10 00 0
	£8 10 00 0

The Administrators give the Estate credit as followeth :

Received of Benjamin Warriner	0 16 00 0

PELATIAH GLOVER,
SAMUEL GLOVER.   } *Admin's.*

February 4, 1739–40. To John Stoddard, Esq., Judge of Probate.

An additional Inventory to the Estate of Mr. Pelatiah Glover, late of Springfield, Dec⁴, viz :

One Acre and one quarter of Land in the Plain field so called, £15. Three acres and a half acre at Paconsuck, £3 10s. 18 10 00 0

as presented to us by Pelatiah Glover and Samuel Glover, Admin".

OBADIAH COOLEY,
JOHN WORTHINGTON, } *Apprais's.*
LUKE HITCHCOCK,

An Additional Account of Debts due from the Estate of Mr. Pelatiah Glover, late of Springfield, Dec⁴.

By a Bond given to Capt. John Gunn . . . £4 00 00 0
To George Masters, £4; and to Lt. Worthington, £1 9s. 3 5 09 03 0
A Note given by John Glover to David Ingersoll . 6 00 00 0

                                  £15 09 03 0

(5) MARY GLOVER, the second and youngest daughter of Rev. Pelatiah and Hannah (Cullick) Glover, was born in Springfield, April 17, 1672, and died in Hartford, Conn., Aug. 19, 1727, in her 55th year. She and her elder brother Pelatiah were the only children who survived the venerable Springfield pastor. She was provided for in her father's will. (See pp. 465, 466.)

She was married, Nov. 7, 1693, to John Haynes, Esq., of Hartford, Ct., and went there to reside. She was, we are informed, an elegant and accomplished woman, and eminently fitted, both by birth and education, to fill with dignity and grace the exalted station which she attained by marriage. Although she had four children, she has left few descendants, and those of other names.

Children of JOHN, Esq., and MARY (GLOVER) HAYNES, born in Hartford, Conn.:

14. Joseph, b. Sept. 14, 1695; graduated at Yale College in the class of 1714, and intended for the law; died unmarried, in Hartford, Sept. 14, 1716, aged 21 years.
15. Sarah,   b. in 1697; d. Nov. 9, 1724, in her 27th year.
16. Jared,   b. in 1699; died young.
+17. Mary Glover, b. in 1703;
          (1st, Elisha Lord, of Hartford;
     m. { 2d, Capt. Rosewell Saltonstall;
          (3d, Thomas Clap, D.D., of New Haven.

JOHN HAYNES, Esq.,* the husband of Mrs.† Mary Glover, was born in Hartford, Conn., in 1669, and died there, Nov. 27, 1713, aged 44 years, leaving a widow (and, it is said, a son and a daughter, viz., Joseph and Mary). He was the eldest son of Rev. Joseph and Sarah (Lord) Haynes. His father was the third pastor of the first Church in Hartford, and a graduate of Harvard College in 1658; died May 24, 1679, in Hartford. His mother was Sarah Lord, daughter of Richard‡ and Sarah Lord, and granddaughter of Thomas and Dorothy Lord, who were among the early settlers of the Connecticut Colony. John Haynes, their son, was sent to Cambridge to be educated, and graduated there in the class of 1689. He was intended for the ministry, and studied divinity with his father at Hartford. After the decease of the Rev. Pelatiah Glover at Springfield, he was called to labor with that Church, and subsequently to

* Gov. Winthrop states, in his journal, that Mr. John Haynes, a gentleman of great estate, came to New England in the Griffin, a ship of 200 tons burthen, commanded by Capt. Gallop.
"May 14, 1634, The Court chose a New Governor, viz. Thomas Dudley, Esq., Mr. Ludlow Deputy, and Mr. John Haynes Assistant. The 3 mo. 6 day, 1634, a General Court was held at Newtown (Cambridge), when Mr. John Haynes was chosen Governor; R. Bellingham, Deputy Governor; Mr. Hough and Mr. Dummer, Assistants." His residence was at Cambridge.
"3d: 2: 1635. Mr. Haynes, one of our Magistrates, removed with his family to Connecticut." The first year after his removal there, it is stated, he became father of the new Colony of Connecticut.
† She was so styled before marriage, on all records, in that day of titles and ranks.
‡ Richard Lord was born in England, about 1611, and probably married there about 1635. He came to New England with his parents and wife Sarah, and died at New London, Ct., May 17, 1662, aged 51 years. He left three children, of whom was Sarah, who married Rev. Joseph Haynes. Mrs. Sarah Haynes died Nov. 15, 1705, aged 67 years. They had three children, of whom was Judge John Haynes, the husband of Mary Glover. His sister, Sarah Haynes, married Rev. James Pierrepont. Sarah Pelrrepont, daughter of Rev. James and Sarah (Haynes) Pierrepont, and niece of Judge Haynes, married the Rev. Jonathan Edwards, of Northampton, and was the mother of the Hon. Pierrepont Edwards (alias Major Sanford), born April 3, 1750, who married for his first wife Frances Ogden, the second daughter of Moses Ogden, of Elizabethtown, New Jersey, in 1679, and had several children. Among her children was Pierrepont, born in 1784, and whom it has been stated married a Deborah Glover, but of what family or lineage has not been ascertained. It is scarcely possible that she could have been a descendant of the Rev. Pelatiah Glover, yet there are slight gleams of evidence that she may have been a descendant by his grandson John Glover, although there is no direct evidence that he ever had any posterity. He died in 1733, intestate, at the age of 42 years. Pelatiah Glover, his father, settled his estate, and nothing appears on the Probate records (as will be seen) of any wife or children; still the conjecture may be right. Another informant states that Deborah Glover was the second wife of the Hon. Pierrepont Edwards, and that after the decease of his first wife, Mrs. Frances (Ogden) Edwards, who died at New Haven, July 7, 1800, he removed to Bridgeport, Conn., married in his old age his housekeeper, who was Deborah Glover, and died there April 5, 1826, aged 76 years. It is hoped the above accounts may lead to some elucidation of the origin of Deborah Glover, whom it seems married either a grandnephew or a more remote relative of the Hon. John and Mary (Glover) Haynes.

fill the vacancy caused by the death of their former pastor. He preached there a short time with eminent success, but declined to settle among them as their minister. He returned to Hartford, and commenced the study of law. He is said to have maintained an honorable position in the colony, as a Lawyer, Judge Advocate, Judge of the Superior Court, and was an assistant and council for the Governor from 1708 until he died, a period of five years. His line of ancestry was highly distinguished—being the son of a minister of Wethersfield and Hartford, and grandson of the first Governor of the Colony of Connecticut, who in 1634 was Governor of Massachusetts.

[*Fourth Generation.*]

(6) PELATIAH GLOVER, the eldest son of Mr. Pelatiah and Hannah (Parsons) Glover, and the third in the regular line of descent bearing the name, was born in Springfield, Aug. 27, 1687, and died there, Jan. 25, 1754, in his 67th year. He possessed a competent landed estate of inheritance, and made accessions to it by purchase.

He was, it is supposed, thrice married, as there are three marriages and intentions recorded of him—two of them in an almost incredibly short space of time. Springfield Records are as follows: "Mr. Pelatiah Glover and Mary Wright, of the Elbows* so called, were married July 4, 1735." They lived probably at or near the Elbows, as the death of Mary does not appear on the Springfield Records. He was published, according to the record of intentions, "to Martha Ould, widow, entered Dec. 14, 1748." And, third, the banns of matrimony were entered by Mr. Pelatiah Glover and the widow Hannah Burt, of Hartford, Ct., March 31, 1749, and notification posted April 1, 1749. To this last wife he was married May 1, 1749; and he lived with her five years, he dying in 1754, as will be seen by his will and other evidence. There is no record to be found of any children by any of the wives, and no proof that he ever had any. Accordingly this line appears, from all that has been gathered, to be extinct.

Dec. 3, 1740, there is recorded a quit-claim deed from Pelatiah

---

* *Elbows.*—The line marked by the Chicopee River through the town of Palmer early bestowed upon that tract the name of the Elbows. It was settled as early as 1727, and afterwards called Palmer.—*Holland's " Western Massachusetts."*

42

Glover to his brother Samuel Glover, of all his lands in Springfield and Brimfield, which said lands were given him by his honored father, Pelatiah Glover, of Springfield, gentleman, deceased. Deed executed April 4, 1740.

The name of Hannah Burt before her first marriage has not been ascertained. She appears to have been thrice married: first, to —————— Burt; second, to Pelatiah Glover, in 1749; and, third, about one year after Mr. Glover's decease, to Noah Brooks, of Springfield June 11, 1755. There appears to have been no other Hannah Glover at that time to whom the record of this last marriage could relate.

Will of Pelatiah Glover, 3d.

In the name of God Amen. This Twenty Fourth day of October Anno Dom* One Thousand Seven Hundred and Fifty three, I Pelatiah Glover of Springfield in the County of Hampshire and in the Province of the Massachusetts Bay in New England, Yeoman, being weak of body but of sound and perfect mind and memory: Thanks be given to God. And therefore calling to mind the mortality of my body and knowing that it is appointed unto all men once to die : I do therefore constitute, ordain and make this my Last Will and Testament. That is to say.

Principally and first of all I recommend my soul into the hands of God that gave it ; and my body I recommend to the Earth to be buried in a decent Christian burial at the discretion of my Executrix hereinafter named.

And as to such worldly Goods and Estate with which God hath been pleased to bless me in this life, I give and bequeathe and dispose thereof in the manner following.

Imp'. I give and bequeathe to Hannah my dear and well beloved wife and to her heirs and assigns forever, All my Real Estate, Lands and Tenements, Edifices and Buildings, and all Rights and Titles in Common and Undivided Lands wheresoever and whatsoever, in the Town of Springfield or elsewhere, she paying all my just debts. That any of my Lands be disposed of, for the payment of my said debts, that, then my Meadow by the Town Street, opposite to the Ferry Lane and my Lot in the Plain field next to the Great River be sold and disposed of for the payment of the same, and I do hereby order and empower my Executrix to sell and dispose of the same accordingly.

Further also my Will is, and I do hereby order that in case my said Wife or her heirs shall at any time after my decease see cause to sell my Home Lot where I now dwell, that then my brother Samuel Glover or his heirs that do or shall possess his new Home Lot where he now dwells, shall have the offer and refusal of my said Home Lot before any other person or persons.

Also I give to my said loving wife all my moveable and personal Estate, Clothing Goods, debts and chattells to dispose of, as she shall see cause.

And I do hereby constitute, ordain and appoint and make my said loving wife Hannah Glover sole Executrix of this my Last Will and Testament. And I do hereby utterly revoke and make null and void all other and former Wills, Testaments, Legacies and bequests by me heretofore made and given, and Executors before made and named.

And I do hereby ratify and confirm this and none other to be my last Will and Testament. In confirmation of all of which I have hereunto set my hand and affixed my seal the day and date above written. (October 24th, 1753.)

Signed, sealed, published and pronounced and declared by the said Pelatiah Glover to be his last Will and Testament, in the presence of Us the subscribers, who signed as witnesses hereto in the presence of the Testator. PELATIAH GLOVER, and a Seal.

> Joshua Lamb,
> David Wright, } *Witnesses.*
> Cornelius Jones,

At a County Court of Probate holden at Northampton, within and for the County of Hampshire, on the second Tuesday of March, Anno Domª 1754, I Timothy Dwight, Esq., Judge of Probate of said Court, the foregoing Will was presented for Probate by the Executrix therein named, and Messrs. Joshua Lamb and David Wright, two of the witnesses of the same, personally appearing made oath that they saw Pelatiah Glover, the Testator, sign, seal, and heard him declare and pronounce the same to be his last Will and Testament. And that he was of sound mind and memory when he did it, and that they, together with Mr. Cornelius Jones, all signed as witnesses to the same in the said Testator's presence.

At the same time, and in as much as there have been sundry objections, by some of the Testator's surviving relatives as to the Testator's capacity at the time of Executing this Will, the Probate of the same Will has been suspended, until the Second Tuesday of October following, and opportunities given them to produce Witnesses and proof of the same; but having hitherto failed to do it, the said Will is now, at a Court of Probate holden at Northampton within and for the County of Hampshire, on the Second Tuesday of October, being the 8th day of said month, Anno Domª 1754, Timothy Dwight, Esq., Judge of said Court, Ratified, approved and confirmed as the last Will and Testament of said Deceased. pr TIMOTHY DWIGHT.

Hampshire ss. Probate office, July 25, 1853. I hereby certify that the foregoing extracts from the Records of said office are truly copied.
SAMUEL F. LYMAN, *Reg. Prob.*

(7) THOMAS GLOVER, the second son of Mr. Pelatiah and Hannah (Parsons) Glover, was born in Springfield, Nov. 16, 1688, and died in Wilbraham, Dec. 30, 1775, aged 87 years. He was never married. He inherited large landed estates from his father, by deeds of gift, bearing dates Dec. 24, 1726, and Dec. 10, 1728.

In 1737, he came in possession of several tracts of land by a quitclaim from his brother Pelatiah Glover and his three sisters. John

Ashley, Esq., and Hannah Ashley his wife in her right, both of West-field; Benjamin Horton, yeoman, and Mary Horton his wife in her right; Pelatiah Glover, glazier; Samuel Glover, yeoman; and Abigail Glover, spinster, all of Springfield, in the County of Hampshire, quit claim their rights in certain parcels of land belonging to their inheritance, to their brother Thomas Glover. Date of deed, Feb. 21, 1737.

He purchased, under date of May 30, 1755, other lands in Springfield; consideration, twenty-seven pounds.

He made the following disposal of his remaining estate, under date of April 6, 1772 : "Thomas Glover, of Wilbraham, in the County of Hampshire, in New England, one of the four sons of Mr. Pelatiah Glover, of Springfield," conveys to John Glover, of Wilbraham, his nephew, son of his brother Samuel Glover, for two thousand pounds, all his lands in Springfield—his home lot, with all the buildings thereon standing—and all his moveable estate, outdoor and indoor, of whatever name, nature or kind, the same to be the property of the said John Glover at his decease, with all his lands in Wilbraham and elsewhere; reserving to himself, during his natural life, the use and income of the whole of said described premises. Signed by himself; and acknowledged, in person, Nov. 3, 1773. He lived three years after this date, and his estate is known to have descended to John Glover his nephew.

(8)   JOHN GLOVER, the third son of Mr. Pelatiah and Hannah (Parsons) Glover, was born in Springfield, Sept. 12, 1690, and died there, March 27, 1733, aged 42 years. It is not known that he was ever married. He was a landholder by inheritance and by deeds of purchase.

From his father, in 1717, he received by deed of gift a home lot of four acres of land for his homestead "as an absolute estate of inheritance." It was situated on the east side of the Great River, at the northerly end of the town of Springfield, on Plot street.

In 1719 he purchased of Henry Wright the tenth part of "a saw mill which now standeth, and is at the place commonly called Sconongonuck, on the River commonly called Chicopy River." It appears that he occupied his homestead and attended to his farm and mill about fourteen years. He may have had a wife and children, but nothing further has been gathered of him, and nothing is known with certainty of any descendants.* He died intestate, and administration was committed to his father, as appears in the following record:

Power of Administration of the Goods, Chattels, Rights and Credits of all and singular of the estate of John Glover, late of Springfield, Dec. intestate, Husbandman, was granted to Mr. Pelatiah Glover of said Springfield, the father of said deceased, and bonds taken for his true performance of said trust. (Hampshire ss. Vol. 5, page 182.) *Northampton, May* 8, 1733.

(9) HANNAH GLOVER, the eldest daughter of Mr. Pelatiah and Hannah (Parsons) Glover, was born in Springfield, Dec. 27, 1693, and died in Westfield.

She was married, Nov. 12, 1735, to John Ashley, son of Robert and Hannah† (Glover) Ashley, of New Haven, who removed to Springfield in 1663, and thence to Westfield. John Ashley, their son, was born in Westfield, June 27, 1669, and died there, April 17, 1759, in his 90th year. By inheritance Hannah Glover was a landholder. In 1737, after the decease of her father, she, with her husband John Ashley, Esq., both of Westfield, conveyed her rights in certain parcels of land, to her brother Thomas Glover, of Wilbraham, deed bearing date Feb. 21, 1737. It is supposed there were no children by this marriage—none having been identified.

JOHN ASHLEY was twice married. First, to Mary Dewey, Sept. 8, 1692, at the age of 23 years. They had five children—viz., Lydia, John, Moses, Ebenezer and Roger. Mrs. Mary Ashley died March 1, 1735; and Nov. 12, of the same year, he married Hannah Glover for his second wife. He was an extensive landholder, and lived on the estate of his inheritance.

(10) MARY GLOVER, second daughter of Mr. Pelatiah and Hannah (Parsons) Glover, was born in Springfield, Aug. 25, 1695, and died there, May 16, 1751, in her 56th year.

She was married, Nov. 8, 1716, to Benjamin Horton. He died in Springfield, Aug. 29th, 1747. They had two children:

18. Benjamin, b. in 1718; married.
19. Mary,　　b. in 1720; died unmarried.

---

* Deborah Glover, who married Pierrepont Edwards, and to whom reference is made in a note on page 480, may have been, as is there intimated, a granddaughter of the above John Glover.

† A daughter of Henry and Helena Glover, of New Haven, Ct.; born there, May 23, 1646, and baptized May 26, 1646, by Rev. John Davenport.

(12) ABIGAIL GLOVER, the third and youngest daughter of
Mr. Pelatiah and Hannah (Parsons) Glover, was born in Springfield,
July 9, 1702, and died there, Aug. 31, 1752, aged 50 years.

She was married, May 3, 1747, to Jonathan Mills, Esq., of Brookfield.   He was the son of Capt. Mills, who formerly lived in Quincy,
and was born there about 1702; graduated at Harvard College in
the class of 1723, and died in Brookfield, in 1773, aged 71 years.

(13) SAMUEL GLOVER, the fifth son of Mr. Pelatiah and
Hannah (Parsons) Glover, was born in Springfield, Dec. 16, 1706,
and died there—date of death not ascertained.

He was a landholder, by inheritance and by purchase.   In 1726
he received a portion of land from his father (see deed of Pelatiah
Glover to his four sons on page 475); also other lands, in 1736,
from his father, by deed of gift, about one year previous to his decease.   In 1740, three years after the decease of Mr. Pelatiah Glover,
he received by quit claim, from John Ashley and Hannah his wife
(alias Hannah Glover in her right), and Benjamin Horton and Mary
Horton (" the said Mary being the daughter of Mr. Pelatiah Glover,
late of Springfield, Gentleman, deceased") in her right, several tracts
of land in Springfield, said lands being their inheritance from the
estate of their honored father the said Mr. Pelatiah Glover; also
from his sister Abigail Glover, spinster, the same, and at the same
time—date of deeds April 4 and April 7, 1740.   In 1755, the 30th
day of May, he confirmed, for twenty-seven pounds, a portion of land
to his brother Thomas Glover, of Wilbraham.

In December, 1765, there appears a conveyance from Capt. Samuel
Day and his wife to Samuel Glover, of Springfield; and at the same
time Thomas Day and wife, of Colchester, Conn., convey to Samuel
Glover a tract of land; which lands have been passed and owned
principally in the male line.

He was married, Dec. 14, 1749, at the age of 43 years, to Joyce
(Newcomb) Jones, widow of ——— Jones, of Springfield.   She was
daughter of Joseph and Joyce (Butler) Newcomb, of Edgartown,
Martha's Vineyard, Mass.; born there about 1712, and died in
Springfield, Oct. 22, 1774.   She was twice married.   First to ———
Jones, of Springfield, and was residing there in 1749, after his death,
and at the time of her marriage with Samuel Glover.   Her father,
Joseph Newcomb, was the son of Andrew and Anna (Bayze) New-

comb, who were married there in 1680, and died between 1701 and 1710. Her mother, Joyce Butler, was a daughter of Capt. John Butler, of Edgartown, one of the early settlers of Dorchester, a son of Nicholas Butler, and came with his parents to New England in 1637. "Nicholas Butler came from Eastwell, in Kent, and was styled yeoman. He embarked with his wife, three children and five servants, at Sandwich (Eng.), in the Hercules, in June, 1637; joined the Church after his arrival, and was made freeman March 14, 1638–39. He had a grant of land at Dorchester Neck in 1637, and in 1647 was proprietor in the Great Lots. The brook which crosses Cottage street was named from him. His wife's name was Joyce. In 1651 he deputed his son John his attorney, and went to Martha's Vineyard, where he died, leaving children. He sold his property in Dorchester, in 1652, to William Ware. He owned land on Duncan's, now Spurr's Hill or Codman Hill." (*Hist. of Dor.*, page 109.) From other sources it has been gathered that he was a man of high respectability and distinction, and had the prefix of Mr., which descended to his sons—viz., John, the grandfather of Mrs. Glover; and Henry, who became a teacher in Dorchester as early as 1648, and of whom it is written that he had previously received the degree of M.A. from the Cambridge University in England. He married, after his arrival here, Anne, a daughter, it is believed, of John Holman, of Dorchester, and was employed in preaching and teaching until the year 1652, at which time he returned to England and settled in the ministry—first at Yeovil, in Somersetshire, and subsequently at Withamfrary, about five miles from Frome, where he died, April 24, 1696, aged 72 years. (See Palmer's *Nonconformist Memorial*, Vol. 2, p. 388.)

Children of SAMUEL and JOYCE (NEWCOMB-JONES) GLOVER:

20. Eleanor, b. Aug. 30, 1750; d. since 1800, unmarried.
+21. John,   b. May   3, 1753; m. Mercy Colton, of Wilbraham.

(17) MARY GLOVER HAYNES, only daughter of the Hon. John and Mary (Glover) Haynes, was born in Hartford, Conn., in 1703, and died at New Haven, Sept. 23, 1769, in her 66th year.

She was thrice married, and had in all five children. May 2, 1723, she was married to Elisha Lord, son of Richard and Sarah Lord, of Hartford; born there, March 15, 1701–2; died April 15, 1725, aged 24 years. He was a lineal descendant of Thomas and Dorothy

Lord, already referred to. Richard Lord, their son, was born in England in 1611, came with his parents to New England with his wife Sarah about 1635, and settled at Hartford. He died in New London, Ct., May 17, 1662. Richard Lord, son of Richard and Sarah Lord, who was born in Hartford in or about 1670, and died there, Jan. 29, 1711–12, aged 42 years, was the father of Mr. Elisha Lord, the first husband of Mary Glover Haynes. They had one son, born in Hartford:

+22. John Haynes, b. Jan. 13, 1725 ; m. Rachel Knowles.

Mrs. Mary (Glover-Haynes) Lord married a second time, April 6, 1727, Capt. Rosewell Saltonstall, with whom she lived eleven years. He was the eldest son of Gov. Gurdon Saltonstall, by Elizabeth Rosewell his second wife, and was born in New London, Conn., Jan. 19, 1701–2; graduated at Harvard College in the class of 1720; married, in 1727, and settled in Brandford, Conn., on an estate which he inherited from his maternal grandfather, William Rosewell. On the west side of this estate is the beautiful Lake Saltonstall, situated in the town of Brandford, and was doubtless named in honor of him. He is described as a man of irreproachable Christian character, amiable in all the relations of life, and was held in high estimation both in New London, his native city, and at Brandford, where he went to reside. He died at New London, Oct. 1, 1738, while there on a visit to his relatives, in his 37th year. They had four children, born in Brandford:

23. Rosewell, b. Aug. 31, 1728 ; grad. Yale Coll. 1751; died unm. at Brandford, Ct., Jan. 25, 1788, aged 60 years 6 mos. After leaving college he is said to have become imbecile, and a guardian was placed over him.
24. Mary, b. in 1730 ; m. Col. Nathan Whiting, of New Haven, Ct. ; grad. Yale Coll. 1743 ; died in 1771.
25. Sarah, b. in 1732 ; m. Jonathan Fitch, of New Haven ; grad. Yale Coll. 1748; became a lawyer, and settled in New Haven ; died there in 1793.
26. Katharine, b. in 1734 ; m. Jonathan Welles, Esq., of Glastenbury, Ct. ; grad. Yale Coll. 1751; studied law, and practised successfully in his native town ; died there in 1792.

Gov. Gurdon Saltonstall, the father of Capt. Rosewell Saltonstall, was born at Haverhill, Mass., in 1666; H. C. 1684; and died in New London, very suddenly, of apoplexy, Sept. 20, 1724, aged about 58 years. He was buried with civil and military honors. His re-

mains were deposited in a tomb which he had caused to be excavated
in the burial yard for himself and family, and in which his second
wife and her infant child had been previously laid. He was intended for a minister of the gospel, and studied divinity after leaving
college. In May, 1688, he received a unanimous call to settle in
New London, Ct. He accepted, and was ordained there, Nov. 19,
1691. For a time he preached successfully.

"He is said to have been an advocate of vigorous ecclesiastical
authority; always striving to exalt the ministerial office, to maintain
its dignity, and to enlarge the powers of ecclesiastical bodies, which
gave him unbounded popularity among his clerical brethren. Such
were his views of law and order, both in Church and State, and of
the discipline to be employed in maintaining them, and such his
regard for official dignity and privilege, that he acquired the' reputation of being severe and imperious, and of seeking self aggrandizement."

Nov. 27, 1707, on the death of Gov. Winthrop, Mr. Saltonstall
was elected his successor, and took the oath of office as Governor of
Connecticut on Jan. 1, 1708. He was very popular as a Governor,
and was successively elected to that office, and continued in it until
his decease, a period of 16 years.

He was thrice married, and had in all ten children—five by his
first, and five by his second wife. By his first wife, Jerusha Richards,
he had no surviving male heir; by his second, Elizabeth Rosewell, he
had four sons, three of whom survived him. In his will he bequeathed the Rosewell estate in Brandford to his eldest son Rosewell, who
settled there; also his manor house and estate in Killingly, near
Pontefract, in Yorkshire, England. To his son Nathaniel Saltonstall, his farm in Cunchencaug (Durham). To his son Gurdon, his
lands at New London; to his three daughters by his first wife, his
estate at Wethersfield, that was their mother's, and also provides
amply for his daughter Katharine by wife Elizabeth Rosewell. He
built a beautiful mansion on the borders of Lake Saltonstall, in
Brandford, which, it is said, was decorated with a variety of antique
ornaments, and the walls adorned with grotesque pictures, Spanish
leather tapestry, &c. The tablet that surrounds his tomb is engraved
with his coat of arms, and the following inscription appears on it:
"Here lyeth ye body of ye Hon. Gurdon Saltonstall, Esq., Governor
of Connecticut, who died Sept. 20, 1724, in the 59th year of his

age." He derived his name Gurdon from his mother's family. His third wife survived him, and died in Boston, Mass. She was a daughter of William and Mary (Lawrence) Whittingham, and widow of William Clark, of Boston.

Madam Saltonstall, the widow of Capt. Rosewell Saltonstall, was married to her third husband, Thomas Clap, D.D., President of Yale College, Feb. 5, 1741. There were no children by this marriage. He was the son of Deacon Stephen Clap, of Scituate, who with his father Thomas Clap came from England to New England in the early settlement of the Colony, previous to 1639, and settled in Scituate about 1640. President Clap was born at Scituate, June 26, 1703, and died there, Jan. 7, 1767, in his 64th year, while on a visit to his native town. He was prepared for college by Rev. Mr. Eels, of Scituate, graduated at Harvard College in 1722, and gave himself to the ministry of the gospel. In 1726 he received a unanimous call from the Church at Windham, Ct., and after preaching there to great acceptance, was ordained as their minister and teacher the same year. He continued in the ministry fourteen years, and in 1739 was elected to fill the office of President of Yale College, at New Haven, and in 1740 accepted the high trust. It is said of him that he became one of the most distinguished men of his time for talents and learning, and was an honor to the office he was called to fill, continuing in the Presidential chair until 1764, a period of twenty-four years, when he tendered his resignation, with the intention of retiring to private life. He subsequently went to visit his relatives and friends at Scituate, where he died, as already stated. His wife survived him about one year. President Stiles, his second successor, ranks him among the first men of the age for learning, and as a philosopher equalled by no person in America, " except the most learned Professor Winthrop." He was succeeded in the office of President of Yale College by the Rev. Naphthali Daggett. Other writers represent him as a Divine of distinguished merit, and highly learned in all the various branches of knowledge, particularly mathematics, astronomy, natural and moral philosophy, history, the civil and canon law; as an earnest and powerful preacher, of exemplary piety, and of remarkable industry and ingenuity. He constructed the first Orrery or Planetarium made in America. Among his published works and manuscripts are the following: "A brief History of Yale College," "A brief History and Vindication of the Doctrines established in the Churches in New England,"

" Two Sermons," and " Upon the Nature and Motions of the Meteors which are above the Atmosphere." He had prepared materials for the history of Connecticut, which collection was carried off by Gen. Tryon, in his expedition against New Haven.

His wife was a woman distinguished for her exalted worth and piety. Her funeral was attended by the Rev. Chauncy Whittlesey, pastor of the first Church in New Haven; and a discourse preached on the occasion of her death, which was printed in 1769 by Thomas and Samuel Green, together with a biographical sketch of her life.

[*Fifth Generation.*]

(21) JOHN GLOVER, youngest child and only son of Samuel and Joyce (Newcomb-Jones) Glover, was born in Wilbraham, May 3, 1753, and died there, July 21, 1830, in his 78th year. He possessed a large landed property, and lived and died on the estate of his inheritance. During the War of the Revolution, when the American troops were stationed on Dorchester Heights, he served as Lieutenant of Infantry, and continued there until Boston was evacuated by the British troops. Subsequently he was commissioned as a Lieutenant of Cavalry, and remained in office until he tendered his resignation.

He was married, in 1778, to Mercy Colton, daughter of Benjamin and Mercy Colton, of Springfield; born there in 1757, and died in Wilbraham, Oct. 1, 1836, aged 79 years. They had twelve children.

Children of JOHN and MERCY (COLTON) GLOVER, born in Wilbraham:

27. Samuel, b. March 24, 1779; d. Feb. 14, 1829, in his 50th year.
+28. Thomas, b. May 28, 1781; m. Flavia Warriner.
29. Pelatiah, } b. in 1783; { d. in 1791.
30. Joyce,   }   { d. soon.
+31. Mary, b. March 28, 1785; m. Trueman Sweet, Hartford, Ct.
+32. Sophia, b. Dec. 29, 1786; m. William Adams, Suffield, Ct.
+33. Roxana, b. Dec. 1, 1788; m. { 1st, Ira Stacey, Belchertown; { 2d, Jason Miller.
+34. John Joseph, b. May 26, 1791; m. Agnes Jane Larkin, widow.
+35. Erastus, b. Feb. 9, 1793; m. Lucinda Bolton, Wilbraham.
+36. Joyce, b. April 12, 1795; m. John Thayer, of Monson.
+37. Ralph, b. Oct. 28, 1797; m. Amelia Evans, New York.
38. Eleanor, b. Sept. 12, 1803; d. Sept. 1, 1805.

(22) JOHN HAYNES LORD, only son of Elisha and Mary Glover (Haynes) Lord, was born in Hartford, Jan. 13, 1725, and died there, in March, 1796, aged 72 years.

He was married, about 1750, to Rachel Knowles, daughter of Capt. John and Rachel (Olcutt) Knowles, of Hartford. No further account of him has been obtained. It is supposed he has descendants residing in Hartford.

[Sixth Generation.]

(28) THOMAS GLOVER, the second son of John and Mercy (Colton) Glover, was born in Wilbraham, May 28, 1781, and died there, Dec. 1, 1849, in his 69th year. He inherited from his father the homestead estate with the ancient mansion, and possessed other landed estates. For many years he kept a public house at his paternal residence.

He was married, Feb. 10, 1803, to Flavia Warriner, daughter of Moses and Mary (Warner) Warriner, of Wilbraham; born there in 1783, and died Nov. 4, 1864, aged 81 years.

Children of THOMAS and FLAVIA (WARRINER) GLOVER, born in Wilbraham:

39. Elmira,   b. Oct. 19, 1803; d. Aug. 19, 1805.
+40. Thomas,   b. Jan. 30, 1806; m. Lydia Knowlton.
+41. Henry,   b. June 12, 1808; m. { 1st, Clarissa Ingraham;
                                      { 2d, Sophronia Hoar;
                                      { 3d, Amanda Arnold.
+42. Elmira,   b. Aug. 11, 1810; m. Roderick Collins, of Ludlow.
+43. Pelatiah, b. Aug. 24, 1816; m. Abiah Allard.
44. Perlin,   b. Nov. 26, 1821; d. Jan. 24, 1823.

(31) MARY GLOVER, the eldest daughter of John and Mercy (Colton) Glover, was born in Wilbraham, March 28, 1785, and died in Hartford, Conn., Sept. 15, 1848, in her 64th year.

She was married, in 1829, to Trueman Sweet, of Hartford, and went there to reside. They had two children, born there as follows:

+45. Mary Anne, b. in 1830; m. James B. Shulters.
46. Caroline,   b. in 1832; m. Norman Boardman; no issue.

(32) SOPHIA GLOVER, the second daughter of John and Mercy (Colton) Glover, was born in Wilbraham, Dec. 29, 1786, and died in Suffield, Conn., July 31, 1839, in her 54th year.

She was married, about 1819, to William Adams, of Suffield, Ct. He died in 1851, aged 58 years. They had four children, and all but one died young or in infancy:

47. Trueman, b. in 1821; d. Oct. 31, 1839, aged 18 years.
48. (Second), b. in 1824; d. in infancy.
49. (Third), b. in 1826; d. in infancy.
50. Elizabeth, b. in 1828; resides in Hartford, Ct.

(33) ROXANNA GLOVER, the third daughter of John and Mercy (Colton) Glover, was born in Wilbraham, Dec. 1, 1788, and is now residing in Williamsburg, Hampshire Co., Mass.

She has been twice married, and has had four children; is now (1867) a widow. She was married, Jan. 10, 1809, to Ira Stacey, son of Mark and Julia (Root) Stacey, of Belchertown, Mass.; born there, May 8, 1789, and died May 20, 1838, aged 49 years. He was an extensive landholder, and occupied himself in agricultural pursuits. They had four children, born in Belchertown, viz.:

+51. John, b. June 15, 1810; m. Betsey Matilda Doolittle, Belchertown.
52. Ira, b. Sept. 6, 1815; d. in 1828, aged 13 years.
+53. Harriet, b. June 3, 1821; m. Hon. Geo. T. Spencer, Saybrook, Ct.
54. Samuel, b. May 27, 1827; m. Terissa Giles, of New Salem; in 1851 removed to Wisconsin, and died there in 1856, aged 29.

Mrs. Roxanna (Glover) Stacey was married, a second time, to Jason Miller, in the year 1844, son of John and Hannah (Root) Miller, of Northampton. He was born in Williamsburg, July 25, 1792, and died there, June 7, 1862, aged nearly 70 years. There were no children by the last marriage.

(34) JOHN JOSEPH GLOVER, the third son of John and Mercy (Colton) Glover, was born in Wilbraham, May 26, 1791, and died at Natchez, Mississippi, Feb. 2, 1828. He was an architect, and fell from the roof of a building, causing his death.

He was married, about 1820, to Agnes Jane Larkin, widow, and had by her three children, as follows:

+55. John George, b. May 8, 1821; m.
56. Mary M., b. Jan. 10, 1823; m. —— McDonald, in 1854.
+57. Francis Larkin, b. July 31, 1825; d. October, 1856, at Natchez.

(35) ERASTUS GLOVER, the fourth son of John and Mercy (Colton) Glover, was born in Wilbraham, Feb. 9, 1793, and died there in 1842.

43

He was married to Lucinda Bolton, of Wilbraham, about 1810.

Children of ERASTUS and LUCINDA (BOLTON) GLOVER, born in Wilbraham:

58. Adaline,   b. in   1812; m. Reuben Underwood.
59. Benjamin, b. Sept. 10, 1814; d. since 1853.
60. Albert,   b. Sept. 8, 1816; d. since 1853.
61. Samuel,   b. Feb.   1, 1824; was a master mariner; drowned, in 1861, when sailing from Washington to New York, aged 37 years; unmarried.

(36)   JOYCE GLOVER, the fourth daughter of John and Mercy (Colton) Glover, was born in Wilbraham, April 12, 1795, and died in Monson, Jan. 19, 1843, in her 48th year.

She was married, in 1815, to John Thayer, of Monson, and went there to reside. He died in Monson, Nov. 13, 1839. They had three children, born in Monson:

62. Edwin, b. in 1817; d. May 21, 1840, aged 23 years.
63. Emery, b. in 1821; d. Jan. 8, 1846, aged 25 years.
64. John, b. in 1824; resides in Springfield.

(37)   RALPH GLOVER, M.D., the fifth and youngest son of John and Mercy (Colton) Glover, was born in Wilbraham, Oct. 28, 1797, and resides in the City of New York. He is a retired physician. He commenced his early education under the instruction of the Rev. Ezra Witter, of the North Parish of Wilbraham, and at the close of the second term entered the academy at Monson, and a few months after left there to attend the academy at Westfield, where he continued during two terms. He then removed to the town of Suffield, in Connecticut, where he continued for one year, to attend a private school under the instruction of the Rev. Ebenezer Gay, the officiating clergyman of that town. In the spring of 1817 he commenced teaching by taking charge of a grammar school in Somerville, the shire town of Somerset County, New Jersey. He closed his engagement in Somerville after one year, returned to his native town, and in the spring of 1818 commenced the study of law, in the office of William Knight, a counsellor at law and practising attorney in that town, and continued his reading one year. Subsequently, in 1819, he went to Palmer, and prosecuted his law studies in the office and under the instruction of James Stebbins, Esq., and at the same time engaged again in teaching a grammar school in that village.

Having completed his law studies, and not finding them congenial to his taste, he suspended study for a short time, before deciding upon any other profession. In the autumn of 1822, he travelled South, and visited a brother at Natchez, Mississippi, arriving there in the winter of 1822. In the following spring he returned to Massachusetts, and having decided upon adopting the profession of medicine, he commenced his studies at Somerville, N. J., and pursued them there for a time. His first course of medical lectures was attended at the Medical College of the Western District of New York, at Fairfield. He continued his medical studies, after the course, with Joseph White, M.D., Professor of Surgery in the College, and the following winter of 1825 attended his last course of medical lectures at Jefferson College, Philadelphia, where he graduated in medicine and surgery in the spring of 1826.

He commenced the practice of his profession in the summer of 1826, at Brentsville, the shire town of Prince William County, in Virginia. An epidemic disease prevailed through that section of the county during the succeeding autumn, which afforded an opportunity to test his medical skill, and he soon found himself engaged in an extensive and very laborious practice, which proved too much for his physical abilities, and near the close of the epidemic he was himself attacked with the disease. This prostrated him for a time, and so impaired his health as to render him unable to endure the hardships of a country physician, and he was compelled to abandon the further practice of his profession in that locality.

At this crisis he received an invitation from a medical friend to join him in opening and establishing a drug store at Harper's Ferry, in Virginia. He acceded to the proposition, and they commenced business there in the spring of 1827; but not having fully recovered from the debilitating effects of his recent sickness, he found himself unable to attend to the business, and continued there but a short time. He disposed of his interest, and returned to his father's in Wilbraham, in the autumn of 1827.

In the spring of 1828, he took up his residence in the City of New York, commencing the practice of his profession there, and continued it until the year 1851, a period of twenty-three years, with only two interruptions. In the winter of 1839, after ten years of uninterrupted practice, his health requiring a change from the confinement and unremitting attention incumbent on its practical duties, he left the city on an excursion to the Southern States. He passed one month in the City of Charleston, S. C.; thence he went to Key West, Florida; thence to Havana, returning through New Orleans, visiting Texas, and returning to New York through New Orleans, St. Louis, Cincinnati, Wheeling and Baltimore. He entered again on his practice with recruited health and with renewed vigor, and continued it until the year 1849, ten years longer. In the autumn of that year he visited California, passed the winter, and returned again to New York in the spring of 1850, resuming his practice and business, and continued it until the spring of 1853. The following autumn he visited England, for the purpose of making inquiries in relation to the Glover genealogy and the English branches of the name, but was prevented from pursuing the subject as extensively as he desired, on account of a severe illness which he endured on his passage out. He however was enabled, by perseverance, to accomplish something, and to make some valuable additions to the collections of the Glover history. On arriving at Liverpool, he proceeded by railway to Chester, a distance of about eighteen miles. He there examined many old wills and ancient documents. He saw and examined the will of Mr. Thomas Glover, which has been printed on page 32; and adds his testimony to the imperfect condition in which it is now found. He describes it as being written on parchment, and much of it nearly destroyed by damp and mould. As there had been a copy taken previous, and brought here in 1848, it was unnecessary for him to obtain another, and he proceeded to London, where he procured the will of Mr. Thomas Glover, grandson of the former (see pages 90 to 95). He was compelled by illness to forego any further investigations, or to collect any more of the Glover history in London, and returned at once to New York.

In the year 1854 he disposed of his professional business in New York, and removed with his family to Wilbraham, in Massachusetts. He was warmly greeted and welcomed back to this place of his birth and boyhood, by the citizens, who conferred on him such offices of trust and honor as were in their power. He was chosen and served as Town Clerk, was commissioned a Justice of the Peace, and elected to other honorary offices in the affairs of the town during his residence there of nearly five years. In the year 1858 he returned again to New York, and is now residing there.

He was married, Feb. 9, 1830, to Amelia Evans, daughter of Dr. Joseph Evans, of New York City; born there in 1808.

Children of Dr. RALPH and AMELIA (EVANS) GLOVER, born in New York City:

+65. Louis Napoleon, b. Feb. 16, 1831 ; d. June 16, 1860, aged 29.
+66. John Joseph,   b. Aug. 15, 1833 ; m. Marguerretta Terhune.
  67. Maria Amelia Caroline, b. Sept. 9, 1836.
  68. Julia Emma,   b. March 4, 1839.
  69. Mary Sweet,   b. Jan. 18, 1841.
  70. Rodolph,   b. Dec. 11, 1843.
  71. Henry Clay,   b. Oct. 20, 1847.

[Seventh Generation.]

(40) THOMAS GLOVER, the eldest son of Thomas and Flavia (Warriner) Glover, was born in Wilbraham, Jan. 30, 1806, and is now residing there. In 1854, and for some years previous, he transacted business and resided in the City of New York. He possesses a competent landed estate.

He was married, Dec. 1, 1831, to Lydia Knowlton, daughter of Nathan and Lydia (Learned) Knowlton. They have had five children, born in New York City.

Children of THOMAS and LYDIA (KNOWLTON) GLOVER:

+72. Jane Eliza,   b. Oct. 20, 1832 ; m. Elisha B. Bloomer.
+73. James Noble, b. Aug. 15, 1835 ; in U. S. service, Fort Warren.
  74. William Henry, b. Dec. 30, 1837 ; d. April 13, 1839.
  75. Harriet Almira, b. Sept. 24, 1845.
  76. Thomas Nathan, b. Oct. 29, 1852.

(41) HENRY GLOVER, the second son of Thomas and Flavia (Warriner) Glover, was born in Wilbraham, June 12, 1808, and is now residing in Brattleboro', Vermont; is a druggist and apothecary. He commenced business in Springfield, Mass., and resided there until 1852, when he removed with his family to Brattleboro,' and established himself in the same business there.

He has been thrice married. First, to Clarissa Ingraham, March 7, 1833, daughter of Ebenezer and Philena Ingraham, of Monson; born there about 1810, and died at Wilbraham, Feb. 1, 1834. Second, April 5, 1836, to Sophronia Hoar, daughter of Nathan and Anna Hoar, of Lebanon, N. Y. She died at Springfield, Feb. 14, 1848. Third, Aug. 8, 1849, to Amanda Arnold, daughter of Samuel and Armitta Arnold, of Somes, Conn.; no issue. By the second marriage there is one son, viz.:

43*

+77. George Henry, b. June 17, 1839.

(42) ELMIRA GLOVER, the second daughter of Thomas and
Flavia (Warriner) Glover, was born in Wilbraham, Aug. 11, 1810,
and died in Ludlow, Sept. 28, 1834, in her 24th year.

She was married, Nov. 27, 1832, to Roderick Collins, of Ludlow.
They had one son:

78. Dwight Marshall, b. in 1834; resides in Pittsfield; is a manufacturer of woolens.

(43) PELATIAH GLOVER, the third son of Thomas and
Flavia (Warriner) Glover, was born in Wilbraham, Aug. 24, 1816,
and resides there at the present time.

He was married, about 1840, to Abiah Allard, a cousin on his
mother's side. She was born, April 9, 1817, and died at Springfield,
Aug. 24, 1861, in her 45th year. They had no children. He enlisted in the volunteer service of the United States at Wilbraham,
Dec. 18, 1861, and was enrolled as a private in the 31st Regiment
of Mass. Vols.; was taken sick at New Orleans, and discharged for
disability, June 22, 1862.

(45) MARY ANNE SWEET, eldest daughter of Trueman and
Mary (Glover) Sweet, was born in Hartford, in 1830, and died there
since 1853.

She was married to James B. Shulters, of Hartford, about 1850.
They have had two children, a son and daughter—names and dates
not reported.

(51) JOHN ·STACEY, the eldest son of Ira and Roxanna
(Glover) Stacey, was born in Belchertown, June 15, 1810, and is
now residing in Syracuse, N. Y. He was graduated at Yale College,
in the class of 1836.

He married Betsy Matilda Doolittle, daughter of the Hon. Mark
and Betsy Matilda (Smith) Doolittle, of Belchertown; born there in
1812, and is still living. Her father graduated at Yale College in
1804, studied the profession of the law, and settled in Belchertown.
He was a native of Westfield, Mass. Her mother was a daughter of
Daniel Smith, Esq., of West Haven, Vermont.

Children of JOHN and BETSEY MATILDA (DOOLITTLE) STACEY:

79. John,   b. in 1845 ; d. in infancy.
80. Sarah Doolittle, b. in 1847 ; d. in infancy.

(53) HARRIET STACEY, third child and only daughter of Ira and Roxanna (Glover) Stacey, was born in Belchertown, June 3, 1821, and is now residing in Corning, N. Y.

She was married, in 1842, to the Hon. George T. Spencer, son of Deacon Spencer, of Saybrook (Deep River Village), Ct.; born there; graduated at Yale College in the class of 1836, and has devoted himself to the study and profession of the law. He has been a member of the State Legislature at Albany, N. Y., and is now in the successful practice of his profession, in Corning, N. Y., as Counsellor at Law and Magistrate, and has attained to a high degree of eminence for his learning and ability. They have had ten children, born in Corning, as follows:

81. ——————————, b. June, 1844 ; d. in 1849, aged 5 years.
82. Emma Roxanna, b. in 1846 ; died same year.
83. George, b. in 1846 ; enrolled in the U. S. Cavalry service, from 1863, and served to the close of the late civil war.
84. Harriet,   b. in 1854 ; is a member of Elmira College, N.Y.
85. Emma Roxanna, b. in 1856 ; is in Elmira College, N. Y.
86. John Stacey, b. in 1858 ; d. in 1862, aged 4 years.
87. Bessie,   b. in 1860.
88. Richard,. b. in 1862 ; d. in 1864, aged 18 months.
89. Carrie, ⎫
90. Hugh, ⎬ b. in 1864.

(55) JOHN GEORGE GLOVER, the eldest son of John Joseph and Agnes Jane (Larkin) Glover, was born in Natchez, Miss., May 8, 1821, and resides at New Orleans, La. He was engaged in an extensive business, and was partner in a large cotton house for several years previous to the breaking out of the rebellion of 1861.

He has been thrice married, and has children, not reported.

(57) FRANCIS L. GLOVER, second and youngest son of John Joseph and Agnes Jane (Larkin) Glover, was born in Natchez, Miss., July 31, 1825, and died there in October, 1856, aged 32 years.

He was never married. He graduated at —— College in Kentucky, adopted the profession of the law, and commenced the practice of his profession in his native city, Natchez, and was in successful practice when he was attacked with consumption, which proved incurable. He was a member of the Masonic brotherhood, and was held in high estimation by all to whom he was known. The following tribute to his memory appeared, a few days after his decease, in a Natchez paper:

Masonic Hall, Oct. 20, 1856. At a special meeting of the Free and Accepted Masons, held this day, the following preamble and resolutions were unanimously adopted:

Whereas, The Grand Architect of the Universe, in the dispensation of an all-wise Providence, has seen fit to remove our lamented friend and brother, Francis L. Glover, from his pilgrimage on earth " to that house not made with hands, eternal in the heavens," and as the unfeigned affection we entertained for him demands from us an expression of our feelings on this mournful occasion; be it therefore

Resolved, That we deeply deplore the loss of our worthy member and brother Francis L. Glover, and will cherish his memory in our hearts, and revere and emulate his virtues. By his death our fraternity is deprived of a member zealous, true and faithful; society, of one who in life discharged with uprightness and fidelity his trust as a man.

Resolved, That the moral rectitude which characterized him in the several relations of life, and his unwearied performance of duties, were worthy tokens of his membership. Stricken in the prime of life, with an incurable disease, with the icy hand of death heavily pressing upon him, he bore his afflictions with christian fortitude, sustained by the high principles inculcated by the order of which he was a member.

Resolved, That we deeply deplore, and sincerely lament the affliction thus sent to the fond mother and other relatives of our late brother, and offer them our sympathy and condolence on the irreparable loss they have sustained.

Resolved, That as a testimony of regard for the memory of our late brother, we will wear the usual badge of mourning for the space of thirty days.

Resolved, That the Secretary be requested to send a copy of these resolutions to the family of the deceased.

J. Queo, *Profilel Secretary.*   A. H. KENDRICK, W.M.

(65) LOUIS N. GLOVER, the eldest son of Dr. Ralph and Amelia (Evans) Glover, was born in the City of New York, Feb. 16, 1831, and died there, June 16, 1860, in his 29th year.

He was never married. He graduated at the Medical Department of the University of the City of New York, in 1851, but the profession of medicine not being congenial to his taste and inclinations, he commenced the study of law, and acquired a knowledge of that profession very rapidly. In 1852 he commenced the practice of his profession as counsellor at law in an office in Wall street. He very soon became known to the professional brethren, was elected as an attorney to the Corporation, and removed to the City Hall. He continued in that connection until his failing health compelled him to retire.

(66) JOHN JOSEPH GLOVER, the second son of Dr. Ralph and Amelia (Evans) Glover, was born in the City of New York, Aug. 15, 1833, and is now residing there. He is a physician, in successful practice. He graduated at the Medical Department of the New York University, in the year 1857.

Dec. 21, 1859, he was married to Marguerretta Terhune, of New York. They have had one son:

91. Charles Ralph, b. Jan. 3, 1864.

[*Eighth Generation.*]

(72) JANE ELIZA GLOVER, the eldest daughter of Thomas and Lydia (Knowlton) Glover, was born Oct. 20, 1832, and is now residing in Wilbraham.

She was married, July 4, 1852, to Elisha B. Bloomer, son of Reuben and Fanny (Mead) Bloomer, of Marlboro', N. Y. They have had five children:

92. Mary Ida, b. Nov. 7, 1853.
93. Cora Ella, b. March 5, 1856.
94. Gerald Glover, b. Feb. 25, 1858.
95. Effie Lydia, b. April 14, 1860.
96. Florence May, b. May 12, 1862.

(73) JAMES NOBLE GLOVER, the eldest son of Thomas and Lydia (Knowlton) Glover, was born in New York, Aug. 15, 1835, and is now (1866) with his regiment at Fort Warren. He was enrolled in the United States service in 1861, and served under Gen. George B. McClellan during all his campaign as commander of the Army of the Potomac. At the battle of Gettysburg, in July, 1863, he was severely wounded by a rifle ball, which passed through his hip and near the bone, dropping into his boot, having spent its force. He was removed to the Philadelphia Hospital, where he remained for three or four months. While there he recovered, and was again able to return to his regiment. He served the balance of the time for which he enlisted, and was again enrolled for another term of three years in 1865.

(77) GEORGE HENRY GLOVER, only son of Henry '
Sophronia (Hoar) Glover, was born in Springfield, June 17, 3,
and is now residing in Brattleboro', Vt.

He was enrolled in the U. S. service at Brattleboro', in 1862, and
served in Capt. Stoughton's Company, 4th Regiment of Vermont
Volunteers, five months, and was discharged on account of failing
health.

———

It will be seen, in the account of the Hon. JOHN GLOVER and his
five sons, which here closes, that their descendants, as far as ascertained and recorded in the preceding pages, amount to two thousand
one hundred and eighty—viz.:

THOMAS	21
HABACKUK	152
NATHANIEL	1911
PELATIAH	96
	2180

PART II.

HENRY GLOVER AND HIS DESCENDANTS.

ELIAS, RALPH, JOSEPH AND RICHARD GLOVER.

HENRY GLOVER AND HIS DESCENDANTS.

HENRY GLOVER, the third son of Thomas and Margery (Deane) Glover (p. 32), was born at Rainhill Parish, in the town of Prescot, Lancashire, England, in 1603; baptized at the Parish Church, Feb. 15, 1603, and came to New England about 1640, as it is supposed, and settled in Dedham. He died in Medfield (a part of the original town of Dedham), in 1655. He had a wife Abigail, whom, it is supposed, came over with him, and likewise children. He was next brother to John, whose history has been given in the First Part of this work, and was three years his junior. Much less is known of his life and character—of his occupation, and other circumstances connected with his residence here, than has been obtained of his elder brother. His name does not appear as frequently on any of the public records of the Colony of New England. It has not been ascertained in what ship he came, or with what emigration he was connected; but it appears highly probable that he came with the Dedham Company. By his father's will he was to receive the sum of £150 in money; and, the mention of him in that document, and the dates of his birth and baptism, are all that have been gathered of his English life. After he came to New England, in 1642, he was admitted townsman in Dedham. He is recorded as a grantee of land from 1642 to 1652, in six different grants from the Dedham proprietors. In 1649 a company was formed for commencing a settlement at Bagashaw, now Medfield, composed of 43 persons, as stated by Mr. Mann in his Annals of Dedham, but only nineteen names are given, and some of those were men with whom Henry Glover was afterwards intimately associated in his business relations; viz., Ralph Wheelock, Thomas Wight and Robert Hinsdale. By other accounts we learn that Medfield was incorporated in 1649, and became a separate town from Dedham, and it is supposable that Mr. Glover went there to reside at that time, and that his grants of land were located in that precinct. Six years after this settlement, in 1655, the notice of his death appears on the Probate Records for

44

Suffolk County; letters of administration being granted to Abigail Glover on the estate of her late husband Henry Glover, and she deposed Nov. 29, 1655. In Vol. 9, fol. 2, is an "Inventory of the goods of Henry Glover of Medfield, deceased the 21 of the 5 month 1655, by Thomas Wight, Robert Hinsdale and Ralph Wheelock."[*] Sum total, £88 05 00 0.

Of his widow Abigail nothing further has been gathered. Whether she married a second time, or died the widow of Henry Glover, is unknown. No record of any Abigail Glover has been found at that period, when, if living here, she would most probably be in some New England town—and nothing has been gathered on which to rest a supposition that she returned, after Mr. Glover's death, to England; yet it is not unreasonable to suppose that she did return, and remain there to the close of her life. Of his children we can only gather an account of a son Henry, who had a wife Hannah. They were in Boston in 1660 to 1665, and had a son Thomas, born there in 1663; and a daughter Hannah, born in 1665. Subsequently they removed to Milton, and had several more children. His history, and that of his descendants, forms the Second Part of these Memorials.

There was a John and Mary Glover living in Boston (on the Common, as their estate has been described) in 1677, whose daughter Hannah married Aaron Beard, of Boston, and came in possession of the estate in 1677. There is much reason to suppose that the above named John Glover was another son of Henry, senior. Other names of Glover have been occasionally found on record, or by tradition, who can claim no other origin but as descendants of some other son whose name cannot now be found.

In 1756 there is a record of names of persons who served in the French War, among whom is a Solomon Glover—enlisted in the volunteer service, Sept. 24, 1755, among the Grafton troops. On page 102, Army Records, is an entry, "Solomon Glover, deceased." It is probable that he died some time about the last of January or in February of 1756, but nothing further is known of him.

---

[*] One of the appraisers of the elder Henry Glover's estate was Ralph Wheelock. The following has been gathered of him: "Ralph Wheelock; A.B. Clare Hall, Cambridge, England, 1626; A.M. 1631; was of Dedham in New England in 1642, and was appointed by the Commissioners to settle small causes at Dedham. Also a Magistrate in 1642; and in October, 1645, he was authorized to solemnize marriages. The marriage of John Crafts, of Roxbury, and Rebecca Wheelock, was one of his first official acts."

[Second Generation.]

(1) HENRY GLOVER, son of Henry and Abigail Glover, was born probably in Dedham, although no record has been found there of his birth. He died in Milton, the 6th day of April, 1714, aged 72 years, and is buried in that town.

The accounts of him are very meagre, there being no record of any baptism or marriage. He lived in Boston as early as 1660, and appears to have continued there about five years. He had a wife Hannah, by whom he had two children, born there, but the earliest period at which he came to Boston has not been ascertained. In 1673–4, Feb. 5, there is an indenture by Henry Glover, of Milton, and Hannah his wife, which conveys a piece of land in that town to David Henshaw, "the said Hannah Glover relinquishing her right of Dower and power of Thirds."

Five years later, June 27, 1679, Henry Glover, of Milton, sold to Ralph Houghton fifty acres of upland on the south side of Neponset River near Brush Hill, being half a lot formerly belonging to Major Atherton and John Henshaw.

Henry Glover was probably a member of some Church, and his wife Hannah was admitted to join the Church at Milton, Aug. 24, 1684, Rev. Peter Thacher, pastor. There has been nothing further gathered of her, excepting the date of her death. She died in Milton, Sept. 20, 1720, and is buried there, in the old burying ground. Her age at death was 79 years, and she was therefore born in 1741. The children of Henry and Hannah Glover were as follows. The two eldest are recorded in Boston, the others in Milton. They are ten in number, six of whom lived to the age of adults, and married:

+ 2. Thomas, b. June 25, 1663; m. Susannah Bradley, Dorchester.
+ 3. Hannah, b. in   1665; m. Thomas Evans, of Dorchester.
  4. Elizabeth, b. April 24, 1667; d. in Milton, April 24, 1752, aged 85 years; unmarried.
+ 5. Henry, b. Aug. 20, 1670; m. Mary Crehore, of Milton.
  6. Sarah, b. Nov. 16, 1672; died young.
  7. Mary, b. Nov. 13, 1674; d. April 6, 1713, aged 39, unm.
+ 8. Abigail, b. June 12, 1677; m. Thomas Ellis, of Milton.
  9. Alice, b. July 20, 1679; d. Sept. 17, 1713, aged 34, unm.
+10. Edward, b. April 26, 1681; m. { 1st, Sarah Gill; 2d, Mary Blake, widow.
  11. Sarah, b. Aug. 5, 1685; d. June 25, 1742, aged 57 years.

The next account gathered of him is a record of a deposition, in Prob. Rec., Vol. 37, pp. 378, 385, which is as follows:

"Boston, April 26, 1692.   Henry Glover, Senior, aged about Fifty years or thereabouts, testifyeth and saith, that having agreed with Capt. Roger Clap to get hay at his farm beyond the Blue Hills; this deponent did get and mow about two loads of grass sometime in August last past.   And when I come with my son to take up the hay, I found it on fire, and finding Richard Thayer, Senior, there, of Brain-tree, I asked him why he burnt my hay ; and Thayer owned that he had burnt the hay, and said it was his ; and I told him we had great damage by having our hay burnt in stacks about three years ago; which was about four loads.   And he Richard Thayer said that he burnt it, and would own it before the Court if he came there ; and that if I made any more, without I agreed with him, it would be burnt as fast as I made it.   Also Henry Glover, Junior, aged about twenty-one years or thereabouts, testifyeth to the above written testimony before us, J. Nyle, S. White, Jacob Nash.   Jan. 26, 1691–2."

Henry Glover died intestate, and his estate was administered on by his wife Hannah, as appears by the following from Vol. 18, p. 50, of Suffolk Probate Records : "Letters of Administration were grant-ed to Hannah Glover and her son Edward Glover, on the estate of her late husband Henry Glover of Milton, Husbandman.   Boston, May 11, 1713–14."

Inventory of the Goods, Chattels, &c. of Henry Glover late of Milton, in the County of Suffolk in New England, lately deceased, Husband-man, the 11 day of May 1713–14, as followeth—

In Housing and Land	£247	00 00 0
Stock and Iron Tools	26	00 00 0
Other Utensils	28	00 00 0
Furniture, Chairs and other Moveables, Books and Wearing apparell, &c.	38	14 00 0
Debts due the estate	3	15 00 0
Amount	£343	09 00 0

Appraised by
          Ephraim Tucker,
          Henry Vose,
          Benjamin Fenno.

Boston, May 13, 1714.   Suffolk ss.   By the Honorable Jonathan Addington, Esq., Judge of Probate of Wills for the County of Suf-folk, Hannah Glover widow and Edward Glover her son, Administra-tors on the estate of Henry Glover late of Milton deceased, intestate, presented the foregoing Instrument, and made Oath that it contains a true and perfect Inventory of the said estate, so far as has come to their knowledge, and that if more do appear they will cause it to be added.   JONA. ADDINGTON, *Judge of Probate.*
          Examined by Paul Dudley.

Settlement of the Estate of Henry Glover, as found in Vol. 18, p. 153, of Probate Records for the County of Suffolk.

This Indenture Octopartite, made on the 8 day of May, Anno Domini 1714, in the 13ᵗʰ year of her Majesty's Reign, between Thomas Glover, Henry Glover, Edward Glover, Thomas Evans and Hannah his wife, Thomas Ellis and Abigail his wife, Elizabeth Glover, Alice Glover, and Sarah Glover, spinsters, children and heirs of Henry Glover late of Milton, in the County of Suffolk and Province of Massachusetts Bay in New England, Husbandman, Deceased ; and Hannah the Relict and Widow of the said deceased Henry Glover ; containing an agreement of their several and respective parts or portions for the division, distribution and settlement of his Real Estate ; consisting of Houses and Lands of the said Deceased who died intestate, in manner as followeth.

That is to say. It is mutually agreed upon, granted and consented to, that the said Hannah Glover, Widow, for her Dower and Thirds shall have and enjoy One Third part of the whole estate in Lands with the East end of the Dwelling House and the North end of the Barn for her use and comfortable support, for, and during the term of her natural life. Further, it is mutually granted, consented to and agreed, that the said Edward Glover, for and in consideration of his pains and tender care of, and for his aged parents for many years past, and for recompense of the same, shall have and enjoy to the use of him and his heirs and assigns forever, Seven Acres of Land lying on the West side of the Farm, over and above a single equal part or portion with other of his brethren and sisters in the remaining part of said farm lying and situated in said Milton as aforesaid.

It is also granted, consented to, and agreed, that Henry Glover aforesaid, in consideration of his Right, Share, and portion of said estate and his disbursements thereupon in building and other improvements, shall be paid by his brother Edward aforenamed, who hath purchased the same, the sum of Sixty pounds in bills of credit of the Province, or in Standard Silver of the rate equivalent. And whereas the Housing and lands of the said Henry Glover the Father are uncapable of being divided and allotted into so many parts and shares as to make each one's Right and Portion therein without prejudicing and spoiling the whole, the said Henry Glover, Thomas Evans and Hannah his wife, Thomas Ellis and Abigail his wife, Elizabeth, Alice and Sarah Glover, parties to these Presents, for and in consideration of the several and respective sums following to be paid them by their brothers Thomas Glover and Edward Glover hereinbefore named, vizt. Sixty pounds to the said Henry by the said Edward and Eighteen pounds apiece to each of the rest in Specie as before named, One part to be paid by the said Thomas and four pounds over and above to the said Henry abovementioned by the said Edward Glover ; have given, granted, bargained, sold, released, quit-claimed and confirmed, and by these Presents for themselves and each and every one of them severally and respectively for themselves and respective heirs, do fully and freely release, quit-claim and confirm unto the said Thomas Glover and Edward Glover and to their heirs and assigns forever, their several Rights, Title, Interest, Prospect, claim or demand in, to and of the whole of their portions of inheritance of the Real estate, housing and

44*

Lands of their said father Henry Glover, whereof he died seized, as well as that at present subject to a division amongst them as assigned to their mother in Dower for the term of her natural life. And the Reversion and Reversions, remainder and remainders of the same with the Appurtenances thereof, to Have and to Hold all the above granted Premises, with the members and privileges thereof to the said Thomas Glover on the one part and the said Edward the other five parts, to be holden by them and their heirs and assigns forever, to their own proper use and behoof forever.

In witness whereof, we the said parties to these Presents have set our hands and seals, this day and year first above written.

> HENRY GLOVER, and a seal,
> THOMAS EVANS and
> HANNAH EVANS,
> THOMAS ELLIS,
> ABIGAIL ELLIS,
> ELIZABETH GLOVER,
> ALICE GLOVER,
> SARAH GLOVER, with their seals.

Signed, sealed and delivered in presence of
> Samuel Withington,
> William Withington.

Suffolk, ss. By the Honble Isaac Addington, Judge of Probate. The parties above named subscribed to the foregoing Instrument personally appeared before me and acknowledged the same to be their free act and deed. Which I do allow and approve as a settlement of the estate in Housing and lands of Henry Glover late of Milton, Husbandman, deceased intestate. ISAAC ADDINGTON, *Judge of Probate.*

Boston, May 14, 1714.

Examined by PAUL DUDLEY, *Register.*

[*Third Generation.*]

(2) THOMAS GLOVER, the eldest son of Henry and Hannah Glover, was born in Boston, June 25, 1663, and died in Milton, Nov. 10, 1715, aged 52 years. He left a widow and two children. "Letters of Administration were granted on the estate of Thomas Glover, late of Milton, to Susannah Glover, his widow and relict, Jan. 19, 1715-16."

Thomas Glover was married to Susannah Bradley, Jan. 1, 1700, by the "worshipful Mr. Bailey." She was the daughter of Nathan and Mary (Evans) Bradley, of Dorchester, who were married there, 17: 5: 1666. Susannah, their daughter, was born in Dorchester, 13: 11: 1669; admitted a member of the Church at Milton, July 21, 1717.

Children of THOMAS and SUSANNAH (BRADLEY) GLOVER, born in Milton:

+12. Samuel, b. April 20, 1702; m. Hepzibah Vose, of Milton.
13. Susannah, b. June 2, 1704; d. Oct. 29, 1715, aged 11 years.

May 10, 1716, the estate of Thomas Glover, late of Milton, was appraised, and an inventory taken and presented to Susannah Glover, widow and relict of the said Thomas Glover, as administratrix, by Henry Vose and John Dickerman.

Thomas Glover died in possession of a house and twenty-four acres of land in Milton, valued at £75. Whole amount of his estate, £124 17s.

May 21, 1716, Samuel Glover, son of Thomas Glover, of Milton, then lately deceased, aged about 15 years, chose John Dickerman, of Milton, to be his guardian. Letters of guardianship were accordingly granted to Mr. Dickerman, who gave bonds for the faithful performance of said trust.

Susannah Glover's name appears on a tax list in Milton, as among those who paid taxes or rates; the latest date found of such payment is in 1718. April 22, 1721, she was married to Caleb Babcock, of Milton, and nothing further has been gathered of her.

(3) HANNAH GLOVER, the eldest daughter of Henry and Hannah Glover, was born in Boston, in 1665, and died in Dorchester, in 1759, in the 94th year of her age.

She was married to Thomas Evans, of Dorchester, March 10, 1686. He was the son of Matthias and Patience (Mead) Evans, of Dorchester, was born there, and died March 16, 1749.

Children of THOMAS and HANNAH (GLOVER) EVANS, born in Dorchester:

14. Hannah, b. Dec. 9, 1689; d. 1696.
15. Thomas, m. Patience Tolman, of Dorchester.
16. Anna, m. Ezekiel Tileston, of Dorchester.
17. Elizabeth, b. Aug. 18, 1697; m.
18. Abigail, b. in 1699; d. in 1739.
19. Mary, b. in 1702.
20. Henry, b. in 1704; d. in 1715.
21. Alice, b. July 11, 1709; m. Henry Woodman.

(5) HENRY GLOVER, the second son of Henry and Hannah Glover, was born in Milton, Aug. 20, 1670, and died in Lebanon, Ct.

He was married, March 1, 1696, to Mary Crehore, daughter of Teague and Mary Crehore, of Milton, and was born there, July 27, 1677, and baptized July 31, by Rev. Peter Thacher, the pastor who married her.   They had five children.

"May 31, 1697, Henry Glover, Junior, in covenant with the Church at Milton, in order for the baptism of his children."

Children of HENRY, Jr., and MARY (CREHORE) GLOVER, born in Milton, and Lebanon, Ct.:

```
 22. Mary,     b. Aug.   6, 1696 ; bap. May   30, 1697.
 23. Hannah,   b. Sept. 24, 1698 ; bap. Sept. 27, 1698.
 24. Elizabeth, b. March 27, 1700 ; bap. March 30, 1700.
+25. Henry,    b. June  20, 1707 ; bap. June  22, 1707.
+26. Thomas,   b. Jan.  28, 1719 ; bap. Jan.  31, 1719 ; m. Joanna
         Swift, of Sandwich.
```

(8)   ABIGAIL GLOVER, fifth daughter of Henry and Hannah Glover, was born in Milton, June 12, 1677, and died there—date not ascertained.

She was married, Feb. 17, 1700, to Thomas Ellis, of Milton. Nothing further has been gathered of him.   They had five children, born in Milton, as follows:

```
 27. Edward, }
 28. Abigail, } b. March  4, 1709–10.
 29. Joshua,  b. Nov.  9, 1712.
 30. John,    b. Feb.  11, 1714–15 ; m. Susanna ——.
 31. Judith,  b. Aug.  25, 1717.
```

(10)   EDWARD GLOVER, the third son of Henry and Hannah Glover, was born in Milton, April 26, 1681, and died there, May 14, 1745, aged 64 years.   He left a widow and six children.

He was twice married.   First, to Sarah Gill, of Milton, April 26, 1718, who died there, Feb. 1, 1740.   By her he had all his children. He was married, second, to Mrs. Mary Blake, widow, of Milton, Oct. 24, 1741, who survived him.   She was a widow a few years, and may have married again.   No date of her death appears on Milton Records.

Edward Glover administered on the estate of his father, and inherited the homestead in Milton.   He also owned lands by purchase. May 20, 1714, he bought a tract of woodland in Milton containing fourteen acres, of Nathaniel Glover, Senior, of Dorchester—bounded on the parallel line of Braintree, westerly on land of Roger Billings. Consideration, fifty pounds. (Suffolk Reg. of Deeds, Vol. 28, fol. 85.)

In May, 1745, letters were granted to John and Edward Glover to administer on the estate of their late father Edward Glover, deceased, intestate, which being fully performed, they were ordered to pay to the widow Mary Glover, the second wife of Edward, Sen., her right of dower, and the brothers and sisters—Moses, Henry, Hannah and Mary—£360 10s. 05d. each; also a further sum of £184 15s. at the reversion of the dower.

Children of EDWARD and SARAH (GILL) GLOVER, born in Milton :

+32. Edward, b. Oct.   26, 1719 ; d. Oct. 2, 1756-7, in his 37th year.
+33. Hannah, b. June 29, 1721 ; m. Jeremiah Phillips, of Milton.
  34. Mary,   b. March 30, 1723 ; d. Dec. 1, 1805, at the house of her niece, Mrs. George Tucker, daughter of her brother Moses Glover, in her 83d year.
+35. John,   b. Jan.   29, 1726 ; m. Abigail Holmes, of Milton.
+36. Moses,   b. Jan.   22, 1730 ; m. Jerusha Crane, of Milton.
+37. Henry,   b. Aug.   22, 1732 ; m. Hannah Lewis, of Dedham.

[*Fourth Generation.*]

(12) SAMUEL GLOVER, only son of Thomas and Susannah (Bradley) Glover, was born in Milton, April 20, 1702, and died there, Aug. 2, 1761, in his 60th year. He was buried in the ancient burial ground in Milton, and has a gravestone. He left a widow and two sons.

He was married, Nov. 22, 1733, to Hepzibah Vose, daughter of Henry* and Elizabeth Vose, of Milton ; born there, Feb. 7, baptized Feb. 10, 1704, and died Sept. 19, 1792, in her 89th year. They both joined the Church in Milton, Nov. 24, 1722-3.

Children of SAMUEL and HEPZIBAH (VOSE) GLOVER, born in Milton :

  38. Samuel, b. Nov. 11, 1735 ; d. Oct. 9, 1760, in his 25th year.
+39. Joshua, b. Feb. 3, 1736-7 ; m. Elizabeth Swift, of Milton.
+40. Thomas, b. Dec. 2, 1745 ; m. Zebiah Vose, of Milton.

---

* Henry Vose, the father of Hepzibah, died in Milton, in 1761. By the executor's account rendered on his estate, July 24, 1761, to Thomas Hutchinson, Judge of Probate of Wills and Estates for Suffolk County, there was found a balance in personal estate of eleven pounds, fourteen shillings and fourpence, which by law was disposed of among the children then living of the said Henry Vose, and to the legal representatives of such as were deceased. The names mentioned are Robert Vose, Joshua Vose, Thomas Vose, Mary Billings, Waitstill Daith, Elizabeth Shaller, Martha Crane, Hepzibah Glover and Burah Billings.

He made a will, July 29, 1761, and appointed his wife Hepzibah executrix. The will was proved Aug. 28, 1761. The following is a copy as recorded on the Probate Records for Suffolk County:

In the name of God Amen. I Samuel Glover of Milton in the County of Suffolk, in his Majestic's Province of Massachusetts Bay in New England, Weaver, being weak of body but of perfect mind and memory, praised be God. And therefore calling to mind the mortality of my body, and knowing it is appointed unto all men once to die, do make and ordain this my last Will and Testament.

And first of all I give and recommend my soul into the hands of God who gave it, hoping for pardon and eternal salvation through the mercy of God and the merits of my Redeemer; and my body I commit to the earth to be buried in a decent manner at the discretion of my Executors hereinafter named.

And as touching such worldly estate as it has pleased God to bless me with in this life, I give, bequeath and demise of the same in manner and form following.

Item. I give, bequeath and demise to my well beloved wife Hepzibah Glover the use and improvement of all my estate both real and personal, except what is hereafter given to my son Joshua Glover, to improve all the time she shall remain my widow; but if she shall marry, my Will is that she shall have her bed with all convenient furniture for the same and she shall acquit my estate both real and personal all of it at the time of her marriage.

I give to my son Joshua Glover at my decease the improvement of one half of my dwelling house, and also the improvement of one half of my cellar and the improvement of my shop and Looms all the time his mother lives and remains my widow. And furthermore my will is, and I bequeath to him my son Joshua Glover one half of all my estate, both real and personal, to him and his heirs and assigns forever after his mother's decease, or, if she shall marry, at the time of her marriage.

My Will is, and I give and bequeath to my son Thomas Glover one half of all my estate both real and personal, to him his heirs and assigns forever, after his mother's decease, or, if she shall marry, at the · time of her marriage.

And also my Will is, that my Executors pay all my just debts and funeral charges,

My Will is, and I do hereby appoint and consitute my well beloved wife Hepzibah Glover and my son Joshua Glover to be my Executors of this my last Will and Testament.

And I do hereby utterly disallow and make void all former Wills and Testaments whatsoever, ratifying and confirming this to be my last Will and Testament. In witness whereof I have hereunto set my hand and seal this 29th day of July, A.D. 1761, and in the first year of the Reign of Our Sovreign Lord King George the Third, King of Great Britain, &c.   SAMUEL GLOVER, and a seal.

Signed, sealed, published and declared in presence of us to be the last Will and Testament of Samuel Glover.
        Justus Soper,
        Moses Glover,
        Benjamin Wadsworth.

(25) HENRY GLOVER, the eldest son of Henry and Mary (Crehore) Glover, was born in Milton, June 20, 1707–8, baptized June 22, and died in Conway, Mass., in 1788, aged 80 years.

He was never married. He removed with his parents to Lebanon, Conn., was a landholder, and paid taxes there. The part of the town in which he lived was soon after set off from Lebanon, and now bears the name of Columbia. It is situated in Tolland County, Conn. Subsequently he went to Colchester, Conn., where it is stated he resided several years, and was a landholder, and a tax-payer. From Colchester he removed, in 1777, to Conway, Mass., and was a landholder there and a tax-payer from 1782 to 1788.

(26) THOMAS GLOVER, the youngest son of Henry and Mary (Crehore) Glover, was born in Lebanon, Conn., at a place called "Old Lebanon Crank," Jan. 28, and baptized Jan. 31, 1719. He removed from Lebanon to the town of Colchester. He was a landholder and owned estates in both places. He subsequently, in 1772, removed to Conway, in Massachusetts, and died there, Oct. 1, 1782, aged 63 years. He owned an estate in Conway, and paid taxes there from 1777 to 1782.

He was married, Feb. 18, 1743, in Lebanon, Ct., to Joanna Swift, of Sandwich, daughter of Thomas and Joanna Swift; born there in 1722, and died in Conway, Dec. 22, 1800, aged 78 years.

Children of THOMAS and JOANNA (SWIFT) GLOVER, born in Lebanon, Ct.:

```
  41. Mary,       b. Nov.  18, 1744.
  42. Joanna,     b. Jan.   1, 1747;  m. Roswell Chamberlain, Conn.
+43. Gamaliel,    b. Oct.   7, 1749;  m. Tabitha Beale, Weymouth.
  44. Marcia,     b. in        1751;  m. David Northup.
  45. Elizabeth,  b. Jan.  27, 1753;  m. Caleb Beale, of Weymouth.
+46. Alexander,   b. March 20, 1756;  m. Sarah Salisbury.
```

(32) EDWARD GLOVER, the eldest son of Edward and Sarah (Gill) Glover, was born in Milton, Oct. 26, baptized Nov. 1, 1719, and died there, Oct. 2, 1757, in his 38th year. In 1745 he served as Lieutenant in the Navy, and was in action at the taking of Louisburg, on June 17, 1745. He returned soon after, and in 1754, during the "French and Indian War," he was enrolled in the army, and in 1756 was appointed Ensign. On the Army Records, Vol. 3 (1756), page

281, is the following: "A muster roll under the command of Capt. Nathaniel Blake, of Milton, Jonathan Fessenden Lieutenant, Edward Glover Ensign, enlisted the following men, viz., Ephraim Mann, Dorchester, and Edward Blake, Boston, 26 years old, glazier—John Cox, Ensign, 21 years old, Bricklayer." He was in the expedition to Fort William Henry in 1756.

He was never married, and but few incidents of his life are recorded. In 1745 he was appointed administrator on the estate of his father, Edward Glover, of Milton, deceased. He served in the Colonial War until within a few months of his decease, when his ill health compelled him to retire from the army to his home in Milton. He died at the house of his brother, John Glover, whom he appointed administrator on his estate. His writing desk, containing his papers and writings, he gave to his youngest brother, Henry Glover, who lived in West Dedham at that time. It is said his papers are still preserved in the same desk in the family of Mr. Edward Glover, a grandson of his brother Henry. Letters of administration on his estate were granted to his brother John, April 19, 1758. March 25, 1760, William Spurr, administered, *De bonis non*, on the estate of Edward Glover, in place of John Glover, deceased.

(33) HANNAH GLOVER, the eldest daughter of Edward and Sarah (Gill) Glover, was born in Milton, June 29, 1721, baptized July 2, and died in Marshfield, Nov. 22, 1772, in her 51st year.

She was married, in 1751, to Jeremiah Phillips, of Milton. They had three children, and perhaps others. The following are the only ones which have been identified with any certainty:

47. Joseph, b. in Milton, April 18, 1753; was a soldier in the War of the Revolution, taken prisoner of war, and died in 1775, aged 22 years.
48. Hannah, b. July 28, 1759; m. Prince Hatch, of Marshfield, Mass., Dec. 18, 1783; removed to Knox, Me., near Belfast.
49. Persis, b. Sept. 27, 1760; m. Robert Cushman, of Marshfield, April, 1785, and died Oct. 25, 1819, aged 59 years.

(35) JOHN GLOVER, the second son of Edward and Sarah (Gill) Glover, was born in Milton, Jan. 29, baptized Feb. 6, 1726, and died there suddenly, Oct. 17, 1759, aged 33 years. He inherited a portion of the landed estate which was the inheritance of his father Edward Glover from Henry Glover his ancestor, and resided on it.

He was married, Aug. 31, 1751, to Abigail Holmes, of Milton, by whom he had four children, the last one posthumous. He was enrolled and served in the army of the French and Indian War, from 1755 to 1756–7, and returned to Milton at the close of the war. In April, 1757, he was appointed to the administration of the estate of his brother Edward Glover. He died before the administration was finished, and the court appointed William Spurr, March 25, 1760, to take his place. Also letters of administration were granted to William Spurr on the estate of John Glover, of Milton, deceased, Nov. 23, 1759.

Children of JOHN and ABIGAIL (HOLMES) GLOVER, born and baptized in Milton:

+50. John, b. May 31, 1753; m. Rachel Littlefield, of Stoughton.
  51. Lemuel, b. Oct. 22, 1754; in the Revolutionary Army from 1778 to 1783; nothing known of him afterwards.
  52. Edward, b. Oct. 19, 1757; in the Revolutionary Army from Aug. 21, 1778, to Sept. 1, 1779; probably never married.
  53. Abijah, b. March 7, 1759–60; died young, it is supposed.

Mrs. ABIGAIL GLOVER, the widow of John Glover, was married a second time, to Benjamin Tilson, of Stoughton, in 1762, and went there to live, in that part of the town bordering on Randolph. The date of her death has not been ascertained.

(36) MOSES GLOVER, the second son of Edward and Sarah (Gill) Glover, was born in Milton, Jan. 22, 1730, baptized the 25th of the same month, and died Nov. 7, 1789, in his 60th year. He was a landholder, and by trade a cordwainer.

He was married, Oct. 5, 1754, to Jerusha Crane, daughter of Henry and Melatiah (Bent) Crane, of Milton; born there, March 25, 1733, and died in Boston, Nov. 14, 1804, at the residence of her son Nathaniel Glover, No. 4 Newbury street, aged nearly 72 years. They had five children. His name is recorded in a memorandum of James Blake, of Dorchester, as having served at Castle William from 1748 to 1753.

Children of MOSES and JERUSHA (CRANE) GLOVER, born in Milton:

+54. Nathaniel, b. April 28, 1755; m. Mary Siders, of Boston.
+55. Ruth, b. Feb. 23, 1757; m. Daniel Spear, of Braintree.
+56. Sarah, b. July 1, 1758; m. George Tucker, of Milton.

+57. Mary,   b. March 20, 1762 ; m. Capt. Charles Gavett, Salem.
 58. Mela,   b. April   5, 1767 ; d. May 13, 1799, in her 33d year.

(37)   HENRY GLOVER, youngest child and third son of Edward
and Sarah (Gill) Glover, was born in Milton, Aug. 22, 1732, baptized
on the 27th of the same month, and died in West Dedham, Aug. 21,
1800.   He owned an estate in West Dedham, and was by trade a
blacksmith.   He was a minor at the decease of his father Edward
Glover.   In August, 1745, letters of guardianship were granted to
William Tucker, of Milton, as guardian to Henry Glover, a minor
aged 13 years.

He was married, Jan. 6, 1754, to Hannah Lewis, daughter of
Ebenezer and Hannah (Gill) Lewis, of West Dedham ; born there,
Aug. 28, 1732, and died Aug. 20, 1807, aged 75 years.

Children of HENRY and HANNAH (LEWIS) GLOVER, born in West
Dedham :

+59. Hannah, b. June 25, 1756 ; m. (second wife) Benjamin French,
      of West Dedham.
+60. Catharine, b. Jan.   3, 1758 ; m. William Clark, W. Needham.
+61. Henry,   b. Aug.   5, 1760 ; m. Rebecca Colburn, Dedham.
 62. Sarah,   b. Jan. 13, 1763 ; d. unm., in 1811, at the house of
      her brother Henry Glover, who administered on her estate.
 63. Jemima, b. Mch 5, 1765 ; m. Benjamin French, Jr., W. Dedham.
 64. Lucy,   b. Aug. 1, 1767.
+65. Edward Lewis, b. March   5, 1770 ; m. Ruth Grout.
+66. Jesse,   b. Nov.   6, 1772 ; m. Deborah Richards, Dover.
+67. David,   b. May   11, 1775 ; m. Tamsan Hall.
 68. Nancy,   b. May   21, 1778 ; d. Dec. 3, 1798, aged 20.

[Fifth Generation.]

(39)   JOSHUA GLOVER, the eldest son of Samuel and Hepzibah (Vose) Glover, was born in Milton, Feb. 3, and baptized Feb. 7,
1736-7, and died Sept. 17, 1788, in his 52d year, leaving a widow
and three children.

He was married, April 21, 1759, to Elizabeth Swift, daughter of
Thomas and Elizabeth (Crehore) Swift, of Milton ; born there about
1740.   The date of her death has not been ascertained, and nothing
further is known of her.

Children of JOSHUA and ELIZABETH (SWIFT) GLOVER, born in
Milton :

69. Hepzibah, b. July   13, 1760; d. Sept. 25, 1775, aged 15 years.

+70. Elizabeth, b. Jan.   25, 1763; m. { 1st, Benjamin Edwards ; 2d, ———— Houghton.

+71. Catharine, b. March 14, 1765; m. Samuel Wheeler.

+72. Joshua,   b. March 11, 1771; m. Susannah Holden, Dorchester.

73. Anne,   b. Sept. 26, 1774; d. Sept. 12, 1775.

Joshua Glover's name is enrolled among those who rendered service to their country in the alarm of April 19, 1775. We find it recorded under that date in the company of Capt. Ebenezer Tucker and Lieut. Ralph Houghton, of Milton.

(40) THOMAS GLOVER, the third and youngest son of Samuel and Hepzibah (Vose) Glover, was born in Milton, Dec. 2, 1745, and died there, of dropsy, in June, 1817, aged 72 years, leaving a widow and six children. He lies buried in the ancient burial yard in Milton.

He was married, Jan. 1, 1766, to Zebiah Vose, daughter of Edward and Abigail Vose, of Milton; born there, Dec. 9, 1744, and died in Boston at the house of her youngest son, Elisha Vose Glover, Sept. 10, 1824, aged 80 years. She was buried at Milton.

Thomas Glover rendered service to his country in the War of the Revolution. His name may be found in Vol. 4, p. 170, of Army Records, under date of June 5, 1780; and also in Vol. 11, p. 199, is this record: "Thomas Glover — Milton — 13 days service — Col. Lemuel Robinson." After he retired from the army he worked at his trade of shoemaking, and resided in Milton.

Children of THOMAS and ZEBIAH (VOSE) GLOVER, born in Milton:

+74. Samuel,   b. April 17, 1767; m. Lois Kilton, of Dorchester.

+75. Rachel,   b. Jan. 30, 1769; m. Nathaniel Ashton, of Boston.

+76. Abigail,   b. Jan. 21, 1770; m. Seth Baggs.*

+77. Susannah, b. Dec. 30, 1771; m. Shepard Bent, of Milton.

+78. Thomas,   b. Jan. 21, 1772; d. at sea.

+79. Elisha Vose, b. Jan. 3, 1785; m. Lydia (Wooley) Cleaveland, widow.

(43) GAMALIEL GLOVER, the eldest son of Thomas and Joanna (Swift) Glover, was born in Lebanon, Conn. (at a place now called Columbia), Oct. 7, 1749, and died in Conway (Ashfield Corner), Mass., of typhoid fever, Oct. 30, 1798, aged 49 years. It is said that he once lived in Colchester, Conn., and removed thence to

---

* This name is now spelled Bangs.

Conway; but the Town and Church Records of Colchester afford no evidence of the fact. He owned a farm in Conway, and paid taxes there in 1772 and previous.

He was married, in 1770, to Tabitha Beale, daughter of Seth and Elizabeth Beale, of Weymouth; born there, and died in Conway (Ashfield Corner), Dec. 11, 1798, about one month after the decease of her husband, and of the same fever.

At a Probate Court holden at Deerfield, in the County of Hampshire, April 2, 1799, letters of administration were granted on the estate of Gamaliel Glover, of Ashfield Corner, Conway, intestate, deceased, to Oliver Root, of Conway, and bonds taken Dec. 4, 1799; rendered insolvent. The estate was sold Dec. 1, 1800.

Children of GAMALIEL and TABITHA (BEALE) GLOVER, born in Conway, Mass.:

+80. Marcia,	b. in	1771;	m. Jeduthan Bartlett, Grafton.
+81. Hannah,	b. in	1772;	m. Joseph Wheeler, of Grafton.
82. Henry,	b. Nov.,	1774;	d. Nov. 12, 1798, aged 24 years.
83. Thomas,	b. in	1776;	m. ; d. in Macedon, N. Y., 1854.
84. Mary,	b. October,	1780;	d. Oct. 26, 1798, aged 18 years.
85. Clarissa,	b. May 1,	1781;	d. May 1, 1799, aged 18 years.
+86. Rachael,	b. in	1783;	m. Osee Crittenden, Phelps, N.Y.
87. Rhoda,	b. in	1785;	m.
88. Lucinda,	} b. in	1787;	{ m.
89. Philomela,			{ d. Dec.1, 1798.
90. Abigail,	b. in	1789;	d. Dec. 7, 1798.
91. Tabitha,	b. in	1790;	d. Dec. 17, 1798.

Thus it appears that near the close of the year 1798, the family of Gamaliel Glover was visited by a distressing sickness, by which Mr. Glover, his wife and six of their children died within a very short space of time. The disease was thought to be typhoid fever.

March 1, 1799, letters of guardianship were granted to Alexander Glover, who was appointed guardian to Clarissa Glover, 18 years; Rhoda Glover, 13 years; Rachael Glover, 11 years; and Lucinda Glover, 9 years, minor children of Gamaliel Glover, then late of Ashfield, deceased.

(46) ALEXANDER GLOVER, the second son and youngest child of Thomas and Joanna (Swift) Glover, was born at Lebanon, Conn., at a place called "Old Lebanon Crank" (now Columbia), March 20, 1756, and died at Phelps, N. Y., Jan. 27, 1826, in his

70th year. He was a landholder, and had owned estates in Colchester, Conn., and in Conway, Mass., previous to his removal to Phelps.

He was married in Conway, Sept. 19, 1781, to Sarah Salisbury, daughter of William and Elizabeth (Beale) Salisbury, of Milton Hill; born there, June 26, 1763, and died at Phelps, N. Y., Feb. 28, 1827, in her 65th year. She was eminently religious, and exemplary in her daily life. "Blessed are the dead who die in the Lord," is inscribed on her gravestone, and in the hearts of all who knew her. Her mother was the daughter of Seth and Elizabeth Beale, of Weymouth. Her father, William Salisbury, was descended from William Salisbury, one of the early settlers of Dorchester.

Children of ALEXANDER and SARAH (SALISBURY) GLOVER, born in Conway, Mass., and Phelps, N. Y.:

+ 92. Philander, b. June 10, 1782; m. { 1st, Polly Melvin, of Phelps ; 2d, Ruhamah Hall.
+ 93. Sarah Salisbury, b. Oct. 11, 1784 ; m. Osee Crittenden, Phelps.
+ 94. Elizabeth, b. April 23, 1787 ; m. Caleb Melvin, Phelps.
+ 95. Alexander, b. March 6, 1789 ; m. { 1st, Abigail R. Powell ; 2d, Clarissa Hawley ; 3d, Eliza F. Tompkins.
  96. Sophronia, b. Aug. 22, 1791 ; m. Jonathan Powell.
  97. Rachel, b. Nov. 22, 1793 ; d. Nov. 3, 1826, aged 33 years.
  98. George Whitfield, b. 5, 1794 ; m. Mary Kingsley.
  99. Charles Williamson, b. March 7, 1796 ; m. Mary A. Powers.
+100. Samuel Stillman, b. Sept. 11, 1798 ; m. Vinera E. Powers.
  101. Polly, } b. May 31, 1801; { m. Henry Powers.
  102. Amelia, } { m. Enoch Eddy.
  103. William Salisbury, b. Oct. 8, 1803 ; d. Oct. 14, 1804.

(50) JOHN GLOVER, the eldest son of John and Abigail (Holmes) Glover, was born in Milton, May 31, 1753, baptized June 3, 1753, and died in Randolph, July 22, 1829, aged 77 years.

He was married, Jan. 6, 1776, to Rachel Littlefield, of Stoughton, Mass., daughter of Moses Littlefield; born there, and died at Grafton, Vt., July 22, 1799.

John Glover resided in Milton a few years after his marriage, and had four children born to him there, their births being recorded on Milton Town Records. He then removed to Lunenburg, Mass., where he lived until about 1790, and had six more children born to him there. He then removed to Grafton, Vt., where he purchased a farm, and resided a few years. His wife Rachel died there, and

45*

several of his children. About the year 1800 he sold his farm in Grafton to his son Edward, for nine hundred dollars, and returned to Milton. Subsequently he bought a farm in Randolph, Mass., whither he removed, and where he resided till he died; and it is said by some that he was there again married, to Betsey Mann.

Children of JOHN and RACHEL (LITTLEFIELD) GLOVER, born in Milton, Mass., and in Grafton, Vt.:

104. Polly,	} b. June 28, 1776;	{ m. —— Derby, Leominster.	
105. Betsey,		{ d. Aug. 30, 1776.	
+106. Edward,	b. July 1, 1777;	m. Hannah Brown, Needham.	
107. John,	b. Dec. 27, 1778.		
108. Lucy,	b. July 2, 1780;	m. —— Evans, Leominster.	
109. Betsey,	b. Mch 27, 1783;	d. March 30, 1807, aged 24.	
+110. Abijah,	b. Sept. 17, 1784;	m. Hannah Hunt, of Milton.	
111. Lemuel,	b. Aug. 20, 1787;	m. Susan ——.	
+112. Benjamin,	b. Dec. 30, 1788;	m. Polly Terry, of Harvard.	
+113. William,	b. Feb. 15, 1790;	m. Betsey Divol, Leominster.	

(54) NATHANIEL GLOVER, the eldest son of Moses and Jerusha (Crane) Glover, was born in Milton, April 28, 1755, and died in Boston, "very suddenly," Oct. 22, 1822, in his 68th year. He was a surveyor of lumber, and resided in Boston.

He was married, Aug. 4, 1780, to Mary Siders, daughter of George P. and Salome Siders, of Germany; born there, March 4, 1762, and died in Boston, June 9, 1833, aged 78 years. Her father, George P. Siders, was born in Germany in 1727, her mother in 1731. They were married there about 1752, and afterwards emigrated to New England, taking with them their children. They settled first at Boston, and died there. He died Nov. 4, 1784, and Mrs. Salome, his wife, died in November, 1788.

Mrs. Mary Glover was a member of the Old South Church, admitted there June 13, 1813.

Children of NATHANIEL and MARY (SIDERS) GLOVER, born in Boston:

+114. William, b. May 27, 1781 ; m. Abigail Peverly, Portsmouth, N. H.
115. Elizabeth,   b. Aug. 14, 1783 ; d. Sept. 8, 1784.
+116. Susannah Siders, b. Jan. 19, 1785 ; m. David Homer, Boston.
117. Nathaniel,   b. May   12, 1787 ; d. Sept. 16, 1788.
118. Sally Siders,   b. Feb. 14, 1789 ; d. Oct.   9, 1791.
119. Lemuel Bent,   b. March 11, 1792 ; d. at Philadelphia, unm.

120. Charles Bradford, b. Nov. 15, 1794 ; d. Oct. 15, 1795.
121. Maria Saloma,   b. Nov. 7, 1796 ; d. March 21, 1798.
122. John Raymond, b. Jan.   1, 1799 ; d. May 16, 1799.
+123. Catharine Bradford, b. Feb. 26, 1800 ; m. William H. Pitcher,
       of London.
124. Nathaniel, b. April 12, 1802 ; went to the W. Indies, where
       he married, and died there or in Florida since 1848 ; no issue
       reported.

(55) RUTH GLOVER, eldest daughter of Moses and Jerusha
(Crane) Glover, was born in Milton, Feb. 23, 1757, and died in
Braintree, Nov. 4, 1793, in her 37th year.

She was married, Nov. 2, 1777, to Daniel Spear, of Braintree, and
went there to reside. Only one child has been reported—a son—
viz.:

125. Lemuel B., b. in 1780 ; d. at South Boston, March 20, 1824,
       aged 40 years.

(56) SARAH GLOVER, the second daughter of Moses and
Jerusha (Crane) Glover, was born in Milton, July 1, 1758, and died
there, May 22, 1833, in her 75th year.

She was married, Jan. 6, 1801, to George Tucker, son of Ebenezer and Mary (———) Tucker, of Milton; born there in June,
1749, and died June 19, 1805, aged 56 years. He was accidentally
killed by falling under the wheel of a loaded wagon. They had one
son, viz.:

+126. Ebenezer George, b. in 1803 ; m. { 1st, Mary Atherton ;
                                        { 2d, Anna T. (Atherton)
                                                Alexander, widow.

(57) MARY GLOVER, the third daughter of Moses and Jerusha
(Crane) Glover, was born in Milton, March 20, 1762, and died in
Salem, April 13, 1799, aged 36 years.

She was married, June 25, 1786, to Capt. Charles Gavett, of
Salem, and went there to reside. They had four children, as follows :

127. Charles Sullivan, b. April 2, 1787 ; d. young.
128. Mary Wallace, b. Oct. 24, 1788 ; m. ——— Onger, and went
       to the West Indies to reside.
129. John Whiting, b. Oct. 27, 1790.
130. Isaac Phillips, b. Sept. 27, 1792.

Mrs. Mary Gavett was a member of the Church at Milton, in full
communion, and the above children were all baptized there.

(59) HANNAH GLOVER, the eldest daughter of Henry and Hannah (Lewis) Glover, was born in West Dedham, June 25, 1756, and died there.

She was married, May 18, 1786, to Benjamin French, of West Dedham, and was his second wife.

Children of BENJAMIN and HANNAH (GLOVER) FRENCH, born in West Dedham:

131. Mary,   b. in 1788.
132. Hannah,   b. in 1790; m. Horatio Gay, of Dedham.
133. Catharine, b. in 1792.
134. Joseph.
135. Lewis.

(60) CATHARINE GLOVER, the second daughter of Henry and Hannah (Lewis) Glover, was born in West Dedham, Jan. 3, 1758, and died in West Needham, about 1800.

She was married, Nov. 14, 1782, to William Clark, of West Needham, and went there to reside. They had seven children, born there, as follows:

136. Rebecca,   b. in Jan., 1784; died, unmarried.
137. Reuben,   b. in 1786; m. { 1st, ——— Kingsbury; 2d, Catharine Tufts.
138. George,   b. in 1788; d. young.
139. Cynthia,   b. in 1790; d. young.
140. Catharine, b. in 1792; m. ——— Park.
141. Calvin,   b. in 1794; d. young.
142. George, 2d, b. in 1797; d. young.

(61) HENRY GLOVER, the eldest son of Henry and Hannah (Lewis) Glover, was born in West Dedham, Aug. 5, 1760, and died there, Oct. 17, 1814, in his 55th year.

He was married, May 3, 1784, to Rebecca Colburn, of Dedham, daughter of Samuel and Nancy (Deane) Colburn; born there, in 1764, died in Pawtucket, R. I., Aug. 1, 1844, and was buried in Dedham. Soon after their marriage, they removed to Needham, and remained there until after the decease of Mr. Glover's father, in August, 1800. They then returned to the old homestead in West Dedham, and in 1812 erected a new house on the spot, and continued there until his death.

Children of HENRY and REBECCA (COLBURN) GLOVER, born in West Dedham and Needham:

+143. Edward,	b. Oct.	10, 1785;	m. Caroline Whitney.
144. Martin,	b. June	14, 1787;	d. Oct. 10, 1793, aged 7.
145. Lucy,	b. June	9, 1789;	d. Oct. 4, 1793, aged 5.
146. Rebecca,	b. June	16, 1791;	d. Aug. 25, 1821, aged 31.
147. Benney,	b. Feb.	27, 1794;	d. Aug. 6, 1814, aged 21.
+148. Martin Colburn,	b. March	26, 1796;	m. Sophronia Bowker.
+149. Lucy,	b. May	14, 1798;	d. Mch 28, 1857, aged 58.
150. Anna,	b. Oct.	21, 1800;	m. Barnard Smith.
+151. Joel,	b. Dec.	26, 1803;	m. { 1st, Nancy Hildreth; 2d, Maria Handley.

(65) EDWARD LEWIS GLOVER, the second son of Henry and Hannah (Lewis) Glover, was born in West Dedham, March 5, 1770, and died at Hawley, Mass., Dec. 14, 1805, aged 36 years.

He was married, about 1795, to Ruth Grout, of Hawley. They had children; the sons went South, and settled there.

Letters of administration were granted on the estate of Edward Glover, of Hawley, to Ruth Glover his widow, who gave bonds as the law directs, June 26, 1806. (Vol. 24, p. 103, Probate Records for Hampshire County.)

(66) JESSE GLOVER, the third son of Henry and Hannah (Lewis) Glover, was born at West Dedham, Nov. 6, 1772, and died in East Cambridge, Jan. 10, 1848, in his 76th year.

He was married, Nov. 18, 1795, to Deborah Richards, daughter of Lemuel and ——— (Battelle) Richards, of Dover. Soon after marriage, they removed to Francestown, N. H., purchased a farm, and lived there many years.

Children of JESSE and DEBORAH (RICHARDS) GLOVER, born in Francestown, N. H.:

152. Rebecca, b. in 1795; m. ——— Pierce, of East Cambridge.
+153. Ira, b. in 1796; m. Sophia Mead, of Waltham.
154. Lydia, b. in 1797; died, shipwrecked on Charleston bar, S. C.
155. Deborah, b. in 1799; m. ——— Waldridge.
+156. Jesse, b. in 1800; d. July 17, 1848, aged 48 years; served in the Navy, in the War of 1812.
+157. Henry, b. in 1802; served in the Navy, in the War of 1812.

(67) DAVID GLOVER, the fourth son of Henry and Hannah (Lewis) Glover, was born in West Dedham, May 11, 1775, and died in Western New York, whither he removed and became a landholder about 1800.

He was married, in 1800, to Tamson Hall, of Conway, Mass.
They had three children, born in West Dedham:

158. Eveline.
159. Louisine.
160. Orville.

He probably had other children, but none have been reported after
his removal from West Dedham.   He lived at one time in Cambridge,
Washington County, N. Y.   It is stated that he subsequently removed
further West.   It is not known in what town he died.

[*Sixth Generation.*]

(70)   ELIZABETH GLOVER, the eldest daughter of Joshua
and Elizabeth (Swift) Glover, was born in Milton, Jan. 25, 1763, and
died in Boston.
She was married, June 1, 1792, to Benjamin Edwards, of Boston,
by whom she had one son:

161. Edward, b. January, 1794; died young.

Mrs. Elizabeth Edwards was married, a second time, to ———
Houghton, in 1800, and had one daughter:

162. Catharine, b. in June, 1801.

(71)   CATHARINE GLOVER, the second daughter of Joshua
and Elizabeth (Swift) Glover, was born in Milton, March 14, 1765,
and died in Cambridgeport.
She was married, April 1, 1786, to Samuel Wheeler, of Dorchester,
and had several children—names not reported.

(72)   JOSHUA GLOVER, only son and fourth child of Joshua
and Elizabeth (Swift) Glover, was born in Milton, March 11, 1771,
and died March 29, 1813.   He was enrolled in the United States
service, in the second war with England, 1812, and served one year,
when he was killed in action.   He left a widow and four children—
all daughters; his name, therefore, extends no further, and must be
classed among the extinct lines.   Letters of administration were
granted on his estate, in April, 1813, to Samuel Swift, of Milton; inventory taken, &c.
He was married, April 30, 1798, by Rev. T. M. Harris, to Susan-

nah Holden, of Dorchester, daughter of Samuel and Hannah (Kilton) Holden; born there, Sept. 11, 1774, and died Sept. 1, 1849, aged 75 years. She lies buried in the ancient cemetery at Dorchester, and has a gravestone.

Children of JOSHUA and SUSANNAH (HOLDEN) GLOVER, born in Dorchester:

+163. Nancy Holden,   b. Sept.   5, 1798; m. Elijah M. Greenwood.
  164. Elizabeth Swift,   b. Aug.   8, 1801; d. in 1865.
+165. Susannah Holden,   b. Jan.   18, 1804; m. Horatio Wood.
  166. Hannah,   b. March   7, 1807.

(74) SAMUEL GLOVER, the eldest son of Thomas and Zebiah (Vose) Glover, was born in Milton, April 17, 1767, and died in Dorchester, March 17, 1830, aged 63 years. He resided in Dorchester, and owned an estate near Meeting-house Hill. He was for many years Overseer of the Town Poor.

He was married, March 1, 1793, to Lois Kilton, of Dorchester, who died there in January, 1847. They had no issue. An adopted child, to whom they gave the name of Warren Glover, lived with them from infancy to mature age, and married, Jan. 29, 1823, Mary Lyon, daughter of Samuel Lyon, of Dorchester. Capt. Warren Glover succeeded to the estate of his adopted father at his decease, and died April 18, 1847. He left a wife and six daughters. His children were born in Dorchester, as follows:

Mary Vose,   b. in 1824; m. ——— Everett.
Eunice Ellen,   b. in 1826; resides in Boston.
Elizabeth,   b. in 1828; d. in 1857.
Caroline,   b. in 1831; m.
Maria Louisa,   b. in 1842.
Emily Frances, b. in 1844.

(75) RACHEL GLOVER, the eldest daughter of Thomas and Zebiah (Vose) Glover, was born in Milton, Jan. 30, 1769, and died in Boston.

She was married, Jan. 3, 1793, to Nathaniel Ashton, of Boston, and went there to reside. They had children, not reported.

(76) ABIGAIL GLOVER, the second daughter of Thomas and Zebiah (Vose) Glover, was born in Milton, Jan. 21, 1770, and died probably in Boston, at what time is unknown.

She was married, April 28, 1795, to Seth Baggs or Bangs, of
Boston, and went there to reside. They were both admitted to join
the Church at Milton, June 5, 1796, and four of their children were
baptized there, as follows. Their births are not recorded on the
Town Records:

   167. David Lenox,   bap. June 5, 1796.
   168. Seth,   bap. Dec. 17, 1799.
   169. Samuel Glover,   bap. Oct. 27, 1800.
   170. Abigail,   bap. June 3, 1802.

(77) SUSANNAH GLOVER, the third daughter of Thomas
and Zebiah (Vose) Glover, was born in Milton, Dec. 30, 1771, and
died in Dorchester.

She was married, in 1795, to Shepard Bent, of Milton, who died
there, Aug. 24, 1828. They had four children, born in Milton, as
follows:

   171. Charles,   b. Dec. 8, bap. Dec. 11, 1796.
   172. Samuel,   b. April 2, bap. April 7, 1799 ; went to the Sand-
       wich Islands and died there.
   173. Lewis,   b. in 1800.
   174. Eunice, m. E. H. R. Ruggles, of Dorchester.

(78) THOMAS GLOVER, the second son of Thomas and Zebiah (Vose) Glover, was born in Milton, Jan. 21, 1772, and died at
sea, date not ascertained. He passed most of his life at sea and in
foreign countries. He visited Lima, in South America; went away
in 1798, when he was 26 years old, and was absent from his home
nine years; returned to Boston and Milton in 1807; remained a few
months, and left again. From this voyage he never returned. It is
believed by his relatives generally that he died at sea. Another
conjecture is that he died at New Orleans. In a burial yard there, a
gravestone has been discovered bearing the inscription of Thomas
Glover, of Massachusetts, which is supposed by some to have been
erected by some friend for him. He was never married, and was
supposed by his surviving relatives to have left a large estate, which
has never been recovered.

(79) ELISHA VOSE GLOVER, sixth child and youngest son
of Thomas and Zebiah (Vose) Glover, was born in Milton, Jan. 3,
1785, and died in Camden, N. J., June 6, 1856, in his 71st year.
He resided in Milton until he attained the age of 21 years. He

then removed to Boston, and was for many years a constable there,
He was also elected and filled other important offices of trust and
honor.   He was a man of strict integrity, and gained many personal
friends by his faithful performance of the duties devolving on him.
A few years before he died, he removed to Camden, N. J., and engaged in the wholesale coal trade.

He was married, Oct. 15, 1812, to Lydia (Wooley) Cleaveland,
widow of Gad Cleaveland, of Dover, Mass.; born there in 1791,
and died in Boston, Jan. 31, 1863, aged 72 years.

Children of ELISHA VOSE and LYDIA (WOOLEY-CLEAVELAND)
GLOVER, born in Boston:

+175. Elisha Vose,   b. May 24, 1813; m. Matilda Bassett.
  176. Thomas Denzer, b. May 15, 1815; d. Sept. 11, 1837, aged 23.
+177. Lydia Louisa,   b. July 29, 1817; m. Ephraim A. Hall.
  178. William Gad,   b. Sept. 15, 1819; d. in California, in 1852.
+179. Samuel, b. Aug.   1, 1821; m. Rebecca D. Lombard, Boston.
+180. Sarah,   b. Jan.   14, 1823; m. Thomas Allen Minard.
  181. Edwin, b. Dec.   25, 1824; m. Lucretia Stone, in California.
+182. John,   b. March 20, 1827; m. Mary Briggs, of Boston.
  183. James Knowles, b. June 10, 1829; drowned in Boston harbor,
           Oct. 29, 1852, in his 23d year.
  184. George, b. Feb.   28, 1831; d. Feb. 5, 1832.
+185. Almira, b. Aug.   6, 1833; m. John Cox, of Dedham.

(80)   MARCIA GLOVER, the eldest daughter of Gamaliel and
Tabitha (Beale) Glover, was born in Conway, Mass., in 1771, and
died there, in 1844, aged 73 years.

She was married to Jeduthan Bartlett, Nov. 19, 1791.   They have
no children reported.

(81)   HANNAH GLOVER, the second daughter of Gamaliel
and Tabitha (Beale) Glover, was born in Conway, in 1772, and died
there in 1846 or '47.

She was married to Joseph Wheeler, of Grafton, Mass.   No children are reported.

(86)   RACHAEL GLOVER, the fifth daughter of Gamaliel and
Tabitha (Beale) Glover, was born in Conway, Mass., in 1783, and died
in Phelps, N. Y., in 1825.

About 1814 she became the second wife of Osee Crittenden, Esq.,
of Phelps, N. Y.   Children not reported.

(92) PHILANDER GLOVER, the eldest son of Alexander and
Sarah (Salisbury) Glover, was born in Conway, Mass., June 10,
1782, and died in Howell, Livingston County, Mich., Nov. 7, 1843,
in his 62d year.

He was twice married. First, to Polly Melvin, Jan. 5, 1804. She
died in Conway, in 1812, and he was married, a second time, to
Ruhamah Hall, in 1814, who died in Howell, Mich., in 1839. He
had two children by his first wife, and five by his second.

Children of PHILANDER and POLLY (MELVIN) GLOVER, born in
Conway and Howell:

186. Lamira, b. July 30, 1807 ; m. Othniel Hall.
+187. Milan, b. Aug. 11, 1811 ; m.

      Children by RUHAMAH HALL:

+188. Wellington Alexander, b. June 6, 1815 ; m. : d. Sept. 17, 1843.
+189. Livingston Maturin, b. Feb. 21, 1819 ; m. Marcia A. Nutting.
+190. Luther Melancthon, b. April 3, 1823 ; m.
191. Mary Jane, b. June 13, 1829 ; m.; no issue ; d. May 27, 1849.
192. Emerson Flavia, b. Jan. 24, 1838 ; m., and resides in Jackson-
      ville, Illinois.

(93) SARAH SALISBURY GLOVER, the eldest daughter of
Alexander and Sarah (Salisbury) Glover, was born in Phelps, N. Y.,
Oct. 11, 1784, and died there, Dec. 15, 1812, aged 28 years.

She was married, Dec. 1, 1808, to Osee Crittenden. She was his
first wife. They had issue, one son, viz.:

193. Cotton.

(94) ELIZABETH GLOVER, the second daughter of Alexander
and Sarah (Salisbury) Glover, was born in Conway, Mass., April 23,
1787, and resides in Phelps, N. Y.

She was married, in 1803, to Caleb Melvin, of Phelps, N. Y., and
had eleven children, born there, as follows:

194. Lyman Melvin, b. in 1805 ; m. A. Arnout.
195. Sarah,   b. in 1807 ; m. Horace Brewster, Greece, N.Y.
196. Harriet,   b in 1809 ; m. Dan Cleaveland, Cleaveland, O.
197. Mary,   b. in 1812 ; m. Amos Ligby ; d. in 1836, aged 24.
198. Larnard, }   b. in 1814 ; d. same year.
199. Warren, }
200. Alexander,   b. in 1817 ; m. Emeline Foster ; is a lawyer.
201. Elizabeth,   b. in 1818 ; d. in Lyons, N. Y., in 1846, aged 28.

202. Fidelia,   b. in 1821 ; d. in Phelps, N. Y., in 1848.
203. Sophronia,   b. in 1824.
204. Thomas J.,   b. in 1826.

(95) ALEXANDER GLOVER, the second son of Alexander and Sarah (Salisbury) Glover, was born in Conway, Mass., March 6, 1789, and resides in Webster, N. Y. He removed from Conway to Phelps, N. Y., and thence to Webster, N. Y. He owns a large landed estate there, which is said to be under high cultivation. For many years he has devoted his attention to agricultural pursuits.

He has been thrice married. First, July 4, 1816, he was married to Abigail Reese Powell, who died Sept. 10, 1837, and by her he had three children, one of whom survives. Second, to Clarissa Hawley, and lived with her 12 years; she died in 1849. There were no children by this marriage. Third, to Mrs. Eliza (Field) Tompkins, widow. They have no issue. She was the daughter of Stephen Salisbury, Esq., of Ypsilanti, Michigan, and a first cousin to Mr. Glover. Stephen Salisbury, her father, was the youngest brother of Sarah Salisbury, the mother of Alexander Glover. The mother of Mrs. Glover was a daughter of the Rev. J. Powell, of the Presbyterian Church in New York City, who emigrated from Wales to that city, and was pastor of a Church there for several years. He afterwards removed to Phelps, N. Y.

Children of ALEXANDER and ABIGAIL REESE (POWELL) GLOVER, born in Phelps, N. Y.:

205. Jonathan Edwards, b. Dec. 5, 1819 ; d. Dec. 23, 1846, aged 27.
206. Mary Ellen,   b. Mch 15, 1812 ; d. young.
+207. William Powell, b. Sept. 7, 1823 ; m. Mary Caroline Hammond.

(98) GEORGE WHITFIELD GLOVER, the third son of Alexander and Sarah (Salisbury) Glover, was born in Conway, Mass., April 5, 1794, and died in Ypsilanti, Michigan, Dec. 26, 1839, in his 46th year.

He was married, April 5, 1820, to Mary Kingsley. They had six children, as follows:

208. Sarah.
209. Anne Eliza.
210. Philander.
211. Diantha.
212. Emily.
213. Minerva.

(99) CHARLES WILLIAMSON GLOVER, the fourth son of Alexander and Sarah (Salisbury) Glover, was born in Conway, Mass., March 7, 1796, and is now residing in Ypsilanti, Michigan.

He was married, Aug. 10, 1825, to Mary A. Powers. They have had seven children, born in Ypsilanti, Michigan—date of birth not reported :

214. Alexander.
215. Sarah.
216. Charles.
217. Carrie.
218. Henry.
219. Aristene.
220. Cephia.

(100) SAMUEL STILLMAN GLOVER, son of Alexander and Sarah (Salisbury) Glover, was born in Conway, Mass., Sept. 11, 1798, and resides in Phelps, N. Y.   He is an extensive landholder.

He was married, April 23, 1817, to Vinera Eglantine Powers daughter of William Powers, Esq., of Mount Vernon, Vt.; born there, July 18, 1802, and married at the age of 15 years. She died in the town of Osceola, Mich., Feb. 14, 1847, in her 45th year. Mr. Glover, since the time of his marriage, has resided in Conway, Mass., Phelps, N. Y., Ypsilanti and Osceola, Mich., and has returned again to Phelps since the decease of his wife.

Children of Samuel Stillman and Vinera Eglantine (Powers) Glover, born in Phelps, N. Y., and Ypsilanti, Mich.:

221. William Powers,   b. March 24, 1818 ; m.
+222. Samuel Worcester, b. Sept.   5, 1821 ; m. Harriet M. Fiske,
          of Lincoln, Mass.
223. Sarah Eglantine, b. Nov. 20, 1826; d. Jan. 23,1849, aged 24.
224. Alanson D.,   b. Aug.   1, 1828.
225. Dennis H.,   b. Dec.   5, 1830 ; m.; d. in Michigan, 1860.
226. Samuel Stillman, b. May   15, 1835 ; m.
227. Daniel W.,   b. May   25, 1837.
228. Vinera Josephine, b. May   21, 1840.
229. George W.,   b. April 20, 1842.
230. Harriet M. A.,   b. March 17, 1844.
231. }
232. } Twins, b. Jan. 15, 1847 ; d. the 24th and 31st of same month.

(106) EDWARD GLOVER, the eldest son of John and Rachel (Littlefield) Glover, was born in Milton, July 1, 1777, and died in Brighton, Dec. 11, 1838. He removed with his parents to Lunen-

burg; thence to Grafton, Vt., and owned a farm in both places. A few years before his decease, he sold his landed estates, came to Brighton, and boarded at a hotel there. His death was caused by a fall from a load of hay which he was assisting his landlord to get into the barn before a shower, which killed him instantly.

He was married to Hannah Brown, of Needham, Mass., in January, 1804. They had ten children.

Children of EDWARD and HANNAH (BROWN) GLOVER, born in Lunenburg, Mass., and Grafton, Vt.:

+233. Joshua,   b. April 2, 1805; m. Elizabeth Boyes, of Grafton.
 234. Mary,   b. Oct. 12, 1807; m. John Shackford, of Grafton.
 235. Benjamin,   b. July 15, 1809; d. July 29, 1809.
 236. Almira,   b. April 30, 1812; m. Joseph Porter, of Brighton.
 237. Elizabeth Brown, b. Nov. 14, 1814; m. Philip Tuttle, Alstead,
                                                            [N. H.
 238. Joanna,   b. March 16, 1816; m. William Minot.
 239. Edward,   b. March 20, 1817; d. Oct. 8, 1817.   [ton.
 240. Adah,   b. Sept. 30, 1820; m. Charles White, Brigh-
 241. Isaac Davis, b. April 8, 1821; d. Aug. 27, 1821.
 242. Martha Lane, b. June 7, 1823; resides in Lowell; unm.

(110) ABIJAH GLOVER, the third son of John and Rachel (Littlefield) Glover, was born in Lunenburg, Mass., Sept. 17, 1784, and died in Milton, May 8, 1833, in his 49th year. He went with his parents to Grafton, Vt., and remained there until he arrived at the age of 21 years, when he returned to Milton.

He was married, May 25, 1807, to Hannah Hunt, a daughter of Joseph and Molly (Littlefield) Hunt, of Milton; born there, July 2, 1790. They resided in Randolph, Mass., about three years after their marriage, owning an estate and paying taxes there. In the summer of 1810 they went to Vermont, and lived there four years, then again returned to Massachusetts and lived in Milton, near Blue Hill, on a landed estate which she inherited from her father, Joseph Hunt.

The widow of Abijah Glover was married, July 15, 1834, to Francis Gooch, of Quincy. She died there, Nov. 9, 1845, in her 55th year. Francis Gooch died in Quincy, in 1863.

Children of ABIJAH and HANNAH (HUNT) GLOVER, born in Randolph, Mass., Vermont (?) and Milton:

243. Hannah,   b. Nov. 20, 1809 ; m. Freeman Gooch, Milton.
244. Abijah Austin, b. July 22, 1811 ; m. Louisa ———, and died
     Oct. 25, 1834, in his 24th year.
245. Syrena Peaks, b. July 12, 1812 ; m. Josiah Hunt, Randolph.
+246. Joseph Hunt, b. Nov. 9, 1814 ; m. Mary Ann Robbins, Salem.
247. Polly Littlefield, b. Feb. 4, 1817 ; d. Dec. 10, 1834, aged 17.
248. Rachel Littlefield, b. May 3, 1819 ; m. Henry Jones.
249. Lucy J.   b. May 12, 1821 ; died young.
+250. John Emery, b. May 10, 1824 ; m. Margaret Allen, Randolph.
251. Sarah Caroline, b. March 20, 1826 ; m. George Pickering.
252. Charlotte Ellen, b. Dec. 31, 1828 ; d. July 11, 1834, aged 6.
253. Olive Rosaline, b. June 3, 1830 ; m. ——— Bates.
+254. Walter Scott, b. April 25, 1832 ; m. Mary Crane, Canton.

(112) BENJAMIN GLOVER, the fifth son of John and Rachel
(Littlefield) Glover, was born in Lunenburg, Dec. 30, 1788, and died
in the United States service, in the second war with England, about
1815. He went with his parents to Grafton, Vt., and resided there
until he attained the age of manhood. He then returned to Massachusetts, and resided in Harvard a few years.

He was married, July 16, 1810, to Polly Terry, of Harvard. In
1812 he enlisted in the United States Army as a soldier, served
through the war, and was drowned while crossing a bridge on his
return home. He left a widow, and a son three years of age :

+255. Ephraim Terry, b. in 1812 ; m. Mary W. Sleeper, Chester, N. H.

The widow of Benjamin Glover was married, a second time, in
1828, to Thomas Livermore, Esq., of Boston, and resides there at
the present time.

(114) WILLIAM GLOVER, the eldest son of Nathaniel and
Mary (Siders) Glover, was born in Boston, May 27, 1781, and died
there at 60 Marion street, Aug. 20, 1853, aged 72 years. He was
an umbrella maker, carried on the business in Boston many years,
and was distinguished for his honesty, industry and uprightness of
conduct.

He was married, April 1, 1801, to Abigail Peverly, of Portsmouth,
N. H.; born there in 1781, and died in Boston, March 12, 1823,
aged 42 years. They had one child, born in Boston :

256. Mary, b. Nov. 29, 1801 ; m. Oliver Stevens.

(116) SUSANNAH SIDERS GLOVER, the second daughter of
Nathaniel and Mary (Siders) Glover, was born in Boston, Jan. 19,
1785, and died there.

She was married, April 21, 1805, to David Homer, of Boston.

Children of DAVID and SUSANNAH SIDERS (GLOVER) HOMER, born in Boston:

257. David.
258. Henry.
259. Charles.
260. George F., m. Frances Homer, of Boston.
261. Caroline.
262. Catharine.
263. Susanna.
264. Mary.

(123) CATHARINE BRADFORD GLOVER, the fifth daughter of Nathaniel and Mary (Siders) Glover, was born in Boston, Feb. 26, 1800, and resides in London, Eng. She was educated in Boston, and adopted the profession of teacher, which she followed a few years; subsequently she accepted the situation of private instructress to the children of her cousin Mrs. Onger, of Salem, accompanied her to the West Indies, and resided with her at St. Pierre, Martinique.

She was married to William H. Pitcher, Dec. 10, 1824. He was born and educated in London, England, and became a lawyer; was afterwards appointed to the office of Consul to the British West Indies, and resided at Martinique at the time of his marriage. The summer following he returned to London, and established himself as a Barrister at law in that city. In 1847 they resided in Russell Square. He died there in 1850.

(126) EBENEZER GEORGE TUCKER, only son of George and Sarah (Glover) Tucker, was born in Milton, in 1803, and resides now in East Boston.

He has been twice married. First, to Mary Atherton, daughter of John and Sarah (Bird) Atherton, of Stoughton; born there, and died in Milton; no issue. He married, second, in 1833, Anna Tisdale (Atherton-Alexander), daughter of Elijah and Ruth (Tisdale) Atherton, of Stoughton, and widow of Capt. Jeduthan Alexander, who was lost at sea in the first voyage after his marriage.

Children of EBENEZER GEORGE and ANNA TISDALE (ATHERTON-ALEXANDER) TUCKER:

265. Henry Vose, b. July 27, 1835; d. Jan. 3, 1861, in 26th year.
266. Edward, b. Sept. 27, 1837; d. Sept. 14, 1841.

Mr. Tucker resided for some years after his marriage in his native town, and filled several important offices there. In 1858 he was appointed to serve in the Custom House, and removed to East Boston.

(143) EDWARD GLOVER, the eldest son of Henry and Rebecca (Colburn) Glover, was born in Needham, Oct. 10, 1785, and died in West Dedham, at the homestead, Feb. 10, 1856, in his 71st year.

He was married, July 13, 1823, to Caroline Whitney, of Dedham. He succeeded to the homestead estate of his father, which was passed to him as an estate of inheritance, and occupied it until his decease in 1856, leaving it to his son Henry Franklin Glover, who is the present incumbent. The estate was first possessed by Henry Glover, the great-grandfather of the present owner, and passed by him, in 1800, to his son Henry, who occupied there until his decease, and passed it to his son Edward. From Edward it passed to his only son and heir apparent, Henry Franklin Glover.

Children of EDWARD and CAROLINE (WHITNEY) GLOVER, born in West Dedham:

267. Henry Franklin, b. April 18, 1824.
268. Abby Frances, b. May 4, 1832.

(148) MARTIN COLBURN GLOVER, the fourth son of Henry and Rebecca (Colburn) Glover, was born in Needham, March 26, 1796, and resides in Scituate, near Hingham. He is an extensive landholder, and formerly kept a public house there, but has retired from that business.

He was married, Dec. 3, 1823, to Sophronia Bowker.

Children of MARTIN COLBURN and SOPHRONIA (BOWKER) GLOVER, born in Scituate:

+269. Martin Colburn, b. Aug. 28, 1824; m. Mary Anne Wellington.
+270. Sophronia Anne, b. July 29, 1826 ; m. John W. Prouty.
 271. Henry,   b. July 29, 1833 ; resides in California, unm.
+272. Catharine Jacobs, b. July 29, 1839 ; m. Charles A. Tilden.
 273. Ellen Jane,   b. Mch 30, 1841 ; m. Morallas Lane, Oct.,'63.
 274. Abby Josephine, b. April 12, 1843 ; a teacher in Boston.
 275. Joseph Warren, b. Mch 18, 1850 ; at school in Hingham.

(149) LUCY GLOVER, the third daughter of Henry and Rebecca (Colburn) Glover, was born in West Dedham, May 14, 1798, and died at Exeter, R. I., March 28, 1857, in her 59th year. She

was never married. She was educated in Dedham, and occupied her-self in teaching for a time in her native town. In the year 1827 she went to the State of Rhode Island, and was engaged in her profes-sion in Pawtucket and vicinity, about twenty years. In 1847 she re-moved her school permanently to Providence, R. I., where she attain-ed an eminence in her calling, was honored with a large patronage, and remained there until within a few months of her decease.

(151) JOEL GLOVER, fifth son and youngest child of Henry and Rebecca (Colburn) Glover, was born in West Dedham, Dec. 26, 1803, baptized Jan. 8, 1804, and resides in East Douglas, Mass. He has been an inhabitant of several towns since he attained his majori-ty—Westford, Concord, Dedham, Bellingham, Millville, and East Douglas since 1857.

He has been twice married, and has had ten children. Nov. 6, 1828, he was married to Nancy Hildreth, who died in Westford, Sept. 30, 1830; and he married, second, Maria Handley. By his first wife he had one daughter:

276. Caroline S., b. Jan. 12, 1829 ; m. Otis Adams, of Chelmsford.

Children of Joel and Maria (Handley) Glover, born in West-ford, Concord, Dedham, Bellingham and Millville:

277. Henry,   b. May   5, 1833.
278. Warren,   b. May   1, 1835.
279. Martha,   b. Aug. 13, 1836.
280. Emily,   b. April 29, 1838.
281. Laura,   b. May   8, 1840.
282. Martin,   b. June 28, 1841 ; d. at Millville, Oct. 22, 1846.
283. Ellen Maria, b. May 13, 1844 ; d. at Millville, Aug. 17, 1844.
284. Maria Ellen, b. Oct. 13, 1845 ; d. at Millville, Aug. 8, 1845.
285. Josephine,   b. Aug. 20, 1848.

(153) IRA GLOVER, the eldest son of Jesse and Deborah (Richards) Glover, was born in the year 1796 in Francestown, N. H., and resided at one time in Waltham.

He was married in Waltham to Sophia Mead, and removed to Orono, Me. Subsequently he removed to Bangor, and in 1852 was keeping a hotel there. It is supposed they have children, but none have been reported.

(156) JESSE GLOVER, the second son of Jesse and Deborah (Richards) Glover, was born in Francestown, N. H., about 1800, and resides now in Lawrence; is a machinist. He served in the Navy in

the second war with England, was honorably discharged, and afterwards resided in West Dedham and Waltham, until he went to Lawrence, where he now resides.

He was married to Martha Bartlett, of Waltham. They have had
children, not reported.

(157) HENRY GLOVER, the third son of Jesse and Deborah
(Richards) Glover, was born in Francestown, N. H., in 1802, and
died in Cambridge, Mass.

He was married to Abby Richer, of Waltham, about 1825, and
had one daughter:

286. Abby, b. in 1830 ; m. ; resides in Waltham.

His widow has since gone to California.

[Seventh Generation.]

(163) NANCY HOLDEN GLOVER, the eldest daughter of
Joshua and Susannah (Holden) Glover, was born in Dorchester, Sept.
5, 1798, and died there, Aug. 24, 1863, in her 65th year.

She was married, Oct. 1, 1829, to Elijah Marble Greenwood, of
Dorchester. They have had four children, viz.:

287. Ellen Eliza, b. Aug. 23, 1830 ; m. Ebenezer Bird, Dorchester,
      Feb. 5, 1860.
288. Susan Emily, b. May 24, 1834 ; d. March 14, 1845, aged 11.
289. Annie Caroline, b. June 16, 1838 ; d. Feb. 3, 1855, aged 18.
290. John Francis, b. Dec. 29, 1841.

(165) SUSANNAH HOLDEN GLOVER, the third daughter
of Joshua and Susannah (Holden) Glover, was born in Dorchester,
Jan. 18, 1804, and is now residing in Boston.

She was married, Jan. 8, 1826, to Horatio Wood, of Boston. They
have had six children, as follows:

291. Elvira Ellen,   b. Sept. 26, 1826 ; m. Samuel Jackson.
292. Charles Augustus, b. Sept. 27, 1828 ; d. July 9, 1832.
293. Henry Holden,   b. Nov. 27, 1829 ; d. May 7, 1831.
294. Susan Emily,   b. Aug. 29, 1830 ; d. July 9, 1832.
295. Susan Glover,   b. Aug. 29, 1833 ; m. Alonzo H. Weaver,
      Feb. 11, 1854.
296. Charles Augustus, b. June 26, 1837 ; m. Adalaide Maria
      Wight, Feb. 2, 1862.

(175) ELISHA VOSE GLOVER, Jr., the eldest son of Elisha
Vose and Lydia (Wooley-Cleaveland) Glover, was born in Boston,
May 24, 1813, and is now residing at Bloomfield Park, near Cam-
den, N. J. His place of business is in Philadelphia, Pa.

He married Matilda Bassett, of Boston, resided there and at East
Boston until after 1853, and removed thence to his present residence.

Children of ELISHA VOSE, Jr., and MATILDA (BASSETT) GLOVER,
born in Boston, and Camden, N. J.:

```
    297. Amelia,          b. June   23, 1841.
 +298. Elisha Vose,       b. Oct.    3, 1843.
    299. Cecelia,         b. June   19, 1845.
    300. George Bassett,  b. April  16, 1847.
    301. Mary Elizabeth,  b. Nov.   25, 1849.
    302. Agnes,           b. Dec.   28, 1851 ; d. in infancy.
    303. Louisa,          b. April  10, 1853.
    304. Edith,           b. in         1855 ; d. in infancy.
    305. Etherlinda,      b. in         1857 ; d. in infancy.
    306. Charles,         b. March 13, 1859 ; d. in infancy.
    307. Geraldine,       b. in         1860 ; d. in infancy.
    308. Lawrence Litchfield, b. May 21, 1862.
```

(177) LYDIA LOUISA GLOVER, the eldest daughter of Elisha
Vose and Lydia (Wooley-Cleaveland) Glover, was born in Boston,
July 29, 1817, and is now residing in South Malden, Mass.

She was married, May 26, 1839, to Ephraim Abbott Hall, son of
Ebenezer and Hannah (Abbott) Hall, of Concord N. H.; born there,
June 27, 1812, and died Aug. 17, 1866, at Oakley Plantation, District
of Charleston, South Carolina, in his 55th year. He was formerly a
resident and transacted business in East Boston. They have had
five children, born in East Boston, as follows:

```
 +309. Ephraim Abbott, b. March 18, 1840 ; m. Eliza M. Fessenden.
    310. Mary Holyoke Pierson, b. July  28, 1841.
    311. Louisa Lydia,    b. Aug. 21, 1842.
    312. Eliza Matilda,   b. Nov. 23, 1843.
    313. Winfield Scott,  b. Sept. 10, 1847.
```

(179) SAMUEL GLOVER, the fourth son of Elisha Vose and
Lydia (Wooley-Cleaveland) Glover, was born in Boston, August 1,
1821, and died there, April 15, 1853, in his 32d year.

He was married, April 15, 1847, to Rebecca D. Lombard, of
Boston, and resided there after his marriage.

Children of SAMUEL and REBECCA D. (LOMBARD) GLOVER, born in Boston:

314. Elizabeth Ruggles, b. March 1, 1848.
315. Emma Cornelia,	b. Feb.	20, 1850.
316. Samuel James,	b. June	20, 1853, posthumous.

(180) SARAH GLOVER, the second daughter of Elisha Vose and Lydia (Wooley-Cleaveland) Glover, was born in Boston, Jan. 14, 1823, and is now (1867) residing there, and is a widow.

She was married, March 8, 1845, to Thomas Allen Minard. They had four children:

317. Clara Derby.
318. Thomas Allen.
319. Elisha Glover.
320. Louisa.

(182) JOHN GLOVER, the sixth son of Elisha Vose and Lydia (Wooley-Cleaveland) Glover, was born in Boston, March 20, 1827, and resides at Jamaica Plain, Roxbury. He was enrolled in the United States service in the late war, and served in the 45th Regiment Mass. Vols., Co. I, from 1861 to 1863.

He was married, July 4, 1848, to Mary Briggs, of Portland, Me.; born there, Oct. 28, 1831, and still living.

Children of JOHN and MARY (BRIGGS) GLOVER, born in Boston:

321. Mary Briggs,	b. March 17, 1849.
322. John,		b. May	31, 1851 ; d. April 25, 1852.
323. Ella Adalaide,	b. May	11, 1854 ; d. Aug. 6, 1866.
324. Louisa Abbott,	b. Aug.	 1, 1858.
325. John,		b. Sept.	13, 1860.
326. Helen A. Stowe,	b. May	28, 1863.
327. Harry W.,		b. Oct.	29, 1865.

(185) ALMIRA GLOVER, the third and youngest daughter of Elisha Vose and Lydia (Wooley-Cleaveland) Glover, was born in Boston, Aug. 5, 1834, and is now residing in Dedham.

She was married, June 13, 1854, to Samuel H. Cox, who was born in Dorchester, Sept. 7, 1830. He is now residing in Dedham, and is postmaster there. They have had three children:

328. Annie D., b. Jan. 26, 1856.
329. Henry C., b. Dec. 17, 1857.
330. Nellie L., b. May 24, 1861.

(187) MILAN GLOVER, the eldest son of Philander and Polly (Melvin) Glover, was born in Conway, Aug. 11, 1811, and resides near Saline, Michigan.

He was twice married. By his first wife he had one daughter:

331. Emma, b. ——— ; lived to the age of womanhood; d. unm.

By his second wife he has had four children:

332. Edward Livingston.
333. Arthur.
334. ———.
335. ———.

(188) WELLINGTON ALEXANDER GLOVER, son of Philander and Ruhamah (Hall) Glover, was born in Howell, Michigan, June 6, 1815, and died there, Sept. 17, 1843, in his 29th year.

He was married, and had two children:

336. Eugene,   d. in infancy.
337. Marcia Annette, d. in infancy.

(189) Rev. LIVINGSTON MATURIN GLOVER, D.D., son of Philander and Ruhamah (Hall) Glover, was born in Howell, Mich., Feb. 21, 1819, and is now residing in Jacksonville, Morgan County, Illinois. He is a clergyman, and obtained his academical education at the Western Reserve College, in Hudson, Ohio, where he graduated in 1840. He was two years a student at the Lane Theological Seminary, where he acquired a knowledge of his profession, and graduated there in 1842. He then became pastor of the Presbyterian Church in Lodi, Michigan, for the six years following, and until 1848, from which time, until the present, he has filled the pastorate of the First Presbyterian Church in Jacksonville, Illinois. Three years since, in 1864, he was honored with the degree of Doctor of Divinity, by Centre College, Kentucky.

He was married, in 1842, to Marcia Anne Nutting, the eldest daughter of Professor Nutting and wife Marcia Manning, of the Western Reserve College, Hudson, Ohio. She was born at Randolph, Vt., Sept. 28, 1821. They have had five children, born in Lodi, Michigan, and Jacksonville, Illinois.

Children of Rev. Dr. LIVINGSTON MATURIN and MARCIA ANNE (NUTTING) GLOVER:

47

338. Mary Amelia,	b. May 11, 1844.
339. Lyman Beecher, b. Feb. 10, 1846; near graduation at Wabash College, Indiana.
340. Martha Nutting, b. April 20, 1851.
341. John Adams,	b. May 16, 1853.
342. William Brown, b. June 22, 1860.

(190)	LUTHER MELANCTHON GLOVER, son of Philander and Ruhamah (Hall) Glover, was born in Howell, Michigan, April 3, 1823, and is residing there at the present time.

He is married, and has a family of four children, as follows:

343. Mattie.
344. Howard.
345. Adalaide.
346. Carrie.

(207)	WILLIAM POWELL GLOVER, the second and youngest son of Alexander and Abigail Reese (Powell) Glover, was born in Webster, Monroe County, N. Y., Sept. 7, 1823, and is now (1867) residing there. He is a landholder, and is engaged in agricultural pursuits.

He was married, in 1847, to Mary Caroline Hammond. They have had three children, born in Webster:

347. Luellen, b. Oct.	23, 1848.
348. Clara,	b. March 20, 1850.
349. Eugene, b. Feb.	9, 1860.

(222)	SAMUEL WORCESTER GLOVER, the second son of Samuel Stillman and Vinera E. (Powers) Glover, was born in Phelps, Ontario Co., N. Y., Sept. 5, 1821, and resides now in Michigan.

He has been twice married. First, to Harriet Maria Fiske, Aug. 22, 1843, by Rev. Edward S. Gregory. She was born in Lincoln, Mass., June 8, 1824. They have lived in Osceola, Michigan, and in Wendell, Mass.

Children of SAMUEL WORCESTER and HARRIET M. (FISKE) GLOVER, born in Osceola, Michigan, and in Shutesbury, Mass.:

350. Harriet Maria,	b. March 17, 1845.
351. Samuel Worcester, b. Dec.	1, 1848 ; d. Jan. 21, 1853.
352. Henry Jerome,	b. July	28, 1851 ; d. Feb.	2, 1852.
353. Irene Genevieve,	b. Aug.	7, 1854.

(233) JOSHUA GLOVER, the eldest son of Edward and Hannah (Brown) Glover, was born in Grafton, Vt., April 2, 1805, and died in Alstead, N. H., Sept. 7, 1853, in his 49th year.

He was married, in 1830, to Elizabeth Boyes, of Grafton, Vt., who died there in 1848.

Children of JOSHUA and ELIZABETH (BOYES) GLOVER:

354. Harriet Newell,   b. in 1831 ; now living.
355. George Pickering, b. in 1834 ; died.
356. Elizabeth Matilda, b. in 1836 ; died.

(246) JOSEPH HUNT GLOVER, the second son of Abijah and Hannah (Hunt) Glover, was born at Blue Hill, Milton, Nov. 9, 1814, and died there, March 31, 1855, in his 41st year. He lived on a landed estate which he inherited from his maternal grandfather, Joseph Hunt, situated in Milton near the Quincy line.

He was married, March 4, 1840, to Mary Ann Robbins, daughter of Jonathan and Mary Ann (Bachelder) Robbins, of Danvers. She was born in Salem, Sept. 20, 1822 ; is a widow, and now residing at the Blue Hill farm.

Children of JOSEPH HUNT and MARY A. (ROBBINS) GLOVER, born at Blue Hill, Milton:

357. Abijah Austin,   b. Nov.   26, 1840 ; resides in Randolph.
358. Joseph Robbins,   b. Dec.   17, 1841 ; resides in Randolph.
359. Mary Ann Robbins, b. March 12, 1843 ; m. John Higgins.
360. Hannah Matilda,   b. Dec.   23, 1844.
361. George Codman,   b. Sept.   9, 1846.
362. John Ira,   b. Oct.   18, 1848.
363. Lucy,   b. Aug.   4, 1849.
364. Martha Copeland, b. July   28, 1851.
365. Ellen Maria,   b. July   15, 1853.

(250) JOHN EMERY GLOVER, the third son of Abijah and Hannah (Hunt) Glover, was born in Milton, at Blue Hill farm, May 10, 1824, and is now residing there.

He was married, Sept. 16, 1854, to Margaret Allen, of Randolph.

Children of JOHN EMERY and MARGARET (ALLEN) GLOVER, born in Milton:

366. Ira Emery,   b. Nov. 3, 1855.
367. John Henry, b. June 16, 1857.

368. Maria Eleanor,   b. Aug. 6, 1859.
369. Mary Evelina,   b. Dec. 3, 1860.
370. Joseph Edward,   b. May 19, 1861.

(254) WALTER SCOTT GLOVER, the fourth son and youngest child of Abijah and Hannah (Hunt) Glover, was born in Milton,
at the Blue Hill farm, April 25, 1832. During the late war he was
enrolled in the United States service, 33d Regt., M. V. M., and was
killed in action in the summer of 1863.

He was married to Mary Crane, of Canton, and resided there at
the time of his enlistment. His widow still remains there. They
had two children, not reported.

(255) EPHRAIM TERRY GLOVER, only son of Benjamin
and Polly (Terry) Glover, was born in Harvard, Mass., in 1812, and
died in Manchester, N. H., since 1842, date of death not ascertained.
He was married, in 1836, to Mary W. Sleeper, of Chester, N. H.

Children of EPHRAIM and MARY W. (SLEEPER) GLOVER, born in
Manchester, N. H.:

371. Mary Livermore,   b. Aug. 6, 1837 ; m.
372. Martha,   b. Nov. 7, 1838.
+373. Thomas Livermore, b. July 10, 1842 ; d. at the Seminary Hos-
       pital, Georgetown, D. C., Sept. 5, 1862, in his 21st year.

(269) MARTIN COLBURN GLOVER, Jr., the eldest son of
Martin Colburn and Sophronia (Bowker) Glover, was born in Scituate,
Mass., Aug. 28, 1824, and died in Medford, Jan. 16, 1864, in his
40th year.

He was married, Oct. 21, 1852, to Mary Anne Wellington, daughter of Isaac Wellington, Esq., of Medford; born there in 1825, and
is now residing there. He was a goldsmith and jeweller, and resided
in Boston for several years after his marriage. He was compelled
to retire from business on account of failing health, and removed with
his family to Medford. Subsequently he visited California, and passed a year, where he so far recovered from his disease (asthma) as to
be able to resume business on his return. His place of business was
288 Washington street, Boston.

Children of MARTIN COLBURN and MARY ANNE (WELLINGTON)
GLOVER, born in Boston and Medford:

374. Francina Wellington, b. Sept. 29, 1853.
375. Annie Wellington, b. Feb. 22, 1856.
376. Mary Wellington, b. Aug. 26, 1858.
377. Luther Wellington, b. Nov. 27, 1861.
378. Adria Wellington, b. April 9, 1863.

(270) SOPHRONIA ANNE GLOVER, the eldest daughter of Martin Colburn and Sophronia (Bowker) Glover, was born in Scituate, July 29, 1826, and is now residing in Pembroke, Mass.

She was married, May 17, 1849, to John W. Prouty, of West Scituate, Mass. They have no children.

(272) CATHARINE JACOBS GLOVER, the second daughter of Martin Colburn and Sophronia (Bowker) Glover, was born in Scituate, July 29, 1839, and is now residing in Pembroke, Mass.

She was married, Dec. 10, 1861, to Charles A. Tilden, of South Scituate, Mass. They have two children, born in Pembroke:

379. Albert Colburn, b. Nov. 27, 1863.
380. Ruth B., b. Nov., 1864.

[Eighth Generation.]

(298) ELISHA VOSE GLOVER, Jr., the eldest son of Elisha Vose and Matilda (Bassett) Glover, was born in Boston, Oct. 3, 1843. In 1862 he was enrolled in the service of the United States at South Malden, as Quartermaster Sergeant to the 32d Regiment of Massachusetts Volunteers, and served a few months, when he was discharged for physical disability, and returned to his father's home in Camden, N. J. He soon recovered his health, and re-entered the service as Lieutenant to Co. A, in the 34th New Jersey Infantry, and served in that office until May 15, 1864, at which time he was promoted to the Captaincy of his company, and served under Gen. A. J. Smith, through the southwestern campaign, participating in the battles of Blakely and Mobile. He was with the first brigade that entered the latter place; retaining the position of Captain while on detached duty, and also, as Assistant Adjutant General, Commissioner for administering the amnesty oath, until Nov. 11, 1865, when by order of the President of the United States he was brevetted Major, and then appointed Colonel of the regiment, for "gallant and meritorious conduct."

47*

(309) EPHRAIM ABBOTT HALL, Jr., the eldest son of Ephraim Abbott and Lydia Louisa (Glover) Hall, was born in Boston, March 18, 1840, and is now residing there.

He was married, in 1860, to Eliza M. Fessenden, daughter of Charles and Eliza B. Fessenden, of South Malden. They have had three children, born in South Malden:

381. Charles Dalton,   b. Sept.   6, 1861.
382. Maria Antoinette, b. Nov.   20, 1862.
383. Ephraim Parker,   b. March 22, 1867.

E. A. Hall, Jr., enlisted in the United States service, July 18, 1861; was promoted Sergeant, Aug. 28, 1861, Co. F, 19th Regiment, Mass. Volunteers. June 18, 1862, he was promoted Sergeant Major; promoted 2d Lieutenant, Oct. 14, 1862; 1st Lieutenant, July 29, 1863; discharged on Surgeon's certificate of disability on account of wounds, April 29, 1864. He had served under Generals Lander, Stone, Dana, Sedgwick, Howard, Webb, Couch and Hancock.

(373) THOMAS LIVERMORE GLOVER, only son of Ephraim and Mary W. (Sleeper) Glover, was born in Manchester, N. H., July 10, 1842, and died at the Seminary Hospital, near Washington, D. C., Sept. 5, 1862. He was educated in Boston, and resided in the family of his step-grandfather, Mr. Thomas Livermore. At the age of 19 years, in 1861, he was enrolled in the United States service, and served in the 1st Regiment of Massachusetts Volunteers, Co. B; at first for three months, subsequently for nine months, and was in all the battles near Washington for those months. August 29, 1862, he was wounded in the spine, and carried from the field to the hospital, where he survived seven days.

A SUPPOSED BRANCH FROM HENRY GLOVER.

THERE was a John Glover living in Boston in 1659, who owned an estate on or near the Common, and continued there until after 1677, a period of 18 years. He had a wife Mary, and had four children born to him who are recorded on the Boston Records. His origin is known only by conjecture, and some slight evidence that he may

have been another son of Henry and Abigail Glover whose history
has been given, and to whom reference is made on page 506. The
time of his death or that of his wife Mary has not been ascertained,
although it is probable they died in Boston, as they made arrangements to continue there during life in the disposal of his property,
as will appear by the document given below. Their children were
as follows:

1. Hannah, b. April 5, 1659; probably m. Aaron Beard.
2. John, b. Feb. 1, 1660; d. April 19, 1660.
3. Mary, b. April 16, 1662.
4. Nathaniel, b. Oct. 6, 1665; d. in infancy.

It will be seen that he left no male heir, and the following disposal
of his estate appears on Suffolk Records, Vol. 11, p. 66, under date
of April 18, 1667.

This writing testifies that we whose names are underwritten, do
witness that we heard John Glover of Boston, Tanner, living upon
the Common, say: He did freely give his housing and land that he
had in Boston to his daughter Hannah Glover, which daughter is now
upon marriage. Whereas the said daughter Hannah and the man that
is about to marry her, to have the aforesaid house and land, as
fully as their own, at the death of him the aforesaid John Glover and
his wife Mary. The said Glover and his wife to have the use of the
best part of the House and land they agree to give their said daughter, to their own use and occupation as long as they both do live.
Only while the aforesaid Glover lives, he gives leave to his aforesaid
daughter Hannah, and her husband that is likely to be, to live in one
of the rooms of the House freely and rent free, and to make use of
the land as much as the aforesaid Glover shall not make use of, for
their own family use. His daughter Hannah and her husband to keep
all the housing in good repair during their father and mother's lives;
and to keep all the fencing firm, and at the death of the aforesaid
Glover and his wife, to have all the housing and land; only to pay
unto Mary Glover another daughter of the aforesaid John Glover,
Twenty pounds. And what moveables is left at their father and
mother's death to be equally divided between the two sisters. Hannah and him that she is about to marry, to have present leave to dwell
in some part of the house and to make present use of the land, and
that free without any rent, as abovementioned. And this was agreed
fully on, by the aforesaid Glover, and his daughter Hannah and her
husband the 18th day of April, 1677.
Testified to by the following witnesses, viz.:

HENRY ROOT,
WILLIAM HAMILTON,
ANDREW LITTLEJOHN,
RICHARD HARDEN.

N. B. The young man's name, that Hannah Glover is about to
marry, is Aaron Beard.

No record of this marriage of Aaron Beard and Hannah Glover has yet been discovered; but the record of the birth of their eldest child has been found, and some other facts gathered in relation to him. "Thomas, the son of Aaron Beard and Hannah his wife, was born 23 September, 1681." Of Aaron Beard very little is known. He was made freeman July 22, 1674. He was at that date said to be of Pemaquid, and took the oath of fidelity in Boston. He had a brother Thomas Beard, who resided in Boston, and died there in 1693. Administration of his estate by his son John Beard, June 13, 1693; inventory taken July 8, 1693. Aaron Beard was by occupation a fisherman, and lived mostly at sea. He died in 1695. No administration of his estate appears on Boston Probate Records. Letters of guardianship were granted to John Carter, of Woburn, Middlesex County, as guardian to Thomas Beard, son of Aaron Beard, July 18, 1695, as follows (Rec., Vol. 13, p. 314):

"Know all men by these Presents that I Thomas Beard son of Aaron Beard, late of Boston within the County of Suffolk in New England, Fisherman, Deceased, being a Minor about 16 years of age, have nominated and appointed, and do hereby nominate and appoint and make choice of my master John Carter of Woburn, in the County of Middlesex in New England, aforesaid, Yeoman, to be my guardian, with full power and authority for me and in my name, to ask, demand and sue for, recover and receive, and take into his possession and custody all such parts and portions of my estate left by my said father or any other ways or means whatsoever may accrue to me on or about his premises, effectually and to all intents and purposes, as I myself might or could do, being of age. Praying that the said John Carter may be accepted and appointed in the same power and trust. Witness my hand and seal, this 18th day of July, 1695.

THOMAS BEARD, and a seal.

Signed, sealed and delivered in presence of
    Jacob Melvin, Edward Turfrey.

Suffolk, ss. By the Hon. William Stoughton, Esq., Judge of Probate, the above named Thomas Beard personally appeared before me, and acknowledged the above letter to be his free Act and Deed, which I do hereby accept, allow and approve.   WILLIAM STOUGHTON.
    Boston, July 18, 1695.
    Examined by Jonathan Addington.

In 1708, thirteen years after the date of the above letter, it appears that Thomas Beard was married to Hannah ———, and made sale of the Boston estate to Thomas Banister. The following is an extract from the deed of sale, which may be found in full on Suffolk Prob. Rec., Vol. 24, fol. 79.

Beard to Banister.

Thomas Beard, of Woburn, in the County of Middlesex, in New England, Husbandman, and Hannah his wife, in consideration of Twenty pounds, sells to Thomas Banister a " Messuage and tenement with all the land on which it stands and is belonging thereto, situated and being in Boston, containing Eighteen acres and one half foot in breadth in front and Eighteen acres and one half foot in the rear. One hundred and nine feet and one half foot in length, running upon a straight line from the front to the rear ; and is butted and bounded by the Common at the North East ; and by the land of Richard Carter at the South East, and by the land of John Cross on the North West, and by the land of the said Richard Carter on the Southwest side. Together with all the Privileges and appurtenances thereunto belonging," &c.   (Signed)   THOMAS BEARD,
      Dec. 3ᵈ, 1708.   HANNAH BEARD.

We gather from the above that he lived in Woburn, was a husbandman, and had a wife Hannah, but have no further knowledge of him.

THE NEW JERSEY GLOVERS.

ELIAS GLOVER, who came to the United States in 1826, and settled in Paterson, New Jersey, states himself to have been descended from Peter Glover, of Prescot, Rainhill Parish, who is noticed on page 37 of these Memorials as Peter (11) the youngest son of Thomas and Margaret (Deane) Glover. The following is the account as rendered to the writer in 1861, by his grandson, Joseph Glover, of Paterson, N. J.

Elias Glover was born in St. Helens, a village about four miles from Prescot, Lancashire, England, in the year 1778. He was the son of Peter and Margaret (Fairhurst) Glover, of that village. Both his father and mother were probably born at Prescot. He had three sisters—Lucy, Alice and Nancy. His father died when he was quite young, and his mother married a second time to ——— Massey. He was himself married, about the year 1801, to Susannah Sharrot, the widow of Isaac Turner, of Prescot, by whom he had five children, as follows:

+1. Margaret, b. Aug. 16, 1802 ; m. William Sanderson.
+2. Mary,   b. March 25, 1804 ; m. Joseph Fletcher, in 1820.
+3. Peter,   b. Oct.   8, 1806 ; m. Alice Owen.
 4. Ellen,   b. in   1808 ; died in infancy.
+5. Maria,   b. Oct.   11, 1809 ; m. John Finden, of Willsbourne.

Elias Glover served his apprenticeship as a machinist at Manchester, in Lancashire, England. In the year 1826 he came with his wife, son Peter, and daughter Maria, to the United States, he and his son having made an engagement with Joseph Marshall to put in the machinery of a factory, called the New York Mills, situated at Whitesboro', in the State of New York. He remained at Whitesboro' about two years, and removed thence to Paterson, N. J., and died there, Jan. 22, 1850, aged 72 years. Susannah his wife died there, Feb. 10, 1853, aged 77 years. She was born at Prescot, about the year 1776.

(1) MARGARET GLOVER, the eldest daughter of Elias and Susannah (Sharrot) Glover, was born at Prescot, England, Aug. 16, 1802, and resided, in 1861, at Paterson, N. J.

She was married, in the year 1820, to William Sanderson, of Cheadle, Stafford Co., England. They came to the United States in the year 1832, and now reside in this country. They have had ten children, as follows:

6. Ann,	b. June 12, 1822.	
7. Jessie,	b. Feb. 17, 1825;	died in 1827.
8. Mary,	b. Nov. 9, 1826.	
9. Elias,	b. April 11, 1829.	
10. Samuel,	b. May 5, 1831.	
11. James,	b. June 19, 1833;	d. Sept. 28, 1834.
12. Susanna,	b. Oct. 15, 1835;	d. March, 1858.
13. Margaret,	b. June 23, 1839.	
14. William,	b. Sept. 29, 1843.	
15. Sarah Hannah,	b. Aug. 28, 1845.	

(2) MARY GLOVER, the second daughter of Elias and Susannah (Sharrot) Glover, was born at Prescot, Eng., March 25, 1804.

She was married, in the year 1820, to Joseph Fletcher, of Brinksway, Cheshire, at the Cheadle Church. They came to the United States in August, 1829. Her husband died soon after his arrival. They resided in Utica, N. Y., and his widow was married again, Feb. 5, 1830, to Frederick Finden, a native of Warwickshire, England. They remained in Utica until the following June, then removed to Paterson, N. J., where they resided in 1861. She had four children by her first husband, Joseph Fletcher, three of whom have died, and one is now living, viz.:

16. Joseph, b. in Brinksway, Cheadle, Dec. 3, 1820.

By her second husband, FREDERICK FINDEN, she has two children:

17. William Frederick, b. in Paterson, July 12, 1831.
18. Henry,   b. in Paterson, Feb. 19, 1839.

(3) PETER GLOVER, the only son of Elias and Susannah (Sharrot) Glover, was born in Prescot, Eng., Oct. 8, 1806, and in 1861 was residing in Aurora, Illinois.

He was married, July 14, 1823, at the Parish Church in Eccleston, Eng., to Alice Owen, daughter of Joseph and Jane Owen, of Manchester. His occupation is a machinist. He served his apprentice-

ship in Stockport, Cheshire, England.   He accompanied his father to
the United States in 1826, to assist in putting in the machinery of
the New York Mills in Whitesboro', N. Y.   He fulfilled his engagement, and remained there one year, and then visited Boston, Mass.,
where he remained eighteen months, and visited and inspected most
of the manufactories in that vicinity.   He then went to Paterson, to
meet his parents, who had removed to that city.   He remained there
for four or five years, and removed with his family to the City of New
York, where he resided until the year 1838.   He removed thence to
Paterson again, and remained until 1851, after the decease of his
father, Elias Glover.   Near the close of the year 1851 he removed
to Susquehanna Depot, on the New York and Erie Railroad, and
remained there until 1854, when he removed thence to Detroit in
Michigan, and resided there until 1856.   He then went to Chicago,
Illinois, and remained a few months superintending the machinery
for the Chicago, Burlington and Quincy Railroad, and when the company removed their shop to Aurora, Illinois, he removed thither,
where he now resides.   He has had eleven children, nine of whom
are living.

Children of PETER and ALICE (OWEN) GLOVER, born in Manchester,
Eng., and New York and Paterson, U. S.   (Names of deceased not
given.)

19. Joseph, b. in New Islington, Manchester, April   4, 1824 ; m.
20. Elias William,   b. in Paterson, N. J.,   Aug.   10, 1831 ; m.
21. Peter,   b. in New York City,   Dec.   6, 1834 ; m.
22. Jane,   b. in New York City,   March 29, 1836 ; m.
23. Frederick,   b. in New York City,   March 27, 1838 ; m.
24. Susan Elizabeth, b. in Paterson, N. J.,   March 15, 1840 ; m.
25. David,   b. in Paterson, N. J.,   Feb.   21, 1842 ;
26. Sarah Ann,   b. in Paterson, N. J.,   Dec.   6, 1845.
27. Alice,   b. in Paterson, N. J.,   Jan.   2, 1848.

(5) MARIA GLOVER, the fourth and youngest daughter of
Elias and Susannah (Sharrot) Glover, was born in Portwood, in
Stockport, Cheshire, England, Oct. 11, 1809, and died in Paterson,
N. J., July 12, 1853.
      She came to the United States in the spring of the year 1826;
was married in Utica, N. Y., July 4, of that year, to John Finden, a
native of Wellsbourne, in Warwickshire, England, by whom she had
eleven children, five of whom were living in 1861.   She removed

from Utica, in the year 1829, to Paterson, and remained there until
the time of her decease. Her children who survived are as follows,
born in Paterson:

28. John Henry,   b. Nov.   14, 1833.
29. Sarah Maria,   b. May   21, 1839.
30. Job Henry,   b. Sept.   14, 1841.
31. William Frederick, b. July   11, 1848.
32. George Ernest,   b. March   10, 1851.

———

The above comprise all of the three generations which have been
reported of Peter Glover, the youngest brother of John and Henry,
numbering in all thirty-two, and with the addition of the three sisters
of Elias Glover may be increased to thirty-five of that branch,
most of whom have lived or are now living in the United States.

·48

MR. RALPH GLOVER.

Mr. Ralph Glover was in New England as early as 1630, and previous to the arrival of Winthrop's fleet. In March of that year he was an inhabitant of Dorchester, and subsequently of Watertown, where he was admitted freeman Oct. 19, 1630. He owned a landed estate in Watertown, and died there before July, 1633. Very few facts have been gathered of him, either as to his English or American life. The prefix of *Mr.* was given to his name on the early records, which shows that he belonged to the distinguished class. He undoubtedly came from Rainhill Parish, Prescot, Lancashire, as the name of Ralph is found there on the Parish Records at a period before his appearance in New England, and has been continued down in many of the Glover families as a Christian name to later generations. Nothing appears on record here to establish definitely his relationships, ancestors or descendants. It is not certainly known whether he was or was not married; but if the former was the case, he was probably married before his emigration. His heirs, if he had any in New England, or his descendants, are as yet unknown to us. He died intestate, and administration was granted on his estate to Thomas Mayhew, of Watertown, as appears on page 120, Vol. 1, of Mass. Col. Records, under date of July 13, 1633.

The following incidents have been found recorded of Mr. Ralph Glover, in the year 1630 (Col. Rec., Vol. 1, pp. 78, 82, 85, 106, 121).

March 22, 1630. Three men to be whipped for stealing three piggs from Mr. Ralph Glover.

Sept. 18, 1630. An Inquisition held and taken on the body of William Bateman, who was set on shore upon a neck of land near Pullen Point, in the Bay of Massachusetts, and being sick and weak was left there with one Ralph Glover, who had a shallop in that place, but they being forced to leave him there, because the wind was contrary, they, on returning home, left him with such provisions as they had, and a fire. But when they returned to their boats on Friday last, they found the said William Bateman dead about high-water mark near their boat and about a stone's cast from the place where they left him ; so the jury brought in that he died by the visitation of God. The above was testified to by the following witnesses.

RALPH GLOVER,
ELIAS MAVERICK,
GILES SEXTON,
JAMES BROWN.

Nov. 30, 1630. At a Court of Assistants holden at Boston. Present the Governor and Deputy Governor and Assistants, viz., Sir Richard Saltonstall, Mr. Ludlow, Mr. Nowell, Mr. Pyncheon, Mr. Coddington and Mr. Bradstreet. It is ordered that Thomas Moulton shall pay unto Mr. Ralph Glover forty shillings before the 8 day of December next; or else be whipped, for the wrong he did Mr. Glover in coming from Plymouth and leaving him without a Pilot.

The next notice of him is under date of June 3, 1634, when it is stated on the records of the General Court at Boston, that

Mr. Thomas Mayhew, being appointed Administrator on the estate of Mr. Ralph Glover Deceased, intestate, hath now exhibited to this Court an inventory of said estate. There is therefore this time given until the first Tuesday in August next for the Creditors of the said Ralph Glover to make their demands of such debts as are due them, or else the said extra shall be divided amongst those that shall come in, and the others shall be excluded.

There is nothing conclusive, apparently, in the foregoing notices of Mr. Ralph Glover, in relation to his family or the manner of disposal of his effects.

Ralph, Ellis and Peter Glover owned estates in Rainhill about the middle of the 18th century, and their names are mentioned in the County History of Lancashire.

In a list of burials at Rainhill Parish Church yard, Prescot, Lancashire, England, the name of Ralph Glover occurs as follows, from 1700 to 1756:

15 April, 1700. Alice daughter of Ralph Glover of Rainhill.
4 May, 1706. Agnes wife of Ralph Glover.
17 March, 1720. Ralph Glover.
8 July, 1720. Alice widow of Ralph Glover.
11 Dec., 1730. Ralph son of Edward Glover and Margery his wife.
30 Jan. Catharine wife of Ralph Glover.

There are notices of a Joseph Glover, mariner, who died in Salem in 1692, and left a will on file, and who may have been a descendant —a grandson, perhaps—of Ralph, as the most diligent searches among records have failed to connect him with any other progenitor who settled in New England at so early a period, and no account of his birth or marriage has yet been discovered. Mr. Savage does not include the above Joseph in his notice of the Glovers of Essex County, of whom there appear to have been several at quite an early period. Tradition, therefore, aided by some remote circumstantial evidence, warrants us in conjecturing that he may have descended from, or was in some way collaterally related to Mr. Ralph Glover, of Rainhill, Dorchester and Watertown. He had, at the date of his will, a wife Elizabeth and an only son Edward. The will is on file at Salem, in the Probate Records for Essex Co. In it, he bequeaths his whole estate, real and personal, to his beloved wife Elizabeth Glover during her life, and afterwards the whole to go to his only son Edward Glover; and no other child is named. The will is witnessed by William Rogers and John Tyler. It was made and signed the 14th day of December, 1692. Inventory taken of the estate June 19, 1693. Amount of property, £34 3 shillings; viz.:

A piece of a house, and little orchard land amounting to £12	£12 03 0	
Household Furniture	22 00 0	
	£34 03 0	

In 1690, two years previous to the above date, the name of Joseph Glover appears among a list of soldiers who served in the expedition against Canada, in Capt. Gallop's company, who are stated to have been mustered from the old Plymouth Colony. However that may be, Joseph Glover formed one of the company in that expedition. In 1695, Elizabeth Glover, widow of Joseph, was admitted to join the First Church in Salem. Five years after that event, Elizabeth Glover was married, July 18, 1700, to Samuel Moulton, son of James Moulton, of Salem; born there, Dec. 25, 1642, and died there. Elizabeth lived to an advanced age, and was legatee to the will of her son in 1747-8. It is not known whether she died in Salem, or at Rehoboth, and the precise date has not been ascertained.

Of the only son Edward, named in the will of Joseph Glover, the facts that have been gathered show that he settled in Rehoboth in the early part of the 18th century, in that part of the town which afterwards took the name of Seekonk; that he was a landholder, was a member of the Church there, and sustained the character of an upright and honest citizen, and an eminent Christian. Cyrus Wheaton, Esq., the present Town Clerk of Rehoboth, in answer to a letter of inquiry in relation to Edward Glover, writes thus under date of Feb. 26, 1861: "I am unable to find, much to my regret, the place where Mr. Glover originated or came from, to this town. He settled in the westerly part of Rehoboth, now Seekonk, and owned a farm on the east side of the Green or Common, near the Meeting

House. In 1719 he, with others, purchased the old and first erected meeting house, for the purpose of having it removed or taken down by a given time, to make way for the erection of a new one. He was an active and prominent man at that time, and had resided there previous to the year 1707. He probably came to Rehoboth at the time or soon after he attained the age of twenty-one years. According to the entries on our Town Records he was married here in the spring of 1707, and died here in the latter part of the year 1747, living here for a period of about forty years. In 1732 he was chosen one of the Seaters to seat the parish in their new three-story meeting house, and was chosen Town Treasurer and one of the Selectmen from 1730 to 1740, and served faithfully and to great acceptance to the town in those offices. He also was elected to other offices of trust and honor. His name is often mentioned among those of other distinguished men in the town on our Records, from which the following dates are copied:

Edward Glover and Dorothea Peck were married April 2, 1707.
Children of Edward Glover and his wife Dorothea:
    Joseph,   b. July 12, 1710.
    Elizabeth, b. Jan. 2, 1711–12. (Probably second of the name.)
    Dorothea, b. Oct. 18, 1715; d. April 1, 1737, aged 22 years.
Dorothea, the wife of Deacon Edward Glover, died Feb. 11, 1737-8.
Mr. Edward Glover and widow Rachel Perrin, both of Rehoboth, were married July 5, 1738.
Dea. Edward Glover died Nov. ye 9th, 1747."

Mr. Wheaton further writes that he has carefully examined the Town Records of Rehoboth under his charge and keeping, and that he has herewith rendered all the births, marriages and deaths found recorded there, relating to Edward Glover and his family. Of Joseph and Elizabeth, the son and daughter of Edward and Dorothea Glover, he does not find any mention after their births. He also says that the name of Glover has disappeared from the town, and has not been known there for the last half century.

In the last will and testament of Edward Glover it is stated that he had a mother, Mrs. Elizabeth Moulton, for whom he provides. This and other circumstances which follow in the disposal of his property, establish the fact that he had no children at that date.

Rev. James O. Barney furnishes the following extracts from the Church Records of Seekonk, anciently Rehoboth:

Edward Glover and Dorothea his wife owned the Covenant June 16, 1709. Their daughter Elizabeth was baptized the same day, and no mention is made of their other children. May 25, 1727, they were received into full communion ; and Oct. 2, 1737, he is first mentioned as Deacon of the Church. The last mention of Dea. Edward Glover on the Church Records is in 1746. The monument in the cemetery says, "Dea. Edward Glover died Nov. 10, 1747, in the 65th year of his age." He gave a silver cup to the Church, bearing this inscription : "The Gift of Deacon Edward Glover, Deceased, to the First Church of Christ in Rehoboth, 1751."

Mr. Barney also adds that the most diligent search has been baffled as to the discovery of his origin, or what branch of Glover he connects with, and that it would be very gratifying to the friends of the Church there, and his successors in office, if more could be known of his previous history. It appears he acquired a competent estate, of which he makes the following disposal by Will, as found recorded on the Probate Records for Bristol County.

Will of Edward Glover, of Rehoboth.

In the name of God, Amen. The Seventh day of September, in the year of our Lord 1747. I Edward Glover of Rehoboth, in the County of Bristol and Province of Massachusetts Bay in New England, Yeoman, being weak of body, but of perfect mind and memory, Thanks be given to God ; and calling to mind the mortality of my body and knowing that it is appointed unto men once to die, do make and ordain this my Last Will and Testament. Principally and first of all I give and recommend my soul into the hands of God who gave. it—hoping through the interest, death, merits and passion of my Saviour Jesus Christ to have full and free pardon and forgiveness of all my sins and to inherit Everlasting Life. And my body I commit to the Earth to be decently buried at the discretion of my Executor hereinafter named, nothing doubting but at the general Resurrection I shall receive the same again by the Mighty Power of God.

And as touching such worldly Estate whereof it hath pleased God to bless me with in this Life, I give, demise, and dispose of the same in manner and form following. That is to say,

Imp. My Will is that all my Lawful debts and funeral charges be paid or discharged by my Executor hereafter named.

Item. I give and bequeathe to my Honoured Mother Elizabeth Moulton a suitable and Honourable support during her natural Life. To be rendered to her out of my Estate by my Executor hereafter named.

Item. I give and bequeathe unto the First Church of Christ in Rehoboth a Silver Cup of the same dimensions and value with one of those thereunto already belonging, to be purchased by my said Executor.

Item. I give and bequeathe to my well beloved nephews, the children of Nathan Peck of Rehoboth Deceased, all my part of that Lott at Brush Plain in said Rehoboth that is in Partnership with them, to be equally divided between them ; and to be to them and to their heirs and assigns forever.

Item. I give and bequeathe unto my well-beloved wife Rachel Glover all my other Estate, both Real and Personal whatsoever and wheresoever to be, to her and her heirs and assigns forever, She or they, performing as above ordered, whom I make and ordain my only and sole Executor of this my last Will and Testament. And I do hereby utterly disallow, revoke and disannul all former Testaments and Wills, Legacies and bequests and Executors by me in any manner of ways before this time named; and bequeathe, ratify and confirm this and no other to be my last will and Testament. In witness whereof, I have hereunto set my hand and seale the day and year above written. EDWARD GLOVER, and a seal.

Signed, sealed, published and declared by the said Edward Glover as his last Will and Testament,

In presence of us the Subscribers,
John Greenwood,
Ezekiel Read,
Thomas Read, Jun'.

Bristol, ss. Dec. 1st, 1747. Then before the Honorable Nathaniel Hubbard, Esq., Judge of the Probate of Wills for and within the County of Bristol, came Mr. John Greenwood, Ezekiel Read and Thomas Read, Jun', Witnesses of the Last Will and Testament of Mr. Edward Glover, Late of Rehoboth Dec'd., and made oath that they were present and did see and hear the said Dec'd sign, seal, publish and declare the within written Instrument to be his Last Will and Testament, and that he was of a sound disposing mind when he did it, and that they all signed in presence of the Testator. NATH'L HUBBARD,
STEPHEN PAINE, *Register.* *Judge of Probate.*

Bristol ss. Nathaniel Hubbard, Esq., duly appointed and commissioned by his Excellency William Shirley, Commander-in-Chief in and over His Majesty's Province of the Massachusetts Bay, by and with the advice and consent of the Council, to be Judge of the Probate of Wills and granting Letters of Administration on the Estates of persons Dec'd, having Goods, Chattels, Rights and Credits in the County of Bristol in the Province aforesaid. To Rachel Glover of Rehoboth in the County of Bristol, aforesaid, Widow. Know ye, that upon the day of the date hereof before me at Rehoboth in the County aforesaid, the Will of your late husband Edward Glover, late of Rehoboth in the County of Bristol aforesaid, Yeoman, Deceased, was proved, approved and allowed, who having while he lived and at the time of his death, Goods, Chattels, Rights and Credits in the County aforesaid and the Probate of the said Will and Power of committing Administration of All and singular the Goods, Chattels, Rights and Credits of the said Deceased and his Will in any manner concerning, is hereby committed to Rachel Glover, sole Executrix of the above named Will; to administer the Estate of the said Dec'd, and to Exhibit the same into the Registry of the Court of Probate for the County aforesaid at or before the 1st day of March next; and also to render a plain account of your administration, on oath, at or before the first day of March, which will be in the year 1748.

In testimony whereof, I have this day set my hand and Seal of the Court of Probate, Dated the 1 day of Dec. 1747.

NATHANIEL HUBBARD,
Judge of Probate of Wills for Bristol County.

REV. JOSEPH GLOVER.

THE name of Rev. JOSEPH GLOVER, Rector of Sutton in Surrey, England, is found among a list of incumbents in the Rectory of Sutton, from 1628 to 1636. In 1636 it is stated he tendered his resignation, with the intention of embarking for New England, which resignation was accepted with "sorrow," and Henry Wyche, A.M., of Cambridge University, was appointed his successor. (Vol. 1, *Hist. Co. of Surrey; English County Histories*, page 487.)

In the Parish Registry is the following entry, under date of June 10, 1636. "Henry Wyche, being a non-resident and Master of Arts in the Cambridge University in England, was inducted into office by Thomas Pope, Knight, to the Rectory of Sutton, after the resignation made of the same Rectory by Joseph Glover, who was much loved by most if not all, and his departure much lamented." After his resignation, he preached some time in London, travelled and visited Lancashire and other counties, preaching and endeavoring to obtain funds for the College which had been already commenced at Cambridge in New England. / But he was destined never to see the accomplishment of his desires with regard to the College, for he died on the voyage over, leaving a widow and five children to "proceed on their lonely way in grief and disappointment."

In Vol. 3, 4th series, of Mass. Historical Collections, page 343, there is the following notice of him: "Amongst the other business that Mr. Winslow had to provide, he had orders from the Church to bring over to New England some able fitt man to be their minister; and accordingly he procured a Godly and worthy man, one Mr. Glover; but it pleased God to cut him off, for when he was prepared for the voyage he fell sick and died." Other writers state that he died on the voyage, which facts seem to prove.

Another account is as follows, gathered from different writers: "In the summer of 1638, Mr. Glover, with his family, embarked in the John of London, bound for New England. He took out with him a printing press, which he intended for Harvard College in Cambridge; and Stephen Daye, a printer, who was to superintend the printing, and three men servants who were bound to work the press for him three years in order to establish the business of printing in the infant Colony." "His heart was wrapt in its progress and advancement; and during the interim of his retirement from the Rectory of Sutton, he had been untiring in his efforts to promote its growth under the influence of an educational system. He contributed unsparingly himself of his wealth and influence, and induced others of his friends, both in England and Holland, to become interested in so noble a cause. Mr. Glover died on the voyage, before reaching the shores of New England. His widow and five children proceeded on the voyage, and arrived in the autumn of 1638. They settled in Cambridge. Stephen Daye, the printer, whom he had engaged to superintend the printing, arrived and set up the press, which was the first printing press in America." "Mr. Glover has been justly styled by historians as the 'Father of the American Press.' The press was set up under the sanction of the Magistrates and Elders, Stephen Daye directing and superintending the whole apparatus, and employing the men whom Mr. Glover had engaged for that purpose. He had it ready for operation, and began business in the first month of 1639." The press first used by Daye became the property of Mr. Glover's heirs in 1656. It has since passed to the possession of the College.

Isaiah Thomas, in his History of Printing, writes of Mr. Glover: "Rev. Jose* Glover, a worthy and wealthy dissenting clergyman of England, may be considered the father of the American Press. He engaged with great earnestness in the settlement of New England, and in particular of the Massachusetts Colony, and attentively pursued such measures for its interest and prosperity as he judged would best promote them. He gave much to Harvard College, and solicited aid from others, both in England and Holland. In the year 1638 he procured a printing press, and engaged a printer to accompany it in

---

* The Christian name of Mr. Glover has been variously spelled by different writers who have noticed him. Mr. Thomas says, "At Harvard it was written Jose." In many other notices of him, by New England writers, it is written Josse, as in the Suffolk Registry of Deeds. Some writers, of later date, have so far corrupted the spelling as to write his name Jesse, which has been the occasion of great confusion. Johnson, who was cotemporary with him, wrote his name Jos', which is an abridgment of Joseph, which was truly his name. Gov. Winthrop gave him his true English name, without contraction or corruption; as in Vol. 1 of Journal, p. 212, he writes thus: "The Printing House was begun by one Daye, at the charge of Mr. Joseph Glover, who died on sea hitherward." But we are no longer in doubt and uncertainty about the spelling of his Christian name, as the English orthography decides it. On the Church Records of Sutton, in Surrey, it is written Joseph, and wherever his name occurs in English Records and in the English County Histories, it is invariably written "Joseph Glover."

a ship bound to New England. Mr. Glover, with his wife and five children, embarked in the same ship, but, unfortunately, he did not live to reach the shores of New England. His widow and children arrived in the autumn of that year, and settled in Cambridge. Rev. Ezekiel Rogers and about sixty families came passengers in the same ship." " His widow, Mrs. Elizabeth Glover, afterwards married the Rev. Henry Dunster, first President of Harvard College."

Mr. Thomas also writes thus: " It is not known whether Mr. Glover had been in New England previous to his embarking for this country in 1638, but I find by the Records of the County of Middlesex that he possessed a valuable real and personal estate in Massachusetts, and that he had two sons and three daughters, viz.: Roger Glover; John Glover, H. C. in 1650, was a physician and settled in Boston; Elizabeth, who married Adam Winthrop; Sarah, who married Deane Winthrop; and Priscilla, who married John Appleton."

The following notices of Mr. Glover's estate and lands in Boston and vicinity are found recorded in the Registry of Deeds for Suffolk County, Vol. 1, p. 254:

Trustees of Glover to Atkinson.

Increase Nowell, William Hibbins, Henry Dunster and George Cooke, Feoffees in trust for the estate of Josse Glover, to Theodore Atkinson of Boston, Feltmaker, viz. Of a certain house and garden in Boston, formerly possessed by Mr. Josse Glover, being bounded by and with Thomas Hawkins on the North, and on the West; and the street on the South and East. Together with three acres of Land lying in the new Field, bounded by and with John Biggs on the East and on the West; and on the Marsh on the North. 29 : 7 : 1645.
Recorded Dec. 13, 1652.   pr   EDWARD RAWSON, *Recorder*.

Vol. 1, p. 66.   Glover's Feoffees to Bennett.

Increase Nowell, William Hibbins and Henry Dunster, Feoffees to the estate of Josse Glover, late of Sutton in the County of Surrey in England, to Samuel Bennett of Lynn, viz. Of a certain Windmill in Lynn, formerly in possession of John Humphrey, Esq. 23 : 31 : 1645.
Recorded 6 : 10 : 1645, by EDWARD RAWSON, *Rec*.

Mr. Glover was twice married. His first wife was Sarah Owfield, daughter of Mr. Roger Owfield, of London (citizen). They had three children, born in Sutton, viz.: Roger, Elizabeth and Sarah. The mother of Sarah Owfield was of Scottish origin, and lived in Edinburgh, Scotland. She died July 10, 1628, aged 30 years, and her husband caused a monument to be erected over her remains, with the following inscription:

Here Underlyeth interred the Corps of that virtuous and religious Gentlewoman and servant of God, Mrs. Sarah Glover, one of the daughters of Mr. Roger Owfield, Citizen of London, Late wife of Mr. Joseph Glover, Rector of Sutton in Surrey, by whom she had three children, viz. Roger, Elizabeth and Sarah. She died July 10, 1628, æ. 30 years. In memory of whom her said husband has caused this monument to be erected, May 24, A.D. 1629.

> This Monument presents unto your view
> A Woman Rare, on whom all Grace divine,
> Truth, Love, Zeal, Piety in Splendid hue
> With Sacred Knowledge, did Splendidly Shine.
> Since then, examples teach; learn you by this,
> To mount the steps of everlasting bliss.

The three children named above, by his first wife:

+1. Roger, b. in Sutton, Eng., 1623; d. at Edenborough, Scotland.
+2. Elizabeth, m. Adam Winthrop, Esq.
+3. Sarah,   m. Deane Winthrop, Esq.

The second wife of Rev. Joseph Glover was Elizabeth Harris, daughter of William Harris, of ——, England, afterwards of Boston, to whom he was married about 1630. By her he had two children, as follows:

+4. Priscilla, m. John Appleton, Esq., of Ipswich.
+5. John,   d. in London, in 1668, unmarried.

Mrs. Elizabeth Glover was married, soon after her arrival at Cambridge, to Rev. Henry Dunster, and died 23: 6: 1643. She was buried in the ancient burial ground at Cambridge, and has a gravestone, much gone to decay. There were no children by this marriage. Mr. Dunster, on his marriage with Mrs. Glover, assumed the charge of her children, was subsequently appointed their guardian, and superintended their education until they were married or arrived at full age. He was also appointed one of the feoffees to the estate of their inheritance. Their mother survived but a few years after her second marriage, and Mr. Dunster married a second time Elizabeth ——, by whom he had several children. She survived him, and died in Cambridge 12: 7: 1690, aged 60 years.

Mr. Glover made his will, which is on file at the Probate office for Middlesex County, and appointed his wife Elizabeth sole executrix of his "last Will and Testament."

In 1639, it was ordered by the General Court at Boston, "that Mr. Thomas Mayhew and Mr. Flint shall set out Mrs. Glover six hundred acres of land on the west side of Concord River."

Under date of Oct. 7, 1640, it is stated that "the six hundred acres formerly granted to Mrs. Elizabeth Glover, to lye on the West side of Sudbury River, it is now granted her on the East side of said River and without the limits of the last addition to the bounds of Sudbury, and between the said bounds and the Great Pond of Cochituate. And by these Presents she shall have Liberty to lay out the same, provided she make a return to the next General Court." The return was not made in 1640. Thomas Mayhew, Peter Noyes and Edmund Rice were appointed to lay out Mrs. Glover's farm, and having faithfully performed the same, made the following report:

We whose names are underwritten have laid out Mrs. Glover's farm as followeth, viz., Sudbury line is the North East Bounds ; the North West bounds is the Great River that issueth out of the Great Pond at Cochituate ; the South East bounds from the place where the little River runs out of the great Pond till you come to the North East end of said Pond, and so to the North West end of the Little Pond, and from thence from the North East end of the said Little Pond ; and from thence to the nearest place of Sudbury line ; according unto the marked trees. Witness hereunto the 7 : 10 : 1644. This is our return of the Court's desire.   THOMAS MAYHEW,
(Mass. Col. Rec., Vol. 2, p. 114.)   PETER NOYES,
                                            EDMUND RICE.

Mrs. Glover became the wife of Rev. Henry Dunster, June 22, 1641 (Camb. Rec.), two years after the grant was made to her by the General Court; but the return was not made and the bounds settled until one year after her decease. The farm was held in trust by Mr. Dunster, guardian for her minor children and feoffee to their estate.

Edmund Rice, Esq., purchased the above described farm of her son John Glover, and it has descended in the Rice families, through many generations, to the present time.

June 18, 1645, it was ordered that Peter Noyes and Edmund Rice be a committee to lay out a farm to Mr. Dunster in the town of Sudbury; and the committee afterwards reported that they had laid out Mr. Dunster's farm as follows : " The land lying between the Ponds, contiguous to Mrs. Glover's farm, being the Southern bounds of this farm."

Mrs. Elizabeth Glover, in 1640, entered a petition, from which the following is an extract, at a Colony Court holden at New Plymouth (Vol. 5, p. 151, Plymouth Col. Rec.):

At a Court of Assistants held at New Plymouth, before William Bradford Esq., Governor of the Plymouth Colony, the following petition was presented and acted upon. "Whereas Mrs. Elizabeth Glover, Widow and Executrix of the last Will and Testament of Joseph Glover Deceased; constituted and appointed Mr. Timothy Hatherly her Attorney to prosecute John Combe of Plymouth, Gentleman, for a debt upon a bond of twelve pounds; now for the ending and deciding thereof, it is concluded and agreed upon, that in Consideration that the said John Combe hath, and in open Court bargained, Sold and assigned, and made over unto Thomas Prince, all his corn now planted and growing about his house at Rooky Nook; To Have and to Hold unto him the said Thomas Prince; and he hath undertaken to pay the said debt unto Mrs. Glover, and either to deliver the sixteen bushels of Wheat and Eighteen bushels of Rye at Mrs. Glover's house at Cambridge in Massachusetts Bay, at, or before the Twentieth day of August next ensuing; or else pay her ten pounds and ten Shillings Sterling. Provided however always that, if the corn be paid as aforesaid, that then, Mrs. Glover shall allow the one half the charges of transportation from hence, to her house at Cambridge. Dated May 5, 1640.

[*Second Generation.*]

(1) ROGER GLOVER, the eldest son and child of Rev. Joseph and Sarah (Owfield) Glover, was born in Sutton, County of Surrey, in England, about 1623, and died in Scotland. As stated by many writers, "He was slain in the Wars at Edenborough in Scotland in the Kingdom of Great Britain," before 1652. At the age of about fourteen years he accompanied his parents to New England, and resided with his mother in Cambridge, both before and after her marriage with President Dunster, and was educated by him. It has not been ascertained at what date he returned to England, but it is probable he left Cambridge soon after or at the time he attained the age of twenty-one years, which would occur in 1645. He made a will, but died before any division could be made of his father's estate accruing to him and the other heirs; some of whom were minors and under guardianship. Application appears to have been made to the General Court for a division of his property in 1652, by Rev. Henry Dunster, "Guardian and Feoffee to the estate of Mr. Josse Glover."

The following is in answer to that petition, as found in Vol. 4, p. 118, of Mass. Col. Rec., under date of Oct. 26, 1652, which renders it certain that Roger Glover died previous to that date, and that he left a will:

49

In answer to the petition of Rev. Henry Dunster, Guardian to the children of Mr. Josse Glover and Feoffee in trust in behalf of Adam Winthrop, the son of Adam Winthrop, Esq. late of Boston Deceased, desiring a Committee may be appointed to view and examine what the estates of Roger and John Glover are, in the hands of the said Henry Dunster, Roger being slain before any division was made, and that so the Will of the said Roger may be justly performed. The Court doth grant the petitioner's request thus far that Mr. John Leverett and Mr. Joseph Hills, Esqs. shall have power to view and examine differences as is desired and make report of their return to the next County Court of Middlesex if it may be ready against the same, or else to the next Court of Middlesex after it. Oct. 26, 1652.

There has been no evidence found on any writing or document here to show that he had any children, or was ever married; but in the County History of Surrey there is an account of a Roger Glover who died and was buried at Cudham, in the County of Kent, in 1722, who may have been a grandson of Rev. Joseph Glover by his son Roger. The following is written of him in the same volume and in connection with the account of his supposed ancestors—Surrey, Vol. 2, p. 437:

Roger Glover purchased of the Norards an estate and other estates of the Greshams. He was buried at Cudham in Kent, 1722. He married Amy Hayward, who was daughter of Richard Hayward of Waldingham. She survived her husband several years, and died Dec. 10, 1750—buried at Cudham. They had children, viz.:
Roger, n. i., buried at Cudham, June 17, 1726.
John, n. i., buried at Cudham, 27 April, 1730.
William, who married Elizabeth Rowed, buried 27 July, 1741, his wife Elizabeth buried there Dec. 29, 1742.
Mary, n. i., buried at Cudham, Jan. 10, 1733.
Anne, married Mr. Thomas Bryant, Gentleman, of Reygate, at St. Stephen's Sepulchre, in London, in 1734; he was buried at Reygate, Aug. 28, 1772, and she was buried there May 28, 1771.

William Glover, who married Elizabeth Rowed, had a daughter Susannah, born at Cottleham. He died in 1776. The daughter married Henry Rowed, Esq., of Cottleham Court Lodge, and died there. She was buried at Cottleham in 1800. Henry Rowed, the husband of Susannah Glover, married a second time, and had Henry Rowed, Jr., a Lieutenant in the British Navy in 1808. He had also one daughter by his first wife Susannah Glover, viz.: Katharine Glover, residing in 1808 in Croyden in Surrey, to whom descended the manor of Cottleham Court Lodge, a description of which has been gathered from another source, and reads in substance as follows:—The Demesne lands of the Manor of Cottleham, called the Manor House of Cottleham Court Lodge, being a good house, near the Church, and four hundred acres of land, were many years ago separated from the Manor and were purchased by Mr. Henry Rowed; from him it descended to his son Henry, who, on the 14th of May, 1765, married Susannah Glover (daughter of William Glover and Elizabeth Rowed), who was his first wife. He settled the estate on her. She died the next year, and he died about 1802, when it came to Katharine Rowed his daughter by that marriage, who was the owner in 1808.

The line of Anne, the supposed daughter of Roger Glover, and who married Mr. Thomas Bryant,* is given as follows: William, son of Mr. Thomas Bryant by his wife Anne, the daughter of Roger Glover, was born January 9, 1734–5; buried at Reygate, May 28, 1780. He was married to Charlotte Cooke, of Reygate, who died in 1769 and was buried there in the family vault, leaving one son, William Bryant, of the third generation, who was born in Reygate, and was living there in 1808.

(2) ELIZABETH GLOVER, the eldest daughter of Rev. Joseph and Sarah (Owfield) Glover, was born in Sutton, in Surrey, England, and died in Boston, N. E.; date of death not ascertained.

She was married, about 1642, to Adam Winthrop, Esq., the sixth child of Gov. John Winthrop, and eldest son and child by his third wife Margaret Tyndale, who was a daughter of Sir John Tyndale, Knight. His maternal grandparents were Sir John Tyndale and Anne Egarton, daughter of Sir Thomas Egarton, Knight. His eldest brother was Governor John Winthrop, of Connecticut, who was born in England, Feb. 12, 1606, and died in Boston, April 6, 1676, aged 70 years. Adam, who married Elizabeth Glover, was born in England, April 7, 1620, and died in Boston, April 4, 1652, aged 32 years.

They had one son, born in Boston, viz.:

+6. Adam, b. in 1647; m.

The inventory of Adam Winthrop's estate was taken Sept. 4, 1652, by Edward Rawson and Thomas Luke. Mrs. Elizabeth Winthrop deposed Jan. 27, 1653. There was due the estate, by bill of sale, a part of the ship Expectation and cargo, more from Mr. Turner and

---

* Probably the descendant of Mr. Thomas Bryant, to whom reference is made on page 36 of these Memorials.

from Mr. Treworthy, from Mr. John Paris, and a negro.   Attested by Edward Rawson, Recorder.

Oct. 19, 1652.   Mrs. Elizabeth Winthrop, the second wife of Adam Winthrop, Esq., late of Boston. Answer to a petition as follows : It is hereby ordered and declared that Adam Winthrop, an orphan of about five years of age, being the only child of Adam Winthrop (Sen.) and grandchild to John Winthrop, Esq., who is the true Proprietor of the Island called Governors Island.   To Have and to Hold to him and his heirs forever.   And that Mrs. Elizabeth Winthrop, the second wife of Adam Winthrop, Esq. Deceased, shall have one full third part of the profits of said Island, during the term of her natural life.   And that Mr. Dunster, Mrs. Elizabeth Winthrop during her Widowhood, Mr. Edward Rawson, Capt. Thomas Clarke and Capt. Richard Davenport are appointed Guardians over the said Adam Winthrop the orphan, to take care of his education ; and also of all his estate, Real and Personal, and to be held accountable for the same unto the said Adam or his guardian whom he shall choose when he comes to the age of fourteen years.   And that administration shall be granted equally of the Goods and Chattels of the late Adam Winthrop Deceased, unto Mrs. Elizabeth Winthrop, Widow, and unto Adam Winthrop the Orphan. (Mass. Col. Rec., Vol. 3, p. 292.)

Mrs. Elizabeth Winthrop was married a second time, 3 : 3 : 1654, to the Hon. John Richards, of Boston, one of his Majesty's Councillors, and one of the most eminent men of his time in the colonies.   He is first mentioned as belonging to Dorchester—was enrolled there as a citizen ; was a member of the Artillery Company in 1644 ; owned lands extensively in Dorchester, Weymouth, and on the Kennebec River ; was the owner of Georgetown, Maine (Island of Arrotheck), which he purchased of the Indian "Robin Hood." He was sometimes styled the "Worshipful." He was a planter, merchant and shipbuilder ; was largely engaged in commercial pursuits and foreign trade, and was one of Boston's most active citizens.

(3)   SARAH GLOVER, the second daughter of Rev. Joseph and Sarah (Owfield) Glover, was born in Sutton, Surrey, England.

She was married, about 1645, to Deane Winthrop, second son of Governor John Winthrop by his third wife Margaret Tyndale, and next brother of Adam who married Elizabeth Glover.   He was born in England, March 16, 1623, and died at Pullen Point, March 16, 1704, aged 81 years.   He owned an estate in Chelsea, and resided there at one time, at another time at Lynn, and also at Pullen Point. They had three children, born in Boston, and perhaps more, viz.:

7. Sarah,   b. Feb. 11, 1657.
8. Margaret, b. July 25, 1660.
9. Deane,   b. May   3, 1665.

Mrs. Sarah (Glover) Winthrop, wife of Deane Winthrop, Esq., died, and he afterwards married Martha Mellows. (See Winthrop Genealogy.)

(4) PRISCILLA GLOVER, third and youngest daughter of Rev. Joseph Glover, and eldest by his second wife Elizabeth Harris, was born in England, and died in Ipswich, Essex County, Mass.

She was married, Oct. 14, 1651, to John Appleton, Esq., of Ipswich, and went there to reside after her marriage. The following entry respecting their marriage is found in the Massachusetts Colonial Records, Vol. 3, p. 248: "It is ordered by the Court that the Rev. Henry Dunster be empowered to marry Mr. John Appleton to Mrs. Priscilla Glover, who have been published according to law." They had children—viz., Priscilla, who married the Rev. Joseph Capen, of Topsfield; and others, all of whom are noticed in the genealogy of the Appletons. Their son, John Appleton, married Elizabeth Rogers, and died in 1739. The descendants of this line are numerous, bearing the name of Appleton and other names by intermarriage.

(5) JOHN GLOVER, M.D., youngest son and child of Rev. Joseph and Elizabeth (Harris) Glover, was born in England, and died in London in 1668. He received his early education under the instruction of Rev. President Dunster, was prepared for College, and graduated at Harvard College in the class of 1650. He returned to England, visited Scotland, studied medicine, took his degree of Doctor of Medicine at Aberdeen in Scotland, and became a physician. Mr. Thomas writes of him that he was a physician, settled in Roxbury and was in practice there at one time; but this is considered doubtful. He may have been a physician there a short time, but there is evidence that he practised in London. In a letter written by him, while in London, to his brother-in-law John Appleton, Esq., of Ipswich, under date of London, March 5, 1655, he says: "I am now come out of Scotland, my grandmother being dead." "My desire is that my sister, your wife, should have all that I have." "I have taken my degrees of Doctor of Physic in Scotland." "Direct

49*

your letter to Dr. Genndaires, Thread Needle street." He names " My father Dunster " in the letter, and signs himself " Your loving brother, J. Glover."

In the year 1656 John Glover was involved in a suit at law with his stepfather, Mr. Dunster. It is probable, but not certain, that he returned to New England while the case was pending, and may have resided in Roxbury and commenced practice there, as has been sometimes stated. Mr. Thomas writes thus of this matter, in his " History of Printing ":

John Glover, after the death of his mother, brought an action or suit against Rev. President Dunster for the recovery of the estate which had belonged to his father and mother, which had been detained by Mr. Dunster, as follows, under date of April 1, 1656. "At a County Court held at Cambridge in the County of Middlesex, John Glover, Gentleman, Plaintiff, against Henry Dunster, Defendant, in an action of the case for an account of the estate, Houses and Lands, Goods and Chattels, Legacies and Gifts or other estate and of right due and belonging unto the said John Glover by the last Will and Testament of his father, the Rev. Jesse Glover, Deceased. or of Elizabeth his wife, or by the last Will and Testament of William Harris, Deceased," &c.

Rev. Henry Dunster met the charge, and responded. " May 8, 1656, Henry Dunster vs. John Glover, case adjourned to August 24 next ensuing." He then filed in Court an account for diet, care and clothing, and all such other expenses as had devolved upon him in the course of the education of Mrs. Glover's five children, from the time he commenced housekeeping with their mother on her marriage with him, to the time when they or any of them were married or ceased to be members of his family. A full account has been given of the items of this bill by Mr. Thomas in the second volume of his " History of Printing."

With some of the elder children this controversy commenced as early as 1652, soon after the decease of Roger Glover.

Nov. 1, 1654, Lieutenant John Appleton petitioned the Court, and was answered as follows :

In answer to the petition of Lieut. John Appleton, It is ordered, that Capt. Atherton and Capt. Morton are hereby appointed to examine the accounts of Mr. Henry Dunster in reference to the estate of Mr. Jesse Glover Deceased, or of what his wife left, or what else may concern the estate contended for by the two eldest sons Roger and John Glover of the said Jesse Glover, or any other whom it may concern, making their report to the next General Court. (Vol. 4, p. 205, Mass. Col. Rec.)

Aug. 25, 1656, a writ was issued against Henry Dunster, in a suit of John Glover in right of Joseph and Elizabeth Glover, both deceased, and in relation to the will of Richard Harris; the house was attached where Richard Kildrick lived, with part of the mill on Mystic River. The following depositions were taken in relation to the matter: The testimony of Sarah Bucknam, aged 84 years, being servant to Mrs. Glover about a year and a quarter; the testimony of Jeanne the wife of Ralph Mousall, servant to Mrs. Glover; the testimony of Stephen Daye and his wife that "there is a jug tipt with Silver and a Silver Salt and a Platter," which were by Mr. Dunster brought into Court as a part of Josse Glover's estate, as also a silver bowl which he left there in Mr. Langhorne's behalf; and the testimony of Edmund Rice, aged about 62 years, that "the house where Robert Wilson (of Sudbury) now dwells, Mr. Dunster's tenant, was built by Mr. Glover."

The case was continued by adjournments until 1657. In Vol. 4, p. 305, of the Colonial Records, it is stated, under date of May 8 of that year, that "It is ordered that Capt. Gookin, Major Atherton, Major Willard and Capt. Edward Johnson are hereby authorized as a committee with full power as the General Court might do, to hear and determine all differences between Mr. Henry Dunster and Mr. Thomas Danforth in behalf of the children of Mr. Josse Glover, and that Capt. Gookin appoint time and place."

Dr. John Glover returned to London; but at what date after the suit commenced has not been satisfactorily ascertained. That he did return and die there, is certain; also that before he left New England he appointed Mr. Thomas Danforth his attorney, who was, after his decease, his administrator. He was never married, and died intestate.

From the Middlesex Court files, page 72, we learn the following, under date of Nov. 3, 1668: "Appleton against Danforth." A writ served upon Thomas Danforth, administrator of the estate of John Glover late of London, gentleman, deceased, by Capt. John Appleton and Priscilla his wife, she being heir to John Glover. 1668: 10: 5, Thomas Danforth, attorney of Dr. John Glover, deceased, states that Mrs. Priscilla Appleton was the reputed daughter of Mr. Josse Glover and Elizabeth his wife, and that Dr. John Glover was her reputed brother.

The result of this suit, which was favorable to Mrs. Appleton, may be found among the Court Records for Middlesex County.

[*Third Generation.*]

(6) ADAM WINTHROP, only son of Adam and Elizabeth (Glover) Winthrop, was born in Boston in 1647, graduated at Harvard College in 1668, and died in Boston in 1700. He rose to distinction in the various offices to which he was appointed. He inherited a large estate from his father; married, and had children—among whom was Adam, the third of the name and line, who married Anne Wainwright, and had Adam the fourth of the name, who graduated at Harvard College in 1724, and died in 1743; also John, who graduated at H. C. in 1732, became a distinguished professor in the College, and died in 1779, leaving descendants. Another Adam, the fifth of this name and descent, was a graduate of H. C. in 1767. Thus the succession of Adam Winthrops in this line was perpetuated to quite a late period.

Answer to Mr. Adam Winthrop's Petition.

March 30, 1683. In answer to the petition of Mr. Adam Winthrop, humbly desiring the favor of the Court, that he being Proprietor of an Island called Governor's Island, falling to him by his Ancestors, which stands charged with two bushels of Apples yearly to the General Court, that the said Rent or acknowledgment may be remitted or a sum equivalent accepted and the said Island fully discharged from the encumbrance aforesaid. The Court grant the said petitioner his request, so that he pay or cause to be paid five pounds in money forthwith by the first opportunity to our agents in England."

RICHARD GLOVER.

RICHARD GLOVER, twenty-four years of age, came from England in the *Assurance*, which sailed from Gravesend in 1635, and settled in Virginia. His name appears among a list of passengers who sailed for Virginia under date of July 16 of that year. They took the oath of allegiance before their embarkation, as the following certificate shows: "These Underwritten names are to be transported to Virginia and embarked in the Assurance—Isaac Bromwell and George Pewsie Masters. Examined before the Minister of the town of Gravesend of their conformity to our Religion. The men having taken the oath of Allegiance and supremacy." The names of Barnes, Brooks, Butler and Lee appear in the list with Richard Glover, and others of the old and distinguished families of Virginia. Richard was born in the year 1611, but in what part of England has not been ascertained. The Records of Lancashire do not give any account of a Richard Glover of so early a date. He was a cotemporary of Richard the poet, who was born in St. Martin's Lane, Cannon street, London, and who descended from a line of Richard Glovers of ancient date. Tradition accords to him at least three sons—one of whom went to South Carolina, where some of his descendants now live. The name is found also in North Carolina and Alabama, all of whom are traceable to the above progenitor.

Very little has been gathered of Richard the emigrant. He settled near James River, in Virginia, and was married soon after his arrival. He owned a plantation, and was ranked among the most wealthy planters of his time. He had a family of children, and has descendants still residing in that State. Others went to Kentucky and the more Southern and the Western States.

Thomas Glover, who from 1664 to 1667 resided in Jamestown, Virginia, is presumed to be a son of Richard. He was a scholar, and a writer of ability and merit. He wrote an account of Virginia, its situation, temperature and productions from personal observation, which was published in Vol. 11 of the Transactions of the Royal Geographical Society.

Two of the descendants of Richard Glover, of the names of William and Robert, were living in the eastern part of Virginia at the time of the Revolution. They were of the Whig party, and had a brother-in-law by the name of Daniel, all of whom were much persecuted for their loyalty by the tories of that day. William, the eldest, married a Miss Harrelson. After the war he removed to New River County, now known as Kanawha County, and noted for its valuable saline springs. While here he was engaged in making salt, and had an extensive business. Subsequently he removed to the Green River country in Kentucky, now known as the " Barrens."

William Glover had six sons born to him in Virginia, by his wife ——— Harrelson, as follows, viz.:

1. Abner,   b. in 1776; d. young, unmarried.
+2. John,   b. in 1778; m. Fanny Taylor.
3. William,   b. in 1780; m. and lived many years near Glasgow, Ky., where he died.
4. Joseph,   b. in 1781; m. and removed to Indiana; died there, leaving children.
5. Weir,   b. in 1783; m. and removed to Indiana; died there, leaving children.
6. Harrelson, married in Kentucky, and died there many years ago, leaving children. Has one son, Joseph Harrelson Glover, now living in Newark, Knox Co., Mo., married, and has a family of children, not reported.

(2)   JOHN GLOVER, the second son of William and ——— (Harrelson) Glover, was born in Virginia in the year 1778, and died in Knox Co., Mo., in the year 1857, aged 79 years.

He was married, about 1812, to Fanny Taylor, daughter of Hon. Samuel Taylor, of ———, Virginia. They had twelve children, ten of whom lived to maturity. He removed from Virginia to Kentucky, about 1825, and lived many years near Harrodsburg, Mercer County, in that State.

Children of JOHN and FANNY (TAYLOR) GLOVER, born in Kentucky:

+ 7. Samuel Taylor, b. in 1813; m. Mildred A. ———.
8. Mary, b. in 1816; d. in 1832, of Asiatic cholera, aged 16 years.
9. Jane, b. in 1818; m. Andrew Kyle, lives near Harrodsburg, Ky.
10. Eliza H., b. in 1819; m. ——— Moore; lives near Newark, Mo.
11. John M., grad. Columbia Coll., Charleston, S. C., 1832; enrolled in U. S. service in 1861, and served as Colonel in the 3d Missouri Vol. Cavalry.

12. Albert D., enrolled in U. S. service as Captain 3d Missouri V. C.
13. Sarah Ann, resides in Knox County, with her widowed mother.
14. William P., resides in Knox County; married, no children.
15. Joseph W., died in Missouri in 1846.
16. James L., died in 1848.
The other two children died in infancy, or at a very early age; names not reported.

(7) SAMUEL TAYLOR GLOVER, the eldest son of John and Fanny (Taylor) Glover, was born in the year 1813, and is now residing in St. Louis, Missouri, having a wife and six children. He is a lawyer of distinguished ability, and in the successful practice of his profession. Many of his public speeches on the great questions which agitated the people of his State from 1860 to 1863, have been printed, and evince his decided opinions as to the proper course to be taken by them during that fearful period. He has been successively a member of the Missouri Legislature as Representative and Senator from St. Louis. In July, 1860, he delivered an able and acceptable address before the citizens of St. Louis, at Turner's Hall, on the respective qualifications and fitness of the four candidates for the office of President of the United States. In June, 1862, he was elected to address the people at the same place on the subject of Emancipation in the State of Missouri.

In the autumn of 1863 he was chosen a candidate for Senator to the Congress of the United States. His character is thus described by an able and distinguished writer in one of the St. Louis papers while speaking of his adaptation to that office: "Another Senator will have to be elected, and so far as our knowledge of the preferences of the people goes, we have heard but one name mentioned in connection with it—the name of the Hon. Samuel T. Glover, of St. Louis. Mr. Glover has been for years favorably known as one of the most distinguished lawyers of our State; devoting his time and talents exclusively to his profession, and until the breaking out of the rebellion had taken but little part in the politics of the country, further than on all fitting occasions to express in a bold and manly way his preferences for men and measures; or if, as he believed, opposed to the welfare and interests of the country, to denounce them with a firmness and independence peculiar to himself. But when the safety of the country was threatened, then and not till then did he rise to the full stature of a great man, and stand forth the Ajax Telamon of the Union party of Missouri. In all the relations of life he

presents a model of manly perfection, worthy the admiration and
imitation of his countrymen, and that man who could know Samuel
T. Glover and fail to admire him and to love him, could not produce
stronger inability to appreciate all that is noble and excellent in our
nature. At this particular time, there is a peculiar fitness in the se-
lection of Mr. Glover for the high and responsible position in connection with which his name has been mentioned. As a Union man
he is as far above suspicion as light is from darkness. In all times and
under all circumstances, even when it was dangerous to avow such
sentiments, no man was ever at a loss to know where he stood—like
a faithful sentinel upon the watch tower, he warned his countrymen
of the coming danger, and no man ever found him despairing or even
desponding of the ultimate results of this war. While others have
quailed before the magnitude of the rebellion, or permitted themselves, from the hope of personal aggrandizement, to float along with
the current of disloyalty, he has been first, last, and all the time, the
firm and consistent friend of his country, and no less firm and consistent in his denunciation of traitors.

"Mr. Glover has been for years identified with the emancipation
policy of Missouri, and has adhered through good and through evil
report to his principles, even at a time when to be an emancipationist in
Missouri was equivalent to signing his own political death warrant;
in that, as in every other act of his life, he has exhibited a stern devotion to principle, which even those who disagreed with him were
bound to respect and admire. This condition of things is, however,
changed, and the party which, but a few years ago, were regarded as
beyond the pale of political preferment, has by the agency of this
rebellion been brought rapidly into public favor, and Mr. Glover
stands to-day the representative man of the emancipationists in Missouri.

"Although a slave owner, and a citizen of a county heretofore the
banner county of slavery in Missouri, we stand to-day the uncompromising advocate of emancipation, not because we are not partial to
the institution of slavery—an institution under which we have been
raised and nurtured—but because we look upon it as a measure absolutely necessary for the true interests of our State. The resources
of our State must be developed, and he who expects those resources
to be developed by the miserable remnant of negroes left in the State,
must be a crazy enthusiast, whose opinions are more worthy a mad-

man than a rational creature. We must trust to the natural influx from the free States to build up our fallen fortunes, and that hope can never be realized so long as Missouri is a slave State.

"Let us, then, in view of all the circumstances that surround us, cast aside the miserable and narrow prejudices which have heretofore controlled our actions as a people, and, anxious only for the permanent good and glory of our country, seek to repair the ruin which has desolated our great State, by elevating to the highest offices in our gift, such men as alone can raise our State to the position she deserves to hold. Such a man is SAMUEL TAYLOR GLOVER."

NORTH AND SOUTH CAROLINA GLOVERS.

ROBERT D. GLOVER was living in Augusta, Georgia, in 1860; owned a plantation there; writes that he was "raised about fifteen miles from Augusta, in Edgefield District, S. C.," and that his brothers and sisters still live there. He can trace no farther back than his grandfather, who was Joseph Glover, who lived and died near Williamsboro', Granville County, N. C., and who had six sons, viz.: William, John, Jacob, Daniel, Robert and David. They all moved to Edgefield, S. C., except Daniel, who retained the homestead in North Carolina and lived and died there. William, John, Jacob and Robert died in South Carolina, at Edgefield; David removed to Kentucky, and died there. There were daughters, but nothing further has been reported of them. The family record was left with Daniel at the homestead. Mr. Glover thinks it probable that his grandfather, Joseph Glover, moved from Virginia to North Carolina, but is not certain. He writes also that his father's name was Robert Glover, and is very desirous that the genealogy of their branch may be traced out.

ROBERT GLOVER, fifth son of Joseph Glover, was born in Williamsboro', Granville Co., N. C., in 1758; removed to Edgefield, S. C., where he died.

He was twice married. First, to Miss Frances Atwood, who died,

50

leaving three children. He was married, second, to Miss Rebecca Jeter and had eight more children.

Children of ROBERT and FRANCES (ATWOOD) GLOVER, born in Edgefield, S. C.:

1. Lucy,   m. James F. Adams; died.
2. Susan,   m. Josiah Lanham; died.
3. Willey.

Children by second wife, REBECCA JETER:

4. Charlotte.
5. Elvira,   m. James Garrett; died 10 months after.
6. Robert D., m. Martha A. Cools.
7. Charles J., m. $\left\{\begin{array}{l}\text{1st, Susan Belcher;}\\\text{2d, Martha Frazier;}\end{array}\right\}$ d. in 1853.
8. David M., m. Frances Bussey, and is still living.
9. Joseph W., d. unmarried.
10. Mary Ann Adaline.
11. William J., m. Emily Collier; lived but a short time after his marriage.

Robert Glover, Esq., died in Edgefield, S. C., July 9, 1822, aged 64 years.

It is stated, also, that William, the eldest son of Joseph Glover, and brother of the above Robert, removed to Edgefield, S. C., married and had fifteen children, who are scattered in the western country.

Mr. Glover also writes that there are two other Glover families living in Edgefield, S. C., who claim kinship, and probably are collateral relatives.

Judge Glover lives in Orangeburg District, S. C. The other family lives in Edgefield, about fifteen miles from Augusta, Ga., viz.: Wade Glover, who died early in the year 1859, and left a family.

Eli Glover, of Monticello, Ga., claims kinship with the Joseph-Robert Glover family. He died in the year 1858. His son, who is a lawyer, bears the name of Richard Glover.

There are two families living in Morgan County, Ga., who bear the name of Glover, and claim relationship with this family. They went to that county from a place in North Carolina, not far from Williamsboro'.

There are two families in Alabama of the name of Glover, viz.: Williamson, who lives in Greene Co.; and Benjamin, who lives at Perrary Bluff, Marengo County, Alabama.

ROBERT D. GLOVER, son of Robert Glover, of Williams-boro', N. C., and Edgefield, S. C., and grandson of Joseph Glover, of Williamsboro', was born in Edgefield, S. C., May 12, 1807; lives in Augusta, Ga.; owns a plantation there. Mrs. Glover, his wife, was born Sept. 25, 1817. They have three sons, born in Augusta, Ga.:

12. Augustus C., b. May 22, 1842.
13. James R., b. June 22, 1845.
14. Lewis L., b. Nov. 27, 1849.

Another account of the Glovers at the South states that William Allen Glover resides now (1861) in Mobile, Alabama. He is the son of Mr. Allen Glover, a planter, born at Cambridge, S. C., and died there in 1840, leaving eight children; had been twice married. He, Mr. Allen Glover, was son of Frederick Glover, who was a son of Benjamin Glover, of Jamestown, Virginia; a descendant of the first Richard Glover of Virginia, in 1635, and was great-grandfather to the informant, Mr. Williamson A. Glover.

The name of Glover appears in many of the Southern and Western cities, and the individuals are presumed to be descended from the Jamestown Richard Glover. But two of the name have been reported as of New England descent, among the settlers there. The following is a list of Glovers, copied from the Charleston (S. C.) Directory for 1859 to 1861:

Glover, Adam B. (Henniker & Glover), house Meeting street.
Francis, planter, house Bull, corner Rutledge street.
George A., saddler, Price Avenue.
H———, widow of A. W., house King street, near Spring.
J. C., house Cannon above Corning street.
S. L., accountant, house 7 Rutledge street.

The Charleston Courier for May, 1861, contained a list of students at Columbia College who volunteered their services in defence of their homes, but were not accepted on account of their youth and inexperience. The name of Leslie Glover appears in that list.

PAGE 113. (5) THOMAS SMITH, baptized at the First Church in Boston, when four days old, May 20, 1678. Married, the first time, by Rev. Samuel Willard. Admitted to the Third Church (Old South), April 28, 1717. Children by wife Sarah Oliver all baptized there.

SARAH OLIVER was baptized at the New Brick Church in Boston, Jan. 7, 1681–2; became a member of Third Church, July 30, 1710.

P. 124. NATHANIEL HUBBARD, Esq., had more children than those found on Braintree Records. After his removal to Dorchester he had, by Elizabeth Nelson his first wife : Sarah, b. in Dorchester in 1715, died the same year; another Sarah, b. in 1716, d. in Rehoboth before 1748; William, b. in 1717, d. in Dorchester 1719; another William, b. in 1721, d. in Rehoboth before 1748; Margaret, b. in 1722, went to Rehoboth, was named in her father's will, probably was married soon after, but to whom is unknown.

Mrs. ELIZABETH HUBBARD, wife of Nathaniel Hubbard, Esq., died in Dorchester in 1724. She was the daughter of Lieutenant-Governor William Tailor, and widow of John Nelson when she became the wife of Judge Hubbard, by whom she had ten children. By his second wife, Mrs. Rebeckah Gore, there was no issue.

P. 134. No. 48. HANNAH SMITH, daughter of Mr. John Smith, merchant, died in Boston in 1772.

P. 235. SUSANNAH ELLISON was cousin to the second wife of Rev. Peter Thacher, the first pastor of the Church at Milton. She was the widow of Rev. John Bayley, at one time assistant minister at the First Church in Boston, subsequently ordained over the Church at Watertown, and died in December, 1693, aged 53. She died in Milton, Sept. 4, 1724. Her origin has not been ascertained. She was born probably in England in 1665, and was perhaps married to Mr. Bayley before coming to New England.

Pp. 236 and 272. No. 48. ELISHA GLOVER's date of birth, from family records, is stated to be Jan. 20, 1728; his baptism is right as printed on page 272.

50*

P. 273. No. 171. ELIZABETH GLOVER was born Feb. 2, not Feb. 21, which has been found to be the date of her baptism.

P. 273. No. 173. JOSIAH GLOVER died August, 1782, the day of the month not known or recorded among family records. He died in New York Harbor, on board the New Jersey Prison Ship.

P. 273. No. 177. Capt. RUSSELL GLOVER, the fifth son of Capt. Elisha and Jerusha (Billings) Glover, was born in Dorchester, June 15, 1776, and died in New York City, June 10, 1840, aged 64 years. He was a skilful navigator and shipmaster, and passed most of his life at sea. At the time of his decease he had retired from business, having acquired a large and valuable property. He became an extensive ship builder and ship owner. The last one built by him, a ship of 900 tons burthen, had not been launched when he died, and was named in honor of him, "Russell Glover." He was never married, and must be added to the lines which are extinct.

P. 292. RUTH (WHEAT-GLOVER) MASON died at the house of her stepson Amos Mason, of Belchertown, Mass.

P. 298. No. 322. GRINDALL RAWSON married Martha Glover, of Windsor, Mass.

P. 300. (123) RICHARD and JANE (CARNES) SALTER had six children. The following Record was taken from the Salter Family Bible, by Mr. Daniel Greenleaf Ingraham, a grandson, and presented to the writer. His letter arrived too late to make the corrections in the proper place:

359. Jane,   b. Aug. 7, 1763; m. Joseph Ingraham, Boston.
360. Richard, b. June 11, 1765; d. Feb. 24, 1767.
361. John,   b. April 13, 1770; m. Elizabeth Rice, of Boston.
     Sarah,   b. April 19, 1772; d. Aug. 31, 1772.
     Edward,   b. April 15, 1776; d. Sept. 5, 1777.
362. Richard, b. Sept. 21, 1779; d. July 13, 1801, at Havana,
        West Indies.

The last named was never married, according to Mr. Ingraham's statement, which is undoubtedly correct, and the marriage of Richard Salter and Sarah Appleton, as given on page 301, must relate to another of the same name.

JANE CARNES, the wife of Richard Salter, was the daughter of John and Sarah ——— Carnes, of Boston; was born there, May 13, 1737, and died Sept. 13, 1812, aged 75 years. Richard Salter died January 14, 1803, and not June 14.

P. 301. MEHETABLE HILL was born in Boston, Jan. 30, 1733–4, and baptized at the New Brick Church, Feb. 3, 1733–4.

P. 305. No. 399. RACHEL HOWE died May 30, 1773.

P. 317. No. 505. ABIGAIL GLOVER married Joseph Thayer, of Randolph, Mass., as stated by a relative.

P. 321. EBENEZER BAKER died in Dorchester, May 24, 1798.

P. 330. No. 649. CHARLOTTE GLOVER died Aug. 10, 1799.

P. 333. MARY, widow of William Glover (204), died in Quincy, January, 1867.

P. 334. No. 705. ELIZABETH NOURSE, born Dec. 17, 1801.

P. 336. (215) JULIA GLOVER was married Feb. 18, 1818, to Benjamin Crabtree, son of Eleazer and Lucy (Train) Crabtree; born in Camden, Me., in 1785, and is now living there. They have no children.

P. 336. Mrs. NANCY (CRABTREE) GLOVER died Sept. 14, 1866.

P. 347. (359) JANE SALTER died in Boston, June 5, 1834. She was at that time the widow of Joseph Ingraham, and was 71 years of age. She was the eldest daughter of Richard and Jane (Carnes) Salter, and was born in Boston, Aug. 7, 1763, as already stated. Her husband, Joseph Ingraham, was the son of Duncan and Susannah (Blake) Ingraham, who resided many years in Concord, and afterwards removed to Boston, where they died. In 1811 they were buried in the Stone Chapel yard on Tremont street, Boston, with others of the Ingraham family. Capt. Joseph Ingraham, their son, was born at Concord or in Boston, in 1762. He was a skilful navigator and shipmaster, and entered the service of the United States as Captain of the U. S. Brig Pickering. He was lost overboard at sea in the year 1800, at the age of 38 years. Capt. Joseph and Jane (Salter) Ingraham had three children, as stated on page 347. The following additional items are copied from the Salter Family Bible, viz.:

857. Joseph, d. Sept. 1, 1787; buried in the Stone Chapel yard.
858. Frederick William, d. April 19, 1822, aged 34 years.
859. Daniel Greenleaf, studied the profession of the law with Rufus G. Amory and Andrew Ritchie, Esqs., from 1809 to 1811.

DANIEL GREENLEAF, after finishing his law studies, chose the profession of teacher, and engaged in that occupation. He continued in it forty years in the City of Boston, preparing boys for college and the counting house, and retired from the business in 1852, and went to Braintree to reside, where he died, Jan. 28, 1867, aged 76 years. About one month before his decease he kindly furnished the writer with the above items of his family, in a letter dated Dec. 22, 1866, with the request that if they were not received until too late to be inserted in the proper place, they might be added in making up additional matter. He states they were taken from the Salter Family Bible, then in his possession.

P. 347. (361) Capt. JOHN SALTER, the second son of Richard and
Jane (Carnes) Salter, did not go to Connecticut, but after the death
of Elizabeth his wife went to sea, as Captain of the ship Boston,
which was bound to the Northwest Coast, where he was killed by the
Indians. A book, bearing the title of Jewett's Narrative, contains a
full account of the expedition to the Northwest Coast and the murder
of Capt. Salter, which occurred March 22, 1803.

P. 348. No. 866. WILLIAM GLOVER died in Quincy, at the house of
Dr. William B. Duggan, Jan. 16, 1867.

P. 357. Mrs. MARY ANNE (HOLDEN) HOWE, wife of (398) George
Howe, died in Dorchester, June 26, 1833, aged 60.

P. 376. No. 1162. AUGUSTUS LAWRENCE BLACKMAN, son of Samuel
and Lois (Glover) Blackman, died July 21, 1858.

P. 376. (626). THOMAS GLOVER died at his residence in Jamaica
Plain (Roxbury), in the autumn of 1866.

P. 391. Children of Rev. EDWARD and (732) SUSANNAH (GLOVER)
FREEMAN :—Julia C., John C., and Fily.

P. 392.   Children of CHARLES R. and (734) RACHEL CRABTREE
(GLOVER) POTTLE :—Anna B. and Helen V.

P. 393. Child of (735) MARSHALL PARKS and MARY (DAGGETT)
GLOVER :—Helen Deborah, b. Feb. 12, 1867.
Marshall P., the father, was elected in January, 1863, Master of
the Amity Lodge of Free and Accepted Masons, and served two years.

P. 393. Children of ORRIS STARRETT and (737) LUCY HILL (GLOVER)
ANDREWS :—Adelaide B., b. June, 1858; Lucy F., b. June, 1860; Jane
M., b. in 1863.

P. 398. No. 1393. GEORGE CLINTON MARTIN, the eldest son of Artemas and Elizabeth Dickerson (Glover) Martin, was born in East Greenwich, Oct. 22, 1808; is now residing in Jackson, Washington Co.,
N. Y. He has had eight children by his wife Mary Leigh, as follows (not before reported) :

George C.,	b. April 9, 1836;	d. same day.
Chloe Elizabeth,	b. April 8, 1837;	d. July 27, 1837.
James Artemas,	b. Jan. 5, 1839;	d. July 22, 1839.
William Henry,	b. Feb. 12, 1841.	
Elizabeth Marian,	b. April 8, 1842;	d. Feb. 11, 1848.
Nancy Jane,	b. Nov. 3, 1844.	
Charlotte Ann,	b. July 1, 1847;	d. Feb. 7, 1848.
Russell Daniel,	b. Aug. 28, 1849;	d. March 26, 1850.

P. 400. No. 1412. DANIEL NELSON BARTON, the eldest son of David and Anna (Glover) Barton, b. April 30, 1824; married Aurilla Sibley, October, 1848, and resides in East Greenwich, N. Y.

P. 402. (835) Dr. WILKES ALLEN graduated at the Baltimore College of Dental Surgery in 1846. His children, three in number, are as follows:

Charles Glover, b. Nov. 21, 1851.
Mary Morrell, b. May 29, 1856.
Harry Monroe, b. July 24, 1858; d. Jan. 9, 1861.

P. 407. No. 1469. NANCY SPRUNG NORCUTT, eldest daughter of Eleazer and Elizabeth (Glover) Norcutt, was born in Dorchester, July 30, 1810, and died in Boston.

She was twice married. First, to William Murphy, who died, leaving four children, as follows:

Elizabeth Norcutt Hammond, b. April 20, 1832; m. Daniel Parker Gage, M.D., Sept. 2, 1857; resides in Lowell; no issue.
Adaline Augusta.
Almira Georgianna.
William Henry Harrison.

She was married, second, to (1463) Thomas B. Vose, and had one child:—George E. A.

P. 407. No. 1471. ELIZABETH BLAKE NORCUTT, the second and youngest daughter of Eleazer and Elizabeth (Glover) Norcutt, was born in Dorchester, in 1812, and is residing at East Cambridge.

She was married, March 31, 1833, to Nathaniel O. Hammond, of Topsfield, Mass. They have had six children, born in East Cambridge, as follows:

Edward, b. Jan. 2, 1834; d. Feb. 28, 1834.
Nathaniel O., b. July 20, 1835; d. June 27, 1837.
Elizabeth, b. May 6, 1838; d. Sept. 11, 1839.
Maria L., b. April 6, 1842; d. March 14, 1844.
William S., b. April 3, 1848; d. July 26, 1849.
Carrie S., b. July 23, 1856; resides with her parents in East Cambridge.

P. 408. No. 1473 (should be 1472). SARAH GLOVER, the eldest daughter of William and Sarah (Sylvester) Glover, was born in Boston,·in 1821, and died there in 1842, leaving no issue.

She was married, in 1842, to Josiah McIntire, of Boston.

P. 408. No. 1475 (should be 1473). ELIZABETH GLOVER, the second daughter of William and Sarah (Sylvester) Glover, was born in Boston, March 24, 1823, and is now residing in Hingham, Mass.

She was married, April 7, 1838, to William H. Jones, of Boston; born in Weymouth, and died in Florida, Sept. 19, 1864. They have had twelve children, eight of whom are living, born in Weymouth and Hingham:

William H. Jones,	b. March 14, 1839;	d. Sept. 5, 1840.
William H. Jones,	b. Jan. 26, 1841;	d. in Washington, D. C., Feb. 12, 1864.
Sarah E.,	b. Aug. 16, 1847;	d. Aug. 16, 1851, in Hing- [ham.
Samuel,	b. Sept. 24, 1849.	
Lizzie M.,	b. May 23, 1852.	
Grace Amelia,	b. Jan. 15, 1854.	
Frederick,	b. Nov. 20, 1855.	
George Bion,	b. Oct. 17, 1857.	
Mary Packard,	b. Sept. 8, 1859.	
Stephen Francis,	b. Jan. 17, 1862.	
Chester Clark,	b. Jan. 7, 1864.	

P. 408. No. 1472 (should be 1475). MARY ANNE GLOVER, the third and youngest daughter of William and Sarah (Sylvester) Glover, was born in Boston, Feb. 14, 1825, and is now residing in East Cambridge. She was married, March 17, 1844, to Chester N. Clark, only son of Nathaniel and Christiana Clark, of Foxborough, Mass.; born there, and is now residing in East Cambridge. They have had three children, born in East Cambridge, as follows:

+Mary Estelle, b. May 8, 1845; m. William G. Fletcher.
  Lilian Maria,   b. April 29, 1851.
  Fannie Mabel, b. Oct. 31, 1864.

(+) MARY ESTELLE CLARK was married, Oct. 20, 1864, to William G. Fletcher, of Cambridge. They have had one child, viz.:
  Willie Chester, b. Sept. 8, 1866.

[William and Sarah (Sylvester) Glover had, besides the above, two children—Eleazer Norcutt and Eliza—both of whom died in infancy.]

P. 436. ANNA AUGUSTA HOLBROOK, wife of (1328) Horatio N. Glover, Jr., was born May 14, 1834.

P. 438. CORDELIA LINFIELD, wife of Charles Glover, No. 1732, died in Randolph, in 1856, aged 22 years and 2 months.

P. 520. No. 83. THOMAS GLOVER, the second son of Gamaliel and Tabitha (Beale) Glover, was born in Conway, Mass., in November, 1777,* and died in Macedon, N. Y., in 1855, aged 78 years.

He was married in 1799, at the age of 22 years, to Rebecca Stuart, daughter of John and Lydia Stuart, of ———; born in 1779. Their children were as follows, born in ———, N. Y.:

Pentha, b. in 1800; m. Osee Crittenden (3d wife) in 1827.
Martha, b. in 1805; m. { 1st, William Billings, in 1824; 2d, William Manchester, in 1844.
Eliza,   b. in 1807.
Mary,   b. in 1809; m. Benjamin Billings, in 1829; d. in 1841.
Harriet, b. in 1817.
Saloma, b. in 1819.

* Another record says born in 1776, and died in 1854, aged 78 years.

GRADUATES OF THE NAME OF GLOVER.

Harvard University.

Page 569.	No.	5.	JOHN, M.D. Aberdeen.	*Physician.*	1650.
" 149.	"	III.	JOHN, Mr.	*Merchant.*	1651.
" 257.	"	35.	NATHANIEL, Mr.	*Merchant.*	1723.
			BENJAMIN STACEY, A.B.	*Lawyer.*	1781.
" 417.	"	393.	LEWIS, Mr.	*Lawyer.*	1824.
" 368.	"	551.	LEWIS JOSEPH, M.D.	*Physician.*	1832.
			CHARLES HENRY.	*Lawyer.*	1845.
" 368.	"	553.	JOHN JEFFERSON, Mr.	*Agriculturist.*	1849.
" 452.	"	1898.	EDWARD WESTON, A.B.	*Lawyer.*	1866.

Brown University.

No.	820.	SAMUEL, A.M.	*Clergyman.*	1808.
"	1401.	SAMUEL, A.M.		1839.

Yale College, and Columbia College, S. C.

ABIEL B.	1816.
JOHN.	1825.
SAMUEL.	1826.

Franklin, N. Y.

HENRY S.	1834.

Columbia College, S. C.

Page 574.	No. 11.	JOHN M.	1832.

Hamilton, N. Y.

SAMUEL.	1820.

Union College, N. Y.

BENNET.	1817.

Waterville College, Me.

Page 337.	No. 219.	WILLARD, A.M.	*Clergyman.*	1825.

Jefferson College, Philadelphia, Pa.

Page 494.   No. 37.   RALPH, M.D.   *Physician.*   1826.

——— *College, Kentucky.*

"   499.   No. 57.   FRANCIS L.   *Lawyer.*

University of the City of New York.

"   500.   No. 65.   LOUIS NAPOLEON.   *Lawyer.*   1851.
"   501.   "   66.   JOHN JOSEPH, M.D.   *Physician.*   1857.

Lane Theological Seminary, Ohio.

"   541.   No. 189.   LIVINGSTON MATURIN, D.D. *Clergyman.*   1842.

The above list is believed to contain all of the name who have graduated at any College in the United States previous to 1842, as stated
in the American Quarterly Register for that year, with a few of later
date. Those printed above without the prefix of numbers, are not
included in this volume, but trace their lineage to other progenitors;
the same, also, of the list of soldiers.

SOLDIERS OF THE NAME OF GLOVER.

At Castle William, Boston Harbor, from 1741 to 1753.

No.		Page.	No.		Page.
(10)	John Glover,	234	(48)	Elisha Glover,	272
(11)	Thomas Glover,	239	(53)	Thomas Glover, Jr.,	275
(13)	John Glover, Tertias,	252	54	Elijah Glover,	279
(38)	Alexander Glover,	263	57	William Glover,	281
(40)	Pelatiah Glover,	263	(58)	James Glover,	281
(46)	Nathaniel Glover,	271	(69)	John Glover, Jr.,	288
(47)	Josiah Glover,	272			

French and Indian War.

No.		Page.	No.		Page.
(32)	Edward Glover,	515	(75)	Samuel Glover,	292
(35)	John Glover,	516	(240)	Thomas Glover,	342
(65)	Robert Glover,	286			

Revolutionary War. From Army Records.

No.		Page.	No.		Page.
(367)	Alexander,	349		Jonathan, Col., *Marblehead.*	
(130)	Alexander,	303		Joseph (probably of Salem).	
	Daniel.		(39)	Joshua,	518
(59)	Ebenezer,	283	(47)	Josiah,	272
(131)	Edward,	304	51	Lemuel,	517
	Elijah.		172	Lewis,	273
(48)	Elisha,	272		Nathan, *Gloucester.*	
(50)	Enoch,	274		Peter, *Beverly.*	
(49)	Ezra,	273	237	Robert,	341
(241)	George,	343	193	William,	326
	Henry.		192	Thomas,	325
	John, Gen., *Marblehead.*		(814)	Thomas,	397
	Jonas.				5 1 ?

Second War with England (1812), as far as ascertained.

No.			No.		Page.
(112)	Benjamin.		(821)	Henry,	399
(72)	Joshua,	526			

Civil War—1861 to 1865.

Massachusetts Volunteers.

No.		Page.	No.		Page.
(1537)	Albert Holden,	446	(1368)	John,	439
(915)	Amasa Stetson,	410		John N.	

51

No.		Page.	No.		Page.
(1295)	Alfred Richardson,	435	(277)	Henry,	537 .
	Benjamin F., *Chelsea.*		(73)	James Noble,	501
	Charles F., *Beverly.*			James H., *Sharon.*	
	Edward William, *Malden.*		(1061)	Joseph Mears,	423
(298)	Elisha V., Jr.,	545	(1060)	John, Jr.,	423
(530)	Erastus Miller,	367	(1075)	Nathaniel E.,	424
(1521)	George, 3d,	446	(43)	Pelatiah,	498
(1455)	George Dodge,	444	(1063)	Samuel Curtis,	423
1173	George Grenville,	377	(373)	Thomas Livermore,	546
	George M., *Beverly.*		(254)	Walter Scott,	544
1518	Harrison,	412	278	Warren,	537
	Hervey B., *Beverly.*		(1559)	William Henry,	423
	Henry, *Beverly.*		(528)	William Sullivan,	366

Connecticut Volunteers.

Martin V. B.	John H.
Henry J.	Louis Henry.
Joseph.	Samuel.

Ohio Volunteers.

Henry, unknown.

INDEX.

CHRISTIAN NAMES OF THE GLOVERS.

Aaron, 343
Abby, 538
Abby Almira, 439
Abby Anne, 386
Abby Caroline, 394
Abby Frances, 536
Abby Josephine, 536
Abiel B., 587
Abigail, 253, 263, 271, 304, 305, 317, 319, 348, 353, 404, 474, 478, 484, 486, 507–510, 512, 517, 519, 527, 583
Abijah, 517, 522, 523
Abijah Austin, 534, 543
Abner, 574
Adah, 533
Adam, 317
Adam B., 579
Adalaide, 412, 542
Adalaide Harriet, 337
Adaline, 494
Adria Wellington, 545
Agnes, 4, 5, 539
Alanson D., 532
Albert, 354, 414, 494
Albert Baxter, 394
Albert D., 575
Albert Henry, 319
Albert Holden, 413, 446, 580
Alexander, 54, 55, 214, 236, 237, 263, 264, 302, 303, 349, 350, 352–354, 400, 402, 407, 408, 410, 521, 531, 532, 580
Alfred Richardson, 387, 435, 590
Alfred Kingsley, 435
Alice, 29, 507, 552
Alice Williams, 444
Almira, 520, 533, 540
Amasa Stetson, 352, 410, 411, 470, 589
Amanda Stetson, 411
Ambrose, 12
Amelia, 449, 521, 539
Andrew, 352, 409, 410
Andrew Warren, 449
Anna, 63, 65–69, 161, 163, 171, 198, 210, 240, 274, 279, 285, 322, 329, 331, 344, 400, 442, 462
Anna Curry, 368
Anna F., 446
Anna Hovey, 394
Anna Maria Stirling, 25
Anne, 20, 21, 23, 259, 260, 299, 365, 430, 451, 560
Anne Augusta, 386
Anne Brazer, 355
Anne Curtis, 317
Anne Eliza, 531
Anne L., 438
Anne Jenkins, 350
Anne W., 423
Annie Wellington, 545

Annis Crane, 386
Annis Turner, 450
Ansel, 354, 415
Ansel Edward, 415
Anson, 354
Aristene, 532
Arthur, 541
Asahel Howe, 332, 385
Augusta, 354
Augustus C., 579
Augustus E., 440
Azor, 353

Benjamin, 485, 494, 522, 533, 534, 570
Benjamin F., 500
Benjamin Franklin, 337, 338, 392, 394, 436, 448
Benjamin Bucey, 587
Benjamin Wadsworth, 74, 285, 337, 365, 394
Benney, 587
Benney, 525
Bethiah, 342, 396, 397, 437, 439
Bethiah B., 451
Bethiah J., 451
Bertie T., 452
Betsey, 522
Bridget, 25

Caroline, 310, 447, 448, 527
Caroline F., 451
Caroline Lewis, 354
Carrie, 532, 542
Carrie S., 452
Catharine, 250, 310
Catharine Bradford, 583, 585
Catharine Kearney, 417
Cecelia, 539
Cephin, 532
Charles, 354, 396, 416, 439, 448, 532, 539, 586
Charles C., 439
Charles F., 590
Charles Gideon, 365
Charles Henry, 597
Charles Howard, 368
Charles H., 432
Charles Joseph, 452
Charles Ralph, 501
Charles Williamson, 521, 532
Charlotte, 330, 597
Chloe, 448
Clara, 542
Clara Ella, 391
Clara Fisher, 336–339
Clara F., 451
Clarissa, 520
Clarence W., 520
Cooke Osborne, 349, 444
Cordelia, 449
Cynthia, 442

Cyrus W., 438

Daniel, 349, 405, 589
Daniel Oliver, 350
Daniel W., 552
David, 437–439, 449, 518, 526, 552
Davis, 325
Deborah, 450, 485, 526
Delight, 271, 319
Dennis H., 552
Diantha, 531
Dilly, 344
Dorothy, 240

Earimira, 320
Ebenezer, 74, 240, 279, 282, 329, 330, 589
Eddie M., 452
Edith, 539
Edmund, 23
Edmund T., 435
Edmund Walter, 385
Edward, 11, 24, 25, 263, 304, 354, 415, 515, 589
Edward Auchmuty, 25
Edward Augustus, 416
Edward Lewis, 519, 526
Edward Livingston, 541
Edward Weston, 452, 587
Edward William, 590
Eleanor, 329, 380, 437, 491
Eli, 578
Elias, 550, 582
Elias W., 552
Elijah, 240, 279, 280, 283, 331, 332, 336, 380, 396, 438, 439, 589
Elijah Anson, 333
Elisha, 236, 271–273, 319, 396, 581, 582, 589
Elisha Vose, 519, 528, 529, 539, 545, 590
Eliza, 318, 352, 379, 586
Eliza Homer, 410
Eliza H., 574
Eliza Lee, 413
Eliza Miller, 318
Eliza Rebecca, 387, 434
Eliza T., 439
Elizabeth, 23, 82, 92, 93, 158, 169, 170, 187, 223, 240, 264, 272–274, 278, 283, 306, 322, 324, 325, 334, 350, 377, 407, 408, 519, 520, 562–565, 592, 585
Elizabeth Barnard, 406, 443
Elizabeth Blanchard, 423
Elizabeth Dickerson, 343, 398
Elizabeth Georgianna, 360
Elizabeth Justina, 424
Elizabeth Lemmon, 363, 411
Elizabeth Matilda, 543
Elizabeth Ruggles, 540
Elizabeth Swift, 227

Ella, 385
Ella Adalakie, 540
Ellen, 25, 31, 35, 408, 550
Ellen Alicia, 25
Ellen Jane, 456
Ellen Maria, 537, 543
Ellis, 555
Ellis Horton, 386
Ellis Morton, 386
Emeline, 337
Emerson Flavia, 530
Emily, 531, 537
Emily Frances, 436, 527
Emily Lincoln, 394
Emma, 541
Emma Cornelia, 540
Emma J., 452
Enoch, 236, 274, 589
Ephraim Terry, 534, 544, 546
Erastus, 491, 493
Erastus Miller, 318, 387, 590
Ernest, 449
Erving, 397, 440
Esther Hallett, 319, 367
Esther Wadsworth, 318
Ethelinda, 530
Eugene, 511, 542
Eunice, 271, 283
Eunice Billings, 333, 387
Eunice Ellen, 527
Evelina, 394, 526
Experience, 253
Ezra, 236, 273, 319, 368, 408, 589

Fannie Maria, 382
Fanny, 321
Francis, 579
Francis A., 438
Francis L., 493, 499, 598
Francina Wellington, 545
Frank Herbert, 368
Frank B., 452
Frank William Thomas, 382, 432
Frederick Pope, 332, 386, 387
Frederick Russell, 391
Frederick Morton, 367
Frederick W., 440

Gamaliel, 515, 519, 520, 586
George, 25, 32, 35-37, 288, 343, 412, 446, 589, 590
George Anson, 416
George Barrett, 539
George Bates, 450
George Church Read, 366
George Clarke, 439, 449
George Codman, 543
George Dodge, 406, 444, 590
George Ernest, 553
George Francis Marion, 449
George Grenville, 337, 590
George Henry, 382, 412, 432, 498, 502
George Pickering, 543
George Quimby, 448
George Stephen, 320, 369
George S., 439
George White, 336, 391
George Whitfield, 521, 531
George Wilson Elsworth, 365
George W., 532
Georgie Eva, 391
Geraldine, 539
Gilmore, 408
Grace Austin, 444
Gratia, 400
Gustavus, 413

Habackuk, 50, 57-60, 70-74, 76, 79, 86-88, 99-107, 176, 196, 465, 470, 502
Hannah, 23, 77-79, 101, 102, 179, 186, 187, 189, 190, 218, 225, 231, 234, 253, 262, 263, 266, 278, 304, 310, 311, 323, 334, 359, 384, 397, 534, 547, 548
Hannah Blake, 411
Hannah Gibbs, 388
Hannah Matilda, 543
Harrelson, 574
Harrison, 412, 590
Harriet, 337, 397, 440, 449, 586
Harriet Almira, 497
Harriet E., 318
Harriet Lincoln, 394
Harriet Louisa, 388
Harriet Maria, 542
Harriet M. A., 532
Harriet Newell, 543
Harriet Wood, 387, 485
Harry W., 549
Helen A. Stowe, 540
Helen Deborah, 584
Henry, 3, 28, 30, 32, 33, 343, 354, 399, 413, 505-510, 515, 516, 532, 536, 537, 549, 590
Henry Clay, 497
Henry Franklin, 536
Henry Jerome, 542
Henry K., 399, 441
Henry S., 587
Henry Winslow, 368
Henrietta D., 394
Hepsibah, 519
Herbert, 435
Herbert Hinckley, 385
Horace Osborne, 444
Horatio Herbert, 359
Horatio Nelson, 338, 393, 436, 586
Howard, 542
Hugh, 5, 11, 399
Hukiah Reed, 450

Ingersoll, 318
Ira, 525, 537
Ira Emery, 543
Irene Genevieve, 542
Isaac B., 440
Isaac Davis, 533
Isaac Howe, 332
Isaac S., 452
Isabella, 442
Israel Eaton, 348, 405

Jacob, 236
James, 24, 25, 240, 251, 283, 288, 325, 342, 396, 436, 589
James Francis, 319, 367
James Gilmore Nichols, 350
James Hovey, 394
James Knowles, 529
James Madison, 333, 388
James Noble, 497, 501, 590
James Otis, 449
James R., 579
James Russell, 336, 391
Jane, 20, 21, 266, 311
Jane Brimmer, 355
Jane Brower, 350
Jane Eliza, 497, 501
Jane Hill, 302
Jarvis, 329, 381
Jemima, 516
Jennie Beale, 413
Jeremiah, 344, 399
Jerusha, 236, 240, 266, 278, 283, 285, 330, 385, 394, 395
Jerusha Eaton, 348
Jesse, 518, 526, 537
Jesse C., 438
Joanna, 18, 515, 533
Johannah, 274, 321
Job Henry, 563
Joel, 525, 536
John, Mr., 33, 39-84, 225, 235, 243, 403, 471, 502

John, 1-10, 50, 59, 65, 67, 70-74, 89, 99, 149-163, 167, 169, 170, 179, 181, 195-210, 221, 234-239, 252-254, 265, 271, 288, 290, 317, 319, 364, 396, 423, 439, 448, 467, 491, 513, 518, 517, 551, 582, 563, 569-571, 587, 589, 590
John Adams, 412, 542
John Bass, 318, 365
John Brazer, 355, 417
John Clough, 240, 283, 332, 336, 355
John Emery, 534, 543
John Francis Garaux, 355, 423
John George, 493, 499
John Henderson, 394
John Henry, 543, 553
John Hill, 302, 345, 405
John H., 442, 451
John Hurlburt, 12
John Ira, 543
John Jackson, 23
John James, 439, 450
John Jefferson, 320, 368, 587
John Joseph, 491, 493, 497, 501, 588
John M., 474, 587
John N., 589
John Nelson, 450
John Raymond, 522
John Stetson, 448
John White, 330, 390
Jonas, 589
Jonathan, 23, 260, 265, 342, 397, 440, 559
Jonathan Edwards, 531
Joseph, 36, 56, 236, 255, 265, 266, 273, 397, 439, 556, 557, 574, 579, 589
Joseph Beale, 354, 414
Joseph Edward, 544
Joseph Hunt, 534, 543
Joseph Lemmon, 412, 445
Joseph Mears, 365, 423, 590
Joseph Robbins, 543
Joseph S., 440, 451
Joseph Stephen, 320
Joseph Warren, 536
Joseph W., 575
Josephine, 537
Josephine Maria, 394
Josephine B., 441
Josiah, 236, 272, 273, 318, 366, 562, 589
Joshua, 518, 519, 526, 533, 543, 569
Joshua Donney, 396, 436
Joshua S., 437, 438
Joyce, 491, 494
Julia, 283, 336, 537, 583
Julia Anne Sophia, 415
Julia Antoinette, 389
Julia Elizabeth, 394
Julia Emma, 497
Julianna Clementina, 366

Keziah, 440
Kirkland, 417

Lamira, 530
Laura, 537
Lawrence Litchfield, 539
Lemuel, 517, 522, 569
Lemuel Bent, 522
Leslie, 579
Leviston, 438, 449
Lewis, 273, 304, 365, 587, 589
Lewis Joseph, 320, 363, 587
Lewis L., 579
Livingston Maturin, 530, 541, 588
Lois, 325, 376
Lois Bent, 283, 333
Loren, 549
Louis Napoleon, 497, 500, 588
Louisa, 332, 384
Louisa Abbott, 541

Louisa Miriam, 400
Louisa M., 451
Louisine, 526
Lucinda, 530
Luchus, 449
Lucretia, 363, 412
Lucy Anne, 405, 442
Lucy Fayette, 366
Lucy Hill, 337, 393
Lucy Jane, 400
Lucy Maria, 412
Lucy Upham, 366
Luellon, 542
Lalie Eva, 391
Luther Melancthon, 530, 542
Luther Wellington, 545
Lydia, 38, 39, 253, 342, 354, 396, 414, 437, 442

Marcey G., 439
Marcia, 518, 520, 529
Marcia Annette, 641
Mactaelie, 318
Margaret, 25, 38, 266, 311, 343, 397, 550, 551
Margaret Anne, 400
Margaret Preston Howe, 354, 414
Marlborough Parsons Stirling Freeman, 25
Maria Ada, 391
Maria Amelia Caroline, 497
Maria Annette, 541
Maria Eleanor, 544
Maria Ellen, 537
Maria Louisa, 527
Maria Saloma, 523
Marshall Parks, 337, 393, 584
Mary, 165, 169, 179, 218, 227, 232, 239, 260, 263, 265, 271, 274, 283, 300, 302, 304, 305, 309, 317, 321, 330, 334, 343, 348, 349, 365, 397, 439, 450, 462, 474, 479, 485, 495, 586
Mary Abby, 441
Mary Amelia, 542
Mary Anna, 450
Mary Anne, 337, 352, 355, 406, 410, 586
Mary Anne Robbins, 543
Mary Briggs, 540
Mary D., 319
Mary Ellen, 531
Mary Elizabeth, 319, 539
Mary Evelina, 544
Mary Field, 317
Mary Georgianna Somerset, 25
Mary Helen, 449
Mary Hill, 336, 389
Mary Jane, 530
Mary Lebaron, 387, 434
Mary Lemmon, 353, 411
Mary Livermore, 544
Mary Louisa, 435
Mary M., 403
Mary Osborne, 349, 406, 443
Mary Rebecca, 388
Mary Selina, 389
Mary Smith, 332
Mary Sweet, 407
Mary Vose, 527
Martha, 283, 288, 334, 361, 537, 554, 586
Martha Copeland, 543
Martha Harriet, 332, 385
Martha Holden, 323, 370
Martha Lane, 533
Martha Maria, 394
Martha Nutting, 542
Martin, 525, 527, 590
Martin Colburn, 525, 536, 544
Mattie, 542
Mehetable, 273, 320
Mela, 518

Mercy Eaton, 348
Milan, 441, 530
Mildred, 3, 12, 17, 18, 23, 25
Mildred Lavinia, 25
Minerva, 531
Minnie Lizzie, 424
Miriam, 263, 399
Moses, 343, 513, 517
Moses Clarke, 344

Nahum, 451
Nancy, 325, 518
Nancy Holden, 527, 538
Nancy Jenkins, 350
Nancy J., 440
Nancy Sprung, 406
Nathan, 589
Nathaniel, 38, 39, 50, 53-55, 58, 59, 65-73, 76-81, 162, 163, 170, 176-198, 203, 218, 220, 227, 257-261, 271, 299, 300-302, 317, 318, 332, 347, 349, 470-473, 517, 522, 523, 587, 589
Nathaniel Ebenezer, 318, 366, 424, 589
Nathaniel S., 437, 447, 448
Nathan Gibbs, 388, 435
Nathan Holbrook, 436
Nellie M., 452
Noah A., 317, 365

Olive, 397
Olive Rosaline, 534
Oliver, 65, 304, 352, 412, 445
Orville, 526
Otis Kimball, 319

Patience, 263, 303
Pelatiah, 218, 263, 453-480, 491, 492, 498, 589, 590
Pentha, 596
Perlin, 492
Peter, 408, 550, 552, 555, 589
Peter Sprung, 350, 408
Phebe Augusta, 365
Phebe Neale, 317, 365
Philander, 521, 530, 531
Philip, 23
Philomela, 520
Phillips, 27
Phinehas Holden, 323, 371
Priscilla, 562, 563, 609

Rachael, 218, 261-264, 276, 304, 305, 326, 521
Rachel, 519, 520, 527, 529
Rachel Crabtree, 337, 392
Rachel Littlefield, 524
Ralph, 554-556, 491, 494, 497, 500, 501, 588
Rebecca, 265, 309, 363, 525
Rebeccah, 51, 90-93
Rebeckah, 82, 98, 102, 278, 332, 386
Rebekah, 304
Rebecca Jones, 412
Reuben, 344, 400
Richard, 3, 25, 28, 573, 574, 578
Ripley, 388
Rhoda, 520
Robert, 5-8, 36, 252, 296-298, 341, 342, 397, 410, 444, 462, 574, 577-579, 589
Robert D., 677, 579
Robert Herald, 11, 25
Robert Martyr, 5-11
Rodolph, 497
Roger, 562, 563, 565-567
Roxanna, 491, 493
Rufus Gardiner, 365
Russell, 273, 582
Ruth, 517, 523
Ruth B., 543
Ruth S., 448

Sally Siders, 522
Saloma, 449, 586
Samuel, 23, 253, 274, 278, 292, 323, 328, 343, 398, 399, 462, 468, 469, 474, 475, 477-479, 486, 487, 491, 494, 511, 513, 514, 587, 589
Samuel Coddington, 23
Samuel Curtis, 317, 365, 423, 590
Samuel Gore, 321
Samuel James, 540
Samuel Jarvis, 382, 432
Samuel Kingsley, 279, 280, 332
Samuel Stillman, 399, 521, 532
Samuel Taylor, 574-577
Samuel Worcester, 532, 542
Samuel Woodward, 394
Sarah, 263, 293, 302, 336, 349, 396, 408, 437-440, 450, 507, 517, 523, 531, 532, 563, 568, 569, 585
Sarah Ann, 575
Sarah Bent, 411
Sarah Caroline, 534
Sarah Eglantine, 532
Sarah Elizabeth, 385
Sarah Hannah, 386
Sarah Lamaine, 449
Sarah Maria, 387, 553
Sarah Salisbury, 521, 530
Sarah Wadsworth, 394
Sarah White, 336, 390
Sewall S., 448
Sibella, 23
Silas Wheelock, 470
Solomon, 506
Sophia, 491, 492
Sophronia, 521
Sophronia Anne, 536, 545
Sophronia Chadbourne, 406
Stephen, 273, 320
Stephen Elisha, 320
Stirling Freeman, 25
Susan, 20-22, 319, 337, 449
Susan Cogswell, 319
Susan Elizabeth, 552
Susan S., 448
Susanna, 26
Susannah, 4, 236, 264, 266, 274, 310, 321, 326, 337, 391, 511, 519, 528
Susannah Holden, 527
Susannah Siders, 522
Syrena Peaks, 522

Tabitha, 520
Theodore Russell, 321
Theodore W., 451
Thomas, 3, 11, 13, 23, 25, 29, 34, 50, 58, 59, 71, 77, 81-97, 161, 179, 254, 240, 252, 275, 277, 278, 287, 288, 325, 342, 370, 386, 396, 397, 520, 584, 586, 589
Thomas B., 419
Thomas Denzer, 529
Thomas Jefferson, 388, 435
Thomas Livermore, 544, 546, 590
Thomas Nathan, 497
Thomas Oliver, 353, 412

Vinera Josephine, 532

Walter Scott, 534, 544, 590
Walter Seymour, 523
Warren, 537, 590
Wier, 574
Willard, 283, 337, 587
Willey, 578
William, 1, 3-5, 8, 9, 20, 22-25, 32, 34, 35, 53, 71, 72, 240, 278, 281, 302, 325, 326, 333, 377, 390, 574, 543-586, 589
William Allen, 579
William Anson, 387
William Bowles, 344, 436
William Charles, 387

William Copeland, 368
William Dwelley, 365
William Earl, 366
William Edward, 366
William Francis Adams, 424
William Franklin, 377, 390
William Flintham, 413
William Frederick, 653
William Gad, 529

William Henry, 364, 423, 590
William H., 439
William Joseph Gleason, 387
William J., 578
William Powell, 531, 542
William Powers, 632
William P., 575
William Salisbury, 521
William Stanley, 423

William Sullivan, 318, 366, 590
William Wood, 319
Williamson, 578
Williamson A., 579
Willie Augustus, 436
Winfield Scott, 365
Winslow Brigham, 319, 357

Zillah, 397

SURNAMES of persons who have intermarried with the Glovers, and all other Surnames mentioned in the Book.

Abercrombie, 390
Abollaram, 25
Abbott, 539, 546
Adams, 40, 235, 255, 271, 278, 284, 285, 296, 308, 318, 321, 324, 320, 329, 330, 337, 338, 339, 344, 367, 380, 381, 395, 401, 402, 460, 491, 493, 537, 578
Addington, 102, 157, 169, 170, 183, 200, 252, 473, 509, 510, 548
Agon, 259
Alden, 33
Aldersey, 40–42
Aldrich, 293
Allard, 492, 498
Allen, 100, 105, 193, 225, 240, 270, 271, 300, 317, 344, 371, 401, 402, 438, 439, 449, 534, 585
Alexander, 523, 535
Ames, 438, 449
Amory, 301, 583
Amos, 426
Anderson, 136, 139, 143, 270
Andrews, 157, 158, 177, 246, 249, 250, 337, 361, 374, 392, 419
Andros, 47, 170
Appleble, 94
Appleton, 17, 96, 157, 402, 562, 563, 569–571, 582
Apsley, 401
Apthorp, 286, 287
Arblaster, 11
Archer, 406, 443
Archibald, 301
Arnold, 41, 42, 240, 285, 332, 338, 339, 383, 394, 395, 492, 497
Armstrong, 364
Armrolde, 94
Arnot, 42; Arnout, 530
Ashley, 22, 474, 475, 484–486
Ashton, 519, 527
Ashurst, 53–55
Ashwood, 63
Aspinwall, 43, 46, 47, 346, 403
Atkins, 202
Atkinson, 246, 562
Atwood, 577, 578
Auchmuty, 192, 194, 195, 235
Audsley, 28
Austin, 353, 411, 444
Avery, 171
Averill, 383

Babbit, 137, 142, 146, 147
Babcock, 99, 149, 238, 230, 280, 322, 330, 332, 333, 354, 370, 382, 387, 414, 417, 433, 511

Bacon, 171
Bailey, 214, 256, 314, 510
Baker, 75, 201, 207, 274, 291, 316, 321, 352, 358, 409, 583
Balch, 322
Baldwin, 297, 391
Balkum, 306
Ball, 78, 90, 91, 93
Ballard, 41, 42
Ballantine, 188, 193–195, 197, 217
Ballen, 25
Ballou, 390
Balston, 199, 200
Bangs, 519, 528
Banks, 433, 434
Banister, 548, 549
Banta, 440, 462
Barber, 460
Bard, 82, 89, 91–95
Barker, 136
Barnard, 118, 211
Barnes, 31, 32, 573
Barney, 557
Barrett, 304, 352, 353
Barrows, 273, 342, 439, 440
Barry, 24
Barsham, 253, 388
Bartlett, 382, 433, 438, 448, 449, 520
Barton, 344, 400, 584
Basin, 109
Bass, 54, 218, 227, 255, 262, 266, 310
Bassett, 323, 529, 539, 545
Batchelder, 543
Battelle, 525
Bateman, 249, 554
Bates, 90, 92, 382, 433, 440, 534
Banry, 313, 314
Baxter, 74, 240, 251, 285, 312, 337–339, 394, 436
Bayley, 131, 581
Bayze, 486
Beale, 304, 336, 353, 354, 413, 414, 515, 520, 521, 529, 585
Beals, 317, 365, 423
Beard, 230, 241, 242, 245, 246, 250, 364, 423, 506, 507, 547–549
Bears, 288
Beck, 385
Beckford, 21
Beers, 415, 447
Bedgood, 115
Belcher, 99, 115, 123, 181, 184, 235, 236, 238, 239, 247, 273, 274, 329, 411, 578
Bell, 345
Bellingham, 45, 50, 53, 68

Bendall, 68, 201, 204
Bennett, 562
Bent, 240, 251, 279, 283–286, 324, 333–335, 340, 341, 352, 376, 377, 430, 517, 519, 528
Beveridge, 335
Biggs, 562
Bill, 236, 265, 309
Billings, 60, 100, 155, 156, 178, 181, 183, 185, 193, 204, 205, 215, 223, 229, 233, 234, 236, 218, 239, 244, 251, 260, 272, 281, 295, 319, 320, 324, 333, 374, 387, 388, 424, 513, 586
Billis, 90, 92
Bird, 123, 236, 263, 274, 278, 304, 321, 323–324, 328, 355–357, 363, 364, 370–373, 416, 421, 422, 424–426, 535, 537
Bisbee, 265, 308, 390, 438, 449, 450
Bishop, 288, 436
Bissett, 270
Blackenburg, 43
Blackman, 179, 192, 197, 236, 272, 270, 325, 324, 330, 331, 372, 376, 378, 382, 385, 431, 433
Blake, 43, 75, 194, 221, 222, 241, 264, 275, 290, 325, 352, 354, 360, 374, 375, 409, 415, 427, 428, 507, 512, 516, 517, 583
Bernard, 153
Blanchard, 115
Bland, 270
Bliss, 456, 458, 473, 474, 478
Bloomer, 497, 501
Boardman, 492
Bodge, 357, 435
Bolton, 32, 383, 491, 494
Bonney, 252, 288, 341, 342, 343, 436–439, 448
Boone, 152
Bore, 342
Bosworth, 448
Bowdoin, 132, 330
Bowen, 237
Bowker, 525, 536, 544, 545
Bowler, 362
Bowman, 131, 261, 263, 301
Boyce, 270
Boyd, 346, 404
Boyes, 513
Boydell, 112, 162
Brabrook, 57
Bradford, 202, 205, 206, 361, 362, 413, 565
Bradley, 398, 507, 510, 511
Bradshaw, 42

Bradstreet, 45, 49, 50, 143, 153, 554
Brackett, 266, 318
Brailing, 94
Bramhall, 131
Branche, 468
Brattle, 114, 461
Brazer, 304, 355, 417
Breck, 75, 159, 180, 185, 478
Breed, 128
Brenton, 103, 117–120, 148
Brewer, 196, 220, 221, 333, 334, 478
Brewster, 530
Bridge, 378, 458
Bridges, 50
Bridgham, 114, 134
Brigham, 339, 366
Briesler, 338
Briggs, 372, 381, 529, 540
Brinley, 292
Brinsmaid, 453
Brookes, 91
Brooks, 57, 432, 482, 573
Broughton, 63
Brown, 266, 283, 291, 329, 351, 443, 460, 522, 564
Browne, 50, 87, 90, 91, 93, 103–105, 146, 162, 153, 286, 341
Brownell, 361
Bromwell, 573
Bruce, 293
Bryant, 36, 355, 416, 439, 450, 566, 567
Buchanan, 270
Buck, 448
Bugbee, 330, 382, 433
Buckminister, 192, 196
Bucknam, 440
Bulfinch, 444
Bullard, 334, 372, 384
Bullock, 211
Bumstead, 311
Bungy, 8
Burbeck, 236, 238, 266–271, 312–316
Burden, 56, 57
Burditt, 405, 448
Burgoyne, 332
Burke, 14, 23, 95, 468
Burleigh, 19
Burnham, 383
Burnet, 270
Burns, 353, 446
Burrill, 326
Burt, 99, 460, 474, 481, 482
Bushrod, 41
Bussey, 105, 297, 578
Butler, 77, 240, 486, 487, 573
Butt, 103, 225, 230
Butterfield, 372
Byfield, 119, 120
Byles, 246, 248
Byram, 57

Cabot, 145
Caine, 237
Calamy, 455
Caldwell, 266, 309, 362
Calvert, 26
Camden, 13–15, 19, 95
Cannon, 157
Capen, 185, 197, 199, 204, 211, 240, 263, 278, 281, 289, 290, 324, 333, 373–376, 386, 411, 427–429
Carey, 119, 281
Carlton, 323, 371
Carnes, 301, 347, 582–584
Carpenter, 126, 267
Carr, 339
Carroll, 311, 363
Carter, 548, 549
Cartwright, 36, 434
Carver, 222
Casno, 78

Cassell, 355
Cathcart, 206, 267, 269
Cecil, 19
Center, 118
Chadbourne, 412, 446
Chalmers, 13
Chalouer, 261
Chamberlain, 135, 248, 515
Chandler, 78, 167, 196, 197, 415
Chapman, 443
Charles, 19
Chardon, 235
Chase, 297
Chauncey, 132, 301
Checkley, 78, 102, 132, 169, 170, 199, 275
Cheever, 235
Childs, 247, 334
Chipman, 307, 440
Chiswell, 82, 90–93, 95, 96
Choate, 158, 236
Christian, 305
Church, 49, 260, 261
Churchill, 343
Clap, 44, 162, 263, 274, 304, 305, 321–321, 342, 358, 479, 490, 508
Clapp, 208, 354, 355, 357, 374, 416, 418, 428
Clark, 100, 162, 202, 280, 281, 307, 327, 343, 460, 472, 490, 518, 524, 586
Clarke, 45, 50, 86, 90, 91, 101–103, 104, 114, 191, 262, 344, 367, 398–400, 439, 558
Cleaveland, 519, 529, 530, 539, 540
Cleverly, 158, 159, 192, 254, 256, 285, 358
Clinton, 584
Clough, 74, 131, 179, 222, 240, 241, 242, 245–250, 272, 275, 277, 279, 280, 347, 430
Coates, 286
Cobb, 113, 325, 376, 398, 415, 447
Cochrane, 218, 264, 305
Coddington, 554
Codman, 129, 136, 143, 487
Coffee, 44
Cogan, 44
Coburn, 340, 518, 524, 536
Colburne, 12
Cole, 95, 397
Coleman, 106, 107, 110
Collier, 328, 355, 578
Collins, 492, 498
Colton, 456, 457, 487, 491–494 ·
Combe, 94, 564
Commee, 237
Concklin, 118
Converse, 43
Cook, 254, 270, 292, 295, 324, 363, 372, 420, 424, 426, 460
Cooke, 12, 105, 233, 234, 562, 567
Cooley, 456, 458, 475, 477, 479
Coolidge, 367
Cools, 578
Cooper, 227, 243, 244, 271, 398, 440, 441, 462
Copeland, 236, 318, 310, 367, 372
Corey, 303, 351, 408, 409
Cornell, 386
Corwin, 103, 114, 129, 133
Cotton, 19, 244, 343
Couch, 202, 646
Cousins, 370
Coverly, 267, 316
Cox, 516, 529, 540
Coye, 253, 291, 292
Crabtree, 283, 336, 337, 383, 391–393, 553, 584
Craddock, 40–42, 128
Crafts, 25, 291
Craghead, 327
Crane, 282, 513, 517, 523, 534, 544

Crehore, 507, 512, 515, 518
Crittenden, 520, 521, 529, 586
Crocker, 171
Crockett, 448
Crooker, 288, 437
Cross, 549
Cullick, 50, 400–462, 407, 479
Culpepper, 22
Cummings, 358, 373
Cunningham, 288, 369
Currier, 378, 431
Curry, 346
Cursette, 257–259
Curtis, 32, 152, 153, 271, 317, 359, 364
Cushing, 250, 336
Cushman, 143, 147, 516

Daggett, 337, 393, 490, 584
Daith, 513
Dame, 370
Damon, 325, 376, 430
Dana, 144, 546
Dane, 400, 444
Danforth, 123, 220, 235, 239, 252, 253, 261, 262, 279, 292, 330, 571
Daniell, 48, 164, 250
Daniels, 255, 297, 384, 443
Darling, 57, 134
Dashwood, 394
Davies, 314, 326
Davis, 90, 93, 291, 351, 354, 864, 387, 422, 434
Davenport, 48, 74, 111, 167, 168, 187, 216, 222, 240, 246, 254, 255, 305, 338, 359, 473, 455, 568
Dawes, 36, 37, 315, 326
Dean, 373
Deane, 30, 31, 33, 35, 37, 38, 209, 250, 524, 560
Dearbon, 137, 314
Deedes, 18
Deering, 372, 373, 425, 426
Dehon, 403
Dell, 84, 85
Deming, 242
Dennie, 110
Dennis, 386
Derby, 12, 14, 15, 522
Derry, 366
Dewey, 465
Dexter, 362
Dickerman, 511
Dickerson, 343, 584
Dill, 412, 445
Dilloway, 247
Dimon, 362
Dingley, 286
Divol, 522
Dixwell, 186, 187
Dodge, 213, 365, 423
Dolbear, 208
Doliver, 136, 139–141
Doolittle, 493, 498, 499
Downes, 115, 116, 160, 242, 246, 270
Downing, 48
Dracot, 9
Drake, 308, 424, 439, 451
Drew, 143, 448, 450
Drury, 334
Duane, 152
Dudley, 45, 47, 50, 107, 109, 141, 384, 480, 508, 510
Dugdale, 19
Duggan, 231, 333, 348, 388, 584
Duguld, 136, 139, 140
Dummer, 187, 480
Dunbar, 265, 314
Duncan, 44, 47, 49, 75, 83, 87, 88, 90, 139, 487, 683
Dunn, 370
Dunnevan, 131
Dunning, 144

Dunster, 562–571
Durant, 403
Durgin, 388
Dwelley, 312, 318, 365, 366
Dwight, 155, 483
Dyer, 255, 294, 332, 385, 370, 433, 434
Dyneley, 95

Eager, 143
Eames, 334
Eanes, 276
East, 131
Eastburn, 402
Eastman, 275
Eastwick, 116
Eaton, 255, 302, 336, 340, 341, 389, 390, 391, 404, 405
Eccleston, 50, 51, 52
Eddy, 386
Edmands, 408
Edmonson, 14, 15
Edwards, 124, 135, 334, 458, 460, 485, 510, 556
Eels, 490
Egerton, 567
Elkins, 137, 142, 144–146
Elliott, 60, 78, 79, 97, 98, 101, 247, 316, 427, 460
Ellis, 206, 448, 507, 509–512
Ellison, 178, 179, 235, 236, 264–266, 581
Elstnche, 18
Elwell, 354, 415
Ely, 388, 415, 447, 458
Emerson, 384
Endicott, 41, 45
Engs, 112
Epes, 240
Euclid, 270
Evans, 441, 491, 493–497, 500, 501, 507, 509–511
Everett, 205, 325, 328, 329, 340, 527

Fairbank, 280, 341
Fairbanks, 222, 324
Farlee, 349
Farrar, 270, 411, 445
Farrington, 265, 307, 361, 356
Farwell, 136, 148
Faxon, 317
Fay, 118, 293, 316, 375, 433
Fayerweather, 102, 103, 237, 286, 287
Fellows, 137, 420
Felt, 383, 411, 444, 415
Felton, 389
Fenno, 279, 285, 320, 339, 382, 395
Fenwick, 461, 462
Fernald, 439
Ferrers, 10
Fessenden, 302, 403, 510, 639, 544
Field, 230, 271, 317, 354, 357, 364, 414, 440, 447
Fifield, 263, 293, 304, 354–356, 446, 447
Fily, 584
Finden, 551, 552
Fisher, 283, 248, 318, 325, 334, 343, 366, 377, 397
Fiske, 354, 409, 532, 542
Fitch, 105, 111, 488
Fitler, 28
Flacks, 420
Flagg, 301
Flavel, 270
Flecker, 217
Fleet, 259
Fletcher, 357, 550, 551, 565, 586
Flint, 284, 562
Flinthnm, 354, 413
Flowers, 11, 18
Foley, 95

Fobes, 483
Folger, 327
Foorde, 41, 42
Foss, 349, 406
Foster, 139, 169, 170, 175, 264, 278, 329, 359, 378, 385, 409, 434, 530
Fowle, 424
Fox, 5, 11
Foye, 103
Franklin, 50, 167, 258, 327
Franklyn, 21
Frazier, 579
Freeman, 23–25, 44, 222, 337, 564
French, 294, 384, 388, 424, 435, 518, 524
Frink, 364, 416
Frost, 111, 322
Frothingham, 43, 44, 371, 424
Fruin, 411
Foxcroft, 40
Fuller, 2, 5, 12, 19, 20, 245, 276, 324, 325, 329, 377, 381, 432, 450

Gage, 299, 385, 585
Gallop, 44, 585
Galpin, 111, 112
Gannett, 250
Gardiner, 308
Garfield, 276
Garnett, 30, 52
Garrett, 578
Gates, 365, 388
Gay, 265, 306, 307, 359, 375, 494, 524
Gaylord, 70
Gaverard, 20, 30
Gavett, 514, 523 .
Gedney, 131, 207
Genndaires, 570
George, 235, 246, 369
Gerrard, 50, 51
Gerrish, 207
Gerry, 331, 383
Gibbs, 123, 141, 333, 398, 435, 441
Gilbert, 87, 334
Gilchrist, 344, 399, 400, 442·
Giles, 493
Gill, 60, 83, 70, 85, 104, 105, 326, 507, 512, 513, 515–518
Gillnm, 87
Gillis, 399, 441
Gilmore, 380, 582, 383
Goddard, 356
Goffe, 48, 88, 248, 249, 277
Goldthwait, 37, 78, 169, 170
Gooch, 533, 534
Goodhue, 158
Goodman, 340
Goodwin, 201
Gookling, 45, 49, 58, 63, 184
Gordon, 366
Gore, 77, 79, 103, 120–123, 173, 220, 273, 320
Goss, 382, 433
Gosling, 95
Gould, 300, 412, 433, 446
Goulding, 99
Gleason, 333, 387, 434, 435
Graham, 349, 507
Grant, 130, 135
Gray, 395, 446
Green, 162, 212, 319, 365, 367, 421, 491
Greenleaf, 347, 582, 583
Greenwood, 266, 309, 389, 527, 537, 559
Gregory, 11, 154, 542
Gresham, 245, 606
Grey, 372
Griggs, 351
Grimes, 252
Grindall, 212
Griswold, 402
Groom, 153

Grout, 518, 525
Guild, 355
Guiteras, 363, 421
Gulliker, 396, 439, 450, 451
Gulliver, 212, 214, 235, 250, 294, 295, 348
Gunn, 479
Gunnison, 56
Gurnell, 63, 164

Hadley, 334
Haggart, 134
Hale, 469
Hall, 144, 146, 147, 167, 170, 171, 180, 185, 208, 209, 214, 220, 225, 250, 278, 299, 328, 360–362, 378, 381, 424, 519, 520, 521, 523, 539, 541, 542, 546
Hallam, 313
Hallett, 319
Halsall, 53
Halsey, 153
Hamilton, 547
Hammatt, 313
Hammond, 407, 542, 585
Hancock, 132, 257, 258, 260, 299, 314, 321
Handley, 525, 537
Hanover, 230
Harden, 547
Hardwick, 312
Harlakenden, 20, 22
Harper, 11, 159, 291
Harrelson, 574, 575
Harrington, 366
Harris, 36, 37, 48, 274, 306, 330, 331, 346, 347, 353, 372, 409, 413, 528, 563, 570
Harrison, 51, 98
Harswell, 26
Hart, 233, 234, 250–252
Hartford, 336, 391
Harwood, 40–42, 211
Hascall, 420
Hastings, 232, 344
Hatch, 230, 253, 264, 275, 281, 356, 418, 516
Hatherly, 565
Haven, 282, 283, 334
Hawes, 278, 325, 328, 329, 349, 375, 380, 381, 386, 407
Hawkins, 47, 178, 562
Hawley, 521
Hawthorne, 49
Hayden, 272, 548
Haynes, 462, 479, 480, 487, 488, 492
Hayward, 25, 72, 150, 201, 202, 204, 310, 506
Heald, 370
Healey, 122
Heard, 301, 398, 441
Hearsey, 304, 355, 356, 406, 416, 417
Heath, 304, 356
Hemmenway, 266
Henchman, 115
Hendricks, 411
Henwage, 19
Henshaw, 144, 185, 506
Henulker, 579
Hewins, 278, 324, 377
Hewson, 42, 50
Hibbins, 45, 60
Hichborn, 143
Higgins, 543
Hildreth, 525, 537
Hill, 44, 61, 240, 263, 283, 301, 302, 333, 336, 348, 349, 374, 582
Hills, 242, 505
Hilton, 264
Himes, 450
Hinckley, 53, 54, 71, 72, 83, 88, 163–172, 180, 198, 206, 217, 227, 234, 235, 256, 369

Hinsdale, 505
Hitchcock, 466, 467, 475, 477, 479
Hix, 219
Hoar, 492, 497
Hobart, 334, 372
Holbrook, 308, 321, 370, 371, 394, 435, 586
Holden, 274, 306, 323, 352, 354, 357, 359, 370, 409, 413, 444, 519, 527, 537, 584
Holland, 53–55, 458, 459
Hollingsworth, 377
466, 467, 469
Hollis, 370
Holmes, 169, 170, 306, 513, 517, 521
Holton, 29
Holyoke, 115, 259, 457, 458, 460
Homer, 527, 522, 534, 535
Homes, 278, 524, 326–328, 332, 352, 372, 377–379, 385, 431
Honeyman, 113
Honnors, 350, 407
Hooker, 212, 458–460
Hooper, 404
Hopkins, 330, 462
Horne, 248
Horton, 178, 179, 235, 236, 238, 239, 271–276, 332, 336
Houghton, 206, 208, 295, 414, 519, 526
Hovey, 157, 158, 536, 635
Howard, 19, 67, 118, 148, 207, 472, 546
Howe, 80, 279, 300, 301, 304, 306, 322, 331, 346, 349, 354, 356–359, 370, 380, 386, 407, 414, 415, 416, 418, 419, 431, 582, 584
Hubbard, 103, 115, 122, 127, 186, 458, 459, 559, 581
Hudibras, 270
Hudson, 25, 43, 56, 59, 96, 99
Huff, 395
Hull, 44, 103
Humfrey, 40, 41
Humphrey, 562
Humphreys, 355
Hunt, 135, 305, 306, 357, 385, 379, 418, 419, 522, 533, 534, 544, 548
Hutchins, 306, 343, 399, 441, 442
Hutchinson, 96, 244, 250, 491, 543
Hyde, 343

Iggledon, 96
Ingersoll, 131, 479
Ingraham, 301, 347, 420, 49 497, 532
Inglee, 858

Jacobs, 378, 394, 431
Jackson, 100, 245, 291, 314, 368, 537
Jaffrey, 127
Jaggard, 19
James, 57
Jameson, 139, 143
Jeffries, 77, 79, 110, 111, 127, 128, 345, 373
Jeffords, 298
Jenkins, 302, 349, 358
Jeter, 878
Jewett, 83, 583, 584
Johnson, 40, 41, 44, 48, 51, 364, 449
Johonnet, 247
Jones, 75, 137, 138, 373, 408, 426, 474, 483, 486, 487, 491, 585
Jordan, 129
Joyce, 486, 487

Kay, 79, 103, 112, 113
Kearney, 556, 417
Keen, 251, 261
Keene, 439, 449
Keith, 321

Kellogg, 132, 432
Kendall, 415
Kendricks, 500
Ketch, 110
Kilby, 109
Kildrick, 571
Kilton, 519, 527
Kimball, 398, 435, 440, 452
King, 152, 220, 266, 432
Kingsbury, 450, 524
Kingsley, 240, 269, 332, 333, 521
Kinsley, 66, 273
Knapp, 153
Kneeland, 346
Knight, 494
Knowles, 488, 492
Knowlton, 492, 497, 501
Knox, 268
Kyle, 574

Lamb, 483
Lamson, 425
Lane, 535
Lancaster, 29, 30, 51
Lancklin, 123
Lander, 546
Langley, 204
Lanham, 548
Lapham, 396
Larkin, 491, 493, 499
Larned, 311, 343
Larr, 401
Larrabee, 131, 438
Lash, 316
Latham, 52, 81
Lathrop, 166, 170
Latimer, 5, 10
Laughton, 328, 390
Lawrence, 395, 490, 584
Laws, 179, 229, 230, 233, 234, 239
Leach, 17, 323
Leadbetter, 190, 191, 278
Learned, 497
Lee, 21, 145, 573
Leeds, 253, 279, 351, 350, 351, 356, 383, 384, 408, 409
Legg, 103
Leggett, 399, 442
Leigh, 396, 584
Leland, 296
Lemmon, 304, 363, 411, 412
Leonard, 221
Leslie, 19
Leverett, 45, 53, 123, 461, 566
Lewis, 115, 304, 330, 349, 352–354, 382, 408, 411, 413, 432, 513, 524
Lidgett, 127
Lidyard, 94
Lighy, 530
Lightman, 90, 93
Lincoln, 417
Lindall, 284
Lindsay, 363, 420
Ling, 125, 270
Litchfield, 411
Little, 120, 238
Littlefield, 517, 521, 522, 532, 534
Littlejohn, 547
Livermore, 213, 534, 546
Lloyd, 13–15
Lombard, 217, 529, 539, 540
Loomis, 276
Lord, 164, 171, 349, 479, 480, 487, 488, 492
Loring, 136, 178, 267
Lothrop, 99
Love, 123
Lovell, 44, 252, 287
Lowden, 289
Lowder, 258
Lowler, 364, 422
Lucas, 90, 93
Ludlow, 44, 480, 584

Luke, 567
Lunt, 340
Lusher, 49, 50
Lyman, 115, 483
Lyndall, 103, 106, 117, 118
Lynde, 196, 276, 282, 331, 383, 384
Lyon, 274, 290, 322, 328, 533, 369, 370, 380, 411, 417, 446, 527

Maccarty, 24, 235
Macomber, 375
Magoon, 396
Malesny, 124
Malbone, 321
Malcolm, 399–401, 440
Mallard, 134
Manchester, 310, 563, 419, 420, 566
Mann, 263, 304, 338, 339, 505, 506, 516, 522
Manning, 256, 399, 441, 541
Manson, 390, 391
Manstrange, 42
Marchant, 255, 306
Marden, 343
Marion, 157, 264
Marsh, 24, 179, 216, 257, 282, 283, 335
Marshall, 308, 375, 440, 452, 550
Marshfield, 456, 458
Marstens, 425
Martin, 24, 343, 398, 448, 584
Mason, 63, 262, 268
Massey, 550
Masson, 307, 361, 419
Masters, 479
Mather, 43, 59, 96, 97, 99, 163, 164, 198, 463, 464, 464, 461
Matthews, 49
Maudsley, 192, 193
Maunsell, 24
Maverick, 44, 564
May, 266, 363, 413, 421–423
Mayhew, 564, 554, 563, 564
Maynard, 286, 340
Mayo, 138
Mayor, 67
Macfarland, 342
McDermot, 25
McIntire, 408
McKean, 271
Mclean, 345, 346
McLellan, 501
McSparrow, 118
Mead, 271, 411, 501, 525, 537
Mears, 365
Melcher, 296, 325, 376
Melvin, 521, 530, 541, 548
Merick, 479
Metcalf, 240, 263, 335, 336
Miles, 151
Miller, 164, 491, 493
Milles, 13, 14, 16–19; 24
Millett, 211
Mills, 474, 486
Millington, 469, 470
Minard, 529, 540
Minot, 111, 273, 319, 320, 368, 523
Mitchell, 163, 440, 449
Monk, 278, 282, 332, 336
Monroe, 344, 349, 402, 403, 406
Montague, 355
Moody, 159, 186
Moore, 35, 36, 318, 381, 574
Move, 206
Morefield, 161
Morey, 373, 426
Morrell, 245, 260, 300, 301, 344–346, 375, 401, 402, 404
Morton, 332, 386, 387, 570
Mosman, 157, 158, 161, 164, 251
Motley, 430
Moull, 18
Moulton, 555–556

Mountfort, 101
Mousall, 98, 99
Moxon, 81, 82, 454, 455-457, 459
Mulliman, 95
Mullens, 24
Miller, 270
Munsley, 124, 125
Munjoy, 131, 132
Murphy, 585
Mutho, 270
Myers, 446
Myles, 112, 328, 379

Nash, 328, 379, 449, 506
Nason, 364
Neal, 346
Neale, 253, 264, 348, 421
Nelson, 124, 551, 584
Newbury, 44, 60, 70
Newcomb, 266, 318, 360, 395, 474, 487, 491
Newcome, 93
Newman, 25, 456
Nichols, 141, 144, 301, 322
Nicholson, 252
Nightingale, 271, 319
Niles, 271
Noble, 241, 350, 407, 501
Norcott, 199, 291, 350, 407, 584, 585
Norton, 205, 253, 409
Nooning, 265, 309, 361
Norrys, 29
Northup, 515
Nott, 411
Nourse, 283, 333, 563
Nowell, 27, 40-43, 554
Noyes, 160, 281, 564
Nunn, 27
Nutting, 530, 541
Nyle, 506

Oakes, 149
Otfield, 40-42
Ogden, 480
Ogle, 352, 410, 644
Olcutt, 492
Oliver, 56, 103, 114, 199, 200, 356, 581
Onger, 523, 535
Ormond, 410, 414, 444
Osborne, 502, 348, 349, 405, 406
Osgood, 138
Otis, 383, 395
Ould, 474, 481
Orfield, 562, 565, 567, 568
Owen, 90, 93, 550-552

Packard, 283, 294, 332, 337, 352, 410, 424, 586
Paddock, 255, 295
Page, 321
Paine, 237, 246, 559
Palfrey, 394
Palmer, 41, 42, 111, 309, 323, 336, 362, 383, 591, 487
Palsgrave, 43
Paris, 568
Park, 384, 387, 424, 524
Parker, 4, 161, 322, 331, 345, 370
Parks, 49
Parmenly, 297
Parshley, 332, 384
Parsons, 460, 462, 473, 474, 481, 482-487
Partridge, 263, 291, 292
Parvel, 102
Passamere, 27
Patch, 286, 340, 386
Patterson, 19
Paul, 196, 224, 320, 369, 376
Payne, 87, 109, 208, 273, 280, 387, 434
Payson, 273

Peabody, 343, 373, 397, 427
Pearce, 573
Pearson, 273, 411
Peck, 310, 557
Perke, 150
Pelton, 165, 185, 206
Pemberton, 134
Penkett, 91
Fenn, 43, 461
Penniman, 99
Pepper, 329
Pepperell, 256
Percival, 24
Perkins, 153, 155, 314
Perne, 212
Perrin, 561
Perry, 40, 41
Peters, 40-42
Peterson, 439, 450, 451
Pettee, 325
Peverly, 522, 534, 545
Phelps, 340
Phillips, 63, 115, 116, 246, 247, 259, 513, 516
Philpot, 18, 21, 22
Phippen, 348, 406
Phipps, 285, 338, 339, 395, 406, 443, 444
Pickering, 534
Pickman, 142
Pierce, 127, 280, 285, 304, 322, 333, 339, 351, 355-360, 375, 386, 419, 525
Pierpont, 123, 480
Pierson, 146
Piggott, 5
Pike, 352
Pimer, 264
Pink, 27
Pinkham, 391
Pinney, 44
Pitcher, 523, 525
Pitman, 204
Pitts, 372
Plaisted, 129
Plummer, 150
Plympton, 286, 341
Pole, 24
Pollard, 246
Pool, 237
Pope, 80, 193, 225, 236, 238, 264, 265, 279, 279, 282, 294, 296, 303, 324-326, 328-334, 352, 353, 359, 361, 385, 410, 430, 435, 560
Porter, 278, 533
Post, 432
Pottle, 337, 392, 554
Powell, 13-15, 246, 521
Power, 25
Powers, 521, 532, 542
Poyntell, 90, 92
Pratt, 101, 351, 406
Prentice, 343, 397
Prescott, 145
Preston, 182, 354, 356
Price, 287
Prichard, 46
Prince, 121, 132, 163, 164, 239, 299, 565
Proctor, 199, 200, 262
Pronk, 359
Prout, 103
Prouty, 414, 536
Pulsifer, 346
Purefoy, 20, 21
Purley, 143
Putnam, 345
Pynchon, 69, 70, 81, 109, 149, 455-457, 460, 466, 469, 473-475, 477, 478, 584
Pynson, 306, 360

Queg, 500 ; Quinn, 24

Quincy, 77, 78, 196, 213, 217, 246
Rand, 207, 208, 299, 344, 460, 462
Randall, 116
Randolph, 59
Ratcliffe, 90, 92
Rawson, 46, 48, 53, 63, 67, 53, 85, 87, 160-166, 161, 162, 167, 182-184, 189, 190, 197, 200-202, 216-217, 229, 235, 237, 254-257, 292, 299, 348, 369, 410, 470-472, 562, 565
Raynolds, 437, 445
Read, 293, 569
Record, 397, 446
Redman, 56
Reed, 318, 364, 423, 424
Remick, 439, 450, 451
Reynardson, 246
Rice, 45, 301, 340, 441, 564, 572
Rich, 376
Richards, 44, 49, 169, 170, 172, 262, 329, 351, 380, 406, 429, 513, 528, 537, 538
Richardson, 383, 437
Richer, 538
Richings, 5
Richman, 4
Richmond, 331
Rideout, 364, 423
Rigbee, 167, 196, 226, 231
Rigby, 32
Ritchie, 583
Roberts, 20, 21, 22
Robertson, 270
Robbins, 427
Robins, 344, 402, 534
Robinson, 63, 135, 205, 364, 382, 386, 396, 405, 419, 442, 519
Rogers, 254, 339, 555
Rollins, 342
Root, 492, 520, 547
Rose, 14, 15, 143, 145
Rosewell, 488, 489
Ross, 139, 364
Rossiter, 44
Roundy, 319, 342, 394
Rowe, 280
Rowed, 566, 567
Rowell, 379
Rowley, 11
Royall, 154
Royston, 96
Rudd, 267, 313
Ruddock, 153
Rudulph, 10
Rugg, 263, 336, 388
Ruggles, 124, 125, 241, 347, 392, 394, 528
Russell, 99, 116, 171, 254, 280, 294, 458, 460
Rust, 157
Ryder, 163, 165
Rysend, 469

Sadler, 293
Salisbury, 269, 521, 530-533
Salter, 54, 215, 226, 256, 292, 300, 301, 347, 582-584
Saltonstall, 40-42, 142, 144-147, 479, 488-490, 564
Sampson, 439, 451
Sanborn, 375
Sanderson, 246, 372, 424, 550, 561
Sanford, 480
Sargeant, 47, 102-104, 113, 136, 141, 144, 149, 205, 206, 464, 470-473
Saunders, 136, 141, 145, 146, 148, 247, 254, 287, 316, 409, 434
Savage, 78, 87, 193, 237, 241, 254, 290, 459, 554
Saville, 512
Sawyer, 349, 364

Saxton, 413
Sayward, 439
Scollay, 130
Scott, 258, 269
Searle, 144
Sears, 351, 409
Seaver, 78, 79, 382
Seaverns, 431
Sedgwick, 446
Seeley, 24
Sever, 288
Sevey, 328, 379
Sewall, 78, 84, 88, 89, 96, 101–108, 160, 161, 211, 241, 259, 826
Seward, 271
Sexton, 554
Shackford, 533
Shaller, 513
Sharrot, 550–552
Sharp, 270
Shattuck, 63, 340
Shaw, 139, 314
Sheafe, 114
Sheepcote, 199, 200
Sheldon, 128
Shepard, 184, 216, 255, 282, 372, 424, 464
Sherborn, 116, 287
Sherburn, 115
Sherman, 285, 439, 441
Shirley, 16, 580
Shrewsbury, 19
Shrimpton, 150
Shusters, 492, 496
Shuman, 359
Shute, 266
Sibley, 400, 584, 585
Siders, 517, 522, 534, 535
Sigourney, 813
Sisben, 146
Simmons, 364, 382, 421, 450
Simonds, 49, 50
Simpson, 111, 112, 213, 240, 299, 395, 307
Sisson, 375
Skinner, 150
Slade, 415
Sleeper, 534, 544, 546
Smith, 44, 57, 63, 77, 99, 102, 136, 137, 151, 152, 159–166, 167, 185, 188, 199, 206, 209, 252, 296, 298, 300, 301, 313, 334, 336, 340, 342, 347, 370, 375, 397, 445, 460, 478, 498, 525, 581
Smythe, 42, 44, 102
Snow, 378, 431
Soley, 260
Somerset, 25
Somes, 270
Soper, 514
Sorrelle, 271, 316, 366
Southcote, 44
Souther, 53
Sparhawke, 43
Spear, 302, 305, 369, 517, 523
Spencer, 493, 499
Spig, 68
Sprague, 455, 456
Sprung, 302, 320, 349, 516, 517
Spurr, 273, 307, 320, 516, 517
Spurriel, 120
Squeb, 42
Stacey, 247, 282, 491, 493, 498, 499
Standish, 288, 342
Stanton, 401, 415, 446
Staples, 439
Starr, 387, 435
Starrett, 337, 592
Stearns, 380
Stebbins, 292, 494
Stephens, 254
Stetson, 282, 266, 336, 342, 390, 399, 431, 447, 448

Stevens, 40–42, 47, 152, 408
Stewart, 400, 416, 442
Stockling, 428
Stockley, 33
Stoddard, 85, 255, 459, 460, 477–479
Stone, 164, 181, 255, 265, 295, 299, 343, 370, 399, 443
Storer, 135
Stoughton, 44, 50, 66, 72, 182, 197, 203, 206, 208, 252, 502, 548, 549
Stowe, 14, 58, 96
Stratton, 435
Strong, 11
Stuart, 586
Stubbs, 303
Studley, 354, 415
Styles, 382
St. Medard, 265, 807
Sumner, 50, 73, 221, 372, 413, 424
Swan, 138, 285, 307, 808, 332, 386, 424
Sweet, 491, 492, 498
Sweetzer, 395
Swift, 248, 429, 513, 515, 518–520, 525
Sylvester, 350, 408, 585

Tailor, 581
Talbee, 309, 361
Talbot, 19, 90, 93, 105, 278, 306, 308, 324
Talcott, 432
Tappan, 327
Target, 134
Taylor, 324, 372, 424, 460, 574, 575, 577
Tenney, 286, 341
Terhune, 497, 501
Terrey, 44, 478, 522, 544
Thacher, 132, 222, 228, 233, 235, 286, 271, 272, 299, 342, 581
Thayer, 78, 160, 285, 319, 334, 339, 356, 364, 367, 583, 372, 433, 491, 494
Thomas, 63, 136, 266, 283, 310, 335, 336, 344, 362, 390, 401, 561
Thompson, 181, 214, 282, 325, 826, 331, 350, 376, 383, 437, 447, 449
Thomson, 82, 89, 90, 92, 93, 96
Thorn, 390
Thornton, 206, 207
Thurston, 299
Thwing, 255, 297
Tiffany, 126
Tilden, 536, 545
Tileston, 182, 185, 197, 231, 301, 302, 350, 511
Tilley, 44
Timmins, 135
Tindale, 536
Tolman, 55, 157, 301, 303, 305, 328, 330, 352, 356, 378, 379, 409, 410, 511
Tomlins, 47
Tompkins, 52
Tompson, 285, 296, 299
Topliff, 182, 296, 350
Torrey, 56, 57, 64, 118, 123, 254
Totman, 316
Tower, 507
Townsend, 128, 191
Tracey, 293
Trafton, 348, 405, 442, 443
Trail, 236
Train, 321, 336, 445, 583
Trask, 324, 424
Tremch, 82, 89–93, 96, 97
Trescott, 278, 329, 382
Treworthy, 568
Trisben, 233, 234
Trott, 164, 171, 227
Trull, 372

Trumbull, 457
Tubbs, 228, 342, 395, 397
Tucker, 121, 222, 240, 284, 333, 334, 508, 517, 519, 523, 535, 536
Tuckerman, 145, 147
Tuffneale, 41
Tufts, 524
Turell, 110, 111
Turfrey, 183, 184, 548
Turner, 144, 147, 309, 312, 333, 342, 549, 567
Turpin, 74, 436
Turpyn, 12
Tuttle, 273, 533
Tyler, 115, 310, 362, 555
Tyley, 109, 111, 112, 119, 120
Tyndall, 567, 568
Tyng, 44, 47, 55, 129, 131, 135, 137, 150, 205, 230
Tyson, 321

Underwood, 494
Upalike, 112
Usher, 127

Valentine, 304, 436
Van Rensselaer, 315
Vantry, 24
Vassall, 40
Veazie, 271, 318, 319, 367
Venn, 40–42
Veren, 117
Vernon, 137, 142
Verrilie, 283, 336
Vinton, 122
Vose, 64–66, 184, 272, 284, 302, 313, 349, 350, 357, 406, 407, 454, 508, 511, 513, 518, 527, 523
519

Wade, 306
Wadsworth, 74, 240, 251, 284, 285, 317, 337, 365, 366, 386, 514
Wakefield, 359
Wakeman, 21
Waldo, 77
Waldridge, 525
Wales, 274, 321, 323, 354, 370
Walker, 57, 100, 254, 435, 438
Walley, 132
Wallis, 359
Wallys, 67
Walton, 131, 254
Ward, 321, 323, 370, 375
Wardwell, 266, 310, 363, 419, 420
Warham, 44, 70
Warner, 492
Warren, 255, 568, 296, 314, 322, 364, 421, 437
Warriner, 466–469, 478, 491, 492, 497, 498
Washburn, 308
Washington, 268, 361
Watkins, 91
Watrous, 90, 93
Watts, 32, 90, 93, 205, 206, 235
Way, 44
Wayland, 338, 409
Wayne, 313, 315
Wear, 131
Weaver, 118, 537
Webb, 40, 55, 132, 187, 212, 294, 313, 337, 375, 428
Webster, 360, 367
Weeks, 190
Weld, 47, 339
Welles, 277, 468
Wellington, 536, 544, 546
Wellman, 94
Wells, 314, 411
Wendell, 129, 130, 135, 138, 139, 143, 247, 270, 271
Wenham, 22
Wentworth, 129, 374

West, 288, 360, 429
Weston, 288, 440, 452
Wheat, 253, 292, 343, 562
Wheaton, 556, 557
Wheeler, 129, 131, 241, 242, 248, 249, 258, 259, 277, 322, 344, 439, 519, 520, 526
Wheelock, 352, 378, 505, 506
Wheelwright, 346, 404, 411
Whetcomb, 40–42
Whipple, 164, 171
Whippo, 171
White, 25, 41, 42, 54, 142, 145, 218, 263, 283, 301, 302, 305, 331, 333, 336, 382, 389–391, 410, 495, 508, 533
Whiting, 96, 451, 488
Whitney, 318, 346, 364, 404, 525, 536
Whittemore, 302, 397, 411, 440, 451, 452
Whitteredge, 417
Whittingham, 490
Whittlesey, 491
Whitwell, 280, 299, 327, 344, 400, 401

Wight, 505, 506, 537
Wightman, 22, 23
Wilbur, 431
Wilde, 307
Wilkins, 45, 46, 237
Wilkinson, 147
Willard, 115, 207, 248, 289, 337, 358, 415, 581
Willey, 383
Williams, 44, 150, 289, 301, 404
Williamson, 35
Willington, 11
Willis, 80, 373, 424, 469
Williston, 477
Willoughby, 13–16
Wilson, 17, 70, 109, 212, 213, 215, 217, 270, 365, 394
Winchester, 255, 291, 295, 378, 431
Winslow, 134, 136, 143, 239, 398, 580, 560
Winter, 135, 143
Winthrop, 39, 43, 47, 56, 57, 102, 141, 155, 480, 489, 490, 561–563, 566–569, 572
Wiswall, 63, 83, 130, 208, 331, 452

Witherell, 288, 342, 406
Withington, 59, 303, 510
Witter, 406
Wolcott, 70
Wolsey, 6
Worden, 171, 388
Wormell, 825
Worthington, 356, 475, 477–479
Wood, 35, 61, 64, 66, 68, 199, 200, 208, 209, 527, 537
Woodfull, 30, 32
Woodman, 338, 340, 511
Woodmansey, 85, 99
Woodruff, 297
Woodward, 273, 320, 360, 370
Wooldridge, 442
Wooley, 519, 539, 540
Wright, 374, 427, 474, 481, 483, 484
Wybourne, 171, 250
Wyche, 560
Wyman, 300, 345, 346, 403, 404

Young, 294, 437, 448, 449
Younge, 41, 42
Younglough, 460

WILLS AND OTHER DOCUMENTS.

CONTRACTS AND AGREEMENTS:
Controversy with Dorchester Proprietors   192
Glover, Hannah and Mary 228
  "   Henry, heirs of 509
  "   John, Settlement and Agreement in relation to undivided lands   76
  "   and daughter Hannah . . 547
  "   Pelatiah, Rev., inhabitants of Springfield with 456
Glovers' Agreement—Newbury Farm . . 71
London Joint Stock Company . . . 41
Rawson, William, and Nathaniel Glover . 182

DEEDS AND INDENTURES:
Clough, John, to Thomas and Elizabeth Glover 247
  "   " to Thomas and Elijah Glover 248, 278
Glover, Anne, to brother Nathaniel . . 214
  "   Heirs to Robert Vose, Senior . . 65
  "   James, to Thomas Shepard . . . 282
  "   John, Mr., to Thomas 61
  "   John, A.M., from Samuel and Anne Myles . . . 151
  "   "   "   " Joseph Curtis . 152
  "   "   "   " William Rawson . 153
  "   " to William Rawson . . 201
  "   " and Mary to Lowell . . 200
  "   " and Mary to John, Senior . 204
  "   Mary, Mrs., to her children . . 167
  "   Mary, to sister Hannah Laws . . 229
  "   " and others to Thomas . . 231
  "   Nathaniel, Sen., from Roger Billings . 156
  "   "   " to Billings (division) 179
  "   "   " to John, his son . 188
  "   "   " to Nathaniel, Jr. (gift) 185
  "   "   " to Thomas & Hannah 187
  "   "   " to Thomas . . 189
  "   "   Jr., to his father . . 220
  "   Pelatiah, Jr., to Nathaniel Glover and William Rawson . . . 470
  "   Ruth 293
  "   Samuel, Capt., from Millington . 469
Glovers to John Glover 236

Laws, Mrs. Hannah, to John Glover . . 233
  "   Mrs. Hannah, to Thomas Glover . 234
Rawson, William, to nephews John and Thomas Glover 216
Wheeler, Elizabeth, to Thomas and Elizabeth Glover 241

DEPOSITIONS:
Blackman, John, and John, Jr. . . . 197
Buckman, Sarah 571
Glover, Henry, Sen. and Junior . . . 506
  "   Nathaniel, Jr. 79
Leadbetter, Henry, and Elizabeth Weeks . 196
Mousall, Joanne 571
Rice, Edmund 571
Seaver, Joshua 78
  "   Shubael 79

ESTATES:
Glover, Henry 509
  "   John, Mr., Dorchester estate . . 53
  "   "   Newbury Farm . . 60
  "   "   Boston estate . . 56
  "   "   Milton 64
  "   "   Common & Undivided Lands 74
  "   Joseph, Rev. 562
Smith, Capt. Thomas 115
  "   Rev. Thomas 130

EPITAPHS:
Glover, Edward 456
  "   John 463
  "   Jane, Lady 21
  "   Richard 24, 26
  "   Robert, Somerset Herald . . . 16
  "   Sarah, Mrs. 563
  "   Susanna, Mrs. 26
  "   William, Sir 20
Hinckley, Mrs. Mary 164
  "   Gov. Thomas 172
Philpot, Susan 22
Roberts, Barne, Esq. 23
Wood, Miriam 569

INVENTORIES:

Burbeck, Col. William 270
Glover, Anna, Mrs. 68
"   Henry 508
"   John, Mr., ... 60
"   John 207
"   Pelatiah, Rev. 468
"   Pelatiah, 2d 475
"   Samuel, Capt. 469
Smith, Capt. Thomas 116

LETTERS:

Adams, Mrs., to her husband, John Adams 313
Glover, Mary, Mrs., to Thomas Fayerweather 287
"   Robert, to   "   "   288
"   Robert (Martyr), to wife Mary . . 7
"   Thomas, to Gov. Hinckley . . . 88

POWERS OF ATTORNEY:

Dawes, Mary, to George Glover . . . 87
Glover, Thomas, to Habackuk 58
Holland, Judith, to Thomas Glover . 84, 85

PETITIONS:

Appleton, Lieut. John 570
Dunster, Rev. Henry 506
Glover, Mrs. Elizabeth 565
Winthrop, Adam 572
"   Mrs. Elizabeth 568

WILLS:

Brenton, Ebenezer, Sen. 119
Burbeck, Col. William 269
Clarke, Mrs. Rebeckah 106
"   Capt. Thomas 110
Cursetle, Mrs. Mary 251
Glover, Edward 558
"   Elizabeth, Mrs. 250
"   Habackuk 100
"   John, Mr. 58
"   John, A.M. 156
"   John 218
"   Nathaniel, Mr. (Boston) . . . 260
"   Pelatiah, Rev. 456
"   Pelatiah, 3d 482
"   Rachel, Mrs. 226
"   Robert 342
"   Samuel 514
"   Thomas (of London) 90
"   Thomas 242
Gore, Capt. John 112
Hubbard, Nathaniel, Esq. 124
Jeffries, John, Esq. 128
Lyndall, Nathaniel, Esq. 118
Salter, Richard, Esq. 263
Smith, Mr. John 134
"   Capt. Thomas 104

ERRATA.

Page 3, line 5, for " affix " read *prefix*.
Pages 3, 5 and 11, for " Monceter " read *Manceter*.
Page 12, line 5, for " power " read *favor*.
Page 14, line 11 from bottom, for " his first " read *the first*.
Page 15, line 16, for " by " read *from*.
Page 33, line 15 from bottom, for " Knawlesby " read *Knowlesby*.
Page 36, line 3 from bottom, for " belief " read *fact*.
Page 36, lines 4 and 5 from bottom, for " abovenamed " read *last named*.
Page 50, line 6 from bottom, for " 1683 " read 1680.
Page 56, line 14 from bottom, for " 1664 " read 1644.
Page 84, line 2 of Deed, for " spinster " read *widow*.
Page 119, should read *Will of Major Ebenezer Brenton, Senior*.
Page 123, last line, for date " 1734 " read 1739.
Page 134, No. 48, Hannah Smith, for " 1762 " read 1772.
Page 141, in note, date of Mrs. Judith Saunders's death should be 1841.
Page 164, line 5, for " 1686 " read 1638.
Page 192, line 3 from bottom, read *Nathaniel Glover, Junior*.
Page 213, last line but one of note, for " Wellcom Rawson " read *William Rawson*.
Page 214, in Anne Rawson's deed, for " Mrs. Nathaniel Glover " read *Mr. Nathaniel Glover*.
Page 239, first line of No. (11), for " third son " read *fifth son*.
Page 255, line 5 of No. (26), for " He " read *William*.
Page 262, No. 125, William Salter born Feb. 8, 1742.
Page 265, line 14, for " Medord " read *Medard*.
Page 267, No. 158, Joseph Burbeck's wife should be *Elizabeth Saunders*.
Page 272, line 7 from bottom, for " Miriam (Davenport) " read *Miriam (Vose)*.
Page 305, No. 400, for " James Robinson " read *Edward Robinson*.
Page 306, No. 418, birth of Martha Fletcher Pope, for " Nov. 1, 1787," read *July 12, 1772*.
Page 317, No. 514, for " Elizabeth Bevice " read *Elizabeth Beals*.
Page 318, No. 518, for " Margaretta N.," read *Margaretta F. G.*
Page 320, No. 560, for " 1817 " read 1816.
Page 321, No. 574, for " Ebenezer " read *Susannah*.
Page 328, No. 637, for " Oct. 3," read *Nov. 3*.
Page 335, No. 714, erase " Zilpah " before Beveridge.
Page 337, last par. of No. (220), add " March 3, 1774," birth of Mehetable Willard Baxter.
Page 357, last line of No. (401), for " July 12, 1772," read *Nov. 1, 1787*.
Page 379, line 3 from bottom, for " 1840 " read 1846.
Page 396, No. 1366, for " Sonney " read *Bonney*.
Page 406, No. (874), the date of death of Sarah Glover should be 1859.
Page 407, No. (886), date of Elizabeth (Glover) Norcutt's death should be 1863.
Page 427, line 8 from bottom, for " Elivenai " read *Elionia*.
Page 436, line 7, insert " Anne (Whitmarsh)" at the blank before Holbrook.
Page 451, No. (1757), Joseph S. Glover, b. March 17, 1813, m. June 2, 1840, d. March 8, 1844, and his wife died Oct. 7, 1849.
Page 452, No. 1898, birth of Edward Weston Glover, Jan. 17, 1842.
Page 452, No. 1899, birth of Charles J., June 5, 1843; enlisted, 1861; discharged, 1865; resides in Amherst.
Page 529, line 12, for " Bassett " read *Barrett*.
Page 539, line 8, for " Bassett " read *Barrett*.